THE HIDDEN HAND

AMERICAN WOMEN WRITERS SERIES

Joanne Dobson, Judith Fetterley, and Elaine Showalter, series editors

ALTERNATIVE ALCOTT
Louisa May Alcott
Elaine Showalter, editor

MOODS
Louisa May Alcott
Sarah Elbert, editor

STORIES FROM THE COUNTRY OF
LOST BORDERS
Mary Austin
Marjorie Pryse, editor

CLOVERNOOK SKETCHES AND
OTHER STORIES
Alice Cary
Judith Fetterley, editor

HOBOMOK AND OTHER WRITINGS
ON INDIANS
Lydia Maria Child
Carolyn L. Karcher, editor

"HOW CELIA CHANGED HER MIND"
AND SELECTED STORIES
Rose Terry Cooke
Elizabeth Ammons, editor

THE LAMPLIGHTER
Maria Susanna Cummins
Nina Baym, editor

RUTH HALL AND OTHER
WRITINGS
Fanny Fern
Joyce Warren, editor

THE ESSENTIAL
MARGARET FULLER
Jeffrey Steele, editor

GAIL HAMILTON: SELECTED WRITINGS
Susan Coultrap-McQuin, editor

A NEW HOME, WHO'LL FOLLOW?
Caroline M. Kirkland
Sandra A. Zagarell, editor

QUICKSAND AND PASSING
Nella Larsen
Deborah E. McDowell, editor

HOPE LESLIE
Catharine Maria Sedgwick
Mary Kelley, editor

THE HIDDEN HAND
E.D.E.N. Southworth
Joanne Dobson, editor

"THE AMBER GODS" AND
OTHER STORIES
Harriet Prescott Spofford
Alfred Bendixen, editor

OLDTOWN FOLKS
Harriet Beecher Stowe
Dorothy Berkson, editor

WOMEN ARTISTS, WOMEN
EXILES: "MISS GRIEF"
AND OTHER STORIES
Constance Fenimore Woolson
Joan Myers Weimer, editor

AMERICAN WOMEN POETS
OF THE NINETEENTH CENTURY:
AN ANTHOLOGY
Cheryl Walker, editor

THE HIDDEN HAND
or,
CAPITOLA THE MADCAP

E.D.E.N. SOUTHWORTH

Edited and with an Introduction by

JOANNE DOBSON

RUTGERS UNIVERSITY PRESS

New Brunswick, New Jersey, and London

Ninth paperback printing, 2009

Library of Congress Cataloging-in-Publication Data

Southworth, Emma Dorothy Eliza Nevitte, 1819–1899.
The hidden hand / by E.D.E.N. Southworth : edited and with an introduction by
Joanne Dobson.
p.   cm.—(The American women writers series)
Bibliography: p.
ISBN 0-8135-1295-6 ISBN 0-8135-1296-4 (pbk.)
I. Dobson, Joanne, 1942– .   II. Title.   III. Series
PS2892.H5   1988   813'.4—dc19   87-22932
CIP

British Cataloging-in-Publication information available

For my daughters, Lisa and Rebecca,
because they share the spirit of Capitola

CONTENTS

ACKNOWLEDGMENTS

I wish to thank Frank Couvares, Susan Harris, and Sandra Zagarell for their very helpful comments on the first version of this Introduction. I am also indebted to Amherst College for the Faculty Research grant that enabled me to investigate the Southworth archives, and to Alan Lebowitz of the Tufts University Department of English for arranging a teaching schedule that helped expedite my work. Jane Tompkins sent me a copy of the hard-to-find first edition of *The Hidden Hand* and Linda Bamber helped track down Shakespeare quotations. My husband, Dave Dobson, and my son, David, served as nonspecialist readers of the Introduction. I especially appreciate the support of Judith Fetterley, Leslie Mitchner, and Elaine Showalter, my colleagues on the American Women Writers series. Elaine's superb work in feminist scholarship has long served as a guiding example. Leslie's imaginative, flexible, and humane editorial style has greatly facilitated my work. Judith provided incisive editorial insight and invaluable personal support for this project. As always, she has been both friend and inspiration.

"I HAVE ALWAYS tried to please the multitude and satisfy the cultured," Emma D. E. N. Southworth wrote to her good friend and publisher Robert Bonner toward the end of her phenomenally successful career as a popular novelist. "I know that I number among my readers some professors of colleges, ministers of the gospel, and senators on the one hand—School boys and girls and little street gamins on the other—& a vast multitude between" (PL, 24 Mar. 1887). And "please the multitude" Southworth did indeed. Beginning in 1846 she published regularly in newspapers and story journals. Her book publications number about sixty (republication of some novels under new titles confuses the count). And the enterprising Bonner, editor of the *New York Ledger,* the best-known of the popular story journals, had her under exclusive contract for over thirty years. Although her success in "satisfying the cultured" is more problematic, depending largely on who is defining "culture" and deciding who has it, Southworth had no mean reputation in her day. Her books were read cross-culturally and enjoyed as much for their moral overtones as for their energetic characters and lively adventures. Among her literary friends she counted such well-known and respected writers as Harriet Beecher Stowe and John Greenleaf Whittier.

Like others of her female contemporaries, however, Southworth has failed to satisfy the cultured of our day, and, until very recently, has appeared in the modern literary arena only as the butt for such dismissive epithets as Herbert Smith's designation of her work as "the veritable archetype of the sentimental." "Perhaps an enlightened readership

grows up, sighing," he elaborates, "by weaning itself from the bathos of
E. D. E. N. Southworth to cut its teeth on the irony and psychology of
Henry James" (19). The fallacies here are widespread in much twentieth-
century literary analysis of nineteenth-century women writers. Critics influenced by the precepts of modernist literature tend to favor exclusively a
literature that *is* ironic and psychological over one possessing other time-
honored qualities of the novel, such as adventure, romance, broad comedy,
and—yes—even sentiment. Further, they tend to reduce to one characteristic a body of fiction which, when viewed in its cultural context, can be
seen, like Southworth's, to be complex.

With Southworth, as with many of her female contemporaries, the
question of literary quality arises immediately. "But is it any good?" is
the first question, Jane Tompkins reminds us, elicited by any mention of
the long forgotten texts of nineteenth-century women writers (ch. 7). Let
me make it clear from the start: Southworth was not Henry James, nor
would she have had any desire to be. She had neither the inclination
nor the privilege. Her forte was not the mastery of stylistics nor the
subtle delineation of human complexities. Rather, it was storytelling.
She was a popular novelist of skill and endurance, whose strength lay in her
ability to render cultural fantasies vividly, in all their fascinating and self-
contradictory complexity. Her strengths and weaknesses had a common
derivation in her desire—in fact pressing need—to please the multitude;
her popularity was literally her bread and butter. Southworth's attempts
to satisfy the cultured, if by cultured we mean the literary elite, are practi-
cally inconsequential in any long-range assessment of the significance of
her work.

In *The Hidden Hand* (first serialized in 1859) Southworth is at her
satiric best: a brilliantly comedic popular analyst of cultural stereotypes
and expectations. In certain other novels, particularly the early ones, she,
in a less light-hearted manner, adeptly and energetically manipulates those
same stereotypes and expectations, particularly as they relate to the
stunted and deprived lives of women, to create an idiosyncratic and still
fascinating melodramatic literary universe. She peoples her novels with
displaced and abused women. As her titles envision them, her female protagonists are deserted wives, discarded daughters, lost heiresses, missing
brides. Displaced and abused as they are, however, these women are for
the most part strong, or able to learn strength. Although Southworth's
advocacy for women certainly has feminist implications for modern readers, her books did not campaign for the rights of women in the openly and

publicly political manner we usually define as feminist. Rather she felt and recorded a deep personal sense of outrage at the oppressions and deprivations of her own life and the lives of the women she saw around her. Her desire to advocate a dignified humanity for women found expression in a fictional arena that did not aspire to literary realism, as we now define that term, but instead reveled in the innumerable imaginative possibilities made available by an overtly fictive universe.

Such an approach has its pitfalls, however. In Southworth's later work her repeated use of conventional depictions of women for the most part came to lack the vitality—the color and fire—of her early novels. As she grew older, more conventionally religious, and less outraged, she looked back on her earlier, more passionate novels with something like embarrassment. In her seventies she wrote to her daughter Lottie about a visit from a Professor Powers: "He told me the first book he ever read was my 'Deserted Wife' which his father a Babtist [sic] minister brought him from Washington. I told him it was a wild story, the work of my younger days. . . . I told him I thought more of my failures in fidelity to the gift and the giver than I did of success" (LOC 27 May 1892).

It is for those "wild stories," however, that we are indebted to Southworth. For if they do not give us a precise and realistic image of women's actual lives in society, they do provide us with a vigorous sense of women's feelings about their existence, and with delightful examples of just what kind of compensatory fantasies served to ease their sense of displacement and loss. Of these fantasies, the heroine of The Hidden Hand, Capitola Le Noir, otherwise known as Cap Black, is the most enticing.

An irreverent ruffian in her early teens, Cap describes herself as "a damsel-errant in quest of adventures." Kidnapped as an infant, Cap has spent her childhood years in Rag Alley, a New York City slum, and her early adolescence in fending for herself on the streets. When her guardian finds her there, she is disguised as a boy, selling newspapers and running odd jobs. Cap has been countersocialized, having, like a street boy, "never been taught obedience or been accustomed to subordination." After she is "rescued" and taken back to her ancestral Virginia, she finds a conventional woman's life stultifying: she is "bored to death" she says "decomposing above ground for want of having my blood stirred." So Cap goes out, as the respectable female reader might long to do but could not, "in search of adventures." Needless to say, the little adventurer finds herself involved in many escapades. She rescues damsels in distress, captures bandits, fights duels, all with insouciance and style.

With her street smarts, irreverence, and pluck, Capitola captivated the popular imagination. The novel was published at full length, by popular demand, three times in the *Ledger* between 1859 and 1883, and was dramatized in forty versions which played internationally. Its eventual book publication in 1888, with the subtitle "Capitola the Madcap," came after years of requests from book publishers for publication rights. Cap is a delightfully irresistible gender-switcher. With the critique of conventional gender definitions implicit in her creation, she fascinated both male and female readers; the *Ledger* was popular with both. She must have appealed, however, particularly to women, for Cap took up her sword and attacked that great humbug that limited their lives—the cultural ethos of feminine "obedience" and "subordination."

EMMA DOROTHY ELIZA NEVITTE SOUTHWORTH lived a life, if not so exciting as Capitola's, in some ways as melodramatic as that of many of her other protagonists. Born in Washington, D.C., on December 26, 1819, Emma was the first child of Captain Charles Le Compte Nevitte, a merchant from Alexandria, Virginia, and Susannah Wailes of St. Mary's County, Maryland. At the time of their marriage, Emma's mother was 15 years old and her father was 45. Although she leaves no record that her parents' marriage was not happy, disparity in age between husband and wife was a situation Southworth often passionately deplored in her novels. Susannah was so young at the time of her marriage that she "could not well be separated" from her mother, and the newly-weds moved into a house on New Jersey Avenue which they shared with her. Emma remembered her grandmother far more than her mother as the dearest friend of her childhood.[1]

That childhood, however, was not a happy memory for the writer. "I was a child of sorrow from the very first year of my life," she said, introducing herself in an autobiographical sketch with as much of a flourish as if she *had* been a character in one of her own novels. "Thin and dark, I had no beauty except a pair of large, wild eyes." The young Emma suffered an eye inflammation from the age of twelve months to three years, which resulted in a temporary loss of vision. At other times, she recalled, she saw the world "through a dim, mysterious 'cathedral light,' in which every object . . . looked larger, vaguer, and more distant and imposing that it really was" (John Hart 211). This period of disturbed sight may well have been a determining factor in the sense of isolation Emma experienced throughout her childhood. A solitary, dreamy child, she felt herself to be "a weird little elf" scorned and neglected by her family, who favored (understandably, she thought) her younger sister Charlotte.

When Emma was four years old, her father, whom she loved deeply, died. She and her sister were baptized into Roman Catholicism at his deathbed, and her last memory of her father was of his laying "his dying hands upon our heads and [blessing] us." Her father's death sent the sensitive child into a state of depression. "For months and even years after, I ruminated on life, death, heaven, and hell, with a painful intensity of thought, impossible to describe" (John Hart 212).

Although her mother's family had been wealthy and her father seemed to have had quite a profitable business at one time, Emma was initiated by his death into the rigors of financial hardship that would plague her for many years. The family of women—the young mother, the grandmother, and the two girls—were left unsupported in an era that offered no employment for middle-class women. On the grandmother's small income they lived frugally in an elegant house that had been rented on a long-term lease by Emma's father, while the grandmother attempted to run a select boarding house. Being "a lady of the lofty old school, [she] never could learn to present a bill" (John Hart 213), and this attempt at self-sufficiency failed.

When Emma was six, her mother married Joshua L. Henshaw of Boston. This second marriage marked a period of profound unhappiness for both Southworth children. Although Emma never detailed Henshaw's mistreatment in any public report, her letters to her daughter Lottie tell of dispossession and actual neglect:

> If they [her own grandchildren] knew what a sad time I and my Sister Charlotte had when we were children[,] how forlorn we were, and how we suffered for everything—though our father left us a large and handsomely furnished house, we would be left to play in a freezing garret and driven away from the fire in the parlor, and never allowed to come to the table until every body else had done & there was very little left for us, hardly ever having a kind word given to us. (LOC, undated letter)

Henshaw, who had been secretary to Daniel Webster, turned to teaching, opening a school in which he and his wife both taught. There Emma, whose emotional deprivation had resulted in an introverted and abstracted personality, "first discovered that she possessed some mental power." She soon became head scholar in her class and developed into an ardent reader, "reading every book of every sort that she could lay her hands on" (*Homestead* 35). Her active imagination was further nourished by long talks with the family's black servants, whose ghost stories, legends, and tales of the family's wealthy past absorbed her attention. Frequent visits to her mother's home country, St. Mary's County, gave her an enduring love for and fascination with the wooded, mountainous countryside of Maryland and Virginia, and she later set many of her novels in that terrain.

At the age of sixteen Emma graduated from her stepfather's school and began a career as a schoolteacher. At twenty-one she married and moved to Wisconsin with her new husband, Frederick Hamilton Southworth, an inventor from Utica, New York. Details of that marriage are sparse—she refused to comment publicly, and probably even privately. In a published autobiographical account she skimmed over those years with an evasive rhetorical maneuver: "Let me pass over in silence the stormy and disastrous days of my wretched girlhood and womanhood—days that stamped upon my brow of youth the furrows of fifty years—let me come at once to the time when I found myself broken in spirit, health, and purse—a widow in fate but not in fact—with my babes looking up to me for a support I could not give them" (John Hart 213). In personal reminiscences she was also evasive; at the age of seventy-five she wrote to her daughter: "I have never told you all about those days. But I will . . . " (LOC, 22 June 1895).

Whether she ever told Lottie the full story or not, we can piece together enough information to know that Southworth returned from Prairie du Chien, Wisconsin, in 1844, pregnant, and with a small, sickly child in hand. Whether her husband was with her at that point or not is not known. Although her grandmother attempted to aid her, her stepfather intervened and she was left, like many a character in her fiction, destitute:

> My one dear, dear, dear friend—my grandmother had been ruthlessly torn away from me. I had only little baby fingers wandering over my bosom and I so starved, that I had not milk enough for her. . . . Yes, there was my dear Mandy—my little 12 year old colored nurse, who used to go out into the woods at night and gather brush to make me a poor fire. . . . In those days I had not a shoe to my foot, except an old pair of india rubbers without shape or linings—"gums" they were called in those days. No fire except from brush Mandy could pick up in the woods. No cradle for my baby, no

rocking chair to rock her. Mr. Henshaw had broken up the only home I had left—my dear grandmother's home and I with my babies was thrown out. It was *then* that S. finally abandoned us and went to Brazil. *Grandmother had supported us until* her home was broken up, and S. had no mind for supporting wife or children. (LOC, 22 June 1895)

After her husband left, Southworth taught in the Washington public schools, a job for which she received about $250 a year, her principal income. It was at this time that she started writing short pieces for newspapers, particularly for the *National Era.* The triple role of mother, teacher, and writer overwhelmed her. She had sole charge of the eighty pupils in her school, her son Richmond was seriously ill, and her salary was inadequate for support of the family:

[M]y time was passed between my housekeeping, my school-keeping, my child's sick-bed, and my literary labours. . . . It was too much for me. It was too much for any human being. My health broke down. I was attacked with frequent hemorrhage of the lungs. Still I persevered. I did my best by my house, my school, my sick child, and my publisher. Yet neither child, nor school, nor publisher received justice. (John Hart 214)

Southworth's literary career had begun during the Christmas season in 1845 when she wrote "The Irish Refugee." This story was published in the *Baltimore Saturday Visitor,* and her second tale in the *National Era.* Her first full-length novel, *Retribution,* was published in the *Era* in 1849, and shortly thereafter in book form by Harper and Brothers in New York. Southworth was launched on a career that would prove her financial salvation. Her description of this initial success reveals in its heightened rhetoric how emotionally important her writing was to her, not as art, but as a profession that would allow her to live with dignity and autonomy in a world that otherwise made no provision for her:

Then my book, written in so much pain, published besides in a newspaper, and, withal, being the *first* work of an obscure and penniless author, was, contrary to all probabilities, accepted by the first publishing house in America, was published and (subsequently) noticed with high favour even by the cautious English reviews. Friends crowded around me—offers for contributions poured in upon me. And I, who six months before had been poor, ill, foresaken, slandered, *killed* by sorrow, privation, toil, and [friendlessness], found myself born as it were into a new life; found independence, sympathy, friendship, and honour, and an occupation in which I could delight. (John Hart 214–15)

Initially Southworth wrote for the *Era* and for the *Saturday Evening Post*. In 1856 she was approached by Robert Bonner with an offer she could not resist: "My own belief is that there is no female author either on this or the other side of the Atlantic, who can write so excellent a story" he told her (PL, 10 Oct. 1856). "*I want to secure all you write . . . and I am willing to pay you your own terms;* or *double as much, at least, as you have ever received from any other newspaper publisher*" (PL, 22 Oct. 1856). Thus began the generous contract with the *Ledger* that sustained Southworth throughout the next thirty years of her professional life. Until 1889 she wrote exclusively for the *Ledger,* providing weekly installments of her novels, which she later published in book form. Bonner was not only employer to Southworth, he served also as friend, advisor, and banker, and to her son Richmond he served as a father, even to the point of offering to buy him a substitute if he were drafted to fight in the Civil War. In 1869 she wrote, thanking Bonner for a Christmas bonus, and for much more.

The first day that you entered my little cottage was a day, *blessed beyond all the other days of my life.* I had some genius in popular writing; but not one bit of business tact. . . . When you came to my cottage, I was dying from the combined effect of overwork and under pay, of anxiety and of actual privation. . . .
[Y]ou came to me, and saved my life. (PL, 26 Dec. 1869)

The many letters from Southworth begging Bonner humbly for some financial favor or thanking him fervently for his generous gifts reveal the paternalistic nature of Bonner's patronage. Southworth most likely made a fortune for Bonner—the circulation of the *Ledger* is said to have doubled when she began to write for him. As a fairly conventional nineteenth-century woman, however, she was far more comfortable with a personal rather than a strictly commercial relationship and couched her financial dealings with him in the terms of friendship rather than of business.

Aside from Bonner, Southworth had many other friends. She was a gregarious and sociable woman. In Prospect Cottage, her home in Georgetown overlooking the Potomac, she hosted government officials, diplomats, and the elite of Washington society as well as writers and other intellectuals at regular Friday evening "conversations." It was with Southworth that Harriet Beecher Stowe stayed when she was in Washington negotiating with the *Era* for the publication of *Uncle Tom's Cabin;* John Greenleaf Whittier oftcn visited her there; and the Bonners sometimes came to stay. Occasionally Southworth found herself overwhelmed by her social life to the detriment of her writing. In March 1863 she wrote to Bonner that she had had "an avalanche of company," but that since Congress had adjourned and the city was quieter she hoped to be able to write more. "I require *solitude,*" she had told him earlier, "to nurse what little genius I have" (PL, 19 Aug. 1862).

Along with her many friendships, Southworth seems to have had for a long while, beginning in the early 1850s, a tender attachment to Henry Hardy, a fellow Washingtonian, a man she told Bonner was "as near Christian perfection as any human being could approach" (PL, 28 May 1862). The status of her marriage in the years after her desertion is hazy. While Southworth was in England between 1859 and 1862, Congress had passed, at Robert Bonner's urging, a Distict of Columbia divorce bill entitled "A Bill for the Relief of Emma Southworth." But with strict Christian rectitude she did not avail herself of it. "I suffered much rather than resort to divorce," she told her daughter in later years (LOC, 2 June 1895). Most likely she supported her husband financially to some degree. According to Southworth's biographer, Regis Boyle, Frederick Southworth was made owner of her story *Kathleen Vernon* as late as 1860 (7). But even while her husband was still alive—according to Boyle he died in Europe sometime in the early 1860s—Southworth seems to have maintained a close relationship with Henry Hardy, and her refusal to avail herself of the opportunity for divorce is still another indication of the conservative side of her multifaceted personality. In 1862, using language that suggests marriage had been a possibility, she wrote to Bonner from London that a permanent break with Hardy had occurred: "As for myself, I shall always remain as I am—E D E N Southworth. So you will never loose [sic] your contributor by her change of name" (PL, 28 May 1862). The wording of this letter is interesting. Southworth's name was a valuable commodity, and the note suggests that financial pragmatism, as well as Christian moralism or romantic disappointment, was on her mind as she made her decision not to divorce and remarry.

In spite of the distractions of a busy and complicated personal and social life, Southworth wrote prolifically. She considered her professional obligations sacred, often staying awake until very late at night to finish her weekly installment by the light of a kerosene lamp. At times she sent

Bonner from forty to sixty pages a week, and she habitually began a new novel as soon as the previous one was finished. Her dedication to her career sometimes seemed to pass the bounds of reason. She and her family were often sick, but she struggled to keep up her installments. In autumn of 1862 she wrote her publisher that she was ill, but expected to be well enough soon to take up her serial. When what she thought were mosquito bites turned out to be smallpox, she promised Bonner that even in this extremity she would not let him down: "The doctor says the disease is not yet at its height, I will therefore to-morrow dictate to my friend a sketch of the remainder of the plot. . . . [Y]ou can get some writer to enlarge on that part and write the story out to its proper length. It was not until this morning that I gave up all hope of finishing the story myself" (PL, 5 Oct. 1862). A week later, after having been desperately ill, she wrote again: "My face, hands and neck are all so frightfully scarred that I shall not be able to show myself for at least three months. . . . This confinement will not however interfere with my writing" (PL, 12 Oct. 1862).

Her husband's desertion forced Southworth far outside the conventional parameters of the domestic woman's sphere, initiating for her a life characterized by success and public acclaim, but also by hardship and personal conflict. At the height of her career she was said to be earning about $6,000 a year, but she maintained her income only by arduous and unceasing literary toil and at the cost of physical health, and ended her life in straitened financial circumstances with little to show for all her labors. She suffered from the weight, she told Bonner, of having had "the life long double burden of man and woman laid upon me" (PL, late 1875). In her letter to Lottie detailing the circumstances of Lottie's birth and her husband's desertion, Southworth concludes by saying "I do forgive but I cannot forget." What she forgave we cannot know for certain; what she did not *forget* is evident in the pages of her multitudinous novels: the hopeless, helpless experience of feminine destitution in a male-dominated society, and the strong resources of the self upon which a woman can draw to overcome even overwhelming odds. As Mary Kelley says, in spite of her reluctance to discuss her marriage and its break-up, "Southworth may have been telling her story to the world throughout her career" (263).

"AMONG ALL THE PEOPLE that I have met," Southworth told a Washington *Post* reporter in 1894, "and they have been very many, and among all the thousands that have written to me, I have never found one who has not read some of my books, and I have never heard of one" (2 Dec. 1894).

Introduction

Southworth was a popular writer in the most accurate sense of the word. Not only did her work find continual favor with an enormous popular audience, but she herself wrote from the vantage point of the people, always bearing in mind the presence of her audience and their desires and preferences. In 1863, when composing a novel more moralistic than her others, she informed her publisher that although she usually wrote for the popular taste, "in this I have a higher aim—popular good." She assured him, however, "I can easily return to my old style, if this should not please the millions" (PL). Conventional pieties, personal passions, and radical departures from gentility intermingle in Southworth's work with an almost confounding sincerity, reflecting not only the author's intimate involvement with the values of her society, but also the complexity and self-contradictions inherent in that culture. She played upon the emotions and fantasies of her audience so very skillfully because in many ways she was one of them. Not self-defined as an artist and not self-consciously transcendent of popular experience, she felt always a profound bond and empathy between herself and her readers. She knew what her audience wanted and she gave it to them. She was a crowd pleaser. If that epithet serves to damn her, she might gladly have considered herself among the damned.

Southworth was not simply a passive recorder of cultural complexities, however. While reflective of popular attitudes, she also reflected upon them. As a talented writer and a woman passionate about the injustices perpetrated upon women in a society that allowed them little other than symbolic power, she inevitably helped shape the popular perception of women's status. Through the skilled manipulation of masculine and feminine stereotypes in her writing, she revealed numerous irreconcilable elements packed within the complex and contradictory concept of gender. Her work focuses almost exclusively on gender and gender relations, and its phenomenal popularity is indicative of the ways in which a culture monitors and modifies itself in this as in other areas. Although I disagree with Alfred Habegger's assertion that *The Hidden Hand* is Southworth's only good novel, his description of the "coherent politics" of this story as a "radicalism of the center, not the fringe" is precise and accurate ("Well-Hidden" 199, 201). Presenting a critique coming from within rather than imposed from without, Southworth bequeaths to us throughout her work a lively record of a nineteenth-century American fascination with the nature and possibilities of gender which enhances the hard data of the historical account.

Introduction

In an era characterized both by feminist agitation (Southworth's first novel was published in 1849, the year after the first Women's Rights Convention in Seneca Falls) and intensive cultural indoctrination regarding woman's exclusively moral nature, selflessness, and domestic inclinations, the popularity of Capitola, the "damsel-errant," points to just what it was about women that both titillated and terrified the American public. Cap was just one in a long line of powerful Southworth heroines, however. From the mousy to the magnificent, for over forty years Southworth's protagonists defined independence, integrity, and personal strength as central to a woman's existence, and these characteristics flourish with particular intensity in atmospheres specifically hostile to them.

Carl Kavanaugh, although a rough mountaineer, speaks for the majority of Southworth's less-than-perceptive male characters when he says in *The Curse of Clifton* (serialized in 1852; published in 1853): "I hate to see strength in women! It don't belong to them, nor grace them, anyhow!"[2] Yet his sister, Kate, the heroine of the novel, fascinates the aristocratic Captain Archer Clifton, even at the age of fourteen, with the rugged quality of her beauty:

> The broad and massive forehead, straight nose, and square, firm jaws, indicated great force of character. But her hair, eyes and lips were beautiful. Her hair, of rich dark brown, with golden lights, rippled around her forehead, shading and softening its stern strength. Her eyes, large and shadowy, with drooping lashes, and her lips sweetly curved, full, and pensively closed, suggested a profound depth of tenderness. (20)

Kate combines the conventional feminine beauties and affectional qualities with an unusual strength. It is this strength that attracts Clifton, although he persistently denies the nature of the attraction: "for the girl did not resemble a flower so much as a hardy pine sapling. No; that look, strength, intellect, and self-balance—in a word, that look of power . . . " (20). The fastidious Captain Clifton is, in spite of himself, captivated.

Woman's "power" is the theme that ties together Southworth's enormous oeuvre. From her first novel *Retribution* (1849), she presents an ongoing investigation of an extensive range of strengths and ambitions embodied in a glorious variorum of female characters. Although often polarized into good and evil characters, her women, especially in the early work, do not fit neat patterns. Larger-than-life characters such as the delightfully narcissistic "wild Irish girl" Britannia O'Riley and the amazonian Gertrude Lion, otherwise known as the "Gerfalcon," appear as early as Southworth's third book, *The Mother-in-Law* (serialized in 1850; published in 1851). The women occasionally have a mythic aura; Gertrude is described as having "the majesty of Juno and the freedom of Diana."[3] The feminist Britomarte Conyers "the man hater, the woman's champion, the marriage renouncer . . . magnificent in the sense of conscious strength, ardor and energy with which she impressed all" is the product of Southworth's later imagination in *Fair Play* (1868) and *How He Won Her* (1869). These works, originally published serially in 1865–66 under the title of "Britomarte, The Man Hater," are the two-volume saga of a woman who, "if law and custom had allowed her freer action and a fairer field, . . . would have influenced the progress of humanity and filled a place in history."[4]

More typical are the less flamboyant but nonetheless powerful heroines created in the conventional, altruistic mode. The plain and mild Hester Dent in *Retribution* is a young woman with an abiding sense of integrity and responsibility, whose primary concern, even in the face of death, is the manumission of her slaves. *The Mother-in-Law* continues what is to be an enduring mode of feminine characterization with the unselfish Susan Somerville, introduced as a young woman who "calmly and deeply enjoyed her life in every vein" (59). Susan comforts and supports Louis Stuart-Gordon, the man she deeply loves, through a number of traumatic experiences, even though he is divorced (temporarily as it turns out) from a woman whom he desperately loves. Betrothed to him at last, Susan renounces her claim magnanimously when she realizes Louis still loves his lost wife.

Malevolent women characters also abound. *Retribution* investigates a beautiful woman's abuse of her sexual attractiveness. The first step in the megalomaniacal career of the ambitious Julliette Summers is to steal Hester Dent's husband. Years later, having become the powerful mistress of a grand duke, she ends her life beheaded in a European coup d'état. For Southworth, the possession and use of power is not inappropriate for women; it is the abuse of power she deplores, particularly as it deprives others of the exercise of free will. In *The Mother-in-Law* she investigates the disastrous effects of a domineering woman's attempts to "gain a life-long ascendancy over the heart and mind of [her daughter]" and force "absolute subjection to her will" (38). Southworth's concern is with the negation of self brought about by a radical and unthinking obedience. The daughter, Louise Armstrong, becomes something less than human in her automated

Introduction

obedience to her mother's will and is immobilized by her mother's power. As a good friend tells her, she has been "confined and fettered so long, that you have lost the use of yourself" (352).

Southworth's enduring concern is the fettering of individuality, and such tampering with personal freedom provides the locus of evil not only for female but for male characters. *The Deserted Wife,* Southworth's second novel (serialized in 1849; published in 1850), is a close study of the deliberate, calculated attempt of a man to destroy the independence of a high-spirited, passionate woman by marrying her and using her love for him to bring her to a state of humiliation and dependency. "I wish you joy of your automaton!",[5] snaps Hagar Churchill to her new husband, Raymond Withers, who induces a wifely "docility" that, as her comment suggests, is neither profound nor permanent.

Although Southworth did become more conventional as she grew older, she did not forget her theme of woman's power and superiority. Her favorite work was *Ishmael* (serialized in 1863–64 as "Self-Made, or Out of the Depths"), an investigation of what she saw as the ideal masculine character. The memory of his dead mother and his reverence for women provide motivation for Ishmael and characterize his life and great public success. And the femininity of Ishmael's character is stressed; he is pious, altruistic, and emotional, and these are obviously qualities Southworth feels men need to learn from women.

Along with her challenge to restrictive roles for women, Southworth is also interesting for her treatment of black characters. An abolitionist and ardent supporter of the Union during the Civil War, she is nonetheless a Southern writer. Most of her novels are set in the South and they contain many black characters, enslaved and free. Unlike most of her Northern contemporaries, Southworth was well acquainted with black men and women. She is not free from the limiting prejudices of her era however. Many of Southworth's black characters are stereotyped in ways offensive to modern readers, and she also partakes of contemporary notions about Jews. In reading her novels, however, one realizes that her mode of characterization is by and large engendered by stereotype. The vast majority of her characters, male and female, black and white, are stock characters straight from the cultural repertoire. The obsequious manservant Wool and the superstitious maidservant Pitapat in *The Hidden Hand,* for instance, are pure, unredeemed cultural schlock, as is the old Jewish pawnbroker who buys Cap's dresses and ringlets when she decides to "become a boy."[6]

With them, as with other black and ethnic characters, she attempts humor through the standard means of humorous names, exaggerated dialect, mispronunciations (Pitapat persistently calls Capitola Miss Caterpillar), facial contortions, and allusion to stereotyped personality traits. These are effects she uses with other minor characters as well; the white house-keeper's name, for instance, is Mrs. Condiment, and she is a tremulous, fainthearted parody of swooning feminine servility.

Southworth's mastery of stereotype allows her—although with race not as often as with gender—subtle and sophisticated manipulations designed to reveal the absurdity of cultural assumptions. In *The Hidden Hand* she twice mocks the contemporary bogeyman of the vicious runaway slave. Out riding alone, against her guardian's explicit orders, Cap meets a sinister fellow—a sinister *white* fellow—with rapacious intentions and disarms him by ingenuously pandering to conventional prejudices; with feigned wide-eyed innocence she pretends to welcome his presence as protection against "runaway negroes and wild beasts." Later when her imperious guardian himself returns from a ride alone, she returns his obsessive worries with a mock scolding in his own idiom: "Didn't you know the jeopardy you placed yourself in riding out alone at this hour? Suppose three or four great runaway negresses had sprung out of the bushes and—and—and—." Here she clearly mocks the culturally pervasive and politically powerful stereotype of the oversexed black male and the helpless Southern belle by reversing the situation to reveal its true nature as an absurd myth of oppression.

As always with Southworth what surprises, delights, and instructs is the redeemed stereotype. To offset Wool and Pitapat, we find such black characters as the proud and self-sufficient Jem Morris in *Ishmael* and *Self-Raised*, the tragic, knowledge-starved Anna in *The Mother-in-Law*, the brilliantly talented singer Erminie in *Retribution*, and the merciful midwife, Nancy Grewell, whose compassion and care save the life of the infant Cap. Further, Southworth's matter-of-fact presentation of the marriage of an attractive interracial couple in *Retribution* displays a strikingly liberal attitude toward intermarriage. Although Southworth does partake in certain ways of the pervasive racism of her era, those black characters who do transcend the realm of the conventional reveal an individuality and authorial warmth congruent with that of her friend Harriet Beecher Stowe and rare among her contemporaries. Southworth's dedication to individual self-realization, especially for women, is a dynamic that overrides all obstacles and gives her a vision of individual freedom at times strangely at odds with the cultural limitations motivating her imagination in other ways.

The readers of E. D. E. N. Southworth, especially in the early years when her writing was at its liveliest, were numerous but not unanimously approving. Many felt a disquieting sense of anxiety about her idiosyncratic vision of life. Although her contemporaries—such as the influential editor of *Godey's Lady's Book,* Sarah Josepha Hale—praised her for her passion and imaginative prowess, some—including Hale herself—were also rendered uneasy by the bold energy of Southworth's depictions of human behavior. Hale accused her of a "freedom of expression that almost borders on impiety," and "an enthusiasm for depicting character as it is actually found . . . beyond the limits prescribed by correct taste or good judgment" (John Hart 215). Henry Peterson, her editor at the *Saturday Evening Post* in the 1850s, chastized her repeatedly for her literary freedom, urging her to "keep up the noble and Christian elements of the story," and to "avoid that vein I so much dislike and fear." "I stand between you and literary perdition," he warned (PL, 26 Dec. 1856). In an era that placed severe constraints particularly upon the expression of women and on the depiction of female characters (Baym, *Novels* ch. 5), Southworth crossed the invisible boundaries of a strict propriety time and again, depicting women, black and white, who challenge the ideals and the restraints placed upon them by the prevailing ethos of white, genteel womanhood.

A vision of feminine freedom empowered this hardworking woman, both in her life and in her imagination. Facing criticism of both the morality and the veracity of her tales, she insisted on the truth of that vision: "Every one of my books was based on incidents in life that I saw, even the most improbable of them. I could tell you stories, true ones, that I have never dared put in my books" (Washington *Post* 2 Dec. 1894). There are truths, she seems to tell us, and then there is truth. And in many of her novels the truth is of woman's integrity and defiance. For her, as for many of her readers, it was obviously a sustaining truth. "It was the saddest time of my life," Southworth tells us about the period during which she wrote *The Hidden Hand*. Her son was sick and her sister was dying. But her imagination focused on the figure of the dauntless Capitola. "'The Hidden Hand' was a true story, or partially true," she told an interviewer from the Washington *Post*. "Capitola was a true picture. Ah, I loved my work as I wrote that!" (2 Dec. 1894)

Introduction

IN 1857, AT THAT low ebb in her personal life, Southworth came across in a New York newspaper "a short paragraph in which it was stated that a little nine-year-old girl dressed in boy's clothing, and selling newspapers, had been arrested. She was homeless and friendless and was sent to some asylum in Westchester County" (LOC, obituary clipping). In that pathetic figure, gender and class mingled in such a way as to germinate in Southworth's mind the concept of an individual free from the usual constraints of cultural gender definitions, which are, of course, class bound as well as sex linked. Her imagination stripped this impoverished waif of the pathos of homelessness, envisioning her, instead, as "home-free"—both literally and idiomatically. Emblematic of a woman's potential, released of the burdens of domesticity and its attendant personal obligations and renunciations, to live freely and self-reliantly, Capitola was also "safe" in the gender game of life.

In *The Hidden Hand,* through a conscious and canny manipulation of cultural stereotypes of the masculine and feminine, Southworth presents a sweeping critique of the limiting nature of codified gender roles. Exaggeration, distortion, reversal: these comic strategies are the weapons in her literary arsenal, and aiming at ideals of masterful masculine dominance and sentimental feminine submission, Southworth fires with unrestrained exuberance. It is not through a polished and sophisticated literary style that Southworth's novel succeeds; while at times witty and engaging, the prose of *The Hidden Hand* more often relies on stock phrases and exaggerated descriptive vocabulary. Neither is Southworth's forte the regionalist realism of some of her sister writers. Instead, she relies on a mastery of storytelling. And, ironically, the success of *The Hidden Hand* lies in the author's conscious and maximized exploitation of those aspects of fiction generally perceived by modern critics to be weaknesses rather than strengths. With a lavish hand she employs conventional plot lines (relying often on startling coincidences for resolution), heavy-handed symbolism (exotic birthmarks, for instance, and descriptive names), and, most particularly, well-defined, easily recognized stereotypes. Part of the popular idiom, these conventional literary elements offered Southworth instantly recognizable vehicles of communication with which to reach and manipulate her numerous readers. Also, they provided a means of reminding both author and reader that they too were "safe" in this exploration of gender possibilities, because the realm in which they were operating was a purely literary one.

In a manifestly fictional universe anything can happen. In such a universe, one that flaunts its fictiveness with a farcical combination of adventure, Gothic melodrama and sentimentality, Southworth grants herself the imaginative space to address the most tabooed subjects. Couched within a humorous idiom—intended to disarm criticism as well as to heighten her critique—is a message of the highest seriousness. Southworth concentrates on the trivialization of women, and *The Hidden Hand* attacks with ridicule a gender ethos that implicitly suggests women are at the disposal of the men who have authority over them. On the one hand Southworth presents Capitola, a model of female autonomy; on the other she shows incarceration, desperation, and sexual oppression as the logical extensions of ideal sentimental feminine docility.

"Cap isn't *sentimental,*" explains her guardian, old Major Ira Warfield (otherwise known as Old Hurricane), to the Rev. Mr. Goodwin, a minister to whom he applies for advice on taming this little hellion he has taken under his wing. "[A]nd if *I* try to be," he continues, "she laughs in my face!" (ch. XXIV) When Southworth conceived Capitola and told her tale in the widely circulated pages of the New York *Ledger,* she was writing at a time when the majority of female literary characters *were* "sentimental"— that is, they were embodiments of the dominant culture's attempt to shape and restrict woman's sphere of activity by defining her as narrowly "moral" in essence, exclusively emotional in constitution, and innately domestic in inclination. As Maria McIntosh stated it in *Woman in America* (1850), woman was to rule "in the little realm of home, our legitimate domain, in the spirit of wisdom and of love" (Baym, *Woman's Fiction* 97). Southworth did not reject this ideology; in fact, she had, in many ways, the utmost respect for it. But she detested the trivialization and exploitation of women which were in actuality a concomitant part of their ideological exaltation. In her creation of Capitola Le Noir—tomboy, adventurer, hero, on the one hand, and fascinating, sexually attractive woman, on the other—Southworth too is laughing in the face of authority. In Cap she skillfully evokes and at the same time reverses the conventions of the sentimental heroine. With doubled effect she taps into a potent cultural mythology, sketching the familiar outlines of the paradigm and simultaneously embodying in that sketch the unique energies of a woman who could not be more unlike her fictional contemporaries.

Ellen Montgomery, in particular would have been known to Southworth. Ellen is the protagonist of Susan Warner's *The Wide, Wide World* (1850), a brilliant and perverse domestic melodrama generally considered to be the first best seller in America. Ellen, the most popular sentimental heroine of her era, is very much the ideal woman of the cultural dream: disposed of by a callous father, she is left to the mercy of strangers and through hardship and the teaching of Christian friends learns to accept passively what life offers her—particularly the manly guidance of the Rev. John Humphries, her future husband—and to leave behind all feelings of rebellion and discontent. Cap, variously described as a "little Napoleon in petticoats," a "hero," a "Tartar," a "damsel-errant," is the direct inverse of this ideal. When left on her own, she does not look to others for help, but, rather, cares for herself. She is far from being subject in any way to the "moral suasion" the Rev. Mr. Goodwin recommends to Major Warfield; instead she plays a sly little joke on the reverend gentleman, leading him to believe she has a lover secreted in her closet, when in reality there is no one there but a neighbor's poodle. Also, she is far from being satisfied with the limited domestic role. In the peace and comfort of her guardian's luxurious home she complains, "Nothing ever happens here! The silence deafens me! the plenty takes away my appetite! the safety makes me low!" (ch. XXIV).

In important ways Capitola nonetheless conforms to the conventional pattern for female protagonists of the era; an abandoned female child, she dwells in the home of a narrow-minded, restrictive guardian, and the narrative takes her from early adolescence to the conventional closure of marriage (Baym, *Woman's Fiction* 11–12). Southworth refers to conventional narratives here only to complicate and subvert the ideology they support, however. In the creation of her protagonist, Southworth makes reference to the paradigmatic Ellen Montgomery. Like Ellen, Cap is not sent to school, is forbidden to ride alone, has a dangerous adventure involving a lonely spot, a sinister man, and a horse, and purchases identical feminine accouterments: a dressing case, a workbox, and a writing desk. Southworth does nod at conventionality: once Cap wanders through the house looking for something to mend; once she lines a pair of slippers. When a young girl is described as having been born "squalling like a wildcat," however, she is guaranteed never to grow up to be yet another model of pious, domestic, sentimental womanhood. Other women in the novel serve as paradigms of feminine virtue. In creating Cap, Southworth turns Ellen Montgomery on her head, and if in so doing she allows the reader to see past the petticoats and glimpse the saucy knickers, well, so much the better.

Capitola's freedom of spirit is directly associated with her upbringing outside the boundaries of middle-class society and of gender expectations, an implicit recognition of the stultifying effects upon women of conventional socialization. As a white child raised by a black laundress in the slums of New York City, as a girl who spends her early adolescence disguised as a boy, Cap has achieved a unique sense of herself and her possibilities. Whereas the docility of other, more genteel, women in the novel leads them to victimization at the hands of the masculine villains of the story, Cap triumphs over all: "From childhood she had been inured to danger, and had never suffered harm; therefore, Cap, like the Chevalier Bayard, was 'without fear and without reproach'" (ch. XLV).

Pierre Terrail, seigneur de Bayard, was an heroic and legendary French soldier of the fifteenth century, and Southworth's mention of him here alludes to a masculine realm of legend, adventure, and heroism. Like a hero of romance Cap is identified as heir to a vast domain by her exotic birthmark: a miniature scarlet hand she bears in the palm of her own left hand. In Southworth's equation of Cap with heroic figures of legend and romance we see one aspect of the skillful manipulation and complication of genre. By placing an heroic protagonist, an adventurer who owes much to the masculine heroes of Walter Scott and Alexandre Dumas, in a feminine sentimental framework, Southworth challenges the limits of genre and stretches imaginative boundaries. The politics of this maneuver are clear: the lives of women are perceived as being as potentially self-reliant and exciting as that of even the most heroic man. Further, Cap not only looks backward to a masculine tradition of the past. Southworth in her creation of Capitola is also very much aware of a contemporary masculine democratic ideal—that of the American "rough," as Walt Whitman had labeled his swaggering poetic persona. And, as Alfred Habegger notes, Cap clearly anticipates the quixotic American heroism of Huckleberry Finn ("Well-Hidden" 201).

Despite allusions to masculine ideals, Cap's childhood is presented, nonetheless, as a parodic intensification of the girlhood hardships of other sentimental heroines, and those hardships are greatly exaggerated. While Ellen Montgomery is sent to a vulgar aunt by an uncaring father, and, further, because of his carelessness, has to travel on a steamboat in October *without her gloves,* Cap is kidnapped at birth by an evil uncle, sold into slavery, shipwrecked, raised in abject poverty, and abandoned in the slums. The patent improbability of these circumstances serves to alert readers that this is not a realistic fiction but, rather, a fantastic universe where the elements of story—of feminine sentiment, of masculine adventure—are primary, taking on a life of their own, and certainly taking precedence over the rigid probabilities of "real life." Yet the novel makes use of its detachment from reality to tell a tale whose underlying truth could not be told so vividly in a realistic mode.

The circumstances of Capitola's early years introduce the major theme of the novel and it is a serious one: the trivialization not only of woman's autonomy, but of woman's very existence, by men. Everyone assumes Cap can be disposed of at will. Her "kidnapping" is really just a benign accidental byproduct of a far worse fate—her uncle Gabriel Le Noir has planned to murder her at birth. At her mother's urging, the black midwife who attends her birth sequesters the infant Cap under her shawl and shows the wicked uncle the body of her still-born brother. The bandit Black Donald, Le Noir's collaborator, is not fooled, but, for profit, sells the midwife and child into slavery. Years later he professes to regret it: "It is so much easier to pinch a baby's nose until it falls asleep, than to stifle a young girl's shrieks and cries" (ch. XXI). In any case, he shows here no hesitation about "stifling" the life of this girl. On their way South, Cap and Nancy Grewell, the midwife, escape drowning in a shipwreck only because they are considered too inconsequential to be saved and are not taken into the lifeboat, which is later swamped. Cap, however, as she asserts over and over again, learns to take care of herself. She is not a disposable woman. Other women, traditionally socialized to obedient passivity, are not so fortunate. They are exploited economically and sexually: deprived of their rightful fortunes, locked in deserted houses, incarcerated in madhouses, abandoned to poverty, threatened with loveless marriages and with rape, all at the will of the men who control their lives.

An aberrant gender socialization, significantly, is Capitola's salvation. In order to survive the dangers facing a homeless waif in the New York of 1845, Cap switches sex. When we first see her at the age of thirteen, she is thriving on the streets. Disguised as a boy, she appears to be "crown prince and heir-apparent to the 'king of shreds and patches,'" but her countenance, is "full of fun, frolic, spirit and courage" (ch. IV). She has learned to live from hand to mouth with the confidence born of autonomy, ability, and pride. Cap's masculine socialization—her education on the streets where she works as a newsboy—allows her to develop the saving characteristics of self-reliance, irreverence, and active, rather than passive, courage.

The motivations for her gender switch are complex, both economic and sexual. When her unofficial guardian, Nancy Grewell (whom Cap knows as Granny), finally saves enough money from her earnings as a laundress to return to Virginia with the intention of exposing the circumstances of Capitola's birth (as yet unknown to the young girl), she leaves Cap in Rag Alley with enough clothes and money to last her for the month she thinks she will be gone. The faithful old woman is long delayed by illness on her voyage and dies after telling her story to Major Warfield. Old Hurricane, who just happens to be Gabriel Le Noir's sworn enemy, then takes upon himself the task of finding Cap and caring for her. In the interim, however, Cap loses her home and is left in very precarious circumstances unprotected on the streets.

As a young girl in nineteenth-century New York Cap is unable to find work. Eventually arrested for the illicit act of saving her life by donning the vestments of masculine privilege, she explains to the Court Recorder her difficulties in finding work as a girl (ch. VI). In its thoroughness, Southworth's delineation of Cap's attempts to support herself stresses the absurdity of contemporary rationales for not employing females. Ingrained habits, false propriety, and a skewed sense of what constitutes masculine dignity combine to doom a healthy and ambitious young girl to death or social parasitism.

This indictment of the economic inequities of a gender-defined society is only one aspect of Southworth's understanding of the deadly dangers facing a female child unaligned with a male protector. As well as starvation and beggary, the pubescent Cap also faces constant sexual peril, and it is this that finally drives her to gender disguise. As she further, and reluctantly, tells the court, she was forced to sleep on the streets:

> "That was a dreadful exposure for a young girl," said the Recorder.
>
> A burning blush flamed up over the young creature's cheek, as she answered:
>
> "Yes, sir, that was the worst of all; that finally drove me to putting on boy's clothes."
>
> "Let us hear all about it."
>
> "Oh, sir, I can't—I—how can I? Well, being always exposed, sleeping out-doors, I was often in danger from bad boys and bad men," said Capitola, and, dropping her head upon her breast, and covering her crimson cheeks with her hands, for the first time she burst into tears and sobbed aloud.
>
> "Come, come, my little man!—my good little *woman,* I mean—don't take it so to heart! You couldn't help it!" said Old Hurricane, with raindrops glittering even in his own stormy eyes.

Introduction

Capitola looked up with her whole countenance flashing with spirit, and exclaimed, "Oh! but I took care of myself, sir! I did, indeed, your honor! You musn't, either you or the old gentleman, dare to think but what I did."

"Oh, of course! of course!" said a bystander, laughing. (ch. VI)

Stressing the prurient interest of Cap's auditors—the fascinated "Let us hear all about it" of the recorder as well as the cynical mockery of the bystander—Southworth suggests that women are twice violated: once in the actual experience of sexual harassment and then again in the recounting of that experience. Everyone assumes the worst, even Old Hurricane, in whose quick forgiveness lies implicit the assumption of female powerlessness in the face of masculine rapacity. But Cap will allow no one to think she is less than virtuous; even if society has conspired in near irresistible ways to create yet another sexual victim, Cap has "taken care of herself" in this as in all other ways.

Capitola, even after she returns to "respectable" society, does not forget the lessons she learned from her gender switch. Refusing to knuckle under to the benign despotism of her new guardian she arouses his wrath over and over again. "You New York hurrah boy!" he fulminates upon one occasion. "you foundling! you vagabond! you vagrant! you brat! you beggar! will you never be a lady!" (ch. LX). And the answer is No. If to be a lady means to be a long suffering passive victim such as Marah Rocke, Old Hurricane's abandoned wife, and the heroine of the sentimental counterplot of the novel, Cap never will succumb. "Liberty," she says, "is too precious a thing to be exchanged for food and clothing" (ch. XXIV).

Southworth's concept of woman's nature displays the doubleness characteristic of much of the writing of conventional women of her era. While sincerely conforming to the precepts of her acculturation (precepts that, not coincidently, will win her personal and professional success), she is nonetheless drawn to a figure of fantasy directly opposed to both the forms and the essence of the ideal. Southworth does not discount the value of such conventional feminine traits as domesticity, self-sacrifice, and religious obedience. By presenting a number of admirable conforming women she seems to say these are admirable traits; they simply should not be taken to the lengths demanded by cultural extremists. Yet, there is something inordinately appealing to her about a girl who can respond breezily to an authoritarian ultimatum in the following mock-apologetic terms: "Sorry . . . not used to being ordered about and don't know how to

xxxiii

submit," and can then proceed gaily to do exactly as she pleases. The doubleness of Southworth's perception is manifested in *The Hidden Hand* in the easy coexistence of Capitola and the other white, middle-class female characters in the same fictional universe. These women serve as foils for Capitola: Marah, the abandoned wife; Clara Day, a young heiress who is the ward of the novel's omnipresent and stereotypically sinister villain, Gabriel Le Noir; and Cap's long-suffering mother, who is discovered at the end of the novel wrongfully incarcerated in a madhouse by, of course, Le Noir.

Southworth genuinely admires these noble women. In her portrayal of Marah, in particular, she delivers a cultural masterstroke. The character of Marah at once satisfies the popular longing for a conforming heroine, deflects criticism aimed at the naughtiness of the nonconforming protagonist, and, ultimately, and perhaps unconsciously on her author's part, creates an example of feminine behavior which, while culturally laudable, in contrast to Capitola seems passive to the point of masochism. Further, as the idealized passive female pawn, Marah provides opportunity for the exercise of what Southworth seems to see as inherently flawed masculine character. The majority of her male characters inadvertently or deliberately place women in situations of peril, displaying character traits ranging from simple insensitivity to pathological brutality. Marah, as a submissive woman, is sexually and economically vulnerable and is abused and exploited in ways that almost destroy her both by her husband, the irascible Major Warfield, and by the novel's villain, Gabriel Le Noir.

Marah is a generation older than Cap, and in her youth was married to the then middle-aged Major Warfield. Reminiscent of Ellen Montgomery's submission to the man who dominates her, Marah gives herself to her husband in "the most perfect self-abandonment to his will." In a fit of unwarranted jealousy, brought about by Gabriel Le Noir's sexual advances to Marah, which she of course rejects, Warfield abandons his young, pregnant bride. The destitute but proud Marah, because her "wifehood and motherhood" are not enough to win her the much-needed help of her wealthy husband, spurns the legal avenues open to her and chooses instead to raise her son in poverty. Marah's truly "womanly" life is characterized by physical deprivation and emotional desperation. According to the physician who comes to see her, she is "starving slowly and in every way! mind, soul and body!" (ch. XIV). Yet Southworth does not denigrate Marah Rocke; although more passive than the typical Southworth heroine, she is for Southworth a paradigmatic and admirable figure. The contrast with Capitola, who thrives in her independent, nonconforming self-reliance, is marked and intentional. Capitola, while admirable and adorable, is an acknowledged anomaly, however. Only her escape from feminine socialization—an escape not shared by her readers or her creator—allows her the peculiar freedom to be her full untrammeled self. Marah is emblematic of the norm, but, ultimately, her presence in the narrative along with that of Cap's mother, incarcerated in a madhouse, and Clara Day, sequestered against her will in Le Noir's isolated mansion, provides evidence of Southworth's understanding that women who accede blindly to conventional expectations will find themselves trivialized, exploited, and abused. While Southworth obviously adores her nonconforming heroine, her true real-life ideal would seem to be a conventional woman who adds to the domestic virtues the integrity and self-reliance of Capitola. "Be cool, firm and alert," says Cap to Clara, "and all will be well!" (ch. XXXIX).

The male characters in *The Hidden Hand* are not exclusively brutal. At one end of the spectrum of Southworth's imaginative perception of masculinity there is room for Dr. Day, the kindly physician who befriends Marah Rocke and gives her son Traverse a start on his medical education. There is room for Traverse, who in many ways is an adaptation of the best qualities of true womanhood to the masculine character. And there is room for Herbert Greyson, the noble young hero who, on the rare occasion when Cap actually needs help, shows up to provide it. These men are peripheral to the action of the novel, however. Southworth reserves her best comic shots for the men who cluster on the other end of the spectrum, and whose characteristics range from pathological selfishness to murderous villainy. The autocratic and chronically infuriated Major Warfield, the villainous Gabriel Le Noir and his bumbling lecherous son Craven, and the dreaded bandit Black Donald: these are the men whose actions shape the lives of the female characters and thus determine the flow of the narrative. Masculine rage, greed, and desire are the imperative forces of Southworth's fictional world, and it is against these that she pits Cap's autonomy and city savvy.

In her portrayal of these men, Southworth turns, literally with a vengeance, to stereotype: the bumptious oldster, the sinister villain, the dashing bandit. She works, to delicious effect, with stock characters, tapping into the underside of cultural notions about masculine nature. The wide dissemination of these figures within the culture indicates that, despite the prevailing notion of masculine superiority, strong suspicion existed in the popular mind that masculine character, unchecked by feminine influence or by Christian precepts, is imperious, rapacious, and greedy. Southworth's gleeful exaggeration of the stereotypes serves to highlight the grotesquery of a social system that puts unilateral power in the hands of such monsters.

The novel opens with an extended analysis of the hedonistic self-ishness of Major Ira Warfield, the retired army officer who becomes Cap's well-meaning but tyrannical guardian. He represents the masculine ideal of masterfulness gone amok. He is described initially as being of "arrogant mind, violent temper and domineering habits," and throughout referred to as a "despot," "a raging lion," and, in the first serialized version, "all Barnum's beasts in one." This is the man who has abandoned his wife because of unfounded suspicions about her fidelity, and has cast off his impoverished widowed sister because she chose to marry a man who "differed with me about the tariff and—the Trinity." Both of these women have children to care for, and Warfield's absolute power over domestic finances leaves them to suffer years of brutal hardship. Although Old Hurricane terrorizes all others who cross his path, Capitola refuses to knuckle under to his demands. Faced with a raging fury and the threat of a beating because she plans to attend a fair against his wishes, Cap disarms the old despot with fearless courage on the one hand, and mockery and humor on the other:

> "Uncle, in all the sorrows, shames and sufferings of my destitute childhood, no one ever dishonored my person with a blow; and if ever you should have the misfortune to forget your manhood so far as to strike me—" she paused, drew her breath hard between her set teeth, grew a shade whiter, while her dark eyes dilated until a white ring flamed around the iris.
>
> "Oh, you perilous witch, what then?" cried Old Hurricane, in dismay.
>
> "Why then," said Capitola, speaking in a low, deep, and measured tone, and keeping her gaze fixed upon his astonished face, "the—first—time—I—should—find—you—asleep—I—would—take—a—razor—and—"
>
> "Cut my throat! I feel you would you terrible termagant!" shuddered Old Hurricane.
>
> "Shave your beard off, smick, smack, smoove!" said Cap, bounding off and laughing merrily as she ran out of the room. (ch. XXV)

Introduction

Old Hurricane is easily subdued by Cap, and his arrogance, selfishness, and bluster moderate under her tuition to the point where the essential humanity of his nature is allowed to shine through, and he is given the opportunity to redeem himself and make up for past mistakes.

Gabriel Le Noir, however, is another matter. Although among his neighbors he is considered to be "a gentleman of irreproachable reputation, in good standing both in the church and in the county" (ch. XXIV), he is in actuality a cloak-swirling, mustache-twirling villain of the first order. A would-be murderer of babies and seducer of virtuous wives, he is also the jailer of both Cap's mother and Clara Day, and usurper of the vast fortune that by rights belongs to Capitola. This blackguard has no humanity. When he feels anything at all, aside from ambition, lust, and greed, it is merely a perverse remorse: "I repeat that I am tortured with remorse!" he tells his crony, Black Donald. "And for what do you suppose?—for those acts of self-preservation that fanatics and fools would stigmatize as crimes? No, my good fellow; but for one 'unacted crime!'" This "unacted crime" is his laxity in allowing the infant Capitola to slip through his fingers: "Donald—I was younger then than now. I—*shrank from bloodshed*," he says in a voice husky with regret (ch. XXI). This man's radical selfishness reinterprets society's moral code so that the crime of murder becomes for him simply an "act of self-preservation."

A more amusing villain is Le Noir's son, Craven, a lecherous fellow of twenty-six, who is "Craven by name and craven by nature." In her portrayal of Gabriel Le Noir, Southworth focuses on the economic exploitation of women; with Craven, the focus is sexual. "From the earliest days of manhood Craven Le Noir had been the votary of vice, which he called pleasure. Before reaching the age of twenty-five he had run the full course of dissipation, and found himself ruined in health, degraded in character and disgusted with life" (ch. XLV). Attracted by Capitola's "diablerie," this charmer develops a passion for her and resolves to "woo, win, and elope with, or forcibly abduct" her. Craven's attempts at "wooing" and "winning" are farcical, but Southworth's treatment of Craven's licentiousness is also serious. His first attempt at matrimony is a forced secret wedding with Clara Day, for whose fortune both he and his father lust. Comforting her with visions of legendary rapists, he assures his unwilling veiled bride, "You will forgive me this, my share in these proceedings after awhile, sweet Clara. The Sabine women did not love the Roman youths the less that they were forcibly made wives by them" (ch. XL). Clara is helpless in the hands of this villainous pair, and that makes their pursuit of her a deadly serious matter. But, what Craven doesn't know as he speaks these words is that underneath the veil is not Clara, but Cap, in yet another of her disguises. It is innocence and obedience that renders women helpless. Cap, who has known all along how to take care of herself turns masculine rapacity into sheer bedroom farce.

The bandit Black Donald (so named, according to local reputation, "for his black soul, black deeds, and . . . for his jet black hair and beard") provides a more interesting representation of masculine sexuality because he is a charming rogue, and Capitola is genuinely fascinated with him. Attraction is one thing, and victimization is another, however, and although Black Donald finally does manage to get into Capitola's bed, it is only at the cost to him of total incapacitation, and, as the pun would suggest, Cap isn't there.

In Chapter XLIX, Black Donald secretes himself in her bedroom one midnight and locks himself in with Cap with the intention of raping and abducting her. Never daunted, she feeds him supper from a tray, deliberately leading him to believe she was expecting another man. "Miss Black," he says, "I am afraid you are not good," and demands a kiss. "I won't!" replies Cap, "until you have done your supper and washed your face. Your beard is full of crumbs!" The scene is comic, but the situation isn't. Like Craven, Black Donald refuses to acknowledge women's sexual autonomy. As on the docks, and as with Craven, Cap refuses to be a sexual victim. "Now, my dear Cap," she tells herself, "if you don't look sharp your hour is come! Nothing on earth will save you, Cap, but your own wits! for if ever I saw mischief in any one's face, it is in that fellow's that is eating you up with his great eyes at the same time that he is laughing at you with his big mouth!"

While Donald undresses and tries to talk Cap into bed, she, admiring this dashing fellow and not wanting to harm him, tries to talk him into repentance. This is an hilarious and compelling scene. The secret to its appeal lies in reversed expectations, in the unsuspected power differential: Donald has the key, he has by far the greater size and strength, he is driven by passion, and he thinks he's got Capitola trapped. In actuality, however, what Cap knows, and what the reader knows, is that she has maneuvered him into a chair placed over the trapdoor that is the central feature of her bedroom. Beneath that door, she has been told, lies a bottomless pit, and she knows that she has the power at any moment to send Black Donald's soul, as she thinks, to eternal perdition. She gives Donald every chance to relent, but when it becomes necessary, does not hesitate to press the spring that sends him hurtling down. Even her strong attraction to this magnificent man is not enough to tempt her into the victim's role.

At 6 feet 8 inches, Black Donald is a stalwart, black-haired, black-bearded outlaw with a "noble and distinguished" air, who wins Cap's sincere admiration from the start. In Black Donald Cap finds her masculine counterpart: a vital, lawless, extraordinary presence whose energies and resourcefulness are boundless. "I *like* him!" says Cap, upon first being questioned about Donald. "I like men whose very names strike terror into the hearts of commonplace people!" (ch. XXII). About Black Donald's villainy we are never certain. Among the country folk he has a reputation as a rapist and murderer, "the awfulest villain that ever went unhung!" But when first in Capitola's presence, disguised as a peddler, he asks the assembled company if Black Donald "may not be so bad after all. Even the devil is not so black as he is painted," and the question is unresolved throughout the novel.

But if Black Donald's generic villainy remains unresolved, his parallels with Capitola are clear. "Our fates are evidently connected!" he says of her. Both are linked with the spirit of misrule, associated with the dark possibilities of human energies uncontrolled by social restraints: he is *Black* Donald; she is Capitola *Black*. Both are presented as shape shifters, winning their way by impersonation and disguise. Her birthmark, the badge of her identity, is the little crimson hand hidden in the palm of her left hand; she says to him at one point that, according to local gossip, *his* "hand is red . . . with crime." And her wedding day is scheduled, significantly enough, for the day of his execution.

Black Donald is present in the text as Cap's double—as a reinforcement of her own wild freedom and primal energy, and, to a slight degree, as a disquieting reminder of the potential for violence and licentiousness present in her own personality. The birthmark of the "hidden hand," from which the book derives its title, is symbolic of a female power that can at times approach a most unfeminine violence. Although Cap is reluctant to harm Donald, she does not flinch from sending him hurtling into bottomless darkness when it becomes necessary. Old Hurricane, when threatened with the razor immediately envisions her slitting his throat. And at one point Cap, in a wild fury at Craven, literally contemplates murder. Cap does not marry Donald; her "blackness" must be modified by a union with her lifelong friend Herbert *Grey*son. But, she does not forget him either.

Introduction

Rescued from the "pit" in Capitola's bedroom, which turns out to be in actuality nothing more terrifying than a dry cellar, Black Donald is condemned to hang for his crimes. On the eve of her wedding, Cap visits Donald in jail, leaving him her pony, the $1000 reward she received for his capture, and the tools he needs to set himself free.

In her vision of a woman free enough of the bonds of feminine decorum to be totally herself, Southworth must resort to the fantasy world made available by the conventions of popular fiction. In this world, although not in reality, Capitola can be at once "outlaw" and heiress. Cap's author knows that the doubleness of her representation offers a titillating vision to her wide reading public. Nowhere is her delight in that doubleness as insistent as in her occasional mock ingenuous "apologies" for the errant behavior of her unruly protagonist. "Reader, I do not defend, far less approve, poor Cap," she says, "I only tell her story and describe her as I have seen her, leaving her to your charitable interpretation" (ch. XVII).

And the audience *was* charitable. Constant demands for the story from the *Ledger*'s readers encouraged Bonner to reprint the serial in 1868 and again, in revised form designed to highlight the presence of Capitola, in 1883. After its first publication as a book in 1888, *The Hidden Hand* was in print well into the twentieth century. In addition, the dramatized version played to crowds in major cities across America. Even in London, which Southworth visited at the time of the initial publication of *The Hidden Hand,* she found Capitola to be the rage; boats and race horses were named after Cap and fashionable women wore "Capitola" hats.

That this pernicious imp so captivated the public imagination indicates that popular culture in the nineteenth century was not as monolithic as modern scholars have tended to think, and that the interests of those cultural arbiters who so narrowly defined woman's nature and role were not uniformly the interests of the populace at large. In the figure of impudent Capitola Le Noir we see clear indication that the dominant ideology of obedient, subordinate womanhood was not unmixed. By mining the popular mood and presenting an attractive and previously unarticulated alternative for the contemporary representation of women, Southworth inevitably influenced imaginative possibilities for gender definition. As much as if she had been a woman's rights activist, she was therefore influential in changing the possibilities of reality for women. A figment of public as well as private fantasy, Capitola represents a figure emergent in the popular imagination, one that was to eventuate as a component of the American flapper of the 1920s and strongly influence the image of the modern self-sufficient woman. To the popular mind the fantasy of a woman who "won't obey . . . except when she likes," who feels that "liberty is too precious a thing to be exchanged for food and clothing," had a healthy fascination. With canny insight into the cultural psyche, Southworth played that fascination for all it was worth.

¹ For information about Southworth's life I have drawn upon the following sources: the Southworth papers at the Library of Congress and at the William R. Perkins Library at Duke University; *Mrs. E. D. E. N. Southworth, Novelist,* a published Masters thesis by Regis Louise Boyle (1939); an autobiographical note in John Seely Hart's *Female Prose Writers of America* (1855), later republished with alterations as a biographical preface to a collection of Southworth's short stories, *The Haunted Homestead* (1860); and Mary Kelley's comprehensive study of nineteenth-century American women writers, *Private Woman, Public Stage.*

² (17). Quotations from *The Curse of Clifton* are taken from an undated reprint edition, Chicago: M. A. Donohue.

³ (142). Quotations from *The Mother-in-Law* are taken from an undated reprint edition, Philadelphia: T. B. Peterson and Bros.

⁴ This quotation from *Fair Play* (4) is taken from an undated reprint edition, New York: A. L. Burt.

⁵ (307). This quotation from *The Deserted Wife* is from an 1855 reprint edition, Philadelphia: T. B. Peterson.

⁶ In the first serialization of *The Hidden Hand,* the pawnbroker is referred to as "the old Jew." In 1883, when she revised the novel for its final serialization, Southworth rethought this designation and changed the character to "the old pawnbroker." The first book edition follows this change, but some later editions were set from the 1859 printing and retain the original.

SELECTED BIBLIOGRAPHY

Primary Sources

ARCHIVAL MATERIAL

The following abbreviations are used in the introduction to designate archival sources:

LOC   Southworth papers, Library of Congress
PL   Southworth papers, William R. Perkins Library, Duke University

WORKS BY EMMA D. E. N. SOUTHWORTH

Novels are listed in order of initial serial publication. Date of serialization precedes book publication data.

Retribution. 1849. New York: Harper and Bros., 1849.
The Deserted Wife. 1849. New York: D. Appleton, 1850.
The Mother-in-Law. 1849–50. New York: D. Appleton, 1851.
The Discarded Daughter. 1851–52. Philadelphia: A. Hart, 1852.
The Curse of Clifton. 1852. Philadelphia: A. Hart, 1853.
India. 1853 (as "Mark Sutherland"). Philadelphia: T. B. Peterson, 1855.
The Lost Heiress. 1853. Philadelphia: T. B. Peterson, 1854.
The Missing Bride. 1854 (as "Miriam the Avenger"). Philadelphia: T. B. Peterson, 1855.
Broken Pledges. 1855. Philadelphia: T. B. Peterson, 1891.
Vivia. 1856. Philadelphia: T. B. Peterson, 1857.
The Hidden Hand. 1859. New York: G. W. Dillingham, 1888.
The Haunted Homestead, and Other Nouvellettes. Philadelphia: T. B. Peterson, 1860.
Ishmael. 1863–64 (as "Self-Made"). Philadelphia: T. B. Peterson, 1876.
Self-Raised. 1863–64 (as "Self-Made"). Philadelphia: T. B. Peterson, 1876.

Fair Play. 1865−66 (as "Britomarte, the Man-Hater"). Philadelphia: T. B. Peterson, 1868.
How He Won Her. 1865−66 (as "Britomarte, the Man-Hater"). Philadelphia: T. B. Peterson, 1869.

WORKS CITED AND FURTHER READINGS

Readers should be aware that treatments of Southworth before the 1970s and the current wave of feminist literary history and criticism are unreliable, tending to consider her condescendingly and with lack of understanding. In general, the most accurate readings of both her life and her works are the more recent ones.

Baym, Nina. *Woman's Fiction: A Guide to Novels by and about Women in America, 1820−1870.* Ithaca: Cornell UP, 1978.
─────. *Novels, Readers, and Reviewers: Responses to Fiction in Antebellum America.* Ithaca: Cornell UP, 1984.
Boyle, Regis Louise. *Mrs. E. D. E. N. Southworth, Novelist.* Washington, D.C.: Catholic U of America P, 1939.
Brown, Herbert Ross. *The Sentimental Novel in America: 1789−1860.* Durham: Duke UP, 1940.
Cowie, Alexander. *The Rise of the American Novel.* New York: American Book Co., 1948.
Dobson, Joanne. "The Hidden Hand: Subversion of Cultural Ideology in Three Mid-Nineteenth-Century Women's Novels." *American Quarterly* 38 (1986): 223−42.
Habegger, Alfred. "A Well-Hidden Hand." *Novel* 14 (1981): 197−212.
─────. *Gender, Fantasy, and Realism in American Literature.* New York: Columbia UP, 1982.
Harris, Susan. "The House That Hagar Built: Houses and Heroines in E. D. E. N. Southworth's *The Deserted Wife.*" *Legacy* 4.2 (1987).
Hart, James D. *The Popular Book.* New York: Oxford UP, 1950.
Hart, John Seely. *Female Prose Writers of America.* 1851. Rpt. Philadelphia: E. H. Butler, 1855.
Kelley, Mary. *Private Woman, Public Stage: Literary Domesticity in Nineteenth-Century America.* New York: Oxford UP, 1984.

Selected Bibliography

Mott, Frank Luther. *Golden Multitudes: The Story of Best Sellers in the United States.* New York: Macmillan, 1947.

Papashvily, Helen Waite. *All the Happy Endings.* New York: Harper, 1956.

Pattee, Fred Lewis. *The Feminine Fifties.* New York: Appleton, 1940.

Smith, Herbert. *The Popular American Novel: 1865–1920.* Boston: Twayne, 1980.

Tompkins, Jane. *Sensational Designs: The Cultural Work of American Fiction, 1790–1860.* New York: Oxford UP, 1985.

Warner, Susan. *The Wide, Wide World.* 1850. Rpt., ed. Jane Tompkins. Old Westbury, N.Y.: Feminist, 1987.

A NOTE ON THE TEXT

THIS EDITION IS SET from the 1888 edition, the first printing of *The Hidden Hand* to appear in book form. Although it largely follows the 1883 serialization, which Southworth revised with an eye to highlighting the presence of Capitola, it differs in both substance and typography from that serialized version and from some later book editions, which seem to have been set from the serialization of 1859. Although this edition reflects Southworth's own changes, it is impossible to know whether she or some later editor is responsible for several altered chapter placements, divisions, and titles that differ from the 1883 version. Typography in the printed edition reflects the editorializing of a contemporary printer, who added many exclamation points not present in the serialized version. Obvious typographical errors, and some glaring inconsistencies (common to nineteenth-century texts), have been silently emended, although period spelling and hyphenization have been preserved to give the flavor of the original.

THE HIDDEN HAND

THE HIDDEN HAND
or,
CAPITOLA THE MADCAP

CONTENTS

CHAPTER I

᥉᥉᥉᥉᥉᥉

"*** Whence is that knocking?
How is't with me when every sound appals me?
*** I hear a knocking
In the south entry! Hark!—more knocking!"
    —*Shakespeare* [1]

HURRICANE HALL is a large old family mansion, built of dark, red sandstone, in one of the loneliest and wildest of the mountain regions of Virginia.

The estate is surrounded on three sides by a range of steep, gray rocks, spiked with clumps of dark evergreens, and called, from its horseshoe form, the Devil's Hoof.

On the fourth side the ground gradually descends in broken rock and barren soil to the edge of the wild mountain stream known as the Devil's Run.

When storms and floods were high, the loud roaring of the wild mountain gorges, and the terrific raging of the torrent over its rocky course, gave to this savage locality its ill-omened names of Devil's Hoof, Devil's Run, and Hurricane Hall.

Major Ira Warfield, the lonely proprietor of the Hall, was a veteran officer, who, in disgust at what he supposed to be ill-requited services, had retired from public life to spend the evening of his vigorous age on this his patrimonial estate. Here he lived in seclusion, with his old-fashioned housekeeper, Mrs. Condiment, and his old family servants and his favorite dogs and horses. Here his mornings were usually spent in the chase, in which he excelled, and his afternoon and evenings were occupied in small convivial suppers among his few chosen companions of the chase or the bottle.

In person Major Warfield was tall and strongly built, reminding one of some old iron-limbed Douglas[2] of the olden time. His features were large and harsh; his complexion dark red, as that of one bronzed by long exposure and flushed with strong drink. His fierce, dark gray eyes were surmounted by thick, heavy black brows, that, when gathered into a frown, reminded one of a thunder cloud, as the flashing orbs beneath them did of lightning. His hard, harsh face was surrounded by a thick growth of iron-gray hair and beard that met beneath his chin. His usual habit was a black cloth coat, crimson vest, black leather breeches, long, black yarn stockings, fastened at the knees, and morocco slippers with silver buttons.

In character Major Warfield was arrogant, domineering and violent—equally loved and feared by his faithful old family servants at home—disliked and dreaded by his neighbors and acquaintances abroad, who, partly from his *house* and partly from his character, fixed upon him the appropriate Nickname of Old Hurricane.

There was, however, other ground of dislike besides that of his arrogant mind, violent temper and domineering habits. Old Hurricane was said to be an old bachelor, yet rumor whispered that there was in some obscure part of the world, hidden away from human sight, a deserted wife and child, poor, forlorn, and heartbroken. It was farther whispered that the elder brother of Ira Warfield had mysteriously disappeared, and not without suspicion of foul play on the part of the only person in the world who had a strong interest in his "taking off." However these things might be, it was known for a certainty that Old Hurricane had an only sister, widowed, sick and poor, who with her son dragged on a wretched life of ill-requited toil, severe privation, and painful infirmity, in a distant city, unaided, unsought and uncared for by her cruel brother.

It was the night of the last day of October, eighteen hundred and forty-five. The evening had closed in dark and gloomy. About dusk the wind arose in the northwest, driving up masses of leaden-hued clouds, and in a few minutes the ground was covered deep with snow, and the air was filled with driving sleet.

As this was All Hallow Eve,[3] the dreadful inclemency of the weather did not prevent the negroes of Hurricane Hall from availing themselves of their capricious old master's permission, and going off in a body to a banjo break-down, held in the negro quarters of their next neighbor.

Upon this evening, then, there was left at Hurricane Hall only Major Warfield; Mrs. Condiment, his little old housekeeper; and Wool, his body-servant.

Early in the evening the old hall was shut up closely to keep out as much as possible the sound of the storm that roared through the mountain chasms, and cannonaded the walls of the house as if determined to force an entrance. As soon as she had seen that all was safe, Mrs. Condiment went to bed and went to sleep.

It was about ten o'clock that night that Old Hurricane, well wrapped up in his quilted flannel dressing-gown, sat in his well-padded easy chair before a warm and bright fire, taking his comfort in his own most comfortable bedroom. This was the hour of the coziest enjoyment to the self-indulgent old Sybarite, who dearly loved his own ease. And indeed every means and appliance of bodily comfort was at hand. Strong oaken shutters and thick heavy curtains at the windows kept out every draft of air, and so deadened the sound of the wind that its subdued moaning was just sufficient to remind one of the stormy weather without in contrast to the bright warmth within. Old Hurricane, as I said, sat well wrapped up in his wadded dressing-gown, and reclining in his padded easy chair, with his head thrown back and his feet upon the fire irons, toasting his shins and sipping his punch. On his right hand stood a little table with a lighted candle, a stack of clay pipes, a jug of punch, lemons, sugar, Holland gin, etc., while on the hearth sat a kettle of boiling water to help to replenish the jug if needful.

On his left hand stood his cozy bedstead with its warm crimson curtains festooned back, revealing the luxurious swell of the full feather bed, and pillows with their snow-white linen, and lambswool blankets inviting repose. Between this bedstead and the corner of the fireplace stood Old Hurricane's ancient body-servant, Wool, engaged in warming a crimson cloth nightcap.

"Fools!" muttered Old Hurricane over his punch—"jacks! they'll all get the pleurisy except those that get drunk! Did they *all* go, Wool?"

"Ebery man, 'oman and chile, sar!—'cept 'tis me and coachman, sar."

"More fools they! And I shouldn't wonder if *you,* you old scarecrow, didn't want to go too!"

"No, Marse——"

"I know better, sir! don't contradict *me!* Well, as soon as I'm in bed, and that won't be long now, you may go!—so that you can get back in time to wait on me to-morrow morning!"

"Thanky, Marse."

"Hold your tongue! You are as big a fool as the rest."

"I take this," said Old Hurricane, as he sipped his punch and

9

smacked his lips—"I take this to be the very quintessence of human enjoyment—sitting here in my soft, warm chair before the fire, toasting my legs, sipping my punch, listening on the one hand to the storm without, and glancing on the other hand at my comfortable bed waiting there to receive my sleepy head. If there is anything better than this in this world, I wish somebody would let me know it."

"It's all werry comfortable indeed, Marse," said the obsequious Wool.

"I wonder now if there is anything on the face of the earth that would tempt *me* to leave my cozy fireside and go abroad to-night? I wonder how large a promise of pleasure or profit or glory it would take now?"

"Much as ebber Congress itse'f could give if it give you a penance for all your sarvins," suggested Wool.

"Yes, and more! for I wouldn't leave my home comforts to-night to ensure not only the pension but the thanks of Congress!" said the old man, replenishing his glass with steaming punch, and drinking it off leisurely.

The clock struck eleven. The old man replenished his glass, and while sipping its contents said:

"You may fill the warming-pan and warm my bed, Wool. The fumes of this fragrant punch are beginning to rise to my head and make me sleepy."

The servant filled the warming-pan with glowing embers, shut down the lid, and thrust it between the sheets, to warm the couch of the luxurious Old Hurricane. The old man continued to toast his feet, sip his punch, and smack his lips. He finished his glass, set it down, and was just in the act of drawing on his woolen nightcap, preparatory to stepping into his well-warmed bed, when he was suddenly startled by a loud ringing of the hall door-bell.

"What the foul fiend can that mean at this time of night!" exclaimed Old Hurricane, dropping his nightcap, and turning sharply around towards Wool, who, warming-pan in hand, stood staring with astonishment. "What does that mean, I ask you?"

"'Deed, I dunno, sar, less it's some benighted traveler in search o' shelter out'n de storm."

"Humph! and in search of supper, too, of course, and everybody gone away or gone to bed but you and me!"

At that moment the ringing was followed by a loud knocking.

"Marse, don't less you and me listen to it, and then we aint 'obliged to sturb ourselves wid answering of it," suggested Wool.

"'Sdeath, sir! do you think that I am going to turn a deaf ear to a stranger that comes to my house for shelter on such a night as this? Go and answer the bell directly."

Not completely cruel

"Yes, sar."

"But stop—look here, sirrah—mind, I am not to be disturbed. If it is a traveler, ask him in, set refreshments before him, and show him to bed. I'm not going to leave my warm room to welcome anybody to-night, please the Lord. Do you hear?"

"Yes, sar," said the darkey, retreating.

As Wool took a shaded taper and opened the door leading from his master's chamber, the wind was heard howling through the long passages ready to burst into the cozy bedroom.

"SHUT THE DOOR, you scoundrel!" roared the old man, folding the skirt of his warm dressing-gown across his knees, and hovering closer to the fire.

Wool quickly obeyed, and was heard retreating down the steps.

"Whew!" said the old man, spreading his hands over the blaze with a look of comfortable appreciation. "What would induce *me* to go abroad on such a night as this? Wind blowing great guns from the north-west—snow falling fast from the heavens, and rising just as fast before the wind from the ground!—cold as Lapland, dark as Erebus! No telling the earth from the sky. Whew!" and to comfort the cold thought, Old Hurricane poured out another glass of smoking punch, and began to sip it.

"How I thank the Lord that I am not a doctor! If I were a doctor now, the sound of that bell at this hour of night would frighten me; I should think some old woman had been taken with the pleurisy, and wanted me to get up and go out in the storm, to turn out of my warm bed to ride ten miles through the snow to prescribe for her. A doctor never can feel sure, even in the worst of weathers, of a good night's rest. But, thank heaven, I am free from all such annoyances, and if I am sure of anything in this world it is of my comfortable night's sleep," said Old Hurricane, as he sipped his punch, smacked his lips and toasted his feet.

At this moment Wool re-appeared.

"SHUT THE DOOR, you villain! Do you intend to stand there holding it open on me all night?" vociferated the old man.

Wool hastily closed the offending portals, and hurried to his master's side.

"Well, sir, who was it rung the bell?"

11

"Please, Marster, sir, it wer' de Reverend Mr. Parson Goodwin."

"Goodwin? Been to make a sick-call, I suppose, and got caught in the snow-storm. I declare it is as bad to be a parson as it is to be a doctor. Thank the Lord *I* am not a parson either; if I were now, I might be called away from my cozy arm-chair and fireside to ride twelve miles to comfort some old man dying of quinsy. Wool, here—help me into bed, pile on more comforters, tuck me up warm, put a bottle of hot water to my feet, and then go and attend to the parson," said the old man, getting up and moving towards his inviting couch.

"Sar! sar! stop, sar, if you *please!*" cried Wool, going after him.

"Why, what does the old fool mean," exclaimed Old Hurricane angrily.

"Sar, de Reverend Mr. Parson Goodwin say how he must see you yourse'f, personable, alone!"

"See *me,* you villain! Didn't you tell him that I had retired?"

"Yes, Marse, I tell him how you wer' gone to bed and asleep more'n an hour ago, and he ordered me to come wake you up, and say how it were a matter o' life and death!"

"Life and death? What have I to do with life and death? *I won't stir!* If the parson wants to see *me,* he will have to come up here and see me in bed," exclaimed Old Hurricane, suiting the action to the word, by jumping into bed and drawing all the comforters and blankets up around his head and shoulders.

childish

"Mus' I fetch his reverence up, sar?"

"Yes, *I* wouldn't get up and go down to see—Washington—SHUT THE DOOR, you rascal, or I'll throw the bootjack at your wooden head!"

Wool obeyed with alacrity, and in time to escape the threatened missile.

After an absence of a few minutes he was heard returning, attending upon the footsteps of another. And the next minute he entered, ushering in the Rev. Mr. Goodwin, the parish minister of Bethlehem, St. Mary's.

"How do you do? How do you do? Glad to see you, sir! glad to see you, though obliged to receive you in bed! Fact is, I caught a cold with this severe change of weather, and took a warm negus and went to bed to sweat it off! You'll excuse me! Wool, draw that easy chair up to my bedside for worthy Mr. Goodwin, and bring him a glass of warm negus! It will do him good after his cold ride!"

"I thank you, Major Warfield! I will take the seat, but not the negus, if you please, to-night."

"Not the negus! Oh, come now, you are joking! Why, it will keep you from catching cold, and be a most comfortable nightcap, disposing you to sleep and sweat like a baby! Of course you spend the night with us?"

"I thank you, no. I must take the road again in a few minutes."

"Take the road again to-night! Why, man alive, it is midnight, and the snow driving like all Lapland!"

"Sir, I am sorry to refuse your proffered hospitality, and leave your comfortable roof to-night, and sorrier still to have to take *you* with me," said the pastor, gravely.

"Take ME with you! No, no, my good sir—no, no, that is too good a joke—ha! ha!"

"Sir, I fear that you will find it a very serious one!—Your servant told you that my errand was one of imminent urgency?"

"Yes, something like life and death——"

"Exactly—down in the cabin near the Punch Bowl, there is an old woman dying——"

"There—I knew it! I was just saying there might be an old woman dying! But, my dear sir, what's that to me? What can I do?"

"Humanity, sir, would prompt you!"

"But, my *dear* sir, how can I help her? I am not a physician to prescribe——"

"She is far past a physician's help!"

"Nor am I a priest to hear her confession——"

"Her confession God has already received."

"Well, and I'm not a lawyer to draw up her will!"

"No sir; but you are recently appointed one of the Justices of the Peace for Alleghany?"

"Yes! well, what of that? That does not comprise the duty of getting up out of my warm bed and going through a snow-storm to see an old woman expire."

"I regret to inconvenience you, sir; but in this instance your duty demands your attendance at the bedside of this dying woman——"

"I tell you I can't go and I won't! Anything in reason, I'll do! Anything I can send, she shall have!—Here! Wool, look in my breeches pocket and take out my purse and hand it! And then go and wake Mrs. Condiment, and ask her to fill a large basket full of everything a poor old dying woman might want, and you shall carry it!"

"Spare your pains, sir! The poor woman is already past all earthly, selfish wants! She only asks your presence at her dying bed."

"But I can't go! I! the idea of turning out of my warm bed and exposing myself to a snow-storm this time of night!"

"Excuse me for insisting, sir; but this is an *official* duty," said the parson, mildly but firmly.

"I'll—I'll throw up my commission to-morrow!" growled the old man.

"To-morrow you may do that! but meanwhile, to-night, being still in the commission of the peace, you are bound to get up and go with me to this woman's bedside."

"And what the demon is wanted of me there?"

"To receive her dying deposition!"

"To receive a dying deposition! Good Heaven! was she murdered, then?" exclaimed the old man, in alarm, as he started out of bed and began to draw on his nether garments.

"Be composed—she was not murdered!" said the pastor.

"Well, then, what is it? Dying deposition! It must concern a crime!" exclaimed the old man, hastily drawing on his coat.

"It *does* concern a crime."

"What crime, for the love of Heaven?"

"I am not at liberty to tell you. She will do that."

"Wool, go down and rouse up Jehu, and tell him to put Parson Goodwin's mule in the stable for the night. And tell him to put the black draught-horses to the close carriage, and light both the front lanterns— for we shall have a dark, stormy road—SHUT THE DOOR, you infernal!— I beg your pardon, parson, but that villain always leaves the door ajar after him."

The good pastor bowed gravely. And the major completed his toilet by the time the servant returned and reported the carriage ready.

It was dark as pitch when they emerged from the hall-door out into the front portico, before which nothing could be seen but two red bull's eyes of the carriage lanterns, and nothing heard but the dissatisfied whinnying and pawing of the horses.

CHAPTER II

THE MASKS

"What are these?
So withered and so wild in their attire
That look not like th' inhabitants of earth
And yet are on't?"
—*Macbeth* [1]

"TO THE DEVIL'S Punch Bowl"—was the order given by Old Hurricane as he followed the minister into the carriage. "And now, sir," he continued, addressing his companion, "I think you had better repeat that part of the church litany that prays to be delivered from 'battle, murder, and sudden death;' [2] for if we should be so lucky as to escape Black Donald and his gang, we shall have at least an equal chance of being upset in the darkness of these dreadful mountains."

"A pair of saddle-mules would have been a safer conveyance, certainly," said the minister.

Old Hurricane knew that, but though a great sensualist, he was a brave man, and so he had rather risk his life in a close carriage than suffer cold upon a sure-footed mule's back.

Only by previous knowledge of the route could any one have told the way the carriage went. Old Hurricane and the minister both knew that they drove, lumbering, over the rough road leading by serpentine windings down that rugged fall of ground to the river's bank, and that then turning to the left by a short bend, they passed in behind that range of horse-shoe rocks that sheltered Hurricane Hall—thus, as it were, doubling their own road. Beneath that range of rocks, and between it and another range, there was an awful abyss or chasm of cleft, torn and jagged rocks, opening as it were from the bowels of the earth, in the shape of a mammoth bowl, in the bottom of which, almost invisible from its great depth, seethed and boiled a mass of dark water of what seemed to be a lost river or a subterranean spring. This terrific phenomenon was called the Devil's Punch Bowl.

Not far from the brink of this awful abyss, and close behind the horse-shoe range of rocks, stood an humble log cabin, occupied by an old free negro, who picked up a scanty living by telling fortunes and showing the way to the Punch Bowl. Her cabin went by name of the Witch's Hut—or Old Hat's cabin. A short distance from Hat's cabin the road became impassable, and the travelers got out, and preceded by the coachman bearing the lantern, struggled along on foot through the drifted snow and against the buffeting wind and sleet to where a faint light guided them to the house.

The pastor knocked. The door was immediately opened by a negro, whose sex from the strange anomalous costume it was difficult to guess. The tall form was rigged out first in a long, red, cloth petticoat, above which was buttoned a blue cloth surtout. A man's old black beaver hat sat upon the strange head and completed this odd attire.

"Well, Hat, how is your patient?" inquired the pastor, as he entered, preceding the magistrate.

"You will see, sir," replied the old woman.

The two visitors looked around the dimly-lighted, miserable room, in one corner of which stood a low bed, upon which lay extended the form of an old, feeble, and gray-haired woman.

kind

"How are you, my poor soul, and what can I do for you now I am here?" inquired Old Hurricane, who in the actual presence of suffering, was not utterly without pity.

"You are a magistrate?" inquired the dying woman.

"Yes, my poor soul."

"And qualified to administer an oath and take your deposition," said the minister.

"Will it be legal—will it be evidence in a court of law?" asked the woman, lifting her dim eyes to the major.

"Certainly, my poor soul! certainly," said the latter, who, by the way, would have said anything to soothe her.

"Send everyone but yourself from the room."

"What, my good soul, send the parson out in the storm? That will never do! Won't it be just as well to let him go up in the corner yonder?"

"No! You will repent it unless this communication is strictly private."

"But—my good soul, if it is to be used in a court of law?"

"That will be according to your own discretion!"

"My dear parson," said Old Hurricane, going to the minister, "would you be so good as to retire?"

"There is a fire in the woodshed, master," said Hat, leading the way.
"Now, my good soul, now! You want first to be put upon your oath?"
"Yes, sir."

The old man drew from his great coat pocket a miniature copy of the Scriptures, and with the usual formalities administered the oath.

"Now then, my good soul, begin—'the truth, the whole truth, and nothing but the truth' you know. But first, your name?"

"Is it possible you don't know me, master?"

"Not I, in faith!"

"For the love of Heaven, look at me and try to recollect me, sir! It is necessary some one in authority should be able to know me," said the woman, raising her haggard eyes to the face of her visitor.

The old man adjusted his spectacles and gave her a scrutinizing look, exclaiming at intervals:

"Lord bless my soul! it is! it aint! it must! it can't be! Granny Grewell, the—the—the—midwife that disappeared from here some twelve or thirteen years ago!"

"Yes, master, I am Nancy Grewell, the ladies' nurse who vanished from sight so mysteriously some thirteen years ago!" replied the woman.

"Heaven help our hearts! And for what crime was it you ran away? Come—make a clean breast of it, woman. You have nothing to fear in doing so, for you are past the arm of earthly law now!"

"I know it, master."

"And the best way to prepare to meet the Divine Judge is to make all the reparation that you can by a full confession!"

"I know it, sir—if I had committed a crime; but I have commited no crime, neither did I run away!"

"What? what? what?—What was it then? Remember, witness, you are on your oath?"

"I know that, sir, and I will tell the truth; but it must be in my own way."

At this moment a violent blast of wind and hail roared down the mountain side and rattled against the walls, shaking the witch's hut, as if it would have shaken it about their ears.

It was a proper overture to the tale that was about to be told. Conversation was impossible until the storm raved past and was heard dying in deep, reverberating echoes from the depths of the Devil's Punch Bowl.

"It was some thirteen years ago," began Granny Grewell, "upon just such a night of storm as this, that I was mounted on my old mule Molly, with my saddle-bags full of dried yarbs, and stilled waters and sich, as I allus carried when I was out 'tendin' on the sick. I was on my way a-going to see a lady as I was sent for to tend.

"Well, master! I'm not 'shamed to say, as I never was afraid of man, beast, *nor* sperrit! and never stopped at going out at all hours of the night, through the most lonesome roads, if so be I was called upon so to do! Still I must say that jest as me and Molly my mule got into that deep, thick, lonesome woods as stands round the old Hidden House in the hollow I did feel queerish; 'case it was the dead hour of the night, and it was said how strange things were seen and hearn, yes, and done too, in that dark, deep, lonesome place! I seen how even my mule Molly felt queer too, by the way she stuck up her ears, stiff as quills. So, partly to keep up my own spirits, and partly to 'courage her, says I, 'Molly,' says I, 'what are ye afeard on? Be a man Molly!' But Molly stepped out cautious, and pricked up her long ears all the same.

"Well, master, it was so dark I couldn't see a yard past Molly's ears, and the path was so narrow and the bushes so thick we could hardly get along! but just as we came to that little creek as they calls the Spout, cause the water jumps and jets along till it empties into the Punch Bowl, and just as Molly was cautiously putting her forefoot into the water, out starts two men from the bushes and seizes poor Molly's bridle!"

"Good heaven!" exclaimed Major Warfield.

"Well, master, before I could cry out one of them willians seized me by the scruff of my neck, and with his other hand upon my mouth, he says:

" 'Be silent, you old fool, or I'll blow your brains out!' "

"And then, master, I saw for the first time that *their faces were covered over with black crape.* I couldn't a-screamed if they'd let me! for my breath was gone and my senses were going along with 'em from the fear that was on me.

" 'Don't struggle; come along quietly and you shall not be hurt,' says the man as had spoke before.

"Struggle! I couldn't a-struggled to a-saved my soul! I couldn't speak! I couldn't breathe! I liked to have a-dropped right offen Molly's back. One on 'em says, says he:

" 'Give her some brandy!' And 'tother takes out a flask and puts it to my lips and says, says he:

" 'Here drink this.'

"Well, master, as he had me still by the scruff o' the neck I couldn't do no other ways but open my mouth and drink it. And as soon as I took a swallow my breath come back and my speech.

"'And oh, gentlemen,' says I, ef it's "*your money or your life*," you mean, I haint it about me! 'Deed 'clare to the Lord-a-mighty I haint! It's wrapped up in an old cotton glove in a hole in the plastering in the chimney-corner at home, and ef you'll spare my life, you can go there and get it,' says I.

"'You old blockhead,' says they, 'we want neither one nor 'tother! Come along quietly and you shall receive no harm. But at the first cry, or attempt to escape—*this* shall stop you!' And with that the willain held the muzzle of a pistol so nigh to my nose that I smelt brimstone, while 'tother one bound a silk hankercher 'round my eyes, and then took poor Molly's bridle and led her along. I couldn't see, in course, and I dassint breathe for fear 'o the pistol. But I said my prayers to myself all the time.

"Well, master, they led the mule on down the path until we comed to a place wide enough to turn, when they turned us 'round and led us back outen the wood, and then round and round, and up and down, and cross ways and length ways, as if they didn't want me to find where they were taking me.

"Well, sir, when they'd walked about in this 'fused way, leadin' of the mule about a mile, I knew we was in the woods again—*the very same woods and the very same path*—I knowed by the feel of the place and the sound of the bushes, as we hit up against them each side, and also by the rumbling of the Spout as it tumbled along toward the Punch Bowl. We went down and down and down, and lower and lower and lower, until we got right down in the bottom of that hollow.

"Then we stopped. A gate was opened. I put up my hand to raise the handkercher and see where I was; but just at that minute I felt the muzzle o' the pistol like a ring of ice right ag'in' my right temple, and the willain growling into my ear:

"'*If you do*——!'

"But I didn't—I dropped my hand down as if I had been shot, and afore I had seen anything, either. So we went through the gate and up a gravelly walk—I knew it by the crackling of the gravel under Molly's feet—and stopped at a horse-block, where one o' them willains lifted me off. I put up my hand again.

"'*Do if you dare,*' says t'other one, with the muzzle of the pistol at my head.

"I dropped my hand like lead. So they lead me on a little way, and then up some steps. I counted them to myself as I went along. They were six. You see, master, I took all this pains to know the house again. Then they opened a door that opened in the middle. Then they went along a passage and up more stairs—there was ten and a turn, and then ten more. Then along another passage, and up another flight of stairs just like the first. Then along another passage and up a third flight of stairs. They was alike.

"Well, sir, here we was at the top o' the house. One o' them willains opened a door on the left side, and t'other said:

"'There—go in and do your duty!' and pushed me through the door, and shut and locked it on me. Good gracious, sir, how scared I was! I slipped off the silk handkercher, and 'feared as I was, I didn't forget to put it in my bosom.

"Then I looked about me. Right afore me on the hearth was a little weeny taper burning, that showed I was in a great big garret with sloping walls. At one end two deep dormer windows, and a black walnut bureau standing between them. At t'other end a great tester bedstead with dark curtains. There was a dark carpet on the floor. And with all there were so many dark objects and so many shadows, and the little taper burned so dimly that I could hardly tell t'other from which, or keep from breaking my nose against things as I groped about.

"And what was in this room for to do? I couldn't even form an idee. But presently my blood ran cold to hear a groan from behind the curtains! then another! and another! then a cry as if some child in mortal agony, saying:

"'*For the love of Heaven, save me!*'

"I ran to the bed and dropped the curtains, and liked to have fainted at what I saw!"

"And what did you see?" asked the magistrate.

"Master, behind those dark curtains I saw a young creature tossing about on the bed, flinging her fair and beautiful arms about, and tearing wildly at the fine lace that trimed her night-dress. But, master, that wasn't what almost made me faint—it was that *her right hand was sewed up in black crape, and her whole face and head completely covered with black crape, drawn down and fastened securely around her throat, leaving only a small slit at the lips and nose to breathe through!*"

"What! take care, woman! remember that you are upon your oath!" said the magistrate.

"I know it, master! And as I hope to be forgiven, I am telling you the truth."

"Go on, then."

"Well, sir, she was a young creature, scarcely past childhood, if one might judge by her small size and soft, rosy skin. I asked her to let me take that black crape from her face and head, but she threw up her hands and exclaimed:

"'Oh, no, no, no! for my life, no!'

"Well, master, I hardly know how to tell you what followed—" said the old woman, hesitating in embarrassment.

"Go right straight on like a car of Juggernaut, woman! Remember—the whole truth!"

"Well, master, in the next two hours there were twins born in that room—a boy and a girl; the boy was dead, the girl living. And all the time I heard the measured tramping of one of them willians up and down the passage outside of that room. Presently the steps stopped, and there was a rap at the door. I went and listened, but did not open it.

"'Is it all over?' the voice asked.

"Before I could answer, a cry from the bed caused me to look round. There was the poor masked mother stretching out her white arms towards me in the most imploring way. I hastened back to her.

"'Tell him—no—no.' she said.

"'Have you got through?' asked the man at the door, rapping impatiently.

"'No, no,' said I, as directed.

"He resumed his tramping up and down, and I went back to my patient. She beckoned me to come close, and whispered:

"'Save my child! the living one I mean! hide her! oh, hide her from him! When he demands the babe, give him the poor little dead one—he cannot hurt that! And he will not know there was another. Oh! hide and save my child!'

"Master, I was used to queer doings, but this was a little the queerest. But if I was to conceal that second child in order to save it, it was necessary to stop its mouth, for it was squalling like a wild cat. So I took a vial of paregoric from my pocket and gave it a drop, and it went off to sleep like an angel. I wrapped it up warm and lay it along with my shawl and bonnet in a dark corner. Just then the man rapped again.

"'Come in, master,' said I.

"'No, bring me the babe,' he said.

"I took up the dead infant. Its mother kissed its brow, and dropped tears upon its little cold face. And I carried it to the man outside.

"'Is it asleep?' the willain asked me.

"'Yes, master'—said I, as I put it, well wrapped up, in his arms— 'very sound asleep.'

"'So much the better,' said the knave, walking away.

"I bolted the door and went back to my patient. With her free hand she seized mine and pressed it to her lips, then held up her left hand and pointed to the wedding ring upon her third finger.

"'Draw it off and keep it,' she said, 'conceal the child under your shawl, and take her with you when you go! save her, and your fortune shall be made.'

"I declare, master, I hadn't time to think, before I heard one of them wretches rap at the door.

"'Come! get ready to go,' he said.

"*She* also beckoned me. I hastened to her. With eager whispers and imploring gestures she prayed me to take her ring and save her child.

"'But *you*,' said I—'who is to attend to you?'

"'I do not know or care! Save *her!*'"

"The rapping continued. I ran to the corner where I had left my things. I put on my bonnet, made a sort of sling around my neck of the silk handkercher, opened the large part of it like a hammock, and laid the little sleeping babe there. I folded my big shawl around my breast, and nobody any the wiser. The rapping was very impatient.

"'I am coming,' said I.

"'*Remember!*' whispered the poor girl.

"'*I will,*' said I, and went and opened the door. There stood t'other willain, with his head covered with black crape. I dreamt of nothing but black-headed demons for six months afterwards.

"'Are you ready?' says he.

"'Yes, your worship,' says I.

"'Come along, then.'

"And binding another silk handkercher round my eyes, he led me along.

"Instead of my mule, a carriage stood near the horse block.

"'Get in,' says he, holding the pistol to my ears by way of argument.

"I got in. He jumped up upon the driver's seat and we drove like the wind. In another direction from that in which we come, in course, for there was no carriage road *there*. The carriage whirled along at such a rate it made me quite giddy. At last it stopped again. The man in the mask got down and opened the door.

"'Where are you taking me?' says I.

"'Be quiet,' says he, 'or——' And with that he put the pistol to my cheek, ordered me to get out, take the bandage from my eyes, and walk before him. I did so, and saw dimly that we were in a part of the country that I was never at before. We were in a dark road through a thick forest. On the left side of the road, in a clearing, stood an old house; a dim light was burning in a lower window.

"'Go on in there,' said the willain, putting the pistol to the back of my head. As the door stood ajar, I went in, to a narrow dark passage, the man all the time at my back. He opened a door on the left side, and made me go into a dark room. Just then the unfortunate child that had been moving restlessly began to wail. Well it might, poor starved thing.

"'What's that?' says the miscreant, under his breath, and stopping short.

"'It ain't nothing, sir,' says I, and 'hush-h-h' to the baby. But the poor little wretch raised a squall.

"'What is the meaning of this?' says he. 'Where did that child come from? Why the demon don't you speak?' And with that he seized me again by the scruff of the neck, and shook me.

"'Oh, master! for the love of heaven, don't,' says I, 'this is only a poor unfortunet infant as its parents wanted to get outen the way, and hired me to take care on. And I have had it wrapped up under my shawl all the time 'cept when I was in your house, when I put it to sleep in the corner.'

"'Humph—and you had that child concealed under your shawl' when I first stopped you in the woods?'

"'In course, master,' says I.

"'Whose is it?'

"'Master,' says I, 'it's——it's a dead secret!' for I hadn't another lie ready.

"He broke out into a rude, scornful laugh, and seemed not half to believe me, and yet not to care about questioning me too closely. He made me sit down then in the dark, and went out and turned the key on me. I wet my finger with the paragoric and put it to the baby's lips to quiet its pains of hunger. Then I heard a whispering in the next room. Now, my eyesight never was good, but to make up for it I believe I had the sharpest ears that ever was, and I don't think anybody could have heard that whispering but me. I saw a little glimmer of light through the chinks that showed me where the door was, and so I creeped up to it, and put my ear to the keyhole. Still they whispered so low that no ears could o' heard them but my sharp ones. The first words I heard good, was a grumbling voice asking:

"'How old?'

"'Fifty—more or less, but strong, active, a good nurse, and a very light mulatto,' says *my* willian's voice.

"'Hum—too old,' says the other.

"'But I will throw the child in.'

"A low, crackling laugh the only answer.

"'You mean *that* would be only a bother. Well, I want to get rid of the pair of them,' said *my* willian, 'so name the price you are willing to give.'

"'Cap'n, you and me have had too many transactions together to make any flummery about this. *You* want to get shet o' them pair. *I* hain't no objections to turning an honest penny. So jest make out the papers— bill o' sale o' the 'oman Kate, or whatsoever her name may be, and the child, with any price you please, so it is only a make-believe price! and I'll engage to take her away, and make the most I can of them in the South— that won't be much, seeing its only an old 'oman and child—scarcely a fair profit on the expense o' takin' o' her out. Now, as money's no object to *you*, Cap'n——'

"'Very well, have your own way, only don't let that woman escape and return, *for if you do*——'

"'I understand, cap'n; but I reckon you needn't threaten, for if you could blow *me*—why I would return you the same favor,' said the other, raising his voice, and laughing aloud.

"'Be quiet, fool, or come away farther—here.' And the two willians moved out of even my hearing.

"I should o' been uneasy, master, if it hadn't been the 'oman they were talking about was named *Kate,* and that warn't my name, which were well beknown to be Nancy.

"Presently I heard the carriage drive away. And almost immediately after the door was unlocked, and a great, big, black-bearded and black-headed beast of a ruffian came in, and says he:

"'Well, my woman, have you had any supper?'

"'No,' said I, 'I hain't; and ef I'm to stay here any length of time, I'd be obleeged to you to let me have some hot water and milk to make pap for this perishing baby.'

24

" 'Follow me,' says he.

"And he took me into the kitchen at the back of the house, where there was a fire in the fireplace, and a cupboard with all that I needed. Well, sir, not to tire you, I made a nursing bottle for the baby, and fed it. And then I got something for my own supper, or rather, breakfast, for it was now near the dawn of day. Well, sir, I thought I would try to get out and look about myself, to see what the neighborhood looked like by daylight; but when I tried the door I found myself locked up, a close prisoner. I looked out of the window, and saw nothing but a little back yard, closed in by the woods. I tried to raise the sash, but it was nailed down. The black-headed monster came in just about that minute, and seeing what I was a-doing of, says he:

" 'Stop that.'

" 'What am I stopped here for?' says I; 'a free 'oman,' says I, 'a-'vented of going about her own business?' says I.

"But he only laughed a loud, crackling, scornful laugh, and went out, turning the key after him.

"A little after sunrise, an old, dried-up, spiteful-looking hag of a woman came in, and began to get breakfast.

" 'What am I kept here for?' says I to her.

"But she took no notice at all; nor could I get so much as a single word outen her. In fact, master, the little 'oman was deaf an' dumb.

"Well, sir, to be short, I was kept in that place all day long, and when night come I was druv into a shay at the point of the pistol, and rattled along as fast as the horses could gallop over a road as I knew nothing of. We changed horses wunst or twict, and just about the dawn of day we come to a broad river with a vessel laying to, not far from the shore.

"As soon as the shay druv down on the sands, the willain as had run away with me puts a pipe to his willainous mouth and blows like mad. Somebody else blowed back from the vessel. Then a boat was put off and rowed ashore. I was forced to get into it and was follered by the willain. We was rowed to the vessel, and I was druv up the ladder on to the decks. And there, master, right afore my own looking eyes, me and the baby was traded off to the captain! It was no use for me to 'splain or 'spostulate! I wan't b'lieved. The willain as had stole me got back into the boat and went ashore. And I saw him get into the shay and drive away. It was no use for me to howl and cry, though I did both, for I couldn't even hear myself for the swearing of the captain and the noise of the crew, as they was a gettin' of the vessel under way. Well, sir, we sailed down that river and out to sea.

"Now, sir, come a strange providence, which the very thoughts of it might convert a heathen! We had been to sea about five days when a dreadful storm riz. Oh, master! the inky blackness of the sky, the roaring of the wind, the raging of the sea, the leaping of the waves, and the rocking of that vessel—and every once in a while, sea and ship all ablaze with the blinding lightning—was a thing to see, not to hear tell of! I tell you, marster, that looked like the wrath of God! And then the cursing and swearing and bawling of the captain and the crew, as they were a-takin' in of sail, was enough to raise one's hair on their head! I hugged the baby to my breast—and went to praying as hard as ever I could pray.

"Presently I felt an awful shock, as if heaven and earth had come together, and then everybody screaming, 'She's struck! She's struck!' I felt the vessel trembling like a live creetur, and the water a pouring in every-where. I hugged the babe and scrambled up the companion-way to the deck. It was pitch dark, and I heard every man rushing towards one side of the vessel.

"A flash of lightning, that made everything as bright as day again, showed me that they were all taking to the boat. I rushed after, calling to them to save me and the baby. But no one seemed to hear me; they were all too busy trying to save themselves and keep others out of the boat, and cursing and swearing and hollering that there was no more room, that the boat would be swamped, and so on. The end was, that all who could crowd into the boat did so. And me and the baby and a poor sailor lad and the black cook were left behind to perish.

"But, marster, as it turned out, we as was left to die were the only ones saved. We watched after that boat with longing eyes, though we could only see it when the lightning flashed. And every time we saw it, it was further off. At last, marster, a flash of lightning showed us the boat as far off as ever we could see her, capsized and beaten hither and thither by the wild waves—its crew had perished.

"Marster, as soon as the sea had swallowed up that wicked captain and crew, the wind died away, the waves fell, and the storm lulled—just as if it had done what it was sent to do and was satisfied. The wreck—where we poor forlorn ones stood—the wreck that had shivered and trembled with every wave that struck it—until we had feared it would break up every minute, became still and firm on its sand-bar, as a house on dry land.

"Daylight came at last. And a little after sunrise we saw a sail bearing down upon us. We could not signal the sail, but by the mercy of Providence, she saw us and lay to, and sent off a boat, and picked us up and took us on board—me and the baby, and the cook and the sailor lad.

"It was a foreign wessel, and we could not understand a word they said, nor they us. All we could do was by signs. But they were very good to us, dried our clothes and gave us breakfast, and made us lie down and rest. And then put about and continued their course. The sailor lad—Herbert Greyson—soon found out and told me they were bound for New York. And, in fact, marster, in about ten days we made that port.

"When the ship anchored below the Battery, the officers and passengers made me up a little bundle of clothes and a little purse of money, and put me ashore, and there I was in a strange city, so bewildered I didn't know which way to turn. While I was a-standing there, in danger of being run over by the omnibuses, the sailor boy came to my side and told me that he and the cook was gwine to engage on board of another 'Merican wessel, and axed me what I was gwine to do. I told him how I didn't know what I should do. Then he said he'd show me where I could go and stay all night, and so he took me into a little by-street to a poor-looking house, where the people took lodgers, and there he left me to go aboard his ship. As he went away he advised me to take care of my money, and try to get a servant's place.

"Well, marster, I aint a gwine to bother you with telling you of how I toiled and struggled along in that great city—first living out as a servant, and afterwards renting a room and taking in washing and ironing—aye! how I toiled and struggled—for—ten—long—years, hoping for the time to come when I should be able to return to this neighborhood, where I was known, and expose the evil deeds of them willains. And for this cause I lived on toiling and struggling, and laying up money, penny by penny. Sometimes I was fool enough to tell my story in the hopes of getting pity and help—but telling my story always made it worse for me! some thought me crazy and others thought me deceitful, which is not to be wondered at, for I was a stranger, and my adventures were indeed beyond belief.

"No one ever helped me but the lad Herbert Greyson. Whenever he came from sea, he sought me out, and made a little present to me or Cap.

"Cap, marster, was Capitola, the child. The reason I gave her that name was because on that ring I had drawn from the masked mother's hand were the two names—Eugene—Capitola.

"Well, marster, the last time Herbert Greyson came home, he gave me five dollars, and that, with what I had saved, was enough to pay my passage to Norfolk.

"I left my little Cap in the care of the people of the house—she was big enough to pay for her keep in work—and I took passage for Norfolk. When I got there I fell ill, spent all my money, and was at last taken to the poorhouse. Six months passed away before I was discharged. And then six more before I had earned and saved money enough to pay my way on here.

"I reached here three days ago, and found a wheatfield growing where my cottage-fire used to burn, and all my old cronies dead, all except Old Hat, who has received and given me shelter. Sir, my story is done— make what you can of it!" said the invalid, sinking down in her bed as if utterly exhausted.

Old Hurricane, whose countenance had expressed emotions as powerful as they were various while listening to this tale, now arose, stepped cautiously to the door, drew the bolt, and coming back bent his head and asked:

"What more of the child?"

"Cap, sir. I have not heard a word of Cap since I left her to try to find out her friends. But any one interested in her might inquire for her at Mrs. Simmons's, laundress, No. 8 Rag Alley."

"You say the names upon that ring were—Eugene—Capitola?"

"Yes, sir, they were."

"Have you that ring about you?"

"No, master. I thought it was best in case of accidents to leave it with the child."

"Have you told her any part of this strange history?"

"No, master, nor hinted it; she was too young for such a confidence."

"You were right! Had she any mark about her person by which she could be identified?"

"Yes, master, a very strange one. In the middle of her left palm was the perfect image of a crimson hand, about half an inch in length. There was also another. Herbert Greyson, to please me, marked upon her forearm in Indian ink her name and birthday—'Capitola, Oct. 31st, 1832.'"

"Right! Now tell me, my good soul, do you know, from what you were enabled to observe, what house that was where Capitola was born?"

"I am on my oath! No, sir, I do not know—but——"

"You suspect?"

The woman nodded.

he know? *Why does he know???*

"It was——" said Old Hurricane, stooping and whispering a name that was heard by no one but the sick woman.

She nodded again, with a look of intense meaning.

"Does your old hostess here, Hat, know or suspect anything of this story?" inquired Major Warfield.

"Not a word! No soul but yourself has heard it!"

"That is right! Still be discreet! If you would have the wicked punished and the innocent protected, be silent and wary. Have no anxiety about the girl! What man can do for her, will I do, and quickly! And now good creature, day is actually dawning. You must seek repose. And I must call the parson in and return home. I will send Mrs. Condiment over with food, wine, medicine, clothing, and every comfort that your condition requires," said Old Hurricane, rising, and calling in the clergyman, with whom he soon after left the hut for home.

They reached Hurricane Hall in time for an early breakfast, which the astonished housekeeper had prepared, and for which their night's adventures had certainly given them a good appetite.

Major Warfield kept his word, and as soon as breakfast was over he dispatched Mrs. Condiment with a carriage filled with provisions for the sick woman. But they were not needed. In a couple of hours the housekeeper returned with the intelligence that the old nurse was dead. The false strength of mental excitement that had enabled her to tell so long and dreadful a tale, had been the last flaring up of the flame of life, that almost immediately went out.

"I am not sorry, upon the whole, for now I shall have the game in my own hands!" muttered Old Hurricane to himself—"Ah! Gabriel Le Noir! better you had cast yourself down from the highest rock of this range and been dashed to pieces below, than have thus fallen into my power!"

CRUEL!

CHAPTER III

THE QUEST

❦❦❦❦❦

"Then did Sir Knight abandon dwelling,
And out he rode."
—*Hudibras*[1]

PURSUANT TO THE orders of Major Warfield, the corpse of the old midwife was the next day after her decease brought over and quietly interred in the family graveyard of Hurricane Hall.

And then Major Warfield astounded his household by giving orders to his housekeeper and his body-servant to prepare his wardrobe and pack his trunks for a long journey to the north.

"What can the major be thinking of, to be setting out for the north at this time of the year?" exclaimed good little Mrs. Condiment, as she picked over her employer's shirts, selecting the newest and warmest to be done up for the occasion.

"Lord A'mighty only knows; but 'pears to me marster's never been right in his head-piece since Hallow-eve night, when he took that ride to the Witch's Hut," replied Wool, who, with brush and sponge, was engaged in rejuvenating his master's outer-garments.

But let his family wonder as they would, Old Hurricane kept his own counsel—only just as he was going away, lest mystery should lead to investigation, and that to discovery, the old man gave out that he was going north to invest capital in bank-stock, and so, quite unattended, he departed.

His servant, Wool, indeed, accompanied him as far as Tip-Top, the little hamlet on the mountain at which he was to meet the eastern stage; but there, having seen his master comfortably deposited in the inside of the coach, and the luggage safely stowed in the boot, Wool was ordered to return with the carriage. And Major Warfield proceeded on his journey alone. This also caused much speculation in the family.

"Who's gwine to make his punch and warm his bed and put his slippers on the hearth and hang his gown to de fire—that's what *I* want to know!" cried the grieved and indignant Wool.

"Oh, the waiters at the taverns where he stops can do that for him," said Mrs. Condiment.

"No, they can't, nuther! they don't know his ways! they don't know nuffin' 'bout him! I 'clare, I think our old marse done gone clean crazy! I shouldn't be s'prised he'd gone off to de norf to get married, and was to bring home a young wife we-dem!"

"Tut! tut! tut! such talk!—that will never do!" exclaimed the deeply-shocked Mrs. Condiment.

"Werry well! all I say is, 'Dem as libs longest will see most!' said Wool, shaking his white head. After which undeniable apothegm the conversation came to a stand.

Meanwhile, Old Hurricane pursued his journey—a lumbering, old-fashioned stage-coach ride—across the mountains, creeping a snail's crawl up one side of the precipice and clattering thunderously down the other at a headlong speed that pitched the back-seat passengers into the bosoms of the front ones, and threatened even to cast the coach over the heads of the horses. Three days and nights of such rugged riding brought the traveler to Washington City, where he rested one night, and then took the cars for New York. He rested another night in Philadelphia, resumed his journey by the first train in the morning, and reached New York about noon.

The crowd, the noise, the hurry and confusion at the wharf almost drove this irascible old gentleman mad!

"No, confound you!"

"I'll see your neck stretched first, you villain!"

"Out of my way or I'll break your head, sirrah!" were some of his responses to the solicitous attentions of cabmen and porters. At length, taking up his heavy carpet-bag in both hands, Old Hurricane began to lay about him, with such effect that he speedily cleared a passage for himself through the crowd. Then addressing a coachman who had not offended, by speaking first, he said:

"Here, sir! Here are my checks! Go get my luggage and take it to the Astor House. Hand the clerk this card, and tell him I want a good room, well warmed. I shall take a walk around the city before going. And hark ye! If one of my trunks is missing, I'll have you hanged, you rogue!"

"Breach of trust isn't a hanging matter in New York, your honor," laughed the hack-man, as he touched his hat and hurried off towards the crowd collected around the baggage car.

Old Hurricane made a step or two, as if he would have pursued and punished the flippancy of the man; but finally thought better of it, picked up his portmanteau and walked up the street slowly, with frequent pauses and bewildered looks, as though he had forgotten his directions, or lost his way, and yet hesitated to inquire of any one for the obscure little alley in which he had been told to look for his treasure.

CHAPTER IV

CAPITOLA

"Her sex a page's dress belied,
Obscured her charms, but could not hide."
—*Scott*[1]

"*PLEASE, SIR,* do you want your carpet-bag carried?" asked a voice near.

Old Hurricane looked around him with a puzzled air, for he thought that a young *girl* had made this offer, so soft and clear were the notes of the voice that spoke.

"It was I, sir! here I am, at your's and everybody's service, sir!" said the same voice.

And turning, Old Hurricane saw sitting astride a pile of boxes at the corner store, a very ragged lad, some thirteen years of age.

"Good gracious!" thought Old Hurricane, as he gazed upon the boy, "this must be crown-prince and heir-apparent to the 'king of shreds and patches.'"[2]

"Well, old gent., you'll know me next time, that's certain!" said the lad, returning the look with interest.

It is probable Old Hurricane did not hear this irreverent speech, for he continued to gaze with pity and dismay upon the ragamuffin before him. He was a handsome boy, too, notwithstanding the deplorable state of his wardrobe. Thick, clustering curls of jet black hair fell in tangled dis-order around a forehead broad, white, and smooth as that of a girl; slender and quaintly-arched black eyebrows played above a pair of mischievous, dark gray eyes, that sparkled beneath the shade of long, thick, black lashes; a little turned-up nose, and red, pouting lips, completed the character of a countenance full of fun, frolic, spirit, and courage.

"Well, governor, if you've looked long enough, maybe you'll take me

33

into service!" said the lad, winking to a group of his fellow newsboys that had gathered at the corner.

"Dear! dear! dear! he looks as if he had never in his life seen soap and water or a suit of whole clothes!" ejaculated the old gentleman; adding, kindly,—"Yes, I reckon I will give you the job, my son!"

"*His son!* Oh, crickey, do you hear *that,* fellows? *His son!* Oh, Lor'! my governor's turned up at last. I'm his son! oh, gemini! But what did I tell you? I always had a sort of impression that I *must* have had a father in some former period of my life; and, behold, here he is! Who knows but I might have had a *mother* also? But that isn't likely. Still, I'll ask him:—How's the old woman, sir?" said the newsboy, jumping off the boxes and taking the carpet-bag in his hand.

"What are you talking about, you infatuated tatterdemalion? Come along! If it weren't for pity, I'd have you put in the pillory!" exclaimed Old Hurricane, shaking his cane at the offender.

"Thanky, sir! I have not had a pillow under my head for a long time!"

"Silence, ragamuffin!"

"Just so, sir! 'a dumb devil is better than a talking one!'" answered the lad, demurely, following his employer.

They went on some distance, Old Hurricane diligently reading the names of the streets at the corners. Presently, he stopped again, bewildered, and after gazing around himself for a few minutes, said:

"Boy!"

"Yes, sir!"

"Do you know such a place as Rag Alley, in Manillo Street?"

"Rag Alley, sir?"

"Yes; a sort of narrow, dark, musty place, with a row of old, tumbledown tenements each side, where poor wretches live all huddled up together, fifty in a house, eh!—I was told I couldn't drive up it in a carriage, so I had to walk! Do you know such a place?"

"Do *I* know such a place! Do *I* know Rag Alley?—oh, my eye! Oh, he! he! he!"

"What are you laughing at *now,* you miscellaneous assortment of variegated pieces?"

"Oh! oh, dear! I was laughing to think how well I knew Rag Alley."

"Humph! you *do* look as if you were born and bred there."

"But, sir, I wasn't."

"Humph! how did you get into life, then?"

"I don't know, governor, unless I was raked up from a gutter by some old woman in the rag-picking line," said the newsboy, demurely.

"Humph! I think that quite likely. But now, do you say that you know where that alley is?"

"Oh, don't set me off again! Oh, he, he, he!—yes, sir, I know."

"Well, then, show me the way, and don't be a fool."

"I'd scorn to be it, sir. This is the way," said the lad, taking the lead.

They walked on several squares, and then the boy stopped, and pointing down a cross-street, said:

"There, governor, there you are!"

"There! Where? Why, that's a handsome street!" said Old Hurricane, gazing up in admiration at the opposite blocks of stately brown stone mansions.

"That's it, hows'ever. That's Rag Alley. 'Taint called Rag Alley *now*, though! It's called Hifalutin Terrace! Them *tenements* you talk of were pulled down more'n a year ago, and these houses put up in their place," said the newsboy.

"Dear! dear! dear! what changes! And what became of the poor tenants?" asked Old Hurricane, gazing in dismay at the inroads of improvements.

"The tenants?—poor wretches! How do I know? Carted away, blown away, thrown away—with the other rubbish—What became of the *tenants?*

> 'Ask of the winds that far around
> With fragments strewed the sea'-ty!

I heard that spouted at a school exhibition once, governor," said the boy, demurely.

"Humph! well, well, the trace is lost! What shall I do?—put advertisements in all the daily papers,—apply at the chief police office. Yes, I'll do *both*," muttered Old Hurricane, to himself. Then, speaking out, he called:

"Boy!"

"Yes, sir.

"Call me a coach."

"Yes, sir." And the lad was off like an arrow to do his bidding.

In a few moments the coach drove up. The newsboy, that was sitting beside the driver, jumped down, and said:

"Here it is, sir."

"Thank you, my son. Here is your fee," said Old Hurricane, putting a silver dollar into the lad's hand.

"What! Lor'! It an't *be!* but it *is!* He must have made a *mistake!* What if he *did,* I don't care. Yes, I do, *too.* 'Honor bright,'" exclaimed the newsboy, looking in wonder and desire and sore temptation upon the largest piece of money he had ever touched in his life.

"Governor!"

"Well, boy," said the old gentleman, with his feet upon the steps of the coach.

"You've been and done and gone and give me a whole dollar by mistake!"

"And why should you think it a mistake, you impertinent monkey?"

"Your honor didn't *mean* it!"

"Why not, you young rascal?—of course I did. Take it and be off with you!" said Old Hurricane, beginning to ascend the steps.

"I'm a great mind to!" said the newsboy, still gazing on the coin with satisfaction and desire; "I'm a *great* mind to! but I *won't!* 'Taint fair.—Governor, I say!"

"What now, you troublesome fellow?"

"Do stop a minute! *Don't* tempt me too hard! 'cause, you see, I aint sure I could keep honest, if I was tempted *too* hard."

"What do you mean now, you ridiculous little ape?"

"I mean I know you're from the country, and don't know no better, and I mustn't impose upon your ignorance."

"*My ignorance,* you impudent villain!" exclaimed the old man, with rising wrath.

"Yes, governor; you haint cut your eye teeth yet! you aint up to snuff! you don't know nothing! Why, *this* is too much for toting a carpetbag a half a dozen squares! and it's very well you fell in with a honest lad like *me,* that wouldn't impose on your innocence! Bless you, the usual price isn't more'n a dime, or if you're rich and generous, a shilling, but———"

"What the deuce do I care for the usual price, you—you—you perfect prodigy of patches!—there, for the Lord's sake, go get yourself a decent suit of clothes. Drive on, coachman!" roared Old Hurricane, flinging an eagle[3] upon the sidewalk, and rolling off in his cab.

"Poor, dear, old gentleman! I wonder where his *keeper* is? How could he have got *loose?* Maybe I'd better go and tell the police! But then I don't know who he is, or where he's gone. But he is *very* crazy, and I'm afraid he'll fling away every cent of his money before his friends can catch him! I know what I'll do! I'll go to the stand and watch for the coach to come back, and ask the driver what he has done with the poor, dear old fellow!" said the newsboy, picking up the gold coin, and putting it into his pocket. And then he started, but with an eye to business, singing out:

"Herald! *Tribune!* *Express!* last account of the orful accident— steamer!" etc., etc., etc., selling his papers as he went on to the coach stand. He found the coachman already there. And to his anxious inquiries as to the sanity of the old gentleman, that Jehu replied:

"Oh, bless your soul, crazy? no! no more'n you or I. He's a real nob! a real Virginian, F. F. V.,⁴ with money like the sands on the seashore. Keep the tin, lad—he knowed what he was a-doin' on."

"Oh! it—it a'most scares me to have so much money!" exclaimed the boy, half in delight, half in dismay; "but to-night I'll have a warm supper, and sleep in a bed once more! And to-morrow a new suit of clothes! So here goes——

"Herald!—*Express*—full account—the horrible murder—Bell street," etc., etc., etc., crying his papers until he was out of hearing.

Never in his life had the newsboy felt so prosperous and happy.

CHAPTER V

THE DISCOVERY

"And at the magistrate's command
They next undid the leathern band
That bound her tresses there,
And raised her felt hat from her head,
And down her slender form there spread
Black ringlets rich and rare."[1]

OLD HURRICANE meanwhile dined at the public table at the Astor, and afterwards went to his room, to rest, smoke and ruminate. And he finished the evening by supping and retiring to bed.

In the morning, after an early breakfast, he wrote a dozen advertisements, and called a coach and rode around to leave them with the various daily papers for immediate publication. Then, to lose no time, he rode up to the Recorder's office to set the police upon the search.

As he was about to enter the front portal, he observed the doorway and passage blocked up with even a larger crowd than usual.

And seeing the coachman who had waited upon him the previous day, he inquired of him—

"What is the matter here?"

"Nothing, your honor, 'cept a boy tuk up for wearing girl's clothes, or a girl took up for wearing boy's, I dunno which," said the man touching his hat.

"Let me pass, then, I must speak to the chief of police," said Old Hurricane, shoving his way into the Recorder's room.

"This is not the office of the chief, sir; you will find him on the other side of the hall," said a bystander.

But before Old Hurricane had gathered the sense of these words, a sight within the office drew his steps thither. Up before the Recorder stood a lad of about thirteen years, who, despite his smart new suit of gray casinet,[2] his long rolling black ringlets, and his downcast and blushing face,

Old Hurricane immediately recognized as his acquaintance of the preceding day, the saucy young tatterdemalion.

Feeling sorry for the friendless boy, the old man impulsively went up to him and patted him on the shoulder, saying:

"What! in trouble, my lad? never mind—never look down! I'll warrant ye an honest lad from what I've seen myself! Come, come! pluck up a spirit! I'll see you through, my lad!"

"'*Lad!*' Lord bless your soul, sir, *he's* no more a lad than you or I. The young rascal is a girl in boy's clothes, sir!" said the officer who had the culprit in custody.

"What—what—what!" exclaimed Old Hurricane, gazing in consternation from the young prisoner to the accuser; "what—what! my newsboy, my saucy little prince of patches, a girl in boy's clothes!!!"

"Yes, sir—a young scoundrel! I actually twigged him selling papers at the Fulton Ferry this morning! A little rascal!"

"A girl in boy's clothes! A *girl!*" exclaimed Old Hurricane, with his eyes nearly starting out of his head.

Just then the young culprit looked up in his face with an expression half melancholy, half mischievous, that appealed to the rugged heart of the old man. Turning around to the policeman, he startled the whole office by roaring out:

"*Girl* is she, sir?—then, demmy, sir! whether a girl in *boy's* clothes, or *men's* clothes, or *soldier's* clothes, or *sailor's* clothes, or, *any* clothes, or NO clothes, sir! treat her with the delicacy due to *woman*hood, sir! aye, and the tenderness owed to *child*hood! for she is but a bit of a poor, friendless, motherless, fatherless *child,* lost and wandering in your great Babylon! No more hard words to *her,* sir—or by the everlasting——"

"Order," put in the calm and dignified Recorder.

Old Hurricane, though his face was still purple, his veins swollen and his eyeballs glaring with anger, immediately recovered himself, turned and bowed to the Recorder and said:

"Yes, sir, I will keep order, if you'll make that brute of a policeman reform his language."

And so saying, Old Hurricane subsided into a seat, immediately behind the child, to watch the examination.

"What'll they do with her, do you think?" he inquired of a bystander.

"Send her *up,* in course."

"*Up?*—where?"

"To Blackwell's Island—to the work'us, in course."

"To the *work*-house—*her,* that *child?*—the wretches! Um-m-m-me! Oh-h-h-h!" groaned Old Hurricane, stooping and burying his shaggy, gray head in his great hands.

He felt his shoulder touched, and looking up saw that the little prisoner had turned around, and was about to speak to him.

"Governor," said the same clear voice that he had even at first supposed to belong to a girl—"Governor, don't you keep on letting out that way! You don't know nothing! You're in the Recorder's Court! If you don't mind your eye, they'll commit you for contempt!"

"Will they? Then they'll do *well,* lad! *lass,* I mean, I plead guilty to contempt. Send a child like *you* to the——! They *shan't do it!* Simply, they *shan't do it!* I—Major Warfield, of Virginia—tell you so, my boy—*girl,* I mean!"

"But, you innocent old lion, instead of freeing *me,* you'll find *yourself* shut up between four walls, and very narrow ones at that, *I* tell you! You'll think yourself in a coffin! Governor, they call it—*The Tombs!*" whispered the child.

"Attention!" said the clerk.

The little prisoner turned and faced the court. And the "old lion" buried his shaggy, gray head and beard in his hands, and groaned aloud.

"Now, then, what is your name, my lad—my *girl,* I should say?" inquired the clerk.

"Capitola, sir."

Old Hurricane pricked up his ears and raised his head, muttering to himself—"*Cap-it-o-la!* That's a very odd name. Can't surely be *two* in the world of the same. *Cap-it-o-la!*—if it should be *my* Capitola, after all? I shouldn't wonder at all! I'll listen, and say nothing." And with this wise resolution Old Hurricane again dropped his head upon his hands.

"You say your name is Capitola—Capitola what?" inquired the clerk, continuing the examination.

"Nothing, sir."

"Nothing! What do you mean?"

"I have no name but Capitola, sir!"

"Who is your father?"

"Never had any that I know, sir."

"Your mother?"

"Never had a mother either, sir, as ever I heard."

40

"Where do you live?"

"About in spots, in the city, sir."

"*Oh—oh—oh!*" groaned Old Hurricane within his hands.

"What is your calling?" inquired the clerk.

"Selling newspapers, carrying portmanteaus and packages, sweeping before doors, clearing off snow, blacking boots, and so on."

"Little odd jobs in general, eh?"

"Yes, sir, anything that I can turn my hand to, and get to do."

"Boy—*girl* I should say—what tempted you to put yourself into male attire?"

"Sir?"

"In boy's clothes, then?"

"Oh, yes—*want, sir*—and—and *danger*, sir," cried the little prisoner, putting her hands to a face crimson with blushes, and for the first time since her arrest upon the eve of sobbing.

"*Oh—oh—oh!*" groaned Old Hurricane from his chair.

"Want? Danger! How is that?" continued the clerk.

"Your honor mightn't like to know."

"By all means. It is, in fact, necessary that you should give an account of yourself," said the clerk.

Old Hurricane once more raised his head, opened his ears, and gave close attention.

One circumstance he had particularly remarked—the language used by the poor child during her examination was much superior to the slang she had previously affected, to support her assumed character of newsboy.

"Well, well—why do you pause? Go on—go on my good boy—*girl* I mean," said the Recorder, in a tone of kind encouragement.

well-educated by nurse

41

CHAPTER VI

A SHORT, SAD STORY

⚜⚜⚜⚜⚜

"Ah! poverty is a weary thing,
It burdeneth the brain.
It maketh even the little child
To murmur and complain."

"IT IS NOT much I have to tell," began Capitola. "I was brought up in Rag Alley and its neighborhood, by an old woman named Nancy Grewell."

"Ah!" ejaculated Old Hurricane.

"She was a washerwoman, and rented one scantily-furnished room from a poor family named Simmons."

"Oh!" cried Old Hurricane.

"Granny, as I called her, was very good to me, and I never suffered cold, nor hunger, until about eighteen months ago, when Granny took it into her head to go down to Virginia."

"Humph!" exclaimed Old Hurricane.

"When Granny went away, she left me a little money and some good clothes, and told me to be sure to stay with the people where she left me, for that she would be back in about a month. But, your honor, that was the very last I ever saw or heard of poor Granny. She never came back again; and by that I know she must have died."

"Ah-h-h!" breathed the old man, puffing fast.

"The first month or two after Granny left, I did well enough. And then, when the little money was all gone, I eat with the Simmons's, and did little odd jobs for my food. But by and by Mr. Simmons got out of work, and the family fell into want, and they wished me to go out and beg for them. *I just couldn't do that,* and so they told me I should look out for myself."

"Were there no customers of your grandmother that you could have applied to for employment?" asked the Recorder.

42

"No, sir. My Granny's customers were mostly boarders at the small taverns, and they were always changing. I did apply to two or three houses where the landladies knew Granny; but they didn't want me."

"*Oh-h-h!*" groaned Major Warfield, in the tone of one in great pain.

why so pained?

"I wouldn't have that old fellow's conscience for a good deal," whispered a spectator, "for, as sure as shooting, that gal's his unlawful child."

"Well—go on. What next?" asked the clerk.

"Well, sir, though the Simmons's had nothing to give me except a crust now and then, they still let me sleep in the house, for the little jobs I could do for them. But at last Simmons got work on the railroad a way off somewhere, and they all moved away from the city."

"And you were left alone?"

"Yes, sir, I was left alone in the empty, unfurnished house. Still it was a *shelter,* and I was glad of it, and I dreaded the time when it would be rented by another tenant, and I should be turned into the street."

"Oh! oh! oh, Lord!" groaned the major.

"But it was never rented again; for the word went around that the whole row was to be pulled down; and so I thought I had leave to stay, at least as long as the *rats* did," continued Capitola, with somewhat of her natural rougish humor twinkling in her dark, gray eyes.

"But how did you get your bread?" inquired the Recorder.

"Did not get it at all, sir. *Bread* was too dear! I sold my clothes, piece by piece, to the old man, over the way, and bought corn meal, and picked up trash to make a fire, and cooked a little mush every day in an old tin can that had been left behind. And so I lived on for two or three weeks. And then when my clothes were all gone—except the suit I had upon my back—and my meal was almost out, instead of making *mush* every day I economized, and made *gruel.*"

"But my boy—*my good girl,* I mean—before you became so destitute, you should have found *some*thing or other to do," said the Recorder.

"Sir, I was trying to get jobs every hour in the day. I'd have done *any*thing honest. I went around to all the houses Granny knew, but they didn't want a girl. Some of the good-natured landlords said, if I was a *boy* now, they could keep me opening oysters, but as I was a *girl,* they had no work for me. I even went to the offices to get papers to sell, but they told me that crying papers was not proper work for a girl. I even went down to the ferry-boats and watched for the passengers coming ashore, and ran and offered to carry their carpet-bags or portmanteaus; but some growled at me, and others laughed at me, and one old gentleman asked me if I thought *he* was a North American Indian, to strut up Broadway with a female behind him carrying his pack. And so, sir, while all the ragged boys I knew could get little jobs to earn bread, I, because I was a girl, was not allowed to carry a gentleman's parcel, or black his boots, or shovel the snow off a shopkeeper's pavement, or put in coal, or do *any*thing that *I* could do just as well as *they*. And so because I was a girl, there seemed to be nothing but starvation or beggary before me."

"Oh, Lord! oh, Lord! that such things should be!" cried Old Hurricane.

"That was *bad*, sir! but there was *worse* behind! There came a day when my meal—even the last dust of it, was gone! Then I kept life in me by drinking water, and by sleeping all I could. At first I could not sleep for the gnawing—gnawing—in my stomach; but afterwards I slept deeply, from exhaustion, and then I'd dream of feasts and the richest sort of food, and of eating such quantities! and really, sir, I seemed to taste it and enjoy it and get the good of it—almost as much as if it was all true! One morning after such a dream I was waked up by a great noise, outside. I staggered upon my feet and crept to the window! and there, sir, were the workmen all outside, a pulling down the house over my head!"

"Good Heaven!" ejaculated Old Hurricane, who seemed to constitute himself the chorus of this drama.

"Sir, they didn't know that I or any one was in the empty house! Fright gave me strength to run down stairs and run out. Then I stopped. Oh! I stopped and looked up and down the street! What should I do? The last shelter was gone away from me!—the house where I had lived so many years and that seemed like a friend to me, was falling before my eyes! I thought I'd just go and pitch myself into the river, and end it all!"

"That was a very wicked thought," said the Recorder.

"Yes, sir, I know it was; and besides, I was dreadfully afraid of being suffocated in the dirty water around the wharf!!!" said Capitola, with a sparkle of that irrepressible humor that effervesced even through all her trouble. "Well, sir, the hand that feeds young ravens kept me from dying that day.[1] I found a five-cent piece in the street, and resolved not to smother myself in the river mud as long as it lasted. So I bought a muffin, ate it, and went down to the wharf to look for a job. I looked all day, but found none, and when night came I went into a lumber-yard and hid myself behind a pile of planks that kept the wind off me, and I went to sleep and dreamed a beautiful dream of living in a handsome house, with friends all around me, and everything good to eat, and drink, and wear!"

"Poor, poor child; but your dream may come true yet!" muttered Old Hurricane to himself.

"Well, your Honor, next day I spent another penny out of my half-dime, and looked in vain for work all day, and slept at night in a broken-down omnibus that had happened to be left on the stand. And so, not to tire your patience, a whole week passed away. I lived on my half-dime, spending a penny a day for a muffin, until the last penny was gone, and sleeping at night wherever I could—sometimes under the front stoop of a house, sometimes in an old broken carriage, and sometimes behind a pile of boxes on the sidewalk!"

"That was a dreadful exposure for a young girl," said the Recorder.

A burning blush flamed up over the young creature's cheek, as she answered: *anger*

"Yes, sir, that was the worst of all; that finally drove me to putting on boy's clothes."

"Let us hear all about it."

"Oh, sir—I can't—I—how can I? Well, being always exposed, sleeping out-doors, I was often in danger from bad boys and bad men," said Capitola, and dropping her head upon her breast, and covering her crimson cheeks with her hands, for the first time she burst into tears and sobbed aloud.

"Come, come, my little man!—my good little *woman,* I mean—don't take it so to heart! You couldn't help it!" said Old Hurricane, with raindrops glittering even in his own stormy eyes.

Capitola looked up with her whole countenance flashing with spirit, and exclaimed, "Oh! but I took care of myself, sir! I did, indeed, your Honor! You mustn't, either you or the old gentleman, dare to think but what I did."

"Oh, of course! of course!" said a bystander, laughing.

Old Hurricane sprung up, bringing his feet down upon the floor with a resound that made the great hall ring again, exclaiming:

"What do you mean by 'of course,' 'of course,' you villain? Demmy! *I'll swear* she took care of herself, you varlet; and if any man dares to hint otherwise, I'll ram his falsehood down his throat with the point of my walking-stick, and make him swallow both!"

"Order, order!" said the clerk.

Old Hurricane immediately wheeled to the right-about, faced and saluted the bench in military fashion, and then said:

"Yes, sir! I'll regard order! but, in the meanwhile, if the court does not protect this child from insult, I must, order or no order!" and with that the old gentleman once more subsided into his seat.

"Governor, don't you be so noisy! You'll get yourself stopped up into a jug next! Why, you remind me of an uproarious old fellow poor Granny used to talk about, that they called Old Hurricane, because he was so stormy!" whispered Capitola, turning towards him.

"Humph! *she's heard of me,* then!" muttered the old gentleman, to himself.

"Well, sir—I mean Miss—go on!" said the clerk, addressing Capitola.

"Yes, sir. Well, your Honor, at the end of five days, being a certain Thursday morning, when I couldn't get a job of work for love nor money, when my last penny was spent for my last roll—and my last roll was eaten up—and I was dreading the gnawing hunger by day, and the horrid perils of the night, I thought to myself *if I were only a boy,* I might carry packages, and shovel in coal, and do lots of jobs by day, and sleep without terror by night! And then I felt bitter against fate for not making me a boy! And so thinking and thinking and thinking, I wandered on until I found myself in Rag Alley, where I used to live, standing right between the pile of broken bricks, plaster, and lumber, that used to be my home, and the old pawn-broker's shop where I sold my clothes for meal. And then, all of a sudden, a bright thought struck me: *and I made up my mind to be a boy!*"

"Made up your mind to be a boy!"

"Yes, sir! for it was so easy! I wondered how I came to be so stupid as not to have thought of it before! I just ran across to the old shop, and offered to swap my suit of girl's clothes, that was good, though dirty, for *any,* even the raggedest suit of boy's clothes he had, whether they'd fit me or not, so they would only stay on me. The old fellow put his finger to his nose, as if he thought I'd been stealing and wanted to dodge the police. So he took down an old, not very ragged, suit that he said would fit me, and opened a door, and told me to go in his daughter's room and put 'em on.

"Well! not to tire your honors, I went into that little back parlor *a girl,* and I came out *a boy,* with a suit of pants and jacket, with my hair cut short and a cap on my head! The pawnbroker gave me a penny roll and a six-pence for my black ringlets."

"All seemed grist that came to his mill!" said Old Hurricane.

"Yes, Governor, he was a dealer in general. Well, the first thing I did was to hire myself to him, at a sixpence a day, and find myself, to shovel in his coal. That didn't take me but a day. So at night he paid me, and I slept in peace behind a stack of boxes. Next morning I was up before the sun, and down to the office of the little penny paper, the 'Morning Star.' I bought two dozen of 'em, and ran as fast as I could to the ferry-boats to sell to the early passengers. Well, sir, in an hour's time I had sold out, and pocketed just two shillings, and felt myself on the high road to fortune!"

"And so that was the way by which you came to put yourself in male attire?"

"Yes, sir! and the only thing that made me feel sorry, was to see what a fool I had been, not to turn to a boy before, when it was so easy! And from that day forth I was happy and prosperous! I found plenty to do! I carried carpet-bags, held horses, put in coal, cleaned sidewalks, blacked gentle-men's boots, and did everything an honest lad could turn his hand to! And so for more'n a year I was as happy as a king, and should have kept on so, only I forgot and let my hair grow, and instead of cutting it off, just tucked it up under my cap; and so this morning, on the ferry-boat, in a high breeze, the *wind blowed off my cap* and the *policeman blowed on me!*"

"'Twasn't altogether her long hair, your honor; for I had seen her before, having known her when she lived with old Mrs. Grewell, in Rag Alley," interrupted the officer.

"You may sit down my child," said the Recorder, in a tone of encouragement.

47

CHAPTER VII

METAMORPHOSIS OF THE NEWSBOY

With caution judge of probability.
Things deemed unlikely, e'en impossible,
Experience oft hath proved to be true.
——*Shakespeare*[1]

"*WHAT SHALL WE* do with her?" inquired the Recorder, *sotto voce,* of a brother magistrate who appeared to be associated with him on the bench.

"Send her to the Refuge," replied the other, in the same tone.

"What are they consulting about?" asked Old Hurricane, whose ears were not of the best.

"They are talking of sending her to the Refuge," answered a bystander.

"Refuge? Is there a Refuge for destitute children in New York? Then Babylon is not so bad as I thought it. What is this Refuge?"

"It is a prison where juvenile delinquents are trained to habits of——"

"A prison! send *her* to a prison! never!" burst forth Old Hurricane, rising and marching up to the Recorder.

He stood hat in hand before him, and said:

"Your Honor, if a proper legal guardian appears to claim this young person, and holds himself in all respects responsible for her, may she not be at once delivered into his hands?"

"Assuredly," answered the magistrate, with the manner of one glad to be rid of the charge.

"Then, sir, I, Ira Warfield, of Hurricane Hall, in Virginia, present myself as the guardian of this girl, Capitola Black, whom I claim as my ward. And I will enter into a recognizance for any sum to appear and prove my right, if it should be disputed. For my personal responsibility, sir, I refer you to the proprietors of the Astor, who have known me many years."

"It is not necessary, Major Warfield: we assume the fact of your responsibility and deliver up the young girl to your charge." *too easy*

"I thank you, sir," said Old Hurricane, bowing low.

Then hurrying across the room where sat the reporters for the press, he said:

"Gentlemen, I have a favor to ask of you—it is that you will altogether drop this case of the boy in girl's clothes—I mean the *girl* in girl's clothes—I declare, I don't know what I mean! nor I shan't, neither, until I see the creature in its proper dress; but this I wish to *request* of you, gentlemen, that you will drop that item from your report, or if you must mention it, treat it with delicacy, as the good name of a young lady is involved."

The reporters, with sidelong glances, winks, and smiles, gave him the required promise, and Old Hurricane returned to the side of his *protégée*.

"Capitola, are you willing to go with me?"

"Jolly willing, governor."

"Then come along, my coach is waiting," said Old Hurricane.

And, bowing to the Court, he took the hand of his charge, and led her forth amid the ill-suppressed jibes of the crowd.

"There's a hoary-headed old sinner!" said one.

"She's as like him as two peas," quoth another.

"Wonder if there's any more belonging to him of the same sort," inquired a third.

Leaving all this sarcasm behind him, Old Hurricane handed his *protégée* into the coach, took the seat beside her, and gave orders to be driven out towards Harlem.

As soon as they were seated in the coach, the old man turned to his charge and said:

"Capitola, I shall have to trust to your girl's wit, to get yourself into your proper clothes again without exciting farther notice."

"Yes, governor."

"My boy, girl, I mean! I am not the governor of Virginia, though if every one had his rights I don't know but I should be! However, I am only Major Warfield," said the old man, naively, for he had not the most distant idea that the title bestowed on him by Capitola, was a mere remnant of her newsboys' slang.

"Now, my lad—pshaw! my lass, I mean, how shall we get you metamorphosed again?"

"I know, gov—major, I mean. There is a shop of ready-made clothing at the 'Needle Woman's Aid,' corner of the next square. I can get out there and buy a full suit."

"Very well! stop at the next corner, driver," called Old Hurricane.

The next minute the coach drew up before a warehouse of ready-made garments.

Old Hurricane jumped out, and leading his charge, entered the shop.

Luckily, there was behind the counter only one person—a staid, elderly, kind-looking woman.

"Here, madam," said Old Hurricane, stooping confidentially to her ear—"I am in a little embarrassment that I hope you will be willing to help me out of for a consideration. I came to New York in pursuit of my ward—this young girl here, whom I found in boy's clothes. I now wish to restore her to her proper dress, before presenting her to my friends, of course. Therefore, I wish you to furnish her with a half a dozen complete suits of female attire, of the very best you have that will fit her. And also to give her the use of a room and of your own aid in changing her dress. I will pay you liberally."

Half suspicious and half scandalized, the worthy woman gazed with scrutiny first into the face of the guardian, and then into that of the ward; but finding in the extreme youth of the one and the advanced age of the other, and in the honest expression of both, something to allay her fears, if not to inspire her confidence, she said:

"Very well, sir. Come after me, young gentleman—young lady, I should say." And calling in a boy to mind the shop, she conducted Capitola to an inner apartment.

Old Hurricane went out and dismissed his coach. When it was entirely out of sight, he hailed another that was passing by empty, and engaged it to take himself and a young lady to the Washington House.

When he re-entered the shop he found the shopwoman and Capitola returned and waiting for him.

Capitola was indeed transfigured. Her bright black hair, parted in the middle, fell in ringlets each side her blushing cheeks; her dark gray eyes were cast down in modesty at the very same instant that her ripe red lips were puckered up with mischief. She was well and properly attired in a gray silk dress, crimson merino shawl, and a black velvet bonnet.

The other clothing that had been purchased was done up in packages and put into the coach.

And after paying the shopwoman handsomely, Old Hurricane took the hand of his ward, handed her into the coach, and gave the order:

"To the Washington House."

The ride was performed in silence.

Capitola sat deeply blushing at the recollection of her male attire, and profoundly cogitating as to what could be the relationship between herself and the gray old man whose claim the Recorder had so promptly admitted. There seemed but one way of accounting for the great interest he took in her fate. Capitola came to the conclusion that the grim old lion before her was no more nor less than—her own father! poor Cap had been too long tossed about New York not to know more of life than at her age she should have known. She had indeed the *innocence* of youth, but not its *simplicity*.

Old Hurricane, on his part, sat with his thick cane grasped in his two knobby hands, standing between his knees, his grizzled chin resting upon it, and his eyes cast down as in deep thought.

And so in silence they reached the Washington House.

Major Warfield then conducted his ward into the ladies' parlor, and went and entered his own and her name upon the books as "Major Warfield and his ward Miss Black," for whom he engaged two bedrooms and a private parlor.

Then leaving Capitola to be shown to her apartment by a chambermaid, he went out and ordered her luggage up to her room, and dismissed the coach.

Next he walked to the Astor House, paid his bill, collected his baggage, took another carriage and drove back to the Washington Hotel.

All this trouble Old Hurricane took to break the links of his action and prevent scandal. This filled up a long forenoon.

He dined alone with his ward in their private parlor.

Such a dinner poor Cap had never even *smelt* before! How intensely she enjoyed it with all its surroundings!—the comfortable room, the glowing fire, the clean table, the rich food, the obsequious attendance, her own genteel and becoming dress, the company of a highly respectable guardian—all, all, so different from anything she had ever been accustomed to, and so highly appreciated.

How happy she felt! how much happier from the contrast of her previous wretchedness! to be suddenly freed from want, toil, fear, and all the evils of destitute orphanage, and to find herself blest with wealth, leisure, and safety, under the care of a rich, good, and kind father! (for such Capitola continued to believe her guardian to be.) It was an incredible thing! It was like a fairy tale!

Something of what was passing in her mind was perceived by Old

Hurricane, who frequently burst into uproarious fits of laughter, as he watched her.

At last, when the dinner and dessert were removed, and the nuts, raisins, and wine placed upon the table, and the waiters had retired from the room and left them alone, sitting one on each side of the fire, with the table and its luxuries between them, Major Warfield suddenly looked up and asked:

"Capitola, whom do you think that I am?"

"Old Hurricane, to be sure! I knew you from Granny's description, the moment you broke out so in the police office," answered Cap.

"Humph! yes, you're right; and it was your granny that bequeathed you to me, Capitola."

"Then she is really dead?"

"Yes. There—don't cry about her. She was very old, and she died happy. Now, Capitola, if you please me, I mean to adopt you as my own daughter."

"Yes, father."

"No, no,—you needn't call me father, you know, because it isn't true. Call me *uncle!* uncle! uncle!"

"Is *that* true, sir?" asked Cap, demurely.

"No, no, no; but it will *do!* it will do! Now, Cap, how much do you know? anything? Ignorant as a horse, I am afraid."

"Yes, sir, even as a *colt.*"

"Can you read at all?"

"Yes, sir. I learned at the Sunday school."

"Cast accounts and write?"

"I can keep your books at a pinch, sir."

"Humph! who taught you these accomplishments?"

"Herbert Greyson, sir."

"Herbert Greyson! I've heard that name before! here it is again. Who *is* that Herbert Greyson?"

"He's second mate on the *Susan,* sir, that is expected in every day."

"Umph! Umph!—take a glass of wine, Capitola?"

"No, sir; I never touch a single drop."

"Why? why? good wine after dinner, my child, is a good thing, let me tell you."

"Ah, sir, my life has shown me too much misery that has come of drinking wine."

"Well, well, as you please. Why, where has the girl run off to?"

exclaimed the old man, breaking off, and looking with amazement at Capitola, who had suddenly started up and rushed out of the room.

In an instant she rushed in again exclaiming:

"Oh, he's come! he's come! I heard his voice!"

"Who's come, you madcap?" inquired the old man.

"Oh, Herbert Greyson! Herbert Greyson! His ship is in, and he has come here! he *always* comes here—most of the sea-officers do!" exclaimed Cap, dancing around until all her black ringlets flew up and down. Then suddenly pausing, she came quietly to his side, and said, solemnly:

"Uncle! Herbert has been at sea three years! he knows nothing of my past misery and destitution, nor of my ever wearing boy's clothes. Uncle, *please* don't tell him, especially of the boy's clothes!" And in the earnestness of her appeal, Capitola clasped her hands and raised her eyes to the old man's face. How soft those gray eyes looked when praying! but for all that, the very spirit of mischief still lurked about the corners of the plump, arch lips.

"Of course I shall tell no one. I am not so proud of your masquerading as to publish it. And as for this young fellow, I shall probably never see him!" exclaimed Old Hurricane.

CHAPTER VIII

HERBERT GREYSON

"A kind, true heart, a spirit high,
That cannot fear and will not bow,
Is flashing in his manly eye
And stamped upon his brow."
—*Halleck* [1]

IN A FEW MINUTES Capitola came bounding up the stairs again, exclaiming, joyously—

"Here he is, uncle! here is Herbert Greyson! Come along Herbert! You must come in and see my new uncle!" And she broke into the room, dragging before her astonished guardian a handsome, dark-eyed young sailor, who bowed, and then stood blushing at his enforced intrusion.

"I beg your pardon, sir," he said, "for bursting in upon you in this way; but——"

"I dragged him here willy-nilly," said Capitola.

"Still, if I had had time to think, I should not have intruded."

"Oh, say no more, sir! You are heartily welcome!" exclaimed the old man, thrusting out his rugged hand and seizing the bronzed one of the youth. "Sit down, sir,—sit down! *Good Lord, how like!*" he added, mentally.

Then, seeing the young sailor still standing blushing and hesitating, he struck his upon the floor and roared out:

"DEMMY, SIT DOWN, SIR! When Ira Warfield *says* sit down, he MEANS sit down!"

"Ira Warfield!" exclaimed the young man, starting back in astonishment—one might almost say in consternation.

"Aye sir! Ira Warfield! that's my name! Never heard any ill of it, did you?"

The young man did not answer, but continued gazing in amazement upon the speaker.

54

"Nor any good of it either, perhaps,—eh, uncle?" archly put in Capitola.

"Silence, you monkey! Well, young man! well, what is the meaning of all this?" exclaimed Old Hurricane, impatiently.

"Oh, your pardon, sir! this was sudden. But you must know I had once a relative of that name—an uncle." *sister's son*

"*And have still, Herbert!* and have still, lad! Come, come, boy! I am not sentimental, nor romantic, nor melo-dramatic, nor anything of that sort. I don't know how to strike an attitude and exclaim—'Come to my bosom, sole remaining offspring of a dear, departed sister,' or any of the like stage-playing. But I tell you, lad, that I like your looks; and I like what I have heard of you from this girl and *another* old woman, now dead; and so—but sit down, *sit down* demmy, SIR, SIT DOWN, and we'll talk over the walnuts and the wine! Capitola, take *your* seat, too!" ordered the old man, throwing himself into his chair. Herbert also drew his chair up.

Capitola resumed her seat, saying to herself,

"Well, well, I am determined not to be surprised at anything that happens, being perfectly clear in my own mind that this is all nothing but a dream. But how pleasant it is to dream that I have found a rich uncle and he has found a nephew, and that nephew is Herbert Greyson! I do believe that I had rather *die* in my sleep than wake from *this* dream!"

"Herbert!" said Old Hurricane, as soon as they had gathered around the table, "Herbert, this is my ward, Miss Black, the daughter of a deceased friend. Capitola, this is the only son of my departed sister."

"*Hem-m-m!* we have had the pleasure of being acquainted with each other before!" said Cap, pinching up her lip, and looking demure.

"But not of really knowing who 'each other' *was*, you monkey! Herbert, fill your glass! Here's to our better acquaintance!"

"I thank you, sir. I never touch wine," said the young man.

"'Never touch wine!' here's *another!* here's a young prig! I don't believe you! yes, I do too! Demmy, sir,—if you never touch *wine* it's because you prefer *brandy!*—Waiter!"

"I thank you, sir. Order no brandy for me. If I never use intoxicating liquors, it is because I gave a promise to that effect to my dying mother!"

"Say no more—say no more, lad! Drink water, if you like. *It won't hurt you!*" exclaimed the old man, filling and quaffing a glass of champagne. Then he said:

"I quarreled with your mother, Herbert, for marrying a man that I *hated*—yes, *hated,* Herbert! for he differed with me about the tariff and—the Trinity! Oh, how I hated him, boy, until he died! and then I wondered in my soul, as I wonder even now, how I ever *could* have been so infuriated against a poor fellow now cold in his grave—as I shall be in time! I wrote to my sister, and expressed my feelings; but somehow or other, Herbert, we never came to a right understanding again. She answered my letter affectionately enough, but she refused to accept a home for herself and child under my roof, saying that she thanked me for my offer, but that the house which had been closed against her husband ought never to become the refuge of his widow. After that we never corresponded, and I have no doubt, Herbert, that she, naturally enough, taught you to dislike me."

"Not so, sir! Indeed, you wrong her! She might have been loyal to my father's memory without being resentful towards you. She said that you had a noble nature, but it was often obscured by violent passions. On her deathbed she bade me, should I ever meet you, to say that she repented her refusal of your offered kindness."

"And *consented* that it should be transferred to her orphan boy?" added Old Hurricane, with the tears like raindrops in his stormy eyes.

"No, sir, she said not so."

"But yet she would not have disapproved a service offered to her son."

"Uncle—since you permit me to call you so—I want nothing. I have a good berth in the *Susan* and a kind friend in her captain."

"You have all your dear mother's pride, Herbert."

"And all his uncle's," put in Cap.

"Hush, magpie! But is the merchant service agreeable to you, Herbert?"

"Not perfectly, sir; but one must be content."

"Demmy, sir, my sister's son *need* not be content unless he has a mind to! And if you prefer the navy——"

"No, sir. I like the navy even less than the merchant service."

"Then *what would* suit you, lad? Come, you have betrayed the fact that you are not altogether satisfied."

"On the contrary, sir, I told you distinctly that I really wanted nothing, and that I must be satisfied."

"And I say demmy, sir, you *shan't* be satisfied, unless you like to! Come, if you don't like the navy, what do you say to the army, eh?

"It is a proud, aspiring profession, sir," said the young man, as his face lighted up with enthusiasm.

"Then, demmy, if you like the army, sir, you shall enter it. Yes, sir. Demmy, the administration, confound them, has not done me justice, but they'll scarcely dare to refuse to send my nephew to West Point, when I demand it."

"To West Point!" exclaimed Herbert, in delight.

"Aye, youngster, to West Point. I shall see to it, when I pass through Washington on our way to Virginia. We start on the early train to-morrow morning. In the meantime, young man, you take leave of your captain, pack up your traps and join us. You must go with me, and make Hurricane Hall your home until you go to West Point."

"Oh, what a capital old governor our uncle is!" exclaimed Cap, jumping up and clapping her hands.

"Sir, indeed you overwhelm me with this most unexpected kindness. I do not know as yet how much of it I ought to accept. But accident will make me, whether or no, your travelling companion for a great part of the way, as I also start for Virginia to-morrow, to visit dear friends there whose house was always my mother's home and mine, and who, since my bereavement, have been to me like a dear mother and brother. I have not seen them for *years* and before I go anywhere else, even to your kind roof, I must go *there,*" said Herbert gravely.

"And who are those dear friends of yours, Herbert, and where do they live? If I can serve them, they shall be rewarded for their kindness unto you, my boy."

"Oh, sir, yes, yes! you can indeed serve them! They are a poor widow and her only son! She has seen better days; but now takes in sewing to support herself and boy. When my mother was living, during the last years of her life, when she also was a poor widow with an only son, they joined their slender means, and took a house and lived together. When my mother died leaving me a boy of ten years old, this poor woman still sheltered and worked for me as for her own son, until ashamed of being a burden to her, I ran away and went to sea!"

"Noble woman! I will make her fortune!" exclaimed Old Hurricane, jumping up and walking up and down the floor.

"Oh, *do,* sir! Oh, *do!* dear uncle. I don't wish you to expend either money or influence upon *my* fortunes; but oh! do educate Traverse! he is such a gifted lad—so intellectual! even his Sunday school teacher says that he is sure to work his way to distinction, although now he is altogether dependent on his Sunday school for his learning. Oh, sir, if you would only educate the son *he'd* make a fortune for his mother!"

"Generous boy, to plead for your friends rather than for yourself! But I am strong enough, thank God, to help you all! You shall go to West Point. Your young friend shall go to school, and then to college," said Old Hurricane, with a burst of honest enthusiasm.

"And where shall I go, sir?" inquired Cap.

harsh "To the lunatic asylum, you imp!" exclaimed the old man; then turning to Herbert, he continued: "Yes, lad, I will do as I say; as for the poor but noble-hearted widow——"

"You'll marry her yourself, as a reward, won't you, uncle?" asked the incorrigible Cap.

"Perhaps I will, you monkey, if it is only to bring somebody home to keep you in order!" said Old Hurricane; then turning again to Herbert, he resumed: "As to the widow, Herbert, I will place her above want."

"Over my head," cried Cap.

"And now, Herbert, I will trouble you to ring for coffee, and after we have had that, I think that we had better separate, and prepare for our journey to-morrow."

Herbert obeyed, and after the required refreshment had been served and partaken of, the little circle broke up for the evening, and soon after retired to rest.

Early the next morning, after a hasty breakfast, the three took their seats in the express train for Washington, where they arrived upon the evening of the same day. They put up for the night at Brown's, and the next day Major Warfield, leaving his party at their hotel, called upon the President, the Secretary of War, and other high official dignitaries, and put affairs in such a train that he had little doubt of the ultimate appointment of his nephew to a cadetship at West Point.

The same evening, wishing to avoid the stage route over the mountains, he took with his party the night boat for Richmond, where in due time they arrived, and whence they took the valley line of coaches that passed through Tip-Top, which they reached upon the morning of the fourth day of their long journey. Here they found Major Warfield's carriage waiting for him, and here they were to separate—Major Warfield and Capitola to turn off to Hurricane Hall, and Herbert Greyson to keep on the route to the town of Staunton.

It was as the three sat in the parlor of the little hotel, where the stage stopped to change horses, their adieus were made.

"Remember, Herbert, that I am willing to go to the utmost extent of my power to benefit the good widow and her son, who were so kind to my nephew in his need. Remember that I hold it a sacred debt that I owe them. Tell them so. And mind, Herbert, I shall expect you back in a week at farthest."

"I shall be punctual, sir! God bless you my dear uncle! you have made me very happy in being the bearer of such glad tidings to the widow and the fatherless. And now I hear the horn blowing—Good-bye, uncle! Good-bye, Capitola. I am going to carry them great joy, such great joy, uncle, as *you* who have everything you want, can scarcely imagine." And, shaking hands heartily with his companions, Herbert ran through the door, and jumped aboard the coach just as the impatient driver was about to leave him behind.

As soon as the coach had rolled out of sight Major Warfield handed Capitola into his carriage that had long been waiting, and took the seat by her side—much to the scandalization of Wool, who muttered to his horses:

"There, I told you so! I said how he'd go and bring home a young wife, and behold he's gone and done it!"

"Uncle!" said Capitola, as the carriage rolled lazily along—"Uncle! do you know you never once asked Herbert the *name* of the widow you are going to befriend, and that he never told you!"

"By George! that is true! how strange! yet I did not seem to *miss* the name. How did it ever happen, Capitola? did he omit it on purpose, do you think?"

"Why, *no,* uncle! he, boy-like, always spoke of them as 'Traverse' and 'Traverse's mother'; and you, like yourself, called her nothing but the 'poor widow,' and the 'struggling mother,' and the 'noble woman,' and so on; and her son, as the 'boy,' the 'youth,' 'young Traverse,' Herbert's 'friend,' etc. I, for my part, had *some* curiosity to see whether you and Herbert would go on talking of them forever, without having to use their surnames. And behold he even went off without naming them!"

"By George! and so he did. It was the strangest oversight. But I'll write as soon as I get home and ask him."

"No, uncle, just for the fun of the thing, wait until he comes back and see how long it will be and how much he will talk of them without mentioning their names."

"Ha! ha! ha! so I will, Cap! so I will. Besides, whatever their names are, it's nothing to me. 'A rose by any other name would smell as sweet,' you know.² And if she is 'Mrs. Tagfoot Waddle,' I shall still think so good a woman exalted as a Montmorencie!—Mind there, Wool! This road is getting rough!"

"Over it now, Marster!" said Wool, after a few heavy jolts—"Over it now, Missus! and de rest of de way is perfectly delightful."

Cap looked out of the window, and saw before her a beautiful piece of scenery—first, just below them, the wild mountain stream of the Demon's Run, and beyond it the wild dell dented into the side of the mountain, like the deep print of an enormous horse's hoof, in the midst of which gleaming redly among its richly tinted autumn woods, stood Hurricane Hall.

CHAPTER IX

MARAH ROCKE

✶✶✶✶✶✶

"There sits upon her matron face
A tender and a thoughtful grace,
Though very still,—for great distress
Hath left this patient mournfulness."

BESIDE AN OLD, rocky road, leading from the town of Staunton, out to the forest-crowned hills beyond, stood alone, a little, gray stone cottage, in the midst of a garden enclosed by a low, moldering stone wall. A few gnarled and twisted fruit trees, long past bearing, stood around the house, that their leafless branches could not be said to shade. A little wooden gate, led up an old paved walk to the front door, on each side of which were large windows.

In this poor cottage, remote from other neighbors, dwelt the friends of Herbert Greyson, the widow Rocke and her son Traverse. ────→ *Capitola's mother*

No one knew who she was, or whence, or why she came. Some fifteen years before she had appeared in the town, clothed in rusty mourning and accompanied by a boy of about two years of age. She had rented that cottage, furnished it poorly, and had settled there, supporting herself and child by needlework.

At the time that Doctor Greyson died and his widow and son were left perfectly destitute, and it became necessary for Mrs. Greyson to look out for an humble lodging where she could find the united advantages of cheapness, cleanliness, and pure air, she was providentially led to inquire at the cottage of the widow Rocke, whom she found only too glad to increase her meagre income by letting half her little house to such unexceptionable tenants as the widow Greyson and her son.

And thus commenced between the two poor young women and the two boys an acquaintance that ripened into friendship, and thence into that devoted love so seldom seen in this world.

61

Their households became united. One fire, one candle and one table served the little family, and thus considerable expense was saved as well as much social comfort gained. And when the lads grew too old to sleep with their mothers, one bed held the two boys and the other accommodated the two women. And despite toil, want, care—the sorrow for the dead and the neglect of the living, this was a loving, contented and cheerful little household. How much of their private history these women might have confided to each other, was not known, but it was certain that they continued fast friends up to the time of the death of Mrs. Greyson. After which the widow Rocke assumed a double burthen, and became a second mother to the orphan boy, until Herbert himself, ashamed of taxing her small means, ran away, as he had said, and went to sea.

Every year had Herbert written to his kind foster-mother, and his dear brother, as he called Traverse. And at the end of every prosperous voyage, when he had a little money he had sent them funds; but not always did these letters or remittances reach the widow's cottage, and long seasons of intense anxiety would be suffered by her for the fate of her sailor boy, as she always called Herbert. Only three times in all these years had Herbert found time and means to come down and see them—and that was long ago. It was many months over two years since they had even received a letter from him. And now the poor widow and her son were almost tempted to think that their sailor boy had quite forsaken them.

It is near the close of a late autumnal evening, that I shall introduce you, reader, into the interior of the widow's cottage.

[margin note: narrational shift]

You enter by the little wooden gate, pass up the moldering, paved walk between the old, leafless lilac bushes, and pass through the front door, right into a large, clean, but poor-looking, sitting-room and kitchen.

Everything was old, though neatly and comfortably arranged about the room: a faded home-made carpet covered the floor, a threadbare crimson curtain hung before the window, a ricketty walnut table, dark with age, sat under the window against the wall; old walnut chairs were placed each side of it; old plated candlesticks, with the silver all worn off, graced the mantel-piece; a good fire—a cheap comfort in that well-wooded country—blazed upon the hearth; on the right side of the fireplace a few shelves contained some well-worn books, a flute, a few minerals and other little treasures belonging to Traverse; on the left hand there was a dresser containing the little delft-ware, tea-service and plates and dishes of the small family.

Before the fire, with her knitting in her hand, sat Marah Rocke, watching the kettle as it hung singing over the blaze, and the oven of biscuits that sat baking upon the hearth.

Marah Rocke was at this time about thirty-five years of age, and of a singularly refined and delicate aspect for one of her supposed rank; her little form, slight and flexible as that of a young girl, was clothed in a poor, but neat, black dress, relieved by a pure white collar around her throat; her jet black hair was parted plainly over her "low, sweet brow," brought down each side her thin cheeks, and gathered into a bunch at the back of her shapely little head; her face was oval, with regular features and pale olive complexion; serious lips, closed in pensive thought, and soft, dark-brown eyes, full of tender affections and sorrowful memories, and too often cast down in meditation beneath the heavy shadows of their long, thick eyelashes, completed the melancholy beauty of a countenance not often seen among the hard-working children of toil.

Marah Rocke was a very hard-working woman, sewing all day long and knitting through the twilight, and then again resuming her needle by candle-light, and sewing until midnight, and yet Marah Rocke made but a poor and precarious living for herself and son—needlework, so ill-paid in large cities, is even worse paid in the country towns, and though the cottage hearth was never cold, the widow's meals were often scant. Lately her son, Traverse, who occasionally earned a trifle of money by doing, "with all his might, whatever his hand could find to do," has been engaged by a grocer in the town to deliver his goods to his customers during the illness of the regular porter; for which, as he was only a substitute, he received the very moderate sum of twenty-five cents a day.

This occupation took Traverse from home at daybreak in the morning, and kept him absent until eight o'clock at night. Nevertheless, the widow always gave him a hot breakfast before he went out in the morning, and kept a comfortable supper waiting for him at night.

It was during the last social meal that the youth would tell his mother all that had occurred in his world outside the home that day, and all that he expected to come to pass the next, for Traverse was wonderfully hopeful and sanguine.

And after supper the evening was generally spent by Traverse in hard study, beside his mother's sewing-stand.

Upon this evening, when the widow sat waiting for her son, he seemed to be detained longer than usual. She almost feared that the biscuits would be burned, or, if taken from the oven, be cold, before he would come to enjoy them; but just as she had looked for the twentieth time at the little black walnut clock that stood between those old plated candlesticks on the mantel-piece, the sound of quick, light, joyous footsteps was heard resounding along the stony street, the gate was opened, a hand laid upon the door-latch, and the next instant entered a youth some seventeen years of age, clad in a homespun suit, whose coarse material and clumsy make could not disguise his noble form or graceful air.

He was like his mother, with the same oval face, regular features, and pale olive complexion, with the same full, serious lips, the same dark tender brown eyes, shaded by long black lashes, and the same wavy, jet black hair—but there was a difference in the character of their faces; where hers showed refinement and melancholy, his exhibited strength and cheerfulness—his loving brown eyes, instead of drooping sadly under the shadow of their lashes, looked you brightly and confidently full in the face—and lastly, his black hair curled crisply around a broad, high forehead, royal with intellect. Such was the boy that entered the room and came joyously forward to his mother, clasping his arm around her neck, saluting her on both cheeks, and then, laughingly claiming his childish privilege of kissing "the pretty little black mole on her throat."

"Will you never have outgrown your babyhood, Traverse?" asked his mother, smiling at his affectionate ardor.

"Yes, dear little mother! in everything but the privilege of fondling you! that feature of babyhood I never *shall* outgrow!" exclaimed the youth, kissing her again with all the ardor of his true and affectionate heart, and starting up to help her set the table.

He dragged the table out from under the window, spread the cloth, and placed the cups and saucers upon it, while his mother took the biscuits from the oven and made the tea; so that in ten minutes from the moment in which he entered the room, mother and son were seated at their frugal supper.

"I suppose, to-morrow being Saturday, you will have to get up earlier than usual to go to the store?" said his mother.

"No, ma'am!" replied the boy, looking up brightly, as if he were telling a piece of good news. "I am not wanted any longer! Mr. Spicer's own man has got well again and returned to work."

"So you are discharged?" said Mrs. Rocke, sadly.

"Yes, ma'am! but just think how fortunate that is! for I shall have a chance to-morrow of mending the fence, and nailing up the gate, and sawing wood enough to last you a week, besides doing all the other little odd jobs that have been waiting for me so long; and then on Monday I shall get more work!"

"I wish I were sure of it!" said the widow, whose hopes had long since been too deeply crushed to permit her ever to be sanguine.

When their supper was over, and the humble service cleared away, the youth took his books and applied himself to study on the opposite side of the table at which his mother sat busied with her needlework. And there fell a perfect silence between them.

The widow's mind was anxious and her heart heavy; many cares never communicated to cloud the bright sunshine of her boy's soul, oppressed hers. The rent had fallen fearfully behind hand, and the landlord threatened, unless the money could be raised to pay him, to seize their furniture and eject them from the premises. And how this money was to be raised, she could not see at all! True, this meek Christian had often in her sad experience proved God's special providence at her utmost need, and now she believed in His ultimate interference, but in what manner He would now interpose she could not imagine, and her faith grew dim, and her hope dark, and her love cold.

While she was revolving these sad thoughts in her mind, Traverse suddenly thrust aside his books, and with a deep sigh, turned to his mother, and said:

"Mother, what *do* you think has ever become of Herbert?"

"I do not know. I dread to conjecture. It has now been nearly three years since we heard from him!" exclaimed the widow, with the tears welling up to her brown eyes.

"You think he has been lost at sea, mother, but I don't! I simply think his *letters* have been lost! And somehow to-night I can't fix my mind on my lessons, or keep it *off* Herbert! He is running in my head all the time! If I were fanciful now, I *should* believe that Herbert was dead and his spirit was about me!—Good heavens mother! whose step is that?" suddenly exclaimed the youth, starting up and assuming an attitude of intense listening, as a firm and ringing step, attended by a peculiar whistling approached up the street and entered the gate.

"It is Herbert! it is Herbert!" cried Traverse, starting across the room and tearing open the door with a suddenness that threw the entering guest forward upon his own bosom, but his arms were soon around the newcomer, clasping him closely there, while he breathlessly exclaimed:

"Oh, Herbert! I am so glad to see you! Oh, Herbert! why didn't you come or write all this long time? Oh, Herbert! how long have you been ashore? I was just talking about you!"

"Dear fellow!—dear fellow! I have come to make you glad at last, and repay all your great kindness; but now let me speak to my second mother," said Herbert, returning Traverse's embrace, and then gently extricating himself and going to where Mrs. Rocke stood up, pale, trembling and incredulous; she had not yet recovered from the great shock of his unexpected appearance.

"Dear mother, won't you welcome me?" asked Herbert, going up to her. His words dissolved the spell that bound her; throwing her arms around his neck and bursting into tears, she exclaimed:

"Oh, my son! my son! my sailor boy! my other child! how glad I am to have you back once more! Welcome?—to be sure you are welcome!—is my own circulating blood welcome back to my heart?—but sit you down and rest by the fire! I will get your supper directly!"

"Sweet mother, do not take the trouble! I supped twenty miles back where the stage stopped."

"And will you take nothing at all?"

"Nothing, dear mother, but your kind hand to kiss again and again!" said the youth, pressing that hand to his lips, and then allowing the widow to put him into a chair right in front of the fire.

Traverse sat on one side of him and his mother on the other, each holding a hand of his, and gazing on him with mingled incredulity, surprise and delight, as if, indeed, they could not realize his presence except by devouring him with their eyes.

And for the next half-hour all their talk was as wild and incoherent as the conversation of long-parted friends suddenly brought together, is apt to be.

It was all made up of hasty questions, hurried one upon another, so as to leave but little chance to have any of them answered, and wild exclamations and disjointed sketches of travel, interrupted by frequent ejaculations; yet through all the widow and her son, perhaps through the quickness of their *love* as well as of their intellect, managed to get some knowledge of the past three years of their "sailor boy's" life and adventures, and they entirely vindicated his constancy when they learned how frequently and regularly he had written, though they had never received his letters.

"And now," said Herbert, looking from side to side, from mother to son, "I have told you all *my* adventures, I am dying to tell you something that concerns *yourselves.*"

"That concerns *us?*" exclaimed mother and son in a breath.

"Yes, ma'am! yes, sir! that concerns you both eminently; but first of all, let me ask how you are getting on at this present time?"

"Oh, as usual," said the widow, smiling, for she did not wish to damp the spirits of her sailor boy; "as usual, of course. Traverse has not been able to accomplish his darling purpose of entering the Seminary yet; but———"

"But I'm getting on quite well with my education for all that," interrupted Traverse; "for I belong to Dr. Day's Bible class in the Sabbath school, which is a class of *young men*, you know! and the doctor is so good as to think that I have some mental gifts worth cultivating, so he does not confine his instructions to me to the Bible class alone, but permits me to come to him in his library at Willow Heights for an hour, twice a week, when he examines me in Latin and Algebra, and sets me new exercises, which I study and write out at night; so that you see I am doing very well."

"Indeed, the doctor, who is a great scholar, and one of the trustees and examiners of the Seminary, says that he does not know any young man *there,* with all the advantages of the institution around him, who is getting along so fast as Traverse is, with all the difficulties he has to encounter. The doctor says it is all because Traverse is profoundly in earnest, and that one of these days he will be———"

"There, mother! don't repeat all the doctor's kind speeches! He only says such things to encourage a poor boy in the pursuit of knowledge under difficulties," said Traverse, blushing and laughing.

—"Will be an honor to his kindred, country and race," said Herbert, finishing the widow's incomplete quotation.

"It was something like that, indeed," she said, nodding and smiling.

"You do me proud!" said Traverse, touching his forelock with comic gravity. "But," inquired he, suddenly changing his tone and becoming serious, "was it not—*is* it not—noble in the doctor to give up an hour of his precious time twice a week, for no other cause than to help a poor, struggling fellow like me up the ladder of learning?"

"I should think it was; but he is not the first noble heart I ever heard of," said Herbert, with an affectionate glance that directed the compliment, "nor is his the last that *you* will meet with. I *must* tell you the good news now."

"Oh, tell it! tell it! have you got a ship of your own, Herbert?"

"No, nor is it about myself that I am anxious to tell you. Mrs. Rocke, you may have heard that I had a rich uncle, whom I had never seen, because, from the time of my dear mother's marriage to that of her death, she and her brother, this very uncle, had been estranged?"

"Yes," said the widow, speaking in a very low tone, and bending her head over her work; "yes, I have heard so; but your mother and myself seldom alluded to the subject."

"Exactly! mother never was fond of talking of him! Well, when I came on shore, and went, as usual, up to the old Washington House, who should I meet with, all of a sudden, but this rich uncle. He had come to New York to claim a little girl whom I happened to know, and who happened to recognize me, and name me to him. Well, I knew him *only* by his name; but he knew me both by my name and by my likeness to his sister, and received me with wonderful kindness, offered me a home under his roof, and promised to get for me an appointment to West Point. Are you not glad?—say, are you not glad?" he exclaimed, jocosely clapping his hand upon Traverse's knee, and then turning around and looking at his mother.

"Oh, yes, indeed I am *very* glad, Herbert!" exclaimed Traverse, heartily grasping and squeezing his friend's hand.

"Yes, yes, I am indeed sincerely glad of your good fortune, dear boy," said the widow; but her voice was very faint, and her head bent still lower over her work.

"Ha! ha! ha! I *knew* you'd be glad for *me;* but now I require you to be glad for *yourselves.* Now listen: When I told my honest old uncle—for he *is* honest, with all his eccentricities—when I told him of what friends you had been to me——"

"*Oh no! you did not! You did not mention* US TO HIM!" cried the widow, suddenly starting up and clasping her hands together, while she gazed in an agony of entreaty into the face of the speaker.

"Why not?—why in the world not? Was there anything improper in doing so?" inquired Herbert, in astonishment, while Traverse himself gazed in amazement at the excessive and unaccountable agitation of his mother.

"Why, mother? Why shouldn't he have mentioned us? Was there anything strange or wrong in that?" inquired Traverse.

"No, oh, no; certainly not!—I forgot, it was so sudden," said the widow sinking back in her chair and struggling for self-control.

"Why, mother, what in the world is the meaning of this?" asked her son.

"Nothing, nothing, boy; only we are poor folks, and should not be forced upon the attention of a wealthy gentleman," she said, with a cold, unnatural smile, putting her hand to her brow and striving to gain composure. Then, as Herbert continued silent and amazed, she said to him:

"Go on—go on—you were saying something about my—about Major Warfield's kindness to you—go on." And she took up her work and tried to sew, but she was as pale as death, and trembling all over at the same time, while every nerve was acute with attention to catch every word that might fall from the lips of Herbert.

"Well," recommenced the young sailor, "I was just saying that when I mentioned you and Traverse to my uncle, and told him how kind and disinterested you had been to me—you being like a mother, and Traverse like a brother,—he was really moved almost to tears! Yes, I declare I saw the raindrops glittering in his tempestuous old orbs, as he walked the floor muttering to himself, 'Poor woman—good, excellent woman.'"

While Herbert spoke, the widow dropped her work without seeming to know that she had done so; her fingers twitched so nervously that she had to hold both hands clasped together, and her eyes were fixed in intense anxiety upon the face of the youth, as she repeated:

"Go on—oh, go on! What more did he say when you talked of us?"

"He said everything that was kind and good. He said that he could not do too much to compensate you for the past."

"Oh! did he say that?" exclaimed the widow, breathlessly.

"Yes—and a great deal more!—that all that he could do for you or your son was but a sacred debt he owed you."

"Oh, he acknowledged it! he acknowledged it! thank heaven! oh, thank heaven! Go on, Herbert! Go on!"

"He said that he would in future take the whole charge of the boy's advancement in life, and that he would place you above want forever; that he would, in fact, compensate for the past by doing you and yours full justice."

"Thank heaven! Oh, thank heaven!" exclaimed the widow, no longer concealing her agitation, but throwing down her work, and starting up and pacing the floor in excess of joy.

"Mother," said Traverse, uneasily, going to her and taking her hand, "mother, what is the meaning of all this? Do come and sit down!"

She immediately turned and walked back to the fire, and resting her hands upon the back of the chair, bent upon them a face radiant with youthful beauty. Her cheeks were brightly flushed, her eyes were sparkling with light, her whole countenance resplendent with joy—she scarcely seemed twenty years of age.

"Mother, tell us what it is," pleaded Traverse, who feared for her sanity.

"Oh, boys, I am so happy! at last! at last! after eighteen years of patient 'hoping against hope!' I shall go mad with joy!"

"Mother," said Herbert, softly.

"Children, I am not crazy! I know what I am saying, though I did not intend to say it! And you shall know, too! But first I must ask Herbert another question: Herbert, are you very sure that he—Major Warfield,—knew who we were?"

"Yes, indeed. Didn't I tell him all about you? Your troubles, your struggles, your disinterestedness, and all your history since ever I knew you?" answered Herbert, who was totally unconscious that he had left Major Warfield in ignorance of one very important fact—her surname.

"Then you are sure he knew who he was talking about?"

"Of course, he did!"

"He could not have failed to do so, indeed! But, Herbert, did he mention any other important fact, that you have not yet communicated to us?"

"No, ma'am."

"Did he allude to any previous acquaintance with us?"

"No, ma'am, unless it might have been in the words I repeated to you—there was nothing else!—except that he bade me hurry to you and make you glad with his message, and return as soon as possible to let him know whether you accept his offers."

"Accept them! accept them! of course I do! I have waited for them for years!—oh! children! you gaze on me as if you thought me mad! I am not so! nor can I now explain myself! for since he has not chosen to be confidential with Herbert, I can not be so prematurely! but you will know all, when Herbert shall have borne back my message to Major Warfield."

It was, indeed, a mad evening in the cottage. And even when the little family had separated and retired to bed the two youths lying together, as formerly, could not sleep for talking; while the widow, on her lonely couch, lay awake for joy.

CHAPTER X

THE ROOM OF THE TRAP-DOOR

"If you have hitherto concealed this sight,
Let it be tenable, in your silence still;
And whatsoever else doth hap to-night,
Give it an understanding, but no tongue."
—*Shakespeare*[1]

CAPITOLA MEANWHILE, in the care of the major, arrived at Hurricane Hall, much to the discomfiture of good Mrs. Condiment, who was quite unprepared to expect the new inmate; and when Major Warfield said:

"Mrs. Condiment, this is your young lady, take her up to the best bedroom, where she can take off her bonnet and shawl," the worthy dame, thinking secretly: "The old fool has gone and married a young wife, sure enough; a mere chit of a child"—made a very deep courtesy, and a very queer cough, and said:

"I'm mortified, Madam, at the fire not being made in the best bedroom; but then I was not warned of *your* coming, Madam!"

"Madam! Is the old woman crazed? This child is no 'madam'! She is Miss Black, my ward, the daughter of a deceased friend!" sharply exclaimed Old Hurricane.

"Excuse me, Miss, I did not know; I was unprepared to receive a young lady. Shall I attend you, Miss Black?" said the old lady in a mollified tone.

"If you please," said Capitola, and arose to follow her.

"Not expecting you, Miss, I have no proper room prepared—most of them are not furnished, and in some, the chimneys are foul; indeed, the only tolerable room I can put you in is the room with the trap-door—if you would not object to it?" said Mrs. Condiment, as with a candle in her hand, she preceded Capitola along the gloomy hall, and then opened a door that led into a narrow passage.

room Capitola was born in

71

"A room with a trap-door?—that's a curious thing; but why should I object to it! I don't at all. I think I should rather like it," said Capitola.

"I will show it to you and tell you about it, and then if you like it, well and good! If not, I shall have to put you in a room that leaks, and has swallows' nests in the chimney," answered Mrs. Condiment, as she led the way along the narrow passages, and up and down dark, black stairs, and through bare and deserted rooms, and along other passages until she reached a remote chamber, opened the door, and invited her guest to enter.

It was a large shadowy room, through which the single candle shed such a faint, uncertain light, that at first Capitola could see nothing but black masses looming up through the darkness.

But when Mrs. Condiment advanced and set the candle upon the chimney-piece, and Capitola's sight accommodated itself to the scene, she saw that upon the right of the chimney-piece stood a tall tester bedstead, curtained with very dark crimson serge; on the left hand, thick curtains of the same color draped the windows. Between these windows, directly opposite the bed, stood a dark mahogany dressing-bureau, with a large looking-glass; a wash-stand in the left-hand corner of the chimney-place; and a rocking-chair and two plain chairs completed the furniture of this room, that I am particular in describing, as upon the simple accident of its arrangement, depended, upon two occasions, the life and honor of its occupant. There was no carpet on the floor, with the exception of a large old Turkey rug which was laid before the fireplace.

"Here, my dear, this room is perfectly dry and comfortable, and we always keep kindlings built up in the fireplace ready to light in case a guest should come," said Mrs. Condiment, applying a match to the wastepaper under the pineknots and logs that filled the chimney. Soon there arose a cheerful blaze that lighted up all the room, glowing on the crimson serge bed-curtains and window-curtains, and flashing upon the large looking-glass between them.

"There, my dear; sit down, and make yourself comfortable," said Mrs. Condiment, drawing up the rocking-chair.

Capitola threw herself into it, and looked around and around the room, and then into the face of the old lady, saying:

"But what about the trap-door?—I see no trap-door!"

"Ah, yes—look!" said Mrs. Condiment, lifting up the rug and revealing a large *drop* some four feet square, that was kept up in its place by a short iron bolt. "Now, my dear, take care of yourself, for this bolt slides very easily, and if, while you happened to be walking across this place, you were to push the bolt back, the trap-door would drop and you fall down— heaven knows where!"

"Is there a cellar under there?" inquired Capitola, gazing with interest upon the door.

"Lord knows, child; I don't! I did once make one of the nigger men let it down, so I could look in it; but, Lord, child, I saw nothing but a great, black, deep vacuity, without bottom or sides! It put such a horror over me, that I never looked down there since, and never want to, I'm sure."

"Ugh! for goodness sake what was the horrid thing made for!" ejaculated Capitola, gazing as if fascinated by the trap.

"The Lord only knows, my dear; for it was made long before ever the house came into the major's family. *But they do say*——" whispered Mrs. Condiment, mysteriously.

"Ah! what do they say?" asked Capitola, eagerly throwing off her bonnet and shawl, and settling herself to hear some thrilling explanation.

Mrs. Condiment slowly replaced the rug, drew another chair to the side of the young girl, and said:

"They do say it was—*a trap for Indians.*"

"A trap for Indians?"

"Yes, my dear. You must know that this room belongs to the *oldest part of the house*. It was all built as far back as the old French and Indian war; but this room belonged to the part that dates back to the first settlement of the country."

"Then I shall like it better than any room in the house, for I doat on old places with stories to them. Go on, please."

"Yes, my dear. Well, first of all, this place was a part of the grant of land given to the *Le Noirs*. And the first owner, old Henri Le Noir, was said to be one of the grandest villains that ever was heard of. Well, you see, he lived out here in his hunting-lodge, which is this part of the house."

"Oh, my! then this very room was a part of the old pioneer hunter's lodge?"

"Yes, my dear, and they do say that he had this place made as a trap for the Indians. You see, they say he was on terms of friendship with the Succapoos, a little tribe of Indians that was nearly wasted away, though among the few that was left there were several braves! Well, he wanted to buy a certain large tract of land from this tribe, and they were all willing to sell it, except these half a dozen warriors, who wanted it for camping-ground. So what does this awful villain do, but lay a snare for them. He makes a great feast in his lodge and invites his red brothers to come to it; and they come. Then he proposes that they stand upon his blanket and all swear eternal brotherhood, which he made the poor souls believe was the right way to do it. Then when they all six stood close together as they could stand, with hands held up touching above their heads, all of a sudden the black villain sprung the bolt, the trap fell, and the six men went down—down, the Lord knows where."

"Oh, that is horrible! horrible!" cried Capitola, "but where do you think they fell to?"

"I tell you the Lord only knows. They say that it is a bottomless abyss, with no outlet but one crooked one miles long that reaches to the Demon's Punch Bowl. But if there *is* a bottom to that abyss, that bottom is strewn with human bones."

"Oh, horrible! most horrible!" exclaimed Capitola.

"Perhaps you are afraid to sleep here by yourself; if so, there's the damp room——"

"Oh, no! oh, no! I am not afraid. I have been in too much deadly peril from the *living* ever to fear the *dead.* No, I like the room, with its strange legend; but tell me, did that human devil escape without punishment from the tribe of the murdered victims?"

"Lord, child, how were they to know of what was done? There wasn't a man left to tell the tale. Besides, the tribe was now brought down to a few old men, women, and children. So, when he showed a bill of sale for the land he wanted, signed by the six braves——'their marks' in six blood-red arrows, there was none to contradict him."

"How was his villainy found out?"

"Well, it was said he married, had a family, and prospered for a long while; but that the poor Succapoos always suspected him, and bore a long grudge, and that when the sons of the murdered warriors grew up to be powerful braves, one night they set upon the house and massacred the whole family except the eldest son, a lad of ten, who escaped and ran away and gave the alarm to the blockhouse, where there were soldiers stationed. It is said that after killing and scalping father, mother, and children, the savages threw the dead bodies down that trap-door. And they had just set fire to the house, and were dancing their wild dance around it, when the soldiers arrived and dispersed the party, and put out the fire."

"Oh, what bloody, bloody days!"

"Yes, my dear, and as I told you before, if that horrible pit *has* any bottom, that bottom is strewn with human skeletons!"

"It is an awful thought——"

"As I said, my dear, if you feel at all afraid you can have another room."

"Afraid—what of? Those skeletons, supposing them to be there, cannot hurt me. I am not afraid of the dead—I only dread the living, and not them much either," said Capitola.

"Well, my dear, you will want a waiting-woman, anyhow, and I think I will send Pitapat to wait on you; she can sleep on a pallet in your room, and be some company."

"And who is Pitapat, Mrs. Condiment?"

"Pitapat? Lord, child, she is the youngest of the housemaids. I've called her Pitapat ever since she was a little one beginning to walk, when she used to steal away from her mother, Dorcas, the cook, and I would hear her little feet coming pit-a-pat, pit-a-pat up the dark stairs up to my room. As it was often the only sound to be heard in the still house, I grew to call my little visitor Pitapat."

"Then let me have Pitapat by all means. I like company, especially company that I can send away when I choose."

"Very well, my dear, and now I think you'd better smooth your hair and come down with me to tea, for it is full time, and the major, as you may know, is not the most patient of men."

Capitola took a brush from her traveling bag, hastily arranged her black ringlets, and announced herself ready.

They left the room, and traversed the same labyrinth of passages, stairs, empty rooms and halls, back to the dining-room, where a comfortable fire burned and a substantial supper was spread.

Old Hurricane took Capitola's hand with a hearty grasp, and placed her in a chair at the side, and then took his own seat at the foot of the table.

Mrs. Condiment sat at the head and poured out the tea.

"Uncle," said Capitola, suddenly, "what is under the trap-door in my room?"

"What! have they put you in *that* room?" exclaimed the old man, hastily looking up.

"There was no other one prepared, sir," said the housekeeper.

"Besides, I like it very well, uncle," said Capitola.

"Humph! humph! humph!" grunted the old man, only half satisfied.

"But uncle, what is under the trap-door?" persisted Capitola, "what's under it?"

"Oh, I don't know—an old cave that was once used as a dry cellar, until an underground stream broke through and made it too damp—so it is said. I never explored it."

"But, uncle, what about the——"

Here Mrs. Condiment stretched out her foot, and trod upon the toes of Capitola so sharply as to make her stop short, while she dexterously changed the conversation by asking the major if he would not send Wool to Tip-Top in the morning for another bag of coffee.

Soon after supper was over, Capitola, saying that she was tired, bade her uncle good-night, and, attended by her little black maid Pitapat, whom Mrs. Condiment had called up for the purpose, retired to her distant chamber. There were already collected her three trunks, which the liberality of her uncle had filled.

As soon as she had got in and locked the door, she detached one of the strongest straps from her largest trunk, and then turned up the rug and secured the end of the strap to the ring in the trap-door. Then she withdrew the bolt, and holding on to one end of the strap, gently lowered the trap, and kneeling, gazed down into an awful black void—without boundaries, without sight, without sounds, except a deep, faint, subterranean roaring as of water.

"Bring the light, Pitapat, and hold it over this place, and take care you don't fall in," said Capitola. "Come, as I've got a 'pit' in my name and you've got a 'pit' in yours, we'll see if we two can't make something of this third 'pit'!"

"'Deed, I'se 'fraid, Miss," said the poor little darkey.

"Afraid! what of?"

"Ghoses."

"Nonsense. I'll agree to lay every ghost you see!"

The little maid approached, candle in hand, but in such a gingerly sort of way, that Capitola seized the light from her hand, and stooping, held it down as far as she could reach, and gazed once more into the abyss. But this only made the horrible darkness "visible";[2] no object caught or reflected a single ray of light—all was black, hollow, void and silent, except the faint, deep, distant roaring as of subterraneous water!

Capitola pushed the light as far down as she could possibly reach, and then yielding to a strange fascination, dropt it into the abyss! It went down, down, down into the darkness, until far below it glimmered out of sight! Then with an awful shudder Capitola pulled up and fastened the trap-door, laid down the rug and said her prayers, and went to bed by the fire-light,—with little Pitapat sleeping on a pallet. The last thought of Cap, before falling to sleep, was:

"It is awful to go to bed over such a horrible mystery; but I *will* be a hero!"

CHAPTER XI

A MYSTERY AND A STORM AT HURRICANE HALL

"Bid her address her prayers to Heaven!
Learn if she *there* may be forgiven;
Its mercy may absolve her yet!
But *here* upon this earth beneath,
There is *no spot* where she and I
Together for an *hour* could breathe!"
—Byron [1]

EARLY THE NEXT morning Capitola arose, made her toilet, and went out to explore the outer walls of her part of the old house, to discover, if possible, some external entrance into the unknown cavity under her room. It was a bright, cheerful, healthy, autumnal morning, well adapted to dispel all clouds of mystery and superstition. Heaps of crimson and golden-hued leaves, glimmering with hoar frost, lay drifted against the old walls, and when these were brushed away by the busy feet and hands of the young girl, they revealed nothing but the old moldering foundation; not a vestige of a cellar-door or window was visible.

Capitola abandoned the fruitless search, and turned to go into the house. And saying to herself:

"I'll think no more of it! I dare say, after all, it is nothing but a very dark cellar without window and with a well, and the story of the murders and of the skeletons, is all moonshine!" She ran into the dining-room, and took her seat at the breakfast table.

Old Hurricane was just then storming away at his factotum Wool for some misdemeanor, the nature of which Capitola did not hear, for upon her appearance, he suffered his wrath to subside in a few reverberating low thunders, gave his ward a grumphy "Good-morning," and sat down to his breakfast.

After breakfast Old Hurricane took his great coat and cocked hat, and stormed forth upon the plantation to blow up his lazy overseer, Mr. Will Ezy, and his idle negroes, who had loitered or frolicked away all the days of their master's absence.

Mrs. Condiment went away to mix a plum pudding for dinner and Cap was left alone.

After wandering through the lower rooms of the house, the stately old-fashioned drawing-room, the family parlor, the dining-room, etc., Cap found her way through all the narrow back passages and steep little staircases back to her own chamber.

The chamber looked quite different by daylight—the cheerful wood fire burning in the chimney right before her, opposite the door by which she entered; the crimson curtained bedstead on her right hand; the crimson draped windows, with the rich old mahogany bureau and dressing-glass standing between them, on her left; the polished, dark oak floor; the rich Turkey rug, concealing the trap-door; the comfortable rocking-chair; the new work-stand; placed there for her use that morning, and her own well-filled trunks standing in the corners, looked altogether too cheerful to associate with dark thoughts.

Besides, Capitola had not the least particle of gloom, superstition or marvelousness in her disposition. She loved old houses and old legends well enough to enjoy them; but was not sufficiently credulous to believe, or cowardly to fear, them.

She had, besides, a pleasant morning's occupation before her, in unpacking her three trunks and arranging her wardrobe and her possessions, which were all upon the most liberal scale, for Major Warfield at every city where they had stopped had given his poor little *protégée* a virtual *carte blanche* for purchases, having said to her:

"Capitola, I'm an old bachelor; I've not the least idea what a young girl requires; all I know is, that you have nothing but your clothes, and must want sewing and knitting needles, and brushes and scissors, and combs and boxes and smelling-bottles and tooth-powder; and *such.* So come along with me to one of those Vanity Fairs they call fancy stores, and get what you want; I'll foot the bill."

And Capitola, who firmly believed that she had the most sacred of claims upon Major Warfield, whose resources she also supposed to be unlimited, did not fail to indulge her taste for rich and costly toys, and supplied herself with a large ivory dressing-case, lined with velvet, and furnished with ivory-handled combs and brushes, silver boxes and crystal bottles; a papier mâché work-box, with gold thimble, needle-case and perforator and gold-mounted scissors and winders; and an ebony writing-desk, with silver-mounted crystal standishes; each of these—boxes and desk—were filled with all things requisite in the several departments. And

The Hidden Hand

now as Capitola unpacked them and arranged them upon the top of the bureau, it was with no small degree of appreciation. The rest of the forenoon was spent in arranging the best articles of her wardrobe in her bureau drawers.

Having locked the remainder in her trunks, and carefully smoothed her hair, and dressed herself in a brown merino, she went down stairs and sought out Mrs. Condiment, whom she found in the housekeeper's little room, and to whom she said:

"Now, Mrs. Condiment, if uncle has any needlework wanted to be done, any buttons to be sewed on, or anything of the kind, just let me have it; I'm just dying to use it!"

"My dear Miss Black——"

"Please to call me Capitola, or even Cap. I never was called Miss Black in my life, until I came here, and I don't like it at all!"

"Well then, my dear Miss Cap, I wish you would wait till tomorrow, for I just came in here in a great hurry to get a glass of brandy out of the cupboard to put in the sauce for the plum pudding, as dinner will be on the table in ten minutes."

With a shrug of her little shoulders, Capitola left the housekeeper's room, and hurried through the central front hall and out at the front door, to look about and breathe the fresh air for a while.

As she stepped upon the front piazza she saw Major Warfield walking up the steep lawn, followed by Wool, leading a pretty, mottled, iron-gray pony, with a side-saddle on his back.

"Ah, I'm glad you're down, Cap! Come! look at this pretty pony! he is good for nothing as a working horse, and is too light to carry *my* weight, and so I intend to give him to you! You must learn to ride," said the old man, coming up the steps.

"Give him to me! I learn to ride! Oh, uncle! Oh, uncle! I shall go perfectly crazy with joy!" exclaimed Cap, dancing and clapping her hands with delight.

"Oh, well, a tumble or two in learning will bring you back to your senses, I reckon!"

"Oh, uncle! oh, uncle! when shall I begin!"

"You shall take your first tumble immediately after dinner, when, being well-filled, you will not be so brittle and apt to break in falling!"

"Oh, uncle! I shall not fall! I feel I sha'n't! I feel I've a natural gift for holding on!"

"Come, come, get in! get in! I want my dinner!" said Old Hurricane, driving his ward in before him to the dining-room, where the dinner was smoking upon the table.

After dinner Cap, with Wool for a riding-master, took her first lesson in equestrianism.

She had the four great requisites for forming a good rider—a well-adapted figure, a fondness for the exercise, perfect fearlessness and presence of mind. She was not once in danger of losing her seat, and during that single afternoon's exercises, she make considerable progress in learning to manage her steed.

Old Hurricane, whom the genial autumn afternoon had tempted out to smoke his pipe in his arm-chair on the porch, was a pleased spectator of her performances, and expressed his opinion that *in time* she would become the best rider in the neighborhood, and that she should have the best riding-dress and cap that could be made at Tip-Top.

Just now, in lack of an equestrian dress, poor Cap was parading around and around the lawn with her head bare and her hair flying, and her merino skirt exhibiting more ankles than grace.

It was while Old Hurricane still sat smoking his pipe and making his comments, and Capitola still ambled around and around the lawn, that a horseman suddenly appeared galloping as fast as the steep nature of the ground would admit, up towards the house, and before they could form an idea of who he was, the horse was at the block, and the rider dismounted and standing before Major Warfield.

"Why, Herbert, my boy! back so soon! We didn't expect you for a week to come! This is sudden, indeed! So much the better! so much the better! Glad to see you, lad!" exclaimed Old Hurricane, getting up and heartily shaking the hand of his nephew.

Capitola came ambling up, and in the effort to spring nimbly from her saddle, tumbled off, much to the delight of Wool, who grinned from ear to ear, and of Old Hurricane, who, with an "I said so," burst into a roar of laughter.

Herbert Greyson sprang to assist her; but before he reached the spot, Cap had picked herself up, straightened her disordered dress, and now she ran to meet and shake hands with him.

There was such a sparkle of joy and glow of affection in the meeting between these two, that Old Hurricane, who saw it, suddenly hushed his laugh, and grunted to himself:

"Humph, humph, humph! I like that; that's better than I could have planned it myself; let *that* go on, and then, Gabe Le Noir, we'll see under what name and head the old divided manor will be held!"

Before his mental soliloquy was concluded, Herbert and Capitola came up to him. He welcomed Herbert again with great cordiality, and then called to his man to put up the horses, and bade the young people follow him into the house, as the air was getting chilly.

"And how did you find your good friends, lad?" inquired Old Hurricane, when they had reached the sitting parlor.

"Oh, very well, sir; and very grateful for your offered kindness; and, indeed, so anxious to express their gratitude, that—that I shortened my visit, and came away immediately to tell you."

"Right, lad, right! You come by the down coach?"

"Yes, sir; and got off at Tip-Top, where I hired a horse to bring me here. I must ask you to let one of your men take him back to Mr. Merry, at the Antlers' Inn, to-morrow."

"Surely, surely, lad! Wool shall do it!"

"And so, Herbert, the poor woman was delighted with the prospect of better times?" said Old Hurricane, with a little glow of benevolent self-satisfaction.

"Oh, yes, sir! delighted beyond all measure!"

"Poor thing! poor thing! See, young folks, how easy it is for the wealthy, by sparing a little of their superfluous means, to make the poor and virtuous happy. And the boy, Herbert, the boy?"

"Oh, sir! delighted for himself, but still more delighted for his mother; for her joy was such as to astonish and even alarm me! Before that, I had thought Marah Rocke a proud woman, but——"

"WHAT—*say that again!*" exclaimed Major Warfield.

"I say that I thought she was a proud woman, but——"

"Thought WHO was a proud woman, sir?" roared Old Hurricane.

"Marah Rocke!" replied the young man, with wonder.

Major Warfield started up, seized the chair upon which he had sat, and struck it upon the ground with such force as to shatter it to pieces; then turning, he strode up and down the floor with such violence that the two young people gazed after him in consternation and fearful expectancy. Presently he turned suddenly, strode up to Herbert Greyson, and stood before him.

His face was purple, his veins swollen until they stood out upon his forehead like cords, his eyes were protruded and glaring, his mouth clenched until the grizzly gray moustache and beard were drawn in, his whole huge frame was quivering from head to foot! It was impossible to tell what passion—whether rage, grief, or shame, the most possessed him, for all three seemed tearing his giant frame to pieces.

For an instant he stood speechless, and Herbert feared he would fall into a fit; but the old giant was too strong for that! For one short moment he stood thus, and in a terrible voice he asked:

"Young man! did you—*did* you know—the SHAME that you dashed into my face, with the name of that woman?"

"Sir, I know nothing but that she is the best and dearest of her sex!" exclaimed Herbert, beyond all measure amazed at what he heard and saw.

"Best and dearest!" thundered the old man—"oh, idiot! is she still a siren, and are you a dupe? But that cannot be! No, sir! it is I whom you *both* would dupe! Ah, I see it all now! *This* is why you artfully concealed her name from me until you had won my promise! It shall not serve either you or her, sir! I break my promise—thus!"—bending and snapping his own cane, and flinging the fragments behind his back—"there, sir! when you can make those ends of dry cedar grow together again, and bear green leaves, you may hope to reconcile Ira Warfield and Marah Rocke! I break my promise sir, as *she* broke——"

The old man suddenly sunk back into the nearest chair, dropped his shaggy head and face into his hands, and remained trembling from head to foot, while the convulsive heaving of his chest, and the rising and falling of his huge shoulders, betrayed that his heart was nearly bursting with such suppressed sobs as only can be forced from manhood by the fiercest anguish.

The young people looked on in wonder, awe and pity; and then their eyes met—those of Herbert silently inquired:

"What can all this mean?"—Those of Capitola as mutely answered: "Heaven only knows."

In his deep pity for the old man's terrible anguish, Herbert could feel no shame nor resentment for the false accusation made upon himself. Indeed, his noble and candid nature easily explained all as the ravings of some heart-rending remembrance. Waiting, therefore, until the violent convulsions of the old man's frame had somewhat subsided, Herbert went to him, and with a low and respectful intonation of voice, said:

"Uncle, if you think that there was any collusion between myself and Mrs. Rocke, you wrong us both. You will remember that when I met you in New York, I had not seen or heard from *her* for years, nor had I then any expectation of ever seeing you. The subject of the poor widow came up between us accidentally, and if it is true that I omitted to call her by *name,* it must have been because we both then felt too tenderly by her to call her anything else but 'the poor widow, the poor mother, the good woman,' and so on—and all this she is still."

The old man without raising his head, held out one hand to his nephew, saying in a voice still trembling with emotion:

"Herbert, I wronged you; forgive me."

Herbert took and pressed that rugged and hairy old hand to his lips, and said:

"Uncle, I do not in the least know what is the cause of your present emotion, but——"

"Emotion! demmy, sir! what do you mean by emotion? Am *I* a man to give way to emotion? Demmy, sir, mind what you say!" roared the old lion, getting up and shaking himself free of all weaknesses.

"I merely meant to say, sir, that if I could possibly be of any service to you, I am entirely at your orders."

"Then go back to that woman and tell her never to dare to utter, or even to *think* my name again, if she values her life!"

"Sir, you do not mean it! and as for Mrs. Rocke, she is a good woman I feel it my duty to uphold!"

"Good! ugh! ugh! ugh! I'll command myself! I'll not give way again. Good! ah, lad, it is quite plain to me now, that you are an innocent dupe. Tell me, now, for instance, do you know anything of that woman's life, before she came to reside at Staunton?"

"Nothing; but from what I've seen of her since, I'm *sure* she always *was* good."

"Did she never mention her former life at all?"

"Never; but, mind! I hold to my faith in her and would stake my salvation on her integrity," said Herbert, warmly.

"Then you'd lose it, lad, that's all; but I have an explanation to make to you, Herbert. You must give me a minute or two of your company alone, in the library, before tea."

And so saying, Major Warfield arose and led the way across the hall to the library, that was immediately back of the drawing-room.

Throwing himself into a leathern chair beside the writing table, he motioned for his companion to take the one on the opposite side. A low fire smoldering on the hearth before them, so dimly lighted the room, that the young man arose again to pull the bell rope; but the other interrupted with:

"No, you need not ring for lights, Herbert: my story is one that should be told in the dark! listen, lad; but drop your eyes, the while!"

"I am all attention, sir!"

"Herbert! the poet says, that:

> 'At thirty man suspects himself a fool,
> *Knows* it at forty and reforms his rule.'[2]

But boy, at the ripe age of forty-five, I succeeded in achieving the most sublime folly of my life! I should have taken a degree in madness, and been raised to a professor's chair in some College of Lunacy! Herbert, at the age of forty-five I fell in love with and married a girl of sixteen, out of a log cabin! merely forsooth, because she had a pretty skin like the leaf of the white japonica, soft, gray eyes like a timid fawn's and a voice like a cooing turtle dove's! because those delicate cheeks flushed, and those soft eyes fell when I spoke to her, and the cooing voice trembled when she replied! because the delicate face brightened when I came, and faded when I turned away! because

> 'She wept with delight when I gave her a smile,
> And trembled with fear at my frown,' etc.

Because she adored me as a sort of god, I loved her as an angel, and married her! married her secretly! for fear of the ridicule of my brother officers, put her in a pastoral log cabin in the woods below the block-house, and visited her there by stealth, like Numa did his nymph in the cave![3] But I was watched, my hidden treasure was discovered—and coveted by a younger and prettier fellow than myself—Perdition! I cannot tell this story in detail! One night I came home very late and quite unexpectedly, and found—this man in my wife's cabin! I broke the man's head and ribs and left him for dead. I tore the woman out of my heart and cauterized its bleeding wounds!—This man was Gabriel Le Noir! Satan burn him forever!—This woman was Marah Rocke, God forgive her! I could have divorced the woman, but as I did not dream of ever marrying again, I did not care to drag my shame before a public tribunal. There! you know all! let the subject sink forever!" said Old Hurricane, wiping great drops of sweat from his laboring brows.

"Uncle! I have heard your story and believe you, of course! But I am bound to tell you, that without even having heard your poor wife's defence, I *believe, and uphold her to be innocent!* I think *you* have been as grossly deceived as she has been fearfully wronged! and that time and providence will prove this!" exclaimed Herbert, fervently.

A horrible laugh of scorn was his only answer, as Old Hurricane arose, shook himself and led the way back to the parlor.

CHAPTER XII

MARAH'S DREAMS

"And now her narrow kitchen walls
Stretched away into stately halls;
The weary wheel to a spinnet turned,
The tallow candle an astral burned;
A manly form at her side she saw,
And joy was duty and love was law."
—*Whittier* [1]

ON THE SAME Saturday morning that Herbert Greyson hurried away from his friend's cottage, to travel post to Hurricane Hall, for the sole purpose of accelerating the coming of her good fortune, Marah Rocke walked about the house with a step so light, with eyes so bright, and cheeks so blooming, that one might have thought that years had rolled backward in their course and made her a young girl again!

Traverse gazed upon her in delight. Reversing the words of the text, he said:

"We must call you no longer Marah (which is bitter), but we must call you Naomi (which is beautiful), mother!"

"Young flatterer!" she answered, smiling and slightly flushing. "But tell me truly, Traverse, am I very much faded? have care, and toil, and grief made me look old?"

"You! old!" exclaimed the boy, running his eyes over her beaming face and graceful form with a look of non-comprehension that might have satisfied her, but did not, for she immediately repeated:

"Yes, do I look old? Indeed, I do not ask from vanity, child! Ah, it little becomes me to be vain; but I do wish to look well in some one's eyes!"

"I wish there was a looking-glass in the house, mother, that it might tell you, you should be called Naomi, instead of Marah!"

"Ah! that is just what *he* used to say to me in the old happy time,—the time in Paradise, before the serpent entered!"

"What 'he,' mother?"

"Your father, boy, of course!"

[handwritten margin note: connects Traverse as O.H.'s son]

That was the first time she had ever mentioned his father to her son, and now she spoke of him with such a flush of joy and hope, that even while her words referred darkly to the past, her eyes looked brightly to the future! All this, taken with the events of the preceding evening, greatly bewildered the mind of Traverse, and agitated him with the wildest conjectures.

"Mother, will you tell me about my father, and also what it is beyond this promised kindness of Major Warfield that has made you so happy!" he asked.

"Not now, my boy! dear boy, not now! I must not, I cannot, I dare not yet! Wait a few days and you shall know all! Oh, it is hard to keep a secret from my boy! but then it is not only my secret, but another's! You do not think hard of me for withholding it now, do you Traverse?" she asked, affectionately.

"No, dear mother, of course I don't. I know you must be right, and I am glad to see you happy."

"Happy! Oh, boy, you don't know how happy I am! I did not think any human being could ever feel so joyful in this erring world, much less I! One cause of this excess of joyful feeling must be from the contrast! else it were dreadful to be so happy!"

"Mother, I don't know what you mean," said Traverse, uneasily, for he was too young to understand these paradoxes of feeling and thought, and there were moments when he feared for his mother's reason.

"Oh, Traverse, think of it! eighteen long, long years of estrangement, sorrow, and dreadful suspense! eighteen long, long, weary years of patience against anger, and loving against hatred, and hoping against despair! your young mind cannot grasp it—your very life is not so long. I was seventeen then; I am thirty-five now. And after wasting all my young years of womanhood in loving, hoping, longing—lo! the light of life has dawned at last."

"God save you, mother!" said the boy, fervently, for her wild, unnatural joy continued to augment his anxiety.

"Ah, Traverse, I dare not tell you the secret now, and yet I am always letting it out; because my heart overflows from its fulness. Ah, boy, many, many weary nights have I lain awake from grief; but last night I lay awake from joy. Think of it."

The boy's only reply to this was a deep sigh. He was becoming seriously alarmed.

"I never saw her so excited. I wish she would get calm," was his secret thought.

Then, with the design of changing the current of her ideas, he took off his coat, and said:

"Mother, my pocket is half torn out, and though there's no danger of my losing a great deal out of it, still I'll get you, please, to sew it in while I mend the fence."

"Sew the pocket! mend the fence! Well," smiled Mrs. Rocke, "we'll do so, if it will amuse you. The mended fence will be a convenience to the next tenant, and the patched coat will do for some poor boy. Ah, Traverse, we must be very good to the poor, in more ways than in giving them what we do not ourselves need, for we shall know what it is to have been poor," she concluded, in more serious tones than she had yet used.

Traverse was glad of this, and went out to his work feeling somewhat better satisfied.

This delirium of happiness lasted intermittently a whole week, during the last three days of which Mrs. Rocke was constantly going to the door and looking up the road, as if expecting some one. The mail came from Tip-Top to Staunton only once a week, on Saturday mornings. Therefore, when Saturday came again, she sent her son to the post office, saying:

"If they do not come to-day, they will surely write."

Traverse hastened with all his speed, and got there so soon that he had to wait for the mail to be opened.

Meanwhile, at home, the widow walked the floor in restless, joyous anticipation, or went to the door and strained her eyes up the road to watch for Traverse, and perhaps for some one else's coming. At last she discerned her son, who came down the road, walking rapidly, smiling triumphantly, and holding a letter up to view.

She ran out of the gate to meet him, seized and kissed the letter, and then, with her face burning, her heart palpitating, and her fingers trembling, she hastened into the house, threw herself into the little low chair by the fire, and opened the letter. It was from Herbert, and read thus:

HURRICANE HALL, Nov. 30th, 1845.
MY DEAREST AND BEST MRS. ROCKE:——May God strengthen you to read the few bitter lines I have to write. Most unhappily, Major Warfield did *not* know exactly who you were, when he promised so much. Upon learning your name he withdrew all his promises. At night, in his library, he told me all your early history. Having heard all, the very worst, I believe you as pure as an angel. So I told him. So I

would uphold with my life, and seal with my death. Trust yet in God, and believe in the earnest respect and affection of your grateful and attached son.

HERBERT GREYSON.

P.S.—For henceforth I shall call you mother.

Quietly she finished reading, pressed the letter again to her lips, reached it to the fire, saw it, like her hopes, shrivel up to ashes, and then she arose, and with her trembling fingers clinging together, walked up and down the floor.

There were no tears in her eyes, but oh, such a look of unutterable woe on her pale, blank, despairing face.

Traverse watched her, and saw that something had gone frightfully wrong; that some awful revolution of fate or revulsion of feeling had passed over her in this dread hour.

Cautiously he approached her, gently he laid his hand upon her shoulder, tenderly he whispered:

"Mother!"

She turned and looked strangely at him, then exclaiming:

"Oh, Traverse, how happy I was this day week!" She burst into a flood of tears.

Traverse threw his arm around his mother's waist, and half-coaxed and half-bore her to her low chair, and sat her in it, and knelt by her side; and embracing her fondly, whispered:

"Mother, don't weep so bitterly. You have *me*, am *I* nothing? Mother, I love you more than son ever loved his mother, or suitor his sweetheart, or husband his wife. Oh, is *my* love nothing, mother?"

Only sobs answered him.

"Mother," he pleaded, "you are all the world to *me*—let me be all the world to *you*. I *can* be it, mother,—I can be it; try me. I will make every effort for my mother, and the Lord will bless us."

Still no answer but convulsive sobs.

"Oh, mother, mother, I will try to do for you more than ever son did for mother, or man for woman before, dear mother, if you will not break my heart by weeping so."

The sobbing abated a little, partly from exhaustion and partly from the soothing influences of the boy's loving words.

"Listen, dear mother, what I will do. In the olden times of chivalry, young knights bound themselves by sacred vows to the service of some

lady, and labored long and perilously in her honor; for her, blood was
spilt—for her, fields were won; but, mother, never yet toiled knight in the
battlefield for his lady-love as I will, in the battle of life, for my dearest
lady—my own mother."

incestuous

She reached out her hand, and silently pressed his.

"Come, come," said Traverse—"lift up your head and smile! We are
young yet, both you and I! for after all you are not much older than your
son! and we two will journey up and down the hills of life together—all in
all to each other; and when at last we are old, as we shall be when you are
seventy-seven and I am sixty—we will leave all our fortune that we shall
have made to found a home for widows and orphans,—as *we were*, and we
will pass out and go to Heaven together."

Now indeed this poor, modern Hagar looked—and smiled at the
oddity of her Ishmael's far-reaching thought.[2]

In that poor household grief might not be indulged. Marah Rocke
took down her work-basket and sat down to finish a lot of shirts, and
Traverse went out with his horse and saw, to look for a job at cutting wood
for twenty-five cents a cord. Small beginnings of the fortune that was to
found and endow asylums! but many a fortune has been commenced
upon less!

Marah Rocke had managed to dismiss her boy with a smile—but
that was the last effort of nature; as soon as he was gone and she found
herself alone, tear after tear welled up in her eyes and rolled down her pale
cheeks; sigh after sigh heaved her bosom!

Ah! the transitory joy of the past week had been but the lightning's
arrowy course *scathing* where it illumined!

She felt as if this last blow, that had struck her down from the height
of hope to the depth of despair, had broken her heart—as if the power of
reaction was gone, and she mourned as one who would not be comforted.

While she sat thus the door opened, and before she was aware of his
presence, Herbert Greyson entered the room and came softly to her side.
Ere she could speak to him, he dropped upon one knee at her feet, bowed
his young head lowly over the hand that he took and pressed to his lips.
Then he arose and stood before her. This was not unnatural or exaggerated—it was his way of expressing the reverential sympathy and compassion he felt for her strange, life-long martyrdom.

"Herbert, you here? why we only got your letter this morning," she
said, in tones of gentle inquiry, as she arose and placed a chair for him.

"Yes, I could not bear to stay away from you, at such a time; I came up in the same mail-coach that brought my letter; but I kept myself out of Traverse's sight, for I could not bear to intrude upon you in the first hour of your disappointment," said Herbert, in a broken voice.

"Oh! that need not have kept you away, dear boy; I did not cry much; I am used to trouble, you know; I shall get over this also—after a little while—and things will go in the old way," said Marah Rocke, struggling to repress the rising emotion that however overcame her, for dropping her head upon her "sailor boy's" shoulder, she burst into a flood of tears and wept plenteously.

"Dear mother, be comforted," he said; "dear mother, be comforted."

CHAPTER XIII

MARAH'S MEMORIES

✿✿✿✿✿

"In the shade of the apple tree again
She saw a rider draw his rein.
And gazing down with a timid grace,
She felt his pleased eyes read her face."
—*Whittier*[1]

"DEAR MARAH, I cannot understand your strong attachment to that
bronzed and grizzled old man, who has besides treated you so barba-
rously," said Herbert.

"Is he bronzed and gray?" asked Marah, looking up with gentle pity
in her eyes and tone.

"Why of course he is. He is sixty-three."

"He was forty-five when I first knew him, and he was very handsome
then—at least I thought him the very perfection of manly strength, and
beauty, and goodness. True, it was the mature, warm beauty of the Indian
summer—for he was more than middle-aged; but it was very genial to the
chilly, loveless morning of my early life," said Marah, dropping her head
upon her hand, and sliding into reminiscences of the past.

"Dear Marah, I wish you would tell me all about your marriage and
misfortunes," said Herbert, in a tone of the deepest sympathy and respect.

"Yes, he was very handsome," continued Mrs. Rocke, speaking more
to herself than to her companion; "his form was tall, full and stately; his
complexion warm, rich and glowing; his fine face was lighted up by a pair
of strong, dark gray eyes, full of fire and tenderness, and was surrounded
by waving masses of jet black hair and whiskers—they are gray now, you
say, Herbert?"

"Gray and grizzled, and bristling up around his hard face, like thorn-
bushes around a rock in winter!" said Herbert, bluntly, for it enraged his
honest but inexperienced boyish heart to hear this wronged woman speak
so enthusiastically.

"Ah! it is winter with him *now,* but *then* it was glorious Indian summer. *He* was a handsome, strong and ardent man. *I* was a young, slight, pale girl, with no beauty but the cold and colorless beauty of a statue; with no learning, but such as I had picked up from a country school; with no love to bless my lonely life—for I was a friendless orphan, without either parents or relatives, and living by sufferance in a cold and loveless home."

"Poor girl!" murmured Herbert, in almost inaudible tones.

"Our log cabin stood beside the military road leading through the wilderness to the Fort where he was stationed. And oh, when he came riding by each day, upon his noble, coal black steed, and in his martial uniform, looking so vigorous, handsome and kingly, he seemed to me almost a god to worship. Sometimes he drew rein in front of the old oak tree that stood in front of our cabin, to breathe his horse, or to ask for a draught of water. I used to bring it to him. Oh! then, when he looked at me, his eyes seemed to send new warmth to my chilled heart; when he spoke, too, his tones seemed to strengthen me; while he stayed, his presence seemed to protect me."

"'Ay, *such* protection as vultures give to doves—covering and devouring them,'" muttered Herbert to himself. Mrs. Rocke, too absorbed in her reminiscences to heed his interruptions, continued:

"One day he asked me to be his wife. I do not know what I answered, or if I answered anything. I only know that when I understood what he meant my heart trembled with instinctive terror at its own excessive joy! We were privately married by the chaplain at the Fort. There were no accommodations for the wives of officers there. And besides, my husband did not wish to announce our marriage, until he was ready to take me to his princely mansion in Virginia."

"Humph!" grunted Herbert, inwardly, for comment.

"But he built for me a pretty cabin in the woods below the Fort, furnished it simply, and hired a half-breed Indian woman to wait on me. Oh, I was too happy! To my wintry spring of life summer had come, warm, rich and beautiful! There is a clause in the marriage service which enjoins the husband to *cherish* his wife. I do not believe many people ever stop to think how much is in that word. He *did*; he cherished my little thin, chill, feeble life, until I became strong, warm and healthful. Oh! even as the blessed sun warms and animates, and glorifies the earth, causing it to brighten with life, and blossom with flowers, and bloom with fruit, so did my husband enrich, and cherish, and bless my life. Such happiness could not and it did not last."

"Of course not," muttered Herbert to himself.

"At first the fault was in myself. Yes, Herbert, it was! you need not look incredulous, or hope to cast all the blame on him! Listen: happy, grateful, adoring as I was, I was also shy, timid, and bashful—never proving the deep love I bore my husband except by the most perfect self-abandonment to his will. All this deep though quiet devotion he understood as mere passive obedience void of love. As this continued he grew uneasy, and often asked me if I cared for him at all, or if it were possible for a young girl like me to love an old man like himself."

"A very natural question," thought Herbert.

"Well, I used to whisper in answer, 'Yes,' and still 'Yes.' But this never satisfied Major Warfield. One day, when he asked me if I cared for him the least in the world, I suddenly answered, that if he were to die I should throw myself across his grave, and lie there until death should release me! whereupon he broke into a loud laugh, saying, 'Methinks the lady doth protest too much.'[2] I was already blushing deeply at the unwonted vehemence of my own words, although I had spoken only as I felt—the very, very truth; but his laugh and his jest so increased my confusion—that—in fine that was the first and last time I ever *did* protest! Like Lear's Cordelia, I was tongue-tied[3]—I had no words to assure him. Sometimes I wept to think how poor I was in resources to make him happy. Then came another annoyance—my name and fame were freely discussed at the Fort."

"A natural consequence," sighed Herbert.

"The younger officers discovered my woodland home, and often stole out to reconnoitre my cabin. Among them was Captain Le Noir, who, after he had discovered my retreat, picked acquaintance with Lura, my attendant. Making the woodland sports his pretext, he haunted the vicinity of my cabin, often stopping at the door to beg a cup of water, which of course was never denied, or else to offer a bunch of partridges, or a brace of rabbits, or some other game, the sports of his gun, which equally of course was never accepted. One beautiful morning in June, finding my cabin door open and myself alone, he ventured unbidden across my threshold, and by his free conversation, and bold admiration, offended and alarmed me. Some days afterwards, in the mess-room at the Fort, being elevated by wine, he boasted among his mess-mates of the intimate terms of friendly acquaintance upon which he falsely asserted that he had the pleasure of standing with 'Warfield's pretty little favorite,' as he insolently called me. When my husband heard of this, I learned for the first time of

95

the terrific violence of his temper. It was awful! It frightened me almost to death. There was a duel, of course. Le Noir was very dangerously wounded—scarred across the face for life, and was confined many weeks to his bed. Major Warfield was also slightly hurt, and laid up at the Fort for a few days, during which I was not permitted to see him."

"Is it possible that even *then* he did not see your danger, and acknowledge your marriage, and call you to his bedside?" inquired Herbert impatiently.

"No! no! if he *had,* all after suffering had been spared! No! at the end of four days he came back to me; but we met only for bitter reproaches on his part, and sorrowful tears on mine. He charged me with coldness, upon account of the disparity in our years, and of preference for Captain Le Noir, because he was 'a pretty fellow.' I knew this was not true of me. I knew that I loved my husband's very footprints better than I did the whole human race besides; but I could not tell him so then. Oh, in those days, though my heart was so full, I had so little power of utterance. There he stood before me! he that had been so ruddy and buoyant, now so pale from loss of blood, and so miserable, that I could have fallen and groveled at his feet in sorrow and remorse at not being able to make him happy!"

"There are some persons whom we can never make happy! It is not in them to be so." commented Herbert.

"He made me promise never to see or to speak to Le Noir again—a promise eagerly given but nearly impossible to keep. My husband spent as much time with me as he possibly could spare from his military duties, and looked forward with impatience to the autumn, when it was thought that he would be at liberty to take me home. He often used to tell me that we should spend our Christmas at his house, Hurricane Hall, and that I should play Lady Bountiful, and distribute Christmas gifts to the negroes, and that they would love me. And oh! with what joy I anticipated that time of honor and safety and careless ease, as an acknowledged wife, in the home of my husband! There, too, I fondly believed our child would be born. All his old tenderness returned for me, and I was as happy if not as wildly joyful, as at first."

"'Twas but a lull in the storm," said Herbert.

"Aye! 'twas but a lull in the storm, or rather *before* the storm! I do think that from the time of that duel, Le Noir had resolved upon our ruin. As soon as he was able to go out, he haunted the woods around my cabin, and continually lay in wait for me. I could not go out even in the company of my maid Lura to pick blackberries and wild plums, or gather forest roses, or to get fresh water at the spring, without being intercepted by Le Noir and his offensive admiration. He seemed to be ubiquitous! He met me everywhere—except in the presence of Major Warfield. I did not tell my husband, because I feared that if I did he would have killed Le Noir, and died for the deed.''

"Humph! it would have been 'good riddance of bad rubbish' in *both* cases!'' muttered Herbert, under his teeth.

"But instead of telling him, I confined myself strictly to my cabin. One fatal day my husband, on leaving me in the morning, said that I need not wait up for him at night, for that it would be very late when he came, even if he came at all. He kissed me very fondly when he went away. Alas! alas! it was the last—last time! At night I went to bed disappointed, yet still so expectant that I could not sleep. I know not how long I had waited thus, or how late it was when I heard a tap at the outer door, and heard the bolt undraw, and a footstep enter, and a low voice asking:

"'*Is she asleep?*' and Lura's reply in the affirmative. Never doubting it was my husband, I lay there in pleased expectation of his entrance. He came in, and began to take off his coat in the dark. I spoke, telling him that there were matches on the bureau. He did not reply, at which I was surprised; but before I could even repeat my words, the outer door was burst violently open, hurried footsteps crossed the entry, a light flashed into my room, my husband stood in the door in full military uniform, with a light in his hand and the aspect of an avenging demon on his brow and——

"HORROR OF HORRORS! the half-undressed man in my chamber was Captain Le Noir! I saw, and swooned away!''

"But you were saved! you were saved!'' gasped Herbert, white with emotion.

"Oh, I was saved, but not from sorrow—not from shame! I awoke from that deadly swoon to find myself alone, deserted, cast away! Oh! torn out from the warmth and light and safety of my home in my husband's heart, and hurled forth shivering, faint and helpless upon the bleak world! and all this in twenty-four hours! Ah! I did not lack the power of expression then! happiness had never given it to me—anguish conferred it upon me! that one fell stroke of fate cleft the rock of silence in my soul, and the fountain of utterance gushed freely forth. I wrote to him—but my letters might as well have been dropped into a well. I went to him, but was spurned away. I prayed him with tears to have pity on our unborn babe; but he laughed aloud in scorn, and called it by an opprobrious name! Letters, prayers, tears, were all in vain. He never *had* acknowledged our marriage, he now declared that he never *would* do so; he discarded me, disowned my child, and forbade us ever to take his name!"

"Oh, Marah! and you but seventeen years of age! without a father or a brother or a friend in the world to take your part! without even means to employ an advocate!" exclaimed Herbert, covering his face with his hands and sinking back.

"Nor would I have used any of these agencies, had I possessed them! If my wifehood and motherhood, my affection and my helplessness, were not advocates strong enough to win my cause, I could not have borne to employ others."

"Oh, Marah, with none to pity or to help! it was monstrous to have abandoned you so!"

"No! hush; consider the overwhelming evidence against me! I considered it even in the tempest and whirlwind of my anguish, and never once blamed and never once was angry with my husband. For I knew—not *he,* but the terrible circumstantial evidence had ruined me!"

"Ay, but did you not explain it to him?"

"How could I, alas! when I did not understand it myself? How Le Noir knew that Major Warfield was not expected home that fatal night—how he got into my house, whether by conspiring with my little maid, or by deceiving her—or lastly, how Major Warfield came to burst in upon him so suddenly, I did not know, and do not to this day!"

"But you told Major Warfield all that you have told me?"

"Oh, yes! again and again, calling Heaven to witness my truth! In vain! '*he had seen with his own eyes,*' he said. Against all I could say or do, there was built up a wall of scornful incredulity, on which I might have dashed my brains out to no purpose!"

"Oh, Marah! Marah! with none to pity or to save!" again exclaimed Herbert.

"Yes," said the meek creature, bowing her head; "God pitied and helped me! First he sent me a son that grew strong and handsome in body, good and wise in soul. Then he kept alive in my heart faith and hope and charity. He enabled me, through long years of unremitting and ill-requited toil, to live on, loving against anger, waiting against time, and hoping against despair!"

"Why did you leave your western home and come to Staunton, Marah?" asked Herbert.

"To be where I could sometimes hear of my husband, without intruding on him. I took your widowed mother in because she was *his* sister, though I never told her who I was, lest *she* should wrong and scorn me, as *he* had done. When she died I cherished you, Herbert, first because you were *his* nephew, but now, dear boy, for your own sake, also."

"And I, while I live, will be a son to you, Madam! I will be your constant friend at Hurricane Hall. He talks of making me his heir. Should he persist in such blind injustice, the day I come into the property, I shall turn it all over to his widow and son. But I do not believe that he *will* persist; I, for my part, still hope for the best."

"I also hope for the best, for whatever God wills is sure to happen, and his will is surely the best! Yes, Herbert, I also hope—*beyond the grave!*" said Marah Rocke, with a wan smile.

The little clock that stood between the tall plated candlesticks on the mantel-piece struck twelve, and Marah rose from her seat, saying:

"Traverse, poor fellow, will be home to his dinner. Not a word to him, Herbert, please! I do not wish the poor lad to know how much he has lost, and above all, I do not wish him to be prejudiced against his father."

"You are right, Marah," said Herbert, "for if he were told, the natural indignation that your wrongs would arouse in his heart, would totally unfit him to meet his father, in a proper spirit, in that event for which I still hope—a future and a perfect family union!"

HERBERT GREYSON remained a week with his friends, during which time he paid the quarter's rent, and relieved his adopted mother of that cause of anxiety. Then he took leave and departed for Hurricane Hall, on his way to Washington City, whence he was immediately going to pass his examination and await his appointment.

CHAPTER XIV

THE WASTING HEART

"Then she took up the burden of life again,
Saying only, 'It might have been.'
Alas for them both, and alas for us all,
Who vainly the dreams of youth recall,
For of all sad words of lips, or pen,
The saddest are these—'It might have been.'"
——*Whittier*[1]

BY THE TACIT consent of all parties, the meteor hope that had crossed and vanished from Marah Rocke's path of life was never mentioned again. Mother and son went about their separate tasks. Traverse worked at jobs all day, studied at night, and went twice a week to recite his lessons to his patron, Doctor Day, at Willow Hill. Marah sewed as usual all day, and prepared her boy's meals at the proper times. But day by day her cheeks grew paler, her form thinner, her step fainter. Her son saw this decline with great alarm. Sometimes he found her in a deep, troubled reverie, from which she would awaken with heavy sighs. Sometimes he surprised her in tears. At such times he did not trouble her with questions that he instinctively felt she could not or would not answer; but he came gently to her side, put his arms about her neck, stooped and laid her face against his breast, and whispered assurances of his "true love," and his boyish hopes of "getting on," of "making a fortune," and bringing "brighter days" for her!

And she would return his caresses, and with a faint smile reply that he "must not mind" her, that she was only "a little low-spirited," that she would "get over it soon."

But as day followed day, she grew visibly thinner and weaker, dark shadows settled under her hollow eyes and in her sunken cheeks. One evening, while standing at the table washing up their little tea-service, she suddenly dropped into her chair and fainted. Nothing could exceed the alarm and distress of poor Traverse. He hastened to fix her in an easy

position, bathed her face and hands in vinegar and water—the only re-
storatives in their meagre stock—and called upon her by every loving
epithet to live and speak to him. The fit yielded to his efforts, and presently, with a few fluttering inspirations, her breath returned and her eyes
opened. Her very first words were attempts to re-assure her dismayed boy.
But Traverse could no more be flattered. He entreated his mother to go at
once to bed. And though the next morning, when she arose, she looked not
worse than usual, Traverse left home with a heart full of trouble. But
instead of turning down the street to go to his work in the town, he turned
up the street towards the wooded hills beyond, now glowing in their gor-
geous autumn foliage, and burning in the brilliant morning sun.

A half hour's walk brought him to a high and thickly-wooded hill,
up which a private road led through a thicket of trees to a handsome
gray stone country seat, situated in the midst of beautifully ornamented
grounds, and known as Willow Heights, the residence of Doctor William
Day, a retired physician of great repute, and a man of earnest piety. He was
a widower with one fair daughter, Clara, a girl of fourteen, then absent at
boarding-school. Traverse had never seen this girl, but his one great admiration was the beautiful Willow Heights, and its worthy proprietor. He
opened the highly ornate iron gate, and entered upon an avenue of willows
that led up to the house, a two-storied edifice of gray stone, with full-
length front piazzas above and below.

Arrived at the door, he rang the bell, which was answered promptly
by a good-humored-looking negro boy, who at once showed Traverse to
the library up stairs, where the good doctor sat at his books. Doctor Day
was at this time about fifty years of age, tall and stoutly built, with a fine
head and face, shaded by soft, bright flaxen hair and beard; thoughtful and
kindly dark blue eyes; and an earnest, penetrating smile, that reached like
sunshine the heart of any one upon whom it shone. He wore a cheerful-
looking flowered chintz dressing-gown corded around his waist; his feet
were thrust into embroidered slippers; and he sat in his elbow-chair at his
reading table, poring over a huge folio volume. The whole aspect of the
man, and of his surroundings, was kindly cheerfulness. The room opened
upon the upper front piazza, and the windows were all up to admit the
bright morning sun and genial air, at the same time that there was a glowing fire in the grate to temper its chilliness. Traverse's soft step across the
carpeted floor was not heard by the doctor, who was only made aware of
his presence by his stepping between the sunshine and his table. Then the

doctor arose, and with his intense smile extended his hands, and greeted the boy with:

"Well, Traverse, lad, you are always welcome! I did not expect you until night, as usual, but as you are here, so much the better! Got your exercise all ready, eh?—Heaven bless you, lad! what is the matter?" inquired the good man suddenly, on first observing the boy's deeply troubled looks.

"My mother, sir! my mother!" was all that Traverse could at first utter.

"Your mother! My dear lad, what about her—is she ill?" inquired the doctor, with interest.

"Oh, sir, I am afraid she is going to die!" exclaimed the boy in a choking voice, struggling hard to keep from betraying his manhood by bursting into tears.

"Going to die—oh! pooh, pooh, pooh, she is not going to die, lad! tell me all about it," said the doctor, in an encouraging tone.

"She has had so much grief, and care, and anxiety, sir—Doctor, is there any such malady as a broken heart?"

"Broken heart?—pooh, pooh! no, my child, no! never heard of such a thing in thirty years' medical experience! Even that story of a porter who broke his heart trying to lift a ton of stone is all a fiction. No such disease as a broken heart. But tell me about your mother!"

"It is of her that I am talking; she has had so much trouble in her life, and now I think she is sinking under it; she has been failing for weeks, and last night, while washing the teacups, she fainted away from the table!"

"Heaven help us, that looks bad," said the doctor.

"Oh, does it? does it, sir? *She* said it was 'nothing much.' Oh, Doctor, don't say she will die! don't! if she were to die—if mother were to die, I'd give right up! I never should do a bit of good in the world, for *she* is all the motive I have in this life! To study hard—to work hard, and make her comfortable and happy, so as to make up to her for all she has suffered, is my greatest wish and endeavor! Oh, don't say mother will die, it would ruin me!" cried Traverse.

"My dear boy, I don't say anything of the sort! I say, judging from your account, that her health must be attended to immediately. And—true I have retired from practice; but I will go and see your mother, Traverse!"

"Oh, sir, if you only would! I came to ask you to do that very thing! I should not have presumed to ask such a favor for any cause but this of my dear mother's life and health, and you will go to see her?"

"Willingly and without delay, Traverse," said the good man, rising immediately and hurrying into an adjoining chamber.

"Order the gig while I dress, Traverse, and I will take you back with me," he added, as he closed the chamber door behind him.

By the time Traverse had gone down, given the necessary orders and returned to the library, the doctor emerged from his chamber, buttoned up in his gray frock coat, and booted, gloved and capped for the ride.

They went down together, entered the gig, and drove rapidly down the willow avenue, slowly through the iron gate and through the dark thicket, and down the wooded hill to the high road, and then as fast as the sorrel mare could trot towards town. In fifteen minutes, the doctor pulled up his gig, at the right-hand side of the road before the cottage gate.

They entered the cottage, Traverse going first in order to announce the doctor. They found Mrs. Rocke, as usual, seated in her low chair by the little fire, bending over her needlework. She looked up with surprise as they came in.

"Mother, this is Doctor Day, come to see you," said Traverse.

She arose from her chair, and raised those soft and timid dark gray eyes to the stranger's face, where they met that sweet, intense smile that seemed to encourage while it shone upon her.

"We have never met before, Mrs. Rocke, but we both feel too much interest in this good lad here to meet as strangers now," said the doctor, extending his hand.

"Traverse gives me every day fresh cause to be grateful to you, sir, for kindness that we can never, never repay," said Marah Rocke, pressing that bountiful hand, and then placing a chair, which the doctor took.

Traverse seated himself at a little distance, and as the doctor conversed with and covertly examined his mother's face, *he* watched the doctor's countenance, as if life and death hung upon the character of its expression. But while they talked, not one word was said upon the subject of sickness or medicine. They talked of Traverse. The doctor assured his mother that her son was a boy of such fine talent, character and promise, that he had already made such rapid progress in his classical and mathematical studies, that he ought immediately to enter upon a course of reading for one of the learned professions.

The mother turned a smile full of love, pride and sorrow upon the fine, intellectual face of her boy, and said:

"You are like the angel in Cole's picture of life.² You point the youth to the far-up temple of fame——"

"And leave him to get there as he can. Not at all madam! Let us see. Traverse, you are now going on eighteen years of age; if you had your choice, which of the learned professions would you prefer for yourself—law, physic, or divinity?"

The boy looked up and smiled, then dropped his head and seemed to reflect.

"Perhaps you have never thought upon the subject. Well, you must take time—you must take time! so as to be firm in your decision when you have once decided," said the doctor.

"Oh, sir, I have thought of it long! and my choice has been long and firmly decided, were I only free to follow it!"

"Speak, lad! What is your choice?"

"Why, don't you *know,* sir? Can't you guess? Why, your *own* profession, *of course,* sir! Certainly sir, I could not think of any other!" exclaimed the boy, with sparkling eyes and flushed cheeks.

"*That's* my own lad!" exclaimed the doctor, enthusiastically seizing the boy's hand with one of his, and clapping the other down upon his palm; for if the doctor had an admiration in the world it was for his own profession. "*That's* my own lad! *My* profession! the *healing* art! why, it is the *only* profession worthy the study of an immortal being. *Law* sets people by the ears together! *Divinity* should never be considered as a profession—it is a divine *mission!* Physic! physic, my boy! The *healing* art! *that's* the profession for you! And I am very glad to hear you declare for it, too; for *now* the way is perfectly clear!"

Both mother and son looked up in surprise.

"Yes, the way is perfectly clear. Nothing is easier! Traverse shall come and read medicine in my office. I shall be glad to have the lad there. It will amuse me to give him instruction occasionally! I have a positive mania for teaching."

"And for doing good! Oh, sir, how have we deserved this kindness at your hands? and how shall we ever, ever repay it?" cried Mrs. Rocke, in a broken voice, while the tears filled her gentle eyes.

"Oh, pooh, pooh! a mere nothing, ma'am! a mere nothing for me to do, whatever it may prove to him. It is very hard, indeed, if I am to be crushed under a cart load of thanks for doing something for a boy I like, when it does not cost me a cent of money, or a breath of effort."

"Oh, sir, your generous refusal of our thanks does but deepen our obligation," said Marah, still weeping.

"Now, my dear madam, will you persist in making me confess that it is all selfishness on my part? I *like* the boy, I tell you! I shall like his bright, cheerful face in my office. I can make him very useful to me, also————"

"Oh, sir! if you can and *will* only make him useful to you————"

"Why, to be sure I can, and will! He can act as my clerk, keep my accounts, write my letters, drive out with me, and sit in the gig while I go in to visit my patients, for though I have pretty much retired from practice, still————"

"Still you visit and prescribe for the sick poor, gratis!" added Marah, feelingly.

"Pooh, pooh! habit, madam, habit! 'ruling passion strong in death,' etc. I can't, for the life of me, keep from giving people bread pills! And now, by the way, I must be off to see some of my patients in Staunton! Traverse, my lad—my young medical assistant, I mean—are you willing to go with me?"

"Oh, sir," said the boy, and here his voice broke down with emotion.

"Come along, then!" laughed the doctor; "you shall drive with me into the village as a commencement."

Traverse got his hat, while the doctor held out his hand to Mrs. Rocke, who, with her eyes full of tears, and her voice faltering with emotion, began again to thank him, when he good-humoredly interrupted her by saying:

"Now, my good little woman, do—pray—hush! I'm a selfish fellow, as you'll see! I do nothing but what pleases my own self, and makes me happy! Good-bye! God bless you, madam!" he cried, cordially shaking her hand. "Come, Traverse," he added, hurriedly striding out of the door and through the yard, to the gate before which the old green gig and sorrel mare were still waiting.

"Traverse, I brought you out again to-day, more especially to speak of your mother and her state of health," said Doctor Day, very seriously, as they both took their seats in the gig and drove on towards the town. "Traverse, your mother is in no immediate danger of death; in fact, she has no disease whatever!"

"Oh, sir, you do not think her ill, then! I thought you did not, from the fact that you never felt her pulse, or gave her a prescription!" exclaimed Traverse, delightedly, for in one thing the lad resembled his mother—he was sensitive and excitable—easily depressed and easily exhilarated.

"Traverse, I said your mother is in no immediate danger of death, for that in fact she has no disease; but yet, Traverse, brace yourself up, for I am about to strike you a heavy blow! Traverse! Marah Rocke is—starving!"

"STARVING! Heaven of Heavens! no! that is not so! it cannot be! My mother starving! oh, horrible! horrible! But, Doctor, it cannot—cannot be! Why, we have two meals a day at our house!" cried the boy, almost beside himself with agitation.

"Lad, there are other starvations beside the total lack of food! there are slow starvations and divers ones! Marah Rocke is starving slowly and in every way! mind, soul and body! her body is slowly wasting from the want of proper nutriment, her heart from the want of human sympathy, her mind from the need of social intercourse. Her whole manner of life must be changed if she is to live at all!"

"Oh, sir, I understand you now! I feel, I feel that you speak the very truth! Something must be done! I must do something. What shall it be? Oh, advise me, sir!"

"I must reflect a little, Traverse," said the doctor, thoughtfully, as he drove along with very slack reins.

"And so, how thoughtless of me! I forgot, indeed I did, sir, when I so gladly accepted your offer for me to read with you, I forgot that if I spent every day reading in your office, my mother would sadly miss the dollar and a half a week I made by doing little odd jobs in town."

"But *I* did not forget it, boy; rest easy upon that score; and now let me reflect how we can best serve your good little mother!" said the doctor, and he drove slowly and thoughtfully along for about twenty minutes before he spoke again, when he said:

"Traverse, Monday is the first of the month. You shall set in with me then. Come to me, therefore, on Monday, and I think by that time, I shall have thought upon some plan for your mother. In the meantime, you may make as much money at jobs as you can, and also you must accept from me for her a bottle or so of port wine and a turkey or two! Tell her, if she demurs, that it is the doctor's prescription, and that for fear of accidents he always prefers to send his own physic!"

"Oh, Doctor Day, if I could only thank you aright!" cried Traverse.

"Pooh, pooh! nonsense! there is no time for it. Here we are at Spicer's grocery store, where I suppose you are again employed. Yes? Well, jump out then. You can still make half a day. Mind, remember on Monday next, December 1st, you enter my office as my medical student, and by that time I shall have some plan arranged for your mother. Good-bye! God bless you lad!" said the good doctor, as he drove off and left Traverse standing in the genial autumn sunshine, with his heart swelling and his eyes overflowing with excess of gratitude and happiness.

CHAPTER XV

CAP'S COUNTRY CAPERS

"A willful elf—an uncle's child.
That half a pet and half a pest,
Was still reproved, endured, caressed
Yet never tamed, though never spoiled."

CAPITOLA AT FIRST was delighted and half incredulous at the great change in her fortunes. The spacious and comfortable mansion of which she found herself the little mistress; the high rank of the veteran officer who claimed her as his ward and niece; the abundance, regularity, and respectability of her new life; the leisure, the privacy, the attendance of servants, were all so entirely different from anything to which she had previously been accustomed, that there were times when she doubted its reality, and distrusted her own identity or her sanity.

Sometimes, of a morning, after a very vivid dream of the alleys, cellars, and gutters, rag-pickers, newsboys, and beggars of New York, she would open her eyes upon her own comfortable chamber, with its glowing fire and crimson curtains, its bright mirror crowning the walnut bureau between them, and would jump up and gaze wildly around, not remembering where she was, or how she came thither.

Sometimes, suddenly started by an intense realization of the contrast between her past and her present life, she would mentally inquire:

"Can this be really *I* myself, and not another? *I*, the little houseless wanderer through the streets and alleys of New York? *I*, the little newsgirl in boy's clothes? *I*, the wretched little vagrant that was brought up before the Recorder, and was about to be sent to the House of Refuge for juvenile delinquents? Can this be *I*, Capitola, the little outcast of the city, now changed into Miss Black, the young lady, perhaps the heiress of a fine old country seat! calling a fine old military officer uncle! having a handsome income of pocket-money settled upon me! having carriages, and horses, and servants to attend me? No; it can't be! it's just impossible. No—I see how it is. I'm crazy, that's what *I* am—crazy! For now I think of it, the last thing I remember of my former life was being brought before the Recorder for wearing boy's clothes. Now I'm sure that it was upon that occasion that I went suddenly mad with trouble, and all the rest is a lunatic's fancy. This fine old country seat, of which I vainly think myself the mistress, is just the pauper mad-house to which the magistrates have sent me. This fine old military officer whom I call my uncle is the head-doctor. The servants who come at my call are the keepers.

"There is no figure out of my past life in my present one, except Herbert Greyson. But, pshaw! *he* is not 'the nephew of his uncle!' he is only my old comrade Herbert Greyson, the sailor lad, who comes here to the mad-house to see me, and out of compassion humors all my fancies.

"I wonder how long they'll keep me here? Forever I hope. Until I get cured I'm sure! I hope they *won't* cure me. I vow I won't *be* cured. It's a great deal too pleasant to be mad, and I'll *stay* so. I'll keep on calling myself Miss Black, and this mad-house my country seat, and the head-doctor my uncle, and the keepers servants until the end of time—so I will. Catch me coming to my senses when it's so delightful to be mad. I'm too sharp for *that*. I didn't grow up in Rag Alley, New York, for nothing."

So, half in jest and half in earnest, Capitola soliloquized upon her change of fortune.

Her education was commenced, but progressed rather irregularly. Old Hurricane bought her books and maps, slates and copy-books, set her lessons in grammar, geography and history, and made her write copies, do sums, and read and recite lessons to him. Mrs. Condiment taught her the mysteries of cutting and basting, back-stitching and felling, hemming and seaming. A pupil as sharp as Capitola soon mastered her tasks, and found herself each day with many hours of leisure, with which she did not know what to do.

These hours were at first occupied with exploring the old house, with all its attics, cuddies, cock-lofts and cellars; then in wandering through the old ornamental grounds, that were, even in winter and in total neglect, beautiful with their wild growth of evergreens; thence she extended her researches into the wild and picturesque country around.

She was never weary of admiring the great forest that climbed the heights of the mountains behind their house; the great bleak precipices of gray rocks seen through the leafless branches of the trees; the rugged falling ground that lay before the house, and between it and the river; and the river itself, with its rushing stream and raging rapids.

Capitola had become as skilful as she had first been a fearless rider. But her rides were confined to the domain between the mountain range and the river; she was forbidden to ford the one or to climb the other. Perhaps if such a prohibition had never been made, Cap would never thought of doing the one or the other; but we all know the diabolical fascination there is in forbidden pleasures for young human nature. And no sooner had Cap been commanded, if she valued her safety, not to cross the water or climb the precipice, than, as a natural consequence, she began to wonder what was in the valley behind the mountain, and what might be in the woods across the river! and she longed, above all things, to explore and find out for herself. She would eagerly have done so, notwithstanding the prohibition; but Wool, who always attended her rides, was sadly in the way; if she could only get rid of Wool, she resolved to go upon a limited exploring expedition.

One day a golden opportunity occurred. It was a day of unusual beauty, when autumn seemed to be smiling upon the earth with her brightest smiles before passing away. In a word, it was Indian summer. The beauty of the weather had tempted Old Hurricane to ride to the county seat on particular business connected with his ward herself.

Capitola, left alone, amused herself with her tasks until the afternoon; then calling a boy, she ordered him to saddle her horse and bring him around.

"My dear, what do you want with your horse? There is no one to attend you; Wool has gone with his master," said Mrs. Condiment, as she met Capitola in the hall, habited for her ride.

"I know that; but I cannot be mewed up here in the old house and deprived of my afternoon ride!" exclaimed Capitola, decidedly.

"But, my dear, you must never think of riding out alone!" exclaimed the dismayed Mrs. Condiment.

"Indeed I shall though!—and glad of the opportunity!" added Cap, mentally.

"But, my dear love, it is improper, imprudent, dangerous."

"Why so?" asked Cap.

"Good gracious, upon every account. Suppose you were to meet with ruffians; suppose—oh, heaven!—suppose you were to meet with—BLACK DONALD!"

"Mrs. Condiment, once for all do tell me who this terrible Black Donald *is?* Is he the Evil One himself, or the Man in the Iron Mask, or the individual that struck Billy Patterson,[1] or—who is he?"

"Who is Black Donald? Good gracious, child, you ask me who is Black Donald?"

"Yes—*who* is he? *where* is he? WHAT is he, that every cheek turns pale at the mention of his name?" asked Capitola.

"Black Donald! Oh, my child, may you never know more of Black Donald than I can tell you. Black Donald is the chief of a band of ruthless desperadoes that infest these mountain roads, robbing mail-coaches, stealing negroes, breaking into houses, and committing every sort of depredation. Their hands are red with murder, and their souls black with darker crimes."

"Darker crimes than murder!" ejaculated Capitola.

"Yes, child, yes—there *are* darker crimes! Only last winter he and three of his gang broke into a solitary house where there was a lone woman and her daughter, and—it is not a story for you to hear, but if the people had caught Black Donald then, they would have burnt him at a stake. His life is forfeit by a hundred crimes. He is an outlaw, and a heavy price is set upon his head."

"And can no one take him?"

"No, my dear; at least, no one has been able to do so yet. His very haunts are unknown, but are supposed to be in concealed mountain caverns."

"How I would like the glory of capturing Black Donald!" said Capitola.

"*You,* child—*you* capture Black Donald! You are crazy."

"Oh, by stratagem I mean, not by force! Oh, how I should like to capture Black Donald!—There's my horse. Good-bye!"

And, before Mrs. Condiment could raise another objection, Capitola ran out, sprang into her saddle, and was seen careering down the hill towards the river as fast as her horse could fly.

"My lord, but the major will be hopping if he finds it out," was good Mrs. Condiment's dismayed exclamation.

Rejoicing in her freedom, Cap galloped down to the water's edge, and then walked her horse up and down along the course of the stream until she found a good fording place. Then gathering up her riding-skirt and throwing it over the neck of her horse, she plunged boldly into the stream, and with the water splashing and foaming all around her, urged him onward until they crossed the river and climbed up the opposite bank. A bridle-path lay before her, leading from the fording place through a deep wood. That path attracted her; she followed it, charmed alike by the solitude of the wood, the novelty of the scene, and her own sense of freedom. But one thought was given to the story of Black Donald, and that was a reassuring one.

fear

"If Black Donald is a mail-robber, then this little bridle-path is far enough off *his* beat."

And so saying, she gaily galloped along, singing as she went, following the narrow path up hill and down dale through the wintry woods. Drawn on by the attraction of the *unknown*, and deceiving herself by the continued repetition of one resolve, namely:

"When I get to the top of the *next* hill, and see what lies beyond, *then* I will turn back," she galloped on and on—on and on—on and on! until she had put several miles between herself and her home, until her horse began to exhibit signs of weariness, and the level rays of the setting sun were striking redly through the leafless branches of the trees.

Cap drew rein on the top of a high, wooded hill, and looked about her. On her left hand the sun was sinking like a ball of fire below the horizon; all around her everywhere were the wintry woods; far away, in the direction whence she had come, she saw the tops of the mountains behind Hurricane Hall, looking like blue clouds against the southern horizon; the Hall itself and the river below were out of sight.

"I wonder how far I am from home?" said Capitola, uneasily; "somewhere between six and seven miles, I reckon. Dear me, I didn't mean to ride so far. I've got over a great deal of ground in these two hours. I shall not get back so soon; my horse is tired to death; it will take me three hours to reach Hurricane Hall. Good gracious, it will be pitch dark before I get there. No, thank heaven, there'll be a moon. But won't there be a row, though! Whew! Well, I must turn about and lose no time. Come, Gyp! get up, Gyp! good horse! we're going home!"

she's scared

And so saying, Capitola turned her horse's head and urged him into a gallop.

She had gone on for about a mile, and it was growing dark, and her horse was again slackening his pace, when she thought she heard the sound of another horse's hoofs behind her. She drew rein and listened, and was sure of it.

Now, without being the least of a coward, Capitola thought of the loneliness of the woods, and the lateness of the hour, her own helplessness, and—Black Donald! And thinking "discretion the better part of valor," she urged her horse once more into a gallop, for a few hundred yards; but the jaded beast soon broke into a trot, and subsided into a walk that threatened soon to come to a stand still.

The invisible pursuer gained on her.

In vain she urged her steed with whip and voice; the poor beast would obey and trot for a few yards, and then fall into a walk.

The thundering footfalls of the pursuing horse were close in the rear.

"Oh, Gyp! is it possible that, instead of my capturing Black Donald, you are going to let Black Donald or somebody else catch *me?*" exclaimed Capitola, in mock despair, as she urged her wearied steed.

In vain! The pursuing horseman was beside her! a strong hand was laid upon her bridle! a mocking voice was whispering in her ear:

"*Whither away so fast, pretty one?*"

CHAPTER XVI

CAP'S FEARFUL ADVENTURE

✻✻✻✻✻✻

> "Who passes by this road so late?
> Companion of the Marjolaine!
> Who passes by this road so late?
> Say! oh, say!"
> —*Old French Song* [1]

OF A NATURALLY STRONG constitution and adventurous disposition, and inured from infancy to danger, Capitola possessed a high degree of courage, self-control, and presence of mind.

At the touch of that ruthless hand, at the sound of that gibing voice, all her faculties instantly collected and concentrated themselves upon the emergency. As by a flash of lightning she saw every feature of her imminent danger—the loneliness of the woods, the lateness of the hour, the recklessness of her fearful companion, and her own weakness. In another instant her resolution was taken and her course determined. So, when the stranger repeated his mocking question:

"Whither away so fast, pretty one?" she answered with animation:

"Oh, I am going home, and so glad to have company; for indeed I was dreadfully afraid of riding alone through these woods to-night!"

"Afraid, pretty one—what of?"

"Oh, of ghosts and witches, wild beasts, runaway negroes and—Black Donald!"

"Then you are not afraid of *me?*"

"Lors! no, indeed! I guess I ain't! why should I be afraid of a respectable-looking gentleman like you, sir?"

"And so you are going home—where *is* your home, pretty one?"

"On the other side of the river; but you need not keep on calling me 'pretty one,' it must be as tiresome to you to repeat it as it is to me to hear it."

"What shall I call you, then, my dear?"

"You may call me Miss Black, or if you are friendly, you may call me Capitola."

"CAPITOLA!" exclaimed the man, in a deep and changed voice, as he dropped her bridle.

"Yes, Capitola! what objection have you got to that? It is a pretty name, isn't it? but if you think it is too long, and if you feel *very* friendly, you may call me Cap."

"Well, then, my pretty Cap, where do you live across the river?" asked the stranger, recovering his self-possession.

"Oh, at a rum old place they call Hurricane Hall, with a rum old military officer they call Old Hurricane," said Capitola, for the first time stealing a sidelong glance at her fearful companion.

It was not Black Donald—that was the first conclusion to which she rashly jumped. He appeared to be a gentlemanly ruffian about forty years of age, well dressed in a black riding suit; black beaver hat drawn down close over his eyes; black hair and whiskers; heavy black eyebrows that met across his nose; drooping eyelashes, and eyes that looked out under the corners of the lids; altogether a sly, sinister, cruel face, a cross between fox and tiger! it warned Capitola to expect no mercy there! After the girl's last words he seemed to have fallen into thought for a moment, and then again he spoke:

"Well, my pretty Cap, how long have you been living at Hurricane Hall?"

"Ever since my guardian, Major Warfield, brought me from the city of New York, where I received my education—(*in the streets*)," she mentally added.

"Humph! why did you ride so fast, my pretty Cap?" he asked, eyeing her from the corner of her eyes.

"Oh, sir, because I was *afraid,* as I told you before; afraid of runaway negroes and wild beasts, and so on—but now with a good gentleman like *you* I don't feel afraid at all; and I'm very glad to be able to walk poor Gyp; because he's tired, poor fellow!"

"Yes, poor fellow!" said the traveler, in a mocking tone, "he *is* tired; suppose you *dismount* and let him rest. Come, I'll get off, too, and we will sit down here by the roadside and have a friendly conversation."

Capitola stole a glance at his face. Yes, notwithstanding his light tone, he was grimly in earnest, there was no mercy to be expected from that sly, sinister, cruel face.

"Come, my pretty Cap, what say you?"

"I don't care if I *do*," she said, riding to the edge of the path, drawing rein, and looking down as if to examine the ground.

"Come, little beauty, must I help you off?" asked the stranger.

"N-n-no," answered Capitola, with deliberate hesitation, "no, this is not a good place to sit down and talk; it's all full of brambles."

"Very well; shall we go on a little further?"

"Oh, yes; but I don't want to ride fast, because it will tire my horse."

"You shall go just as you please, my angel," said the traveler.

"I wonder whether this wretch thinks me very simple or very depraved—he must have come to one or the other conclusion," thought Capitola.

They rode on very slowly for a mile further, and then having arrived at an open glade, the stranger drew rein, and said:

"Come, pretty lark, hop down! here's a nice place to sit and rest."

"Very well, come help me off!" said Capitola, pulling up her horse—then, as by a sudden impulse, she exclaimed, "I don't like *this* place either! it's right on the top of the hill! so windy! and just see how rocky the ground is! No! I'll not sit and rest *here,* and that I tell you!"

"I am afraid you are trifling with me, my pretty bird! take care! I'll not be trifled with!" said the man.

"I don't know what you mean by *trifling* with you, any more than the dead. But I'll not sit down there on those sharp rocks, and so I tell you. If you will be civil and ride along with me until we get to the foot of the hill, I know a nice place, where we can sit down and have a *good* talk, and I will tell you all my travels, and you shall tell me all yours."

"Ex-actly—and where is that nice place?"

"Why, in the valley at the foot of the hill."

"Come! come on, then."

"Slowly, slowly!" said Capitola—"I won't tire my horse."

They rode over the hill, down the gradual descent, and on towards the centre of the valley.

They were now within a quarter of a mile of the river, on the opposite side of which was Hurricane Hall and—*safety!* The stranger drew rein, saying:

"Come, my cuckoo! here we are at the bottom of the valley! now or never!"

"Oh! now, of course! you see I keep my promise," answered Capitola, pulling up her horse.

The man sprang from his saddle and came to her side.

116

"Please to be careful, now, don't let my riding-skirt get hung in the stirrup," said Capitola, cautiously disengaging her drapery, rising in the saddle and giving the stranger her hand. In the act of jumping, she suddenly stopped and looked down, exclaiming:

"Good gracious! how very damp the ground is here in the bottom of the valley!"

"More objections, I suppose, my pretty one! but they won't serve you any longer. I am bent upon having a cozy chat with you, upon that very turf!" said the stranger, pointing to a little cleared space among the trees beside the path.

"Now, don't be cross; just see how damp it is there; it would spoil my riding-dress, and give me my death of cold."

"*Humph,*" said the stranger, looking at her with a sly, grim, cruel resolve.

"I'll tell you what it is," said Cap, "I'm not witty nor amusing, nor will it *pay* to sit out in the night air to hear *me* talk; but since you wish it, and since you were so good as to guard me through these woods, and since I *promised,* why, damp as it is, I will even get off and talk with you!"

"That's my birdling."

"But hold on one minute. Is there nothing you can get to put there for me to sit on—no stump, nor dry stone?"

"No, my dear, I don't see any."

"Could you not turn your hat down and let me sit on that?"

"Ha, ha, ha! why, your weight would crush it as flat as a flounder!"

"Oh! I know now!" exclaimed Capitola, with sudden delight. "You just spread your saddle-cloth down there, and that will make a beautiful seat, and I'll sit and talk with you so nicely—only you must not want me to stay long, because if I don't get home soon I shall catch a scolding."

"You shall neither catch a scolding nor a cold on my account, pretty one!" said the man, going to his horse to get the saddle-cloth.

"Oh, don't take off the saddle; it will detain you too long," said Cap, impatiently.

"My pretty Cap, I cannot get the cloth without taking it off," said the man, beginning to unbuckle the girth.

"Oh, yes you can! you can draw it from under!" persisted Cap.

"Impossible, my angel!" said the man, lifting off the saddle from his horse and laying it carefully by the roadside.

Then he took off the gay, crimson saddle-cloth, and carried it into the little clearing and began carefully to spread it down.

Now was Cap's time. Her horse had recovered from his fatigue. The stranger's horse was in the path before her. While the man's back was turned, she raised her riding-whip, and with a shout, gave the front horse a sharp lash that sent him galloping furiously ahead. Then instantaneously putting whip to her own horse, she started into a run.

Hearing the shout, the lash, and the starting of the horses, the baffled villain turned and saw that his game was lost! He had been outwitted by a child! He gnashed his teeth and shook his fist in rage.

Turning, as she wheeled out of sight, Capitola—I'm sorry to say—put her thumb to the side of her nose, and whirled her fingers into a semi-circle, in a gesture more expressive than elegant.

CHAPTER XVII

ANOTHER STORM AT HURRICANE HALL

"At this, Sir Knight grew high in wroth,
And lifting hands and eyes up both,
Three times he smote on stomach stout,
From whence, at length, fierce words broke out."
—*Hudibras*

THE MOON was shining full upon the river and household beyond, when Capitola dashed into the water, and amid the sparkling and leaping of the foam, made her way to the other bank, and rode up the rugged ascent. On the outer side of the lawn wall, the moonbeams fell full upon the little figure of Pitapat, waiting there.

"Why, Patty, what takes *you* out so late as this?" asked Capitola, as she rode up to the gate.

"Oh, Miss Caterpillar, I'se waitin' for you! Ole Marse is dreadful, *he* is! jes fit to burst the shingles offen the roof with swearing! So I come out to warn you, so you can steal in the back way and go to your rooms so he won't see you, and I'll go and send Wool to put your horse away, and then I'll bring you up some supper, and tell Ole Marse how you've been home ever so long, and gone to bed with a werry bad head-ache."

"Thank you, Patty. It is perfectly astonishing, how easy lying is to you. You really deserve to have been born in Rag Alley. But I won't trouble the Recording Angel to make another entry against you on my account."

"Yes, Miss," said Pitapat, who thought that her mistress was complimenting her.

"And now, Patty, stand out of my way. I'm going to ride straight up to the horse-block, dismount, and walk right into the presence of Major Warfield!" said Capitola, passing through the gate.

"Oh, Miss Caterpillar, don't! don't! he'll kill you, so he will!"

"Who's afeared?" muttered Cap to herself, as she put her horse to his mettle, and rode gaily through the evergreens, up to the horse-block where she sprang down lightly from her saddle.

Gathering up her train with one hand and tossing back her head, she swept along toward the house with the air of a young princess.

There was a vision calculated to test her firmness. Reader! did you ever see a raging lion tearing to and fro the narrow limits of his cage, and occasionally shaking the amphitheatre with his tremendous, roar? or a furious bull tossing his head and tail, and ploughing up the earth with his hoofs as he careered back and forth between the boundaries of his pen? If you have seen and noted these mad brutes, you may form some faint idea of the frenzy of Old Hurricane, as he stormed up and down the floor of the front piazza.

Cap had just escaped an actual danger of too terrible a character to be frightened now by sound and fury. Composedly she walked up into the porch, and said:

"Good evening, uncle."

The old man stopped short in his furious strides, and glared upon her with his terrible eyes.

Cap stood fire without blenching, merely remarking:

"Now I have no doubt that in the days when you went battling, that look used to strike terror into the heart of the enemy, but it doesn't into mine, somehow!"

"Miss!" roared the old man, bringing down his cane with a resounding thump upon the floor; "Miss!! how *dare* you have the impudence to face me, much less the—the—the assurance!—the effrontery!—the audacity! the *brass* to speak to me!"

"Well, I declare," said Cap, calmly untying her hat, "this is the first time I ever heard it was impudent in a little girl to give her uncle good evening."

The old man trotted up and down the piazza two or three turns, then stopping short before the delinquent, he struck his cane down upon the floor with a ringing stroke, and thundered:

"Young woman! tell me instantly, and without prevarication, where you have been?"

"Certainly, sir; 'going to and fro in the earth, and walking up and down in it!'" said Cap, quietly.

"Flames and furies, that is no answer at all! Where have you been?" roared Old Hurricane, shaking with excitement.

"Look here, uncle, if you go on that way you'll have a fit presently!" said Cap, calmly.

"WHERE HAVE YOU BEEN!" thundered Old Hurricane.

"Well, since you will know—just across the river, and through the woods and back again!"

"And didn't I forbid you to do that, minion? and how *dare* you disobey me? *You, the creature of my bounty! you,* the miserable little vagrant that I picked up in the alleys of New York, and tried to make a young lady of; but an old proverb says—'You can't make a silken purse out of a pig's ear!' How dare *you,* you little beggar disobey your benefactor!—a man of my age, character and position?—I—I——" Old Hurricane turned abruptly, and raged up and down the piazza.

All this time Capitola had been standing quietly, holding up her train with one hand and her riding hat in the other. At this last insult she raised her dark gray eyes to his face with one long, indignant, sorrowful gaze, then turning silently away, and entering the house, she left Old Hurricane to storm up and down the piazza until he had raged himself to rest.

Reader! I do not defend, far less approve, poor Cap! I only tell her story and describe her as I have seen her, leaving her to your charitable interpretation.

Next morning Capitola came down into the breakfast-room with one idea prominent in her hard little head—to which she mentally gave expression:

"Well as I like that old man, he must not permit himself to talk to me in *that* indecent strain, and so he must be made to know."

When she entered the breakfast-room, she found Mrs. Condiment already at the head of the table, and Old Hurricane at the foot. He had quite got over his rage, and turned around blandly to welcome his ward, saying:

"Good-morning, Cap."

Without taking the slightest notice of the salutation, Cap sailed on to her seat.

"Humph! did you hear me say, '*Good-morning*,' Cap?"

Without paying the least attention, Capitola reached out her hand and took a cup of coffee from Mrs. Condiment.

"Humph! Humph! GOOD-MORNING, Capitola!" said Old Hurricane, with marked emphasis. Apparently without hearing him, Cap helped herself to a buckwheat cake, and daintily buttered it.

"Humph! humph! humph! well, as you said yourself, 'a dumb devil is better than a speaking one!'" ejaculated Old Hurricane, as he sat down and subsided into silence.

Doubtless the old man would have flown into another passion, had that been possible; but, in truth, he had spent so much vitality in rage number *one,* that he had none left to sustain rage number *two.* Besides, he knew it would be necessary to blow up Bill Ezy, his lazy overseer, before night, and perhaps saved himself for that performance. He finished his meal in silence, and went out.

Cap finished hers; and, 'tempering justice with mercy,' went up stairs to his room, and looked over all his appointments and belongings to find what she could do for his extra comfort; and found a job in newly lining his warm slippers, and the sleeves of his dressing-gown.

They met again at the dinner-table.

"How do you do, Cap?" said Old Hurricane, as he took his seat.

Capitola poured out a glass of water and drank it in silence, and without looking at him.

"Oh! very well! 'a dumb devil, etc.,'" exclaimed Old Hurricane, addressing himself to his dinner. When the meal was over they again separated. The old man went to his study to examine his farm books, and Capitola back to her chamber to finish lining his warm slippers.

Again at tea they met.

"Well, Cap, is 'the dumb devil' cast out yet?" he said, sitting down.

Capitola took a cup of tea from Mrs. Condiment and passed it on to him in silence.

"Humph, not gone yet, eh?—poor girl! how it must try you!" said Old Hurricane.

After supper the old man found his dressing-gown and slippers before the fire all ready for his use.

"Cap, you monkey! you did this," he said, turning around. But Capitola had already left the room.

Next morning at breakfast there was a repetition of the same scene. Early in the forenoon Major Warfield ordered his horses, and, attended by Wool, rode up to Tip-Top. He did not return either to dinner or tea, but as that circumstance was not unusual it gave no one uneasiness. Mrs. Condiment kept his supper warm, and Capitola had his dressing-gown and slippers ready.

She was turning them before the fire when the old man arrived. He came in quite gayly, saying:

"Now, Cap, I think I have found a *talisman* at last to cast out that 'dump devil.' I heard you wishing for a watch the other day. Now, as devils belong to eternity, and have no business with *time*, of course the sight of this little time-keeper must put yours to flight!" and so saying he laid upon the table, before the eyes of Capitola, a beautiful little gold watch and chain. She glanced at it, as it lay glittering and sparkling in the lamp-light, and then turned abruptly and walked away.

"Humph! that's always the way the devils do! fly when they can't stand shot!"

Capitola deliberately walked back, laid a paper over the little watch and chain, as if to cover its fascinating sparkle and glitter, and said:

"Uncle, your bounty is large, and your present is beautiful; but there is something that poor Capitola values more than that——"

She paused, dropped her head upon her bosom, a sudden blush flamed up over her face, and teardrops glistened in her downcast eyes; she put both hands before her burning face for a moment, and then dropping them, resumed:

"Uncle! you rescued me from misery, and perhaps, *perhaps* early death! you have heaped benefits and bounties upon me without measure! you have placed me in a home of abundance, honor and security! for all this, if I were not grateful, I should deserve no less than death! But, uncle, there is a sin that is worse, or at least more *ungenerous,* than ingratitude! it is to put a helpless fellow creature under heavy obligations, and then treat that grateful creature with undeserved contempt and cruel unkindness!" Once more her voice was choked with feeling.

For some reason or other, Capitola's tears, perhaps because they were so rare, always moved Old Hurricane to his heart's centre; going towards her softly he said:

"Now, my dear, now my child, now my little Cap, you *know* it was all for your own good! Why, my dear, I never for one instant regretted bringing you to the house, and I wouldn't part with you for a kingdom! Come now, my child, come to the heart of your old uncle."

Now the soul of Capitola naturally abhorred sentiment! If ever she gave way to serious emotion, she was sure to avenge herself by being more capricious than before. Consequently flinging herself out of the caressing arms of Old Hurricane, she exclaimed:

"Uncle! I won't be treated with both kicks and half-pennies by the same person—and so I tell you. I'm not a cur to be fed with roast-beef and beaten with a stick! nor, nor, nor a Turk's slave to be caressed and oppressed as her master likes!—Such abuse as you heaped upon me, I never heard—no, not even in Rag Alley."

"Oh, my dear, my dear, for Heaven's sake forget Rag Alley."

"I won't! I vow I'll go back to Rag Alley, for a very little more! Freedom and peace are even sweeter than wealth and honors!"

"Ah, but I wouldn't let you, my little Cap."

"Then I'd have you up before the nearest magistrate, to show by what right you detained me! Ah, ha! I wasn't brought up in New York for nothing!"

"Whee-ew! and all this because, for her own good, I gave my own niece and ward a little gentle admonition."

"Gentle admonition! Do you call *that* gentle admonition? Why, uncle, you are enough to frighten most people to death with your fury! You are a perfect dragon! a griffin! a Russian bear! a Bengal tiger! a Numidian lion! I declare if I don't write and ask some menagerie man to send a party down here to catch you for his show. You'd *draw*, I tell you!"

"Yes! especially with *you* for a keeper to stir me up once in a while with a long pole!"

"And that I'd engage to do—*cheap!*"

The entrance of Mrs. Condiment with the tea-tray put an end to the controversy. It was, as yet, a drawn battle.

"And what about the watch, my little Cap?"

"Take it back, uncle, if you please."

"But they won't have it back! it has got your initials engraved upon it—look here," said the old man, holding the watch to her eyes.

"C. L.N. Those are not my initials," said Capitola, looking up with surprise.

"Why, so they are not! the blamed fools have made a mistake!—but you'll have to take it, Cap."

"No, uncle, keep it for the present," said Capitola, who was too honest to take a gift that she felt she did not deserve, and yet too proud to confess as much.

Peace was proclaimed—for the present.

Alas! 'twas but of short continuance. During these two days of coolness and enforced quietude Old Hurricane had gathered a store of bad humors that required expenditure.

So the very next day something went wrong upon the farm, and Old Hurricane came storming home, driving his overseer, poor, old, meek Billy Ezy and his man Wool, before him.

Billy Ezy was whimpering; Wool was sobbing aloud; Old Hurricane was roaring at them both as he drove them on before him—swearing that Ezy should go and find himself a new home, and Wool should go and seek another master.

And for this cause Old Hurricane was driving them on to his study, that he might pay the overseer his last quarter's salary, and give the servant a written order to find a master.

He raged past Capitola in the hall, and meeting Mrs. Condiment at the study door, ordered her to bring in her account book directly, for that he would not be imposed upon any longer, but meant to drive all the lazy, idle, dishonest eye-servants[1] and time-servers[2] from the house and land!

"What's the matter now?" said Capitola meeting her.

"Oh, child, he's in his terrible tantrums again! He gets into these ways every once in a while, when a young calf perishes, or a sheep is stolen, or anything goes amiss, and then he abuses us all for a pack of loiterers, sluggards and thieves, and *pays* us off and *orders* us off. We don't go, of course, because we know he doesn't mean it; still it is very trying to be talked to so. Oh! I should go, but, Lord, child! he's a bear, but we love him."

Just as she spoke the study door opened, and Bill Ezy came out sobbing, and Wool lifting up his voice and fairly roaring.

Mrs. Condiment stepped out of the parlor door.

"What's the matter, you blockhead?" she asked of Wool.

"Oh! Boo-hoo-woo! Ole Marse been and done and gone and guv me a line to find an—an—another—Boo-hoo-woo!" sobbed Wool, ready to break his heart.

"Give you a line to find another Boo-hoo-woo! I wouldn't do it if I were you, Wool!" said Capitola.

"Give me the paper, Wool," said Mrs. Condiment, taking the "permit" and tearing it up, and adding:

"There! now you go home to your quarter, and keep out of your old master's sight until he gets over his anger, and then you know very well that it will be all right. There! go along with you."

Wool quickly got out of the way, and made room for the overseer, who was snivelling like a whipped school-boy, and to whom the housekeeper said:

"I thought *you* were wiser than to take this so to heart, Mr. Ezy!"

"Oh, mum! what could you expect?—an old sarvint as has sarved the major faithful these forty years, to be discharged at sixty-five! *Oh! hoo-ooo-oo!*" whimpered the overseer.

"But then you have been discharged so often, you ought to be used to it by this time! you get discharged just as Wool gets sold—about once a month! but do you ever go?"

"Oh, mum! but he's in airnest this time! 'deed he is, mum! *terrible* in airnest! and all about that misfortnet bob-tail colt getting stole! I know how it wur some of Black Donald's gang as done it! As if I could always be on my guard against *they* devils! And he *means* it this time, mum! He's *terrible* in airnest!"

"Tut! he's *always* in earnest for as long as it lasts! Go home to your family and to-morrow go about your business, as usual."

Here the study bell rang violently and Old Hurricane's voice was heard calling—"Mrs. Condiment! Mrs. Condiment!"

"Oh, lor! he's coming!" cried Bill Ezy, running off as fast as age and grief would let him.

"Mrs. Condiment! Mrs. Condiment!" called the voice.

"Yes, sir! yes!" answered the housekeeper, hurrying to obey the call.

Capitola walked up and down the hall for half an hour, at the end of which Mrs. Condiment came out "with a smile on her lip and a tear in her eye," and saying:

"Well, Miss Capitola, I'm paid off and discharged also!"

"What for?"

"For aiding and abetting the rebels! in a word, for trying to comfort poor Ezy and Wool."

"And are you going?"

"Certainly not! I sha'n't budge! I would not treat the old man so badly as to take him at his word!" and, with a strange smile, Mrs. Condiment hurried away just in time to escape Old Hurricane, who came raving out of the study.

"Get out of my way, you beggar!" he cried, pushing past Capitola, and hurrying from the house.

"Well, I declare, that *was* pleasant!" thought Cap, as she entered the parlor.

"Mrs. Condiment, what will he say when he comes back and finds you all here still?" she asked.

"Say?—nothing. After this passion is over, he will be so exhausted that he will not be able to get up another rage in two or three days."

"Where has he gone?"

"To Tip-Top; and alone, too; he was so mad with poor Wool that he wouldn't even permit him to attend."

"Alone? has he gone alone! *Oh, won't I give him a dose when he comes back?*" thought Capitola.

Meanwhile Old Hurricane stormed along towards Tip-Top, lashing off the poor dogs that wished to follow him, and cutting at every living thing that crossed his path. His business at the village was to get bills printed and posted, offering an additional reward for the apprehension of "the marauding outlaw Black Donald." That day, he dined at the village tavern—"The Antlers," by Mr. Merry—and differed, disputed, or quarrelled, as the case might be, with every man whom he happened to come in contact with.

Towards evening he set off for home. It was much later than his usual hour of returning; but he felt weary, exhausted, and indisposed to come into his own dwelling where his furious temper had created so much unhappiness. Thus, though it was very late, he did not hurry; he almost hoped that every one might be in bed when he should return. The moon was shining brightly when he passed the gate and rode up the evergreen avenue to the horse-block in front of the house. There he dismounted and walked up into the piazza, where a novel vision met his surprised gaze.

It was Capitola, walking up and down the floor, with rapid, almost masculine strides, and apparently in a state of great excitement.

"Oh, is it you, my little Cap? Good-evening, my dear," he said, very kindly.

Capitola "pulled up" in her striding walk, wheeled around, faced him, drew up her form, folded her arms, threw back her head, set her teeth, and glared at him.

"What the demon do you mean by *that?*" cried Old Hurricane.

"SIR!" she exclaimed, bringing down one foot with a sharp stamp—"SIR, how *dare* you the impudence to *face* me, much less the—the—the—the brass! the *bronze!* the COPPER! to speak to me?"

"Why, what in the name of all the lunatics in Bedlam does the girl mean? Is she crazy?" exclaimed the old man, gazing upon her in astonishment.

Capitola turned and strode furiously up and down the piazza, and then, stopping suddenly and facing him, with a sharp stamp of her foot, exclaimed:

"OLD GENTLEMAN, tell me instantly, and without prevarication, where have you been?"

"To the demon with you! what do you mean? Have you taken leave of your senses?" demanded Old Hurricane.

Capitola strode up and down the floor a few times, and stopping short and shaking her fist, exclaimed:

'DIDN'T you know, you headstrong, reckless, desperate, frantic veteran! _didn't you know the jeopardy in which you placed yourself by riding_ out alone at this hour? Suppose three or four great runaway negresses had sprung out of the bushes—and—and—"

She broke off, apparently for want of breath, and strode up and down the floor; then, pausing suddenly before him, with a stern stamp of her foot and a fierce glare of her eye, she continued:

"You shouldn't have come back _here_ any more! No dishonored old man should have entered the house of which _I_ call myself the mistress!"

"Oh, I take! I take! ha! ha! ha! Good, Cap, good! You are holding up the glass before me; but your mirror is not quite large enough to reflect 'Old Hurricane,' my dear—_I owe you one,_" said the old man, as he passed into the house, followed by his capricious favorite.

CHAPTER XVIII

THE DOCTOR'S DAUGHTER

"Oh, her smile, it seemed half holy,
As if drawn from thoughts more far,
Than our common jestings are.
And if any painter drew her,
he would paint her unaware
With a halo round her hair."
—E. B. *Browning* [1]

ON THE APPOINTED day, Traverse took his way to Willow Heights, to keep his tryst and enter upon the medical studies in the good doctor's office. He was anxious also to know if his patron had as yet thought of any plan by which his mother might better her condition. He was met at the door by little Mattie, the parlor maid, who told him to walk right up stairs into the study, where his master was expecting him.

Traverse went up quietly and opened the door of that pleasant study-room, to which the reader has already been introduced, and the windows of which opened upon the upper front piazza.

Now, however, as it was quite cold, the windows were down, though the blinds were open, and through them streamed the golden rays of the morning sun that fell glistening upon the fairy hair and white raiment of a young girl, who sat reading before the fire.

The doctor was not in the room, and Traverse in his native modesty was just about to retreat, when the young creature looked up from her book, and seeing him, arose with a smile, and came forward, saying:

"You are the young man whom my father was expecting, I presume. Sit down, he has stepped out, but will be in again very soon."

Now, Traverse being unaccustomed to the society of young ladies felt excessively bashful when suddenly coming into the presence of this refined and lovely girl. With a low bow and a deep blush he took the chair she placed for him.

With natural politeness, she closed her book and addressed herself to entertaining him.

129

"I have heard that your mother is an invalid, I hope she is better?"

"I thank you—yes, ma'am—Miss," stammered Traverse, in painful embarrassment. Understanding the timidity of the bashful boy, and seeing that her efforts to entertain only troubled him, she placed the newspapers on the table before him, saying:

"Here are the morning journals if you would like to look over them, Mr. Rocke," and then she resumed her book.

"I thank you, Miss," replied the youth, taking up a paper, more for the purpose of covering his embarrassment, than for any other.

Mr. Rocke! Traverse was seventeen years of age, and had never been called Mr. Rocke before! This young girl was the very first first to compliment him with the manly title, and he felt a boyish gratitude to her and a harmless wish that his well-brushed Sunday suit of black was not quite so rusty and threadbare, tempered by an innocent exultation in the thought that no gentleman in the land could exhibit fresher linen, brighter shoes or cleaner hands than himself.

But not many seconds were spent in such egotism. He stole a glance at his lovely companion sitting on the opposite side of the fireside—he was glad to see that she was already deeply engaged in reading, for it enabled him to observe her, without embarrassment or offence. He had scarcely dared to look at her before, and had no distinct idea of her beauty.

There had been for him only a vague, dazzling vision of a golden-haired girl in floating white raiment, wafting the fragrance of violets as she moved, and with a voice sweeter than the notes of the cushat dove as she spoke.

Now he saw that the golden hair flowed in ringlets around a fair, roseate face, soft and bright with feeling and intelligence. As her dark blue eyes followed the page, a smile intense with meaning deepened the expression of her countenance. That intense smile!—it was like her father's, only lovelier—more heavenly. That intense smile! It had, even on the old doctor's face, an inexpressible charm for Traverse—but on the lovely young face of his daughter it exercised an ineffable fascination. So earnest and so unconscious became the gaze of poor Traverse that he was only brought to a sense of propriety by the opening of the door, and the entrance of the doctor, who exclaimed:

"Ah! here already, Traverse! that is punctual!—This is my daughter Clara, Traverse! Clara, this is Traverse, you've heard me speak about!—But, I dare say, you've already become acquainted," concluded the doctor, drawing his chair up to the reading-table, sitting down and folding his dressing-gown around his limbs.

"Well, Traverse, how is the little mother?" he presently inquired.

"I was just telling Miss Day that she was much better, sir," said Traverse.

"Ah, ha! ah, ha!" muttered the doctor to himself—"that's kitchen physic—roast turkey and port wine! and moral medicine, hope! and mental medicine, sympathy."

"Well, Traverse," he said aloud, "I have been racking my brain for a plan for your mother—and to no purpose! Traverse, your mother should be in a home of peace, plenty and cheerfulness!—I can speak before my little Clara here! I never have any secrets from *her*—Your mother wants good living, cheerful company, and freedom from toil and care! The situation of gentleman's or lady's housekeeper in some home of abundance, where she would be esteemed as a member of the family, would suit her; but where to find such a place! I have been inquiring—without mentioning her name, of course—among all my friends, but not one of them wants a housekeeper, or knows a soul who does want one, and so I am 'at sea on the subject.' I'm ashamed of myself for not succeeding better!"

"Oh, sir, do not do yourself so great injustice," said Traverse.

"Well, the fact is after boasting so confidently that I would find a good situation for Mrs. Rocke, lo and behold! I have proved myself as yet *only* a boaster!"

"Father," said Clara, turning upon him her sweet eyes.

"Well, my love?"

"Perhaps Mrs. Rocke would do us the favor to come *here* and take charge of *our* household."

"Eh! what! I never thought of that! I never had a housekeeper in my life!" exclaimed the doctor.

"No, sir, because you never *needed* one before, but now we really *do*. Aunt Moggy has been a very faithful and efficient manager, although she is a colored woman; but she is getting very old."

"Yes, and deaf, and blind, and careless! I know she is! I have no doubt in the world she scours the coppers with the table napkins, and washes her face and hands in the soup tureen."

"*Oh father!*" said Clara.

"Well, Clara, at least she wants looking after."

"Father, she wants rest in her old age."

"No doubt of it! no doubt of it!"

"And, father, I intend, of course, in time, to be your housekeeper; but having spent all my life at a boarding-school, I know very little about domestic affairs, and I require a great deal of instruction; so I really do think that there is no one needs Mrs. Rocke's assistance more than we do, and if she will do us the favor to come, we cannot do better than engage her."

"To be sure! to be sure! Lord bless my soul! to think it should never have entered my stupid old head, until it was put there by Clare! Here was I searching blindly all over the country for a situation for Mrs. Rocke, and wanting her all the time more than any one else! That's the way, Traverse, that's the way with us all, my boy! While we are looking away off yonder for the solution of our difficulties, the remedy is all the time lying just under our noses!"

"But so close to our eyes, father, that we cannot see it!" said Clara.

"Just so, Clare! just so! You are always ahead of me in ideas! Now, Traverse, when you go home this evening you shall take a note to your mother, setting forth our wishes—mine and Clara's; if she accedes to them she will make us very happy."

With a good deal of manly strength of mind Traverse had all his mother's tenderness of heart. It was with difficulty that he could keep back his tears or control his voice, while he answered:

"I remember reading, sir, that the young queen of England[2] when she came to her throne wished to provide handsomely for an orphan companion of her childhood; and seeing that no office in her household suited the young person, she created one for her benefit. Sir, I believe you have made one for my mother."

"Not at all! not at all! If she doesn't come to look after our housekeeping, old Moggy will be greasing our griddles with tallow candle ends next! If you don't believe me, ask Clara! ask Clara!"

Not "believe" him! If the doctor had affirmed that the moon was made of moldy cheese, Traverse would have deemed it his duty to stoutly maintain that astronomical theory. He felt hurt that the doctor should use such a phrase.

"Yes, indeed, we really do need her, Traverse," said the doctor's daughter.

"Traverse!" It had made him proud to hear her call him, for the first time in his life, "Mr. Rocke," but it made him deeply happy to hear her call him "Traverse." It had such a sisterly sound coming from this sweet creature. How he wished that she really *were* his sister! but then the idea of that fair, golden-haired, blue-eyed, white-robed angel being the sister of such a robust, rugged, sun-burned boy as himself! The thought was so absurd, extravagant, impossible, that the poor boy heaved an unconscious sigh.

"Why, what's the matter, Traverse? What are you thinking of so intently?"

"Of your great goodness, sir, among other things."

"Tut! let's hear no more of that. I please myself," said the doctor; "and now, Traverse, let's go to work decently and in order; but first let me settle *this* point: if your good little mother determines in our favor, Traverse, then of course *you* will live with us also, so I shall have my young medical assistant always at hand. That will be very convenient; and then we shall have no more long, lonesome evenings, Clara, shall we, dear? And now, Traverse, I will mark out your course of study, and set you to work at once."

"Shall I leave the room, father?" inquired Clara.

"No, no, my dear; certainly not. I have not had you home so long as to get tired of the sight of you yet. No, Clare, no; you are not in our way—is she, Traverse?"

"Oh, sir, the idea——" stammered Traverse, blushing deeply to be so appealed to.

In his way! why a pang had shot through his bosom at the very mention of her going.

"Very well, then; here, Traverse—here are your books; you are to begin with this one; keep this Medical Dictionary at hand for reference. Bless me! it will bring back my own student days to go over the ground with you, my boy."

Clara took her work-box and sat down to stitch a pair of dainty wristbands for her father's shirts.

The doctor took up the morning papers.

Traverse opened his book and commenced his readings. It was a quiet but by no means a dull circle. Occasionally Clara and her father exchanged words, and once in a while the doctor looked over his pupil's shoulder, or gave him a direction.

Traverse studied *con amore* and with intelligent appreciation. The presence of the doctor's lovely daughter, far from disturbing him, calmed and steadied his soul into a state of infinite content. If the presence of the beautiful girl was ever to become an agitating element, the hour had not yet come.

So passed the time until the dinner-bell rang.

By the express stipulation of the doctor himself, it was arranged that Traverse should always dine with his family. After dinner an hour, which the doctor called a digestive hour, was spent in loitering about, and then the studies were resumed.

At six o'clock in the evening Traverse took leave of the doctor and his fair daughter and started for home.

"Be sure to persuade your mother to come, Traverse," said Clara.

"She will not need persuasion; she will be only too glad to come, Miss," said Traverse, with a deep bow, turning and hurrying away towards home. With "winged feet" he ran down the wooded hill and got into the highway and hastened on with such speed that in half an hour he reached his mother's little cottage. He was all agog with joy and eagerness to tell her the good news.

CHAPTER XIX

THE RESIGNED SOUL

"This day be bread and peace my lot;
    All else beneath the sun
Thou knowest if best bestowed or not,
    And let thy will be done."
                    —*Pope*[1]

POOR MARAH ROCKE had schooled her soul to resignation; had taught herself just to do the duty of each day as it came, and leave the future—where indeed it must always remain—in the hands of God. Since the doctor's delicate and judicious kindness had cherished her life, some little health and cheerfulness had returned to her.

Upon this particular evening of the day upon which Traverse entered upon his medical studies, she felt very hopeful.

The little cottage fire burned brightly; the hearth was swept clean; the tea-kettle was singing over the blaze; the tiny tea-table, with its two cups and saucers, and two plates and knives, was set; everything was neat, comfortable and cheerful for Traverse's return. Marah sat in her little low chair, putting the finishing touches to a set of fine shirts.

She was not anxiously looking for her son; for he had told her that he should stay at the doctor's until six o'clock; therefore she did not expect him until seven.

But so fast had Traverse walked that just as the minute hand pointed to half-past six, the latch was raised and Traverse ran in—his face flushed with joy.

The first thing he did was to run to his mother, fling his arms around her neck, and kiss her. Then he threw himself into his chair to take breath.

"Now then, what's the matter, Traverse? You look as if somebody had left you a fortune."

"And so they have, or as good as done so!" exclaimed Traverse, panting for breath.

135

"What in the world do you mean?" exclaimed Marah, her thoughts naturally flying to Old Hurricane, and suggesting his possible repentance or relenting.

"Read that, mother, read that!" said Traverse, eagerly putting a note in her hand.

She opened it, and read:

WILLOW HEIGHTS—Monday.

DEAR MADAM:—My little daughter Clara, fourteen years of age, has just returned from boarding-school to pursue her studies at home. Among other things, she must learn domestic affairs, of which she knows nothing. If you will accept the position of housekeeper and matronly companion of my daughter, I will make the terms such as shall reconcile you to the change. We shall also do all that we can to make you happy. Traverse will explain to you the details. Take time to think of it, but if possible let us have your answer by Traverse, when he comes to-morrow. If you accede to this proposition you will give my daughter and myself sincere satisfaction. Yours truly,

WILLIAM DAY

Marah finished reading, and raised her eyes, full of amazement, to the face of her son.

"Mother!" said Traverse, speaking fast and eagerly, "they say they really cannot do without you. They have troops of servants, but the old cook is in her dotage and does all sorts of strange things—such as frying buckwheat cakes in lamp-oil and the like."

"Oh, hush! what exaggeration!"

"Well, I don't *say* she does *that* exactly, but she isn't equal to her situation, without a housekeeper to look after her; and they want you very much indeed."

"And what is to become of *your* home, if I break up?" suggested the mother.

"Oh, that is the very best of it! The doctor says if you consent to come, that I must also live there, and that then he can have his medical assistant always at hand, which will be very convenient."

Marah smiled dubiously.

"I do not understand it; but one thing I do know, Traverse: there is not such a man as the doctor appears in this world more than once in a hundred years."

"Not in a thousand years, mother! and as for his daughter—oh, you should see Miss Clara, mother! Her father calls her Clare—Clare Day—how the name suits her! She is so fair and bright! with such a warm, thoughtful, sunny smile that goes right to your heart! Her face is indeed like a clear day, and her beautiful smile is the sunshine that lights it up!" said the enthusiastic youth, whose admiration was as yet too simple and single-hearted and unselfish to tie his tongue.

The mother smiled at his earnestness—smiled without the least misgiving; for to her apprehension the youth was still a boy, to wonder at and admire beauty without being in the least danger of having his peace of mind disturbed by love. And as yet her idea of him was just.

"And mother, of course you will go," said Traverse.

"Oh, I do not know. The proposition was so sudden and unexpected, and is so serious and important that I must take time to reflect," said Mrs. Rocke, thoughtfully.

"How much time, mother? Will until to-morrow morning do? It must, little mother, because I promised to carry your consent back with me. Indeed I did mother!" exclaimed the impatient boy.

Mrs. Rocke dropped her head upon her hand, as was her custom when in deep thought. Presently she said:

"Travy, I'm afraid this is not a genuine offer of a situation of house-keeper. I'm afraid that it is only a ruse to cover a scheme of benevolence, and that they don't really want me, and I should only be in their way."

"Now, mother, I do assure you, they do want you! Think of that young girl and elderly gentleman—can either of them take charge of a large establishment like that of Willow Heights?"

"Well argued, Traverse; but granting that they need a housekeeper, how do I know I would suit them?"

"Why you may take their own words for that, mother."

"But how can they know? I am afraid they would be disappointed."

"Wait until they complain, mother."

"I don't believe they ever would."

"I don't believe they ever would have cause."

"Well, granting also that I should suit them——"

The mother paused and sighed. Traverse filled up the blank by saying:

"I suppose you mean if you should suit them, they might not suit you."

"No, I do not mean that! I am sure they would suit me! but there is one in the world, who may one day come to reason and take bitter umbrage at the fact that *I* should accept a subordinate situation in any household," murmured Mrs. Rocke, almost unconsciously.

"Then that 'one in the world,' whoever he, she, or *it* may be, had better place you above the necessity, or else hold his, her, or its tongue!—Mother, *I* think that goods thrown in our way by Providence had better be accepted, leaving the consequences to Him!"

"Traverse, dear, I shall pray over this matter to-night, and sleep on it; and He to whom even the fall of a sparrow² is not indifferent will guide me," said Mrs. Rocke; and here the debate ended.

The remainder of the evening was spent in laudation of Clara Day, and in writing a letter to Herbert Greyson, at West Point, in which all these laudations were reiterated, and in the course of which Traverse wrote these innocent words—"I have known Clara Day scarcely twelve hours, and I admire her as much as I love you! and oh, Herbert! if you could only rise to be a major-general and marry Clara Day, I should be the happiest fellow alive!" Would Traverse as willingly dispose of Clara's hand a year or two after this time? I trow not!

The next morning after breakfast Mrs. Rocke gave in her decision.

"Tell the doctor, Traverse," she said, "that I understand and appreciate his kindness; that I will not break up my humble home as yet; but I will lock up my house and come a month on trial; if I can perform the duties of the situation satisfactorily, well and good! I will remain; if not, why then, having my home still in possession, I can return to it."

"Wise little mother! she will not cut down the bridge behind her!" exclaimed Traverse, joyfully, as he bade his mother good-bye for the day, and hastened up to Willow Heights with her answer. This answer was received by the good doctor and his lovely daughter with delight as unfeigned as it was unselfish. They were pleased to have a good housekeeper; but they were far better pleased to offer a poor struggling mother a comfortable and even luxurious home.

On the next Monday morning, Mrs. Rocke having completed all her arrangements, and closed up her house, entered upon the duties of her new situation.

Clara gave her a large and airy bed-chamber for her own use, communicating with a smaller one for the use of her son; besides this, as housekeeper, she had of course the freedom of the whole house.

Traverse watched with anxious vigilance to find out whether the efforts of his mother really improved the condition of the housekeeping, and was delighted to find that the coffee was clearer and finer flavored; the bread whiter and lighter; the cream richer, the butter fresher, and the beefsteak juicier than he had ever known them to be on the doctor's table; that on the dinner-table, from day to day, dishes succeeded each other in a well-ordered variety and well-dressed style—in a word, that in every particular, the comfort of the family was greatly enhanced by the presence of the housekeeper, and that the doctor and his daughter knew it.

While the doctor and the student were engaged in the library, Clara spent many hours of the morning in Mrs. Rocke's company learning the arts of domestic economy and considerably assisting her in the preparation of delicate dishes.

In the evening the doctor, Clara, Mrs. Rocke, and Traverse gathered around the fire as one family—Mrs. Rocke and Clara engaged in needle-work, and the doctor or Traverse in reading aloud, for their amusement, some agreeable book. Sometimes Clara would richly entertain them with music—singing and accompanying herself upon the piano.

An hour before bedtime the servants were always called in, and general family prayer offered up.

Thus passed the quiet, pleasant, profitable days. Traverse was fast falling into a delicious dream, from which, as yet, no rude shock threatened to wake him. Willow Heights seemed to him Paradise, its inmates angels, and his own life—beatitude!

CHAPTER XX

THE OUTLAW'S RENDEZVOUS

☙☙☙☙☙☙

"Our plots fall short like darts which rash hands throw
With an ill aim, and have too far to go;
Nor can we long discoveries prevent;
God is too much about the innocent!"
—*Sir Robert Howard*[1]

"*THE OLD ROAD* Inn," described in the dying deposition of poor Nancy Grewell, was situated some miles from Hurricane Hall, by the side of a forsaken turnpike in the midst of a thickly wooded, long and narrow valley, shut in by two lofty ranges of mountains.

Once this turnpike was lively with travel, and this inn gay with custom; but, for the last twenty-five years, since the highway had been turned off in another direction, both road and tavern had been abandoned, and suffered to fall to ruin. The road was washed and furrowed into deep and dangerous gullies, and obstructed by fallen timber; the house was disfigured by mouldering walls, broken chimneys and patched windows.

Had any traveler lost himself, and chanced to have passed that way, he might have seen a little, old, dried-up woman, sitting knitting at one of the windows. She was known by those who were old enough to remember her and her home as Granny Raven, the daughter of the last proprietor of the inn. She was reputed to be dumb, but none could speak with certainty of the fact. In truth, for as far back as the memory of the "oldest inhabitant" could reach, she had been feared, disliked and avoided, as one of malign reputation; indeed, the ignorant and superstitious believed her to possess the "evil eye," and to be gifted with "second sight."

But of late years as the old road and the old inn were quite forsaken, so the old beldame was quite forgotten.

It was one evening, a few weeks after Capitola's fearful adventure in the forest, that this old woman carefully closed up every door and window in the front of the house, stopping every crevice through which a ray of light might gleam and warn that impossible phenomenon—a chance traveler, on the old road, of life within the habitation.

Having, so to speak, hermetically sealed the front of the house, she betook herself to a large back kitchen.

This kitchen was strangely and rudely furnished—having an extra broad fireplace with the recesses on each side of the chimney filled with oaken shelves, laden with strong pewter plates, dishes and mugs; all along the walls were arranged rude, oaken benches; down the length of the room, was left, always standing, a long deal table, capable of accommodating from fifteen to twenty guests.

On entering this kitchen Granny Raven struck a light, kindled a fire, and began to prepare a large supper.

Nor did this old beldame look unlike the ill-omened bird whose name she bore, in her close clinging black gown, and flapping black cape and hood, and with her sharp eyes, hooked nose and protruding chin.

Having put a large sirloin of beef before the fire, she took down a pile of pewter plates and arranged them along on the sides of the table; then to every plate she placed a pewter mug. A huge wheaten loaf of bread, a great roll of butter and several plates of pickles were next put upon the board, and when all was ready the old woman sat down to the patient turning of the spit.

She had not been thus occupied more than twenty minutes when a hasty, scuffling step was heard at the back of the house, accompanied by a peculiar whistle, immediately under the window.

"That's 'Headlong Hal,' for a penny! He never can learn the cat's tread!" thought the crone, as she arose and withdrew the bolt of the back door.

A little, dark-skinned, black-eyed, black-haired, thin and wiry man came hurrying in, exclaiming:

"How now, old girl—supper ready?"

She shook her head, pointed to the roasting beef, lifted up both hands with the ten fingers spread out twice, and then made a rotary motion with one arm.

"Oh—you mean it will be done in twenty turns; but hang me if I understand your dumb show half the time.—Have none of the men come yet?"

She put her fingers together, flung her hands wildly apart in all direc-

The Hidden Hand

tions, brought them slowly together again, and pointed to the supper table.

"Um!—that is to say they are dispersed about their business, but will all be here to-night?"

She nodded.

"Where's the cap'n?"

She pointed over her left shoulder upwards—placed her two hands out broad from her temples—then made a motion as of lifting and carrying a basket, and displaying goods.

"Humph! humph! gone to Tip-Top to sell goods disguised as a peddler!"

She nodded. And before he could put another question, a low, soft *mew* was heard at the door.

"There's Stealthy Steve!—he might walk with hobnailed high-lows over a gravelly road, and you would never hear his footfall," said the man, as the door noiselessly opened and shut, and a soft-footed, low-voiced, subtile-looking mulatto entered the kitchen, and gave good evening to its occupants.

"Ha! I'm devilish glad you've come, Steve, for hang me if I'm not tired to death trying to talk to this crone, who, to the charms of old age and ugliness, adds that of dumbness. Seen the cap'n?"

"No, he's gone out to hear the people talk, and find out what they think of him."

Hal burst into a loud and scornful laugh, saying—"I should think it would not require much seeking to discover that!"

Here the old woman came forward, and, by signs, managed to inquire whether he had brought her "the tea."

Steve drew a packet from his pocket, saying, softly,

"Yes, mother, when I was in Spicer's store I saw this lying with other things on the counter, and remembering you, quietly put it into my pocket."

The old crone's eyes danced; she seized the packet, patted the excellent thief on the shoulder, wagged her head deridingly at the delinquent one, and hobbled off to prepare her favorite beverage.

While she was thus occupied the whistle was once more heard at the door, followed by the entrance of a man decidedly the most repulsive-looking of the whole party—a man one having a full pocket would scarcely like to meet on a lonely road in a dark night. In form he was of Dutch proportions, short but stout; with a large, round head covered with stiff, sandy hair; broad, flat face; coarse features; pale, half-closed eyes, and an expression of countenance strangely made up of elements as opposite as they were forbidding—a mixture of stupidity and subtilty, cowardice and ferocity, caution and cruelty. His name in the gang was Demon Dick, a sobriquet of which he was eminently deserving and characteristically proud.

He came in sulkily, neither saluting the company nor returning their salutations. He pulled a chair to the fire, threw himself into it, and ordered the old woman to draw him a mug of ale.

"Dick's in a bad humor to-night," murmured Steve, softly.

"When was he ever in a good one?" roughly broke forth Hal.

"H-sh!" said Steve, glancing at Dick, who, with a hideous expression, was listening to the conversation.

"There's the cap'n!" exclaimed Hal, as a ringing footstep sounded outside, followed by the abrupt opening of the door and entrance of the leader.

Setting down a large basket, and throwing off a broad-brimmed Quaker hat and broad-skirted overcoat, Black Donald stood roaring with laughter.

Black Donald, from his great stature, might have been a giant walked out of the age of fable into the middle of the nineteenth century. From his stature alone he might have been chosen leader of this band of desperadoes. He stood six feet eight inches in his boots, and was stout and muscular in proportion. He had a well-formed, stately head, fine aquiline features, dark complexion, strong, steady, dark eyes, and an abundance of long, curling black hair and beard that would have driven to despair a Broadway beau, broken the heart of a Washington belle, or made his own fortune in any city of America as a French count or a German baron! He had decidedly "the air noble and distinguished."

While he threw his broad brim in one direction and his broad coat in another and gave way to peals of laughter, Headlong Hal said:

"Cap'n, I don't know what you think of it; but I think it just as churlish to laugh alone as to get drunk in solitude."

"Oh, you shall laugh! Wait until I tell you! But first, answer me: Does not my broad-skirted gray coat and broad-brimmed gray hat make me look about twelve inches shorter and broader?"

"That's so, Cap'n!"

"And when I bury my black beard and chin deep down in this drab neckcloth, and pull the broad brim low over my black hair and eyes, I look as mild and respectable as William Penn."

"Yes, verily, friend Donald," said Hal.

"Well, in this meek guise I went peddling to-day."

"Aye, Cap'n we knew it; and you'll go once too often."

"I *have* gone just once too often."

"I knew it."

"We said so."

"D——n!" were some of the ejaculations as the members of the band sprang to their feet and handled secret arms.

"Pshaw! put up your knives and pistols! There is no danger; I was not traced; our rendezvous is still a secret for which the government would pay a thousand dollars!"

"How, then, do you say that you went once too often, Cap'n?"

"It *was* accurate. I *should* have said that I had gone for the last time, for that it would not be safe to venture again. Come—I must tell you the whole story;—but in the meantime let us have supper. Mother Raven, dish the beef. Dick, draw the ale. Hal, cut the bread. Steve, carve. Bestir yourselves, burn you! or you shall have no story!" exclaimed the captain, flinging himself into a chair at the head of the table.

When his orders had been obeyed, and the men were gathered around the table, and the first draught of ale had been quaffed by all, Black Donald asked:

"Where do you think I went peddling to-day?"

"Devil knows," said Hal.

"That's a secret between the Demon and Black Donald," said Dick.

"Hush! he's about to tell us," murmured Steve.

"Wooden heads! you'd never guess, I went—I went to—Do you give it up? I went right straight into the lion's jaws—not only into the very clutches, but into the very teeth, and down the very throat of the lion! and have come out as safe as Jonas from the whale's belly!—in a word, I have been up to the county seat where the court is now in session, and sold cigar-cases, snuff-boxes and smoking caps to the grand and petit jury, and a pair of gold spectacles to the learned judge himself!"

"No!"

"No!!"

"No!!!" exclaimed Hal, Steve and Dick in a breath.

"Yes! and moreover, I offered a pair of patent steel spring handcuffs to the sheriff, John Keepe, in person, and pressed him to purchase them, assuring him that he would have occasion for their use if ever he caught that grand rascal, Black Donald!"

"'Ah! the atrocious villain, if I thought I should ever have the satisfaction of springing them upon *his* wrists, I'd buy them at my own proper cost!' said the sheriff, taking them in his hands, and examining them curiously.

"'Ah! he's a man of Belial,[2] that same Black Donald!—thee'd better buy the handcuffs, John,' said I.

"'Nay, friend, I don't know; and as for Black Donald, we have some hopes of taking the wretch at last!' said the simple gentleman.

"'Ah, verily, John, that's a good hearing for peaceful travelers like myself,' said I.

"'Excellent! excellent! for when that fell marauder once swings from a gallows———'

"'His neck will be broken, John!'

"'Yes, friend; yes, probably; after which honest men may travel in safety! Ah! never have I adjusted a hempen cravat about the throat of any aspirant for such an honor with less pain than I shall officiate at the last toilet of Black Donald!'

"'If thee catch him?'

"'Exactly friend, if I catch him; but the additional reward offered by Major Warfield, together with the report that he often frequents our towns and villages in disguise, will stimulate people to renewed efforts to discover and capture him,' said the sheriff.

"'Ah! that will be a great day for Alleghany. And when Black Donald is hanged, I shall make an effort to be present at the solemnity *myself!*'

"'Do friend,' said the sheriff, 'and I will see to getting you a good place for witnessing the proceedings.'

"'I have no doubt thee will, John—a very good place! and I assure thee, that there will not be one present more interested in those proceedings than *myself,*' said I.

"'Of course that is very natural; for there is no one more in danger from these marauders than men of your itinerant calling. Good heavens! it was but three years ago a peddler was robbed and murdered in the woods around the Hidden House.'

"'Just so, John,' said I; 'and it's my opinion that often when I've been traveling along the road at night Black Donald hasn't been *far off!* But tell me, John, so that I may have a chance of earning that thousand dollars—what disguises does this son of Moloch[3] take?'

"'Why, friend, it is said that he appears as a Methodist missionary, going about selling tracts; and sometimes as a knife-grinder, and sometimes simulates your calling as a peddler!' said the unsuspicious sheriff.

"I thought, however, it was time to be off, so I said, 'thee had better let me sell thee those handcuffs, John. Allow me! I will show thee their beautiful machinery! Hold out thy wrists, if thee pleases, John.'

"The unsuspicious officer, with a face brimful of interest, held out his wrists for experiment.

"I snapped the ornaments on them in a little less than no time, and took up my pack and disappeared before the sheriff had collected his faculties and found out his position."

"Ha, ha, ha! haw, haw, haw! ho, ho, ho!" laughed the outlaws, in every key of laughter—"and so our captain, instead of being pinioned by the sheriff, turned the tables and actually manacled his honor! Hip, hip, hurrah! three times three for the merry captain, that manacled the sheriff!"

"Hush, burn you! there's some one coming!" exclaimed the captain, rising and listening. "It is Le Noir, who was to meet me here to-night on important business."

CHAPTER XXI

GABRIEL LE NOIR

🐦🐦🐦🐦🐦

"Naught's had! all's spent!
When our desires are gained without content."
—*Shakespeare*[1]

"THE COLONEL!" exclaimed the three men in a breath, as the door opened and a tall, handsome and distinguished-looking gentleman, wrapped in a black military coat, and having his black beaver pulled low over his brow, strode into the room.

All arose upon their feet to greet him as though he had been a prince.

With a haughty wave of his hand, he bade them resume their seats, and beckoning their leader, said:

"Donald, I would have a word with you."

"At your command, Colonel," said the outlaw, rising and taking a candle and leading the way into the adjoining room, the same in which fourteen years before old Granny Grewell and the child had been detained.

Setting the candle upon the mantel-piece, Black Donald stood waiting for the visitor to open the conversation; a thing that the latter seemed in no hurry to do, for he began walking up and down the room in stern silence.

"You seem disturbed, Colonel," at length said the outlaw.

"I *am* disturbed—*more* than disturbed! I am suffering!"

"*Suffering,* Colonel!"

"Aye!—suffering!—from what, think you?—the pangs of remorse!"

"Remorse! ha-ha-ha-ha-ha!" laughed the outlaw till all the rafters rang.

"Aye, man, you may laugh! but I repeat that I am tortured with remorse!—and for what do you suppose?—for those acts of self-

147

preservation that fanatics and fools would stigmatize as crimes? No, my good fellow; but for one 'unacted crime!'"

"I told your honor so!" cried the outlaw, triumphantly.

"Donald, when I go to church, as I do constantly, I hear the preacher prating of repentance; but, man, I never knew the meaning of the word until recently!"

"And I can almost guess what it is that has enlightened your honor!" said the outlaw.

"Yes! it is that miserable old woman and babe! Donald, in every vein of my soul, I repent not having silenced them both forever while they were yet in my power!"

"Just so, Colonel; the dead never come back; or, if they do, are not recognized as property-holders in this world! I wish your honor had taken my advice, and sent that woman and child on a longer journey."

"Donald—I was younger then than now. I—*shrank from bloodshed,*" said the man, in a husky voice.

"Bah! superstition. Bloodshed!—blood is shed every day! 'We kill to live,' say the butchers. *So do we!* Every creature preys upon some other creature weaker than himself—the big beasts eat up the little ones; artful men live on the simple; so be it! the world was made for the strong and cunning; let the weak and foolish look to themselves!" said the outlaw, with a loud laugh.

While he spoke, the visitor resumed his rapid, restless striding up and down the room. Presently he came again to the side of the robber, and whispered:

"Donald, that girl has returned to the neighborhood, brought back by old Warfield. My son met her in the woods a month ago, fell into conversation with her—heard her history, or as much of it as she herself knows. Her name is Capitola! she is the living image of her mother. How she came under the notice of old Warfield—to what extent he is acquainted with her birth and rights—what proofs may be in his possession, I know not. All that I have discovered, after the strictest inquiry that I was enabled to make, is this: that the old beggar-woman that died and was buried at Major Warfield's expense, was no other than Nancy Grewell, returned—that the night before she died she sent for Major Warfield, and had a long talk with him, and that shortly afterwards the old scoundrel traveled to the North and brought home this girl."

"Humph! it is an ugly business, your honor, especially with your honor's little prejudice against——"

"Donald! this is no time for weakness! I have gone too far to stop— Capitola must die!"

"That's so, Colonel; the pity is that it wasn't found out fourteen years ago. It is so much easier to pinch a baby's nose until it falls asleep, than to stifle a young girl's shrieks and cries! Then the baby would not have been missed; but the young girl will be sure to be inquired after."

"I know that there will be additional risk; but there shall be the larger compensation, larger than your most sanguine hopes would suggest. Donald, listen!" said the colonel, stooping and whispering low—"the day that you bring me undeniable proof that Capitola Le Noir is dead you finger one thousand dollars!"

C .L. N!

"Ha-ha-ha!" laughed the outlaw, in angry scorn—"Capitola Le Noir is the sole heiress of a fortune—in land, negroes, coal-mines, iron-foundries, railway shares and bank-stock, of half a million of dollars—and you ask me to get her out of your way for a thousand dollars! I'll do it! you know I will! ha-ha-ha!"

"Why, the government doesn't value your whole carcass at more than I offer you for the temporary use of your hands, you villain!" frowned the colonel.

"No ill names, your honor! Between *us* they are like kicking guns— apt to recoil!"

"You forget that you are in my power."

"I remember that your honor is in mine! Ha-ha-ha! The day Black Donald stands at the bar, the honorable Colonel Le Noir will probably be beside him."

"Enough of this! Confound you, do you take me for one of your pals?"

"No, your worship! my pals are too poor to hire their work done; but then they are brave enough to do it themselves."

"Enough of this, I say! Name the price of this new service!"

"Ten thousand dollars—five thousand in advance—the remainder when the deed is accomplished."

"Extortioner!—shameless, ruthless extortioner!"

"Your honor *will* fall into that vulgar habit of calling ill names!—it isn't worth while; it doesn't pay. If your honor doesn't like my terms you needn't employ me; what is certain is that I cannot work for less."

"You take advantage of my necessities."

"Not at all; but the truth is, Colonel, that I am tired of this sort of life, and wish to retire from active business. Besides, every man has his ambition, and I have mine. I wish to emigrate to the glorious West, settle, marry, turn my attention to politics, be elected to Congress, then to the Senate, then to the Cabinet, then to the White House; for success in which career, I flatter myself nature and education have especially fitted me. Ten thousand dollars will give me a fair start. Many a successful politician, your honor *knows,* has started on less character and less capital!"

To this impudent slander the colonel made no answer; with his arms folded, and his head bowed upon his chest, he walked moodily up and down the length of the apartment; then muttering, "Why should I hesitate?" he came to the side of the outlaw, and said:

"I agree to your terms; accomplish the work, and the sum shall be yours. Meet me here on to-morrow evening to receive the earnest money. In the meantime, in order to make sure of the girl's identity, it will be necessary for you to get sight of her beforehand at her home, if possible; find out her habits and her haunts—where she walks, or rides—when she is most likely to be alone, and so on. Be very careful! A mistake might be fatal."

"Your honor may trust me."

"And now good-bye; remember, to-morrow evening," said the colonel, as, wrapping himself closely in his dark cloak, and pulling his hat low over his eyes, he passed out by the back passage-door, and left the house.

"Ha! ha-ha! Why does that man think it needful to *look* so villainous! If *I* were to go about in such a bandit-like dress as *that,* every child I met would take me for—what I am," laughed Black Donald, returning to his comrades.

During the next hour other members of the band dropped in, until some twenty men were collected together in the large kitchen around the long table, where the remainder of the night was spent in revelry.

CHAPTER XXII

THE SMUGGLER AND CAPITOLA

"Come buy of me! come buy! come buy!
Buy, lads, or else the lasses cry;
I have lawns as white as snow;
Silk as black as e'er was crow;
Gloves as sweet as damask roses;
Veils for faces; musk for noses;
Pins and needles made of steel;
All you need from head to heel."
　　　　　—*Shakespeare*[1]

"IF I AM not allowed to walk or ride out alone I shall 'gang daft.' I know I shall. Was ever such a dull, lonesome, hum-drum place as this same Hurricane Hall?" complained Cap, as she sat sewing with Mrs. Condiment in the housekeeper's room.

"You don't like this quiet country life?" inquired Mrs. Condiment.

"No; no better than I do a quiet country grave-yard. I don't want to return to dust before my time, I tell you," said Cap, yawning dismally over her work.

"I HEAR YOU, VIXEN!" roared the voice of Old Hurricane, who presently came storming in and saying:

"If you want a ride go and get ready quickly and come with me; I am going down to the water-mill, please the Lord, to warn Hopkins off the premises, worthless villain! had my grain there since yesterday morning, and hasn't sent it home yet! shan't stay in my mill another month. Come, Cap, be off with you and get ready!"

The girl did not need a second bidding, but flew to prepare herself, while the old man ordered the horses.

In ten minutes more Capitola and Major Warfield cantered away.

They had been gone about two hours, and it was almost time to expect their return, and Mrs. Condiment had just given orders for the tea-table to be set, when Wool came into her room and said there was a sailor at the hall-door with some beautiful foreign goods which he wished to show to the ladies of the house.

"A sailor, Wool, a sailor with foreign goods for sale? <u>I am *very* much</u> <u>afraid he's one of these smugglers I've heard tell of; and I'm not sure about</u> <u>the right of buying from smugglers!</u> However, I suppose there's no harm in looking at his goods. You may call him in, Wool," said the old lady, tampering with temptation.

"He *do* <u>look like a smudgeler, dat's a fact</u>," said Wool, whose ideas of the said craft were purely imaginary.

"I don't know him to be a smuggler, and it's wrong to judge, particularly beforehand," said the old lady, nursing ideas of rich silks and satins, imported free of duty and sold at half price, and trying to deceive herself.

While she was thus thinking, the door opened, and Wool ushered in a stout, jolly-looking tar, dressed in a wide pea-jacket, duck trowsers and tarpaulin hat, and carrying in his hand a large pack. He took off his hat and scraped his foot behind him, and remained standing before the housekeeper, with his head tied up in a red bandanna handkerchief, and his chin sunken in a red comforter that was wound around his throat.

"Sit down, my good man, and rest while you show me the goods," said Mrs. Condiment, who, whether he were smuggler or not, was inclined to show the traveler all lawful kindness.

The sailor scraped his foot again, sat down on a low chair, put his hat on one side, drew the pack before him, untied it, and first displayed a rich, golden-hued fabric, saying:

"Now here, ma'am, is a rich China silk I bought in the streets of Shanghai, where the long-legged chickens come from; come, now, I'll ship it off cheap——"

"Oh, that is a great deal too gay and handsome for an old woman like me," said Mrs. Condiment.

"Well, ma'am, <u>perhaps there's young ladies in the fleet?</u> Now this would rig out a smart young craft as gay as a clipper! Better take it, ma'am. I'll ship it off cheap."

"Wool," said Mrs. Condiment, turning to the servant, "go down to the kitchen and call up the house-servants; perhaps they would like to buy something."

As soon as Wool had gone, and the good woman was left alone with the sailor, she stooped and said:

"I did not wish to inquire before the servantman, but, my good sir, I do not know whether it is right to buy from you."

"Why so, ma'am?" asked the sailor, with an injured look.

"Why, I am afraid—I am *very* much afraid you risk your life and liberty in an unlawful trade."

"Oh, ma'am, on my soul these things are honestly come by, and you have no right to accuse me!" said the sailor, with a look of subdued indignation.

"I know I haven't, and meant no harm; but did these goods pass through the custom-house?"

"Oh, ma'am, now, that's not a fair question!"

"It is as I suspected, I cannot buy from you, my good friend; I do not judge you; I don't know whether smuggling is right or wrong; but I know that it is unlawful, and I cannot feel free to encourage any man in a traffic in which he risks his life and liberty, poor fellow!"

"Oh, ma'am," said the sailor, evidently on the brink of bursting into laughter—"if we risk our lives, sure it's our own business, and if you've no scruples on your *own* account you needn't have any on *ours!*"

While he was speaking the sound of many shuffling feet was heard along the passage, and the room was soon half filled with colored people come in to deal with the sailor.

"You may *look* at these goods; but you must not buy anything."

"Lor', missus, why?" asked Little Pitapat.

"Because I want you to lay out all your money with my friend Mr. Crash, at Tip-Top."

"But after de good gemman has had de trouble?" said Pitapat.

"He shall have his supper and a mug of ale and go on his journey," said Mrs. Condiment.

The sailor arose and scraped his foot behind him in acknowledgment of this kindness, and began to unpack his wares and display them all over the floor.

And while the servants in wonder and delight examined these treasures and inquired their prices, a fresh, young voice was heard carolling along the hall, and the next moment Capitola, in her green riding-habit and hat, entered the room.

She turned her mischievous gray eyes about, pursed up her lips, and asked Mrs. Condiment if she were about to open a fancy bazaar.

"No, my dear Miss Capitola. It is a sailor with foreign goods for sale," answered the old lady.

"A sailor with foreign goods for sale! umph! yes! I know. Isn't he a smuggler?" whispered Capitola.

"Indeed, I'm afraid so, my dear! In fact he don't deny it!" whispered back the matron.

"Well, *I* think it's strange a man that smuggles can't lie!"

"Well, I don't know, my dear; maybe he thinks it's no harm to smuggle, and he *knows* it would be a sin to lie. But where is your uncle, Miss Capitola?"

"Gone around to the stable to blow Jem up for mounting him on a lame horse; he swears Jem shall find another master before to-morrow's sun sets. But now I want to talk to that bold buccaneer. Say you, sir! Show me your foreign goods; I'm very fond of smugglers myself!"

"You are right, my dear young lady! *You* would give poor sailors some little chance to turn an honest penny."

"Certainly! brave fellows! Show me that splendid fabric that shines like cloth of gold."

"This, my young lady, is a real, genuine China silk; I bought it myself in my last cruise in the streets of Shanghai, where the long-legged chickens——"

"And fast young men come from! I know the place. I've been all along there!" interrupted Capitola, her gray eyes glittering with mischief.

"This, you will perceive, young lady, is an article that cannot be purchased anywhere except——"

"From the manufactory of foreign goods in the city of New York, or from their traveling agents."

"Oh, my dear young lady, how you wrong me! This article came from——"

"The factory of Messrs. Hocus & Pocus, corner of Cant and Come-it street, city of Gotham!"

"Oh, my dear young lady——"

"Look here, my brave buccaneer, I know all about it. I told you I'd been along there!" said the girl; and turning to Mrs. Condiment, she said: "See here, my dear, good soul if you want to buy that 'India' silk that you are looking at so longingly, you may do it with a safe conscience. True, it never passed through the custom-house—because it was made in New York. I know all about it! *All* these 'foreign goods' are manufactured at the north and sent by agents all over the country. These agents dress and talk like sailors, and assume a mysterious manner on purpose to be suspected of smuggling—because they know well enough fine ladies will buy much quicker and pay much more, if they only fancy they are cheating Uncle Sam, in buying foreign goods from a smuggler at half price!"

"So, then, you are not a smuggler, after all!" said Mrs. Condiment, looking almost regretfully at the sailor.

"Why, ma'am, you know I told you you were accusing me wrongfully."

"Well, but really, now, there was something about you that looked sort of suspicious."

"What did I tell you! a look put on on purpose," said Cap.

"Well—he knows that if he wanted to pass for a smuggler, it didn't take *here,*" said Mrs. Condiment.

"No—*that* it didn't!" muttered the object of these commentaries.

"Well, my good man, since you are, after all, an honest peddler, just hand me that silk, and don't ask me an unreasonable price for it, because I'm a judge of silks, and I won't pay more than it is worth," said the old lady.

"Madam, I leave it to your own conscience. You shall give me just what you think it's worth."

"Humph! that's too fair by half. I begin to think this fellow is worse than he seems!" said Capitola to herself.

After a little hesitation a price was agreed upon, and the dress bought.

Then the servants received permission to invest their little change in ribbons, handkerchiefs, tobacco, snuff, or whatever they thought they needed. When the purchases were all made, and the peddler had done up his diminished pack and replaced his hat upon his head and was preparing to leave, Mrs. Condiment said:

"My good man, it is getting very late, and we do not like to see a traveler leave our house at this hour; pray remain until morning, and then, after an early breakfast, you can pursue your way in safety."

"Thank you, kindly, ma'am, but I must be far on my road to-night," said the peddler.

"But, my good man, you are a stranger in this part of the country, and don't know the danger you run," said the housekeeper.

"Danger, ma'am, in this quiet country!"

"Oh, dear, yes, my good man, particularly with your valuable pack—oh, my good gracious!" cried the old lady, with an appalled look.

"Indeed, ma'am, you—you make me sort of uneasy! What danger can there be for a poor, peaceful peddler pursuing his path?"

"Oh, my good soul, may Heaven keep you from—BLACK DONALD!"

"Black Donald—who's he?"

"Oh, my good man, he's the awfulest villain that ever went unhung!"

The Hidden Hand

"Black Donald! Black Donald! never heard that name before in my life! Why is the fellow called *Black* Donald?"

"Oh, sir, he's called Black Donald for his black soul, black deeds, and—and—also, I believe, for his jet black hair and beard."

"Oh, my countrymen, what a falling *up* was there!" exclaimed Capitola, at this anti-climax.

"And how shall I keep from meeting this villain?" asked the peddler.

"Oh, sir, how can I tell you? You never can form an idea where he is or where he isn't! Only think, he may be in our very midst any time, and we not know it. Why, only yesterday the desperate villain handcuffed the very sheriff in the very courtyard! Yet I wonder the sheriff did not know him at once! For my own part, I'm sure *I* should know Black Donald the minute I clapped my two looking eyes on him!"

"Should you, ma'am?"

"Yes, indeed, by his long, black hair and beard! They say it is half a yard long. Now a man of such a singular appearance as *that* must be easily recognized!"

"Of course! Then you never met this wretch face to face?"

"Me! *me!* am I standing here alive? Do you suppose I should be standing here if ever I had met that demon? Why, man, I never leave this house, even in the day-time, except with two bull-dogs and a servant, for fear I should meet Black Donald! I know if ever I should meet that demon, I should drop dead with terror. I feel I should!"

"But maybe now, ma'am, the man may not be so bad, after all. Even the devil is not so black as he is painted."

"The devil may *not* be, but Black Donald *is*."

"What do *you* think of this outlaw, young lady?" asked the peddler, turning to Capitola.

"Why, I *like* him!" said Cap.

"You do?"

"Yes, I *do!* I like men whose very names strike terror into the hearts of commonplace people!"

"Oh, Miss Black!" exclaimed Mrs. Condiment.

"Yes, I *do*, ma'am. And if Black Donald were only as honest as he is brave, I should quite *adore* him! so there! And if there is one person in the world I long to see, it is Black Donald."

"Do you *really* wish to see him?" asked the peddler, looking intently into the half earnest, half satirical face of the girl.

156

"Yes, I *do* wish to see him above all things."

"And do you know what happened to the rash girl who wished to see the devil?"

"No—what did?"

"She saw him!"

"Oh, if that's all, I dare it! and if wishing will bring me the sight of this notorious outlaw, lo! I wish it. I wish it. I wish to see Black Donald," said Capitola.

The peddler deliberately arose and put down his pack and his hat; then he suddenly tore off the scarf from his neck and the handkerchief from his head, lifted his chin and shook loose a great, rolling mass of black hair and beard; drew himself up, struck an attitude, called up a look, and exclaimed:

"Behold Black Donald!"

With a piercing shriek, Mrs. Condiment swooned and fell to the floor; the poor negroes, men and maids, were struck dumb and motionless with consternation; Capitola gazed for one lost moment in admiration and curiosity; in the meantime Black Donald quickly resumed his disguises, took up his pack and walked out of the room.

Capitola was the first to recover her presence of mind; the instinct of the huntress possessed her; starting forward, she exclaimed:

"Pursue him! catch him! come with me! Cowards! will you let a robber and murderer escape!" and she ran out and overtook the outlaw in the middle of the hall. With the agile leap of a little terrier she sprang up behind him, seized the thick collar of his pea-jacket with both hands, and drawing up her feet, hung there with all her weight, crying:

"Help! murder! murder! help! Come to my aid! I've caught Black Donald!"

He could have killed her instantly in any one of a dozen ways! He could have driven in her temples with a blow of his sledge-hammer fist; he could have broken her neck with the grip of his iron fingers; he only wished to shake her off without hurting her—a difficult task, for there she hung, a dead weight, at the collar of his coat at the back of his neck.

"Oh, very well!" he cried, laughing aloud. "Such adhesiveness I never saw! You stick to me like a wife to her husband. So, if you won't let go, I shall have to take you along, that's all! So here I go, like Christian with his bundle of sin on his back."

And loosing the upper button of his pea-jacket so as to give him more breath, and putting down his peddler's pack to relieve himself as much as possible, the outlaw strode through the hall-door, down the steps, and down the evergreen avenue leading to the woods.

Capitola, still clinging to the back of his coat-collar, with her feet drawn up, a dead weight, and still crying:

"Help! murder! I've caught Black Donald, and I'll *die* before I'll let him go."

"You're determined to be an outlaw's bride, that's certain. Well I've no particular objection," cried Black Donald, roaring with laughter as he strode on.

It was "a thing to see, not hear"—that brave, rash, resolute imp clinging like a terrier, or a crab, or a briar, on to the back of that gigantic ruffian, whom, if she had no strength to stop, she was determined not to release.

They had nearly reached the foot of the descent when a great noise and hallooing was heard behind them. It was the negroes, who, having recovered from their panic, and armed themselves with guns, pistols, swords, pokers, tongs, and pitch-forks, were now in hot pursuit.

And cries of "Black Donald!" "Black Donald!" "Black Donald!" filled the air.

"I've got him! I've got him! help! help! quick! quick!" screamed Capitola, clinging closer than ever.

Though still roaring with laughter at the absurdity of his position, Black Donald strode on faster than before and was in a fair way of escape, when lo! suddenly coming up the path in front of him, he met—

OLD HURRICANE!!!

As the troop of miscellaneously-armed negroes running down the hill were still making eve "hideous" with yells of "Black Donald!" "Black Donald!" and Capitola still clinging and hanging on at the back of his neck continued to cry: "I've caught him! I've caught him! help! help!" something like the truth flashed in a blinding way upon Old Hurricane's perceptions.

Roaring forth something between a recognition and defiance, the old man threw up his fat arms, and as fast as age and obesity would permit, ran up the hill to intercept the outlaw.

There was no time for trifling now! The army of negroes was at his heels; the old veteran in his path; the girl clinging a dead weight to his jacket behind. An idea suddenly struck him which he wondered had not done so before—quickly unbuttoning and throwing off his garment he dropped both captor and jacket behind him on the ground.

And before Capitola had picked herself up, Black Donald, bending his huge head and shoulders forward and making a battering-ram of himself, ran with all his force and butted Old Hurricane in the stomach, pitched him into the horse-pond, leaped over the park fence and disappeared in the forest.

What a scene! what a row followed the escape and flight of the famous outlaw!

Who could imagine, far less describe it!—a general tempest in which every individual was a particular storm.

There stood the baffled Capitola, extricating her head from the pea-jacket, and with her eyes fairly flashing out *sparks* of anger, exclaiming:

"Oh, wretches! wretches, that you are! if you'd been worth *salt* you could have caught him while I clung to him so!"

There wallowed Old Hurricane, spluttering, floundering, half-drowning, in the horse-pond, making the most frantic efforts to curse and swear as he struggled to get out.

There stood the crowd of negroes brought to a sudden stand by a panic of horror at seeing the dignity of their master so outraged.

And most frenzied of all, there ran Wool around and around the margin of the pond, in a state of violent perplexity how to get his master out without half-drowning himself.

"*Blurr-urr-rr! flitch! filch! Blurr-ur!* spluttered and sneezed and strangled Old Hurricane, as he floundered to the edge of the pond. *Blurr-urr-rr!* Help me out, you scoundrel! I'll break every bone in your—*flitch!*—body! Do you hear me—*ca-snish!*—villain you! *flitch! flitch! ca-snish! oh-h!*"

Wool, with his eyes starting from his head, and his hair standing up with horrors of all sorts, plunged at last into the water and pulled his old master up upon his feet.

"*Ca-snish! ca-snish! blurr-rr! flitch!*—what are you gaping there for as if you'd raised the devil, you crowd of born fools!" howled Old Hurricane, as soon as he could get the water out of his mouth and nose—"what are you standing there for?—after him! after him, I say! Scour the woods in every direction! His freedom to any man who brings me Black Donald, dead or alive!—Wool!"

"Yes, sir," said that functionary who was busying himself with squeezing the water out of his master's garments.

"Wool, let me alone! take the fleetest horse in the stable! ride for your life to the Court House! Tell Keepe to have new bills posted everywhere, offering an additional five hundred dollars for the apprehension of that—that—that"—for the want of a word strong enough to express himself, Old Hurricane suddenly stopped, and for lack of his stick to make silence emphatic, he seized his gray hair with both hands and groaned aloud.

Wool waited no second bidding, but flew to do his errand.

Capitola came to the old man's side, saying:

"Uncle, hadn't you better hurry home—you'll take cold."

"Cold?—*Cold!* demmy! I never was so hot in my life!" cried the old man; "but demmy! you're right! run to the house, Capitola, and tell Mrs. Condiment to have me a full suit of dry clothes before the fire in my chamber. Go, child! every man-jack is off after Black Donald, and there is nobody but you, and Condiment, and the housemaids to take care of me. Stop, look for my stick first; where did that black demon throw it?—demmy! I'd as well be without my legs!"

Capitola picked up the old man's cane and hat, and put the one on his head and the other in his hand, and then hastened to find Mrs. Condiment, and tell her to prepare to receive her half-drowned patron. She found the old lady scarcely recovered from the effects of her recent fright, but ready on the instant to make every effort on behalf of Old Hurricane, who presently after arrived dripping wet at the house.

Leaving the old gentleman to the care of his housekeeper, we must follow Black Donald.

Hatless and coatless, with his long black hair and beard blown by the wind, the outlaw made tracks for his retreat—occasionally stopping to turn and get breath, and send a shout of laughter at his baffled pursurers.

That same night, at the usual hour, the gang met at their rendezvous, the deserted inn, beside the old road through the forest. They were in the midst of their orgies around the supper-table, when the well-known ringing step of the leader sounded under the back windows without, the door was burst open, and the captain, hatless, coatless, with his dark elf locks flying, and every sign of haste and disorder, rushed into the room.

He was met by a general rising and outcry:—"Hi! hillo! what's up?" exclaimed every man, starting to his feet and laying hands upon secret arms, prepared for instant resistance.

For a moment Black Donald stood with his leonine head turned and looking back over his stalwart shoulders, as if in expectation of pursuit, and then, with a loud laugh, turned to his men, exclaiming:

"Ho! you thought me followed! So I have been! but not as close as hound to heel!"

"In fact, Captain, you look as if you'd but escaped with your skin this time!" said Hal.

"Faith! the captain looks well peeled!" said Stephen.

"Worse than that, boys! worse than that! Your chief has not only lost his pack, his hat and his coat, but—his *heart!* Not only are the outworks battered, but the citadel itself is taken! Not only has he been captured, but *captivated!* and all by a little minx of a girl!—Boys, your chief is in love!" exclaimed Black Donald, throwing himself into his seat at the head of the table, and quaffing off a large draught of ale.

"Hip! hip! hurraw! three times three for the Captain's love!" cried Hal, rising to propose the toast, which was honored with enthusiasm.

"Now tell us all about it, Captain. Who is she? where did you see her? is she fair or dark? tall or short? thin or plump? what's her name? and is she kind?" asked Hal.

"First guess where I have been to-day."

"You and your demon only know!"

"I guess they also know at Hurricane Hall, for it is there I have been!"

"Well, then, why didn't you go to perdition at once?" exclaimed Hal, in a consternation that was reflected in every countenance present.

"Why, because when I go *there* I intend to take you all with me and remain!" answered Black Donald.

"Tell us about the visit to Hurricane Hall," said Hal.

Whereupon Black Donald commenced, and concealing only the motive of his visit, gave his comrades a very graphic, spicy and highly colored narrative of his adventure at Hurricane Hall, and particularly of his "passages at arms" with the little witch, Capitola, whom he described as:

"*Such a girl!* slender, petite, lithe, with bright, black ringlets dancing around a little face full of fun, frolic, mischief and spirit, and eyes quick and vivacious as those of a monkey, darting hither and thither from object to object."

"The Captain *is* in love, sure enough," said Steve.

"Bravo! here's success to the Captain's love!—*She's* a brick!" shouted the men.

"Oh, she *is,*" assented their chief, with enthusiasm.

"Long life to her! three times three for the pretty witch of Hurricane Hall!" roared the men, rising to their feet and raising their full mugs high in the air, before pledging the toast.

"*That* is all very well, boys; but I want more substantial compliments than words—*Boys! I must have that girl!*"

"Who doubts it, Captain?—of course you will take her at once if you want her," said Hal, confidently.

"But, I must have *help* in taking her."

"Captain, I volunteer for one!" exclaimed Hal.

"And I, for another," added Steve.

"And *you,* Dick?" inquired the leader, turning towards the sullen man, whose greater atrocity had gained for him the name of Demon Dick.

"What is the use of volunteering when the captain has only to *command,*" said this individual, sulkily.

"Ah! when the enterprise is simply the robbing of a mail-coach, in which you all have equal interest, then, indeed, your captain has only to command, and you to obey; but *this* is a more delicate matter of entering a lady's chamber and carrying her off for the captain's arms, and so should only be entrusted to those whose feelings of devotion to the captain's person prompt them to volunteer for the service," said Black Donald.

"How elegantly our captain speaks! he ought to be a lawyer," said Steve.

"The captain knows I'm with him for everything," said Dick, sulkily.

"Very well, then! for a personal service like this, a delicate service requiring devotion, I should scorn to give *commands!* I thank you for your offered assistance, my friends, and shall count on you three, Hal, Stephen and Richard, for the enterprise," said the captain.

"Ay! ay! ay!" said the three men in a breath.

"For the time and place and manner of the seizure of the girl, we must reflect. Let us see! there is to be a fair in the village next week, during the session of the court. Old Hurricane will be at court as usual. And for one day, at least, his servants will have a holiday to go to the fair. They will not get home until the next morning. The house will be ill-guarded. We must find out the particular day and night when this shall be so. Then you three shall watch your opportunity, enter the house by stealth, conceal yourselves in the chamber of the girl, and at midnight, when all is quiet, gag her and bring her away."

"Excellent!" said Hal.

"And mind, no liberty except the simple act of carrying her off is to be taken with your captain's prize," said the leader, with a threatening glare of his lion-like eye.

"Oh, no! no! not for the world! She shall be as sacred from insult as though she were an angel and we saints," said Hal, both the others assenting.

"And now not a word more. We will arrange the further details of this business hereafter," said the captain, as a peculiar signal was given at the door.

Waving his hand for the men to keep their places, Black Donald went out and opened the back passage-door, admitting Colonel Le Noir.

"Well," said the latter, anxiously.

"Well, sir, I have contrived to see her; come into the front room and I will tell you all about it," said the outlaw, leading the way into the old parlor that had been the scene of so many of their conspiracies.

"*Does Capitola Le Noir still live?*" hoarsely demanded the colonel, as the two conspirators reached the parlor.

"Still live? yes; 'twas but yesterday we agreed upon her death. Give a man time. Sit down, Colonel; take this seat! we will talk the matter over again."

With something very like a sigh of relief, Colonel Le Noir threw himself into the offered chair.

Black Donald drew another chair up and sat down beside his patron.

"Well, Colonel, I have contrived to see the girl as I told you," he began.

"But you have not done the deed; when will it be done?"

"Colonel, my patron, be patient. Within twelve days I shall claim the last instalment of the ten thousand dollars agreed upon between us for this job."

"But why so long? since it is to be done, why not have it over at once?" said Colonel Le Noir, starting up and pacing the floor impatiently.

"Patience, my Colonel. The cat may play with the mouse most delightfully before devouring it."

"What do you mean?"

"My Colonel, I have seen the girl under circumstances that have fired my heart with an uncontrollable desire for her———"

"Ha-ha-ha!" scornfully laughed the colonel. "Black Donald, the mail-robber, burglar, outlaw, the subject of the grand passion!"

"Why not, my Colonel. Listen, you shall hear, and then you shall judge whether or not you yourself might not have been fired by the fascination of such a witch!" said the outlaw, who straightway commenced and gave his patron the same account of his visit to Hurricane Hall that he had already related to his comrades.

The colonel heard the story with many a "pish," "tush" and "pshaw," and when the man had concluded the tale, he exclaimed:

"Is that all? Then we may continue our negotiations—*I* care not. Carry her off! marry her! do as you please with her! only at the end of all— *kill her!*" hoarsely whispered Le Noir.

"That is just what I intend, Colonel."

"That will do if the event be certain; but it must be certain. I cannot breathe freely while *my brother's heiress lives!* whispered Le Noir.

"Well, Colonel, be content; here is my hand upon it. In six days Capitola will be in my power. In twelve days *you* shall be out of *hers.*"

"It is a bargain," said each of the conspirators in a breath, as they shook hands and parted—Le Noir to his home and Black Donald to join his comrades' revelry.

CHAPTER XXIII

THE BOY'S LOVE

"Endearing! endearing!
Why so endearing
Are those soft, shining eyes,
Through their silk fringe peering?
They love thee! they love thee!
Deeply, sincerely;
And more than aught else on earth
Thou lovest them dearly!"
—*Motherwell* [1]

WHILE THESE DARK conspiracies were hatching elsewhere, all was comfort, peace and love in the doctor's quiet dwelling.

Under Marah Rocke's administration the business of the household went on with the regularity of clock-work. Every one felt the advantage of this improved condition.

The doctor often declared that for his part he could not for the life of him think how they had ever been able to get along without Mrs. Rocke and Traverse.

Clara affirmed that however the past might have been, the mother and son were a present and future necessity to the doctor's comfort and happiness.

The little woman herself gained rapidly both health and spirits and good looks. Under favorable circumstances, Marah Rocke, even at thirty-six, would have been esteemed a first-rate beauty; and even now she was pretty, graceful, and attractive to a degree that she herself was far from suspecting.

Traverse advanced rapidly in his studies, to the ardent pursuit of which he was urged by every generous motive that could fire a human bosom: affection for his mother, whose condition he was anxious to elevate; gratitude to his patron, whose great kindness he wished to justify; and admiration for Clara, whose esteem he was ambitious to secure.

He attended his patron in all his professional visits; for the doctor

165

said that actual experimental knowledge formed the most important part of a young medical student's education.

The mornings were usually passed in reading in the library; the middle of the day in attending the doctor in his professional visits, and the evenings were passed in the drawing-room with the doctor, Clara, and Mrs. Rocke. And if the morning's occupation was the most earnest and the day's the most active, the evening's relaxation with Clara and music and poetry was certainly the most delightful. In the midst of all this peace and prosperity, a malady was creeping upon the boy's heart and brain that in his simplicity and inexperience he could neither understand nor conquer.

Why was it that these evening fireside meetings with the doctor's lovely daughter, once such unalloyed delight, were now only a keenly pleasing pain? Why did his face burn and his heart beat and his voice falter when obliged to speak to her? Why could he no longer talk of her to his mother, or write of her to his friend Herbert Greyson? Above all, why had his favorite daydream of having his dear friends Herbert and Clara married together grown so abhorrent as to sicken his very soul?

in love

Traverse himself could not have answered these questions. In his ignorance of life he did not know that all his strong, ardent earnest nature was tending towards the maiden by a power of attraction seated in the deepest principles of being and of destiny.

Clara in her simplicity did not suspect the truth; but tried in every innocent way to enliven the silent boy, and said that he worked too hard, and begged her father not to let him study too much.

Whereupon the doctor would laugh, and bid her not be uneasy about Traverse—that the boy was all right and would do very well. Evidently the doctor, with all his knowledge of human nature, did not perceive that his *protégé* was in process of forming an unadvisable attachment for his daughter and heiress.

Mrs. Rocke, with her woman's tact and mother's forethought, saw all. She saw that in the honest heart of her poor boy unconsciously there was growing up a strong, ardent, earnest passion for the lovely girl with whom he was thrown in such close, intimate, daily association and who was certainly not indifferent in her feelings towards him; but whom he might never, never hope to possess.

She saw this daily growing, and trembled for the peace of both. She wondered at the blindness of the doctor who did not perceive what was so plain to her own vision. Daily she looked to see the eyes of the doctor open and some action taken upon the circumstances; but they did *not* open to the evil ahead, for the girl and boy! For morning after morning their hands would be together tying up the same vines, or clearing out the same flower bed; day after day at the doctor's orders Traverse attended Clara on her rides; night after night their blushing faces would be bent over the same sketch book, chess board, or music sheet.

"Oh! if the doctor cannot and will not see, what shall I do? what ought I to do?" said the conscientious little woman to herself, dreading above all things, and equally for her son and the doctor's daughter, the evils of an unhappy attachment, which she, with her peculiar temperament and experience, believed to be the worst of sorrows, a misfortune never to be conquered or outlived.

"Yes! it is even better that we should leave the house, than that Traverse should become hopelessly attached to Clara; or, worse than all, that he should repay the doctor's great bounty by winning the heart of his only daughter," said Marah Rocke to herself; and so "screwing her courage to the sticking place" she took an opportunity one morning early while Traverse and Clara were out riding, to go into the study to speak to the doctor.

As usual he looked up with a smile to welcome her as she entered; but her downcast eyes and serious face made him uneasy, and he hastened to inquire if she was not well, or if anything had happened to make her anxious, and at the same time he placed a chair, and made her sit in it.

"Yes, I am troubled, Doctor, about a subject that I scarcely know how to break to you," she said, in considerable embarrassment.

"Mrs. Rocke, you know I am your friend, anxious to serve you! Trust in me, and speak out!"

"Well, sir," said Marah, beginning to roll up the corner of her apron, in her embarrassment, "I should not presume to interfere, but you do not see! gentlemen, perhaps, seldom do until it is too late." She paused, and the good doctor turned his head about, listening first with one ear and then with the other, as if he thought by attentive hearing he might come to understand her incomprehensible words.

"Miss Clara has the misfortune to be without a mother, or an aunt, or any lady relative———"

"Oh! yes! I know it my dear madam; but then I am sure you conscientiously try to fill the place of a matronly friend and adviser to my daughter," said the doctor, striving after light.

"Yes, sir, and it is in view of my duties in this relation that I say—*I and Traverse ought to go away.*"

"You and Traverse go away! My good little woman you ought to be more cautious how you shock a man at my time of life! fifty is a very apoplectic age to a full blooded man, Mrs. Rocke! But now that I have got over the shock, tell me why you fancy that you and Traverse ought to go away."

"Sir, my son is a well-meaning boy——"

"A high-spirited, noble-hearted lad!" put in the doctor. "I have never seen a better!"

"But granting all that to be, what I hope and believe it is—true, still Traverse Rocke is not a proper or desirable daily associate for Miss Day."

"Why?" curtly inquired the doctor.

"If Miss Clara's mother were living, sir, she would probably tell you that young ladies should never associate with any except their equals of the opposite sex," said Marah Rocke.

"Clara's dear mother, were she on earth, would understand and sympathize with me, and esteem your Traverse as I do, Mrs. Rocke," said the doctor, with moist eyes and a tremulous voice.

"But oh, sir, exceeding kind as you are to Traverse, I dare not, in duty, look on and see things going the way in which they are, and not speak and ask your consent to withdraw Traverse!"

"My good little friend," said the doctor, rising and looking kindly and benignantly upon Marah. "My good little woman, 'sufficient unto the day is the evil thereof!' Suppose you and I trust a little in Divine Providence, and mind our own business?"

"But, sir, it seems to be a part of our business to watch over the young and inexperienced, that they fall into no snare."

"And also to treat them with 'a little wholesome neglect' that our over officiousness may plunge them into none!"

"I wish you would comprehend me, sir!"

"I do, and applaud your motives; but give yourself no further trouble! leave the young people to their own honest hearts and to Providence. Clara, with all her softness, is a sensible girl! and as for Traverse, if he is one to break his heart from an unhappy attachment, I have been mistaken in the lad, that is all!" said the doctor, heartily.

Mrs. Rocke sighed, and saying—"I deemed it my duty to speak to you, sir; and having done so, I have no more to say," she slightly curtsied and withdrew.

"He does not see! his great benevolence blinds him! In his wish to serve us he exposes Traverse to the most dreadful misfortune—the misfortune of becoming hopelessly attached to one far above him in station, whom he can never expect to possess!" said Marah Rocke to herself, as she retired from the room.

"I must speak to Traverse himself, and warn him against this snare," she said, as she afterwards ruminated over the subject.

And accordingly that evening, when she had retired to her chamber and heard Traverse enter the little adjoining room where he slept, she called him in and gave him a seat, saying that she must have some serious conversation with him.

The boy looked uneasy, but took the offered chair and waited for his mother to speak.

"Traverse," she said, "a change has come over you recently that may escape all other eyes but those of your mother; she, Traverse, cannot be blind to anything that seriously affects her boy's happiness."

"Mother, I scarcely know what you mean," said the youth in embarrassment.

"Traverse, you are beginning to think too much of Miss Day."

"Oh, mother!" exclaimed the boy, while a violent blush overspread and empurpled his face! Then in a little while and in faltering tones he inquired—"Have I betrayed in any way, that I do?"

"To no one but to me, Traverse, to me whose anxiety for your happiness makes me watchful; and now, dear boy, you must listen to me! I know it is very sweet to you, to sit in a dark corner, and gaze on Clara, when no one, not even herself, witnesses your joy, and to lie awake and think and dream of her, when no eye but that of God looks down upon your heart; and to build castles in the air for her and for you; all this I know is very sweet: But, Traverse, it is a sweet *poison,* fatal if indulged in, fatal to your peace and integrity."

"Oh, my mother!—oh, my mother! what are you telling me!" exclaimed Traverse, bitterly.

"Unpalatable truths, dear boy, but necessary antidotes to that sweet poison of which you have already tasted too much."

"What would you have me to do, my mother?"

"Guard your acts and words, and even *thoughts;* forbear to look at, or speak to, or think of Clara, except when it is unavoidable—or if you do, regard her as she *is*—one so far beyond your sphere as to be forever unattainable!"

"Oh, mother, I never once dreamed of such presumption as to think of—of——" The youth paused, and a deep blush again overspread his face.

"I know you have not indulged presumptuous thoughts as yet, my boy, and it is to warn you against them, while yet your heart is in some measure within your own keeping, that I speak to you. Indulge your imagination in no more sweet reveries about Miss Day, for the end thereof will be bitter humiliation and disappointment. Remember also that in so doing you would indulge a sort of treachery against your patron, who in his great faith in your integrity had received you in the bosom of his family, and admitted you to an almost brotherly intimacy with his daughter. Honor his trust in you, and treat his daughter with the distant respect due to a princess."

"I will, mother. It will be hard, but I will! Oh, an hour ago I did not dream how miserable I should be now!" said Traverse, in a choking voice.

"Because I have pointed out to you the gulf towards which you were walking blindfold!"

"I know it. I know it now, mother," said Traverse, as he arose and pressed his mother's hand and hurried to his own room.

The poor youth did his best to follow out the line of conduct prescribed for him by his mother. He devoted himself to his studies and to the active service of his patron. He avoided Clara as much as possible and, when obliged to be in her company, he treated her with the most respectful reserve.

Clara saw and wondered at this change of manner, and began to cast about in her own mind for the probable cause of his conduct.

"I am the young mistress of the house," said Clara to herself, "and I know I owe to everyone in it consideration and courtesy; perhaps I may have been unconsciously lacking in these towards Traverse, whose situation would naturally render him very sensitive to neglect. I must endeavor to convince him that none was intended." And so resolving, Clara redoubled all her efforts to make Traverse, as well as others, happy and comfortable.

But happiness and comfort seemed for the time to have departed from the youth. He saw her generous endeavors to cheer him, and while adoring her amiability, grew still more reserved.

This pained the gentle girl, who, taking herself seriously to task, said:

"Oh, I must have deeply wounded his feelings in some unconscious way! and if so how very cruel and thoughtless of me! how could I have done it? I cannot imagine; but I know I shall not allow him to continue unhappy if I can prevent it. I will speak to him about it."

And then in the candor, innocence and humility of her soul, she followed him to the window where he stood in a moody silence, and said, pleasantly:

"Traverse, we do not seem to be so good friends as formerly. If I have done anything to offend you, I know that you will believe me when I say that it was quite unintentional on my part and that I am very sorry for it, and hope you will forget it."

"You, you, Miss Day! you say anything to displease—*anybody!* Any one become displeased with *you!*" exclaimed the youth, in a tremulous enthusiasm that shook his voice and suffused his cheeks.

"Then if you are not displeased, Traverse, what *is* the matter, and why do you call me Miss Day instead of Clara?"

"Miss Day, because it is right that I should. You are a young lady— the only daughter and heiress of Doctor Day of Willow Heights, while I am——."

"*His friend,*" said Clara.

"The son of his housekeeper," said Traverse, walking away.

Clara looked after him in dismay for a moment, and then sat down and bent thoughtfully over her needlework.

From that day Traverse grew more deeply in love and more reserved than before. How could it be otherwise, domesticated, as he was, with this lovely girl, and becoming daily more sensible of her beauty, goodness and intelligence? Yet he struggled against his inevitable attachment as a great treachery. Meantime he made rapid progress in his medical studies. It was while affairs were in this state that one morning the doctor entered the study holding the morning paper in his hand. Seating himself in his leathern arm-chair, at the table, he said:

"I see, my dear Traverse, that a full course of lectures is to be commenced at the medical college in Washington, and I think that you are sufficiently far advanced in your studies to attend them with great advantage—what say you?"

"Oh, sir!" said Traverse, upon whom the proposition had burst quite unexpectedly—"I should indeed be delighted to go, if that were possible."

"There is no *if* about it, my boy; if you wish to go you shall do so. I have made up my mind to give you a professional education, and shall not stop half-way."

"Oh, sir, the obligation—the overwhelming obligation you lay upon me!"

"Nonsense, Traverse! it is only a capital investment of funds! If I were a usurer, boy, I could not put out money to a better advantage! You will repay me, by and by, with compound interest; so just consider all that I may be able to do for you as a loan to be repaid when you shall have achieved success."

"I am afraid, sir, that that time will never——"

"No you are not!" interrupted the doctor—"and so don't let modesty run into hypocrisy. Now put up your books and go and tell your good little mother to get your clothes all ready for you to go to Washington, for you shall start by the next coach."

Much surprise it created in the little household by the news that Traverse was going immediately to Washington to attend the medical lectures. There were but two days to prepare his wardrobe for the journey. Mrs. Rocke went cheerfully to work; Clara lent her willing and skilful aid, and at the end of the second day his clothes, in perfect order, were all neatly packed in his traveling trunk.

And on the morning of the third day Traverse took leave of his mother and Clara, and for the first time left home to go out into the great world. Doctor Day accompanied him in the old green gig as far as Staunton, where he took the stage.

As soon as they had left the house Marah Rocke went away to her own room to drop a few natural tears over this first parting with her son. Very lonely and desolate the mother felt as she stood weeping by the window, and straining her eyes to catch a distant view of the old green gig that had already rolled out of sight.

While she stood thus in her loneliness and desolation, the door silently opened, a footstep softly crossed the floor, a pair of arms was put around her neck, and Clara Day dropped her head upon the mother's bosom and wept softly.

Marah Rocke pressed that beautiful form to her breast, and felt with dismay that the doctor's sweet daughter already returned her boy's silent love!

CHAPTER XXIV

CAPITOLA'S MOTHER

"A woman like a dew-drop she was purer than the purest,
  And her noble heart the noblest, yes, and her sure faith the surest;
And her eyes were dark and humid like the depth in depth of lustre
  Hid i' the harebell, while her tresses, sunnier than the wild grape's
    cluster,
  Gushed in raven-tinted plenty down her cheeks' rose-tinted marble:
  Then her voice's music—call it the well's bubbling, the birds'
warble."
    —*Browning* [1]

"CAP?"

"Sir!"

"What the blazes is the matter with you?"

"What the *blazes?* You better say what the dust and ashes! I'm bored to death! I'm blue as indigo! There never *was* such a rum old place as this, or such a rum old uncle as you!"

"Cap! how often have I told you to leave off this Bowery boy talk *Rum!* bah!" said old Hurricane.

"Well, it *is* rum then! Nothing ever happens here! The silence deafens me! the plenty takes away my appetite! the safety makes me low!"

"*Hum!* you are like the Bowery boys in times of peace, 'spoiling for a fight.'"

"Yes, I *am!* just decomposing above ground for want of having my blood stirred, and I wish I was back in the Bowery! Something was always happening *there!* One day a fire, the next day a fight, another day a fire and a fight together."

"Umph! and you to run with the engine!"

"Don't talk about it, uncle! It makes me homesick!—every day something glorious to stir one's blood! Here *nothing* ever happens, hardly! It has been three days since I caught Black Donald; ten days since you blowed up the whole household! Oh! I wish the barns would catch on fire! I wish thieves would break in and steal! I wish Demon's Run would only rise to a flood and play the demon for once! *Oh—yah—oo!*" said Cap,

173

opening her mouth with a yawn, wide enough to threaten the dislocation of her jaws.

"Capitola," said the old man, very gravely, "I am getting seriously uneasy about you. I know I am a rough old soldier, quite unfit to educate a young girl, and that Mrs. Condiment can't manage you, and—*I'll consult Mr. Goodwin!*" he concluded, getting up and putting on his hat, and walking out of the breakfast-room, where this conversation had taken place.

Cap laughed to herself—"I hope it is not a sin! I know I should die of the blues if I couldn't give vent to my feelings—and tease uncle!"

Capitola had scarcely exaggerated her condition. The monotony of her life affected her sprits; the very absence of the necessity of thinking and caring for herself, left a dull void in her heart and brain; and as the winter waned, the annual spring fever of lassitude and dejection to which mercurial organizations like her own are subject, tended to increase the malady that Mrs. Condiment termed "a lowness of spirits."

At his wit's end, from the combined feelings of his responsibility and his helplessness in his ward's case, Old Hurricane went and laid the matter before the Rev. Mr. Goodwin.

Having reached the minister's house, and found him alone and disengaged in the library, Old Hurricane first bound him over to strict secrecy, and then "made a clean breast of it;" told him where Capitola had been brought up, and under what circumstances he had found her!

The honest country clergyman was shocked beyond all immediate power of recovering himself—so shocked, in fact, that Old Hurricane, fearing he had gone too far, hastened to say:

"But mind, on my truth as a man, my honor as a soldier, and my faith as a Christain, I declare that that wild, reckless, desolate child has passed unscathed through the terrible ordeal of destitution, poverty and exposure! She *has,* sir! She is as innocent as the most daintily sheltered young heiress in the county! she *is,* sir! and I'd cut off the tongue and ears of any man that said otherwise."

"I do not say otherwise, my friend! but I say that she has suffered a frightful series of perils."

"She has come out of them safe, sir! I know it by a thousand signs!— what I fear for her is the *future!* I can't manage her! She won't obey me, except when she likes! she has never been taught obedience or been accustomed to subordination, and don't understand either! She rides and walks out alone in spite of all I can do or say! If she were a boy, I'd thrash her! But what can I do with a *girl?*" said Old Hurricane, in despair.

"Lock her up in her chamber until she is brought to reason," suggested the minister.

"Demmy, she'd jump out of the window and break her neck! or hang herself in her garters! or starve herself to death! you don't know what an untamable thing she is! Some birds, if caged, beat themselves to death against the bars of their prison! she is just such a wild bird as that!"

"Humph! it is a difficult case to manage; but you should not shrink from responsibility; you should be firm with her."

"That's just what I *can't* be with the witch, confound her! she is such a wag, such a droll, such a mimic; disobeys me in such a mocking, cajoling, affectionate way! I could not give her pain if her soul depended on it."

"Then you should talk to her! try moral suasion."

"Yes, if I could only get her to be serious long enough to listen to me! But you see Cap isn't *sentimental!* and if *I* try to be, she laughs in my face!"

"But then is she so insensible to all the benefits you have conferred upon her?—will not gratitude influence her?"

"Yes; so far as repaying me with a genuine affection, fervent caresses and careful attentions to my little comforts can go! but Cap evidently thinks that the restriction of her liberty is too heavy a price to pay for protection and support! The little rogue! Think of her actually threatening, in her good-humored way, to cite me before the nearest justice to show cause why I detain her in my house!"

"Well, you could easily do that, I suppose, and she could no longer oppose your authority."

"No, that is just what I *couldn't do!*—I couldn't show any legal right to detain Capitola."

"Humph, that complicates the case very much."

"*Yes;* and much more than you think! for I wish to keep Capitola until she is of legal age. I do not wish that she should fall into the hands of her perfidious guardian until I shall be able to bring legal proof of his perfidy."

"Then it appears that this girl has received foul play from her friends?"

"Foul play! I should think so! Gabriel Le Noir has very nearly put his neck into a halter."

"Gabriel Le Noir! Colonel Le Noir! Our neighbor!" exclaimed the minister.

"Exactly so!—Parson! you have given me your word as a Christian minister to be silent forever concerning this interview or until I give you leave to speak of it."

"Yes, Major, and I repeat my promise; but indeed, sir, you astound me!"

"Listen! and let astonishment rise to consternation. I will tell you who Capitola is. You, sir, have been in this neighborhood only ten years, and consequently you know Gabriel Le Noir only as the proprietor of Hidden House, a widower with one grown son——"

"And as a gentlemen of irreproachable reputation, in good standing both in the church and in the county."

"Exactly. A man that pays his pew-rent, gives good dinners, and takes off his hat to women and clergymen. Well, sir, this gentleman of irreproachable manners and morals—this citizen of consideration in the community—this member in good standing with the Church has qualified himself for a twenty years' residence in the penitentiary, even if not for the exaltation of a hangman's halter."

"Sir, I am inexpressibly shocked to hear you say so; and I must still believe that there is some great mistake."

"Wait until I tell you: I, Ira Warfield, have known Gabriel Le Noir as a villain for the last eighteen years. I tell you so without scruple, and hold myself ready to maintain my words in field or forum, by sword or law. Well, having known him so long, for such a knave, I was in no manner surprised to discover some six months ago that he was also a criminal, and only needed exposure to become a felon."

"Sir, sir, this is strong language!"

"I am willing to back it with 'life, liberty, and sacred honor,' as the Declaration of Independence has it. Listen: Some sixteen years ago, before you came to take this pastoral charge, the Hidden House was occupied by old Victor Le Noir, the father of Eugene the heir, and of Gabriel the present usurper. The old man died, leaving a will to this effect: the landed estate, including the coal and iron-mines, the Hidden House, and all the negroes, stock, furniture and other personal property upon the premises, to his eldest son Eugene, with this proviso; that if Eugene should die without issue, the landed estate, house, negroes, etc., should descend to his younger brother Gabriel. To Gabriel he left his bank-stock and blessing."

"An equitable will," observed the minister.

"Yes; but hear. At the time of his father's death Eugene was traveling in Europe. On receiving the news he immediately returned home, bringing with him a lovely young creature, a mere child, that he presented to his astounded neighbors as Madame Eugene Le Noir. I declare to you there was one simultaneous outcry of shame, that he should have trapped into matrimony a creature so infantile—for she was scarcely fourteen years of age."

"It was indeed highly improper," said the minister.

"So thought all the neighborhood; but when they found out how it happened, disapproval was changed to commendation. She was the daughter of a French patriot. Her father and mother had both perished on the scaffold in the sacred cause of liberty; she was thrown helpless, friendless, and penniless upon the cold charity of the world; Providence cast her in the way of our sensitive and enthusiastic young traveler. He pitied her; he loved her; and was casting about in his own mind how he could help without compromising her, when the news of his father's illness summoned him home. Then, seeing no better way of protecting her, after a little hesitation on account of her tender years, he married her and brought her with him."

"Good deeds, we know, must be rewarded in heaven, since on earth they are so often punished."

"He did not long enjoy his bride. She was just the most beautiful creature that ever was seen—with a promise of still more glorious beauty in riper years. I have seen handsome women and pretty woman, but Madame Eugene Le Noir was the only perfectly beautiful woman I ever saw in my long life. My own aged eyes seemed 'enriched' only to look at her. She adored Eugene, too—any one could see that. At first she spoke English in 'broken music,' but soon her accent became as perfect as if she had been native-born—how could it have been otherwise when her teacher and inspirer was Love? She won all hearts with her loveliness!—Humph! hear me, an old fool—worse, an Old Hurricane, betrayed into discourse of love and beauty, merely by the remembrance of Madame Eugene Le Noir! Ah, bright exotic flower! she did not bloom long. The bride had scarcely settled down into the wife when one night Eugene Le Noir did not come home as usual. The next day his dead body, with a bullet in his brain, was found in the woods around the Hidden House. The murderer was never discovered. Gabriel Le Noir came in haste from the military post where he had been stationed. Madame Eugene was never seen abroad after the death of her husband. It was reported that she had lost her reason—a consequence that surprised no one. Eugene having died without issue, and his young widow being mad, Gabriel, by the terms of his father's will, stepped at once into the full possession of the whole property."

"Something of all this I have heard before," said the minister.

"Very likely; for these facts and *falsehoods* were the common property of the neighborhod. But what you have *not* heard before, and what is *not* known to any now living, except the criminals, the victims and myself, is, that three months after the death of her husband, Madame Eugene Le Noir gave birth to twins—one living, one dead. The dead child was privately buried; the living one, together with the nurse that was the sole witness of the birth, was abducted."

"Great heaven, can this be true!!" exclaimed the minister, shocked beyond all power of self-control.

"True as gospel! I have proof enough to carry conviction to any honest breast—to satisfy any caviller—except, a court of justice. You shall hear. You remember the dying woman whom you dragged me out in the snow-storm to see—blame you!"

"Yes."

"*She* was the abducted nurse, escaped and returned! It was to make a deposition to the facts I am about to relate, that she sent you to fetch me," said Old Hurricane; and with that he commenced and related the whole dark history of crime comprised in the nurse's dying deposition. They examined the instrument together, and Old Hurricane again related, in brief, the incidents of his hurried journey to New York; his meeting and identifying Capitola, and bringing her home in safety to his house.

"And thus," said the old man, "you perceive that this child whose birth was feloniously concealed, and who was cast away to perish among the wretched beggars, thieves and street-walkers of New York, is really the only living child of the late Eugene Le Noir, and the sole inheritrix of the Hidden House, with its vast acres of fields, forests, iron and coal-mines, water-powers, steam-mills, furnaces and foundries—wealth that I would not undertake to estimate within a million of dollars!—all of which is now held and enjoyed by that usurping villain, Gabriel Le Noir!"

"But," said the minister, gravely, "you have, of course, commenced proceedings on the part of your *protégée.*"

"Listen. I will tell you what I have done. When I first brought Cap home, I was moved not only by the desire of wreaking vengeance upon a most atrocious miscreant who had done ME an irreparable injury, but also by sympathy for the little witch who had won my heart at first sight. Therefore you may judge I lost no time in preparing to strike a double blow which should ruin my own mortal enemy, and reinstate my favorite in her rights. With this view, immediately on my return home I sent for Breefe, my confidential attorney, and laid the whole matter before him."

"And he——"

"To my dismay he told me that though the case was clear enough, it was not sufficiently strong, in a legal point of view, to justify us in bringing suit; for that the dying deposition of the mulatto nurse could not be received as evidence in our courts."

"You knew *that* before, sir, I presume."

"Of course I did; but I thought it was a lawyer's business to get over such difficulties; and I assure you, parson, that I flew into a passion, and cursed court and law and lawyers to my heart's content! I would have quarreled with old Breefe, then and there, only Breefe *won't* get excited. He very cooly advised me to keep the matter close, and my eye open, and gather all the corroborative testimony I could find, and that in the meantime he would reflect upon the best manner of proceeding."

"I think, Major Warfield, that his counsel was wise and disinterested. But tell me, sir, of the girl's mother! Is it not astonishing; in fact, is it not perfectly incomprehensible, that so lovely a woman as you have represented her to be, should have consulted to the concealment, if not to the destruction of her own legitimate offspring."

"Sir, to *me* it is not incomprehensible at all! She was at once an orphan and a widow; a stranger in a strange land; a poor, desolate, brokenhearted child, in the power of the cunningest and most unscrupulous villain that the Lord ever suffered to live! I wonder at nothing that he might have deceived or frightened her into doing!"

"Heaven forgive us! Have I known that man for ten years to hear this account of him at last! But tell me, sir, have you really any true idea of what has been the fate of the poor young widow?"

"No—not the slightest. Immediately after his brother's funeral, Gabriel Le Noir gave out that Madame Eugene had lost her reason through excessive grief, soon after which he took her with him to the North, and upon his return alone, reported that he had left her in a celebrated Lunatic Asylum. The story was probable enough, and received universal belief. Only *now* I do not credit it, and do not know whether the widow be living or dead; or if living, whether she be mad or sane; if dead, whether she came to her end by fair means or *foul!*"

"Merciful Heaven, sir! you do not mean to say——"

"Yes, I *do* mean to say; and if you would like to know what is on my private mind I'll tell you. I believe that Madame Eugene Le Noir has been treacherously made away with by the same infernal demon at whose instigation her husband was murdered and her child stolen."

The minister seemed crushed beneath the overwhelming weight of this communication; he passed his hand over his brow, and thence down his face, and signed deeply; for a few moments he seemed unable to reply, and when he spoke it was only to say:

"In this matter, Major Warfield, I can offer you no counsel better than that of your confidential attorney—follow the light that you have, until it lead you to the full elucidation of this affair, and may Heaven grant that you may find Colonel Le Noir less guilty than you apprehend."

"Parson!—humbug! When charity drivels it ought to be turned off by justice! I *will* follow the little light I have! I suspect from the description, that the wretch who at Le Noir's instance carried off the nurse and child was no other than the notorious Black Donald. I have offered an additional thousand dollars for his apprehension, and if he is taken he will be con-demned to death, make a last dying speech and confession, and give up his accomplices, the accomplished Colonel Le Noir among the rest!"

"If the latter really *was* an accomplice, there could be no better way of discovering the fact than to bring this Black Donald to justice; but I greatly fear that there is little hope of that."

"Aye, but there *is!* Listen! the long impunity enjoyed by this desper-ado has made him daring to fatuity! Why, I was within a hair's breadth of capturing him *myself* a few days ago."

"Ha! is it possible?" asked the minister, with a look of surprise and interest.

"Aye, was I! And you shall hear all about it!" said Old Hurricane. And upon that he commenced and told the minister the adventure of Capitola with Black Donald at Hurricane Hall.

The minister was amazed, yet could not forbear to say:

"It seems to me, however, that it was Capitola who was within a hair's breadth of capturing this notorious desperado!"

"Pooh! she clung to him like the reckless lunatic that she is; but lord, he would have carried her off on his back if it had not been for ME."

The minister smiled a little to himself and then said:

"This *protégée* of yours is a very remarkable girl, as interesting to me in her character, as she is in her history; her very spirit, courage and insubordination make her singularly hard to manage and apt to go astray. With your permission I will make her acquaintance, with the view of seeing what good I can do her."

"Pray, do so, for then you will be better able to counsel me how to manage the capricious little witch, who if I attempt to check her in her wild and dangerous freedom of action, tells me plainly that liberty is too

precious a thing to be exchanged for food and clothing, and that rather
than live in bondage, she would throw herself upon the protection of the
court!—if she does *that* the game is up! Le Noir, against whom we can as
yet prove nothing, would claim her as his niece and ward, and get her into
his power for the purpose of making away with *her,* as he did with her
father and mother."

"Oh! for heaven's sake, sir, no more of that until we have further
evidence," said the minister, uneasily, adding—"I will see your very interesting *protégée* to-morrow."

"Do! do! to-morrow, to-day, this hour, anytime!" said Major Warfield, as he cordially took leave of the pastor.

CHAPTER XXV

CAP'S TRICKS AND PERILS

✤✤✤✤✤✤

"I'll be merry and free,
    I'll be sad for naebody;
Naebody cares for me,
    I cares for naebody."
                    —*Burns* [1]

THE NEXT DAY, according to agreement, the pastor came and dined at Hurricane Hall. During the dinner he had ample opportunity of observing Capitola.

In the afternoon Major Warfield took an occasion of leaving him alone with the contumacious young object of his visit.

Cap, with her quick perceptions, instantly discovered the drift and purpose of this action, which immediately provoked all the mischievous propensities of her elfish spirit.

"Uncle means that I shall be lectured by the good parson: if he preaches to me, *won't* I humor him 'to the top of his bent?'—that's all!" was her secret resolution, as she sat demurely, with pursed-up lips, bending over her needlework.

The honest and well-meaning old country clergyman hitched his chair a little nearer to the perverse young rebel, and, *gingerly,*—for he was half afraid of his questionable subject,—entered into conversation with her.

To his surprise and pleasure, Capitola replied with the decorum of a young nun.

Encouraged by her manner, the good minister went on to say how much interested he felt in her welfare; how deeply he compassionated her lot in never having possessed the advantage of a mother's teaching; how anxious he was by his counsels to make up to her as much as possible such a deficiency.

Here Capitola put up both her hands and dropped her face upon them.

Still farther encouraged by this exhibition of feeling, Mr. Goodwin went on. He told her that it behooved *her,* who was a motherless girl, to be even more circumspect than others, lest through very ignorance she might err; and in particular he warned her against riding or walking out alone, or indulging in any freedom of manners that might draw upon her the animadversions of their very strict community.

"Oh, sir, I know I have been very indiscreet, and I am very miserable!" said Capitola, in a heart-broken voice.

"My dear child, your errors have hitherto been those of ignorance only, and I am very pleased to find how much your good uncle has been mistaken; and how ready you are to do strictly right when the way is pointed out!" said the minister, pleased to his honest heart's core that he had made this deep impression.

A heavy sigh burst from the bosom of Capitola.

"What is the matter, my dear child?" he said, kindly.

"Oh, sir, if I had only known you before!" exclaimed Capitola, bitterly.

"Why, my dear?—I can do you just as much good now."

"Oh, no, sir! it is too late! *it is too late!*"

"It is never too late to do well."

"Oh, yes, sir, it is for me! Oh, how I wish I had had your good counsel before! it would have saved me from so much trouble!"

"My dear child, you make me seriously uneasy! do explain yourself," said the old pastor, drawing his chair closer to hers, and trying to get a look at the distressed little face that was bowed down upon her hands, and veiled with her hair—"Do tell me, my dear, what is the matter?"

"Oh, sir, I'm afraid to tell you! you'd hate and despise me! you'd never speak to me again!" said Capitola, keeping her face concealed.

"My dear child," said the minister, very gravely and sorrowfully, "whatever your offense has been, and you make me fear that it has been a very serious one, I invite you to confide it to me, and having done so I promise however I may mourn the sin, not to 'hate,' or 'despise,' or forsake the sinner. Come, confide in me."

"Oh, sir, I daren't! indeed I daren't!" moaned Capitola.

"My poor girl!" said the minster, "if I am to do you any good, it is absolutely necessary that you make me your confidant."

"Oh, sir, I have been a very wicked girl! I daren't tell you *how* wicked I have been!"

"Does your good uncle know or suspect this wrong-doing of yours?"

"Uncle! Oh, no, sir! He'd turn me out of doors. He'd kill me! Indeed he would, sir. Please don't tell him!"

"You forget, my child, that *I* do not know the nature of your offence," said the minister, in a state of painful anxiety.

"But I'm going to inform you, sir! and, oh, I hope you will take pity on me and tell me what to do; for though I dread to speak, I can't keep it on my conscience any longer, it is such a heavy weight on my breast!"

"Sin always *is,* my poor girl!" said the pastor, with a deep groan.

"But, sir, you know I had no mother, as you said yourself."

"I know it, my poor girl, and am ready to make every allowance," said the old pastor, with a deep sigh, not knowing what next to expect.

"And—and—I hope you will forgive me, sir! but—*but he was so handsome I couldn't help liking him!*"

"MISS BLACK!" cried the horrified pastor.

"There! I *knew* you'd just go and bite my head off the very first thing! Oh dear, what shall I do!" sobbed Capitola.

The good pastor, who had started to his feet, remained gazing upon her in a panic of consternation, murmuring to himself:

"Good angels! I am fated to hear more great sins than if I were a prison chaplain!" Then going up to the sobbing delinquent, he said:

"Unhappy girl! who is this person of whom you speak?"

"H—h—h—him that I met when I went walking in the woods!" sobbed Capitola.

"Heaven of Heavens! this is worse than my very worst fears!—Wretched girl! tell me instantly the name of this base deceiver!"

"He—he—he's no base deceiver; he—he—he's very amiable and good-looking; and—and—and that's why I liked him so much; it was all my fault, not his, poor, dear fellow!"

"His name?" sternly demanded the pastor.

"Alf—Alf—Alfred," wept Capitola.

"Alfred *whom?*"

"Alfred Blen—Blen—Blenheim!"

"Miserable girl! how often have you met this miscreant in the forest?"

"I—don't—know!" sobbed Capitola.

"Where is the wretch to be found now?"

"Oh, please don't hurt him, sir! Please don't! He—he—he's *hid in the closet in my room.*"

A groan that seemed to have rent his heart in twain burst from the minister, as he repeated in deepest horror:

"In your room! (Well! I must prevent murder being done!) Did you not know, you poor child, the danger you ran by giving this young man private interviews; and, above all, admitting him to your apartment? Wretched girl! better you'd never been born than ever so to have received a man!"

"Man? *man?* MAN?—I'd like to know what you mean by *that,* Mr. Goodwin!" exclaimed Capitola, lifting her eyes flashing through their tears.

"I mean the man to whom you have given these private interviews."

"*I!*—I give private interviews to a man! Take care what you say, Mr. Goodwin! I won't be insulted! no not even by *you!*"

"Then if you are not talking of a man, who or what in the world *are* you talking about?" exclaimed the amazed minister.

"Why, Alfred, the Blenheim poodle that strayed away from some of the neighbor's houses, and that I found in the woods and brought home and hid in my closet, for fear he would be inquired after, or uncle would find it out, and make me give him up! I knew it was wrong, but then he was so pretty———"

Before Capitola had finished her speech, Mr. Goodwin had seized his hat, and rushed out of the house in indignation, nearly overturning Old Hurricane, whom he met on the lawn, and to whom he said:

"Thrash that girl as if she were a bad boy—for she richly deserves it!"

"There what did I say! now you see what a time I have with her! she makes me sweat, I tell you!" said Old Hurricane, in triumph.

"Oh, oh, oh," groaned the sorely tried minister.

"What is it now?" inquired Old Hurricane.

The pastor took the major's arm, and while they walked up and down before the house, told how he had been 'sold' by Capitola, ending by saying:

"You will have to take her firmly in hand."

"I'll do it," said Old Hurricane. "I'll do it."

The pastor then called for his horse, and resisting all his host's entreaties to stay to tea, took his departure.

Major Warfield re-entered the house, resolving to say nothing to

Capitola for the present, but to seize the very first opportunity of punishing her for this flippancy.

The village fair had commenced on Monday. It had been arranged that all Major Warfield's family should go, though not all upon the same day. It was proposed that on Thursday, when the festival should be at its height, Major Warfield, Capitola and the house-servants should go. And on Saturday, Mrs. Condiment, Mr. Ezy and the farm-servants should have a holiday for the same purpose.

Therefore upon Thursday morning all the household bestirred themselves at an unusually early hour, and appeared before breakfast in their best Sunday's suit.

Capitola came down to breakfast in a rich, blue silk carriage dress, looking so fresh, blooming and joyous, that it went to the old man's heart to disappoint her; yet Old Hurricane resolved, as the pastor had told him to "be firm," and once for all by inflicting punishment to bring her to a sense of her errors.

"There, you need not trouble yourself to get ready, Capitola, you shall not go to the fair with us" he said, as Cap, took her seat.

"Sir!" exclaimed the girl, in surprise.

"Oh, yes! you may stare! but I'm in earnest! you have behaved very badly! you have deeply offended our pastor! you have no reverence, no docility, no propriety, and I mean to bring you to a sense of your position by depriving you of some of your indulgences! and in a word, to begin, I say you shall not go to the fair today!"

"You mean, sir, that I shall not go with *you,* although you promised that I should," said Cap, cooly.

"I mean you shall not *go at all,* demmy!"

"I'd like to know who'll prevent me," said Cap.

"*I* will, Miss Vixen! Demmy, I'll not be set at naught by a beggar!—Mrs. Condiment! leave the room, mum, and don't be sitting there listening to every word I have to say to my ward. Wool, be off with yourself, sir! what do you stand there gaping and staring for?—be off, or—" the old man looked around for a missile, but before he found one the room was evacuated except by himself and Capitola.

"Now, minion!" he began as soon as he found himself alone with the little rebel:

"I did not choose to mortify you before the servants, but once for all, I will have you to understand that I intend to be obeyed!" And Old Hurricane "gathered his brows like a gathering storm."

186

"Sir, if you were really my uncle, or my father, or my legal guardian, I should have no choice but to obey you; but the same fate that made me desolate made me *free!* a freedom that I would not exchange for any gilded slavery!" said Cap, gaily.

"Pish! tush! pshaw! I say I will have no more of this nonsense! I say I will be obeyed," cried Old Hurricane, striking his cane down upon the floor—"and in proof of it I order you immediately to go and take off that gala dress and settle yourself down to your studies for the day."

"Uncle, I will obey you as far as taking off this dress goes, for since you won't give me a seat in your carriage I shall have to put on my habit and ride Gyp," said Cap, good humoredly.

"WHAT!! do you dare to hint that you have the slightest idea of going to the fair against my will?"

"Yes, sir," said Cap, gaily—"sorry it's against your will, but can't help it! not used to being ordered about and don't know how to submit, and so I'm going!"

"Ungrateful girl! actually meditating disobedience *on the horse I gave her!*"

"Easy now, uncle—fair and easy! I did not sell my free will for Gyp! I wouldn't for a thousand Gyps! He was a free gift!" said Capitola, beginning an impatient little dance about the floor.

"Come here to me! Come—here—to—me!" exclaimed the old man, peremptorily, rapping his cane down upon the floor with every syllable.

Capitola danced up to him, and stood, half smiling, and fingering and arranging the lace of her under-sleeves.

"Listen to me, you witch! Do you intend to obey me or NOT!"

"NOT!" said Cap, good-humoredly, adjusting her cameo bracelet, and holding up her arm to see its effect.

"You will not! Then demmy, Miss, I shall know how to make you!" thundered Old Hurricane, bringing the point of his stick down with a sharp rap.

"Eh!" cried Capitola, looking up in astonishment.

"Yes, Miss, *that's* what I said! MAKE YOU!"

"I should like to know how," said Cap, returning to her cool good-humor.

"You would, would you? Demmy, I'll tell you! I have broken haughtier spirits than yours in my life. Would you know how?"

"Yes," said Capitola, indifferently, still busied with her bracelets.

"Stoop, and I will whisper the mystery."

Capitola bent her graceful head to hear.

"*With the rod!*" hissed Old Hurricane, maliciously.

Capitola sprang up as if she had been shot, wave after wave of blood tiding up in burning blushes over neck, face and forehead, then turning abruptly, she walked off to the window.

Old Hurricane, terrified at the effect of his rude, rash words, stood excommunicating himself for having been provoked to use them, nor was the next aspect of Capitola one calculated to re-assure his perturbed feelings.

She turned around; her face was as white and still as marble, except her glittering eyes, that, half sheathed under their long lashes, flashed like stilettoes; raising her head and keeping her eyes fixed upon him, with the slow and gliding motion, and the deep and measured voice that scarcely seemed to belong to a denizen of earth, she approached and stood before him, and spoke these words:

"Uncle, in all the sorrows, shames and sufferings of my destitute childhood, no one ever dishonored my person with a blow; and if ever you should have the misfortune to forget your manhood so far as to strike me——" she paused, drew her breath hard between her set teeth, grew a shade whiter, while her dark eyes dilated until a white ring flamed around the iris.

"Oh, you perilous witch, what then?" cried Old Hurricane, in dismay.

"Why then," said Capitola, speaking in a low, deep, and measured tone, and keeping her gaze fixed upon his astonished face, "the—first—time—I—should—find—you—asleep—I—would—take—a—razor—and——"

"Cut my throat! I feel you would you terrible termagant!" shuddered Old Hurricane.

"*Shave your beard off smick, smack, smoove!*" said Cap, bounding off and laughing merrily as she ran out of the room.

In an instant she came bounding back, saying: "Uncle! I will meet you at the fair! *au revoir! au revoir!*" and kissing her hand, she danced away and ran off to her room.

"She'll kill me! I know she will! If she don't in one way she will in another! Whew! I'm perspiring at every pore. Wool! Wool, you scoun-drel!" exclaimed the old man, jerking the bell-rope as if he would have broken the wires.

"Yes, sir! here I am, marse!" exclaimed that worthy, hastening in, in a state of perturbation, for he dreaded another storm.

"Wool! go down to the stables and tell every man there, that if any of them allows a horse to be brought out for the use of Miss Black to-day, I'll flay them alive, and break every bone in their skins! Away with you!"

"Yes, sir!" cried the shocked and terrified Wool, hurrying off to convey his panic to the stables.

Old Hurricane's carriage being ready, he entered it and drove off for the fair.

Next, the house-servants (with the exception of Pitapat, who was commanded to remain behind and wait upon her mistress) went off in a wagon.

When they were all gone, Capitola dressed herself in her riding-habit, and sent Pitapat down to the stables to order one of the grooms to saddle Gyp and bring him up for her.

Now when the little maid delivered this message, the unfortunate grooms were filled with dismay—they feared their tyrannical little mistress almost as much as their despotic old master, who in the next change of his capricious temper might punch all their heads for crossing the will of his favorite, even though in doing so they had followed his directions. An immediate private consultation was the consequence, and the result was that the head groom came to Pitapat, told her that he was sorry, but that Miss Black's pony had fallen lame.

The little maid went back with this answer.

When she was gone the head groom, calling to his fellows, said:

"That young gal ain't a-gwine to be fooled either by old marse or we! She'll be down here herself nex' minute and have the horse walked out. Now we must have him lame a little. Light a match here, Jem, and I'll burn him foot."

This was immediately done. And sure enough, while poor Gyp was still smarting with his burn, Capitola came, holding up her riding train and hurrying to the scene, and asking indignantly:

"Who dares to say that my horse is lame? Bring him out here this instant that I may see him."

The groom immediately took poor Gyp and led him limping to the presence of his mistress.

At the sight Capitola was almost ready to cry with grief and indignation.

"He was not lame last evening. It must have been your carelessness, you good-for-nothing set of loungers! And if he is not well enough to take me to the fair to-morrow, at least, I'll have the whole set of you lamed for life!" she exclaimed, angrily, as she turned off and went up to the house—not caring so much, after all, for her own personal disappointment as for Old Hurricane's triumph.

Cap's ill-humor did not last long. She soon exchanged her riding-habit for a morning wrapper, and took her needlework and sat down to sew by the side of Mrs. Condiment in the housekeeper's room.

The day passed as usual, only that just after sunset Mrs. Condiment, as a matter of precaution, went all over the house securing windows and doors before nightfall. Then, after an early tea, Mrs. Condiment, Capitola and the little maid, Pitapat, gathered around the bright little wood fire that the chilly spring evening made necessary in the housekeeper's room. Mrs. Condiment was knitting, Capitola stitching a bosom for the Major's shirts, and Pitapat winding yarn from a reel.

The conversation of the three females left alone in the old house naturally turned upon subjects of fear—ghosts, witches and robbers.

Mrs. Condiment had a formidable collection of accredited stories of apparitions, warnings, dreams, omens, etc., all true as gospel. There was a haunted house, she said, in their own neighborhood—the Hidden House. It was well authenticated that ever since the mysterious murder of Eugene Le Noir, unaccountable sights and sounds had been seen and heard in and about the dwelling. A traveler, a brother officer of Colonel Le Noir, had slept there once, and 'in the dead waste and middle of the night' had had his curtains drawn by a lady, pale and passing fair, dressed in white, with flowing hair, who, as soon as he attempted to speak to her, fled. And it was well known that there was no lady about the premises.

Another time old Mr. Ezy himself, when out after coons, and coming through the woods near the house, had been attracted by seeing a window near the roof lighted up by a strange blue flame; drawing near, he saw within the lighted room a female clothed in white, passing and repassing the window.

Another time, when old Major Warfield was out with his dogs, the chase led him past the haunted house, and as he swept by he caught a glimpse of a pale, wan, sorrowful female face pressed against the window-pane of an upper room, which vanished in an instant.

"But might not that have been some young woman staying at the house?" asked Capitola.

"No, my child, it is well ascertained that since the murder of Eugene

Le Noir and the disappearance of his lovely young widow, no white female has crossed the threshold of that fatal house," said Mrs. Condiment.

"*Disappearance* did you say? Can a lady of condition *disappear* from a neighborhood and no inquiry be made for her?"

"No, my dear, there was inquiry, and it was answered plausibly that Madame Eugene was insane and sent off to a lunatic asylum; but there are those who believe that the lovely lady was privately made way with," whispered Mrs. Condiment.

"How dreadful! I did not think such things happened in a quiet country neighborhood. Something like that occurred, indeed, in New York, within my own recollection, however," said Capitola—who straightway commenced and related the story of Mary Rogers,[2] and all other stories of terror that memory supplied her with.

As for poor little Pitapat, she did not presume to enter into the conversation, but with her ball of yarn suspended in her hand, her eyes started until they threatened to burst from their sockets, and her chin dropped until her mouth gaped wide open, she sat and swallowed every word, listening with a thousand-audience power.

By the time they had frightened themselves pretty thoroughly the clock struck eleven, and they thought it was time to retire.

"Will you be afraid, Mrs. Condiment?" asked Capitola.

"Well, my dear, if I am, I must try to trust in the Lord and overcome it, since it is no use to be afraid. I have fastened up the house well and I have brought in Growler, the bull-dog, to sleep on the mat outside of my bed-room door, so I shall say my prayers and try to go to sleep. I dare say there is no danger, only it seems lonesome like for us three women to be left in this big house by ourselves."

"Yes," said Capitola: "but as you say there is no danger; and as for *me,* if it will give you any comfort or courage to hear me say it, I am not the *least* afraid, although I sleep in such a remote room, and have no one but Patty, who, having no more heart than a hare, is not near such a powerful protector as Growler."

And, bidding her little maid to take up the night-lamp, Capitola wished Mrs. Condiment good-night, and left the housekeeper's room.

CHAPTER XXVI

THE PERIL AND THE PLUCK OF CAP

✥✥✥✥✥✥

"Who that had seen her form so light
   For swiftness only turned,
Would e'er have thought in a thing so slight,
   Such a fiery spirit burned?"

VERY DREARY looked the dark and silent passages as they went on towards Capitola's distant chamber.

When at last they reached it, however, and opened the door, the cheerful scene within quite reanimated Capitola's spirits. The care of her little maid had prepared a blazing wood fire that lighted up the whole room brightly glowing on the crimson curtains of the bed and the crimson hangings of the windows opposite, and flashing upon the high mirror between them.

Capitola having secured her room in every way, stood before her dressing-bureau and began to take off her collar, under-sleeves, and other small articles of dress. As she stood there, her mirror, brilliantly lighted up by both lamp and fire, reflected clearly the opposite bed, with its warm crimson curtains, white coverlet, and little Pitapat flitting from post to post, as she tied back the curtains or smoothed the sheets.

Capitola stood unclasping her bracelets, and smiling to herself at the reflected picture—the comfortable nest in which she was so soon to curl herself up in sleep. While she was sitting thus, she tilted the mirror downwards a little for her convenience, and looking into it again:

Horror! what did she see reflected there? Under the bed a pair of glaring eyes, watching her from the shadows.

A sick sensation of fainting came over her; but mastering the weakness, she tilted the glass a little lower, until it reflected all the floor, and looked again.

Horrors on horrors! there were three stalwart ruffians armed to the teeth, lurking in ambush under her bed.

The deadly inclination to swoon returned upon her; but with a heroic effort she controlled her fears, and forced herself to look.

Yes, there they were! It was no dream, no illusion, no nightmare— there they were, three powerful desperadoes, armed with bowie knives and revolvers, the nearest one crouching low, and watching her with his wolfish eyes, that shone like phosphorus in the dark.

What should she do? The danger was extreme, the necessity of immediate action imminent, the need of perfect self-control absolute. There was Pitapat flitting about the bed in momentary danger of looking under it. If she should, their lives would not be worth an instant's purchase. Their throats would be cut before they should utter a second scream. It was necessary, therefore, to call Pitapat away from the bed, where her presence was as dangerous as the proximity of a lighted candle to an open powder-barrel.

But how to trust her voice to do this? A single quaver in her tones would betray her consciousness of their presence to the lurking robbers and prove instantly fatal.

Happily, Capitola's pride in her own courage came to her aid.

"Is it possible," she said to herself, "that after all, I am a coward and have not even nerve and will enough to command the tones of my own voice. Fie on it! Cowardice is worse than death."

And summoning all her resolution she spoke up, glibly:

"Patty, come here and unhook my dress."

"Yes, Miss, I will just as soon as I get your slippers from unnerneaf of de bed."

"I don't want them! come here this minute and unhook my dress, I can't breathe! Plague take those country dressmakers, they think the tighter they screw one up the more fashionable they make one appear! Come, I say, and set my lungs at liberty."

"Yes, Miss, in one minute," said Pitapat; and to Capitola's unspeakable horror the little maid stooped down and felt along under the side of the bed, from the head post to the foot post, until she put her hands upon the slippers and brought them forth. Providentially, the poor little wretch had not for an instant put her stupid head under the bed, or used her eyes in the search!—that was all that saved them from instant massacre.

"Here dey is, Caterpillar! I knows how yer foots mus' be as much out of breaf wid yer tight gaiters as your waise is long of yer tight dress."

"Unhook me!" said Capitola, tilting up the glass lest the child should see what horrors were reflected there.

The little maid began to obey, and Capitola tried to think of some plan to escape their imminent danger. To obey the natural impulse—to fly from the room would be instantly fatal! they would be followed and murdered in the hall, before they could possibly give the alarm. And to whom could she give the alarm when there was not another creature in the house except Mrs. Condiment?

While she was turning these things over in her mind it occurred to her that "man's extremity is God's opportunity." Sending up a silent prayer to heaven for help at need, she suddenly thought of a plan—it was full of difficulty, uncertainty and peril, affording not one chance in fifty of success, yet the only possible plan of escape. It was to find some plausible pretext for leaving the room without exciting suspicion, which would be fatal. Controlling her tremors, and speaking cheerfully, she asked:

"Patty, do you know whether there were any of those nice quince tarts left from dinner?"

"Lor! yes, miss, a heap on 'em. Ole Mis' put 'em away in her cubbed."

"Was there any baked custard left?"

"Lors, yes, Miss Caterpillar! dere was nobody but wedens three, and think I could eat up all as was left?"

"I don't know but you might. Well, is there any pear-sauce?"

"Yes, Miss, a big bowl full."

"Well, I wish you'd go down and bring me up a tart, a cup of custard and a spoonful of pear-sauce. Sitting up so late makes me as hungry as a wolf. Come, Patty, go along."

" 'Deed, Miss, Ise 'fraid!" whimpered the little maid.

"Afraid of what, you goose?"

" 'Fraid of meeting a ghose in the dark places."

"Pooh! you can take the light with you. I can stay here in the dark well enough."

"Deed, Miss, I'so 'fraid!"

"What with the candle, you blockhead!"

"Lors, Miss, de candle wouldn't be no 'tection. I'd see de ghoses all de plainer wid de candle!"

"What a provoking, stupid dolt! you're a proper maid! afraid to do my bidding! afraid of *ghosts,* forsooth. Well! I suppose I shall have to go myself; plague on you for an aggravating thing! There! take the candle and come along!" said Capitola, in a tone of impatience.

Pitapat took up the light, and stood ready to accompany her mistress. Capitola humming a gay tune, went to the door and unlocked and opened it.

She wished to withdraw the key, so as to lock it on the other side and secure the robbers, and insure the safety of her own retreat; but to do this without betraying her purpose and destroying her own life seemed next to impossible. Still singing gaily she ran over in her mind with the quickness of lightning every possible means by which she might withdraw the key silently, or without attracting the attention of the watching robbers. It is difficult to say what she would have done, had not chance instantly favored her.

At the same moment that she unlocked and opened the door, and held the key in her hand, fearful of withdrawing it, Pitapat, who was hurrying after her with the candle, tripped and fell against a chair with a great noise, under cover of which Capitola drew forth the key.

Scolding and pushing Pitapat out before her, she closed the door with a bang; with the quickness of lightning she slipped the key in the keyhole, and turned the lock—covering the whole with loud and angry railing against poor Pitapat, who silently wondered at this unhappy change in her mistress's temper, but ascribed it all to hunger, muttering to herself:

"Ise offen hern tell how people's cross when dere empty! Lors knows ef I don't fetch up a whole heap o' wittles ebery night for Miss Caterpillar from dis time forred, so I will, 'deed me!"

So they went on through the long passages and empty rooms, Capitola carefully locking every door behind her, until she got down stairs into the great hall.

"Now, Miss Caterpillar, ef you wants quint tart, an' pear sass, and baked cusset, an' all dem, you'll jest has to go an' wake Ole Mis' up; case dey's in her cubbud an' she's got the keys," said Pitapat.

"Never mind, Patty, you follow me," said Capitola, going to the front hall-door, and beginning to unlock it and take down the bars and withdraw the bolts.

"Lors, Miss, what is yer adoin' of?" asked the little maid, in wonder, as Capitola opened the door and looked out.

"I am going out a little way, and you must go with me."

" 'Deed, Miss, I'se 'fraid."

"Very well, then; stay here in the dark until I come back, but don't go to my room, because you might meet a ghost on the way!"

"Oh, Miss, I daren't stay here—indeed I daren't!"

"Then you'll have to come along with me, and so no more about it," said Capitola, sharply, as she passed out from the door. The poor little maid followed, bemoaning the fate that bound her to so capricious a mistress.

Capitola drew the key from the hall-door and locked it on the outside. Then clasping her hands and raising her eyes to Heaven, she fervently ejaculated:

"Thank God! oh, thank God that we are safe!"

"Lors, Miss, was we in danger?"

"We are not now, at any rate, Pitapat. Come along," said Capitola, hurrying across the lawn towards the open fields.

"Oh, my goodness, Miss, where *is* yer agoin' of?—don't less run so fur from home dis lonesome, wicked, onlawful hour o' de night," whimpered the distressed little darkey, fearing that her mistress was certainly crazed.

"Now, then, what are you afraid of?" asked Capitola, seeing her hold back.

"Lors, Miss, *you* knows—everybody knows—Brack Dunnel!"

"Patty, come close, listen to me; don't scream—Black Donald and his men are up there at the house, in my chamber, under the bed," whispered Capitola.

Pitapat could not scream, for, though her mouth was wide open, her breath was quite gone. Shivering with fear, she kept close to her mistress's heels, as Capitola scampererd over the fields.

A run of a quarter of a mile brought them to the edge of the woods, where, in its little garden, stood the overseer's house.

Capitola opened the gate, hurried through the little front yard, and rapped loudly at the door.

This startled the house dog into furious barking, and brought old Mr. Ezy, with his night-capped head, to the window to see what was the matter.

"It is I, Capitola, Mr. Ezy—Black Donald and his men are lurking up at the house," said our young heroine, commencing in an eager and hurried voice, and giving the overseer an account of the manner in which she had discovered the presence of the robbers and left the room without alarming them.

The old man heard with many cries of astonishment, ejaculations of prayer, and exclamations of thanksgiving! And all the while his head was bobbing in and out of the window, as he pulled on his pantaloons or buttoned his coat.

"And oh" he said, at last, as he opened the door to Capitola, "how providential that Mr. Herbert Greyson is arrove."

"Herbert Greyson! Herbert Greyson arrived! Where is he then?" exclaimed Capitola, in surprise and joy.

"Yes, sartin. Mr. Herbert arrove about an hour ago, and thinking you all were abed and asleep at the Hall, he just stopped in with us all night. I'll go and see, I doubt if he's gone to bed yet," said Mr. Ezy, withdrawing into the house.

"Oh, thank Heaven! thank Heaven!" exclaimed Capitola, just as the door opened and Herbert sprang forward to meet her with a——

"Dear Capitola I am so glad to come to see you."

"Dear Herbert! Herbert! just fancy you have said that a hundred times over, and that I have replied to the same words a hundred times—for we haven't a moment to spare," said Capitola, shaking his hands, and then, in an eager, vehement manner, recounting her discovery and escape from the robbers whom she had locked up in the house.

"Go now," she said, in conclusion, "and help Mr. Ezy to rouse up and arm the farm hands, and come immediately to the house. I am in an agony lest my prolonged absence should excite the robbers' suspicion of my ruse, and that they should break out and perhaps murder poor Mrs. Condiment. Her situation is awful, if she did but know it! For the love of mercy, hasten!"

Not an instant more of time was lost. Mr. Ezy and Herbert Greyson, accompanied by Capitola and Patty, hurried at once to the negro quarters, roused up and armed the men with whatever was at hand, and enjoining them to be as stealthy as cats in their approach, set out swiftly for the Hall, where they soon arrived.

"Take off all your shoes, and walk lightly in your stocking feet—do not speak—do not breathe—follow me as silent as death," said Herbert Greyson, as he softly unlocked the front door and entered the house.

Silently and stealthily they passed through the middle hall, up the broad stair-case, and through the long narrow passage and steep stairs that led to Capitola's remote chamber.

There at the door they paused awhile to listen.

All was still within.

Herbert Greyson unlocked the door, withdrew the key, and opened it and entered the room, followed by all the men. He had scarcely time to close the door and lock it on the inside, and withdraw the key, before the robbers, finding themselves surprised, burst out from their hiding-place and made a rush for the passage; but their means of escape had been already cut off by the forethought of Herbert Greyson.

A sharp conflict ensued.

Upon first being summoned to surrender, the robbers responded by a hailstorm of bullets from their revolvers, followed instantly by a charge of bowie knives. This was met by an avalanche of blows from pick-axes, pokers, pitch-forks, sledge-hammers, spades and rakes, beneath which the miscreants were quickly beaten down and overwhelmed.

They were then set upon and bound with strong ropes brought for the purpose by Mr. Ezy.

When they were thus secured hand and foot, Capitola, who had been a spectator of the whole scene, and exposed as much as any other to the rattle of the bullets, now approached and looked at the vanquished.

Black Donald certainly was not one of the party, who were no other than our old acquaintances, Hal, Steve, and Dick of the band.

Each burglar was conveyed to a separate apartment, and a strong guard set over him.

Then Herbert Greyson, who had received a flesh wound in his left arm, returned to the scene of the conflict to look after the wounded. Several of the negroes had received gun-shot wounds of more or less importance. These were speedily attended to. Mrs. Condiment, who had slept securely through all the fight, was now awakened by Capitola, and cautiously informed of what had taken place, and assured that all danger was now over.

The worthy woman, as soon as she recovered from the consternation into which this news had plunged her, at once set about succoring the wounded. Cots and mattresses were made up in one of the empty rooms, and bandages and balsams prepared.

And not until all who had been hurt were made comfortable, did Herbert Greyson throw himself upon horseback, and ride off to the county seat to summon the authorities, and to inform Major Warfield of what had happened.

No one thought of retiring to bed at Hurricane Hall that night.

Mrs. Condiment, Capitola and Patty sat watching by the bedsides of the wounded.

Bill Ezy and the men who had escaped injury mounted guard over the prisoners.

Thus they all remained until sunrise, when the major, attended by the deputy-sheriff and half a dozen constables, arrived. The night ride of several miles had not sufficed to modify the fury into which Old Hurricane had been thrown by the news Herbert Greyson had aroused him from sleep to communicate. He reached Hurricane Hall in state of excitement that his factotum Wool characterized as "boiling." But "in the very torrent, tempest, and whirlwind of his passion," he remembered that to rail at the vanquished, wounded and bound was unmanly, and so he did not trust himself to see or speak to the prisoners.

They were placed in a wagon, and under a strong escort of constables, were conveyed by the deputy-sheriff to the county seat, where they were securely lodged in jail.

But Old Hurricane's emotions of one sort or another were a treat to see! He bemoaned the sufferings of the poor wounded men; he raved at the danger to which his "women-kind" had been exposed, and he exulted in the heroism of Capitola, catching her up in his arms and crying out:

"Oh, my dear Cap! my heroine! my queen! and it was you against whom I was plotting treason! ninny that I was! you that have saved my house from pillage and my people from slaughter! Oh, Cap, what a jewel you are, my dear."

To all of which Capitola, extricating her curly head from his embrace, cried only:

"Bother."

Utterly refusing to be made a lioness of, and firmly rejecting the grand triumph.

The next day Major Warfield went up to the county seat to attend the examination of the three burglars, whom he had the satisfaction of seeing fully committed to prison to await their trial at the next term of the criminal court, which would not sit until October; consequently the prisoners had the prospect of remaining in jail some months, which Old Hurricane declared to be "some satisfaction."

CHAPTER XXVII

SEEKING HIS FORTUNE

"A wide future smiles before him,
    His heart will beat for fame,
And he will learn to breathe with love
    The music of a name,
Writ on the tablets of his heart
    In characters of flame."
                        —*Sargent*

WHEN THE WINTER'S course of medical lectures at the Washington College was over, late in the spring, Traverse Rocke returned to Willow Heights.

The good doctor gave him a glad welcome, congratulating him upon his improved appearance and manly bearing.

Clara received him with blushing pleasure, and Marah Rocke with all the mother's love for her only child.

He quickly fell into the old pleasant routine of his country life; resumed his arduous studies in the doctor's office, his work in the flower-garden, and his morning rides and evening talk with the doctor's lovely child.

Not the least obstacle was set in the way of his association with Clara; yet Traverse, grown stronger and wiser than his years would seem to promise, controlled both his feelings and his actions, and never departed from the most respectful reserve, or suffered himself to be drawn into that dangerous familiarity to which their constant companionship might tempt him.

Marah Rocke, with maternal pride, witnessed his constant self-control, and encouraged him to persevere. Often in the enthusiasm of her heart, when they were alone, she would throw her arm around him, and push the dark curls from his fine forehead, and gazing fondly on his face, exclaim:

"That is my noble-hearted boy. Oh, Traverse, God will bless you. He only tries you now to strengthen you."

Traverse always understood these vague words, and would return her embrace with all his boyish ardor, and say:

"God *does* bless me now, mother. He blesses me so much, in so many, many ways, that I should be worse than a heathen not to be willing to bear cheerfully *one* trial."

And so Traverse would "reck his own read," and cultivate cheerful gratitude as a duty to God and man.

Clara, also, now, with her feminine intuition, comprehended her reserved lover, honored his motives, and rested satisfied with being so deeply loved, trusting all their unknown future to heaven.

The doctor's appreciation and esteem for Traverse increased with every new unfolding of the youth's heart and intellect, and never did master take more pains with a favorite pupil, or father with a beloved son, than did the doctor to push Traverse on in his profession. The improvement of the youth was truly surprising.

Thus passed the summer in healthful alternation of study and exercise.

When the season waned, late in the autumn, he went a second time to Washington to attend the winter's course of lectures at the Medical College.

The doctor gave him letters recommending him as a young man of extraordinary talents and of excellent moral character, to the particular attention of several of the most eminent professors.

His mother bore this second parting with more cheerfulness, especially as the separation was enlivened by frequent letters from Traverse, full of the history of the present and the hopes of the future.

The doctor did not forget from time to time to jog the memories of his friends, the professors of the medical college, that they might afford his *protégé* every facility and assistance in the prosecution of his studies.

Towards spring Traverse wrote to his friends that his hopes were sanguine of obtaining his diploma at the examination to be held at the end of the session. And when Traverse expressed this hope, they who knew him so well felt assured that he had made no vain boast.

And so it proved, for early in April Traverse Rocke returned home with a diploma in his pocket.

Sincere was the joyful sympathy that met him.

The doctor shook him cordially by the hands, declaring that he was the first student he ever knew to get his diploma at the end of only three years' study.

Clara, amid smiles and blushes, congratulated him.

And Mrs. Rocke, as soon as she had him alone, threw her arms around his neck and wept for joy.

A few days Traverse gave up solely to enjoyment of his friends' society, and then growing restless, he began to talk of opening an office and hanging out a sign in Staunton.

He consulted the doctor upon this subject. The good doctor heard him out, and then caressing his own chin and looking over the tops of his spectacles, with good-humored satire, he said:

"My dear boy, you have confidence enough in me by this time to bear that I should speak plainly to you?"

"Oh, Doctor Day, *just say whatever you like,*" replied the young man, fervently.

"Very well, then, I shall speak *very* plainly—to wit: you'll never succeed in Staunton—no, not if you had the genius of Galen and Esculapius, Abernethy, and Benjamin Rush put together."[1]

"My dear sir, why?"

"Because, my son, it is written that 'a prophet hath no honor in his own city!'[2] Of our blessed Lord and Savior the contemptuous Jews said, 'Is not this Jesus, the carpenter's son?'"

"Oh, I understand you, sir," said Traverse, with a deep blush, "you mean that the people who used some years ago to employ me to put in their coal and saw their wood and run their errands, will never trust me to look at their tongues and feel their pulses and write prescriptions."

"That's it, my boy; you've defined the difficulty. And now I'll tell you what you are to do, Traverse—you must go to the West, my lad."

"Go to the West, sir! leave my mother! leave you! leave——"

He hesitated, and blushed.

——"*Clara?* Yes, my son; you must go to the West, leave your mother, leave me and leave Clara; it will be best for all parties. We managed to live without our lad, when he was away at his studies in Washington, and we will try to dispense with him longer if it be for his own good."

"Ah, sir, but *then* absence had a limitation, and the hope of return sweetened every day that passed; but if I go to the West to settle it will be without the remotest hope of returning!"

"Not so, my boy—not so; for just as soon as Doctor Rocke has established himself in some thriving Western town, and obtained a good practice, gained a high reputation and made himself a home—which, as he is a fast young man in the best sense of the phrase, he can do in a very few years—he may come back here and carry to his Western home—his mother," said the doctor, with a mischievous twinkle of his eyes.

"Doctor Day, I owe you more than a son's honor and obedience. I will go wherever you think it best that I should," said Traverse, earnestly.

"No more than I expected from all my previous knowledge of you, Traverse. And I, on my part, will give you only such counsel as I should give my own son, had Heaven blessed me with one. And now, Traverse, there is no better season for emigration than the spring, and no better point to stay and make observations at than St. Louis. Of course, the place of your final destination must be left for future consideration. I have influential friends at St. Louis to whom I will give you letters."

"Dear sir, to have matured this plan so well you must have been kindly thinking of my future this long past," said Traverse, gratefully.

"Of course! of course! Who has a better right? Now go and break this plan to your mother."

Traverse pressed the doctor's hand and went to seek his mother. He found her in his room busy among his clothing. He begged her to stop and sit down while he talked to her. And when she had done so, he told her the doctor's plan. He had almost feared that his mother would meet this proposition with sighs and tears.

To his surprise and pleasure, Mrs. Rocke received the news with an encouraging smile, telling him that the doctor had long prepared her to expect that her boy would very properly go and establish himself in the West; that she should correspond with him frequently, and as soon as he should be settled, come and keep house for him.

Finally she said that, anticipating this emergency, she had, during her three years' residence beneath the doctor's roof, saved three hundred dollars, which she should give her boy to start with.

The tears rushed to the young man's eyes.

"For your dear sake, mother, only for *yours,* may they become three hundred *thousand* in my hands," he exclaimed.

Preparations were immediately commenced for Traverse's journey.

As before, Clara gladly gave her aid in getting ready his wardrobe. As he was to about to make his debut as a young physician in a strange city, his mother was anxious that his dress should be faultless, and therefore put the most delicate needlework upon all the little articles of his outfit. Clara volunteered to mark them all. And one day, when Traverse happened to be alone with his mother, she showed him his handkerchiefs, collars and linen beautifully marked in minute embroidered letters.

"I suppose, Traverse, that you being a young man, cannot appreciate the exquisite beauty of this work," she said.

"Indeed, but I can, mother. I did not sit by your side so many years while you worked without knowing something about it. This is wonderful. The golden thread with which the letters are embroidered is finer than the finest silk I ever saw," said Traverse, admiringly, to please his mother, whom he supposed to be the embroideress.

"Well, they may be," said Mrs. Rocke, "for that golden thread of which you speak is Clara's golden hair, which she herself has drawn out and threaded her needle with, and worked into the letters of your name."

Traverse suddenly looked up, his color went and came, he had no words to reply.

"I told you because I thought it would give you pleasure to know it, and that it would be a comfort to you when you are far away from us; for Traverse, I hope that by this time you have grown strong and wise enough to have conquered yourself, and to enjoy dear Clara's friendship *aright!*"

"Mother," he said, sorrowfully, and then his voice broke down, and without another word he turned and left the room.

To feel how deeply and hopelessly he loved the doctor's sweet daughter—to feel sure that she perceived and returned his dumb, despairing love—and to know that duty, gratitude, honor commanded him to be silent, to tear himself away from her and make no sign was a trial almost too great for the young heart's integrity. Scarcely could he prevent the internal struggle betraying itself upon his countenance. As the time drew near for his departure self-control grew difficult and almost impossible. Even Clara lost her joyous spirits, and despite all her efforts to be cheerful, grew so pensive that her father, without seeming to understand the cause, gaily rallied her upon her dejection.

Traverse understood it and almost longed for the day to come when he should leave this scene of his love and his sore trial.

One afternoon, a few days before he was to start, Doctor Day sent for Traverse to come to him in his study. And as soon as they were seated comfortably together at the table, the doctor put into the young man's hand a well-filled pocket-book; and when Traverse, with a deep and painful blush, would have given it back, he forced it upon him with the old argument:

"It is only a loan, my boy. Money put out at interest. Capital well and satisfactorily invested. And now listen to me. I am about to speak to you of that which is much nearer your heart——"

Traverse became painfully embarrassed.

"Traverse," resumed the doctor, "I have grown to love you as a son, and to esteem you as a man. I have lived long enough to value solid integrity far beyond wealth or birth, and when that integrity is adorned and enriched by high talents, it forms a character of excellence not often met with in this world. I have proved both your integrity and your talents, Traverse, and I am more than satisfied with you; I am proud of you, my boy."

Traverse bowed deeply, but still blushed.

"You will wonder," continued the doctor, "to what all this talk tends. I will tell you. Traverse, I have long known your unspoken love for Clara, and I have honored your scruples in keeping silent, when silence must have been so painful. Your trial is now over, my son. Go and open for yourself an honorable career in the profession you have chosen and mastered, and return, and Clara shall be yours."

Traverse, overwhelmed with surprise and joy at this incredible good fortune, seized the doctor's hand, and in wild and incoherent language tried to express his gratitude.

"There, there," said the doctor, "go and tell Clara all this, and bring the roses back to her cheeks, and then your parting will be the happier for this hope before you."

"I must speak. I must speak first," said the young man, in a choking voice. "I must tell you some little of the deep gratitude I feel for you, sir. O! when I forget all that you have done for me, 'may my right hand forget her cunning!'[3] May God and man forget me! Doctor Day, the Lord helping me for your good sake, I WILL be all that you have prophesied and hope and expect of me. For your sake, for Clara's and my mother's, I WILL bend every power of my mind, soul and body to attain the eminence you desire for me. In a word, the Lord giving me grace, I will become worthy of being your son and Clara's husband."

"There, there, my dear boy, go and tell Clara all that," said the doctor, pressing the young man's hand and dismissing him.

Traverse went immediately to seek Clara, whom he found sitting alone in the parlor.

She was bending over some delicate needlework, that Traverse knew by instinct was intended for himself.

Now, had Traverse foreseen from the first the success of his love, there might possibly have been the usual shyness and hesitation in declaring himself to the object of his affection. But although he and Clara had long deeply and silently loved and understood each other, yet neither had dared to hope for so improbable an event as the doctor's favoring their attachment, and now, under the exciting influence of the surprise, joy and gratitude with which the doctor's magnanimity had filled his heart, Traverse forgot all shyness and hesitation, and stepping quickly to Clara's side, and dropping gently upon one knee, he took her hand, and bowing his head upon it, said:

"Clara, my own, own Clara! your dear father has given me leave to tell you at last how much and how long I have loved you," and then he arose and sat down beside her.

The blush deepened upon Clara's cheek, tears filled her eyes, and her voice trembled as she murmured:

"Heaven bless my dear father! He is unlike every other man on earth."

"Oh, he is! he is!" said Traverse, fervently,—"and, dear Clara, never did a man strive so hard for wealth, fame or glory, as I shall strive to become 'worthy to be called his son.'"

"Do Traverse, do dear Traverse. I want you to honor even his very highest drafts upon your moral and intellectual capacities. I know you are 'worthy' of his high regard now, else he never would have chosen you as his son—but I am ambitious for you Traverse. I would have your motto be— Excelsior![4] higher!" said the doctor's daughter.

"And you, dear Clara, may I venture to hope that you do not disapprove of your father's choice, or reject the hand that he permits me to offer you?" said Traverse; for though he understood Clara well enough, yet like all honest men, he wanted some definite and practical engagement.

"There is my hand, my *heart* was yours long ago," murmured the maiden in a tremulous voice.

He took and pressed that white hand to his heart, looked hesitatingly and pleadingly in her face for an instant, and then drawing her gently to his bosom, sealed their betrothal on her pure lips.

Then they sat side by side, and hand in hand, in a sweet silence for a few moments, and then Clara said:

"You have not told your mother yet. Go and tell her, Traverse; it will make her so happy. And, Traverse, I will be a daughter to her, while you are gone. Tell her that, too."

"Dear girl, you have always been as kind and loving to my mother as it was possible to be—how can you ever be more so than you have been?"

"I shall find a way," smiled Clara.

Again he pressed her hand to his heart and to his lips, and left the room to find his mother. He had a search before he discovered her at last in the drawing-room, arranging it for their evening fireside gathering.

"Come, mother, and sit down by me on this sofa, for I have glorious tidings for your ear. Dear Clara sent me from her own side to tell you."

"Ah! still thinking, always thinking, madly thinking of the doctor's daughter. Poor, poor boy!" said Mrs. Rocke.

"Yes! and always intend to think of her to the very end of my life, and beyond, if possible. But come, dear mother, and hear me explain," said Traverse; and as soon as Mrs. Rocke had taken the indicated seat, Traverse commenced and related to her the substance of the conversation between the doctor and himself in the library, in which the former authorized his addresses to his daughter, and also his own subsequent explanation and engagement with Clara.

Mrs. Rocke listened to all this, in unbroken silence, and when, at length, Traverse had concluded his story, she clasped her hands and raised her eyes, uttering fervent thanksgivings to the fountain of all mercies.

"You do not congratulate me, dear mother."

"Oh, Traverse! I am returning thanks to Heaven on your behalf. Oh, my son! my son! but that such things as these are Providential, I should tremble to see you so happy. So I will not presume to congratulate. I will pray for you."

"Dear mother, you have suffered so much in your life, that you are incredulous of happiness. Be more hopeful and confiding. The Bible says: 'There remaineth now these three, Faith, Hope and Charity, but the greatest of all is Charity.'[5] You have Charity enough, dear Mother; try to have more Faith and Hope, and you will be happier. And look; there is Clara coming this way; she does not know that we are here. I will call her. Dear Clara, come in and convince my mother; she will not believe in our happiness," said Traverse, going to the door and leading his blushing and smiling betrothed into the room.

"It may be that Mrs. Rocke does not want me for a daughter-in-law," said Clara, archly, as she approached and put her hand in that of Marah.

"Not want you, my own darling," said Marah Rocke, putting her arm around Clara's waist, and drawing her to her bosom; "not want you? You know I am just as much in love with you as Traverse himself can be. And I have longed for you, my sweet, longed for you as an unattainable blessing, ever since that day when Traverse first left us and you came and laid your bright head on my bosom and wept with me."

"And now if we *must* cry a little when Traverse leaves us, we can go and take comfort in being miserable together, with a better understanding of our relations," said Clara, with an arch smile.

"Where are you all?—Where is *everybody*—that I am left wandering about the lonely house like a poor ghost in Hades?" said the doctor's cheerful voice in the passage without.

"Here father! here we are! a family party wanting only *you* to complete it," answered his daughter, springing to meet him.

The doctor came in smiling, pressed his daughter to his bosom, shook Traverse cordially by the hand, and kissed Marah Rocke's cheek. That was his way of congratulating himself and all others, on the betrothal.

The evening was passed in unalloyed happiness.

Let them enjoy it. It was their last of comfort—that bright evening.

Over that household was already gathering a cloud, heavy and dark with calamity—calamity that must have overwhelmed the stability of any faith which was not as theirs was—stayed upon God.

CHAPTER XXVIII

A PANIC IN THE OUTLAW'S DEN

☙☙☙☙☙☙

"Imagination frames events unknown,
In wild, fantastic shapes of hideous ruin,
And what it fears creates!"
　　—*Hannah More* [1]

"Dark doubt and fears, o'er other spirits lower,
But touch not his, who every waking hour,
Has one fixed hope and always feels its power."
　　—*Crabbe* [2]

UPON THE VERY same night that the three robbers were surprised and captured by the presence of mind of Capitola at Hurricane Hall, Black Donald, disguised as a negro, was lurking in the woods around the mansion, waiting for the coming of the three men with their prize.

But as hour after hour passed and they came not, the desperado began heartily to curse their sloth—for to no other cause was he enabled to attribute the delay, as he knew the house, the destined scene of the outrage, to be deserted by all for the night, except by the three helpless females.

As night waned and morning began to dawn in the East, the chief grew seriously uneasy, at the prolonged absence of his agents—a circumstance that he could only account for upon the absurd hypothesis that those stupid brutes had suffered themselves to be overtaken by sleep in their ambuscade.

While he was cursing their inefficiency, and regretting that he had not himself made one of the party, he wandered in his restlessness to another part of the woods, on the opposite side of the house.

He had not been long here before his attention was arrested by the trampling of approaching horsemen. He withdrew into the shade of the thicket and listened while the travelers went by.

The party proved to consist of Old Hurricane, Herbert Greyson, and the sheriff's officers, on their way from the town to Hurricane Hall, to take the captured burglars into custody. And Black Donald, by listening attentively, gathered enough from their conversation to know that his men had been discovered and captured by the heroism of Capitola.

"That girl again!" muttered Black Donald to himself. "She is doomed to be my destruction, or I hers. Our fates are evidently connected! Poor Steve! poor Dick! poor Hal! Little did I think that your devotion to your captain would carry you into the very jaws of death!—Pshaw! hang it! let boys and women whine. I must act!"

And with this resolution Black Donald dogged the path of the horsemen until he had reached that part of the woods skirting the road opposite the park gate. Here he hid himself in the bushes to watch events. Soon from his hiding-place he saw the wagon approach, containing the three men, heavily ironed and escorted by a strong guard of county constables and plantation negroes, all well armed, and under the command of the sheriff and Herbert Greyson.

"Ha, ha, ha! they must dread an attempt on our part of rescue, or they never would think of putting such a formidable guard over three wounded and handcuffed men!" laughed Black Donald to himself.

"Courage, my boys," he muttered. "Your chief will free you from prison or share your captivity. I wish I could trumpet that into your ears at this moment, but prudence, 'the better part of valor,'³ forbids, for the same words that would encourage you would warn your captors into greater vigilance." And so saying Black Donald let the procession pass, and then made tracks for his retreat.

It was broad daylight when he reached the old inn. The robbers, worn out with waiting and watching for the captain and his men with the fair prize, had thrown themselves down upon the kitchen floor, and now lay in every sort of awkward attitude, stretched out or doubled up in heavy sleep. The old beldame had disappeared—doubtless she had long since sought her night lair.

Taking a poker from the corner of the fireplace, Black Donald went around among the sleeping robbers and stirred them up, with vigorous punches in the ribs and cries of:

"Wake up! dolts! blockheads! wake up! You rest on a volcano about to break out! You sleep over a mine about to be exploded! Wake up, sluggards that you are! Your town is taken! Your castle is stormed! The enemy is at your throats with drawn swords! Ah, brutes! will you wake then! or shall I have to lay it on harder?"

"What the demon!"

"How now?"

"What's this?" were some of the ejaculations of the men as they slowly and sulkily roused themselves from their heavy slumber.

"The house is on fire; the ship's sinking; the cars have run off the track; the boiler's burst; and the devil's to pay," cried Black Donald, accompanying his words with vigorous punches of the poker into the ribs of the recumbent men.

"What the foul fiend ails you, Captain? Have you got the girl, and drunk too much liquor on your wedding night?" asked one of the men.

"No, Mack, I have not got the girl. On the contrary, the girl, blame her, has got three of my best men in custody. In one word, Hal, Dick and Steve are safely lodged in the county jail."

"WHAT!"

"Perdition!"

"Here's a go!" were the simultaneous exclamations of the men as they sprung upon their feet.

"In the fiend's name, Captain, tell us all about it," said Mac, anxiously.

"I have no time to talk much, nor you to tarry long. It was all along of that blamed witch, Capitola," said Black Donald, who then gave a rapid account of the adventure, and the manner in which Capitola entrapped and captured the burglars, together with the way in which he himself came by the information.

"I declare one can't help liking that girl. I should admire her even if she should put a rope about my neck," said Mac.

"She's a *brick,*" said another, with emphasis.

"She's some punkins, now, I tell you," assented a third.

"I am more than ever resolved to get her into my possession. But in the meantime, lads, we must evacuate the old inn; it is getting too hot to hold us."

"Aye, Captain!"

"Aye, lads! listen! we must talk fast, and act promptly! the poor fellows up there in jail are game, I know. They would not willingly peach: but they are badly wounded: if one of them should have to die, and be blessed with a psalm-singing parson to attend him—no knowing what he may be persuaded to confess. Therefore, let us quickly decide upon some new rendezvous that will be unsuspected, even by our poor caged birds. If any of you have any place in your eye, speak."

"We would rather hear what you have to say, Captain," said Mac; and all the rest assented.

"Well, then, you all know the Devil's Punch Bowl."

"Aye, do we, Captain."

"Well, what you do *not* know! what nobody knows but myself is *this*—that about half way down that awful chasm, in the side of the rock, is a hole, concealed by a clump of evergreens; that hole is the entrance to a cavern of enormous extent—let that be our next rendezvous. And now, avaunt! fly! scatter! and meet me in the cavern to-night, at the usual hour. Listen—carry away all our arms, ammunition, disguises, and provisions—so that no vestige of our presence may be left behind. As for dummy, if they can make *her* speak, the cutting out of her tongue was lost labor!—Vanish!"

"But our pals in prison," said Mac.

"They shall be *my* care. We must lie low for a few days, so as to put the authorities off their guard; then if our pals recover from their wounds, and have proved game against Church and State, I shall know what measures to take for their deliverance. No more talk now! prepare for your flitting and fly!"

The captain's orders were obeyed, and within two hours from that time no vestige of the robbers' presence remained in the deserted old inn. If any sheriff's officer had come there with a search-warrant, he would have found nothing suspicious; he would have seen only a poor old dumb woman, busy at her spinning-wheel; and if he had questioned her, would only have got smiles and shakes of the head for an answer; or the exhibition of coarse country gloves and stockings of her own knitting, which she would, in dumb show, beg him to purchase.

Days and weeks passed, and the three imprisoned burglars languished in jail, each in a separate cell.

Bitterly each in his heart complained of the leader that had, apparently, deserted them in their direst need. And if neither betrayed him, it was probably because they could not do so without deeply criminating themselves, and for no better motive.

There is said to be "honor among thieves." It is, on the face of it, untrue; there can be neither honor, confidence nor safety among men whose profession is crime. The burglars, therefore, had no confidence in their leader, and secretly and bitterly reproached him for his desertion of them.

Meanwhile the annual camp-meeting season approached. It was rumored that a camp-meeting would be held in the wooded vale below Tip-Top, and soon this report was confirmed by announcements in all the county papers. And all who intended to take part in the religious festival or have a tent on the ground, began to prepare provisions—cooking meat and poultry, baking bread, cakes, pies, etc. And preachers from all parts of the country were flocking into the village to be on the spot for the commencement.

Mrs. Condiment, though a member of another church, loved in her soul the religious excitement—"the warming up," as she called it, to be had at the camp-meeting! But never in the whole course of her life had she taken part in one, except so far as riding to the preaching in the morning and returning home in the evening.

But Capitola, who was as usual in the interval between her adventures bored half to death with the monotony of her life at Hurricane Hall,—and praying not against but wishing for—fire, floods or thieves, or anything to stir her stagnant blood, heard of the camp-meeting, and expressed a wish to have a tent on the camp-ground and remain there from the beginning to the end, to see all that was to be seen; hear all that was to be heard; feel all that was to be felt; and learn all that was to be known.

And as Capitola, ever since her victory over the burglars, had been the queen regnant of Hurricane Hall, she had only to express this wish to have it carried into immediate effect.

Old Hurricane himself went up to Tip-Top and purchased the canvas and set two men to work under his own immediate direction to make the tent.

And as Major Warfield's campaigning experience was very valuable here, it turned out that the Hurricane Hall tent was the largest and best on the camp-ground. As soon as it was set up under the shade of a grove of oak trees, a wagon from Hurricane Hall conveyed to the spot the simple and necessary furniture, cooking materials and provisions. And the same morning the family carriage, driven by Wool, brought out Major Warfield, Mrs. Condiment, Capitola and her little maid Patty.

The large tent was divided into two compartments—one for Major Warfield and his man Wool—the other for Mrs. Condiment, Capitola and Patty.

As the family party stepped out of the carriage, the novelty, freshness and beauty of the scene called forth a simultaneous burst of admiration. The little snow-white tents were dotted here and there through the woods, in beautiful contrast with the greenness of the foliage; groups of well-dressed and cheerful-looking men, women and children were walking about; over all smiled a morning sky of cloudless splendor. The preachings and the prayer-meetings had not yet commenced. Indeed, many of the brethren were hard at work in an extensive clearing, setting up a rude pulpit, and arranging rough benches to accommodate the women and children of the camp congregation.

Our party went into their tent, delighted with the novelty of the whole thing, though Old Hurricane declared that it was nothing new to his experience, but reminded him strongly of his campaigning days.

Wool assented, saying that the only difference was, there were no ladies in the old military camp.

I have neither time or space to give a full account of this camp-meeting. The services commenced the same evening. There were preachers of more or less fervor of piety and eloquence of utterance. Old Christians had their "first love" revived; young ones found their zeal kindled, and sinners were awakened to a sense of their sin and danger. Every Christian there said the season had been a good one.

In the height of the religious enthusiasm, there appeared a new preacher in the field. He seemed a man considerably past middle age, and broken down with sickness or sorrow. His figure was tall, thin and stooping, his hair white as snow, his face pale and emaciated, his movements slow and feeble, and his voice low and unsteady. He wore a solemn suit of black, that made his thin form seem of skeleton proportions, a snow-white neckcloth, and a pair of great round iron-rimmed spectacles that added nothing to his good looks.

Yet this old, sickly and feeble man seemed one of fervent piety and of burning eloquence. Every one sought his society; and when it was known that Father Gray was to hold forth, the whole camp congregation turned out to hear him.

It must not be supposed that in the midst of this great revival, those poor "sinners above all sinners," the burglars imprisoned in the neighboring town were forgotten; no, they were remembered, prayed for, visited, and exhorted. And no one took more interest in the fate of these men than good Mrs. Condiment, who, having seen them all on that great night at Hurricane Hall, and having with her own kind hands plastered their heads and given them possets, could not drive out of her heart a certain compassion for their miseries.

No one either admired Father Gray more than did the little old housekeeper of Hurricane Hall, and as her table and her accommodations were the best on the camp-ground, she often invited and pressed good Father Gray to rest and refresh himself in her tent. And the old man, though a severe ascetic, yielded to her repeated solicitations, until at length he seemed to live there altogether.

One day Mrs. Condiment, being seriously exercised upon the subject of the imprisoned men, said to Father Gray, who was reposing himself in the tent:

"Father Gray, I wished to speak to you, sir, upon the subject of those poor, wretched men who are to be tried for their lives at the next term of the criminal court. Our ministers have all been to see them, and talked to them, not one of the number can make the least impression on them, or bring them to any sense of their awful condition."

"Ah! that is dreadful," sighed the aged man.

"Yes, dreadful, Father Gray. Now I thought if *you* would only visit them, you could surely bring them to reason."

"My dear friend, I would willingly do so, but I must confess to you a weakness, a great weakness of the flesh—I have a natural shrinking from men of blood. I know it is sinful, but indeed I cannot overcome it."

"But, my dear Father Gray, a man of *your* experience knows full well that if you cannot overcome that feeling, you should act in direct opposition to it. And, I assure you, there is no danger. Why, even *I* should not be at all afraid of a robber when he is double-ironed and locked up in a cell, and I should enter guarded by a pair of turnkeys."

"I know it, my dear lady, I know it; and I feel that I ought to overcome this weakness or do my duty in its despite."

"Yes, and if *you* would consent to go, Father Gray, I would not mind going with you myself, if *that* would encourage you any."

"Of course it would, my dear friend; and if you will go with me, and if the brethren think that I could do any good, I will certainly endeavor to conquer my repugnance, and visit these imprisoned men."

It was arranged that Father Gray, accompanied by Mrs. Condiment, should go to the jail upon the following morning; and accordingly they set out immediately after breakfast. A short ride up the mountain brought them to Tip-Top, in the centre of which stood the jail. It was a simple structure of gray stone, containing within its own walls the apartments occupied by the warden. To these, Mrs. Condiment, who was the leader in the whole matter, first presented herself, introducing Father Gray as one of the preachers of the camp-meeting, a very pious man, and very effective in his manner of dealing with hardened offenders.

"I have heard of the Reverend Mr. Gray, and his powerful exhortations," said the warden, with a low bow; "and I hope he may be able to make some impression on these obdurate men, and induce them, if possible, to 'make a clean breast of it,' and give up the retreat of their band. Each of them has been offered a free pardon on condition of turning State's evidence, and each has refused."

"Indeed; have they done so, case-hardened creatures?" mildly inquired Father Gray.

"Aye, have they! but you, dear sir, may be able to persuade them to do so."

"I shall endeavor—I shall endeavor," said the mild old man.

The warden then requested the visitors to follow him, and led the way up stairs to the cells.

"I understand that the criminals are confined separately?" said Mr. Gray to the warden.

"No, sir; they were so confined at *first,* for better security; but as they have been very quiet, and as since those rowdies that disturbed the camp-meeting have been sent to prison, and filled up our cells, we have had to put those three robbers into one cell!"

"I'm afraid, I—" began the minister, hesitating.

"Father Gray is nervous, good Mr. Jailer; I hope there's no danger from those dreadful men—all of them together—for I promised Father Gray that he should be safe, myself," said Mrs. Condiment.

"Oh, ma'am, undoubtedly; they are double-ironed," said the warden, as he unlocked a door and admitted the visitors into rather a darkish cell, in which were the three prisoners.

Steve, the mulatto, was stretched upon the floor in a deep sleep.

Hal was sitting on the side of the cot, twiddling his fingers.

Dick sat crouched up in a corner, with his head against the wall.

"Peace be with you, my poor souls," said the mild old man, as he entered the cell.

"You go to the demon!" said Dick, with a hideous scowl.

"Nay, my poor man, I came in the hope of saving you from that enemy of souls."

"Here's another! There's three comes reg'lar! here's the fourth! Go it, old fellow! We're gettin' used to it! It's gettin' to be entertainin'! It's the only diversion we have in this blamed hole!" said Hal.

"Nay, friend, if you use profane language, I cannot stay to hear it," said the old man.

"*Yaw-aw-aw-*ow!" yawned Steve, half rising and stretching himself. "What's the row? I was just dreaming our captain had come to deliver us—*yaw-aw-aw-ooh!* it's only another parson?" and with that, Steve turned himself over and settled to sleep.

"My dear Mr. Jailer—do you think that these men are safe?—for if you do, I think we had better leave excellent Mr. Gray to talk to them alone—he can do them so much good, if he has them all to himself," said Mrs. Condiment, who was, in spite of all her previous boasting, beginning to quail and tremble under the hideous glare of Demon Dick's eyes.

"N-no! n-no! n-no!" faltered the preacher, nervously taking hold of the coat of the warden.

"You go along out of this! the *whole* on you. I'm not a wild beast in a cage to be stared at!" growled Demon Dick, with a baleful glare that sent Mrs. Condiment and the preacher, shuddering to the cell door.

"Mr. Gray, I do assure you, sir, there is no danger! the men are double-ironed, and malignant as they may be, they can do you no harm. And if you *would* stay and talk to them you might persuade them to confession and do the community much service," said the warden.

"I—I—I'm no coward! But—but—but—" faltered the old man, tremblingly approaching the prisoners.

"I understand you, sir. You are in bad health, which makes you nervous."

"Yes, yes, Heaven forgive me; but if you, Mr. Jailer, and this good lady here, will keep within call, in case of accidents, I don't mind if I do remain and exhort these men, for a short time," said the old man.

"Of course we will. Come, Mrs. Condiment, mum! there's a good bench in the lobby, and I'll send for my old woman, and we three can have a good talk while the worthy Mr. Gray is speaking to the prisoners," said the warden, conducting the housekeeper from the cell.

As soon as they had gone, the old man went to the door and peeped after them, and having seen that they went to the extremity of the lobby to a seat under an open window, he turned back to the cell, and going up to Hal, said in a low voice:

"Now, then, is it possible that you do not know me!"

Hal stopped twiddling his fingers and looked up at the tall, thin, stooping figure, the gray hair, the white eyebrows and the pale face, and said gruffly:

"No! May the demon fly away with me if I ever saw you before!"

"Nor you, Dick?" inquired the old man, in a mild voice, turning to the one addressed.

"*No,* burn you! nor want to see you now!"

"Steve! Steve!" said the old man, in a pitiful voice, waking the sleeper. "Don't *you* know me either!"

"Don't bother me," said that worthy, giving himself another turn and another settle to sleep.

"Dolts! blockheads! brutes! do you know me now?" growled the visitor, changing his voice.

"Our Captain!"

"Our Captain!"

"Our Captain!" they simultaneously cried.

"*Hush,* sink your souls! Do you want to bring the warden upon us?" growled Black Donald, for it was unquestionably him in a new metamorphosis.

"Then all I have to say, Captain, is that you have left us here a blamed long time!"

"And exposed you to sore temptation to peach on me! Couldn't help it, lads! couldn't help it! I waited until I could do something to the *purpose!*"

"Now, may Satan roast me alive if I know what you have done to turn yourself into an old man! Burn my soul! if I should know you now, Captain, if it wa'n't for your voice," grumbled Steve.

"Listen, then, you ungrateful, suspicious wretches! I did for you what no captain ever did for his men before. I had exhausted all manner of disguises, so that the authorities would almost have looked for me in an old woman's gown! See, then, what I did: I put myself on a month's regimen of vegetable diet, and kept myself in a cavern, until I grew as pale and thin as a hermit! Then I shaved off my hair, beard, moustaches and eyebrows! Yes, blame you, I sacrificed all my beauty to your interests! Fate helps those who help themselves. The camp-meeting gathering together hosts of people and preachers, gave me the opportunity of appearing without exciting inquiry. I put on a gray wig, a black suit, assumed a feeble voice, stooping gait, and a devout manner, and—became a popular preacher at the camp-meeting!"

"Captain, you're a brick! you are, indeed! I do not flatter you" said Hal. It was a sentiment in which all agreed.

"I had no need of further machination," continued the captain; "they actually gave me the game! I was urged to visit you here—forced to remain alone and talk with you!" laughed Black Donald.

"And now, Captain, my jewel! my treasure! my sweetheart that I love with 'a love passing the love of woman!'[4] how is your reverence going to get us out?"

"Listen!" said the Captain, diving into his pockets. "You must get yourselves out!—this prison is by no means strongly fastened, or well guarded. Here are files to file off your fetters; here are tools to pick the locks, and here are three loaded revolvers to use against any of the turn-keys who might discover and attempt to stop you. To-night, however, is the last of the camp-meeting, and the two turnkeys are among *my* hearers! I shall keep them all night! Now you know what to do. I must leave you. Dick, try to make an assault on me that I may scream—but first conceal your tools and arms."

Hal hid the instruments, and Dick, with an awful roar, sprang at the visitor, who ran to the grating, crying:

"Help! help!"

The warden came hurrying to the spot.

"Take 'im out o' this, then!" muttered Dick, sulkily, getting back into his corner.

"Oh, what a wretch!" said Mrs. Condiment.

"I shall be glad when he's once hanged," said the jailer.

"I—I—fear that I can do them but little good, and—and I would rather not come again, being sickly and nervous," faltered Father Gray.

"No, my dear good sir. *I* for one shall not ask you to risk your precious health for such a set of wretches. They are Satan's own! You shall come home to our tent and lie down to rest, and I will make you an egg-caudle that will set you up again," said Mrs. Condiment, tenderly, as the whole party left the cell.

That day the outrageous conduct of the imprisoned burglars was the subject of conversation, even dividing the interest of the religious excitement.

But the next morning the whole community was thrown into a state of consternation by the discovery that the burglars had broken jail and fled, and that the notorious outlaw, Black Donald, had been in their very midst, disguised as an elderly field preacher.

CHAPTER XXIX

THE VICTORY OVER DEATH

🜂🜂🜂🜂🜂

"'Glory to God! to God!' he saith,
'Knowledge by suffering entereth,
And life is perfected in death.'"
—*E. B. Browning* [1]

ONE MORNING, in the gladness of his heart, Doctor Day mounted his horse and rode down to Staunton, gaily refusing to impart the object of his ride to any one, and bidding Traverse stay with the women until he should return.

As soon as the doctor was gone, Traverse went into the library to arrange his patron's books and papers.

Mrs. Rocke and Clara hurried away to attend to some little mystery of their own invention, for the surprise and delight of the doctor and Traverse. For the more secret accomplishment of their purpose, they had dismissed all attendance, and were at work alone in Mrs. Rocke's room. And here Clara's sweet, frank and humble disposition was again manifest, for when Marah would arise from her seat to get anything, Clara would forestall her purpose, and say:

"Tell me—tell *me* to get what you want, just as if I were your child, and you will make me feel so well—*do* now!"

"You are very good, dear Miss Clara, but—I would rather not presume to ask you to wait on me," said Marah, gravely.

"*Presume!* what a word from you to me; please don't use it ever again, nor call me *Miss Clara.* Call me 'Clara' or 'child,' *do, mamma,*" said the doctor's daughter; then suddenly pausing, she blushed and was silent.

Marah gently took her hand, and drew her into a warm embrace.

It was while the friends were conversing so kindly in Marah's room, and while Traverse was still engaged in arranging the doctor's books and papers, that one of the men-servants rapped at the library door, and without waiting permission to come in, entered the room with every mark of terror in his look and manner.

"What is the matter?" inquired Traverse, anxiously rising.

"Oh, Mr. Traverse, sir! the doctor's horse has just rushed home to the stables all in a foam, without his rider."

"Good Heaven!" exclaimed Traverse, starting up and seizing his hat; "follow me immediately; hurry to the stables and saddle my horse, and bring him up instantly! We must follow on the road the doctor took, to see what has happened! Stay! on your life, breathe not a word of what has occurred! I would not have Miss Day alarmed for the world!" he concluded, hastening down stairs attended by the servant.

In five minutes from the time he left the library, Traverse was in the saddle, galloping towards Staunton, and looking attentively along the road as he went. Alas! he had not gone far, when, in descending the wooded hill, he saw lying doubled up helplessly on the right side of the path, the body of the good doctor!

With an exclamation between a groan and a cry of anguish, Traverse threw himself from his saddle and kneeled beside the fallen figure, gazing in an agony of anxiety upon the closed eyes, pale features and contracted form, and crying:

"Oh, heaven have mercy! Doctor Day! oh, Doctor Day!—can you speak to me?"

The white and quivering eyelids opened and the faltering tongue spoke:

"Traverse—get me home—that I may see—Clara before I die."

"Oh, must this be so! must this be so! Oh, that I could die for you, my friend! my dear, dear friend!" cried Traverse, wringing his hands in such anguish as he had never known before.

Then feeling the need of self-control and the absolute necessity of removing the sufferer, Traverse repressed the swelling flood of sorrow in his bosom and cast about for the means of conveying the doctor to his house. He dreaded to leave him for an instant, and yet it was necessary to do so, as the servant whom he had ordered to follow him, had not yet come up.

While he was bathing the doctor's face with water from a little stream beside the path, John, the groom, came riding along, and seeing his fallen master, with an exclamation of horror, sprang from his saddle and ran to the spot.

"John," said Traverse, in a heart-broken tone, "mount again and

ride for your life to the house! have—a cart—yes! that will be the easiest
conveyance! have a cart got ready instantly with a feather-bed placed in it,
and the gentlest horse harnessed to it, and drive it here to the roadside at
the head of this path. Hasten for your life! say not a word of what has
happened lest it should terrify the ladies! Quick! quick! on your life!"

Again, as the man was hurrying away, the doctor spoke, faintly
murmuring:

"For heaven's sake—do not let—poor Clara be shocked!"

"No, no, she shall not be; I warned him, dear friend. How do you
feel?—can you tell where you are hurt?"

The doctor feebly moved one hand to his chest and whispered:

"*There,* and in my back."

Traverse, controlling his own great mental agony, did all that he
could to soothe and alleviate the sufferings of the doctor, until the arrival
of the cart that stopped on the road at the head of the little bridle-path
where the accident happened. Then John jumped from the driver's seat
and came to the spot where he tenderly assisted the young man in raising
the doctor and conveying him to the cart and laying him upon the bed.
Notwithstanding all their tender care in lifting and carrying him, it was but
too evident that he suffered greatly in being moved. Slowly as they proceeded, at every jolt of the cart, his corrugated brows and blanched and
quivering lips told how much agony he silently endured.

Thus at last they reached home. He was carefully raised by the bed
and borne into the house and upstairs to his own chamber, where, being
undressed, he was laid upon his own easy couch. Traverse sent off for other
medical aid, administered a restorative, and proceeded to examine his
injuries.

"It is useless, dear boy, useless all! you have medical knowledge
enough to be as sure of that as I am. Cover me up, and let me compose
myself before seeing Clara, and while I do so, go you and break this news
gently to the poor child!" said the doctor, who, being under the influence
of the restorative, spoke more steadily than at any time since his fall.

Traverse, almost broken-hearted, obeyed his benefactor, and went to
seek his betrothed, praying the Lord to teach him how to tell her this
dreadful calamity and to support her under its crushing weight.

As he went slowly, wringing his hands, he suddenly met Clara with
her dress in disorder and her hair flying, just as she had run from her room
while dressing for dinner. Hurrying towards him, she exclaimed:

"Traverse, *what* happened? for the good Lord's sake tell me quickly! the house is all in confusion! every one is pale with affright! no one will answer me! your mother just now ran past me out of the store-room, with her face as white as death! Oh, *what* does it all mean?"

"Clara, love, come and sit down, you are almost fainting—oh, Heaven support us!" murmured Traverse, as he led the poor girl to the hall sofa.

"Tell me! tell me!" she said.

"Clara—your father—"

"My father! Oh no, no; do not say any harm has happened to my father! do not, Traverse, do not!"

"Oh, Clara, try to be firm, dear one!"

"My father! oh, my father! he is DEAD!" shrieked Clara, starting up wildly to run—she knew not whither.

Traverse sprang up and caught her arm, and drawing her gently back to her seat, said:

"No, dear Clara, no—not so bad as that! he is living."

"Oh, thank Heaven for so much! what is it, then Traverse? He is ill?—oh, let me go to him."

"Stay, dear Clara! compose yourself first! You would not go and disturb him with this frightened and distressed face of yours—let me get you a glass of water," said Traverse, starting up and bringing the needed sedative from an adjoining room.

"There, Clara, drink that, and offer a silent prayer to Heaven to give you self-control."

"I will! oh, I must, for his sake. But, tell me, Traverse, is it—is it as I fear—as *he* expected—apoplexy?"

"No, dear love, no; he rode out this morning and his horse got frightened by the van of a circus-company that was going into the town, and——"

"——And ran away with him and threw him! Oh, Heaven! oh, my dear father!" exclaimed Clara, once more clasping her hands wildly, and starting up.

Again Traverse promptly but gently detained her, saying:

"You promised me to be calm, dear Clara, and you must be so before I can suffer you to see your father."

Clara sank into her seat and covered her face with her hands, murmuring in a broken voice:

"How can I be? Oh, how can I be, when my heart is wild with grief and fright? *Traverse!* was he—was he—oh! I dread to ask you! Oh! was he much hurt?"

"Clara, love, his injuries are internal. Neither he nor I yet know their full extent. I have sent off for two old and experienced practitioners from Staunton. I expect them every moment. In the meantime, I have done all that is possible for his relief."

"Traverse," said Clara, very calmly, controlling herself by an almost superhuman effort; "Traverse, I will be composed; you shall see that I will; take me to my dear father's bedside; it is there that I ought to be!"

"That is my dear, brave, dutiful girl! Come, Clara," replied the young man, taking her hand, and leading her up to the bed-chamber of the doctor. They met Mrs. Rocke at the door, who tearfully signed them to go in as she left it.

When they entered and approached the bedside, Traverse saw that the suffering but heroic father must have made some superlative effort before he could have reduced his haggard face and writhing form to its present state of placid repose, to meet his daughter's eyes and spare her feelings.

She, on her part, was no less firm. Kneeling beside his couch, she took his hand and met his eye composedly as she asked:

"Dear father, how do you feel now?"

"Not just so easy, love, as if I had laid me down here for an afternoon's nap, yet in no more pain than I can very well bear."

"Dear father, what can I do for you?"

"You may bathe my forehead and lips with cologne, my dear," said the doctor, not so much for the sake of the reviving perfume, as because he knew it would comfort Clara to feel that she was doing something, however slight, for him.

Traverse stood upon the opposite side of the bed fanning him.

In a few moments Mrs. Rocke re-entered the room, announcing that the two old physicians from Staunton, Doctor Dawson and Doctor Williams, had arrived.

"Show them up, Mrs. Rocke; Clara, love, retire while the physicians remain with me," said Doctor Day.

Mrs. Rocke left the room to do his bidding. And Clara followed and sought the privacy of her own apartment, to give way to the overwhelming grief which she could no longer resist.

As soon as she was gone the doctor also yielded to the force of the suffering that he had been able to endure silently in her presence, and writhed and groaned in agony, that wrung the heart of Traverse to behold.

Presently the two physicians entered the room, and approached the bed, with expressions of sincere grief at beholding their old friend in such a condition, and a hope that they might speedily be able to relieve him.

To all of which the doctor, repressing all exhibitions of pain, and holding out his hand in a cheerful manner, replied:

"I am happy to see you in a friendly way, old friends, I am willing also that you should try what you—what you can do for me—but I warn you that it will be useless. A few hours or days of inflammation, fever and agony; then the ease of mortification; then dissolution."

"Tut, tut," said Williams, cheerfully, "we never permit a patient to pronounce a prognosis upon his own case."

"Friend, my horse ran away, stumbled and fell upon me, and rolled over me in getting up; the viscera is crushed within me; breathing is difficult; speech painful; motion agonizing;—but you may examine and satisfy yourselves," said Dr. Day, still speaking cheerfully, though with great suffering.

His old friends proceeded gently to the examination, which resulted in their silently and perfectly coinciding in opinion with the patient himself.

Then, with Dr. Day and Traverse, they entered into a consultation, and agreed upon the best palliatives that could be administered; and begging that if in any manner, professionally or otherwise, they could serve their suffering friend, at any hour of the day or night, they might be summoned, they took leave.

As soon as they had gone, Clara, who had given way to a flood of tears, and regained her composure, rapped for admittance.

"Presently, dear daughter, presently," said the doctor, who then beckoning Traverse to stoop low, said:

"Do not let Clara sit up with me to-night; I foresee a night of great anguish, which I may not be able to repress, and which I would not have her witness. Promise you will keep her away."

"I promise," faltered the almost broken-hearted youth.

"You may admit her now," said the doctor, composing his convulsed countenance as best he could, lest the sight of his suffering should distress his daughter.

Clara entered and resumed her post at the side of the bed.

Traverse left the room to prepare the palliatives for his patient.

The afternoon waned. As evening approached, the fever, inflammation and pain arose to such a degree, that the doctor could no longer forbear betraying his excessive suffering, which was, besides, momentarily increasing; so he said to Clara:

"My child, you must now leave me and retire to bed. I must be watched by Traverse alone to-night."

And Traverse seeing her painful hesitation, between her extreme reluctance to leave him, and her wish to obey him, approached and murmured:

"Dear Clara, it would distress him to have you stay; he will be much better attended by me alone."

Clara still hesitated; and Traverse, beckoning his mother to come and speak to her, left her side.

Mrs. Rocke approached her and said:

"It must be so, dear girl, for you know that there are some cases in which sick men should be watched by men only, and this is one of them. I myself shall sit up to-night in the next room, within call."

"And may I not sit there beside you?" pleaded Clara.

"No, my dear love; as you can do your father no good, he desires that you should go to bed and rest. Do not distress him by refusing."

"Oh, and am I to go to bed and sleep while my dear father lies here suffering?—I cannot! Oh, I cannot!"

"My dear, yes, you must; and if you cannot sleep, you can be awake and pray for him."

Here the doctor, whose agony was growing unendurable, called out:

"Go, Clara! go at once, my dear."

She went back to the bedside and pressed her lips to his forehead, and put her arms around him and prayed:

"Oh, my dear father, may the blessed Saviour take you in his pitying embrace and give you ease to-night. Your poor Clara will pray for you as she never prayed for herself!"

"May the Lord bless you, my sweet child," said the doctor, lifting one hand painfully and laying it in benediction on her fair and graceful head.

Then she arose and left the room, saying to Mrs. Rocke as she went:

"Oh, Mrs. Rocke, only last evening we were so happy!—But if we have received good things at the hand of God, why should we not receive evil?"

"Yes, my child; but remember nothing is really evil that comes from His good hand," said Mrs.Rocke, as she attended Clara to the door.

His daughter had no sooner gone out of hearing than the doctor gave way to his irrepressible groans.

At a sign from Traverse Mrs. Rocke went and took up her position in the adjoining room.

Then Traverse subdued the light in the sick chamber, arranged the pillows of the couch, administered a sedative, and took up his post beside the bed, where he continued to watch and nurse the patient with un-wearied devotion.

At the dawn of day, when Clara rapped at the door, the doctor was in no condition to be seen by his daughter.

Clara was put off with some plausible excuse.

After breakfast his friends the physicians called and spent several hours in his room. Clara was told that she must not come in while they were there. And so, by one means and another, the poor girl was spared from witnessing those dreadful agonies which, had she seen them, must have so bitterly increased her distress.

In the afternoon, during a temporary mitigation of pain, Clara was admitted to see her father. But in the evening as his sufferings augmented, she was again, upon the same excuse they had used the preceding evening, dismissed to her chamber.

Then passed another night of suffering, during which Traverse never left him for an instant.

Towards morning the fever and pain abated, and he fell into a sweet sleep. About sunrise he awoke quite free from suffering. Alas! it was the ease he had predicted—the ease preceding dissolution.

"It is gone forever now, Traverse, my boy, thank God my last hours will be sufficiently free from pain to enable me to set my house in order. Before calling Clara in, I would talk to you alone. You will remain here until all is over?"

"Oh, yes, sir! yes, I would do anything on earth—anything for you, I would lay down my life this hour, if I could do so to save you from this bed of death."

famous last words

"Nay, do not talk so; your life belongs to others—to Clara and your mother. God doeth all things well. Better the ripened ear should fall, than the budding germ. I do not feel it hard to die, dear Traverse. Though the journey has been very pleasant, the goal is not unwelcome. Earth has been very sweet to me, but Heaven is sweeter."

"Oh! but we love you so! we love you so! you have so much to live for!" exclaimed Traverse, with an irrepressible burst of grief.

"Poor boy, life is too hopeful before you to make you a comforter by a deathbed. Yes, Traverse, I have much to live for, but more to die for. Yet not voluntarily would I have left you, though I know that I leave you in the hands of the Lord, and with every blessing and promise of his bountiful providence. Your love will console my child. My confidence in you makes me easy in committing her to your charge.

"Oh, Doctor Day, may the Lord so deal with my soul eternally, as I shall discharge this trust," said Traverse, earnestly.

"I know you will be true—I wish you to remain here with Clara and your mother for a few weeks, until the child's first violence of grief shall be over. Then you had best pursue the plan we laid out. Leave your good mother here to take care of Clara, and go you to the West, get into practice there, and at the end of a few years return and marry Clara. Traverse, there is one promise I would have of you."

"I give it before it is named, dear friend," said Traverse, fervently.

"My child is but seventeen; she is so gentle that her will is subject to that of all she loves, especially to yours. She will do anything in conscience that you ask her to do. Traverse, I wish you to promise me that you will not press her to marriage until she shall be at least twenty years old. And———"

"Oh, sir, I promise! Oh, believe me, my affection for Clara is so pure and so constant, as well as so confiding in her faith and so solicitous for her good, that, with the assurance of her love, and the privilege of visiting her and writing to her, I could wait many years if needful."

"I believe you, my dear boy. And the very promise I have asked of you is as much for your sake as for hers. No girl can marry before she is twenty without serious risk of life, and almost certain loss of health and beauty; that so many do so is one reason why there are such numbers of sickly and faded young wives. If Clara's constitution should be broken down by prematurely assuming cares and burdens of matrimony, you would be as unfortunate in having a sickly wife, as she would be in losing her health."

"Oh, sir, I promise you, that no matter how much I may wish to do so, I will not be tempted to make a wife of Clara, until she has attained the age you have prescribed. But at the same time, I must assure you that such is my love for her, that if accident should now make her an invalid for life she would be as dear—as dear—yes, much dearer to me if possible on that very account; and if I could not marry her for a wife, I should marry her only for the dear privilege of waiting on her night and day—Oh, believe this of me, and leave your dear daughter with an easy mind to my faithful care!" said Traverse, with a boyish blush suffusing his cheeks and tears filling his eyes.

"I do, Traverse! I do!—and now to other things."

"Are you not talking too much, dear friend!"

"No, no, I must talk while I have time. I was about to say that long ago, my will was made. Clara, you know, is the heiress of all I possess. You, as soon as you become her husband, will receive her fortune with her. I have made no reservation in her favor against you; for he to whom I can entrust the charge of my daughter's person, happiness and honor, I can also entrust with her fortune."

"Dear sir, I am glad, for Clara's sake, that she has a fortune; as for me, I hope you will believe that I would have gladly dispensed with it and worked for dear Clara all the days of my life."

"I do believe it. But this will was made, Traverse, three years ago, before any of us anticipated the present relations between you and my daughter, and while you were both still children. Therefore, I appointed my wife's half brother, Clara's only male relative, Colonel Le Noir, as her guardian. It is true, we have never been very intimate; for our paths in life widely diverged; nor has my Clara seen him within her recollection; for since her mother's death, which took place in her infancy, he has never been at our house. But he is a man of high reputation and excellent character. I have already requested Doctor Williams to write for him, so that I expect he will be here in a very few days. When he comes, Traverse, you will tell him that it is my desire that my daughter shall continue to reside in her present home, retaining Mrs. Rocke as her matronly companion. I have requested Doctor Williams to tell him the same thing, so that in the mouths of two witnesses my words may be established."

Now, Traverse had never in his life before heard the name of Colonel Le Noir; and therefore was in no position to warn the dying father who placed so much confidence in the high reputation of his brother-in-law, that his trust was miserably misplaced—that he was leaving his fair daughter and her large fortune to the tender mercies of an unscrupulous villain and a consummate hypocrite. So he merely promised to deliver the message with which he was charged by the dying father, for his daughter's guardian, and added that he had no doubt that Clara's uncle would consider that message a sacred command and obey it to the letter.

As the sun was now well up, the doctor consented that Mrs. Rocke and his daughter should be admitted.

Marah brought with her some wine-whey, that her patient drank, and from which he received temporary strength.

Clara was pale but calm; one could see at a glance that the poor girl was prepared for the worst, and had nerved her gentle heart to bear it with patience.

"Come hither, my little Clara," said the doctor as soon as he had been revived by his whey.

Clara came and kissed his brow, and sat beside him with her hands clasped in his.

"My little girl, what did our Saviour die for? First to redeem us, and also to teach us by his burial and resurrection that death is but a falling asleep in this world and an awakening in the next. Clara, after this, when you think of your father, do not think of him as lying in the grave; for he will not be there in his vacated body, no more than he will be in the trunk with his cast-off clothes. As the coat is the body's covering, so the body is the soul's garment and it is the *soul* that is the innermost and real man; it is my soul that is *me;* and that will not be in the earth but in Heaven! therefore do not think of me gloomily as lying in the grave, but cheerfully as living in Heaven—as living there with God and Christ and his saints, and with your mother, Clara, the dear wife of my youth, who has been waiting for me these many years. Think of me as being happy in that blessed society. Do not fancy that it is your duty to grieve, but on the contrary know that it is your duty to be as cheerful and happy as possible. Do you heed me, my daughter?"

"Oh, yes! yes, dear father!" said Clara, heroically repressing her grief.

"Seek for yourself, dear child, a nearer union with Christ and God. Seek it, Clara, until the spirit of God shall bear witness with your spirit that you are as a child of God! so shall you, as you come to lie where I do now, be able to say of your life and death, as I say with truth of mine—The journey has been pleasant, but the goal is blessed!———"

The doctor pressed his daughter's hand, and dropped suddenly into an easy sleep.

Mrs. Rocke drew Clara away, and the room was very still.

Sweet, beautiful and lovely as is the deathbed of a Christian, we will not linger too long beside it.

All day the good man's bodily life ebbed gently away. He spoke at intervals as he had strength given him, words of affection, comfort, and counsel to those around him.

Just as the setting sun was pouring his last rays into the chamber, Doctor Day laid his hand upon his child's head and blessed her. Then, closing his eyes, he murmured softly: "'Lord Jesus, into thy hands I resign my spirit;'" and with the sweet, deep, intense smile that had been so lovely in life, now so much lovelier in death, his pure spirit winged its flight to the realms of eternal bliss!

CHAPTER XXX

THE ORPHAN

"Let me die, father! I fear, I fear
    To fall in earth's terrible strife!"
"Not so, my child, for the crown must be won
    In the battle-field of life."
        —*Life and Death*

"HE HAS GONE to sleep again," said Clara, with a sigh of relief.

"He has gone to Heaven, my child," said Marah Rocke, softly.

The orphan started, gazed wildly on the face of the dead, turned ghastly pale, and with a low moan and suffocating sob, fell fainting into the motherly arms of Mrs. Rocke.

Marah beckoned Traverse, who lifted the insensible girl tenderly in his arms, and preceded by his mother, bore her to her chamber and laid her upon the bed.

Then Marah dismissed Traverse to attend to the duties owed to the remains of the beloved departed, while she herself stayed with Clara, using every means for restoration.

Clara opened her eyes at length, but in reviving to life also returned to grief. Dreadful to witness was the sorrow of the orphan girl. She had controlled her grief in the presence of her father, and while he lingered in life, only to give way now to its overwhelming force. Marah remained with her, holding her in her arms, weeping with her, praying for her, doing all that the most tender mother could do to soothe, console and strengthen the bleeding young heart.

The funeral of Dr. Day took place the third day from his decease, and was attended by all the gentry of the neighboring town and the county, in their own carriages, and by crowds who came on foot to pay the last tribute of respect to their beloved friend.

He was interred in the family burial ground, situated on a wooded hill up behind the homestead, and at the head of his last resting-place was afterwards erected a plain obelisk of white marble, with his name and the date of his birth and death, and the following inscription:

"HE IS NOT HERE, BUT IS RISEN."[1]

"When dear Clara comes to weep at her father's grave, these words will send her away comforted, and with her faith renewed," had been Traverse Rocke's secret thought, when giving directions for the inscription of this inspiring text.

On the morning of the day succeeding the funeral, while Clara, exhausted by the violence of her grief, lay prostrate upon her chamber couch, Mrs. Rocke and Traverse sat conversing in that once pleasant, now desolate, morning reading room.

"You know, dear mother, that by the doctor's desire, which should be considered sacred, Clara is still to live here, and you are to remain to take care of her. I shall defer my journey West until everything is settled to Clara's satisfaction, and she has in some degree recovered her equanimity. I must also have an interview and a good understanding with her guardian, for whom I have a message."

"Who *is* this guardian of whom I have heard you speak more than once, Traverse?" asked Marah.

"Dear mother, will you believe that I have forgotten the man's name; it was an uncommon name that I never heard before in my life, and, in the pressure of grief upon my mind, its exact identity escaped my memory; but that does not signify much, as he is expected hourly; and when he announces himself, either by card or word of mouth, I shall know, for I shall recognize the name the moment I see it written or hear it spoken. Let me see—it was something like Des Moines, De Vaughn, De Saule—or something of that sort. At all events, I'm sure I shall know it again the instant I see or hear it. And now, dear mother, I must ride up to Staunton to see some of the doctor's poor sick, that he left in my charge for as long as I stay here. I shall be back by three o'clock. I need not ask you to take great care of that dear suffering girl upstairs," said Traverse, taking his hat and gloves for a ride.

"I shall go and stay with her as soon as she wakes," answered Mrs. Rocke.

And Traverse, satisfied, went his way.

He had been gone perhaps an hour, when the sound of a carriage was heard below in the front of the house, followed soon by a loud rapping at the hall door.

"It is dear Clara's guardian," said Marah Rocke, rising and listening.

Soon a servant entered and placed a card in her hand, saying:

"The gentleman is waiting in the hall below, and asked to see the person that was in charge here, ma'am. So I fotch the card to *you*."

"You did right, John. Show the gentleman up here," said Marah; and as soon as the servant had gone she looked at the card, but failed to make it out. The name was engraved in Old English text, and in such a complete labyrinth, thicket and network of ornate flourishes, that no one who was not familiar at once with the name and the style could possibly have distinguished it.

"I do not think my boy would know *this* name at sight!" was Marah's thought, as she twirled the card in her hand, and stood waiting the entrance of the visitor, whose step was now heard coming up the stairs. Soon the door was thrown open, and the stranger entered.

Marah, habitually shy in the presence of strangers, dropped her eyes before she had fairly taken in the figure of a tall, handsome, dark-complexioned, distinguished-looking man somewhat past middle age, and arrayed in a rich military cloak, and carrying in his hand a military cap.

The servant who admitted him had scarcely retired, when Marah looked up, and her eyes and those of the stranger met—and—

"MARAH ROCKE!!!"

"COLONEL LE NOIR!!!"

Burst simultaneously from the lips of each.

Le Noir first recovered himself, and holding out both hands, advanced towards her with a smile as if to greet an old friend.

But Marah, shrinking from him in horror, turned and tottered to the farthest window, where leaning her head against the sash, she moaned:

"Oh, my heart! my heart! is *this* the wolf to whom my lamb must be committed!"

As she moaned these words, she was aware of a soft step at her side and a low voice murmuring:

"Marah Rocke, yes! the same beautiful Marah that as a girl of fifteen, twenty years ago, turned my head, led me by her fatal charms into the very jaws of death! the same lovely Marah with her beauty only ripened by time and exalted by sorrow."

With one surprised, indignant look, but without a word of reply,

Mrs. Rocke turned and walked composedly towards the door with the intention of quitting the room.

Colonel Le Noir saw and forestalled her purpose by springing forward, turning the key, and standing before the door.

"Forgive me, Marah, but I must have a word with you before we part," he said, in those soft, sweet, persuasive tones he knew so well how to assume.

Marah remembered that she was an honorable matron and an honored mother, that as such, fears and tremors and self-distrust in the presence of a villain, would not well become her; so calling up all the gentle dignity latent in her nature, she resumed her seat, and signing to the visitor to follow her example, she said, composedly:

"Speak on, Colonel Le Noir,—remembering, if you please, to *whom* you speak."

"I *do* remember, Marah! remember but too well!"

"They call me Mrs. Rocke who converse with me, sir."

"Marah, why this resentment? Is it possible that you can still be angry? Have I remained true to my attachment *all these years,* and sought you *throughout the world* to find this reception at last?"

"Colonel Le Noir, if this is all you had to say it was scarcely worth while to have detained me," said Mrs. Rocke, calmly.

But it is *not* all, my Marah. Yes, *I call you mine* by virtue of the strongest attachment man ever felt for woman. Marah Rocke, you were the only woman who ever inspired me with a feeling worthy to be called a passion——"

"——Colonel Le Noir, how dare you blaspheme this house of mourning by such sinful words! You forget where you stand and to whom you speak."

"I forget nothing, Marah Rocke, nor do I violate this sanctuary of sorrow,"—here he sunk his voice below his usual low tones—"when I speak of the passion that maddened my youth and withered my manhood—a passion whose intensity was its excuse for all extravagances and whose enduring constancy is its final, full justification."

Before he had finished this sentence, Marah Rocke had calmly arisen and pulled the bell-rope.

"What do you mean by that, Marah?" he inquired.

Before she replied, a servant, in answer to the bell, came to the door and tried the latch; and, finding it locked, rapped.

With a blush that mounted to his forehead, and with a half-suppressed imprecation, Colonel Le Noir went and unlocked the door, and admitted the man.

"John," said Mrs. Rocke, quietly, "show Colonel Le Noir to the apartment prepared for him, and wait his orders."

And, with a slight nod to the guest, she went calmly from the room.

Colonel Le Noir, unmindful of the presence of the servant, stood gazing in angry mortification after her. The flush on his brow had given way to the fearful pallor of rage or hate, as he muttered inaudibly:

"Insolent beggar! contradiction always confirms my half-formed resolutions; years ago I swore to possess that woman, and I will do it, if it be only to keep my oath and humble her insolence. She is *very* handsome still; she shall be my slave."

Then, perceiving the presence of John, he said:

"Lead the way to my room, sirrah, and then go and order my fellow to bring up my portmanteau."

John devoutly pulled his forelock as he bowed low, and then went out, followed by Colonel Le Noir.

Marah Rocke meanwhile had gained the privacy of her own chamber, where all her firmness deserted her.

Throwing herself into a chair, she clasped her hands and sat with blanched face and staring eyes, like a marble statue of despair.

"Oh, what shall I do? while this miscreant remains here? this villain whose very presence desecrates the roof and dishonors me? I would instantly leave the house but that I must not abandon poor Clara.

"I cannot claim the protection of Traverse, for I would not provoke him to wrath or run him into danger; nor indeed would I even permit my son to dream such a thing possible as that his mother could receive insult.

"Nor can I warn Clara of the unprincipled character of her guardian, for if she knew him as he is, she would surely treat him in such a way as to get his enmity—his dangerous, fatal enmity—doubly fatal since her person and property are legally at his disposal. Oh, my dove, my dove! that you should be in the power of this vulture. What shall I do, oh, Heaven!"

Marah dropped on her knees and finished her soliloquy with prayer. Then, feeling composed and strengthened, she went to Clara's room.

She found the poor girl lying awake and quietly weeping.

"Your guardian has arrived, love," she said, sitting down beside the bed and taking Clara's hand.

"Oh, must I get up and dress to see a stranger?" sighed Clara, wearily.

"No, love, you need not stir until it is time to dress for dinner; it will answer quite well if you meet your guardian at table," said Marah, who had particular reasons for wishing that Clara should first see Colonel Le Noir with other company to have an opportunity of observing him well and possibly forming an estimate of his character (as a young girl of her fine instincts might well do) before she should be exposed in a *tête-à-tête* to those deceptive blandishments he knew so well how to bring into play.

"That is a respite! Oh, dear Mrs. Rocke, you don't know how I dread to see any one!"

"My dear Clara, you must combat grief by prayer, which is the only thing that can overcome it," said Marah.

Mrs. Rocke remained with her young charge as long as she possibly could, and then she went down stairs to oversee the preparation of dinner.

And it was at the dinner-table that Marah, with the quiet and gentle dignity for which she was distinguished, introduced the younger members of the family to the guest, in these words:

"Your ward, Miss Day, Colonel Le Noir."

The Colonel bowed deeply, and raised the hand of Clara to his lips, murmuring some sweet, soft, silvery and deferentially inaudible words of condolence, sympathy, and melancholy pleasure, from which Clara, with a gentle bend of her head, withdrew to take her seat.

"Colonel Le Noir, my son, Doctor Rocke," said Marah, presenting Traverse.

The colonel stared superciliously, bowed with ironical depth, said he was "much honored," and turning his back on the young man, placed himself at the table.

During the dinner he exerted himself to be agreeable to Miss Day and Mrs. Rocke, but Traverse he affected to treat with supercilious neglect, or ironical deference.

Our young physician had too much self-respect to permit himself to be in any degree affected by this rudeness. And Marah, on her part, was glad, so that it did not trouble Traverse, that Le Noir should behave in this manner, so that Clara should be enabled to form some correct idea of his disposition.

When dinner was over, Clara excused herself and retired to her room, whither she was soon followed by Mrs. Rocke.

"Well, my dear, how do you like your guardian?" asked Marah, in a tone as indifferent as she could make it.

"I do not like him at all," exclaimed Clara, her gentle blue eyes flashing with indignation through their tears; "I do not like him at all, the scornful, arrogant, supercilious—Oh! I do not wish to use such strong language, or to grow angry when I am in such deep grief; but my dear father *could not* have known this man, or he *never would* have chosen him for my guardian! *do* you think he would, Mrs. Rocke?"

"My dear, your excellent father must have thought well of him, or he never would have intrusted him with so precious a charge. Whether your father's confidence in this man will be justified as far as *you* are concerned, time will show. Meanwhile, my love, as the guardian appointed by your father, you should treat him with respect; but so far as *reposing any trust in him goes, consult your own instincts!*"

"I shall! and I thank heaven that I have not got to go and live with Colonel Le Noir!" said Clara, fervently.

Mrs. Rocke sighed. She remembered that the arrangement that permitted Clara to live at her own home with her chosen friends was but a verbal one, not binding upon the guardian and executor, unless he chose to consider it so.

Their conversation was interrupted by the entrance of a servant with a message from Colonel Le Noir, expressing a hope that Miss Day felt better from her afternoon's repose, and desiring the favor of her company in the library.

Clara returned an answer pleading indisposition, and begging upon that account to be excused.

At tea, however, the whole family met again. As before, Colonel Le Noir exerted himself to please the ladies, and treated the young man with marked neglect. This conduct offended Miss Day to such a degree that she, being a girl of truth in thought, word and deed, could only exhibit towards the guest the most freezing politeness that was consistent with her position as hostess, and she longed for the time to come that should deliver their peaceful home and loving little circle from the unwelcome presence of this arrogant intruder.

"How can he imagine that I can be pleased with his deference and courtesy and elaborate compliments, when he permits himself to be so rude to Traverse? I hope Traverse will tell him of our engagement, which will, perhaps, suggest to him the propriety of reforming his manners, while he remains under a roof of which Traverse is the destined master!" said

Clara to herself, as she arose from the table, and with a cold bow, turned to retire from the room.

"And will not my fair ward give me a few hours of her company this evening?" inquired Colonel Le Noir, in an insinuating voice, as he took and pressed the hand of the doctor's orphan daughter.

"Excuse me, sir; but except at meal times, I have not left my room since"—here her voice broke down—she could not speak to him of her bereavement, or give way, in his presence, to her holy sorrow. "Besides, sir," she added, "Doctor Rocke, I know, has expressed to you his desire for an early interview."

"My fair young friend, Doctor Rocke, as you style the young man, will please be so condescending as to tarry the leisure of his most humble servant," replied the colonel, with an ironical bow in the direction of Traverse.

"Perhaps, sir, when you know that Doctor Rocke is charged with the last uttered will of my dear father, and that it is of more importance than you are prepared to anticipate, you may be willing to favor us all by granting this 'young man' an early audience," said Clara.

"The last uttered will! I had supposed that the will of my late brother-in-law was regularly drawn up and executed and in the hands of his confidential attorney at Staunton."

"Yes, sir, so it is; but I refer to my father's last dying wishes, his verbal directions entrusted to his confidential friend, Doctor Rocke," said Clara.

"Last verbal directions, entrusted to Doctor Rocke. Humph! humph! this would require corroborative evidence," said the colonel.

"Such corroborative evidence can be had, sir," said Clara, coldly; "and as I know that Doctor Rocke has already requested an interview for the sake of an explanation of these subjects, I must also join my own request to his, and assure you that by giving him an early opportunity of coming to an understanding with you, you will greatly oblige me."

"Then, undoubtedly, my sweet young friend, your wishes shall be commands——Eh! you—sir! Doctor—What's your name!—meet me in the library at ten o'clock to-morrow morning," said Le Noir, insolently.

"I have engagements, sir, that will occupy me between the hours of ten and three—before or after that period I am at your disposal," said Traverse, coldly.

"Pardieu! It seems to me that I am placed at yours!" replied the colonel, lifting his eyebrows; "but as I am so placed by the orders of my fair little tyrant here, so be it!—at nine to-morrow I am your most obedient servant!"

"At nine then, sir, I shall attend you," said Traverse, with a cold bow.

Clara slightly courtesied and withdrew from the room, attended by Mrs. Rocke.

Traverse, as the only representative of host, remained for a short time with his uncourteous guest, who, totally regardless of his presence, threw himself into an arm-chair, lighted a cigar, took up a book, and smoked and read.

Whereupon Traverse, seeing this, withdrew to the library to employ himself with finishing the arranging and tying up of certain papers, left to his charge by Doctor Day.

CHAPTER XXXI

THE ORPHAN'S TRIAL

"We met ere yet the world had come
To wither up the springs of youth,
Amid the holy joys of home,
And in the first warm blush of youth.
We parted as they never part
Whose tears are doomed to be forgot;
On, by what agony of heart,
Forget me not!—forget me not!"
—*Anonymous*

AT NINE O'CLOCK the next morning Traverse went to the library to keep his tryst with Colonel Le Noir.

Seated in the doctor's leathern chair, with his head thrown back, his nose erect, and his white and jeweled hand caressing his mustachioed chin, the colonel awaited the young man's communication.

With a slight bow, Traverse took a chair and drew it up to the table, seating himself, and after a little hesitation, commenced, and in a modest and self-respectful manner, announced that he was charged with the last verbal instructions from the doctor to the executor of his will.

Colonel Le Noir left off caressing his chin for an instant, and with a wave of his dainty hand, silently intimated that the young man should proceed.

Traverse then began and delivered the dying directions of the late doctor, to the effect that his daughter Clara Day should not be removed from her paternal mansion, but that she should be suffered to remain there, retaining as a matronly companion, her old friend Mrs. Marah Rocke.

"Umm! umm! very ingenious, upon my word," commented the colonel, still caressing his chin.

"I have now delivered my whole message, sir, and have only to add that I hope, for Miss Day's sake, there will be no difficulty thrown in the way of the execution of her father's last wishes, which are also, sir, very decidedly her own," said Traverse.

241

"Umm—doubtless they are—and also *yours* and your worthy *mother's.*

"Sir, Miss Day's will in this matter is certainly *mine.* Apart from the consideration of *her* pleasure, *my* wishes need not be consulted. As soon as I have seen Miss Day made comfortable, I leave for the Far West," said Traverse, with much dignity.

"Umm—and leave mamma here to guard the golden prize until your return, eh?" sneered the colonel.

"Sir, I do not—*wish* to understand you," said Traverse with a flushed brow.

"Possibly not, my excellent young friend," said the colonel, ironically; then rising from his chair and elevating his voice he cried—"But *I*, sir, understand *you* and your *mother* and your pretty *scheme,* perfectly! Very ingenious invention these 'last verbal instructions.' Very pretty plan to *entrap* an *heiress;* but it shall not avail you—adventurers that you are!— This afternoon, Sauter, the confidential attorney of my late brother-in-law, will be here with the will, which shall be read in the presence of the assembled household. If these last verbal directions are to be found duplicated in the *will,* very good! they shall be obeyed!—if *not,* they shall be discredited."

During this speech, Traverse stood with kindling eyes and blazing cheeks, scarcely able to master his indignation; yet, to his credit be it spoken, he did 'rule his own spirit' and reply with dignity and calmness.

"Colonel Le Noir, my testimony in regard to the last wishes of Dr. Day can, if necessary, be supported by other evidence—though I do not believe that *any* man who did not *himself* act in habitual disregard of truth, would wantonly question the veracity of *another.*

"Sɪʀ!—this to me!" exclaimed Le Noir, growing white with rage, and making a step towards the young man.

"Yes, Colonel Le Noir, *that to you!* and *this in addition:*—you have presumed to charge my mother (in connection with myself) with being an adventuress! with forming dishonorable 'schemes!' and in so charging her, Colonel Le Noir, you utter a *falsehood.*"

"Sɪʀʀᴀʜ!" cried Le Noir, striding towards Traverse and raising his hand over his head—with a fearful oath—"retract your words, or——"

Traverse calmly drew himself up, folded his arms, and replied coolly:

"I am no *brawler,* Colonel Le Noir; the pistol and the bowie knife are as strange to my hands as abusive epithets and profane language are to my lips; nevertheless, instead of retracting my words, I repeat and reiterate them. If you charge my mother with conspiracy, you utter a *falsehood*. As her son, I am in duty bound to say as much."

"VILLAIN!" gasped Le Noir, shaking his fist and choking with rage; "VILLAIN! you shall repent this in every vein of your body!"

Then seizing his hat, he strode from the room.

"Boaster!" said Traverse to himself, as he also left the library by another door.

Clara was waiting for him in the little parlor below.

"Well, well, dear Traverse?" said she, as he entered. "You have had the explanation with my guardian, and—he makes no objection to carrying out the last directions of my father, and our own wishes?—he is willing to leave me here?"

"My dear girl, Colonel Le Noir defers all decision until the reading of the will, which is to take place this afternoon," said Traverse, unwilling to add to her distress by recounting the disgraceful scene that had just taken place in the library.

"Oh! these delays! these delays! Heaven give me patience! Yet I do not know why I should be so uneasy! It is only a form! Of course, he will regard my father's wishes."

"I do not see well how he can avoid doing so, especially as Doctor Williams is another witness to them, and I shall request the doctor's attendance here this afternoon. Dear Clara, keep up your spirits! A few hours, now, and all will be well," said Traverse, as he drew on his gloves and took his hat to go on his morning round of calls.

An early dinner was ordered, for the purpose of giving ample time in the afternoon for the reading of the will.

Owing to the kindly forbearance of each member of this little family, their meeting with their guest at the table was not so awkward as it might have been rendered. Mrs. Rocke had concealed the insults that had been offered her. Traverse had said nothing of the affronts put upon him. So that each, having only their own private injuries to resent, felt free in forbearing. Nothing but this sort of prudence on the part of individuals rendered their meeting around one board possible.

While they were still at the table, the attorney, Mr. Sauter, with Doctors Williams and Dawson, arrived, and was shown into the library.

And very soon after the dessert was put upon the table, the family left it, and, accompanied by Colonel Le Noir, adjourned to the library. After the usual salutations, they arranged themselves along each side of an extension table, at the head of which the attorney placed himself.

In the midst of a profound silence the will was opened and read. It was dated three years before.

The bulk of his estate, after the paying of a few legacies, was left to his esteemed brother-in-law, Gabriel Le Noir, in trust for his only daughter, Clara Day, until the latter should attain the age of twenty-one, at which period she was to come into possession of the property. Then followed the distribution of the legacies. Among the rest the sum of a thousand dollars left to his young friend, Traverse Rocke, and another thousand to his esteemed neighbor, Marah Rocke. Gabriel Le Noir was appointed sole executor of the will, trustee of the property, and guardian of the heiress.

At the conclusion of the reading Mr. Sauter folded the document and laid it upon the table.

Colonel Le Noir arose, and said:

"The will of the late Doctor Day has been read in your presence. I presume you all heard it, and that there can be no mistake as to its purport. All that remains now is to act upon it. I shall claim the usual privilege of twelve months before administering upon the estate or paying the legacies. In the meantime, I shall assume the charge of my ward's person, and convey her to my own residence, known as the Hidden House. Mrs. Rocke," he said, turning towards the latter, "your presence and that of your young charge is no longer required here. Be so good as to prepare Miss Day's traveling trunks, as we set out from this place to-morrow morning."

Mrs. Rocke started, looked wistfully in the face of the speaker, and seeing that he was in determined earnest, turned her appealing glances toward Traverse and Doctor Williams.

As for Clara, her face, previously blanched with grief, was now flushed with indignation. In her sudden distress and perplexity, she knew not at once what to do. Whether to utter a protest or continue silent— whether to leave the room or remain. Her embarrassment was relieved by Traverse, who, stooping, whispered to her:

"Be calm, love; all shall be well. Doctor Williams is about to speak."

And at that moment Doctor Williams arose, and said:

"I have, Colonel Le Noir, to endorse a dying message from Doctor Day, entrusted to my young friend here to be delivered to you, to the effect that it was his last desire and request that his daughter, Miss Clara Day, should be permitted to reside during the term of her minority in this her patrimonial home, under the care of her present matronly friend,

Mrs. Marah Rocke. Doctor Rocke and myself are here to bear testimony to these, the last wishes of the departed—which wishes, I believe, also express the desires of his heiress."

"Oh, yes! yes!" said Clara, earnestly. "I do very much desire to remain in my own home among my own familiar friends. My dear father only consulted my comfort and happiness when he left these instructions."

"There can be therefore no reason why Miss Day should be disturbed in her present home," said Traverse.

Colonel Le Noir smiled grimly, saying:

"I am sorry, Doctor Williams, to differ with you, or to distress Miss Day! But if, as she says, her lamented father consulted her pleasure, in those last instructions, he certainly consulted nothing else—not the proprieties of conventionalism, the opinion of the world, nor the future welfare of his daughter. Therefore, as a man of Doctor Day's high position and character, in his sane moments, never could have made such a singular arrangement, I am forced to the conclusion that he could not, at the time of giving those instructions, have been in his right mind. Consequently, I cannot venture to act upon any 'verbal instructions,' however well attested, but shall be guided in every respect by the will, executed while yet the testator was in sound body and mind."

"Doctor Rocke and myself are both physicians competent to certify that, at the time of leaving these directions, our respected friend was perfectly sound in mind at least," said Doctor Williams.

"That, sir, I repeat, I contest. And acting upon the authority of the will, I shall proceed to take charge of my ward as well as of her estate. And as I think this house, under all the circumstances, a very improper place for her to remain, I shall convey her without delay to my own home. Mrs. Rocke, I believe I requested you to see to the packing of Miss Day's trunks."

"Oh, heaven, shall this wrong be permitted," ejaculated Marah.

"Mrs. Rocke, I will not go unless absolutely forced to do so by a decree of the court! I shall get Doctor Williams to make an appeal for me to the Orphans' Court," said Clara, by way of encouraging her friend.

"My dear Miss Day, that, I hope, will not be required. Colonel Le Noir acts under a misapprehension of the circumstances. We must enter into more explanations with him. In the meantime, my dear young lady, it is better that you should obey him, for the present, at least, so far as retiring from the room," said Doctor Williams.

Clara immediately arose, and requesting Mrs. Rocke to accompany her, withdrew from the library.

Doctor Williams then said:

"I advised the retirement of the young lady, having a communication to make, the hearing of which in a mixed company, might have cost her an innocent blush. But first I would ask you, Colonel Le Noir—what are those circumstances to which you allude which render Miss Day's residence here, in her patrimonial mansion with her old and faithful friends, so improper?" inquired Doctor Williams, courteously.

"The growing intimacy, sir, between herself and a very objectionable party—this young man Rocke!" replied Colonel Le Noir.

"Ah! and is that all?"

"It is enough, sir!" said Colonel Le Noir, loftily.

"Then, suppose I should inform you, sir, that this young man, Doctor Rocke, was brought up and educated at Doctor Day's cost, and under his own immediate eye?"

"Then, sir, you would only inform me that an eccentric gentleman of fortune had done—what eccentric gentlemen of fortune *will* sometimes do—educated a pauper."

At this opprobious epithet, Traverse, with flushed face started to his feet.

"Sit down, my boy, sit down; leave me to deal with this man," said Doctor Williams, forcing Traverse back into his seat. Then turning to Colonel Le Noir, he said:

"But, suppose, sir, that such was the estimation in which Doctor Day held the moral and intellectual worth of his young *protégé,* that he actually gave him his daughter?"

"I cannot suppose an impossibility, Doctor Williams," replied Colonel Le Noir, haughtily.

"Then, sir, I have the pleasure of startling you a little by a prodigy, that you denominate an impossibility! Clara Day and Traverse Rocke were bethrothed with full knowledge and cordial approbation of the young lady's father!"

"Impossible! preposterous! I shall countenance no such ridiculous absurdity!" said Colonel Le Noir, growing red in the face.

"Miss Day, Doctor Rocke, Mrs. Rocke, and myself are witnesses to that fact."

"The young lady and the young man are parties immediately concerned—they cannot be received as witnesses in their own case; Mrs. Rocke is too much in their interest for her evidence to be taken; you, sir, I consider the dupe of these cunning conspirators—mother and son," replied Colonel Le Noir, firmly.

"Tut," said Doctor Williams, almost out of patience, "I do not depend upon the words of Miss Day and her friends, although I hold their veracity to be above question; I had Doctor Day's dying words to the same effect. And he mentioned the existing bethrothal as the very reason why Clara should remain here in the care of her future mother-in-law."

"Then, sir, that the doctor should have spoken and acted *thus,* is only another and a stronger reason for believing him to have been deranged in his last moments! You need give yourself no further trouble! I shall act upon the authority of this instrument which I hold in my hand," replied Colonel Le Noir, haughtily.

"Then, as the depository of the dying man's last wishes and as the next friend of his injured daughter, I shall make an appeal to the Orphans' Court," said Doctor Williams, coldly.

"You can do as you please about that; but in the meanwhile, acting upon the authority of the will, I shall tomorrow morning set out with my ward for my own home."

"There may be time to arrest that journey," said Doctor Williams, arising and taking his hat to go.

In the passage he met Mrs. Rocke.

"Dear Doctor Williams," said Mrs. Rocke, earnestly, "pray come up to poor Clara's room, and speak to her, if you can possibly say anything to comfort her; she is weeping herself into a fit of illness at the bare thought of being, so soon after her dreadful bereavement, torn away from her home and friends."

"Tut! tut! no use in weeping! all will yet be right!"

"You have persuaded that man to permit her to remain here, then?" said Marah gladly.

"Persuaded *him!* no, nor even undertaken to do so! I never saw him before to-day, yet I would venture to say, from what I have now seen of him, that he never was *persuaded* by any agent except his own passions and interests, to any act whatever. No, I have endeavored to show him that we have *law* as well as justice on our side, and even now I am afraid I shall have to take the case before the Orphans' Court before I can convince him. He purposes removing Clara to-morrow morning. I will endeavor to see the

Judge of the Orphans' Court to-night, take out a *habeas corpus,* ordering Le Noir to bring his ward into court, and serve it on him as he passes through Staunton on his way home."

"But is there no way of preventing him from taking Clara away from the house to-morrow morning?"

"No *good* way. No, Madam, it is best that all things should be done decently and in order. I advise you, as I shall also advise my young friends, Traverse and Clara, not to injure their own cause by unwise impatience or opposition. We should go before the Orphans' Court with the very best aspect."

"Come, then, and talk to Clara. She has the most painful antipathy to the man who claims the custody of her person, as well as the most distressing reluctance to leaving her dear home and friends; and all this, in addition to her recent heavy affliction, almost overwhelms the poor child," said Mrs. Rocke, weeping.

"I will go at once and do what I can to soothe her," said Doctor Williams, following Mrs. Rocke, who led him up to Clara's room.

They found her prostrate upon her bed, crushed with grief.

"Come, come, my dear girl, this is too bad! It is not like the usual noble fortitude of our Clara," said the old man, kindly taking her hand.

"Oh, Doctor, forgive—forgive me! but my courage must have been very small, for I fear it is all gone. But then, indeed, everything comes on me at once. My dear, dear father's death; then the approaching departure and expected long absence of Traverse! All that was grievous enough to bear; and now to be torn away from the home of my childhood, and from the friend that has always been a mother to me, and by a man, from whom every true, good instinct of my nature teaches me to shrink. I, who have always had full liberty in the house of my dear father, to be forced away against my will by this man, as if I were his slave!" exclaimed Clara, bursting into fresh tears of indignation and grief.

"Clara, my dear, dear girl! this impatience and rebellion is so unlike your gentle nature, that I can scarcely recognize you for the mild and dignified daughter of my old friend! Clara, if the saints in Heaven could grieve at anything, I should think your dear father would be grieved to see you thus!" said the old man in gentle rebuke, that immediately took effect upon the meek and conscientious maiden.

"Oh! I feel—I feel that I am doing very wrong, but I cannot help it. I scarcely know *myself* in this agony of mingled grief, indignation and terror, yes, *terror,* for every instinct of my nature teaches me to distrust and fear that man, in whom my father must have been greatly deceived before he could have intrusted him with the guardianship of his only child!"

"I think that quite likely," said the old man, "yet, my dear, even in respect to your dear father's memory, you must try to bear this trial patiently."

"Oh, yes! I know I must! Dear father, if you can look down and see me now, forgive your poor Clara, her anger and her impatience. She will try to be worthy of the rearing you have given her, and to bear even this great trial, with the spirit worthy of your daughter!" said Clara, within her own heart, then speaking up, she said, "You shall have no more reason to reprove me, Doctor Williams."

"That is my brave girl! That is my dear Clara Day! And now, when your guardian directs you to prepare youself for your journey, *obey him*— go with him without making any objection. I purpose to arrest your journey at Staunton with a *habeas corpus* that he dare not resist, and which shall compel him to bring you into the Orphans' Court! There our side shall be heard, and the decision will rest with the judge."

"And all will be well! Oh, say that, sir! to give me the courage to act with becoming docility," pleaded Clara.

"I have not a doubt in this world that it *will* all be right! for however Colonel Le Noir may choose to disregard the last wishes of your father, as attested by myself and young Rocke, I have not the least idea that the judge will pass them over! On the contrary, I feel persuaded that he will confirm them by sending you back here to your beloved home."

"Oh, may heaven grant it," said Clara. "You do indeed give me new life!"

"Yes, yes, be cheerful, my dear; trust in Providence, and expect nothing short of the best. And now I dare not tarry longer with you, for I must see the judge at his house this night! Good-bye, my dear! keep up a good heart!" said the old man, cheerfully, pressing her hand and taking his leave.

Mrs. Rocke accompanied him to the hall-door.

"My dear Madam, keep up *your* spirits also for the sake of your young charge! Make her go to bed early! To-morrow, when she thinks she is about to be torn from you forever, remind her in her ear that I shall meet the carriage at Staunton with a power that shall turn the horses' heads."

And so saying, the worthy gentleman departed.

As Marah Rocke looked after him, she also saw with alarm that Colonel Le Noir had mounted his horse and galloped off in the direction of Staunton, as if impelled by the most urgent haste.

She returned to the bedside of Clara, and left her no more that night. As the colonel did not return to supper, they, the family party, had their tea in Clara's room.

Late at night Mrs. Rocke heard Colonel Le Noir come into the house and enter his chamber.

Poor Clara slept no more that night; anxiety, despite of all her efforts, kept her wide awake. Yet, though anxious and wakeful, yet by prayer and endeavor she had brought her mind into a patient and submissive mood, so that when a servant knocked at her door in the morning with a message from Colonel Le Noir that she should be ready to set forth immediately after breakfast, she replied that she should obey him, and without delay she arose and commenced her toilet.

All the family met for the last time around the board. The party was constrained. The meal was a gloomy one. On rising from the table Colonel Le Noir informed his ward that his traveling carriage was waiting, and that her baggage was already on, and requested her to put on her bonnet and mantle, and take leave of her servants.

Clara turned to obey. Traverse went to her side, and whispered:

"Take courage, dear love; my horse is saddled; I shall ride in attendance upon the carriage, whether that man likes it or not; nor lose sight of you for one moment until we meet Williams with his *habeas corpus.*"

"Nor even then, dear Traverse! nor even then! You will attend me to the court and be ready to take me back to this dear, dear home!" murmured Clara, in reply.

"Yes, yes, dear girl. There, be cheerful," whispered the young man, as he pressed her hand and released it.

Colonel Le Noir had been a silent but frowning spectator of this little scene, and now that Clara was leaving the room, attended by Mrs. Rocke, he called the latter back, saying:

"You will be so kind as to stop here a moment, Mrs. Rocke, and you also, young man."

The mother and son paused to hear what he should have to say.

"I believe it is the custom here, in discharging domestics, to give a month's warning, or, in lieu of that, to pay a month's wages in advance. There, woman, is the money. You will oblige me by leaving the house to-day, together with your son and all your other trumpery—as the premises are put in charge of an agent, who will be here this afternoon, clothed with authority to eject all loiterers and intruders."

While the colonel spoke, Marah Rocke gazed at him in a panic from which she seemed unable to rouse herself, until Traverse gravely took her hand, saying:

"My dear mother, let me conduct you from the presence of this man, who does not know how to behave himself towards women. Leave me to talk with him, and do you, dear mother, go to Miss Day, who I know is waiting for you."

Marah Rocke mechanically complied, and allowed Traverse to lead her from the room.

When he returned, he went up to Colonel Le Noir, and standing before him and looking him full and sternly in the face, said, as sternly:

"Colonel Le Noir, my mother will remain *here* and abide the decision of the Orphans' Court; until *that* has been pronounced, she does not *stir* at your or any man's bidding."

"Villain! out of my way!" sneeered Le Noir, endeavoring to pass him.

"Sir, in consideration of your age, which should be venerable, your position which should prove you honorable, and of this sacred house of mourning in which you stand, I have endeavored to meet all the insults you have offered me with forbearance. But, sir, I am here to defend my mother's rights and to protect her from insult. And I tell you plainly that you have affronted her for the very last time. One more *word* or *look* of insult levelled at Marah Rocke, and neither your age, position, nor this sacred roof shall protect you from personal chastisement at the hands of her son."

Le Noir, who had listened in angry scorn, with many an ejaculation of contempt, now at the conclusion which so galled his pride, broke out furiously, with:

"Sir, you are a bully! If you were a gentleman I could *call you out*."

"And I should not come if you did, sir. Dueling is un-Christian, barbarous and abominable in the sight of God and all good men. For the rest you may call me anything you please; but do not again insult my mother, for if you do, I shall hold it a Christian duty to teach you better manners," said Traverse, cooly taking his hat and and walking from the room.

He mounted his horse, and stood ready to attend Clara to Staunton.

Colonel Le Noir ground his teeth in impotent rage, muttering:

"Take care, young man. I shall live to be revenged upon you yet for these affronts!"

And his dastard heart burned with the fiercer malignity that he had not dared to meet the eagle eye or encounter the strong arm of the upright and stalwart young man. Gnashing his teeth with ill-suppressed fury, he strode into the hall just as Mrs. Rocke and Clara in her traveling dress, descended the stairs.

Clara threw her arms around Mrs. Rocke's neck, and weeping, said:

"Good-bye! dear, best friend! good-bye! Heaven grant it may not be for long. Oh, pray for me that I may be sent back to you!"

"May the Lord have you in His holy keeping, my child! I shall pray until I hear from you!" said Marah, kissing and releasing her.

Colonel Le Noir then took her by the hand, led her out, and put her into the carriage.

Just before entering, Clara had turned to take a last look at her old home; all, friends and servants, noticed the sorrowful, anxious, almost despairing look of her pale face, which seemed to ask:

"Ah, shall I ever, ever return to you, dear old home, and dear, familiar friends?"

In another instant, she had disappeared within the carriage—which immediately rolled off.

As the carriage was heavily laden, and the road was in a very bad condition, it was a full hour before they reached the town of Staunton. As the carriage drew up for a few moments before the door of the principal hotel, and Colonel Le Noir was in the act of stepping out, a sheriff's officer, accompanied by Dr. Williams, approached, and served upon the Colonel a writ of *habeas corpus,* commanding him to bring his ward, Clara Day, into court.

Colonel Le Noir laughed scornfully, saying:

"And do any of you imagine this will serve your purposes? Ha! ha! the most that it can do will be to delay my journey for a few hours, until the decision of the judge, which will only serve to confirm my authority beyond all future possibility of questioning."

"We will see that," said Dr. Williams.

"Drive to the court-house," ordered Colonel Le Noir.

And the carriage, attended by Traverse Rocke, Dr. Williams, and the sheriff's officer, each on horseback, drove thither.

And now, reader, I will not trouble you with a detailed account of this trial. Clara, clothed in deep mourning, and looking pale and terrified, was led into the court-room on the arm of her guardian. She was followed closely by her friends, Traverse Rocke and Dr. Williams, each of whom whispered encouraging words to the orphan.

As the court had no pressing business on its hands, the case was immediately taken up, the will was read and attested by the attorney, who had drawn it up, and the witnesses who had signed it. Then the evidence of Dr. Williams and Dr. Rocke was taken concerning the last verbal instructions of the deceased. The case occupied about three hours, at the end of which the judge gave a decision in favor of Colonel Le Noir.

This judgment carried consternation to the heart of Clara and all her friends.

Clara herself sank nearly fainting in the arms of her old friend, the venerable Dr. Williams.

Traverse, in bitterness of spirit, approached and bent over her.

Colonel Le Noir spoke to the judge.

"I deeply thank your honor for the prompt hearing and equally prompt decision of this case, and I will beg your honor to order the sheriff and his officers to see your judgment carried into effect, as I foresee violent opposition, and wish to prevent trouble."

"Certainly. Mr. Sheriff, you will see that Colonel Le Noir is put in possession of his ward and protected in that right until he shall have placed her in security," said the judge.

Clara, on hearing these words, lifted her head from the old man's bosom, nerved her gentle heart, and in a clear, sweet, steady voice, said:

"It is needless precaution, your honor; my friends are no law-breakers; and since the Court has given me into the custody of my guardian, I do not dispute its judgment—I yield myself up to Colonel Le Noir."

"You do well, young lady," said the judge.

"I am pleased, Miss Day, to see that you understand and perform your duty; believe me, I shall do all that I can to make you happy," said Colonel Le Noir.

Clara replied by a gentle nod; and then, with a slight blush mantling her pure cheeks, she advanced a step, and placed herself immediately in front of the judge, saying:

"But there is a word that I would speak to your honor."

"Say on, young lady," said the judge.

And as she stood there in her deep mourning dress, with her fair hair unbound and floating softly around her pale, sweet face, every eye in that court was spell-bound by her almost unearthly beauty. Before proceeding with what she was about to say she turned upon Traverse a look that brought him immediately to her side.

"Your honor," she began, in a low, sweet, clear tone, "I owe it to Doctor Rocke here present, who has been sadly misrepresented to you, to say (what under less serious circumstances my girl's heart would shrink from avowing so publicly) that I *am* his betrothed wife—sacredly betrothed to him by almost the last act of my dear father's life. I hold this engagement to be so holy that no earthly tribunal can break or disturb it. And while I bend to your honor's decision, and yield myself to the custody of my legal guardian for the period of my minority, I here declare to all who may be interested, that I hold my hand and heart irrevocably pledged to Doctor Rocke, and that, as his betrothed wife, I shall consider myself bound to correspond with him regularly, and to receive him as often as he shall seek my society, until my majority, when I and all that I posess will become his own. And those words I force myself to speak, your honor, both in justice to my dear lost father and his friend Traverse Rocke, and also to myself, that hereafter no one may venture to accuse me of clandestine proceedings, or distort my actions into improprieties, or in any manner call in question the conduct of my father's daughter." And, with another gentle bow, Clara retired to the side of her old friend.

"You are likely to have a troublesome charge in your ward," said the sheriff apart to the colonel, who shrugged his shoulders by way of reply.

The heart of Traverse was torn by many conflicting passions, emotions and impulses; there was indignation at the decision of the court; grief for the loss of Clara, and dread for her future!

One instant he felt a temptation to denounce the guardian as a villain and to charge the judge with being a corrupt politician, whose decisions were swayed by party interests.

The next moment he felt an impulse to catch Clara up in his arms, fight his way through the crowd and carry her off. But all these wild emotions, passions and impulses he succeeded in controlling.

Too well he knew that rage, do violence, or commit extravagances as he might, the law would take its course all the same.

While his heart was torn in this manner, Colonel Le Noir was urging the departure of his ward. And Clara came to her lover's side and said, gravely and sweetly:

"The law, you see, has decided against us, dear Traverse! let us bend gracefully to a decree that we cannot annul; it cannot at least, alter our sacred relations; nor can anything on earth shake our steadfast faith in each other; let us take comfort in that, and in the thought that the years will surely roll round at length and bring the time that shall re-unite us."

"Oh, my angel-girl! my angel-girl! your patient heroism puts me to the blush, for my heart is crushed in my bosom and my firmness quite gone!" said Traverse, in a broken voice.

"You will gain firmness, dear Traverse. 'Patient!' *I* patient! you should have heard me last night! I was so impatient that Doctor Williams had to lecture me. But it would be strange if one did not learn *something* by suffering. *I* have been trying all night and day to school my heart to submission, and I hope I have succeeded, Traverse. Bless me and bid me good-bye."

"The Lord forever bless and keep you, my own dear angel, Clara!" burst from the lips of Traverse: "the Lord abundantly bless you!"

"*And you!*" said Clara.

"Good-bye! good-bye!"

"Good-bye."

And thus they parted.

Clara was hurried away and put into the carriage by her guardian.

Ah! no one but the Lord knew how much it had cost that poor girl to maintain her fortitude during that trying scene. She had controlled herself for the sake of her friends. But now, when she found herself in the carriage, her long strained nerves gave way—she sank exhausted and prostrated into the corner of her seat, in the utter collapse of woe.

But leaving the travelers to pursue their journey, we must go back to Traverse.

Almost broken-hearted, Traverse returned to Willow Heights to convey the sad tidings of his disappointment to his mother's ear.

Marah Rocke was so overwhelmed with grief at the news, that she was for several hours incapable of action.

The arrival of the house-agent was the first event that recalled her to her senses.

She aroused herself to action, and assisted by Traverse, set to work to pack up her own and his wardrobe, and other personal effects.

And the next morning Marah Rocke was re-established in her cottage.

And the next week, having equally divided their little capital, the mother and son parted—Traverse, by her express desire, keeping to his original plan, set out for the Far West.

CHAPTER XXXII

OLD HURRICANE STORMS

"At this sir knight flamed up with ire!
His great chest heaved, his eyes flashed fire,
The crimson that suffused his face,
To deepest purple now gave place." [1]

WHO CAN DESCRIBE the frenzy of Old Hurricane upon discovering the fraud that had been practiced upon him by Black Donald?

It was told him the next morning in his tent, at his breakfast table, in the presence of his assembled family, by the Reverend Mr. Goodwin.

Upon first hearing it, he was incapable of anything but blank staring, until it seemed as though his eyes must start from their sockets!

Then his passion, "not loud but deep," found utterance only in emphatic thumps of his walking-stick upon the ground.

Then as the huge emotion worked upwards, it broke out in grunts, groans and inarticulate exclamations.

Finally it burst forth as follows:

"Ugh! ugh! ugh! Fool! dolt! blockhead! *brute* that I've been!—I wish somebody would punch my wooden head!—I didn't think the demon himself could have deceived me so! Ugh!—Nobody *but* the demon *could* have done it. And he *is* the demon! the very demon himself!—he does not *disguise* he *transforms* himself. Ugh! ugh! ugh! that I should have been such a donkey."

"Sir, compose yourself, we are all liable to suffer deception," said Mr. Goodwin.

"Sir," broke forth Old Hurricane, in fury—"that wretch has *eaten at my table! has drunk wine with me!! has slept in my bed!!!* Ugh! ugh!! ugh!!!"

"Believing him to be what he seemed, sir, you extended to him the rights of hospitality; you have nothing to blame yourself with!"

256

places him below slaves

"Demmy, sir, I did *more* than that!—I have coddled him up with negusses! I've pampered him up with possets[2] and put him to sleep in my own bed! Yes, sir! and more!—look there at Mrs. Condiment, sir, the way in which SHE worshipped that villain was a sight to behold," said Old Hurricane, jumping up and stamping around the tent in fury.

"Oh, Mr. Goodwin, how could *I* help it when I thought he was such a precious saint?" whimpered the old lady.

"Yes, sir, when 'his Reverence' would be tired with delivering a long-winded mid-day discourse, Mrs. Condiment, sir, would take him into her own tent, make him lie down on her own sacred cot, and set my niece to bathing his head with cologne and *her* maid to fanning him, while *she herself* prepared an iced sherry cobbler for his Reverence. Aren't you ashamed of yourself, Mrs. Condiment, mum," said Old Hurricane, suddenly stopping before the poor old woman, in anger and scorn.

"Indeed I'm sure if I'd know it was Black Donald, I'd no more have suffered *him* inside my tent than I would have Satan."

"Demmy, mum, you had Satan there as well. Who but Satan could have tempted you all to disregard *me,* your lawful lord and master, as you every one of you did for the wretch's sake. Hang it, parson, I wasn't the master of my own house, nor the head of my own family. Precious Father Gray was. Black Donald was. Oh, you shall hear," cried Old Hurricane, in a frenzy.

"Pray, sir, be patient and do not blame the woman for being no wiser than you were yourself," said Mr. Goodwin.

"Tah! tah! tah! one act of folly is a contingency to which any man may for once in his life be liable, but folly is a woman's normal condition. You shall hear, you shall hear. Hang it, sir, everybody had to give away to Father Gray, everything was for Father Gray. *Precious* Father Gray. *Excellent* Father Gray. *Saintly* Father Gray. It was Father Gray here and Father Gray there, and Father Gray everywhere and always. He ate with us all day and slept with us all night. The coolest cot in the dryest nook of the tent at night, the shadiest seat at the table by day, were always for his Reverence, the nicest tit-bits of the choicest dishes, the middle slices of the fish, the breast of the young ducks, and the wings of the chickens, mealiest potatoes, the juciest tomatoes, the tenderest roasting ear, the most delicate custards and the freshest fruit always for his Reverence. *I* had to put up with the necks of poultry, and the tails of fishes, watery potatoes, specked apples, and scorched custards; and if I dared to touch anything better before his precious Reverence had eaten and was filled, Mrs. Condiment, there, would look as sour as if she had bitten an unripe lemon, and Cap would tread on my gouty toe. Mrs. Condiment, mum, I don't know how you can look me in the face," said Old Hurricane, savagely—a very unnecessary reproach, since poor Mrs. Condiment had not ventured to look any one in the face since the discovery of the fraud of which she, as well as others, had been an innocent victim.

"Come, come, my dear Major, there is no harm done to you or your family; therefore take patience," said Mr. Goodwin.

"Demmy, sir; I beg your pardon parson, I *won't* take patience. You don't know. Hang it, man, at last they got me to give up one half of my own blessed bed to his precious Reverence—the *best* half which the fellow always took, right out of the middle, leaving me to sleep on both sides of him if I could. Think of it: *me,* Ira Warfield, sleeping between the sheets, night after night, with Black Donald! Ugh! ugh! ugh! Oh, for some lethean draught, that I might drink and forget. Sir, I *won't* be patient! patience would be a sin. Mrs. Condiment, mum, I desire that you will send in your account and supply yourself with a new situation. You and I cannot agree any longer. You'll be putting me to bed with Beelzebub next!" exclaimed Old Hurricane, beside himself with indignation.

Mrs. Condiment sighed, and wiped her eyes under her spectacles.

The worthy minister, seriously alarmed, came to him, and said:

"My dear, dear Major, do not be unjust—consider, she is an old faithful domestic, who has been in your service forty years—whom you could not live without. I say it under advisement—*whom you could not live without!*"

"Hang it, sir, not live *with.* Think of her helping to free the prisoners— actually taking Black Donald—*precious Father Gray*—into their cell, and leaving them together to hatch their—I beg your pardon—*horrid* plots."

"But, sir, instead of punishing the innocent victim of his deception, let us be merciful and thank the Lord that, since those men *were* delivered from prison, they were freed without bloodshed; for remember that neither the warden, nor any of his men, nor any one else, has been personally injured."

"Hang it, sir! I wish they had cut all our throats, to teach us more discretion," broke forth Old Hurricane.

"I am afraid that the lesson so taught would have come too late to be useful," smiled the pastor.

"Well, it hasn't come too late now. Mrs. Condiment, mum, mind what I tell you: as soon as we return to Hurricane Hall, send in your accounts and seek a new home. I am not going to suffer myself to be set at naught any longer," exclaimed Old Hurricane, bringing down his cane with an emphatic thump.

The sorely troubled minister was again about to interfere, when, as the worm, if trodden upon, will turn, Mrs. Condiment herself spoke up, saying:

"Lor, Major Warfield, sir, there were others deceived besides *me,* and as for myself, I never can think of the risk I've run without growing cold all over."

"Serves you right, mum, for your officiousness and obsequiousness, and toadying to—*precious Mr. Gray!* serves you doubly right for famishing me at my own table."

"Uncle," said Capitola, "'Honor bright!' 'Fair play is a jewel.' If you and I, who have seen Black Donald before, failed to recognize that stalwart athlete in a seemingly old and sickly man, how could you expect Mrs. Condiment to do so, who never saw him but once in her life, and then was so much frightened that she instantly fainted?"

"Pah! Pah! Pah! Cap, hush!! You, all of you disgust me, except Black Donald! I begin to respect *him!* Confound me, if I don't take in all the offers I have made for his apprehension; I'll nominate him to represent us in the National Congress!—for, of all the fools that ever I have met in my life, the people of this county are the greatest! and fools should at least be represented by one clever man—and Black Donald is the very fellow! He is decidedly the ablest man in this congressional district."

"Except yourself, dear uncle!" said Capitola.

"Except nobody, *Miss* Impudence! least of all *me!* The experience of the last week has convinced me that I ought to have a cap and bells awarded me by public acclamation!" said Old Hurricane, stamping about in fury.

The good minister finding that he could make no sort of impression upon the irate old man, soon took his leave, telling Mrs. Condiment that if he could be of any service to her in her trouble, she must be sure to let him know.

At this Capitola and Mrs. Condiment exchanged looks; and the old lady thanking him for his kindness, said that if it should become necessary, she should gratefully avail herself of it.

That day the camp-meeting broke up.

Major Warfield struck tents, and with his family and baggage returned to Hurricane Hall.

On their arrival, each member of the party went about his or her own particular business.

Capitola hurried to her room to take off her bonnet and shawl. Pitapat, before attending her young mistress, lingered below to astonish the housemaids with accounts of "Brack Dunnel, dress up like an ole parson, an 'ceiving eberybody, even old Marse!"

Mrs. Condiment went to her store-room to inspect the condition of her newly put up preserves and pickles, lest any of them should have "worked" during her absence.

And Old Hurricane, attended by Wool, walked down to his kennels and his stables to look after the well-being of his favorite hounds and horses. It was while going through this interesting investigation that Major Warfield was informed—principally by overhearing the gossip of the grooms with Wool—of the appearance of a new inmate of the Hidden House—a young girl, who, according to their description, must have been the very pearl of beauty.

Old Hurricane pricked up his ears. Anything relating to the "Hidden House" possessed immense interest for him.

"Who is she, John?" he inquired of the groom.

"Deed I dunno, sir, only they say she's a bootiful young creature, fair as any lily, and dressed in deep mourning."

"Humph! humph! humph! another victim! ten thousand chances to one, another victim! Who told you this, John?"

"Why, Marse, you see Tom Griffith, the Reverend Mr. Goodwin's man, he's very thick long of Davy Hughs, Colonel Le Noir's coachman. And Davy he told Tom how one day last month his marse ordered the carriage, and went two or three day's journey up the country beyant Staunton, where he stayed a week and then came home, fetching along with him in the carriage this lovely young lady, who was dressed in the deepest mourning and wept all the way. They 'spects how she's an orphan, and has lost all her friends by the way she takes on."

"Another victim! My life on it, another victim! Poor child! she had better be dead than in the power of that atrocious villain and consummate hypocrite!" said Old Hurricane, passing on to the examination of his favorite horses, one of which, the swiftest in the stud, he found galled on the shoulders. Whereupon he flew into a towering passion, abusing his unfortunate groom, by every opprobrious epithet blind fury could suggest, ordering him as he valued whole bones, to vacate the stable instantly, and never dare to set foot on his premises again, as he valued his life, an order which the man meekly accepted and immediately disobeyed, muttering to himself:

"Humph! if we took ole marse at his word, there'd never be a man or 'oman left on the 'state,"—knowing full well that his tempestuous old master would probably forget all about it, as soon as he got comfortably seated at the supper table of Hurricane Hall, towards which the old man now trotted off.

Not a word did Major Warfield say at supper in regard to the new inmate of the Hidden House, for he had particular reasons for keeping Cap in ignorance of a neighbor, lest she should insist upon exchanging visits and being "sociable."

But it was destined that Capitola should not remain a day in ignorance of the interesting fact.

That night when she retired to her chamber, Pitapat lingered behind, but presently appeared at her young mistress's room door with a large waiter on her head, laden with meat, pastry, jelly and fruit, which she brought in and placed upon the work-stand.

"Why, what on the face of earth do you mean by bringing all that load of victuals into my room to-night? Do you think I am an ostrich or cormorant, or that I am going to entertain a party of friends," asked Capitola, in astonishment, turning from the wash-stand, where she stood bathing her face.

" 'Deed, I dunno, Miss, whedder you'se an ostrizant or not, but I knows I don't 'tend for to be 'bused any more 'bout wittels, arter findin' out how cross empty people can be! *Dere dey is!* You can eat um or leab um alone, Miss Caterpillar!" said little Pitapat, firmly.

Capitola laughed. "Patty," she said, "you are worthy to be called my waiting-maid!"

"And lors knows Miss Caterpillar, if it was *de wittels* you was a-frettin' arter, you ought to a-told me before! Lors knows dere's wittels enough!"

"Yes, I'm much obliged to you, Patty, but now I am not hungry, and I do not like the smell of food in my bedroom, so take the waiter out and set it on the passage table until morning."

Patty obeyed, and came back smiling and saying:

"Miss Caterpillar, has you hern de news?"

"What news, Pat?"

"How us has got a new neighbor—a bootiful young gal—as bootiful as a pictor in a gilt-edged Chrismas book! wid a snowy skin, and sky-blue eyes, and glistenin' goldy hair like de princess you was a readin' me about, all in deep mournin' and a weepin' and a weepin' all alone down dere in dat wicked, lonesome, outlawful ole haunted place, the Hidden House, along of old Colonel Le Noir and old Dorkey Knight, and the ghost as draws people's curtains of a night, just for all the worl' like dat same princess in de ogre's castle!"

"What on earth is all this rigmarole about? Are you dreaming or romancing?"

"I'm a telling on you de bressed trufe! Dere's a young lady a livin' at de Hidden House!"

"Eh! is that really true, Patty?"

"True as preaching, Miss."

"Then I am very glad of it! I shall certainly ride over and call on the stranger," said Capitola, gaily.

"Oh, Miss Cap! oh, Miss, don't you do no sich thing! Ole Marse kill me! I heerd him t'reaten all de men and maids, how if dey telled you anything 'bout de new neighbor, how he'd skin dem alive!"

"Won't he skin you?" asked Cap.

"No, Miss, not 'less you 'form ag'in me, case he didn't tell me not to tell you, case you see he didn't think how I knowed! But leastways, I know from what I heard, old Marse wouldn't have you to know nothin' 'bout it, no, not for de whole worl'."

"He does not want me to call at the Hidden House! That's it! Now why doesn't he wish me to call there? I shall have to go in order to find out, and so I will," thought Cap.

CHAPTER XXXIII

CAP'S VISIT TO THE HIDDEN HOUSE

"And such a night 'she' took the road in
As ne'er poor sinner was abroad in.
The wind blew as 'twad blawn its last;
The rattling showers rose on the blast;
The speedy gleams the darkness swallowed;
Loud, deep and long the thunder bellowed;
That night a child might understand
That de'il had business on his hand."
                    —Burns [1]

A WEEK PASSED before Capitola carried her resolution of calling upon the inmate of Hidden House into effect. It was in fact, a hot, dry, oppressive season, the last few days of August, when all people, even the restless Capitola, preferred the coolness and repose of indoors. But that she should stay at home more than a week was a moral and physical impossibility. So on Thursday afternoon, when Major Warfield set out on horseback to visit his mill, Capitola ordered her horse saddled and brought up that she might take an afternoon's ride.

"Now please, my dear child, don't go far," said Mrs. Condiment, "for besides that your uncle does not approve of your riding alone, you must hurry back to avoid the storm."

"Storm, Mrs. Condiment, why, bless your dear old heart, there has not been a storm these four weeks!" said Capitola, almost indignant that such an absurd objection to a long ride should be raised.

"The more reason, my child, that we should have a very severe one when it does come, and I think it will be upon us before sunset; so I advise you to hurry home."

"Why, Mrs. Condiment! there's not a cloud in the sky!"

"So much the worse, my dear. The blackest cloud that ever gathered is not so ominous of mischief as this dull, coppery sky and still atmosphere; and if forty years' observation of weather signs goes for anything, I tell you that we are going to have the awfulest storm that ever gathered in the heavens! Why, look out of that window! the very birds and beasts know it, and instinctively seek shelter!—look at that flock of crows flying home!

see the dumb beasts come trooping towards their sheds! Capitola, you had better give up going altogether, my dear."

"There! I thought all this talk tended to keeping me within doors! but I can't stay, Mrs. Condiment! Good Mrs. Condiment, I can't!"

"But, my dear, if you should be caught out in the storm!"

"Why, I don't know but I should like it! What harm could it do me? I'm not soluble in water—rain won't melt me away! I think, upon the whole, I rather prefer being caught in the storm!" said Cap, perversely.

"Well, well, there's no need of that; you may ride as far as the river's bank and back again in time to escape, if you choose," said Mrs. Condiment, who saw that her troublesome charge was bent upon the frolic.

And Cap, seeing her horse approach, led by one of the grooms, ran up stairs, donned her riding-habit, hat and gloves, ran down again, sprang into her saddle, and was off, galloping away towards the river before Mrs. Condiment could add another word of warning.

She had been gone about an hour when the sky suddenly darkened, the wind rose and the thunder rolled in prelude to the storm.

Major Warfield came skurrying home from the mill, grasping his bridle with one hand, and holding his hat on with the other.

Meeting poor old Ezy in the shrubbery, he stormed out upon him with:

"What are you lounging there for, you old idiot! you old sky-gazing lunatic! don't you see that we are going to have an awful blow? Begone with you, and see that the cattle are all under shelter. Off, I say, or,"—he rode towards Bill Ezy, but the old man, exclaiming:

"Yes, sir! yes, sir! in coorse, sir!" ducked his head, and ran off in good time.

Major Warfield quickened his horse's steps and rode to the house, dismounted, and threw the reins to the stable-boy, exclaiming:

"My beast is dripping with perspiration—rub him down well, you knave, or I'll impale you!"

Striding into the hall, he threw down his riding-whip, pulled off his gloves, and called:

"Wool! Wool, you scoundrel, close every door and window in the house; call all the servants together in the dining-room; we're going to have one of the worst tempests that ever raised."

Wool flew to do his bidding.

"Mrs. Condiment, mum," said the old man, striding into the sitting-room—"Mrs. Condiment, mum, tell Miss Black to come down from her room until the storm is over; the upper chambers of this old house are not safe in a tempest. Well, mum, why don't you go, or sent Pitapat?"

"Major Warfield, sir, I'm very sorry, but Miss Black has not come in yet," said Mrs. Condiment, who for the last half hour had suffered extreme anxiety upon account of Capitola.

"Not come in yet! Demmy, mum! do you tell me she has *gone out?*" cried Old Hurricane, in a voice of thunder, gathering his brows into a dark frown, and striking his cane angrily upon the floor.

"Yes, sir, I am sorry to say she rode out about an hour ago and has not returned," said Mrs. Condiment, summoning all her firmness to meet Old Hurrican's "roused wrath."

"MA'AM! you venture to stand there before MY face and tell ME composedly that you permitted Miss Black to go off alone in the face of such a storm as this!" roared Old Hurricane.

"Sir, I could not help it," said the old lady.

"Demmy, mum, you *should* have helped it. A women of *your* age stand there and tell me that she could not prevent a young creature like Capitola from going out alone in a storm!"

"Major Warfield, could *you* have done it?"

"Me? Demmy, I should think so, but that is not the question. You——"

He was interrupted by a blinding flash of lightning, followed immediately by an awful peal of thunder and a sudden fall of rain.

Old Hurricane sprang up as though he had been shot off his chair, and trotted up and down the floor exclaiming:

"And she! she out in all this storm! Mrs. Condiment, mum, you deserve to be ducked! Yes, mum, you do! Wool! Wool! you diabolical villain!"

"Yes, marse, yes, sir, here I is!" exclaimed that officer, in trepidation, as he appeared in the doorway. "De windows and doors, sir, is all fastened close, and de maids are all in the dining-room as you ordered, and——"

"Hang the maids, and the doors and windows, too! who the demon cares about them? How dared you, you knave, permit your young mistress to ride, unattended, in the face of such a storm, too! Why didn't you go with her, sir?"

" 'Deed, marse——"

"Don't ' 'deed marse' *me,* you atrocious villain! Saddle a horse quickly, inquire which road your mistress took, and follow and attend her home safely—after which, I intend to break every bone in your skin, sirrah! So———"

Again he was interrupted by a dazzling flash of lightning, accompanied by a deafening roll of thunder, and followed by a flood of rain.

Wool stood appalled at the prospect of turning out in such a storm, upon such a fruitless errand.

"Oh, you may stare, and roll up your eyes! but I *mean* it, you varlet! So be off with you!—go! I don't care if you should be drowned in the rain, or blown off the horse, or struck by lightning. I hope you *may* be, you knave, and I shall be rid of *one* villain! OFF, you varlet, or———" Old Hurricane lifted a bronze statuette to hurl at Wool's delinquent head, but that functionary dodged and ran out in time to escape a blow that might have put a period to his mortal career.

But let no one suppose that honest Wool took the road that night. He simply ran down stairs and hid himself comfortably in the lowest regions of the house, there to tarry until the storms, social and atmospheric, should be over.

Meanwhile the night deepened—the storm raged without, and Old Hurricane raged within.

The lightning flashed, blaze upon blaze, with blinding glare. The thunder broke, crash upon crash, with deafening roar. The wind gathering all its force cannonaded the old walls as though it would batter down the house. The rain fell in floods. In the midst of all, the Demon's Run, swollen to a torrent, was hard like the voice of a "roaring lion, seeking whom he might devour." [2]

Old Hurricane strode up and down the floor, groaning, swearing, threatening, and at every fresh blast of the storm without, breaking forth into fury.

Mrs. Condiment sat crouched in a corner, praying fervently every time the lightning blazed into the room, longing to go and join the men and maids in the next apartment, yet fearing to stir from her seat lest she should attract Old Hurricane's attention, and draw down upon herself the more terrible thunder and lightning of his wrath. But to escape Old Hurricane's violence was not in the power of mortal man or woman. Soon her very stillness exasperated him, and he broke forth upon her with:

"Mrs. Condiment, mum, I don't know how you can *bear* to sit there so quietly and listen to this storm, knowing that the poor child is exposed to it?"

"Major Warfield, would it do any good for me to jump up and trot up and down the floor, and go on as you do, even supposing I had the strength?" inquired the meek old lady, thoroughly provoked at his injustice.

"I'd like to see you show a little more feeling. You are a perfect barbarian. Oh, Cap, my darling, where are you now? Heavens! what a blast was that! enough to shake the house about our ears! I wish it would— blamed if I don't.

"Oh, Major, Major, don't say such awful things nor make such awful wishes," said the appalled old lady; "you don't know what you might bring down upon us."

"No, nor care; if the old house should tumble in, it would bury under its ruins a precious lot of good-for-nothing people, unfit to live. Heavens! what a flash of lightning! Oh, Cap, Cap, my darling, where are you in this storm? Mrs. Condiment, mum, if any harm comes to Capitola this night, I'll have you indicted for manslaughter."

"Major Warfield, if it is all on Miss Black's account that you are raving and raging so, I think it is quite vain of you; for any young woman caught out in a storm would know enough to get into shelter; especially would Miss Black, who is a young lady of great courage and presence of mind, as we know. She has surely gone into some house to remain until the storm is over," said Mrs. Condiment, soothingly.

This speech, so well intended, exasperated Old Hurricane more than all the rest. Stopping and striking his cane upon the floor, he roared forth:

"Hang it, mum! hold your foolish old tongue! You know nothing about it. Capitola is exposed to more serious dangers than the elements. Perils of all sorts surround her. She should never, rain or shine, go out alone. Oh, the little villain! the little wretch! the little demon! if EVER I get her safe in this house again, WON'T I lock her up and keep her on bread and water until she learns to behave herself!"

Here again a blinding flash of lightning, a deafening peal of thunder, a terrific blast of wind and flood of rain suddenly arrested his speech.

"Oh, my Cap! my dear Cap! I needn't threaten you! I shall never have the chance to be cruel to you again—never. You will perish in this terrible storm, and then—and then my tough old heart will break, it will—it will, Cap. But demmy, before it does, I will break the necks of every man and women in this house, old and young. Hear it, Heaven and earth, for I'll do it!"

All things must have an end. So, as the hours passed on, the storm having spent all its fury, gradually grumbled itself into silence.

Old Hurricane also raged into a state of exhaustion so complete, that when the midnight hour struck he could only drop into a chair and murmur:

"Twelve o'clock, and no news of her yet!"

And then unwillingly he went to bed, attended by Mrs. Condiment and Pitapat instead of Wool, who was supposed to be out in search of Capitola, but who was, in fact, fast asleep on the floor of a dry cellar.

Meanwhile, where did this midnight hour find Capitola?

CHAPTER XXXIV

THE HIDDEN HOLLOW

X X X X X

"On every side the aspect was the same,
All ruined, desolate, forlorn and savage,
No hand or foot within the precinct came
To rectify or ravage!
Here Echo never mocked the human tongue;
Some weighty crime that Heaven could not pardon,
A secret curse on that old Building hung
And its deserted Garden!"
　　　　—*Hood's Haunted House* [1]

CAP WAS A BIT of a Don Quixote.[2] The stirring incidents of the last few months had spoiled her; the monotony of the last few weeks had bored her; and now she had just ridden out in quest of adventures.

The Old Hidden House, with its mysterious traditions, its gloomy surroundings and its haunted reputation, had always possessed a powerful attraction for one of Cap's adventurous spirit. To seek and gaze upon the sombre house, of which, and of whose inmates, such terrible stories had been told or hinted, had always been a secret desire and purpose of Capitola.

And now the presence there of a beautiful girl near her own age was the one last item that tipped the balance, making the temptation to ride thither outweigh every other consideration of duty, prudence and safety. And having once started on the adventure, Cap felt the attraction drawing her towards the frightful hollow of the Hidden House growing stronger with every step taken thitherward.

She reached the banks of the "Demon's Run," and took the left-hand road down the stream until she reached the left point of the Horse-Shoe Mountain, and then going up around the point, she kept close under the back of the range until she had got immediately in the rear of the round bend of the "Horse Shoe," behind Hurricane Hall.

"Well," said Cap, as she drew rein here, and looked up at the lofty ascent of gray rocks that concealed Hurricane Hall, "to have had to come such a circuit around the outside of the 'Horse Shoe,' to find myself just at the back of our old house, and no farther from home than this! There's as many doubles and twists in these mountains as there are in a lawyer's discourse! There! Gyp, you needn't turn back again and pull at the bridle, to tell me that there is a storm coming up and that you want to go home! I have no more respect for your opinion than I have for Mrs. Condiment's. Besides, you carry a damsel-errant in quest of adventures, Gyp! and so you must on, Gyp! you must on!" said Capitola, forcibly pulling her horse's head around, and then taking a survey of the downward path.

It was a scene fascinating from its very excess of gloom and terror!

It was a valley so deep and dark as to merit the name of the hollow, or hole, but for its great extent and its thick growth of forest, through which spectral-looking rocks gleamed, and moaning waters could be heard but not seen.

"Now, somewhere in that thick forest, in the bottom of that vale, stands the house—well called the Hidden House, since not a chimney of it can be seen even from this commanding height! But I suppose this path that leads down into the valley may conduct me to the building! Come along, Gyp! You needn't turn up your head and pull at the bit! You've got to go! I am bound this night to see the outside of the Hidden House, and the window of the haunted chamber at the very least," said Cap, throwing her eyes up defiantly towards the darkening sky, and putting whip to her unwilling horse.

As the path wound down into the valley the woods were found deeper, thicker and darker. It occupied all Cap's faculties to push her way through the overhanging and interlacing branches of the trees.

"Good gracious," she said, as she used her left arm rather vigorously to push aside the obstructions to her path, "one would think this were the enchanted forest containing the castle of the sleeping beauty, and I was the knight destined to deliver her! I'm sure it wouldn't have been more difficult."

Still deeper fell the path, thicker grew the forest and darker the way.

"Gyp, I'm under the impression that we shall have to turn back yet," said Cap dolefully, stopping in the midst of a thicket so dense that it completely blockaded her farther progress in the same direction. Just as she came to this very disagreeable conclusion she spied an opening on her left, from which a bridle-path struck out. With an exclamation of joy, she immediately turned her horse's head and struck into it. This path was very rocky, but in some degree clearer than the other, and she went on quickly, singing to herself, until gradually her voice began to be lost in the sound of many rushing waters.

"It must be the Devil's Punch Bowl I am approaching," she said to herself, as she went on.

She was right. The roaring of the waters grew deafening, and the path became so rugged with jagged and irregularly piled rocks, that Cap could scarcely keep her horse upon his feet in climbing over them. And suddenly, when she least looked for it, the great natural curiosity—the Devil's Punch Bowl—burst upon her view.

It was an awful abyss, scooped out as it were from the very bowels of the earth, with its steep sides rent open in dreadful chasms, and far down in its fearful depths a boiling whirlpool of black waters.

Urging her reluctant steed through a thicket of stunted thorns and over a chaos of shattered rocks, Capitola approached as near as she safely could to the brink of this awful pit. So absorbed was she in gazing upon this terrible phenomenon of natural scenery that she had not noticed in the thicket on her right a low hut that, with its brown-green moldering colors, fell so naturally in with the hue of the surrounding scenery as easily to escape observation. She did not even observe that the sky was entirely overcast, and the thunder was muttering in the distance. She was aroused from her profound reverie by a voice near her asking:

"Who are you that dares to come without a guide to the Devil's Punch Bowl?"

Capitola looked around, and came nearer screaming than she ever had been in her life, upon seeing the apparition that stood before her. Was it man, woman, beast or demon? She could not tell. It was a very tall, spare form, with a black cloth petticoat tied around the waist, a blue coat buttoned over the breast, and a black felt hat tied down with a red handkerchief, shading the darkest old face she had ever seen in her life.

"Who are you, I say, who comes to the Devil's Punch Bowl without leave or license?" repeated the frightful creature, shifting her cane from one hand to the other.

"I? I am Capitola Black, from Hurricane Hall; but who, in the name of all the fates and furies are you?" inquired Capitola; who, in getting over the shock, had recovered her courage.

"I am Harriet, the Seeress of Hidden Hollow!" replied the apparition, in a melo-dramatic manner that would not have discredited the Queen of Tragedy herself. "You have heard of me?"

"Yes, but I always heard you called Old Hat the Witch," said Cap.

"The world is profane—give me your hand," said the beldame, reaching out her own to take that of Capitola.

"Stop! is your hand clean? It looks very black."

"Cleaner than yours will be when it is *stained with blood,* young maiden."

"Tut!—if you insist on telling my fortune, tell me a pleasant one, and I will pay you double," laughed Capitola.

"The fates are not to be mocked. Your destiny will be that which the stars decree. To prove to you that I know this, I tell you that you are not what you have been."

"You've hit it this time, old lady, for I was a baby once, and now I am a young girl," said Cap, laughing.

"You will not continue to be that which you are now!" pursued the hag, still attentively reading the lines of her subject's hand.

"Right again! for if I live long enough, I shall be an old woman."

"You bear a name that you will not bear long."

"I think that quite a safe prophecy, as I haven't the most distant idea of being an old maid."

"This little hand of yours—this dainty woman's hand—will be—red with blood."

"Now, do you know, I don't doubt *that* either? I believe it altogther probable that I shall have to cook my husband's dinner and kill the chickens for his soup."

"Girl, beware! you deride the holy stars!—and already they are adverse to you!" said the hag, with a threatening glare.

"Ha-ha-ha! I *love* the beautiful stars, but do not *fear* them. I fear only Him who made the stars!"

"Poor butterfly, listen and beware!—you are destined to imbrue that little hand in the life current of one who loves you the most of all on earth. You are destined to rise by the destruction of one who would shed his heart's best blood for you," said the beldame, in an awful voice.

Capitola's eyes flashed. She advanced her horse a step or two nearer the witch, and raised her riding-whip, saying:

"I protest if you were only a man, I should lay this lash over your wicked shoulders until my arms ached! How dare you? Faith, I don't wonder that in the honest old times such pests as you were cooled in the ducking pond! Good gracious, that must have made a hissing and spluttering in the water, though!"

"Blasphemer! pay and be gone!"

"*Pay you!* I tell you I would if you were only a man! but it would be sinful to pay a wretched old witch in the only way *you* deserve to be paid!"

said Cap, flourishing her riding-whip before a creature tall enough and strong enough to have doubled up her slight form together and hurled it into the abyss.

"Gold! gold!" said the hag, curtly, holding out black and talon-like fingers, which she worked convulsively.

"Gold! gold indeed! for such a wicked fortune! not a penny!" said Cap.

"Ho! your're stingy; you do not like to part with the yellow demon that has bought the souls of all your house!"

"Don't I?—you shall see! There! if you want gold, go fish for it from the depth of the whirlpool," said Cap, taking her purse and casting it over the precipice.

This exasperated the crone to frenzy.

"Away! Begone!" she cried, shaking her long arm at the girl. "Away! Begone! the fate pursues you! the badge of blood is stamped upon your palm!"

"'Fee—faw—fum!'—" said Cap.

"Scorner! Beware! the curse of the crimson hand is upon you!"

—"'I smell the blood of an Englishman'—" continued Cap.

"Derider of the fates, you are foredoomed to crime!"

—"'Be he alive or be he dead, I'll have his brains to butter my bread!'" concluded Cap.

"Be Silent!" shrieked the beldame.

"I won't," said Cap, "because you see, if we are in for the *horrible*, I can beat you hollow at *that!*

> 'Avaunt! and quit my sight!
> Let the earth hide thee!
> Thy bones are marrowless! Thy blood is cold!
> Thou hast no speculation in those eyes
> Which thou dost glare with!'[3]

"Begone! you're doomed! doomed! doomed!" shrieked the witch, retreating into her hut.

Cap laughed and stroked the neck of her horse, saying:

"Gyp, my son, that was Old Nick's wife who was with us just this instant; and now, indeed, Gyp, if we are to see the Hidden House this afternoon, we must get on."

And so saying, she followed the path that wound half around the Punch Bowl, and then along the side of a little mountain torrent called the spout,—which, rising in an opposite mountain, leaped from rock to rock, with many a sinuous turn, as it wound through the thicket that immediately surrounded the Hidden House—until it finally jetted through a subterranean channel into the Devil's Punch Bowl.

Capitola was now, unconsciously, upon the very spot where, seventeen years before, the old nurse had been forcibly stopped and compelled to attend the unknown lady.

As Capitola pursued the path that wound lower and lower into the dark valley, the gloom of the thicket deepened. Her thoughts ran on all the horrible traditions connected with the Hidden House and Hollow—the murder and robbery of the poor peddler; the mysterious assassination of Eugene Le Noir; the sudden disappearance of his youthful widow; the strange sights and sounds reported to be heard and seen about the mansion; the spectral light at the upper gable window; the white form seen flitting through the chamber; the pale lady that in the dead of night drew the curtains of a guest that once had slept there; and above all, Capitola thought of the beautiful, strange girl, who was an inmate of that sinful and accursed house. And while these thoughts absorbed her mind, suddenly in a turning of the path, she came full upon the gloomy building.

CHAPTER XXXV

THE HIDDEN HOUSE

"The very stains and fractures on the wall,
Assuming features solemn and terrific,
Hinting some tragedy of that old hall
Locked up in hieroglyphic!
Prophetic hints that filled the soul with dread;
But to one gloomy window pointing mostly,
The while some secret inspiration said,
That chamber is the ghostly!"
—*Hood*

THE HIDDEN HOUSE was a large, irregular edifice, of dark red sandstone, with its walls covered closely with the clinging ivy that had been clipped away only from a few of the doors and windows, and its roof overshadowed by the top branches of gigantic oaks and elms that clustered around and nearly concealed the building.

It might have been a long-forsaken house for any sign of human habitation that was to be seen about it. All was silent, solitary and gloomy.

As Capitola drew up her horse to gaze upon its sombre walls, she wondered which was the window at which the spectral light and ghostly face had been seen. She soon believed that she had found it.

At the highest point of the building, immediately under the sharp angle of the roof, in the gable end nearest to view, was a solitary window. The ivy that clung tightly to the stone, covering every portion of the wall at this end, was clipped away from that high-placed, dark and lonely window by which Capitola's eyes were strangely fascinated.

While thus she gazed in wonder, interest and curiosity, though without the least degree of superstitious dread, a vision flashed upon her sight, that sent the blood from her ruddy cheek to her brave heart and shook the foundations of her unbelief!

For while she gazed, suddenly that dark window was illumined by a strange, unearthly light that streamed forth into the gloomy evening air, and touched with blue flame the quivering leaves of every tree in its brilliant line! In the midst of this lighted window appeared a white female face wild with woe! And then the face suddenly vanished and the light was swallowed up in darkness!

Capitola remained transfixed!

"Great Heaven!" she thought, "can these things really be! Have the ghostly traditions of this world truth in them at last? When I heard this story of the haunted window I thought some one had surely imagined or invented it! Now I have seen for myself! but if I were to tell what I have seen not one in a hundred would believe me!"

While these startling thoughts disturbed her usual well-balanced mind, a vivid flash of lightning, accompanied by a tremendous peal of thunder and a heavy fall of rain, roused her into renewed activity.

"Gyp, my boy, the storm is upon us sure enough! We shall catch it all around! get well drowned, beaten and buffeted here and well abused when we get home. Meantime, Gyp, which is the worst, the full fury of the tempest or the mysterious terrors of the haunted house!"

Another blinding flash of lightning, a stunning crash of thunder, a flood of rain and tornado of wind decided her.

"We'll take the haunted house, Gyp, my friend. That spectral lady of the lighted window looked rather in sorrow than in anger, and who knows but the ghosts may be hospitable? So gee up, Dobbin," said Capitola, and urging her horse with one hand and holding on her cap with the other, she went on against wind and rain until she reached the front of the old house.

Not a creature was to be seen; every door and window was closely shut. Dismounting Capitola led her horse under the shelter of a thickly leaved old oak tree, secured him and then holding up her saturated skirt with one hand and holding on her cap with the other, she went up some mouldering stone steps to an old stone portico, and seizing the heavy iron knocker of a great black oak double door, she knocked loudly enough to awaken all the mountain echoes.

She waited a few minutes for an answer, but receiving none, she knocked again more loudly than before. Still there was no reply. And growing impatient, she seized the knocker with both hands and exerting all her strength, made the welkin ring again.

This brought a response. The door was unlocked and angrily jerked open, by a short, squarely formed, beetle-browed, stern-looking woman, clothed in a blackstuff gown and having a stiff muslin cap upon her head.

"Who are you? What do you want here?" harshly demanded this

woman, whom Capitola instinctively recognized as Dorky Knight, the morose housekeeper of the Hidden House.

"Who am I? What do I want? Old Nick fly away with you, it's plain enough to be seen who I am and what I want. I am a young woman caught out in the storm, and I want shelter!" said Cap indignantly. And her words were endorsed by a terrific burst of the tempest in lightning, thunder, wind and rain.

"Come in then and when you ask favors learn to keep a civil tongue in your head," said the woman sternly, taking the guest by the hand and pulling her in, and shutting and locking the door.

"Favors! plague on you for a bearess! I ask no favor! every storm-beaten traveler has a right to shelter under the first roof that offers and none but a curmudgeon would think of calling it a *favor!* And as for keeping a civil tongue in my head, I'll do it when you set me the example!" said Cap.

"Who are you?" again demanded the woman.

"Oh, I see you are no Arabian in your notions of hospitality!—Those pagans entertain a guest without asking him a single question; and though he were their bitterest foe, they consider him, while he rests beneath their tent, sacred from intrusion."

"That's because they *are* pagans," said Dorky. "But as I am a Christian, I'd thank you to let me know who it is that I have received under *this* roof."

"My name," said our heroine impatiently "is Capitola Black! I live with my uncle, Major Warfield, at Hurricane Hall. And now, I should thank your ladyship to send some one to put away my horse, while you yourself accommodate me with dry clothes."

While our saucy little heroine spoke the whole aspect of the dark-browed woman changed.

"Capitola—Capitola," she muttered, gazing earnestly upon the face of the unwelcome guest.

"Yes! Capitola! that is my name; you never heard anything against it, did you?"

For all answer the woman seized her hand, and while the lightning flashed, and the thunder rolled, and the wind and rain bent down, she drew her the whole length of the hall before a back window that overlooked the neglected garden, and regardless of the electric fluid that incessantly blazed upon them, she held her there and scrutinized her features.

"Well! I like this! upon my word, I do!" said Cap, composedly.

Without replying the strange woman seized her right hand, forcibly opened it, gazed upon the palm, and then flinging it back with a shudder, exclaimed:

"Capitola, what brought you under this roof! Away! Begone! Mount your horse and fly while there is yet time."

"What! expose myself again to the storm? I won't and that's flat," said Cap.

"Girl! girl! there are worse dangers in the world than any to be feared from thunder, lightning, rain, or wind."

"Very well, then, when I meet them, it will be time enough to deal with them! Meanwhile the stormy night and my soaked clothing are very palpable evils, and as I see no good end to be gained by my longer enduring them, I will just beg you to stop sooth-saying—(as I have had enough of that from another old witch)—and be so good as to permit me to change my clothes."

"It is madness! You shall not stay here," cried the woman, in a harsh voice.

"And I tell you I *will!* You are not the head of the family, and I do not intend to be turned out by you."

While she spoke, a servant crossed the hall, and the woman, whisking Capitola around until her back was turned, and her face concealed, went to speak to the new-comer.

"When will your master be here?" Capitola heard her inquire.

"Not to-night; he saw the storm rising and did not wish to expose himself; he sent me on to say that he would not be here until morning; I was caught as you see! I am dripping wet," replied the man.

"Go change your clothes at once, then, Davy."

"Who is that stranger?" asked the man, pointing to Capitola.

"Some young woman of the neighborhod, who has been caught out in the tempest. But you had better go and change your clothes than to stand here gossiping," said the woman harshly.

"I say," said the man, "the young woman is a God-send to Miss Clara; nobody has been to see her yet; nobody ever visits this house unless they are driven to it; I don't wonder the colonel and our young master pass as much as ten months in the year away from home, spending all the summer at the watering places, and all the winter in New York or Washington."

"Hold your tongue! what right have *you* to complain? You always attend them in their travels!"

"True; but you see for this last season, they have both been staying *here,* old master to watch the heiress, young master to court her, and as I have no interest in *that* game, I find the time hang heavy on my hands," complained the man.

"It will hang heavier if you take a long fit of illness by standing in wet clothes," muttered the woman.

"Why, so 'twill, missus! so here goes," assented the man, hurrying across the hall and passing out through the door opposite that by which he entered.

Dorcas returned to her guest.

Eyeing her closely for a while, she at length inquired:

"Capitola, how long have you lived at Hurricane Hall?"

"So long," replied Cap, "that you must have heard of me. I, at least, have often heard of Mother Dorky Knight!"

"And heard no good of her."

"Well, *no,* to be candid with you, I never did," said Cap.

"And much harm of her?" continued the woman, keeping her stern black eyes fixed upon those of her guest.

"Well, *yes*—since you ask me, I have heard pretty considerable harm!" answered Cap, nothing daunted.

"Where did you live before you came to Hurricane Hall?" asked Dorcas.

"Where I learned to fear God, to speak the truth, and to shame the devil!" replied Cap.

—"And to force yourself into people's houses against their will!"

"There you are again! I tell you that when I learn from the head of this household that I am unwelcome, then I will retreat, and not until then! And now I demand to be presented to the master."

"To Colonel Le Noir?"

"Yes."

"I cannot curse you with 'the curse of a granted prayer!' Colonel Le Noir is away."

"Why do you talk so strangely?" inquired Capitola.

"It is my whim. Perhaps my head is light."

"I should think it was, excessively so! Well—as the master of the house is away, be good enough to present me to the mistress!"

"What mistress? there is no mistress here!" replied Dorcas, looking around in strange trepidation.

"I mean the young lady, Colonel Le Noir's ward. In lieu of any other lady, *she,* I suppose, may be considered the mistress of the house!"

"Humph! well, young girl, as you are fully resolved to stand your ground, I suppose there is nothing to do but to put up with you!" said Dorcas.

"And put up my horse," added Cap.

"He shall be taken care of! But mind, you must depart early in the morning," said Dorcas, sternly.

"Once more, and for the last, Mother Cerberus, I assure you I do not acknowledge your authority to dismiss me," retorted Capitola, "so show me to the presence of your mistress!"

"Perverse, like all the rest! Follow me!" said the housekeeper, leading the way from the hall towards a back parlor.

CHAPTER XXXVI

THE INMATE OF THE HIDDEN HOUSE

紫紫紫紫紫

"There is a light around her brow,
A holiness in those dark eyes,
That show, though wandering earthward now,
Her spirit's home is in the skies."
—*Moore* [1]

PUSHING OPEN the door, Dorcas Knight exclaimed:

"Here is a young lady, Miss Black, from Hurricane Hall, come to see you, Miss Day."

And having made this announcement, the woman retired and shut the door behind her.

And Capitola found herself in a large, dark, gloomy, wainscotted room, whose tall, narrow windows afforded but little light, and whose immense fireplace and blackened furniture seemed to belong to a past century.

The only occupant of this sombre apartment was a young girl, seated in pensive thought beside the central table. She was clothed in deep mourning, which only served to throw into fairer relief the beauty of her pearly skin, golden hair and violet eyes.

The vision of her mourning robes and melancholy beauty so deeply impressed Capitola that almost for the first time in her life she hesitated, from a feeling of diffidence, and said gently:

"Indeed, I fear that this is an unwarranted intrusion on my part, Miss Day."

"You are very welcome," replied the sweetest voice Capitola had ever heard, as the young girl arose and advanced to meet her. "But you have been exposed to the storm. Please come into my room and change your clothes," continued the young hostess as she took Cap's hand and led her into an adjoining room.

The storm was still raging; but these apartments being in the central portion of the strong old house, were but little exposed to the sight or sound of its fury.

There was a lamp burning upon the mantel-piece, by the light of which the young girl furnished her visitor with dry clothing, and assisted her to change—saying as she did so:

"I think we are about the same size, and that my clothes will fit you; but I will not offer you mourning habiliments; you shall have this lilac silk."

"I am very sorry to see *you* in mourning," said Capitola, earnestly.

"It is for my father," replied Clara, very softly.

As they spoke, the eyes of the two young girls met. They were both good physiognomists and intuitive judges of character. Consequently, in the full meeting of their eyes, they read, understood and appreciated each other.

The pure, grave and gentle expression of Clara's countenance, touched the heart of Capitola.

The bright, frank, honest face of Cap recommended her to Clara.

The very opposite traits of their equally truthful characters attracted them to each other.

Clara conducted her guest back into the wainscotted parlor, where a cheerful fire had been kindled to correct the dampness of the air. And here they sat down unmindful of the storm that came much subdued through the thickness of the walls. And, as young creatures, however tried and sorrowful, will do, they entered into a friendly chat. And before an hour had passed Capitola thought herself well repaid for her sufferings from the storm and the rebuff, in having formed the acquaintance of Clara Day.

She resolved, let Old Hurricane rage as he might, henceforth she would be a frequent visitor to the Hidden House.

And Clara, for her part, felt that in Capitola she had found a frank, spirited, faithful neighbor who might become an estimable friend.

While they were thus growing into each other's favor, the door opened and admitted a gentleman of tall and thin figure, and white and emaciated face, shaded by a luxuriant growth of glossy black hair and beard. He could not have been more than twenty-six, but prematurely broken by vice, he seemed forty years of age. He advanced, bowing, towards the young women.

As Capitola's eyes fell upon this new-comer it required all her presence of mind and power of self-control to prevent her from starting or otherwise betraying herself—for in this stranger she recognized *the very man who had stopped her upon her night ride!* She did, however, succeed in banishing from her face every expression of consciousness. And when Miss Day courteously presented him to her guest, saying merely:

"My cousin, Mr. Craven Le Noir, Miss Black,"—Capitola arose and curtsied as composedly as if she had never set eyes upon his face before.

He, on his part, evidently remembered *her,* and sent one stealthy, keen and scrutinizing glance into her face; but finding that imperturbable, he bowed with stately politeness, and seemed satisfied that she had not identified him as her assailant.

Craven Le Noir drew his chair to the fire, seated himself, and entered into an easy conversation with Clara and her guest. Whenever he addressed Clara there was a deference and tenderness in his tone and glance that seemed very displeasing to the fair girl, who received all these delicate attentions with coldness and reserve. These things did not escape the notice of Capitola, who mentally concluded that Craven Le Noir was a lover of Clara Day, but a most unacceptable one.

When supper was announced, it was evidently hailed by Clara as a great relief. And after the meal was over, she arose and excused herself to her cousin, by saying that her guest, Miss Black, had been exposed to the storm, and was doubtless very much fatigued and that she would show her to her chamber.

Then taking a night-lamp she invited Capitola to come, and conducted her to an old-fashioned upper chamber, where a cheerful fire was burning on the hearth. Here the young girls sat down before the fire and improved their acquaintance by an hour's conversation. After which Clara arose, and saying:

"I sleep immediately below your room, Miss Black. If you should want anything, rap on the floor, and I shall hear you and get up."

She wished her guest a good night's rest, and retired from the room.

Cap was disinclined to sleep; a strange, superstitious feeling which she could neither understand nor throw off, had fallen upon her spirits.

She took the night-lamp in her hand and got up to examine her chamber. It was a large, dark, oak-panelled room, with a dark carpet on the floor, and dark green curtains on the windows and the bedstead. Over the mantel-piece hung the portrait of a most beautiful black-haired and black-eyed girl of about fourteen years of age, but upon whose infantile brow fell the shadow of some fearful woe. There was something awful in the despair "on that face, so young," that bound the gazer in an irresistible

and most painful spell. And Capitola remained standing before it transfixed, until the striking of the hall-clock aroused her from her enchantment. Wondering who the young creature could have been, what had been
her history, and above all what had been the nature of that fearful woe that
darkened like a curse her angel brow, Capitola turned almost sorrowfully
away, and began to prepare for bed.

She undressed, put on the delicate night-clothes Clara had provided
for her use, said her evening prayers—looked under the bed—a precaution
taken ever since the night upon which she had discovered the burglars—
and finding all right, she blew out her candle and lay down. She could not
sleep—many persons of nervous or mercurial temperaments cannot do so
the first night in a strange bed. Cap was very mercurial, and the bed and
room in which she lay were very strange; for the first time since she had
had a home to call her own, she was unexpectedly staying all night away
from her friends, and without their having any knowledge of her where-
abouts; she was conjecturing, half in fear and half in fun, how Old Hurricane was taking her escapade, and what he would say to her in the
morning! She was wondering to find herself in such an unforeseen position
as that of a night-guest in the mysterious Hidden House—wondering
whether this were the guest-chamber in which the ghost appeared to the
officer, and these were the very curtains that the pale lady drew at night.
While her thoughts were thus running over the whole range of circumstances around her singular position, sleep overtook Capitola, and speculation was lost in brighter visions.

How long she had slept and dreamed she did not know, when something gently awakened her. She opened her eyes calmly—to meet a vision
that, brave as she was, nearly froze the blood in her warm veins!

Her chamber was illuminated with an intense blue flame that lighted
up every portion of the apartment with a radiance bright as day; and in the
midst of this effulgence moved a figure clothed in white—a beautiful,
pale, spectral woman, whose large, motionless black eyes, deeply set in her
death-like face, and whose long, unbound black hair, fallen upon her white
raiment, were the only marks of color about her marble form.

Paralyzed with wonder, Capitola watched this figure as it glided
about the chamber. The apparition approached the dressing-table, seemed
to take something thence, and then gliding towards the bed—to Capitola's inexpressible horror—drew back the curtains and bent down and
gazed upon her! Capitola had no power to scream, to move, or to avert her
gaze from those awful eyes that met her own, until at length, as the spectral

head bent lower, she felt the pressure of a pair of icy lips upon her brow, and closed her eyes!

When she opened them again the vision had departed and the room was dark and quiet.

There was no more sleep for Capitola. She heard the clock strike four, and was pleased to find that it was so near day. Still the time seemed very long to her who lay there wondering, conjecturing and speculating on the strange adventure of the night.

When the sun arose, she left her restless bed, bathed her excited head, and proceeded to dress herself. When she had finished her toilet, with the exception of putting on her trinkets, she suddenly missed a ring that she prized more than she did all her possessions put together—it was a plain gold band, bearing on the inner side the inscription—*Capitola—Eugene*—and which she had been enjoined by her old nurse never to part from but with life. She had, in her days of destitution, suffered the extremes of cold and hunger—had been upon the very brink of death from starvation or freezing, but without ever dreaming of sacrificing her ring. And now for the first time it was missing. While she was still looking anxiously for the lost jewel the door opened, and Dorcas Knight entered the room, bearing on her arm Capitola's riding-dress, which had been well dried and ironed.

"Miss Capitola, here is your habit; you had better put it on at once, as I have ordered breakfast an hour sooner than usual, so that you may have an early start."

"Upon my word, you are very anxious to get rid of me; but not more so than I am to depart" said Capitola, still pursuing her search.

"Your friends, who do not know where you are, must be very uneasy about you. But what are you looking for?"

"A ring—a plain gold circle with my name and that of another inscribed on it, and which I would not lose for the world. I hung it on a pin, on this pin-cushion, last night before I went to bed—I would swear I did! and now it is missing," answered Cap, still pursuing her search.

"If you lost it in this room, it will certainly be found," said Dorcas Knight, putting down the habit and helping in the search.

"I am not so *sure* of that. There was some one in my room last night."

"Some one in your room!" exclaimed Dorcas in dismay.

"Yes; a dark-haired woman, all dressed in white."

Dorcas Knight gave two or three angry grunts, and then harshly exclaimed:

"Nonsense! Woman, indeed! There is no such woman about the house! There are no females here except Miss Day, myself, and you—not even a waiting-maid or cook."

"Well," said Cap, "if it was not a woman, it was a ghost, for I was wide awake and I saw it with my own eyes."

"Fudge; you've heard that foolish story of the haunted room, and you have dreamed the whole thing."

"I tell you I didn't. I saw it. Don't I know?"

"I say you dreamed it! There is no such living woman here; and as for a ghost, *that* is all folly! And I *must* beg, Miss Black, that you will not distress Miss Day by telling her this strange dream of yours. She has never heard the ridiculous story of the haunted room, and as she lives here in solitude, I would not like her to hear of it."

"Oh, I will say nothing to disquiet Miss Day. But it was no *dream.* It was *real,* if there is any reality in this world."

There was no more said. They continued to look for the ring, but in vain. Dorcas Knight, however, assured her guest that it should be found and returned, and that—breakfast waited. Whereupon Capitola went down to the parlor, where she found Clara awaiting her presence to give her a kindly greeting.

"Mr. Le Noir never gets up until very late, and so we do not wait for him," said Dorcas Knight, as she took her seat at the head of the table, and signed to the young girls to gather around it.

After breakfast, Capitola, promising to come again soon, and inviting Clara to return her visit, took leave of her entertainers and set out for home.

"Thank Heaven I have got her off in time and safety!" muttered Dorcas Knight, in triumph.

✻✻✻✻✻

"Must I give way and room for your rash choler
Shall I be frighted when a madman stares?
Go show your slaves how choleric you are!
And make your bondsmen tremble! I'll not blench."
    —*Shakespeare* [1]

IT HAPPENED that about sunrise that morning, Wool awoke in the cellar, and remembered that upon the night previous his master had commanded him to sally forth in the storm and seek his young mistress, and had forbidden him, on pain of broken bones, to return without bringing her safe. Therefore, what did the honest soul do but to steal out to the stables, saddle and mount a horse, and ride back to the house just as Mrs. Condiment had come out into the poultry-yard to get eggs for breakfast.

"Missus Compliment, ma'am, Ise been out all night in search of Miss Caterpillar, without finding of her. Is she come back, ma'am?"

"Lor! no, indeed, Wool. I'm very anxious, and the major is taking on dreadful. But I hope she is safe in some house. But, poor Wool, *you* must have had a dreadful time out all night in the storm, looking for her."

"Awful, Missus Compliment, ma'am, awful!" said Wool.

"Indeed, I know you had, my poor creature. Come in and get some warm breakfast," said the kind old lady.

"I daren't, Missus Compliment. Old marse forbid me to show my face to him until I fotch Miss Caterpillar home safe," said Wool, turning his horse's head as if to go. In doing so, he saw Capitola galloping towards the house, and with an exclamation of joy, pointed her out to the old lady, and rode on to meet her.

"Oh, Miss Caterpillar, Ise so glad I've found you. Ise done been out looking for you all night long!" exclaimed Wool, as he met her.

Capitola pulled up her horse, and surveyed the speaker with a comical expression, saying:

"'Been out all night looking for me!' Well, I must say, you seem in a fine state of preservation for a man who has been exposed to the storm all night. You have not a wet thread on you!"

"Lor, Miss, it rained till one o'clock, and then the wind riz and blowed till six, and blowed me dry!" said Wool, as he sprang off his horse, and helped his young mistress to alight.

Then, instead of taking the beasts to the stable, he tied them to the tree, and hurried into the house, and up stairs to his master's room, to apprise him of the return of the lost sheep, Capitola.

Old Hurricane was lying awake, tossing, groaning, and grumbling with anxiety.

On seeing Wool enter, he deliberately raised up and seized a heavy iron candlestick, and held it ready to hurl at the head of that worthy, whom he thus addressed:

"Ah, you have come, you atrocious villain. You know the conditions. If you have dared to show your face without bringing your young mistress——"

"Please, marse, I wur out looking for her all night!"

"Have you brought her!" thundered Old Hurricane, rising up.

"Please, marse, yes sir. I done found her and brought her home safe."

"Send her up to me," said Old Hurricane, sinking back with a sigh of infinite relief.

Wool flew to do his bidding.

In five minutes Capitola entered her uncle's chamber.

Now Old Hurricane had spent a night of almost intolerable anxiety upon his favorite's account, bewailing her danger and praying for her safety; but no sooner did he see her enter his chamber safe and sound, and smiling, than indignation quite mastered him, and jumping out of the bed in his night-gown, he made a dash straight at Capitola.

Now, had Capitola run, there is little doubt but that, in the blindness of his fury, he would have caught and beat her then and there. But Cap saw him coming, drew up her tiny form, folded her arms, and looked him directly in the face.

This stopped him, but like a mettlesome old horse suddenly pulled up in full career, he stamped, and reared, and plunged with fury, and foamed, and spluttered, and stuttered before he could get words out.

"What do you mean, you vixen, by standing there and popping your great gray eyes out at me? Are you going to bite, you tigress? What do you mean by facing me at all?" he reared, shaking his fist within an inch of Capitola's little pug nose.

"I am here because you sent for me, sir," was Cap's unanswerable rejoinder.

"'Here because I sent for you!' humph! humph! humph! and come dancing and smiling into my room as if you had not kept me awake all the live long night—yes! driven me within one inch of a brain fever! Not that I cared for you, you limb of Old Nick! not that I cared for you, except to wish with all my heart and soul that something or other had happened to you, you vagrant! Where did you spend the night, you lunatic?"

"At the Hidden House, where I went to make a call on my new neighbor, Miss Day, and where I was caught in the storm."

"I wish to heaven you had been caught in a man-trap and had all your limbs broken, you—you—you—OH!" ejaculated Old Hurricane, turning short and trotting up and down the room. Presently he stopped before Capitola, and rapping his cane down upon the floor, demanded:

"WHO did you see at that accursed place, you—you—you infatuated maniac?"

"Miss Day, Mr. Le Noir, Mrs. Knight, and a man-servant—name unknown," coolly replied Cap.

"And the head demon, where was he."

"Uncle, if by the head demon you mean Old Nick, I think it quite likely, from present appearances, that he passed the night at Hurricane Hall."

"I mean—Colonel Le Noir!" exclaimed Old Hurricane, as if the name choked him.

"Oh! I understand that *he* had that day left home."

"Umph! Oh! Ah! that accounts for it! that accounts for it," muttered Old Hurricane to himself—then, seeing Capitola was wistfully regarding his face, and attending to his muttered phrases, he broke out upon her with:

"Get out of this—this—this——" he meant to say "get out of this house," but a sure instinct warned him that if he should speak thus, Capitola, unlike the other members of his household, would take him at his word.

"Get out of this room, you vagabond!" he vociferated.

And Cap, with a curtsey and a kiss of her hand, danced away.

Old Hurricane stamped up and down the floor, gesticulating like a demoniac, and vociferating:

"She'll get herself burked,[2] kidnapped, murdered, or what not! I'm sure she will! I know it! I feel it! It's no use to order her *not* to go; she would be *sure* to disobey! and go ten times as often, for the very reason that she was forbidden! What the demon shall I do?—Wool! Wool! Wool, you brimstone villain, come here!" he roared, going to the bell-rope and pulling it until he broke it down.

Wool ran in with his hair bristling, his teeth chattering, and his eyes starting.

"Come here to me, you varlet! Now listen: You are to keep a sharp look-out after your young mistress. Whenever she rides abroad, you are to mount a horse and ride after her, and keep your eyes open, for if you only once lose sight of her, you knave, do you know what I shall do to you, eh?"

"N—n—no, marse" stammered Wool, pale with apprehension.

"I should cut your eyelids off to improve your vision! Look to it, sir, for I shall keep my word. And now come and help me to dress," concluded Old Hurricane.

Wool, with chattering teeth, shaking knees, and trembling fingers, assisted his master in his morning toilet, meditating the while whether it were not better to avoid impending dangers by running away.

And, in fact, between his master and his mistress, Wool had a hot time of it. The weather, after the storm had cleared the atmosphere, was delightful, and Cap rode out that very day. Poor Wool kept his eyeballs metaphorically "skinned," for fear they should be treated literally so— held his eyes wide open, lest Old Hurricane should keep his word, and make it impossible for him ever to shut them.

When Cap stole out, mounted her horse and rode away, in five minutes from the moment of starting she heard a horse's hoofs behind her, and presently saw Wool gallop to her side.

At first Cap bore this good-humoredly enough, only saying:

"Go home, Wool, I don't want you. I had much rather ride alone."

To which the groom replied:

"It is ole Marse's orders, Miss, as I should wait on you."

Capitola's spirit rebelled against this; and suddenly turning upon her attendant, she indignantly exclaimed:

"Wool, I don't want you, sir! I insist upon being left alone! and I order you to go home, sir!"

Upon this Wool burst into tears and roared.

Much surprised, Capitola inquired of him what the matter was.

For some time, Wool could only reply by sobbing, but when he was able to articulate he blubbered forth:

"It's nuf to make anybody go put his head underneaf of a meat-ax, so it is!"

"What *is* the matter, Wool?" again inquired Capitola.

"How'd *you* like to have your eyelids cut off?" howled Wool, indignantly.

"*What!*" inquired Capitola.

"Yes, I axes how'd *you* like to have *your* eyelids cut off?—Case that's what ole marse t'reatens to do long o' *me,* if I don't follow arter you and keep you in sight!—And now you forbids of me to do it, and—and—I'll go and put my head right underneaf of a meat-ax!"

Now Capitola was really kind-hearted, and well knowing the despotic temper of her guardian, she pitied Wool, and after a little hesitation, she said:

"Wool, so your old master says if you don't keep your eyes on me, he'll cut your eyelids off?"

"Ye—ye—yes, Miss," sobbed Wool.

"Did he say if you don't listen to me he'd cut your ears off?"

"N—n—no, Miss."

"Did he swear if you didn't talk to me he'd cut your tongue out?"

"N—n—no, Miss."

"Well, now, stop howling, and listen to me. Since at the peril of your eyelids you are obliged to keep me in sight, I give you leave to ride just within view of me; but no nearer, and you are never to let me see or hear you, if you can help it, for I like to be alone."

"I'll do anything in this world for peace, Miss Caterpillar," said poor Wool.

And upon this basis the affair was finally settled. And no doubt Capitola owed much of her personal safety to the fact that Wool kept his eyes open!

While these scenes were going on at Hurricane Hall, momentous events were taking place elsewhere, which require another chapter for their development.

CHAPTER XXXVIII

ANOTHER MYSTERY AT THE HIDDEN HOUSE

"Hark! what a shriek was that of fear intense,
Of horror and amazement!
What fearful struggle to the door, and thence,
With mazy doubles, to the casement!"[1]

AN HOUR AFTER the departure of Capitola, Colonel Le Noir returned to
the Hidden House, and learned, from his man David, that upon the preceding evening a young girl, of whose name he was ignorant, had sought
shelter from the storm and passed the night at the mansion.

Now Colonel Le Noir was extremely jealous of receiving strangers
under his roof—never during his short stay at the Hidden House going
out into company, lest he should be obliged in return to entertain visitors.
And when he learned that a strange girl had spent the night beneath his
roof, he frowningly directed that Dorcas should be sent to him.

When his morose manager made her appearance, he harshly demanded the name of the young woman she had dared to receive beneath
his roof.

Now, whether there is any truth in the theory of magnetism or not, it
is certain that Dorcas Knight, stern, harsh, resolute woman that she was
towards all others, became as submissive as a child, in the presence of
Colonel Le Noir.

At his command she gave him all the information he required, not
even withholding the fact of Capitola's strange story of having seen the
apparition of the pale-faced lady in her chamber, together with the subsequent discovery of the loss of her ring.

Colonel Le Noir sternly reprimanded his domestic manager for her
neglect of his orders, and dismissed her from his presence.

Another Mystery at the Hidden House

The remainder of the day was passed by him in moody thought. That evening he summoned his son to a private conference in the parlor—an event that happily delivered poor Clara Day from their presence at her fireside.

That night Clara, dreading lest at the end of the interview they might return to her society, retired early to her chamber, where she sat reading until a later hour, when she went to bed and found transient forgetfulness of trouble in sleep.

She did not know how long she had slept, when she was suddenly and terribly awakened by a woman's shriek sounding from the room immediately overhead, in which, upon the night previous, Capitola had slept.

Starting up in bed, Clara listened.

The shriek was repeated—prolonged and piercing, and was accompanied by a muffled sound of struggling that shook the ceiling overhead.

Instinctively springing from her bed, Clara threw on her dressing-gown and flew to the door, but just as she turned the latch to open it, she heard a bolt slipped on the outside and found herself a prisoner in her own chamber.

Appalled, she stood and listened.

Presently there came a sound of footsteps on the stairs and a heavy muffled noise as of some dead weight being dragged down the stair-case, and along the passage. Then she heard the hall door cautiously opened and shut. And finally she distinguished the sound of wheels rolling away from the house.

Unable longer to restrain herself, she rapped and beat upon her own door, crying aloud for deliverance.

Presently the bolt was withdrawn, the door jerked open and Dorcas Knight, with a face of horror, stood before her.

"What is the matter? Who was that screaming? In the name of mercy what has happened?" cried Clara, shrinking in abhorrence from the ghastly woman.

"Hush! it is nothing! there were two tom-cats screaming and fighting in the attic and they fought all the way down stairs, rolling over and over each other. I've just turned them out," faltered the woman, shivering as with an ague fit.

"What—what was that—that went away in the carriage?" asked Clara, shuddering.

"The Colonel, gone to meet the early stage at Tip-Top, to take him to Washington. He would have taken leave of you last night, but when he came to your parlor you had left it."

"But—but—*there is blood upon your hand, Dorcas Knight!*" cried Clara, shaking with horror.

"I—I know—The cats scratched me as I put them out," stammered the stern woman, trembling almost as much as Clara herself.

These answers failed to satisfy the young girl, who shrank in terror and loathing from that woman's presence, and sought the privacy of her own chamber, murmuring:

"What has happened? What has been done, oh, heaven! Oh, heaven, have mercy on us some dreadful deed has been done in this house, to-night!"

There was no more sleep for Clara. She heard the clock strike every hour from one to six in the morning, when she arose and dressed herself and went from her room, expecting to see upon the floor and walls, and upon the faces of the household, signs of some dreadful tragedy enacted upon the previous night.

But all things were as usual—the same dark, gloomy and neglected magnificence about the rooms and passages, the same reserved, sullen and silent aspect about the persons.

Dorcas Knight presided as usual at the head of the breakfast table, and Craven Le Noir at the foot. Clara sat in her accustomed seat at the side, midway between them.

Clara shuddered in taking her cup of coffee from the hand of Dorcas, and declined the wing of fowl that Craven Le Noir would have put upon her plate.

Not a word was said upon the subject of the mystery of the preceding night, until Craven Le Noir, without venturing to meet the eyes of the young girl, said:

"You look very pale, Clara!"

"Miss Day was frightened by the cats last night," said Dorcas.

Clara answered never a word. The ridiculous story essayed to be palmed off upon her credulity in explanation of the night's mystery, had not gained an instant's belief.

She knew that the cry that had startled her from sleep, had burst in strong agony from human lips.

That the helpless weight she had heard dragged down the stairs and along the whole length of the passage, was some dead or insensible human form!

That the blood she had seen upon the hand of Dorcas Knight, was— oh, heaven, her mind shrank back appalled with horror, at the thought which she dared not entertain! She could only shudder, pray and trust in God.

CHAPTER XXXIX

CAP FREES THE CAPTIVE

✿✿✿✿✿

"Hold daughter! I do spy a kind of hope,
Which craveth as desperate an execution
As that is desperate, which we would prevent
And if thou darest, I'll give the remedy!
Hold, then! go home, be merry, give consent
To marry Paris! Wednesday is to-morrow!"
—*Shakespeare*[1]

AS THE AUTUMN weather was now very pleasant, Capitola continued her rides, and without standing upon ceremony, repeated her visit to the Hidden House. She was as usual followed by Wool, who kept a respectful distance, and who during his mistress's visit remained outside in attendance upon the horses.

Capitola luckily was in no danger of encountering Colonel Le Noir, who since the night of the mysterious tragedy had not returned home; but had gone to and settled in his winter quarters at Washington City.

But she again meet Craven Le Noir, who, contrary to his usual custom of accompanying his father upon his annual migrations to the metropolis, had upon this occasion remained home in close attendance upon his cousin, the wealthy orphan.

Capitola found Clara the same sweet, gentle and patient girl, with this difference only—that her youthful brow was now overshadowed by a heavy trouble which could not wholly be explained by her state of orphanage, or her sorrow for the dead—it was too full of anxiety, gloom and terror to have reference to the past alone.

Capitola saw all this, and trusting in her own powers, would have sought the confidence of the poor girl, with the view of soothing her sorrows and helping her out of her difficulties; but Miss Day, candid upon all other topics was strangely reserved upon this subject, and Capitola, with all her eccentricity, was too delicate to seek to intrude upon the young mourner's sanctuary of grief.

296

But a crisis was fast approaching which rendered further concealment difficult and dangerous, and which threw Clara for protection upon
the courage, presence of mind and address of Capitola.

Since Clara Day had parted with her betrothed and taken up her
residence beneath her guardian's roof, she had regularly written both to
Traverse at St. Louis, and to his mother at Staunton. But she had received
no reply from either mother or son. And months had passed filling the
mind of Clara with anxiety upon their account.

She did not for one moment doubt *their* constancy; alas! it required
but little perspicacity on her part to perceive that the letters on either side
must have been intercepted by the Le Noirs—father and son!

Her great anxiety was lest Mrs. Rocke and Traverse, failing to hear
from her, should imagine that she had forgotten them. She longed to
assure them she had not! But how should she do this?—It was perfectly
useless to write and send the letter to the post-office by any servant at the
Hidden House, for such a letter so sent would be sure to find its way—not
into the mail bags, but—into the pocket of Colonel Le Noir.

Finally, Clara resolved to entrust honest Cap with so much of her
story as would engage her interest and cooperation, and then confide to
her care the letter to be placed in the post-office. Clara had scarcely come
to this resolution ere, as we said, an imminent crisis obliged her to seek the
further aid of Capitola.

Craven Le Noir had never abated his unacceptable attentions to the
orphan heiress. Day by day, on the contrary, to Clara's unspeakable distress, these attentions grew more pointed and alarming.

At first she had received them coldly and repulsed them gently; but
as they grew more ardent and devoted she became colder and more reserved, until at length by maintaining a freezing hauteur, at variance with
her usually sweet temper, she sought to repel the declaration that was ever
ready to fall from his lips.

But notwithstanding her evident abhorence of his suit, Craven Le
Noir persisted in his purpose.

And so, one morning, he entered the parlor and finding Clara alone,
he closed the door, seated himself beside her, took her hand and made a
formal declaration of love and proposal of marriage, urging his suit with all
the eloquence of which he was master.

Now Clara Day, a Christian maiden, a recently bereaved orphan and
an affianced bride, had too profound a regard for her duties towards God,

her father's will, and her betrothed husband's rights, to treat this attempted invasion of her faith in any other than the most deliberate, serious and dignified manner.

"I am very sorry, Mr. Le Noir, that it has at length come to this. I thought I had conducted myself in such a manner as totally to discourage any such purpose as this which you have just honored me by disclosing. Now, however, that the subject may be set at rest forever, I feel bound to announce to you that my hand is already plighted," said Clara, gravely.

"But my fairest and dearest love, your little hand *cannot* be plighted without the consent of your guardian, who would never countenance the imprudent pretensions which I understand to be made by the low-born young man to whom, I presume, you allude. That engagement was a very foolish affair, my dear girl, and only to be palliated upon the ground of your extreme childishness at the time of its being made. You must forget the whole matter, my sweetest love, and prepare yourself to listen to a suit more worthy of your social position," said Craven Le Noir, attempting to steal his arm around her waist.

Clara coldly repelled him, saying:

"I am at a loss to understand, Mr. Le Noir, what act of levity on my part has given you the assurance to offer me this affront!"

"Do you call it an affront, fair cousin, that I lay my hand and heart, and fortune, at your feet?"

"I have called your act, sir, by its gentlest name. Under the circumstances, I might well have called it an outrage!"

"And what may be those circumstances that convert an act of—adoration—into an outrage, my sweet cousin?"

"Sir, you know them well! I have not concealed from yourself or my guardian that I am the affianced bride of Doctor Rocke, nor that our troth was plighted with the full consent of my dear father," said Clara, gravely.

"Tut, tut, tut, my charming cousin, that was mere child's play—a school-girl's romantic whim; do not dream that your guardian will ever permit you to throw yourself away upon that low-bred fellow!"

"Mr. Le Noir, if you permit yourself to address me in this manner, I shall feel compelled to retire. I cannot remain here to have my honored father's will and memory, and the rights of my betrothed, insulted in my person!" said Clara, rising to leave the room.

"No stay! forgive me, Clara! pardon me, gentlest girl, if, in my great love for you, I grow impatient of any other claim upon your heart, especially from such an unworthy quarter! Clara, you are a mere child, full of generous, but romantic sentiments, and dangerous impulses! You require extra vigilance and firm exercise of authority on the part of your guardians to save you from certain self-destruction! And some day, sweet girl, you will thank us for preserving you from the horrors of such a mésalliance," said Craven Le Noir, gently detaining her.

"I tell you, Mr. Le Noir, that your manner of speaking of my betrothal is equally insulting to myself, Doctor Rocke, and my dear father, who never would have plighted our hands had *he* considered our prospective marriage a mésalliance."

"Nor do I suppose he ever *did* plight your hands—while in his right senses."

"Oh, sir! this has been discussed before! I beg of you to let the subject drop forever, remembering that I hold myself sacredly betrothed to Traverse Rocke, and ready—when, at my legal majority, he shall claim me—to redeem my plighted faith by becoming his wife."

"Clara! this is madness! it must not be endured, nor shall not! I have hitherto sought to win your heart by showing you the great extent of my love! but be careful how you scorn that love, or continue to taunt me with the mention of an unworthy rival! For though I use *gentle means,* should I find them fail of their purpose, I shall know how to avail myself of harsher ones."

Clara disdained reply, except by permitting her clear eye to pass over him from head to foot, with an expression of consuming scorn that scathed him to the quick.

"I tell you to be careful, Clara Day! I come to you armed with the authority of your legal guardian, my father, Colonel Le Noir, who will forestall your foolish purpose of throwing yourself and your fortune away upon a beggar, even though to do so he strain his authority and coerce you into taking a more suitable companion," said Craven Le Noir, rising impatiently, and pacing the floor. But no sooner had he spoken those words than he saw how greatly he had injured his cause, and repented them. Going to Clara and intercepting her as she was about to leave the room, he gently took her hand, and dropping his eyes to the floor with a look of humility and penitence, he said:

"Clara, my sweet cousin, I know not how sufficiently to express my sorrow at having been hurried into harshness towards you;—towards you whom I love more than my own soul, and whom it is the fondest wish of my heart to call—wife! I can only excuse myself for this, or any future extravagance of manner, by my excessive love for you and the jealousy that maddens my brain at the bare mention of my rival. That is it, sweet girl! Can you forgive one whom love and jealousy have hurried into frenzy?"

"Mr. Le Noir, the Bible enjoins me to forgive injuries. I shall endeavor, when I can, to forgive you; though for the present, my heart is still burning under the sense of wrongs done towards myself and those whom I love and esteem, and the only way in which you can make me forget what has just passed, will be—*never to repeat the offence.*" And with these words, Clara bent her head and passed from the room.

Could she have seen the malignant scowl and gesture with which Craven Le Noir followed her departure, she would scarcely have trusted his expressions of penitence.

Lifting his arm above his head, he fiercely shook his fist after her, and exclaimed:

"Go on, insolent girl, and imagine that you have humbled me! but the tune shall be changed by this day month! for before that time, whatever power the law gives the husband over his wife and her property, shall be mine over you and your possessions! Then we shall see who shall be insolent! Then we shall see whose proud blue eye shall day after day dare to look up and rebuke me! Oh! to get you into my power, my girl! not that I *love* you, moon-faced creature! but I *want your possessions!* which is quite as strong an incentive."

Then he fell into thought. He had an ugly way of scowling and biting his nails when deeply brooding over any subject, and now he walked slowly up and down the floor with his head upon his breast, his brows drawn over his nose, and his four fingers between his teeth, gnawing away like a wild beast, while he muttered:

"She is not like the other one! she has more sense and strength! she will give us more trouble. We must continue to try fair means a little longer! It will be difficult, for I am not accustomed to control my passions even for a purpose! Yet—penitence and love are the only cards to be played to this insolent girl for the present. *Afterwards*——*!*"

Here his soliloquy muttered itself into silence, his head sunk deeper upon his breast, his brows gathered lower over his nose, and he walked and gnawed his nails like a hungry wolf.

The immediate result of his cogitation was that he went into the library and wrote off a letter to his father, telling him all that had transpired between himself and Clara, and asking his further counsel.

He despatched this letter, and waited an answer.

During the week that ensued before he could hope to hear from

Colonel Le Noir, he treated Clara with marked deference and respect.

And Clara on her part did not tax his forbearance by appearing in his presence oftener than she could possibly avoid.

At the end of the week the expected letter came. It was short and to the purpose. It ran thus:

> WASHINGTON, DEC. 14, 18—.
>
> MY DEAR CRAVEN:—You are losing time. Do not hope to win the girl by the means you propose. She is too acute to be deceived and too firm to be persuaded. We must not hesitate to use the only possible means by which we can coerce her into compliance. I shall follow this letter by the first stage-coach; and, before the beginning of the next month, Clara Day shall be your wife.
>
> Your affectionate father,
>
> C. LE NOIR, Esq., Hidden House.   GABRIEL LE NOIR.

When Craven Le Noir read this letter, his thin white face and deep-set eyes lighted up with triumph. But Craven Le Noir huzzaed before he was out of the woods. He had not calculated upon Capitola.

The next day Colonel Le Noir came to the Hidden House. He arrived late in the afternoon.

After refreshing himself with a bath, a change of clothing, and a light luncheon, he went to the library where he passed the remainder of the evening in a confidential conference with his son. Their supper was ordered to be served up to them there. And for that one evening Clara had the comfort of taking her tea alone.

The result of this conference was that the next morning, after breakfast, Colonel Le Noir sent for Miss Day to come to him in the library.

When Clara, nerving her gentle heart to resist a sinful tyranny, entered the library, Colonel Le Noir arose and courteously handed her to a chair; and then, seating himself beside her, said:

"My dear Clara, the responsibilities of a guardian are always very onerous, and his duties *not* always very agreeable, especially when his ward is the sole heiress of a large property and the object of pursuit by fortune-hunters and manœuverers, male and female. When such is the case, the duties and responsibilities of the guardian are augmented a hundred fold."

"Sir, this cannot be so in *my* case; since you are perfectly aware that my destiny is—humanly speaking—already decided," replied Clara, with gentle firmness.

"As *how*, I pray you, my fair ward?"

"You cannot possibly be at a loss to understand, sir. You have been already advised that I am betrothed to Dr. Rocke, who will claim me as his wife upon the day that I shall complete my twenty-first year."

"Miss Clara Day, no more of that I beseech you. It is folly, perversity, frenzy! But, thanks to the wisdom of legislators, the law very properly invests the guardian with great latitude of discretionary power over the person and property of his ward—to be used, of course, for that ward's best interest. And thus, my dear Clara, it is my duty, while holding this power over you, to exercise it for preventing the possibility of your *ever,* either now or at any future time, throwing yourself away upon a mere adventurer. To do this, I must provide you with a suitable husband. My son, Mr. Craven Le Noir, has long loved and wooed you. He is a young man of good reputation and fair prospects. I entirely approve his suit; and as your guardian, I command you to receive him for your destined husband."

"Colonel Le Noir, this is no time 'for bated breath and whispered humbleness.' I am but a simple girl of seventeen, but I understand your purpose and that of your son just as well as though I were an old man of the world! *You* are the fortune-hunters and manœuverers! It is the *fortune* of the wealthy heiress and friendless orphan that you are in pursuit of! But that fortune, like my hand and heart, is already promised to one I love; and to speak very plainly to you, I would *die* ere I would disappoint *him* or wed your *son!*" said Clara, with invincible firmness.

"*Die, girl?*—there are worse things than death in the world!" said Colonel Le Noir, with a threatening glare.

"I know it! and *one* of the worst things in the world would be a union with a man I could neither esteem nor even endure!" exclaimed Clara.

Colonel Le Noir saw that there was no use in further disguise. Throwing off, then, the last restraint of good breeding, he said:

"And there are still more terrible evils for a woman than to be the wife of one she 'can neither esteem nor endure!'"

Clara shook her head in proud scorn.

"There are evils, to escape which, such a woman would go down upon her bended knees to be made the wife of such a man!"

Clara's gentle eyes flashed with indignation!

"Infamous!" she cried. "You slander all womanhood in my person!"

"The evils to which I allude are—comprised in—a life of dishonor!" hissed Le Noir, through his set teeth.

"This to my father's daughter?" exclaimed Clara, growing white as death at the insult.

"Aye, my girl! it is time we understood each other! You are in my power, and _I intend to coerce you to my will!_"

These words, accompanied as they were by a look that left no doubt upon her mind that he would carry out his purpose to any extremity, so appalled the maiden's soul that she stood like one suddenly struck with catalepsy.

The unscrupulous wretch then approached her and said:

"I am going now to the county-seat to take out a marriage license for you and my son. I shall have the carriage at the door by six o'clock this evening, when I desire that you shall be ready to accompany us to church, where a clerical friend will be in attendance to perform the marriage ceremony!—Clara Day, if you would save your honor, look to this!"

All this time Clara had neither moved, nor spoken, nor breathed. She had stood cold, white and still, as if turned to stone.

"Let no vain hope of escape delude your mind. The doors will be kept locked; the servants are all warned not to suffer you to leave the house. Look to it, Clara, for the rising of another sun shall see my purposes accomplished!"

And with these words the atrocious wretch left the room. His departure took off the dreadful spell that had paralyzed Clara's life; her blood began to circulate again; breath came to her lungs and speech to her lips.

"Oh, Lord," she cried; "Oh, Lord, who delivered the children from the fiery furnace, deliver thy poor handmaiden now from her terrible foes." [2]

While thus she prayed, she saw upon the writing table before her a small penknife. Her cheeks flushed and her eyes brightened as she seized it:

"This! this!" she said, "this small instrument, is sufficient to save me! Should the worst ensue—I know where to find the carotid artery, and even such a slight puncture as my timorous hand could make would set my spirit free. Oh, my father! oh, my father! you little thought when you taught your Clara the mysteries of anatomy, to what fearful use she would put your lessons.—And would it be right?—Oh, would it be right? One may desire death; but can anything justify suicide?—Oh, Father in Heaven, guide me! guide me!" cried Clara, falling upon her knees and sobbing forth this prayer of agony!

Soon approaching footsteps drew her attention. And she had only time to rise and put back her damp, dishevelled hair from her tear-stained face, before the door opened and Dorcas Knight appeared, and said:

"Here is this young woman come again!"

And rudely ushering in Capitola, she closed the door and retreated.

"I declare, Miss Day," said Cap, laughing, "you have the most accomplished, polite and agreeable servants here that ever I met with! Think with what a courteous welcome this woman received me—'Here you are again!' she said. 'You'll come once too often for your good, and that I tell you.' I answered that *every* time I came it appeared to be once too often for her liking. She rejoined—'The Colonel has come home, and he don't like company, so I advise you to make your call a short one.' I assured her that I should measure the length of my visit by the breadth of my will—But good angels, Clara! what is the matter? You look worse than death!" exclamed Capitola, noticing for the first time the pale, wild, despairing face of her companion.

Clara clasped her hands as if in prayer, and raised her eyes with an appealing gaze into Capitola's face.

"Tell me, dear Clara, what is the matter? how can I help you? what shall I do for you?" said our heroine.

Before trusting herself to reply, Clara gazed wistfully into Capitola's eyes, as though she would have read her soul.

Cap did not blench, nor for an instant avert her own honest, gray orbs; she let Clara gaze straight down through those clear windows of the soul into the very soul itself, where she found only truth, honesty and courage.

The scrutiny seemed to be satisfactory, for Clara soon took the hand of her visitor, and said:

"Capitola, I will tell you. It is a horrid, horrid story, but you shall know all. Come with me to my chamber."

Cap pressed the hand that was so confidingly placed in hers, and accompanied Clara to her room, where, after the latter had taken the precaution to lock the door, the two girls sat down for a confidential talk.

Clara, like the author of Robin Hood's Barn, "began at the beginning" of her story, and told everything—her betrothal to Traverse Rocke; the sudden death of her father; the decision of the Orphans' Court; the departure of Traverse for the Far West; her arrival at the Hidden House; the interruption of all her epistolary correspondence with her betrothed and his mother; the awful and mysterious occurrence of that dreadful night when she suspected some heinous crime had been committed; and finally of the long, unwelcome suit of Craven Le Noir, and the present attempt to force him upon her as a husband.

Cap listened very calmly to this story, showing very little sympathy, for there was not a bit of sentimentality about our Cap.

"And now," whispered Clara, while the pallor of horror overspread her face, "by threatening me with a fate worse than death, they would drive me to marry Craven Le Noir!"

"Yes, I know I would," said Cap, as if speaking to herself, but by her tone and manner clothing these simple words in the very keenest sarcasm.

"What would you do, Capitola?" asked Clara, raising her tearful eyes to the last speaker.

"Marry Mr. Craven Le Noir, and thank him, too!" said Cap. Then suddenly changing her tone, she exclaimed:

"I wish—oh how I wish it was only me in your place—that it was only me they were trying to marry against my will!"

"What would you do?" asked Clara, earnestly.

"What would I do? Oh! wouldn't I make them know the difference between their Sovereign Lady and Sam the Lackey? If I had been in your place, and the dastard Le Noir had said to me what he said to you, I do believe I should have stricken him dead with the lightning of my eyes! But what shall you do, my poor Clara?"

"Alas! alas! see here! this is my last resort!" replied the unhappy girl, showing the little penknife.

"Put it away from you! put it away from you!" exclaimed Capitola, earnestly; "suicide is never, never justifiable! God is the lord of life and death! He is the only judge whether a mortal's sorrows are to be relieved by death, and when he does not himself release you, he means that you shall live and endure. That proves that suicide is never right, let the Roman pagans have said and done what they pleased. So no more of that. There are enough other ways of escape for you."

"Ah! what are they? You would give me life by teaching me how to escape!" said Clara, fervently.

"The first and most obvious means that suggests itself to my mind," said Cap, "is to—run away."

"Ah! that is impossible! The servants are warned; the doors are all locked; I am watched!"

"Then the next plan is equally obvious; consent to go with them to the church, and when you get there, denounce them, and claim the protection of the clergyman!"

"Ah! dear girl, that is still more impracticable. The officiating clergyman is their friend; and even if I could consent to act a deceitful part, and should go to church as if to marry Craven, and upon getting there, denounce him, instead of receiving the protection of the clergyman, I should be restored to the hands of my legal guardian, and be brought back here to meet a fate worse than death," said Clara, in a tone of despair.

Capitola did not at once reply, but fell into deep thought, which lasted many minutes. Then, speaking more gravely than she had spoken before, she said:

"There is but one plan of escape left! your only remaining chance, and that full of danger."

"Oh! why should I fear danger? What evil can befall me so great as that which now threatens me?" said Clara.

"This plan requires on your part great courage, self-control and presence of mind."

"Teach me, teach me, dear Capitola. I will be an apt pupil!"

"I have thought it all out, and will tell you my plan. It is now eleven o'clock in the forenoon, and the carriage is to come for you at six this evening, I believe?"

"Yes! yes!"

"Then you have seven hours in which to save yourself. And this is my plan: First, Clara, you must change clothes with me, giving me your suit of mourning and putting on my riding habit, hat and veil. Then leaving me here in your place, you are to pull the veil down closely over your face and walk right out of the house. No one will speak to you, for they never do to me. When you have reached the yard, spring upon my horse and put whip to him for the village of Tip-Top. My servant, Wool, will ride after you, but not speak to you or approach near enough to discover your identity—for he has been ordered by his master to keep me in sight, and he has been forbidden by his mistress to intrude upon her privacy. You will reach Tip-Top by three o'clock, when the Staunton stage passes through. You may then reveal yourself to Wool, give my horse into his charge, get into the coach and start for Staunton. Upon reaching that place, put yourself under the protection of your friends, the two old physicians, and get them to prosecute your guardian for cruelty and flagrant abuse of authority. Be cool, firm and alert, and all will be well!"

Clara, who had listened to this little Napoleon in petticoats with breathless interest, now clasped her hands in a wild ecstasy of joy, and exclaimed:

"I will try it! Oh, Capitola, I will try it! Heaven bless you for the counsel!"

"Be quick, then, change your dress, provide yourself with a purse of money, and I will give you particular directions how to make a short-cut for Tip-Top! Ha, ha, ha! when they come for the bride she will be already rolling on the turnpike between Tip-Top and Staunton."

"But you! Oh, you, my generous deliverer?"

"I shall dress myself in your clothes and stay here in your place to keep you from being missed, so as to give you full time to make your escape."

"But, you will place yourself in the enraged lion's jaws. You will remain in the power of two men who know neither justice nor mercy, who in their love or their hate fear neither God nor man. Oh, Capitola, how can I take an advantage of your generosity, and leave you here in such extreme peril? Capitola, I cannot do it."

"Well, then, I believe you must be anxious to marry Craven Le Noir."

"Oh, Capitola."

"Well, if you are not, hurry and get ready; there is no time to be lost."

"Never mind me. *I* shall be safe enough. *I* am not afraid of the Le Noirs. Bless their wigs, I should like to see them make *me* blench. On the contrary, I desire above all things to be pitted against those two. How I shall enjoy their disappointment and rage. Oh, it will be a rare frolic."

While Capitola was speaking she was also busily engaged doing. She went softly to the door and turned the key in the lock, to prevent any one from looking through the keyhole, murmuring as she did it:

"I wasn't brought up among the detective policemen for nothing."

Then she began to take off her riding-habit. Quickly she dressed Clara, superintending all the details of her disguise as carefully as though she were the costumer of a new debutante. When Clara was dressed, she was so nearly of the same size and shape of Capitola, that from behind no one would have suspected her identity.

"There, Clara, tuck your light hair out of the way; pull your cap over your eyes; gather your veil down close; draw up your figure, throw back your head; walk with a little springy sway and swagger, as if you didn't care a damson for anybody, and—there! I declare, nobody could tell you from me," exclaimed Capitola, in delight, as she completed the disguise and the instructions of Clara.

307

Then Capitola dressed herself in Clara's deep mourning robes. And then the two girls sat down to compose themselves for a few minutes, while Capitola gave new and particular directions for Clara's course and conduct, so as to ensure, as far as human foresight could do it, the safe termination of her perilous adventure. By the time they had ended their talk the hall clock struck twelve.

"There, it is full time you should be off. Be calm, be cool, be firm, and God bless you, Clara. Dear girl, if I were only a young man, I would deliver you by the strength of my own arm, without subjecting you to inconvenience or danger," said Cap, gallantly, as she led Clara to the chamber door, and carefully gathered her thick veil in close folds over her face, so as entirely to conceal it.

"Oh, may the Lord in Heaven bless and preserve and reward you, my brave, my noble, my heroic Capitola!" said Clara, fervently, with the tears rushing to her eyes.

"Bosh," said Cap. "If you go doing the sentimental you won't look like me a bit, and that will spoil all. There, keep your veil close, for it's windy you know; throw back your head, and swing yourself along with a swagger, as if you didn't care a—hem! for anybody, and—there you are," said Cap, pushing Clara out and shutting the door behind her.

Clara paused an instant to offer up one short fervent prayer for her success and Capitola's safety, and then following her instructions, went on.

Nearly all girls are clever imitators, and Clara readily adopted Capitola's light, springy, swaying walk, and met old Dorcas Knight in the hall, without exciting the slightest suspicion of her identity.

"Humph," said the woman; "so you are going. I advise you not to come back again."

Clara threw up her head with a swagger, and went on.

"Very well, you may scorn my words, but if you know your own good, you'll follow my advice," said Dorcas Knight, harshly.

Clara threw up her head and passed out.

Before the door Wool was waiting with the horses. Keeping her face closely muffled, Clara went to Capitola's pony. Wool came and helped her into the saddle saying:

"Yer does right, Miss Cap, to keep your face kivered; it's awful windy, aint it though? I kin scarcely keep the hat from blowing offen my head."

With an impatient jerk after the manner of Capitola, Clara signified that she did not wish to converse. Wool dropped obediently behind, mounted his horse, and followed at a respectful distance, until Clara turned her horse's head and took the bridle-path towards Tip-Top. This move filled poor Wool with dismay. Riding towards her, he exclaimed:

" 'Deed, Miss Cap, yer mus' scuse me for speakin' now. Whar de mischief *is* yer a'goin' to?"

For all answer Clara, feigning temper of Capitola, suddenly wheeled her horse, elevated her riding-whip, and galloped upon Wool in a threatening manner.

Wool dodged and backed his horse with all possible expedition—exclaiming in consternation:

"Dar! Dar, Miss Cap, I won't go for to ax you any more questions—no—not if yer rides straight to Old Nick or Black Donald!"

Whereupon receiving this apology in good part, Clara again turned her horse's head and rode on her way.

Wool followed, bemoaning the destiny that kept him between the two fierce fires of his old master's despotism and his young mistress's caprice, and muttering:

"I know old marse and dis young gal am going to be the death of me. I knows it jes' as well as nuffin at all. I 'clare to man, if it ain't nuff to make anybody go heave themselves right into a grist mill and be ground up at once."

Wool spoke no more until they got to Tip-Top, when Clara, still closely veiled, rode up to the stage office just as the coach, half filled with passengers, was about to start. Springing from her horse, she went up to Wool, and said:

"Here, man, take this horse back to Hurricane Hall. Tell Major Warfield that Miss Black remains at the Hidden House in imminent danger. Ask him to ride there and bring her home. Tell Miss Black, when you see her, that I reached Tip-Top safe and in time to take the coach. Tell her I will never cease to be grateful. And now, here is a half eagle for your trouble. Good-bye, and God bless you." And she put the piece in his hand and took her place in the coach, which immediately started.

As for Wool!!!—From the time that Clara had thrown aside her veil and began to speak to him, he had stood staring and staring—his consternation growing and growing—until it had seemed to have turned him into stone—from which state of petrification he did not recover until he saw the stage-coach roll rapidly away, carrying off—whom? Capitola,

Clara, or the Evil One?—Wool could not have told which! He presently astounded the people about the stage office by leaving his horse and taking to his heels after the stage-coach, vociferating:

"Murder! murder! help! help! stop thief! stop thief! stop the coach! stop the coach!"

"What is the matter, man?" said a constable, trying to head him.

But Wool incontinently ran over the officer, throwing him down and keeping on his headlong course, hat off, coattail streaming, and legs and arms flying like the sails of a windmill, as he tried to overtake the coach, crying:

"Help! Murder! Head the horses! Stop the coach! Old Marse told me not to lose sight of her! Oh, for hebben's sake, good people, stop the coach!"

When he got to a gate, instead of taking time to open it, he rolled himself summerset-like right over it. When he met man or woman, instead of turning from his straight course, he knocked them over and passed on, garments flying, and legs and arms circulating with the velocity of a wheel.

The people whom he successively met and overthrew in his course, picking themselves up, and getting into the village, reported that there was a furious madman broke loose, who attacked every one he met.

And soon every man and boy in the village who could mount a horse started in hot pursuit. *Only* race horses would have beaten the speed with which Wool ran, urged on by fear. It was nine miles on the turnpike road from Tip-Top that the horsemen overtook and surrounded Wool, who seeing himself hopelessly environed fell down upon the ground and kicked, swearing that he would not be taken alive to have his eyelids cut off!

It was not until after a desperate resistance that he was finally taken, bound, put in a wagon and carried back to the village, where he was recognized as Major Warfield's man, and a messenger was dispatched for his master.

And not until he had been repeatedly assured that no harm should befall him, did Wool gain composure enough to say, amid tears of cruel grief and fear:

"Oh, marsers, my young missuss, Miss Black, done been conjured and bewitched and turned into somebody else, right afore my own two looking eyes, and gone off in dat coach! 'deed she is, and ole marse kill me! 'deed he will, gemmen. He went and ordered me not to take my eyes offen her, and no more I didn't. But what good that do, when she turned to somebody else, and went off right afore my two looking eyes! But old marse won't listen to reason! He'll kill me, I know he will!" whimpered Wool, refusing to be comforted.

CHAPTER XL

CAP IN CAPTIVITY

✻✻✻✻✻

"I lingered here and rescue planned
For Clara and for me."
—*Scott* [1]

MEANWHILE HOW fared it with Capitola in the Hidden House?

"I am in for it now!" said Cap, as she closed the door behind Clara; "I am in for it now! This *is* a jolly imprudent adventure! What will Wool do when he discovers that he has 'lost sight' of me? What will uncle say when he finds out what I've done? Whe—ew! Uncle will explode! I wonder if the walls at Hurricane Hall will be strong enough to stand it? Wool will go mad! I doubt if he will ever do a bit more good in this world!

"But above all, I wonder what the Le Noirs, father and son, WILL say when they find that the heiress has flown, and a 'beggar,' as uncle flatters me by calling me, will be here in her place! Whe—ew—ew—ew! There will be a tornado! Cap, child, they'll murder you! that's just what they'll do! They'll kill and eat you, Cap, without any salt! or they may lock you up in the haunted room to live with the ghost, Cap, and that would be worse!

"Hush! here comes Dorcas Knight! Now I must make believe I'm Clara, and do the sentimental up brown!" concluded Capitola, as she seated herself near the door where she could be heard, and began to sob softly.

Dorcas rapped.

Cap sobbed in response.

"Are you coming to luncheon, Miss Day?" inquired the woman.

"Ee—*hee!* Ee—*hee!* Ee—*hee!* I do not want to eat," sobbed Cap, in a low and smothered voice. Any one would have thought she was drowned in tears.

312

"Very well—just as you like," said the woman, harshly, as she went away.

"Well, I declare," laughed Cap, "I did that quite as well as an actress could! But now what am I to do? How long can I keep this up? Heigh-ho! 'let the world slide!' I'll not reveal myself until I'm driven to it, for when I do—! Cap, child, you'll get chawed right up!"

A little later in the day Dorcas Knight came again, and rapped at the door.

"Eh—*hee!* Ee—*hee!* Ee—*hee!*" sobbed Cap.

"Miss Day, your cousin, Craven Le Noir, wishes to speak with you alone."

"Ee—*hee!* Ee—*hee!* Ee—*hee!* I cannot see him," sobbed Cap, in a low and suffocating voice.

The woman went away and Cap suffered no other interruption until six o'clock, when Dorcas Knight once more rapped, saying:

"Miss Day, your uncle is at the front door with the carriage, and he wishes to know if you are ready to obey him."

"Ee—*hee!* Ee—*hee!* Ee—*hee!*—te—te—tell him yes!" sobbed Cap, as if her heart would break.

The woman went off with this answer, and Capitola hastily enveloped her form in Clara's large black shawl, put on Clara's black bonnet, and tied her thick mourning veil closely over her face.

"A pretty bridal dress this! but, however, I suppose these men are no more particular about my costume than they are about their own conduct," said Cap.

She had just drawn on her gloves when she heard the footsteps of two men approaching. They rapped at the door.

"Come in," she sobbed, in a low, broken voice, that might have belonged to any girl in deep distress, and she put a white cambric handkerchief up to her eyes and drew her thick veil closely over her face.

The two Le Noirs immediately entered the room. Craven approached her, and whispered, softly:

"You will forgive me this, my share in these proceedings after awhile, sweet Clara. The Sabine women did not love the Roman youths the less that they were forcibly made wives by them."

"Ee—*hee!* Ee—*hee!* Ee—*hee!*" sobbed Cap, entirely concealing her face in her white cambric handkerchief under her impenetrable veil.

"Come, come! we lose time," said the elder Le Noir. "Draw her arm within yours, Craven, and lead her out."

The young man did as he was directed, and led Cap from the room. It was now quite dark—the long dreary passage was only dimly lighted by a hanging lamp, so that with the care she took there was scarcely a possibility of Capitola's being discovered. They went on, Craven Le Noir whispering hypocritical apologies, and Cap replying only by sobs.

When they reached the outer door, they found a close carriage drawn up before the house.

To this Craven Le Noir led Capitola, placed her within and took the seat by her side. Colonel Le Noir placed himself on the front seat opposite them, and the carriage was driven rapidly off.

An hour's ride brought the party to an obscure church in the depths of the forest, which Capitola recognized by the cross on its top to be a Roman Catholic Chapel.

Here the carriage drew up and the two Le Noirs got out and assisted Capitola to alight.

They then led her into the church, which was dimly illumined by a pair of wax candles burning before the altar. A priest in his sacerdotal robes was in attendance. A few country people were scattered thinly about among the pews, at their private devotions.

Guarded by Craven Le Noir on the right, and Colonel Le Noir on the left, Capitola was marched up the aisle and placed before the altar.

Colonel Le Noir then went and spoke apart to the officiating priest, saying, in a tone of dissatisfaction:

"I told you, sir, that as our bride was an orphan, recently bereaved, and still in deep mourning, we wished the marriage ceremony to be strictly private, and you gave me to understand, sir, that at this hour, the chapel was most likely to be vacant. Yet here I find half a score of people. How is this?"

"Sir," replied the priest, "it is true, that at this hour of the evening, the chapel *is* most likely to be vacant, but it is not therefore certain to be so, nor did I promise as much. Our chapel is, as you know, open at all hours of the day and night, that all who please may come and pray. These people that you see are hard-working farm laborers, who have no time to come in the day, and who are now here to offer their evening prayers and, also, some of them to examine their consciences preparatory to confession. They can certainly be no interruption to the ceremony."

"Egad, I don't know that," muttered Colonel Le Noir between his teeth.

As for Cap the sight of other persons present in the chapel filled her heart with joy and exultation, inasmuch as it ensured her final safety. And so she just abandoned herself to the spirit of frolic that possessed her, and anticipated with the keenest relish the denouement of her strange adventure.

"Well, what are we waiting for? Proceed, sir, proceed," said Colonel Le Noir, as he took Cap by the shoulders and placed her on the left side of his son, while he himself stood behind ready to 'give the bride away.'

The ceremony immediately commenced.

The prologue beginning—"Dearly Beloved, we are gathered together here," etc., etc., etc., was read.

The solemn exhortation to the contracting parties commencing—"I require and charge ye both, as ye shall answer in the dreadful day of judgment when the secrets of all hearts shall be disclosed, that if either of you know any just cause or impediment why ye may not lawfully be joined together," etc., etc., etc., followed.

Capitola listened to all this with the deepest attention, saying to herself—"Well, I declare, this getting married is really awfully interesting. If it were not for Herbert Greyson, I'd just let it go right straight on to the end, and see what would happen next."

While Cap was making these mental comments the priest was asking the bridegroom:

"Wilt thou have this woman to be thy wedded wife," etc., etc., etc., etc., "so long as ye both shall live?"

To which Craven Le Noir, in a sonorous voice responded:

"I will."

"*Indeed* you will? We'll see that presently," said Cap, to herself.

The priest then turning towards the bride, inquired:

"Wilt thou have this man to be thy wedded husband," etc., etc., etc., "so long as ye both shall live?"

To which the bride, throwing aside her veil, answered firmly:

"No! not if he were the last man and I the last woman on the face of the earth, and the human race were about to become extinct, and the angel Gabriel came down from above to ask it of me as a personal favor."

The effect of this outburst, this revelation, this explosion, may be imagined but can never be adequately described.

The priest dropped his book, and stood with lifted hands and open mouth and staring eyes as though he had raised a ghost!

The two Le Noirs simultaneously sprang forward, astonishment, disappointment and rage contending in their blanched faces!

"Who are you, girl?" exclaimed Colonel Le Noir.

"Capitola Black, your honor's glory!" she replied making a deep courtesy.

"What the foul fiend is the meaning of all this?" in the same breath inquired the father and son.

Cap put her thumb to the side of her nose and whirling her four fingers, replied:

"It means, your worships' excellences, that—you—can't—come it! it's no go! this chicken won't fight! It means that the fat's in the fire, and the cat's out of the bag! It means confusion! distraction! perdition! and a tearing off of our wigs! It means the game's up, the play's over, villainy is about to be hanged, and virtue about to be rewarded, and the curtain is going to drop, and the principal performer—that's I—is going to be called out amid the applause of the audience!" Then suddenly changing her mocking tone to one of great severity, she said:

"It means that you have been outwitted by a girl; it means that your proposed victim has fled, and is by this time in safety. It means that you two, precious father and son would be a pair of knaves if you had sense enough; but, failing in that, you are only a pair of fools."

By this time the attention of the few persons in the church was aroused. They all arose to their feet to look and listen, and some of them left their places and approached the altar. And to these latter Capitola now suddenly turned and said, aloud:

"Good people, I am Capitola Black, the niece and ward of Major Ira Warfield, of Hurricane Hall, whom you all know; and now I claim your protection while I shall tell you the meaning of my presence here."

"Don't listen to her! she is a maniac!' cried Colonel Le Noir.

"Stop her mouth!" cried Craven, springing upon Capitola, and holding her tightly in the grasp of his right arm, while he covered her lips and nostrils with his large left hand.

Capitola struggled so fiercely to free herself that Craven had enough to do to hold her, and so was not aware of a ringing footstep coming up the aisle, until a stunning blow dealt from a strong arm covered his face with blood, and stretched him out at Capitola's feet.

Cap flushed, breathless, and confused, looked up, and was caught to the bosom of Herbert Greyson, who, pale with concentrated rage, held her closely, and inquired:

"Capitola, what violence is this which has been done you?—Explain, who is the aggressor?"

"Wai—wai—wait until I get my breath!—there! that was good. That villain has all but strangled me to death. Oh, Herbert, I'm so delighted you've come! How is it that you always drop right down at the right time and on the right spot?" said Cap, while gasping for breath.

"I will tell you another time. Now I want an explanation."

"Yes, Herbert, I also wish to explain—not only to you, but to these gaping good people. Let me have a hearing!" said Cap.

"She is mad—absolutely mad!" cried Colonel Le Noir, who was assisting his son to rise.

"SILENCE, SIR!" thundered Herbert Greyson, advancing towards him with uplifted and threatening hand.

"Gentlemen, gentlemen! *pray* remember that you are within the walls of a church!" said the distressed priest.

"Craven, this is no place for us—let us go and pursue our fugitive ward," whispered Colonel Le Noir to his son.

"We might as well; for it is clear that all is over here," replied Craven.

And the two baffled villains turned to leave the place. But Herbert Greyson, speaking up, said:

"Good people! prevent the escape of those men until we hear what this young lady has to say, that we may judge whether to let them go or to take them before a magistrate."

The people flew to the doors and windows and secured them, and then surrounded the two Le Noirs, who found themselves prisoners.

"Now Capitola, tell us how it is that you are here?" said Herbert Greyson.

"Well, that elder man," said Cap, "is the guardian of a young heiress, who was betrothed to a worthy young man, one Dr. Traverse Rocke."

"My friend," interrupted Herbert.

"Yes, Mr. Greyson, your friend. The engagement was approved by the young lady's father, who gave them his dying blessing. Nevertheless, in the face of all this, this 'guardian' here, appointed by the Orphans' Court to take charge of the heiress and her fortune, undertakes, for his own ends, to compel the young lady to break her engagement and marry his own son. To drive her to this measure, he does not hesitate to use every species of cruelty. This night he was to have forced her to this altar. But in the interval, to-day, I chanced to visit her at the house where she was confined. Being informed by her of her distressing situation, and having no time to help her in any better way, I just changed clothes with her. She escaped unsuspected in my dress. And those two heroes there, mistaking me for

317

her, forced me into a carriage and dragged me hither to be married against my will. And instead of catching an heiress, they caught a Tartar—that's all! And now, Herbert, let the two poor wretches go hide their mortification, and do you take me home, for I am immensely tired of doing the sentimental, making speeches, and piling up the agonies."

While Cap was delivering this long oration, the two Le Noirs had made several essays to interrupt and contradict her, but were effectually prevented by the people, whose sympathies were all with the speaker. Now, at Herbert Greyson's command, they released the culprits, who, threatening loudly, took their departure.

Herbert then led Capitola out, and placed her upon her own pony, Gyp, which, to her unbounded astonishment, she found there in charge of Wool, who was also mounted upon his own hack.

Herbert Greyson threw himself into the saddle of a third horse, and the three took the road to Hurricane Hall.

"And now," said Capitola, as Herbert rode up to her side, "for Mercy's sake tell me, before I go crazy with conjecture, how it happened that you dropped down from the sky at the very moment and on the very spot where you were needed? and where did you light upon Wool and the horses?"

"It is very simple when you come to understand it," said Herbert, smiling. "In the first place, you know I graduated at the last Commencement?"

"Yes."

"Well, I have just received a lieutenant's commission in a regiment that is ordered to join General Scott in Mexico."

"Oh, Herbert, that *is* news, and I don't know whether to be in despair or in ecstacy!" said Cap, ready to laugh or cry as a feather's weight might tip the scales in which she balanced Herbert's new honors with his approaching perils.

"If there's any doubt about it, I decidedly recommend the latter emotion!" said Herbert, laughing.

"When do you go?" inquired Cap.

"Our regiment embarks for Baltimore on the first of next month. Meanwhile I got leave of absence to come and spend a week with my friends at home."

"Oh, Herbert, I—I am in a quandary! But you haven't told me yet how you happened to meet with Wool and to come here just in the nick of time."

"I am just going to do so. Well, you see, Capitola, I came down in the stage to Tip-Top, which I reached about three o'clock. And there I found Wool in the hands of the Philistines, suspected of being mad, from the manner in which he raved about losing sight of you. Well, of course, like a true knight, I delivered my lady's squire, comforted and re-assured him, and made him mount his own horse and take charge of yours. After which I mounted the beast that I had hired to convey me to Hurricane Hall, and we set off thither. I confess that I was excessively anxious on your account, for I could make nothing whatever of Wool's wild story of your supposed metamorphosis. I thought it best to make a circuit, and take the Hidden House in our course, to make some inquiries there as to what had really happened. I had got a little bewildered between the dark night and the strange road, and seeing the light in the church, I had just ridden up to inquire my way, when to my astonishment I saw you within, before the altar, struggling in the grasp of that ruffian. And you know the rest. And now let us ride on quickly, for I have a strong presentiment that Major Warfield is suffering the tortures of a lost soul through anxiety upon your account," concluded Herbert Greyson.

"Please, Marse Herbert and Miss Cap, don't you tell ole marse nuffen 'tall 'bout my loosin' sight of you," pleaded Wool.

"We shall tell your old master all about it, Wool, for I would not have him miss the pleasure of hearing this adventure upon any account; but I promise to bear you harmless through it," said Herbert, as they galloped rapidly towards home.

They reached Hurricane Hall by eight o'clock, and in good time for supper. They found Old Hurricane storming all over the house, and ordering everybody off the premises, in his fury of anxiety upon Capitola's account. But when the party arrived, surprise at seeing them in the company of Herbert Greyson, quite revolutionized his mood, and forgetting to rage, he gave them all a hearty welcome.

And when after supper was over, and they were all gathered around the comfortable fireside, and Herbert related the adventures and feats of Capitola at the Hidden House, and in the Forest Chapel, the old man grasped the hand of his favorite, and with his stormy old eyes full of rain, said:

"You deserve to have been a man, Cap! Indeed you do, my girl!"

That was his highest style of praise.

Then Herbert told his own little story of getting his commission and being ordered to Mexico.

"God bless you, lad, and save you in the battle, and bring you home with victory!" was Old Hurricane's comment.

Then seeing that the young people were quite worn out with fatigue, and feeling not averse to his own comfortable couch, Old Hurricane broke up the circle, and they all retired to rest.

CHAPTER XLI

AN UNEXPECTED VISITOR AT MARAH'S COTTAGE

"'Friend, wilt thou give me shelter here?'
The stranger meekly saith;
'My life is haunted; evil men
Are following on my path.'"

MARAH ROCKE sat by her lonely fireside.

The cottage was not changed in any respect since the day upon which we first of all found her there. There was the same bright, little wood fire; the same clean hearth, and the identical faded carpet on the floor. There was the dresser with its glistening crockery-ware on the right, and the shelves with Traverse's old school-books on the left of the fireplace.

The widow herself had changed in nothing except that her clean, black dress was threadbare and rusty, and her patient face whiter and thinner than before.

And now there was no eager restlessness; no frequent listening and looking towards the door. Alas! she could not now expect to hear her boy's light and springing step and cheerful voice as he hurried home at eventide from his daily work. Traverse was far away at St. Louis undergoing the cares and trials of a friendless young physician trying to get into practice. Six months had passed since he took leave of her, and there was as yet no hope of his returning even to pay a visit.

So Marah sat very still and sad, bending over her needlework, without ever turning her head in the direction of the door. True, he wrote to her every week. No Wednesday ever passed without bringing her a letter written in a strong, buoyant and encouraging strain. Still she missed Traverse very sadly. It was dreary to rise up in the empty house every morning; dreary to sit down to her solitary meals, and drearier still to go to bed in her lonely room without having received her boy's kiss and heard his cheerful good-night. And it was her custom every night to read over Traverse's last letter before retiring to bed.

It was getting on towards ten o'clock when she folded up her work and put it away, and drew her boy's latest epistle from her bosom to read. It ran as follows:

St. Louis, Dec. 1, 184—.

My Dearest Mother:——I am very glad to hear that you continue in good health, and that you do not work too hard, or miss me too sadly. It is the greatest comfort of my life to hear good news of you, sweet mother. I count the days from one letter to another, and read every last letter over daily until I get a new one. You insist upon my telling you how I am getting on, and whether I am out of money. I am doing quite well, ma'am, and have some funds left! I have quite a considerable practice. It is true that my professional services are in request only among the very poor, who pay me with their thanks and good wishes. But I am very glad to pay off a small part of the great debt of gratitude I owe to the benevolent of this world by doing all that I can in my turn for the needy. And even if I had never myself been the object of a good man's benevolence, I should still have desired to serve the indigent; "for whoso giveth to the poor lendeth to the Lord,"[1] and I "like the security." Therefore, sweet mother of mine, be at ease, for I am getting on swimmingly—*with one exception.* Still I do not hear from our Clara. Six months have now passed, during which, despite of the seeming silence, I have written to her every week; but not one letter or message have I received from her in return! And now you tell me also that you have not received a single letter from her either. I know not what to think. Anxiety upon her account is my one sole trouble. Not that I wrong the dear girl by one instant's doubt of her constancy—no; my soul upon her truth! if I could do that, I should be most unworthy of her love. No, mother, you and I know that Clara is true. But, ah, we do not know to what sufferings she may be subjected by Le Noir, who I firmly believe has intercepted all our letters. Mother, I am about to ask a great, perhaps an unreasonable, favor of you. It is to go down into the neighborhood of the Hidden House, and make inquiries, and try to find out Clara's real condition. If it be possible, put yourself into communication with her, and tell her that I judge her heart by my own and have the firmest faith in her constancy, even though I have written to her every week for six months, without ever having received an answer. I feel that I am putting you to expense and trouble, but my great anxiety about Clara, which I am sure you share, must be my excuse. I kiss your dear and honored hands: and remain ever,

Your loving son and faithful servant,

TRAVERSE ROCKE.

"I must try to go. It will be an awful expense, because I know no one down there, and I shall have to board at the tavern at Tip-Top while I am making inquiries—for I dare not approach the dwelling of Gabriel Le Noir!" said Marah Rocke, as she folded up her letter, and replaced it in her bosom.

Just at that moment she heard the sound of wheels approach, and a vehicle of some sort draw up to the gate, and some one speaking without.

She went to the door, and listening, heard a girlish voice say:

"A dollar?—Yes, certainly; here it is. There you may go now."

She recognized the voice, and with a cry of joy jerked the door open just as the carriage rolled away. And the next instant Clara Day was in her arms.

"Oh, my darling! my darling! my darling! is this really you? Really, really you, and no dream?" cried Marah Rocke, all in a flutter of excitement, as she strained Clara to her bosom.

"Yes, it is I, sweet friend; come to stay with you a long time, perhaps," said Clara, softly, returning her caresses.

"Oh, my lamb! my lamb! what a joyful surprise! I do think I shall go crazy! Where did you come from, my pet? Who came with you? When did you start? Did Le Noir consent to your coming? And how did it happen?—But, dear child, how worn and weary you look. You must be very tired. Have you had supper? Oh, my darling! come and lie down on this soft lounge, while I put away your things and get you some refreshment," said Marah Rocke, in a delirium of joy, as she took off Clara's hat and sacque, and laid her down to rest on the lounge, which she wheeled up near the fire.

"Oh, my sweet, we have been so anxious about you! Traverse and myself. Traverse is still at St. Louis, love, getting on slowly. He has written to you every week, and so indeed have I, but we neither of us have so much as one letter in reply. And yet neither of us ever doubted your true heart, my child. We knew that the letters must have been lost, miscarried, or intercepted," said Marah, as she busied herself putting on the tea-kettle.

"They must indeed, since my experience in regard to letters exactly corresponds with yours. I have written every week to both of you, yet never received one line in reply from either," said Clara.

"We knew it: we said so. Oh, those Le Noirs! those Le Noirs! But, my darling, you are perfectly exhausted, and though I have asked you a half an hundred questions, you shall not reply to one of them, nor talk a bit more until you have rested and had refreshment. Here, my love, here is Traverse's last letter. It will amuse you to lie and read it while I am getting tea," said Marah, taking the paper from her bosom and handing it to Clara, and then placing the stand with the light near the head of her couch, that she might see to read it without rising.

And while Clara, well pleased, perused and smiled over her lover's letter, Marah Rocke laid the cloth and spread a delicate repast of tea, milk-toast and poached eggs, of which she tenderly pressed her visitor to partake.

And when Clara was somewhat refreshed by food and rest, she said:

"Now, dear mamma, you will wish to hear how it happens that I am with you to-night."

"Not unless you feel quite rested, dear girl."

"I am rested sufficiently for the purpose, besides I am anxious to tell you. And oh, dear mamma! I could just now sit in your lap, and lay my head upon your kind, soft bosom so willingly."

"Come then, Clara. Come, then my darling," said Marah, tenderly; holding out her arms.

"No, no, mamma, you are too little, it would be a sin," said Clara, smiling; "but I will sit by you and put my hand in yours, and rest my head against your shoulder while I tell you all about it."

"Come then, my darling," said Marah Rocke.

Clara took the offered seat, and when she was fixed to her liking, she commenced and related to her friend a full history of all that had occurred to her at the Hidden House, from the moment that she had first crossed its threshold to the hour in which, through the courage and address of Capitola, she was delivered from imminent peril.

"And now," said Clara, in conclusion, "I have come hither in order to get Dr. Williams to make one more appeal for me to the Orphans' Court. And when it is proved what a traitor my guardian has been to his trust, I have no doubt that the judge will appoint some one else in his place, or at least see that my father's last wish in regard to my residence is carried into effect."

"Heaven grant it, my child! Heaven grant it! Oh, those Le Noirs! those Le Noirs! were there ever in the world before such ruthless villains and accomplished hypocrites!" said Marah Rocke, clasping her hands in the strength of her emotions.

A long time yet they talked together, and then they retired to bed, and still talked until they fell asleep in each other's arms.

The next morning the widow arose early, gazed a little while with delight upon the sleeping daughter of her heart, pressed a kiss upon her cheek so softly as not to disturb her rest, and then, leaving her still in the deep, sweet sleep of wearied youth, she went down stairs to get a nice breakfast.

Luckily a farmer's cart was just passing the road before the cottage on its way to market.

Marah took out her little purse from her pocket, hailed the driver, and expended half of her little store in purchasing two young chickens, some eggs, and some dried peaches, saying to herself:

"Dear Clara always had a good appetite, and healthy young human nature must live substantially, in spite of all its little heart-aches."

While Marah was preparing the chicken for the gridiron, the door at the foot of the stairs opened, and Clara came in, looking, after her night's rest, as fresh as a rosebud.

"What! up with the sun, my darling!" said Marah, going to meet her.

"Yes, mamma. Oh! it is so good to be here with you in this nice, quiet place, with no one to make me shudder. But you must let me help you, mamma. See! I will set the table and make the toast."

"Oh, Miss Clara——"

"Yes, I will! I have been ill-used and made miserable, and now you must pet me, mamma, and let me have my own way, and help you to cook our little meals and to make the house tidy, and afterwards to work those button-holes in the shirts you were spoiling your gentle eyes over last night. Oh! if they will only let me stay here with you and be at peace, we shall be very happy together, you and I!" said Clara, as she drew out the little table and laid the cloth.

"My dear child, may the Lord make you as happy as your sweet affection would make me!" said Marah.

"We can work for our living together," continued Clara, as she gaily flitted about from the dresser to the table, placing the cups and saucers and plates—"you can sew the seams and do the plain hemming, and I can work the button-holes and stitch the bosoms, collars and wrist-bands. And 'if the worst comes to the worst,' we can hang out our little shingle before the cottage gate, inscribed with:

MRS. ROCKE AND DAUGHTER,
SHIRT MAKERS.

Orders executed with neatness and despatch.

"We'd drive a thriving business, mamma, I assure you," said Clara, as she sat down on a low stool at the hearth and began to toast the bread.

"I trust in Heaven that it will never come to that with you, my dear."

"Why? why, mamma? why should I not taste of toil and care as well as others a thousand times better than myself? Why should not I work as well as you and Traverse, mamma? I stand upon the broad platform of human rights, and I say I have just as good a right to work as others," said Clara, with a pretty assumption of obstinacy, as she placed the plate of toast upon the board.

"Doubtless, dear Clara, you may *play* at work just as much as you please; but heaven forbid you should ever have to *work* at work!" replied Mrs. Rocke, as she placed the coffee-pot and the dish of broiled chicken on the table.

"Why, mamma? I do not think that is a good prayer at all. That is a wicked, proud prayer, Mrs. Marah Rocke. Why shouldn't your daughter really toil as well as other people's daughters, I'd like to be informed?" said Clara, mockingly, as they both took their seats at the table.

"I think, dear Clara, that you must have contracted some of your eccentric little friend Capitola's ways, from putting on her habit. I never before saw you in such gay spirits," said Mrs. Rocke, as she poured out the coffee.

"Oh, mamma, it is but the glad rebound of the free bird! I am so glad to have escaped from that dark prison of the Hidden House, and to be here with you! But tell me, mamma, is my old home occupied?"

"No, my dear; no tenant has been found for it. The property is in the hands of an agent to let; but the house remains quite vacant and deserted."

"Why is that?" asked Clara.

"Why, my love, for the strangest reason. The foolish country people say that since the doctor's death, the place has been haunted."

"Haunted!"

"Yes, my dear, so the foolish people say, and they get wiser ones to believe them."

"What exactly *do* they say? I hope——I hope they do not trifle with my dear father's honored name and memory?"

"Oh, no, my darling——no; but they say that although the house is quite empty and deserted by the living, strange sights and sounds are heard and seen by passers-by at night. Lights appear at the upper windows from which pale faces look out."

"How very strange!" said Clara.

"Yes, my dear, and these stories have gained such credence that no one can be found to take the house."

"So much the better, dear mamma, for if the new judge of the Orphans' Court should give a decision in our favor, as he must when he hears the evidence, old and new, you and I can move right into it, and need not then enter the shirtmaking line of business."

"Heaven grant it, my dear. But now, Clara, my love, we must lose no time in seeing Doctor Williams, lest your guardian should pursue you here and give you fresh trouble."

Clara assented to this, and they immediately arose from the table, cleared away the service, put the room in order, and went up stairs to put on their bonnets——Mrs. Rocke lending Clara her own best bonnet and shawl. When they were quite ready, they locked up the house and set out for the town.

It was a bright, frosty, invigorating winter's morning, and the two friends walked rapidly until they reached Doctor Williams' house.

The kind old man was at home, and was much surprised and pleased to see his visitors. He invited them into his parlor, and when he had heard their story, he said:

"This is a much more serious affair than the other. We must employ counsel. Witnesses must be brought from the neighborhood of the Hidden House. You are aware that the late judge of the Orphans' Court has been appointed to a high office under the government at Washington. The man that has his place is a person of sound integrity who will do his duty. It remains only for us to prove the justice of our cause to his satisfaction, and all will be well."

"Oh, I trust in Heaven that it will be," said Marah, fervently.

"You two must stay in my house until the affair is decided. You *might* possibly be safe from real injury; but you could not be free from molestation in your unprotected condition at the cottage," said Doctor Williams.

Clara warmly expressed her thanks.

"You had better go home now and pack up what you wish to bring, and put out the fire and close up the house, and come here immediately.

"In the meantime I will see your dear father's solicitor and be ready with my report by the time you get back," said Doctor Williams, promptly taking his hat to go.

Mrs. Rocke and Clara set out for the cottage which they soon reached.

Throwing off her bonnet and shawl, Clara said:

"Now, mamma, the very first thing I shall do will be to write to Traverse, so that we can send the letter by today's mail, and set his mind at rest. I shall simply tell him that our mutual letters have failed to reach their destination, but that I am now on a visit to you, and that while I remain here nothing can interrupt our correspondence. I shall not speak of the coming suit, until we shall see how it will end."

Mrs. Rocke approved this plan, and placed writing materials on the table. And while the matron employed herself in closing up the rooms, packing up what was needful to take with them to the doctor's, and putting out the fire, Clara wrote and sealed her letter. They then put on their bonnets, locked up the house, and set out. They called at the post-office just in time to mail their letter, and they reached the doctor's house just as he himself walked up to the door, accompanied by the lawyer. The latter greeted the daughter of his old client, and her friend, and they all went into the house together.

In the doctor's study the whole subject of Clara's flight and its occasion was talked over, and the lawyer agreed to commence proceedings immediately.

CHAPTER XLII

"'Tis hardly in a body's power,
To keep at times frae being sour,
    To see how things are shared;
How best o' chiels are whiles in want,
While coofs and countless thousands rant,
    And ken na how to wear't."
        —*Burns*[1]

LEAVING CLARA DAY and Marah Rocke in a home of safety, plenty and kindness, in the old doctor's house, we must run down to Hurricane Hall, to see what mischief Cap has been getting into since we left her! In truth, none. Cap had had such a surfeit of adventures, that she was fain to lie by and rest upon her laurels. Besides, there seemed just now nothing to do—no tyrants to take down, no robbers to capture, no distressed damsels to deliver, and Cap was again in danger of "spoiling for a fight." And then Herbert Greyson was at the Hall—Herbert Greyson whom she vowed always *did* make a Miss Nancy of her! And so Cap had to content herself for a week with quiet mornings of needlework at her work-stand, with Herbert to read to or talk with her; sober afternoon rides, attended by Herbert and Old Hurricane; and hum-drum evenings at the chessboard, with the same Herbert, while Major Warfield dozed in a great "sleepy hollow"[2] of an arm-chair.

One afternoon when they were out riding through the woods beyond the Demon's Run, a sheriff's officer rode up, and bowing to the party, presented a suspicious-looking document to Capitola, and a similar one to Herbert Greyson. And while Old Hurricane stared his eyes half out, the parties most interested opened the papers, which they found to be rather pressing invitations to be present at a certain solemnity at Staunton. In a word, they were subpœnaed to give testimony in the case of Williams vs. Le Noir.

"Here's a diabolical dilemma!" said Old Hurricane to himself, as soon as he learned the purport of these documents; "here I shall have to bring Cap into court face to face with that demon to bear witness against him. Suppose, losing one ward he should lay claim to another! Ah, but he can't without foully criminating himself. Well, well, we shall see!"

While Old Hurricane was cogitating, Cap was exulting.

"Oh, *won't* I tell all I know! Yes, and more too!" she exclaimed, in triumph.

"'More too!' oh! hoity-toity! never say more too!" said Herbert, laughing.

"I will, for I'll tell all I suspect!" said Cap galloping on ahead, in her eagerness to get home and pack up for her journey.

The next day Old Hurricane, Herbert Greyson, Capitola, Pitapat and Wool went by stage to Staunton. They put up at the Planters' and Farmers' Hotel, whence Herbert Greyson and Capitola soon sallied forth to see Clara and Mrs. Rocke. They soon found the doctor's house, and were ushered into the parlor in the presence of their friends.

The meeting between Capitola and Clara and between Mrs. Rocke and Herbert was very cordial. And then Herbert introduced Capitola to Mrs. Rocke, and Cap presented Herbert to Clara. And they all entered into conversation upon the subject of the coming lawsuit, and the circumstances that led to it. And Clara and Capitola related to each other all that had happened to each after their exchanging clothes and parting. And when they had laughed over their mutual adventures and misadventures, Herbert and Capitola took leave and returned to their hotel.

Herbert Greyson was the most serious of the whole family. Upon reaching the hotel he went to his own room, and fell into deep reflection. And this was the course of his thoughts:

"Ira Warfield and Marah Rocke are here in the same town! brought hither upon the same errand! to-morrow to meet in the same court-room! And yet not either of them suspects the presence of the other. Mrs. Rocke does not know that in Capitola's uncle she will behold Major Warfield! He does not foresee that in Clara's matronly friend he will behold Marah Rocke. And Le Noir, the cause of all their misery, will be present also. What will be the effect of this unexpected meeting? Ought I not to warn one or the other?—Let me think—No! for were I to warn Major Warfield he would absent himself. Should I drop a hint to Marah she would shrink from the meeting. No, I will leave it all to Providence; perhaps the sight of her sweet, pale face and soft appealing eyes, so full of constancy and truth, may touch that stern old heart. Heaven grant it may!" concluded Herbert Greyson.

At an early hour Dr. Williams appeared, having in charge Clara Day, who was attended by her friend Mrs. Rocke. They were accommodated with seats immediately in front of the judge.

Very soon afterwards Major Warfield, Herbert Greyson and Capitola entered, and took their places on the witness's bench, at the right side of the court-room.

Herbert watched Old Hurricane, whose eyes were spellbound to the bench where sat Mrs. Rocke and Clara. Both were dressed in deep mourning, with their veils down and their faces towards the judge. But Herbert dreaded every instant that Marah Rocke should turn her head and meet that fixed, wistful look of Old Hurricane. And he wondered what strange instinct it could be that rivetted the old man's regards to that unrecognized woman.

At last, to Herbert's great uneasiness, Major Warfield turned and commenced questioning him:

"Who is that woman in mourning?"

"Hem—m—that one with the flaxen curls under her bonnet is Miss Day."

"I don't mean the *girl,* I mean the woman sitting by her?"

"That is—hem—hem!—that is Doctor Williams sitting——"

Old Hurricane turned abruptly around and favored his nephew with a severe, scrutinizing gaze—demanding:

"Herbert, have you been drinking so early in the morning?— Demmy, sir! Is that great, stout, round-bodied, red-faced old Doctor Williams a little woman?—I see him sitting on the right of Miss Day. I didn't refer to him. I referred to that still, quiet little woman sitting on her left, who has never stirred hand or foot since she sat down there. Who is she?"

"That woman?—oh!—she?—yes—ah, let me see—she is a— Miss Day's companion!" faltered Herbert.

"To the demon with you! who does not see *that?*—But who is she? What is her name?" abruptly demanded Old Hurricane.

"Her name is a—a—Did you ever see her before, sir?"

"I don't know. That is what I am trying to remember. But, sir, will you answer my question?"

"You seem very much interested in her."

"You seem very much determined not to let me know who she is! Hang it, sir! will you or will you not, tell me that woman's name?"

"Certainly," said Herbert; "her name is——" He was about to say Marah Rocke, but moral indignation overpowered him, and he paused.

"Well, well, her name is what?" impatiently demanded Old Hurricane.

"*Mrs. Warfield!*" answered Herbert doggedly.

And just at that unfortunate moment Marah turned her pale face and beseeching eyes around and met the full gaze of her husband!

In an instant her face blanched to marble and her head sank upon the railing before her bench. Old Hurricane was too dark to grow pale, but his bronzed cheek turned as gray as his hair, which fairly lifted itself on his head. Grasping his walking-stick with both his hands, he tottered to his feet, and muttering:

"I'll murder you for this, Herbert!" he strode out of the court-room.

Marah's head rested for about a minute on the railing before her, and when she lifted it again, her face was as calm and patient as before.

This little incident had passed without attracting attention from any one except Capitola, who, sitting on the other side of Herbert Greyson, had heard the little passage of words between him and her uncle, and had seen the latter start up and go out, and who now turning to her companion, inquired:

"What is the meaning of all this, Herbert?"

"It means—Satan! And now attend to what is going on. Mr. Sauter has stated the case, and now Stringfellow, the attorney for the other side, is just telling the judge that he stands there in the place of his client, Lieutenant Colonel Le Noir, who, being ordered to join General Taylor in Mexico, is upon the eve of setting out and cannot be here in person."

"And is that true? Won't he be here?"

"It seems not. I think he is ashamed to appear after what has happened, and just takes advantage of a fair excuse to absent himself."

"And is he really going to Mexico?"

"Oh, yes. I saw it officially announced in this morning's papers. And, by-the-by, I am very much afraid he is to take command of our regiment and be my superior officer!"

"Oh, Herbert, I hope and pray not! I think there is wickedness enough packed up in that man's body to sink a squadron or lose an army!"

"Well, Cap, such things will happen. Attention! There's Sauter ready to call his witnesses." And, in truth, the next moment Capitola Black was called to the stand.

Cap took her place and gave her evidence *con amore,* and with such *vim* and such expressions of indignation, that Stringfellow reminded her she was there to give testimony, and not to plead the cause.

Cap rejoined that she was perfectly willing to do *both!* And so she continued not only to tell the facts, but to express her opinions as to the motives of Le Noir, and give her judgment as to what should be the decision of the court.

Stringfellow, the attorney for Colonel Le Noir, evidently thought that in this rash, reckless, spirited witness, he had a fine subject for sarcastic cross-examination! But he reckoned "without his host." He did not know Cap! He too, "caught a Tartar." And before the cross-examination was concluded, Capitola's apt and cutting replies had overwhelmed him with ridicule and confusion, and done more for the cause of her friend than all her partisans put together!

Other witnesses were called to corroborate the testimony of Capitola, and still others were examined to prove the last expressed wishes of the late William Day, in regard to the disposal of his daughter's person during the period of her minority.

There was no effective rebutting evidence, and after some hard arguing by the attorneys on both sides, the case was closed, and the judge deferred his decision until the third day thereafter.

The parties then left the court and returned to their several lodgings.

Old Hurricane gave no one a civil word that day. Wool was an atrocious villain, an incendiary scoundrel, a cut-throat, and a black demon. Cap was a beggar, a vagabond, and a vixen. Herbert Greyson was another beggar, besides being a knave, a fop and an impudent puppy. The innkeeper was a swindler, the waiters thieves, the whole world was going to ruin, where it well deserved to go, and all mankind to the demon—as he hoped and trusted they would!

And all this tornado of passion and invective arose just because he had unexpectedly met in the court-room the patient face and beseeching eyes of a woman, married and forsaken, loved and lost, long ago!

Was it strange that Herbert, who had so resented his treatment of Marah Rocke, should bear all his fury, injustice and abuse of himself and others with such compassionate forbearance? But he not only forbore to resent his own affronts, but also besought Capitola to have patience with the old man's temper, and apologized to the host, by saying that Major

333

Warfield had been very severely tried that day, and when calmer, would be the first to regret the violence of his own words.

Marah Rocke returned with Clara to the old doctor's house. She was more patient, silent and quiet than before. Her face was a little paler, her eyes softer, and her tones lower—that was the only visible effect of the morning's unexpected *rencontre*.

The next day but one all the parties concerned assembled at the court-house to hear the decision of the judge. It was given as had been anticipated in the favor of Clara Day, who was permitted in accordance with her father's approved wishes, to reside in her patrimonial home, under the care of Mrs. Marah Rocke. Colonel Le Noir was to remain trustee of the property, with directions from the court immediately to pay the legacies left by the late Doctor Day to Marah Rocke and Traverse Rocke, and also to pay to Clara Day, in quarterly instalments, from the revenue of her property, an annual sum of money, sufficient for her support.

This decision filled the hearts of Clara and her friends with joy. Forgetting time and place, she threw herself into the arms of Marah Rocke and wept with delight. All concerned in the trial then sought their lodgings.

Clara and Mrs. Rocke returned to the cottage to make preparations for removing to Willow Heights.

Doctor Williams went to the agent of the property to require him to give up the keys, which he did without hesitation.

Old Hurricane and his party packed up, to be ready for the stage to take them to Tip-Top the next day.

But that night a series of mysterious events were said to have taken place at the deserted house at Willow Heights, that filled the whole community with superstitious wonder. It was reported by numbers of gardeners and farmers, who passed that road on their way to early market, that a perfect witches' sabbath had been held in that empty house all night! That lights had appeared flitting from room to room; that strange, weird faces had looked out from the windows; and wild screams had pierced the air!

The next day when this report reached the ears of Clara, and she was asked by Doctor Williams whether she would not be afraid to live there, she laughed gaily and bade him try her.

Cap who had come over to take leave of Clara, joined her in her merriment, declared that she, for her part, doted on ghosts and that after

Herbert Greyson's departure, she should come and visit Clara and help her to entertain the spectres.

Clara replied that she should hold her to her promise. And so the friends kissed and separated.

That same day saw several removals.

Clara and Mrs. Rocke took up their abode at Willow Heights, and seized an hour even of that busy time, to write to Traverse and apprise him of their good fortune.

Old Hurricane and his party set out for their home, where they arrived before nightfall.

And the next day but one Herbert Greyson took leave of his friends and departed to join his company on their road to glory.

CHAPTER XLIII

BLACK DONALD

"Feared, shunned, belied ere youth had lost her force,
He hated men too much to feel remorse,
And thought the vice of wrath a sacred call,
To pay the injuries of some on all.

"There was a laughing devil in his sneer,
That caused emotions both of rage and fear;
And where his frown of hatred darkly fell,
Hope, withering, fled, and mercy sighed farewell!"
　　　　—*Byron*[1]

HERBERT GREYSON had been correct in his conjecture concerning the cause of Colonel Le Noir's conduct in absenting himself from the trial, or appearing there only in the person of his attorney. A proud, vain, conceited man, full of Joseph Surfaceisms,[2] he could better have borne to be arraigned upon the charge of murder than to face the accusation of baseness that was about to be proved upon him. Being reasonably certain as to what was likely to be the decision of the Orphans' Court, he was not disappointed in hearing that judgment had been rendered in favor of his ward and her friends. His one great disapppointment had been upon discovering the flight of Clara. For when he had ascertained that she had fled, he knew that all was lost—and lost through Capitola—the hated girl for whose destruction he had now another and a stronger motive—revenge.

In this mood of mind, three days before his departure to join his regiment, he sought the retreat of the outlaw. He chose an early hour of the evening as that in which he should be most likely to find Black Donald.

It was about eight o'clock when he wrapped his large cloak around his tall figure, pulled his hat low over his sinister brows, and set out to walk alone to the secret cavern in the side of the Demon's Punch Bowl.

The night was dark and the path dangerous; but his directions had been careful, so that when he reached the brink of that awful abyss, he knew precisely where to begin his descent with the least danger of being precipitated to the bottom.

And by taking a strong hold upon the stunted saplings of pine and cedar that grew down through the clefts of the ravine, and placing his feet firmly upon the points of projecting rocks, he contrived to descend the inside of that horrible abyss, which from the top seemed to be fraught with certain death to any one daring enough to make the attempt.

When about half way down the precipice he reached the clump of cedar bushes growing in the deep cleft, and concealing the hole that formed the entrance to the cavern.

Here he paused, and looking through the entrance into a dark and apparently fathomless cavern, he gave the peculiar signal whistle, which was immediately answered from within by the well-known voice of the outlaw chief, saying:

"All right, my Colonel. Give us your hand. Be careful now; the floor of this cavern is several feet below the opening."

Le Noir extended his hand into the darkness within and soon felt it grasped by that of Black Donald, who, muttering: "Slowly, slowly, my Colonel!" succeeded in guiding him down the utter darkness of the subterranean descent until they stood upon the firm bottom of the cavern.

They were still in the midst of a blackness that might be felt, except that from a small opening in the side of the rock a light gleamed. Towards this second opening Black Donald conducted his patron.

And stooping and passing before him, led him into an inner cavern, well lighted and rudely fitted up. Upon a large natural platform of rock, occupying the centre of the space, were some dozen bottles of brandy or whiskey, several loaves of bread and some dried venison. Around this rude table, seated upon fragments of rock, lugged thither for the purpose, were some eight or ten men of the band, in various stages of intoxication. Along the walls were piles of bearskins, some of which served as couches for six or seven men, who had thrown themselves down upon them in a state of exhaustion or drunken stupor.

"Come, boys, we have not a boundless choice of apartments here, and I want to talk to my Colonel. Suppose you take your liquor and bread and meat into the outer cavern, and give us the use of this one for an hour," said the outlaw.

The men sullenly obeyed and began to gather up the viands. Demon Dick seized one of the lights to go after them.

"Put down the glim. Satan singe your skin for you! Do you want to bring a hue and cry upon us?—Don't you know a light in the outer cavern can be seen from the outside?" roared Black Donald.

Dick sulkily set down the candle and followed his comrades.

"What are you glummering about? confound you! You can see to eat and drink well enough and find your way to your mouth in the dark, you brute!" thundered the captain.

But as there was no answer to this, and the men had retreated and left their chief with his visitor alone, Black Donald turned to Colonel Le Noir, and said:

"Well, my patron, what great matter is it that has caused you to leave the company of fair Clara Day for our grim society?"

"Ah, then it appears you are not aware that Clara Day has fled from us! has made a successful appeal to the Orphans' Court, and been taken out of our hands?" angrily replied Colonel Le Noir.

"Whe—ew! My Colonel, I think I could have managed that matter better. I think if I had had that girl in my power as you had, she should not have escaped me!"

"Bah! bah! bah! stop boasting since it was through *your* neglect—yours! yours!—that I lost this girl."

"*Mine!*" exclaimed Black Donald, in astonishment.

"Aye, yours! for if you had done your duty, performed your engagement, kept your word, and delivered me from this fatal Capitola, I had not lost my ward, nor my son his wealthy bride!" exclaimed Le Noir, angrily.

"Capitola! Capitola again! What on earth had she to do with the loss of Clara Day?" cried Black Donald in wonder.

"Everything to do with it, sir! By a cunning artifice she delivered Clara from our power; actually set her free and covered her flight until she was in security!"

"That girl again! Ha-ha-ha-ha-ha! Ho-ho-ho-ho-ho!" laughed and roared Black Donald, slapping his knees.

Le Noir ground and gnashed his teeth in rage, muttering hoarsely:

"Yes! you may laugh, confound you, since it is granted those who win to do so! you may laugh! for you have done me out of five thousand dollars, and what on earth have you performed to earn it?"

"Come, come, my Colonel! fair and easy! I don't know which is vulgarest, to betray loss of temper or love of money, and you are doing both! However, it is between friends! But how the demon did that girl, that *capital* Capitola, get Clara off from right under your eyes?"

"By changing clothes with her! confound you! I will tell you all about it," replied Le Noir, who thereupon commenced and related the whole stratagem by which Capitola freed Clara, including the manner in which she accompanied them to the church and revealed herself at the altar.

Black Donald threw himself back and roared with laughter, vigorously slapping his knees and crying:

"That girl! that *capital* Capitola! I would not sell my prospect of possessing her for double your bribe!"

"Your 'prospect!' Your prospect is about as deceptive as a *fata morgana!*[3] What have you been doing, I ask you again, towards realizing this prospect, and earning the money you have already received?"

"Fair and easy, my Colonel! Don't let temper get the better of justice! What have I been doing towards earning the money you have already paid me!—In the first place, I lost my time and risked my liberty watching around Hurricane Hall. Then, when I had identified the girl, and the room she slept in, by seeing her at her window, I put three of my best men in jeopardy to capture her! Then, when she, the witch! had captured *them,* I sacrificed all my good looks, transmogrifying myself into a frightful old field preacher, and went to the camp-meeting to watch, among other things, for an opportunity of carrying her off! The sorceress!—she gave me no such opportunity! I succeeded in nothing except in fooling the wiseacres and getting admitted to the prison of my comrades, whom I furnished with instruments by which they made their escape. Since that time we have had to lie low—yes, literally—*to lie low*—to keep out of sight, to burrow under ground! in a word, to live in this cavern!"

"And since which you have abandoned all intention of getting the girl and earning the five thousand dollars," sneered Le Noir.

"Earning the *remaining* five thousand, you mean, Colonel! The *first* five thousand I consider I have already earned. It was the last five thousand that I was to get when the girl should be disposed of."

"Well?"

"Well, I have not given up, either the intention of earning the money, or the hope of getting the girl; in truth, I had rather lose the money than the girl. I have been on the watch almost continually; but though I suppose she rides out frequently, I have not yet happened to hit upon her in any of her excursions. At last, however, I have fixed upon a plan of getting the witch into my power. I shall trust the execution of that plan to no one but *myself!* But I must have time."

"Time! perdition, sir! delay in this matter is fraught with danger! Listen, sir! How Warfield got possession of this girl, or the knowledge of her history I do not kow, except that it was through the agency of that accursed hag, Nancy Grewell!—but that he has her, and that he knows all about her, is but too certain! That he has not at present legal proof enough to establish her identity and her rights before a court of justice, I infer from the fact of his continuing inactive in the matter. But who can foresee how soon he may obtain all the proof that is necessary to establish Capitola's claims, and wrest the whole of this property from me? Who can tell whether he is not now secretly engaged in seeking and collecting such proof!—therefore, I repeat, that the girl must immediately be got rid of— Donald! rid me of that creature and the day that you prove to me her death, I will double your fee!"

"Agreed, my Colonel, agreed. I have no objection to your doubling, or even quadrupling my fee! you shall find me in that as in all other matters, perfectly amenable to reason. Only I must have time. Haste would ruin us. I repeat that I have a plan by which I am certain to get the girl into my possession. A plan, the execution of which I will intrust to no other hands but my own. But I conclude as I began—I must have time!"

"And how much time?" exclaimed Le Noir, again losing his patience.

"Easy my patron. That I cannot tell you. It is imprudent to make promises, especially to you, who will take nothing into consideration, when they cannot be kept," replied Black Donald, coolly.

"But, sir, do you not know that I am ordered to Mexico, and must leave within three days!—I would see the end of this before I go!" angrily exclaimed Le Noir.

"Softly, softly, my child, the Colonel!—'Slow and sure!' 'Fair and easy goes far in a day!'"

"In a word, will you do this business for me, and do it promptly?"

"Surely, surely, my patron! But I insist upon time!"

"But I go to Mexico in three days!"

"All honor go with you my Colonel! Who would keep his friend from the path of glory?"

"Perdition, sir, you trifle with me!"

"Perdition, certainly, Colonel. There I perfectly agree with you; but the rest of your sentence is wrong; I don't trifle with you!"

"What in the fiend's name do you mean?"

"Nothing in the name of any absent friend of ours! I mean simply that you may go to—Mexico."

"And—my business———"

———"Can be done just as well, perhaps better, without you! Recollect, if you please, my Colonel, that when you were absent with Harrison in the West, your *great business was done here without you!* And done better for that very reason! No one ever suspected your agency in that matter. The person most benefited by the death of Eugene Le Noir was far enough from the scene of his murder!"

"*Hush!* Perdition seize you! Why do you speak of things so long past!" exclaimed Le Noir, growing white to his very lips.

"To jog your worship's memory, and suggest that your honor is the last man who ought to complain of this delay, since it will be very well for you to be in a distant land, serving your country, at the time that your brother's heiress, whose property you illegally hold, is got out of your way."

"There is something in that," mused Le Noir.

"There is *all* in that!"

"You have a good brain, Donald!"

"What did I tell you?—I ought to have been in the cabinet, and mean to be too. But Colonel, as I mean to conclude *my* part of the engagement, I should like, for fear of accidents, that you conclude yours—and settle with me before you go."

"What do you mean?"

"That you should fork over to me the remaining five thousand."

"I'll see you at the demon first," passionately exclaimed Le Noir.

"No you won't; for in that case you'd have to make way with the girl, yourself; or see Old Hurricane make way with all your fortune."

"Wretch, that you are!"

"Come, come, Colonel, don't let's quarrel. The Kingdom of Satan divided against itself cannot stand. Do not let us lose time by falling out. *I* will get rid of the girl! *You*, before you go, must hand over the tin, lest you should fall in battle and your heirs dispute the debt. Shell out, my Colonel. Shell out, and never fear. Capitola shall be a wife and Black Donald a widower, before many weeks shall pass."

"I'll do it. I have not time for disputation, as you know; and you profit by the knowledge. I'll do it, though under protest," muttered Le Noir, grinding his teeth.

"That's my brave and generous patron," said Black Donald, as he arose to attend Le Noir from the cavern. "That's my magnificent Colonel of cavalry. The man who runs such risks for you, should be very handsomely remunerated."

CHAPTER XLIV

GLORY!

✻✻✻✻✻✻

"What Alexander sighed for,
What Cæsar's soul possessed,
What heroes, saints have died for,
Glory!"

WITHIN THREE DAYS after this settlement with Black Donald, Colonel Le
Noir left home to join his regiment, ordered to Mexico.

He was accompanied by his son, Craven Le Noir, as far as Baltimore,
from which port the reinforcements were to sail for New Orleans, *en route*
for the seat of war.

Here, at the last moment, when the vessel was about to weigh
anchor, Craven Le Noir took leave of his father and set out for the Hidden House.

And here Colonel Le Noir's regiment was joined by the company of
new recruits, in which Herbert Greyson held a commission as lieutenant,
and thus the young man's worst forebodings were realized, in having for a
traveling companion and superior officer, the man of whom he had been
destined to make a mortal enemy, Colonel Le Noir. However, Herbert
soon marked out his course of conduct, which was to avoid Le Noir as
much as was consistent with his own official duty, and when compelled to
meet him, to deport himself with the cold ceremony of a subordinate to a
superior officer.

Le Noir, on his part, treated Herbert with an arrogant scorn amount-
ing to insult, and used every opportunity afforded him by his position to
wound and humiliate the young lieutenant.

After a quick and prosperous voyage they reached New Orleans,
where they expected to be farther reinforced by a company of volunteers
who had come down the Mississippi river from St. Louis. These volunteers

were now being daily drilled at their quarters in the city, and were only waiting the arrival of the vessel to be enrolled in the regiment.

One morning, a few days after the ship reached harbor, Herbert Greyson went on shore to the military rendezvous to see the new recruits exercised. While he stood within the enclosure watching their evolutions under the orders of an officer, his attention became concentrated upon the form of a young man of the rank and file, who was marching in a line with many others having their backs turned towards him. That form and gait seemed familiar—under the circumstances in which he saw them again— painfully familiar. And yet he could not identify the man. While he gazed, the recruits, at the word of command, suddenly wheeled and faced about. And Herbert could scarcely repress an exclamation of astonishment and regret.

That young man in the dress of a private soldier was Clara Day's betrothed, the widow's only son, Traverse Rocke! While Herbert continued to gaze in surprise and grief, the young recruit raised his eyes, recognized his friend, flushed up to his very temples, and cast his eyes down again. The rapid evolutions soon wheeled them around, and the next order sent them into their quarters.

Herbert's time was also up, and he returned to his duty.

The next day Herbert went to the quarters of the new recruits, and sought out his young friend, whom he found loitering about the grounds. Again Traverse blushed deeply as the young lieutenant approached. But Herbert Greyson, letting none of his regret appear, since now it would be worse than useless, in only serving to give pain to the young private, went up to him cordially and shook his hands, saying:

"Going to serve your country, eh, Traverse? Well, I am heartily glad to see you, at any rate."

"But heartily sorry to see me here, enlisted as a private in a company of raw recruits, looking not unlike Falstaff's ragged regiment?"

"Nay, I did not say that, Traverse. Many a private in the ranks has risen to be a general officer," replied Herbert, encouragingly.

Traverse laughed good-humoredly, saying:

"It does not look much like that in my case. This dress," he said, looking down at his coarse, ill-fitting uniform, cow-hide shoes, etc.— "this dress, this drilling, these close quarters, coarse food, and mixed company, is enough to take the military ardor out of anyone."

"Traverse, you talk like a dandy, which is not at all your character. Effeminacy is not your vice."

343

"Nor any other species of weakness, do you mean? Ah, Herbert! your aspiring, hopeful, confident old friend is considerably taken down in his ideas of himself, his success, and life in general. I went to the West with high hopes. Six months of struggling against indifference, neglect, and accumulating debts, lowered them down. I carried out letters and made friends, but their friendship began and ended in wishing me well. While trying to get into profitable practice I got into debt. Meanwhile I could not hear from my betrothed in all those months. An occasional letter from her might have prevented this step. But troubles gathered around me, debts increased, and——"

"Creditors were cruel. It is the old story, poor boy!"

"No; my only creditors were my landlady and my laundress, two poor widows who never willingly distressed me, but who occasionally asked for 'that little amount' so piteously, that my heart bled to lack it to give them. And as victuals and clean shirts were absolute necessaries of life, every week my debts increased. I could have faced a prosperous male creditor, and might, perhaps, have been provoked to bully such an one, had he been inclined to be cruel; but I could not face poor women, who after all, I believe, are generally the best friends a struggling young man can have; and so, not to bore a smart young lieutenant with a poor private's antecedents——"

"Oh, Traverse——"

——"I will even make an end of my story. 'At last there came a weary day when hope and faith beneath the weight gave way.' And hearing that a company of volunteers was being raised to go to Mexico, I enlisted, sold my citizen's wardrobe and my little medical library, paid my debts, made my two friends, the poor widows, some acceptable presents, sent the small remnant of the money to my mother, telling her that I was going farther south to try my fortune, and—here I am!"

"You did not tell her that you had enlisted?"

"No."

"Oh, Traverse! how long ago was it that you left St. Louis?"

"Just two weeks."

"Ah! if you had only had patience for a few days longer!" burst unaware from Herbert's bosom. In an instant he was sorry for having spoken thus, for Traverse, with all his soul in the eyes, asked eagerly:

"Why—why, Herbert? What do you mean?"

"Why, you should know that I did not come direct from West Point, but from the neighborhood of Staunton and Hurricane Hall."

"Did you? oh, did you? Then you may be able to give me news of Clara and my dear mother!" exclaimed Traverse, eagerly.

"Yes, I am—pleasant news," said Herbert, hesitating in a manner in which no one ever hesitated before in communicating good tidings.

"Thank Heaven! oh, thank Heaven! What is it, Herbert? How is my dear mother getting on? Where is my best Clara?"

"They are both living together at Willow Heights, according to the wishes of the late Doctor Day. A second appeal to the Orphans' Court, made in behalf of Clara by her next friend, Doctor Williams, about a month ago, proved more successful. And if you had waited a few days longer before enlisting and leaving St. Louis, you would have received a letter from Clara to the same effect, and one from Doctor Williams, apprising you that your mother had received her legacy, and that the thousand dollars left you by Doctor Day had been paid into the Agricultural Bank, subject to your orders."

"Oh, Heaven! had I but waited three days longer!" exclaimed Traverse, in such acute distress that Herbert hastened to console him by saying:

"Do not repine, Traverse. These things go by fate. It was your destiny—let us hope it will prove a glorious one."

"It was my IMPATIENCE!" exclaimed Traverse. "It was my IMPATIENCE! Doctor Day always faithfully warned me against it—always told me that most of the errors, sins and miseries of this world arose from simple impatience, which is want of faith. And now I know it! and now I know it! What had I, who had an honorable profession, to do with becoming a private soldier?"

"Well, well, it is honorable at least to serve your country," said Herbert, soothingly.

"If a foreign foe invaded her shores, yes; but what had I to do with invading another's country?—enlisting for a war of the rights and wrongs of which I know no more than anybody else does! Growing impatient because fortune did not at once empty her cornucopia upon my head! Oh, fool!"

"You blame yourself too severely, Traverse. Your act was natural enough and justifiable enough, much as it is to be regretted," said Herbert, cheerfully.

"Come, come, sit on this plank bench beside me—if you are not ashamed to be seen with a private who is also a donkey—and tell me all about it. Show me the full measure of the happiness I have so recklessly squandered away," exclaimed Traverse, desperately.

"I will sit beside you and tell you everything you wish to know,—on condition that you stop berating yourself in a manner that fills me with indignation," replied Herbert, as they went to a distant part of the dusty enclosure and took their seats upon a rude bench.

"Oh, Herbert, bear with me; I could dash my wild, impatient head against a stone wall!"

"That would not be likely to clear or strengthen your brains," said Herbert, who thereupon commenced and told Traverse the whole history of the persecution of Clara Day at the Hidden House; the interception of her letters; the attempt made to force her into a marriage with Craven Le Noir; her deliverance from her enemies by the address and courage of Capitola; her flight to Staunton and refuge with Mrs. Rocke; her appeal to the court; and finally her success and her settlement under the charge of her matronly friend at Willow Heights.

Traverse had not listened patiently to this account. He heard it with many bursts of irrepressible indignation and many involuntary starts of wild passion. Towards the last he sprang up and down, chafing like an angry lion in his cage.

"And this man," he exclaimed, as Herbert concluded,—"This demon—this beast—is now commanding officer! the colonel of our regiment!"

"Yes," replied Herbert, "but as such you must not call him names; military rules are despotic: and this man who knows your person and knows you to be the betrothed of Clara Day, whose hand and fortune he covets for his son will leave no power, with which his command invests him, untried, to ruin and destroy you! Traverse, I say these things to you, that being 'forewarned' you may be 'forearmed.' I trust that you will remember your mother and your betrothed, and for *their* dear sakes practice every sort of self-control, patience and forbearance under the provocations you may receive from our colonel. And in advising you to do this, I only counsel that which I shall myself practice. I, too, am under the ban of Le Noir for the part I played in the church in succoring Capitola, as well as for happening to be 'the nephew of my uncle,' Major Warfield, who is his mortal enemy."

"I?—will I not be patient, after the lesson I have just learned upon the evils of its opposite? Be easy on my account, dear old friend. I will be as patient as Job, meek as Moses, and long suffering as—my own sweet mother!" said Traverse, earnestly.

The drum was now heard beating to quarters, and Traverse, wringing his friend's hand, left him.

Herbert returned to his ship full of one scheme, of which he had not spoken to Traverse lest it should prove unsuccessful. This scheme was to procure his free discharge before they should set sail for the Rio Grande. He had many influential friends among the officers of his regiment, and he was resolved to tell them as much as was delicate, proper and useful for them to know of the young recruit's private history in order to get their co-operation.

Herbert spent every hour of this day and the next, when off duty, in this service of his friend. He found his brother-officers easily interested, sympathetic and propitious. They united their efforts with his own to procure the discharge of the young recruit; but in vain! the power of Colonel Le Noir was opposed to their influence, and the application was peremptorily refused.

Herbert Greyson did not sit down quietly under this disappointment, but wrote an application, embodying all the facts of the case to the Secretary of War, got it signed by all the officers of the regiment and despatched it by the first mail.

Simultaneously he took another important step for the interest of his friend. Without hinting any particular motive he had begged Traverse to let him have his photograph taken, and the latter, with a laugh, at the lover-like proposal, had consented. When the likeness was finished, Herbert sent it by express to Major Warfield, accompanied by a letter describing the excellent character and unfortunate condition of Traverse, praying the Major's interest in his behalf, and concluded by saying:

"You cannot look upon the accompanying photograph of my friend and any longer disclaim your own express image in your son."

How this affected the action of Old Hurricane will be seen hereafter.

Traverse, knowing nothing of the efforts that had been, and were still being made for his discharge, suffered neither disappointment for failure of the first, nor anxiety for the issue of the last.

He wrote to his mother and Clara, congratulating them on their good fortune; telling them that he, in common with many young men of St. Louis, had volunteered for the Mexican War; that he was then at New Orleans, *en route* for the Rio Grande, and that they would be pleased to know that their mutual friend, Herbert Greyson, was an officer in the same regiment of which he himself was at present a private, but with strong hopes of soon winning his epaulettes. He endorsed an order for his mother to draw the thousand dollars left him by Doctor Day; and he advised her to redeposit the sum in her own name, for her own use in case of need. Praying God's blessing upon them all, and begging their prayers for himself, Traverse concluded his letter, which he mailed the same evening.

And the next morning the company was ordered on board, and the whole expedition set sail for the Rio Grande.

Now we might just as easily as not accompany our troops to Mexico and relate the feats of arms there performed, with the minuteness and fidelity of an eye-witness, since we have sat at dinner-tables where the heroes of that war have been honored guests, and where we have heard them fight their battles over till "thrice the foe was slain, and thrice the field was won."

We might follow the rising star of our young lieutenant, as by his own merits and other's mishaps he ascended from rank to rank, through all the grades of military promotion, but we need not, because the feats of Lieutenant—Captain—Major and Colonel Greyson, are they not written in the chronicles of the Mexican War?

_We_ prefer to look after our little domestic heroine, our brave little Cap, who, when women have their rights, shall be a lieutenant-colonel herself. Shall she not, gentlemen?

IN ONE FORTNIGHT from this time, while Mrs. Rocke and Clara were still living comfortably at Willow Heights, and waiting anxiously to hear from Traverse, whom they still supposed to be practicing his profession at St. Louis, they received his last letter written on the eve of his departure for the seat of war. At first the news overwhelmed them with grief, but then they sought relief in faith, answered his letter cheerfully, and commended him to the infinite mercy of God.

CHAPTER XLV

CAP CAPTIVATES A CRAVEN

"He knew himself a villain, but he deemed
The rest no better than the thing he seemed:
And scorned the best as hypocrites who hid
Those deeds the bolder spirits plainly did,
He knew himself detested, but he knew
The hearts that loathed him crouched and—dreaded too."

THE UNREGENERATE human heart is perhaps the most inconsistent thing in all nature; and in nothing is it more capricious than in the manifestations of its passions; and in no passion is it so fantastic as in that which it miscalls love—but which is really often only appetite.

From the earliest days of manhood Craven Le Noir had been the votary of vice, which he called pleasure. Before reaching the age of twenty-five he had run the full course of dissipation, and found himself ruined in health, degraded in character, and disgusted with life.

Yet in all this experience his heart had not been once agitated with a single emotion that deserved the name of passion. It was colder than the coldest.

He had not loved Clara; though, for the sake of her money, he had courted her so assiduously. Indeed, for the doctor's orphan girl, he had from the first, conceived a strong antipathy. His evil spirit had shrunk from her pure soul with the loathing a fiend might feel for an angel. He had found it repugnant and difficult, almost to the extent of impossibility, for him to pursue the courtship to which he was only reconciled by a sense of duty to—his pocket.

It was reserved for his meeting with Capitola, at the altar of the Forest Chapel to fire his clammy heart, stagnant blood, and sated senses, with the very first passion that he had ever known. Her image, as she stood there at the altar with flashing eyes, and flaming cheeks, and scathing tongue, defying him, was ever before his mind's eye. There was something about that girl so spirited, so piquant and original, that she impressed even his apathetic nature as no other woman had ever been able to do. But what, most of all, attracted him to Capitola was her *diablerie!* He longed to catch that little savage to his bosom and have her at his mercy. The aversion she had exhibited towards him only stimulated his passion.

Craven Le Noir, among his other graces, was gifted with inordinate vanity. He did not in the least degree despair of overcoming all Capitola's dislike to his person, and inspiring her with a passion equal to his own.

He knew well that he dared not present himself at Hurricane Hall, but he resolved to waylay her in her rides, and there to press his suit. To this he was urged by another motive almost as strong as love—namely, avarice.

He had gathered thus much from his father—that Capitola Black was supposed to be Capitola Le Noir, the rightful heiress of all that vast property in land, houses, iron and coal-mines, foundries and furnaces, railway shares, &c., and bank-stocks, from which his father drew the princely revenue that supported them both in their lavish extravagance of living.

As the heiress, or rather the rightful owner, of all this vast fortune, Capitola was a much greater "catch" than poor Clara with her modest estate had been. And Mr. Craven Le Noir was quite willing to turn the tables on his father by running off with the great heiress, and step from his irksome position of dependent upon Colonel Le Noir's often ungracious bounty to that of the husband of the heiress and the master of the property. Added to that was another favorable circumstance, namely, whereas he had had a strong personal antipathy to Clara, he had as strong an attraction to Capitola, which would make his course of courtship all the pleasanter.

In one word, he resolved to woo, win, and elope with, or forcibly abduct, Capitola Le Noir, marry her, and then turn upon his father and claim the fortune in right of his wife. The absence of Colonel Le Noir in Mexico favored his projects, as he could not fear interruption.

Meanwhile our little madcap remained quite unconscious of the honors designed her. She had cried every day of the first week of Herbert's absence; every alternate day of the second; twice in the third; once in the fourth; not at all in the fifth, and the sixth week she was quite herself again, as full of fun and frolic and as ready for any mischief or deviltry that might turn up.

She resumed her rides, no longer followed by Wool, because Old

Hurricane, partly upon account of his misadventure in having had the misfortune inadvertently "to lose sight of" his mistress upon that memorable occasion of the metamorphosis of Cap into Clara, and partly because in the distant absence of Le Noir, did not consider his favorite in danger.

He little knew that a subtle and unscrupulous agent had been left sworn to her destruction, and that another individual, almost equally dangerous, had registered a secret vow to run off with her.

Neither did poor Cap, when rejoicing to be free from the dogging attendance of Wool, imagine the perils to which she was exposed, nor is it even likely that if she had she would have cared for them in any other manner than as promising piquant adventures. From childhood she had been inured to danger, and had never suffered harm; therefore, Cap, like the Chevalier Bayard, was "without fear and without reproach."[1]

Craven Le Noir proceeded cautiously with his plans, knowing that there was time enough, and that all might be lost by haste. He did not wish to alarm Capitola.

The first time he took occasion to meet her in her rides, he merely bowed deeply, even to the flaps of his saddle, and with a melancholy smile passed on.

"Miserable wretch, he is a mean fellow to want to marry a girl against her will, no matter how much he might have been in love with her; and I am very glad I balked him! Still, he looks so ill and unhappy that—I can't help pitying him!" said Cap, looking compassionately at his white cheeks and languishing eyes, and little knowing that the illness was the effect of dissipation, and that the melancholy was assumed for the occasion.

A few days after this, Cap again met Craven Le Noir, who again, with a deep bow and sad smile, passed her.

"Poor fellow! he richly deserved to suffer, and I hope it may make him better, for I am right down sorry for him; it must be so dreadful to lose one we love! but it was *too* base in him to let his father try to compel her to have him! Suppose, now, Herbert Greyson was to take a fancy to another girl, would *I* let uncle go to him and put a pistol to his head, and say, 'Cap is fond of you, you varlet! and demmy, sir! you shall marry none but her, or receive an ounce of lead in your stupid brains!' No, I'd scorn it! I'd forward the other wedding! I'd make the cake and dress the bride, and—then maybe I'd break—no, I'm blamed if I would!! I'd not break my heart for anybody! Set them up with it, indeed! Neither would my dear, darling, sweet, precious Herbert treat me so! And I'm a wretch to think of it!" said

Cap, with a rich, inimitable unction, as, rejoicing in her own happy love, she cheered Gyp and rode on.

Now Craven Le Noir had been conscious of the relenting and compassionate looks of Capitola, but he did not know that they were only the pitying regards of a noble and victorious nature over a vanquished and suffering wrong-doer. However, he still determined to be cautious, and not ruin his prospects by precipitate action, but to "hasten slowly."

So the next time he met Capitola he raised his eyes with one deep, sad, appealing gaze to hers, and then bowing profoundly, passed on.

"Poor man!" said Cap, to herself, "he bears no malice towards me for depriving him of his sweetheart, that's certain! and badly as he behaved, I suppose it was all for love; for I don't know how any one could live in the same house with Clara and not be in love with her. I should have been so myself, if I'd been a man, I know!"

The next time Cap met Craven, and saw again that deep, sorrowful, appealing gaze, as he bowed and passed her, she glanced after him, saying to herself:

"Poor soul, I wonder what he means by looking at me in that piteous manner?—I can do nothing to relieve him. I'm sure if I could, I would. 'But the way of transgressors is hard,' Mr. Le Noir, and he who sins must suffer!"

For about three weeks their seemingly accidental meetings continued in this silent manner, so slowly did Craven made his advances. Then feeling more confidence, he made a considerably long step forward.

One day, when he guessed that Capitola would be out, instead of meeting her as heretofore, he put himself in her road, and riding slowly toward a five-barred gate, allowed her to overtake him.

He opened the gate, and bowing, held it open until she had passed.

She bowed her thanks and rode on; but presently, without the least appearance of intruding—since *she* had overtaken *him*—he was at her side;—and speaking with downcast eyes and deferential manner, he said:

"I have long desired an opportunity to express the deep sorrow and mortification I feel, for having been hurried into rudeness towards an estimable young lady at the Forest Chapel. Miss Black, will you permit me now to assure you of my profound repentance of that act, and to implore your pardon."

"Oh, *I* have nothing against you, Mr. Le Noir. It was not *I* whom you were intending to marry against my will! and as for what you said and did to *me,* ha-ha! I had provoked it, you know, and I also afterwards paid it in kind! It was a fair fight, in which I was victor; and victors should never be vindictive!" said Cap, laughing, for though knowing him to have been violent and unjust, she did not suspect him of being treacherous and deceitful, or imagine the base designs concealed beneath his plausible manner. Her brave, honest nature could understand a brute and a despot, but not a traitor.

"Then like frank enemies who have fought their fight out, yet bear no malice towards each other, we may shake hands and be friends, I hope!" said Craven, replying in the same spirit in which she had spoken.

"Well, I don't know about that, Mr. Le Noir! Friendship is a very sacred thing, and its name should not be lightly taken on our tongues. I hope you will excuse me if I decline your proffer," said Cap—who had a well of deep, true, earnest feeling beneath her effervescent surface.

"What! you will not even grant a repentant man your friendship, Miss Black?" asked Craven, with a sorrowful smile.

"I wish you well, Mr. Le Noir. I wish you a *good* and therefore a *happy* life; but I cannot give you friendship, for that means a great deal."

"Oh, I see how it is! You cannot give your friendship where you cannot give your esteem. Is it not so?"

"Yes," said Capitola, "that is it; yet I wish you so well that I wish you might grow worthy of higher esteem than mine."

"You are thinking of my—yes, I will not shrink from characterizing that conduct as it deserves—my unpardonable violence towards Clara. Miss Black, I have mourned that sin from the day that I was hurried into it until this. I have bewailed it from the very bottom of my heart," said Craven, earnestly fixing his eyes with an expression of perfect truthfulness upon those of Capitola.

"I am glad to hear you say so," said Cap.

"Miss Black, please to hear this in palliation—I will not presume to say in defense of my conduct; I was driven to frenzy by a passion of contending love and jealousy, as violent and maddening as it was unreal and transient. But that delusive passion has subsided, and among the unmerited mercies for which I have to be thankful is that, in my frantic pursuit of Clara Day, I was not cursed with success. For all the violence into which that frenzy drove me I have deeply repented. I can never forgive myself, but—cannot you forgive me?"

"Mr. Le Noir, I have nothing for which to forgive you. I am glad that you have repented towards Clara, and I wish you well, and that is really all that I can say."

"I have deserved this, and I accept it," said Craven, in a tone so mournful that Capitola, in spite of all her instincts, could not choose but pity him.

He rode on, with his pale face, downcast eyes and melancholy expression, until they reached a point at the back of Hurricane Hall where their paths diverged.

Here Craven, lifting his hat and bowing profoundly, said, in a sad tone:

"Good evening, Miss Black!"

And turning his horse's head, took the path leading down into the Hidden Hollow.

"Poor young fellow! he must be very unhappy down in that miserable place! but I can't help it! I wish he would go to Mexico with the rest," said Cap, as she pursued her way homeward.

Not to excite her suspicion, Craven Le Noir avoided meeting Capitola for a few days, and then threw himself in her road, and as before, allowed *her* to overtake *him*.

Very subtilely he entered into conversation with her, and guarding every word and look, took care to interest without alarming her. He said no more of friendship, but a great deal of regret for wasted years and wasted talents in the past, and good resolutions for the future.

And Cap listened good-humoredly. Capitola being of a brave, hard, firm nature, had not the sensitive perceptions, fine intuitions, and true insight into character that distinguished the more refined nature of Clara Day—or at least, she had not these delicate faculties in the same perfection. Thus her undefined suspicions of Craven's sincerity were overborne by a sort of noble benevolence which determined her to think the best of him which circumstances would permit.

Craven, on his part, having had more experience, was much wiser in the pursuit of his object; he had also the advantage of being in earnest; his passion for Capitola was sincere, and not, as it had been in the case of Clara, simulated; he believed, therefore, that when the time should be ripe for the declaration of his love, he would have a much better prospect of success—especially as Capitola, in her ignorance of her own great fortune, must consider his proposal the very climax of disinterestedness.

After three more weeks of riding and conversing with Capitola, he had, in his own estimation, advanced so far in her good opinion as to make it perfectly safe to risk a declaration. And this he determined to do upon the very first opportunity.

Chance favored him.

One afternoon Capitola, riding through the pleasant woods skirting the back of the mountain range that sheltered Hurricane Hall, got a fall, for which she was afterward inclined well to cuff Wool.

It happened in this way: she had come to a steep rise in the road, and urged her pony into a hard gallop, intending, as she said to herself, to "storm the height," when suddenly, under the violent strain, the girth, ill-fastened, flew apart, and Miss Cap was on the ground, buried under the fallen saddle.

With many a blessing upon the carelessness of the grooms, Cap picked herself up, put the saddle on the horse and was engaged in drawing under the girth when Craven Le Noir rode up, sprang from his horse, and with anxiety depicted on his countenance, ran to the spot inquiring:

"What is the matter?—No serious accident, I hope and trust, Miss Black?"

"No; those wretches in uncle's stable did not half buckle the girth, and as I was going in a hard gallop up the steep, it flew apart and gave me a tumble, that's all!" said Cap, desisting a moment from her occupation to take breath.

"You were not hurt?" inquired Craven, with deep interest in his tone.

"Oh, no!—there was no harm done except to my riding-skirt, which has been torn and muddled by the fall," said Cap, laughing, and resuming her efforts to tighten the girth.

"Pray permit me," said Craven, gently taking the end of the strap from her hand; "this is no work for a lady, and is besides beyond your strength."

Capitola thanking him, withdrew to the side of the road and seating herself upon the trunk of a fallen tree, began to brush the dirt from her habit.

Craven adjusted and secured the saddle with great care, patted and soothed the pony, and then approaching Capitola in the most deferential manner, stood before her and said:

"Miss Black, you will pardon me, I hope, if I tell you that the peril I had imagined you to be in, has so agitated my mind as to make it impossible for me longer to withhold a declaration of my sentiments"—here his voice that had trembled throughout his disclosure now really and utterly failed him.

Capitola looked up with surprise and interest; she had never in her life before heard an explicit declaration of love from anybody. She and Herbert somehow had always understood each other very well, without ever a word of technical love-making passing between them; so Capitola did not exactly know what was coming next.

Craven recovered his voice; and encouraged by the favorable manner in which she appeared to listen to him, actually threw himself at her feet and seizing one of her hands, with much ardor and earnestness and much more eloquence than any one would have credited him with, poured forth the history of his passion and his hopes.

"Well, I declare!" said Cap, when he had finished his speech and was waiting in breathless impatience for her answer, "this is what is called a declaration of love and a proposal for marriage, is it!—It is downright sentimental, I suppose, if I had only the sense to appreciate it! It is as good as a play! pity it is lost upon me!"

"Cruel girl! how you mock me!" cried Craven, rising from his knees and sitting beside her.

"No, I don't! I'm in solemn earnest! I say it is first rate! do it again! I like it!"

"Sarcastic and merciless one, you glory in the pain you give! But if you wish again to hear me say I love you, I will say it a dozen—yes, a hundred times over if you will only admit that you could love me a little in return!"

"Don't! that would be too tiresome! Two or three times is quite enough! Besides, what earthly good could my saying 'I love you,' do?"

"I might persuade you to become the wife of one who will adore you to the last hour of his life!"

"Meaning *you!*"

"Meaning *me,* the most devoted of your admirers!"

"That isn't saying much, since I haven't got any but you!"

"Thank fortune for it! Then I am to understand, charming Capitola, that at least your hand and your affections are free," said Craven, joyfully.

"Well, now, I don't know about that. Really, I can't positively say! but it strikes me, if I were to get married to anybody else, there's *somebody* would feel quecrish!"

"No doubt there are many whose secret hopes would be blasted, for so charming a girl could not have passed through this world without having won many hearts, who would keenly feel the loss of hope, in her marriage! But what if they do, my enchanting Capitola? You are not responsible for any one having formed such hopes!"

"Fudge!" said Cap. "*I'm* no belle! never was! never can be! have neither wealth, beauty, nor coquetry enough to make me one! *I've* no lovers or admirers to break their hearts about me, one way or another; but there is one honest fellow—hem! never mind; I feel as if I belonged to somebody else; that's all. I am *very* much obliged to you, Mr. Le Noir, for your preference, and even for the beautiful way in which you have expressed it, but—I belong to somebody else."

"Miss Black," said Craven, somewhat abashed but not discouraged, "I think I understand you! I presume that you refer to the young man who was your gallant champion in the Forest Chapel."

"The one that made your nose bleed!" said the incorrigible Cap. ——

"Well, Miss Black, from your words it appears that this is by no means an acknowledged, but only an understood engagement, which cannot be binding upon either party! Now a young lady of your acknowledged good sense——"

"I never had any more good sense than I have had admirers," interrupted Cap.

Craven smiled.

"I would not hear your enemy say that," he replied, then resuming his argument he said:

"You will really understand, Miss Black, that the vague engagement of which you speak, where there is want of fortune on *both* sides, is no more prudent than it is binding. On the contrary, the position which it is my pride to offer you, is considered an enviable one, even apart from the devoted love that goes with it. You are aware that I am the sole heir of the Hidden House estate, which with all its dependencies is considered the largest proprietary, as my wife would be the most important lady in the county."

Cap's lip curled a little; looking askance at him, she answered:

"I really am very much obliged to you, Mr. Le Noir, for the distinguished honor that you designed for me. I should highly appreciate the magnanimity of a young gentleman, the heir of the wealthiest estate in the neighborhood, who deigns to propose marriage to the little beggar that I acknowledge myself to be. I regret to be obliged to refuse such dignities, but—I belong to another!" said Capitola, rising and advancing towards her horse.

Craven would not risk his success by pushing his suit farther at this sitting.

Very respectfully lending his assistance to put Capitola into her saddle, he said he hoped at some future, and more propitious time, to resume the subject. And then with a deep bow he left her, mounted his horse and rode on his way.

He did not believe that Capitola was more than half in earnest, or that any girl in Capitola's circumstances would do such a mad thing as to refuse the position he offered her.

He did not throw himself in her way often enough to excite her suspicion that their meetings were preconcerted on his part, and even when he did not overtake her or suffer her to overtake him, he avoided giving her offense by pressing his suit until another good opportunity should offer. This was not long in coming.

One afternoon he overtook her and rode by her side for a short distance when finding her in unusually good spirits and temper, he again renewed his declaration of love and offer of marriage.

Cap turned around in her saddle and looked at him with astonishment for a full minute before she exclaimed:

"Why, Mr. Le Noir, I gave you an answer more than a week ago. Didn't I tell you 'no'? What on earth do you mean by repeating the question?"

"I mean, bewitching Capitola, not to let such a treasure slip out of my grasp if I can help it?"

"I never was in your grasp that I know of!" said Cap, whipping up her horse and leaving him far behind.

Days passed before Craven thought it prudent again to renew and press his suit. He did so upon a fine September morning, when he overtook her riding along the banks of the river. He joined her, and in the most deprecating manner besought her to listen to him once more. Then he commenced in a strain of the most impassioned eloquence and urged his love and his proposal.

Capitola stopped her horse, wheeled around and faced him, looking him full in the eyes, while she said:

"Upon my word, Mr. Le Noir, you remind me of an anecdote told of young Sheridan. When his father advised him to take a wife and settle, he replied by asking *whose* wife he should take! Will nobody serve your purpose, but somebody else's sweetheart?—I have told you that I belong to a brave young soldier who is fighting his country's battles in a foreign land, while you are lazing here at home, trying to undermine him! I am ashamed of you, sir! and ashamed of myself for talking with you so many times! Never do you presume to accost me on the highways, or anywhere else, again! Craven by name and craven by nature, you have once already felt the weight of Herbert's arm. Do not provoke its second descent upon you! You are warned!" and with that Capitola, with her lips curled, her eyes flashing and her cheeks burning, put whip to her pony and galloped away.

Craven Le Noir's thin, white face grew perfectly livid with passion.

"I will have her yet! I have sworn it, and by fair means or by foul, I will have her yet!" he exclaimed, as he relaxed his hold upon his bridle and let his horse go on slowly, while he sat with his brows gathered over his thin nose, his long chin buried in his neckcloth, and his nails between his teeth, gnawing like a wild beast, as was his custom when deeply cogitating.

Presently he conceived a plan so diabolical that none but Satan himself could have inspired it! This was to take advantage of his acquaintance and casual meetings with Capitola, so to malign her character, as to make it unlikely that any honest man would ever risk his honor by taking her to wife; that thus the way might be left clear for himself; and he resolved if possible to effect this in such a manner—namely, by jests, innuendoes, and sneers, that it should never be directly traced to a positive assertion on his part. And in the meantime he determined so to govern himself in his deportment towards Capitola as to arouse no suspicion, give no offense and if possible win back her confidence.

It is true that even Craven Le Noir, base as he was, shrank from the idea of smirching the reputation of the woman of whom he wished to make a wife; but then he said to himself that in that remote neighborhood the scandal would be of little consequence to him who as soon as he should be married, would claim the estate of the Hidden House in right of his wife, put it in charge of an overseer, and then with his bride start for Paris, the paradise of the epicurean, where he designed to fix their principal residence.

Craven Le Noir was so pleased with his plan that he immediately set about putting it in execution. Our next chapter will show how he succeeded.

CHAPTER XLVI

CAP'S RAGE

"Is he not approved to the height of a villain, who hath slandered, scorned, dishonored thy kinswoman! Oh! that I were a man for his sake, or had a friend who would be one for mine!"
—*Shakespeare* [1]

AUTUMN BROUGHT the usual city visitors to Hurricane Hall to spend the sporting season and shoot over Major Warfield's grounds. Old Hurricane was in his glory, giving dinners and projecting hunts.

Capitola also enjoyed herself rarely, enacting with much satisfaction to herself and guests her new role of hostess, and not unfrequently joining her uncle and his friends in their field sports.

Among the guests there were two who deserve particular attention, not only because they had been for many years annual visitors of Hurricane Hall, but more especially because there had grown up between them and our little madcap heroine a strong mutual confidence and friendship. Yet no three persons could possibly be more unlike than Capitola and the two cousins of her soul, as she called these two friends. They were both distant relatives of Major Warfield, and in right of this relationship invariably addressed Capitola as "Cousin Cap."

John Stone, the elder of the two, was a very tall, stout, squarely-built young man, with a broad, good-humored face, fair skin, blue eyes, and light hair. In temperament he was rather phlegmatic, quiet and lazy. In character he was honest, prudent and good-tempered. In circumstances he was a safe banker, with a notable wife and two healthy children. The one thing that was able to excite his quiet nerves was the *chase,* of which he was as fond as he could possibly be of an amusement. The one person who agreeably stirred his rather still spirits was our little Cap, and that was the secret of his friendship for her.

Edwin Percy, the other, was a young West Indian, tall and delicately formed, with a clear olive complexion, languishing, dark-hazel eyes, and dark, bright-chestnut hair and beard. In temperament he was ardent as his clime. In character, indolent, careless and self-indulgent. In condition he was the bachelor of a sugar plantation of a thousand acres. He loved not the chase, nor any other amusement requiring exertion. He doted upon swansdown sofas with springs, French plays, cigars and chocolate. He came to the country to find repose, good air, and an appetite. He was the victim of constitutional ennui that yielded to nothing but the exhilaration of Capitola's company; that was the mystery of his love for her, and doubtless the young Creole would have proposed for Cap had he not thought it too much trouble to get married, and dreaded the bustle of a bridal. Certainly Edwin Percy was as opposite in character to John Stone as they both were to Capitola, yet great was the relative attraction among the three. Cap impartially divided her kind offices as hostess between them.

John Stone joined Old Hurricane in many a hard day's hunt, and Capitola was often of the party.

Edwin Percy spent many hours on the luxurious lounge in the parlor, where Cap was careful to place a stand with chocolate, cigars, wax matches and his favorite books.

One day Cap had had what she called "a row with the governor," that is to say, a slight misunderstanding with Major Warfield; a very uncommon occurrence, as the reader knows, in which that temperate old gentleman had so freely bestowed upon his niece the names of "beggar, foundling, brat, vagabond and vagrant," that Capitola, in just indignation, refused to join the birding party, and taking her game-bag, powder-flask, shot-horn and fowling-piece, and calling her favorite pointer, walked off, as she termed it, "to shoot herself." But if Capitola's by no means sweet temper had been tried that morning, it was destined to be still more severely tested before the day was over.

Her second provocation came in this way: John Stone, another deserter of the birding party, had that day betaken himself to Tip-Top upon some private business of his own. He dined at the Antlers in company with some sporting gentlemen of the neighborhood, and when the conversation naturally turned upon field sports, Mr. John Stone spoke of the fine shooting that was to be had around Hurricane Hall, when one of the gentlemen, looking straight across the table to Mr. Stone, said:

"Ahem!—that pretty little huntress of Hurricane Hall—that niece, or ward, or mysterious daughter of Old Hurricane, who engages with so much enthusiasm in your field sports over there, is a girl of very free and easy manners, I understand!—a Diana in nothing but her love of the chase!"

"Sir! it is a base calumny! and the man who endorses it is a shameless slanderer! There is my card! I may be found at my present residence, Hurricane Hall," said John Stone, throwing his pasteboard across the table, and rising to leave it.

"Nay, nay," said the stranger, laughing and pushing the card away. "I do not endorse the statement; I know nothing about it. I wash my hands of it," said the young man. And then upon Mr. Stone's demanding the author of the calumny, he gave the name of Mr. Craven Le Noir, who, he said, had "talked in his cups" at a dinner party recently given by one of his friends.

"I pronounce—publicly, in the presence of all these witnesses, as I shall presently to Craven Le Noir himself—that he is a shameless miscreant, who has basely slandered a noble girl! You, sir, have declined to endorse those words; henceforth decline to *repeat* them! For after this I shall call to a severe account any man who ventures, by word, gesture or glance, to hint this slander, or in any other way deal lightly with the honorable name and fame of the lady in question. Gentlemen, I am to be found at Hurricane Hall, and I have the honor of wishing you a more improving subject of conversation, and—a very good afternoon," said John Stone, bowing and leaving the room.

He immediately called for his horse and rode home.

In crossing the thicket of woods between the river and the rising ground in front of Hurricane Hall, he overtook Capitola, who, as we have said, had been out alone with her gun and dog, and was now returning home with her game-bag well laden.

Now, as John Stone looked at Capitola, with her reckless, free and joyous air, he thought she was just the sort of a girl unconsciously to get herself and friends into trouble. And he thought it best to give her a hint to put an abrupt period to her acquaintance, if she had even the slightest, with the heir apparent of the Hidden House.

While still hesitating how to begin the conversation, he came up with the young girl, dismounted, and leading his horse, walked by her side, asking carelessly:

"What have you bagged, Cap?"

"Some partridges. Oh, you should have been out with me and Sweetlips! we've had *such* sport! But, anyhow, you shall enjoy your share of the spoils! Come home, and you shall have some of these partridges broiled for supper, with currant sauce—a dish of my own invention, for uncle's sake, you know! he's such a gourmand!"

"Thank you, yes, I am on my way home now. Hem-m! Capitola, I counsel you to cut the acquaintance of our neighbor, Craven Le Noir."

"I have already done so; but—what in the world is the matter, that you should advise me thus?" inquired Capitola, fixing her eyes steadily upon the face of John Stone, who avoided her gaze as he answered:

"The man is not a proper associate for a young woman."

"I know that, and have cut him accordingly; but, cousin John, there is some reason for your words, that you have not expressed; and as they concern me, now I insist upon knowing what they are."

"Tut! it is nothing," said the other, evasively.

"John Stone, I know better! and the more you look down and whip your boot, the surer I am that there is something I ought to know, and I *will* know!"

"Well, you termagant! have your way!—he has been speaking lightly of you—that's all! nobody minds *him; his* tongue is no scandal."

"John Stone, what has he said?" asked Capitola, drawing her breath *hardly* between her closed teeth.

"Oh, now, why should you ask?—It is nothing; it is not proper that I should tell you," replied the gentleman, in embarrassment.

"'It is nothing,' and yet 'it is not proper that you should tell me!' How do you make that out? John Stone! leave off lashing the harmless bushes and listen to me!—I have to live in the same neighborhood with this man, after you have gone away, and I insist upon knowing the whole length and breadth of his baseness and malignity, that I may know how to judge and punish him!" said Capitola, with such grimness of resolution that Mr. Stone, provoked at her perversity, answered:

"Well, you willful girl, listen!" And commencing, he mercilessly told her all that had passed at the table.

To have seen our Cap, then! Face, neck and bosom were flushed with the crimson tide of indignation!

"You are sure of what you tell me, Cousin John?"

"The man vouches for it."

"He shall bite the dust!"

"What?"

"The slanderer shall bite the dust!"

Without more ado, down was thrown gun, game-bag, powder-flask and shot-horn, and bounding from point to point over all the intervening space, Capitola rushed into Hurricane Hall, and without an instant's delay ran straight into the parlor, where her epicurean friend, the young Creole, lay slumbering upon the lounge.

With her face now livid with concentrated rage, and her eyes glittering with that suppressed light peculiar to intense passion, she stood before him and said:

"Edwin! Craven Le Noir has defamed your cousin! get up and challenge him!"

"What did you say, Cap?" said Mr. Percy, slightly yawning.

"Must I repeat it? Craven Le Noir has defamed my character—challenge him!"

"That would be against the law, coz; they would indict me, sure!"

"You—you—you lie there and answer me in that way! *Oh,* that I were a man!"

"Compose yourself, sweet coz, and tell me what all this is about. Yaw-oo!—really I was asleep when you first spoke to me."

"Asleep! had you been *dead* and in your *grave,* the words that I spoke should have roused you like the trump of the archangel!" exclaimed Capitola, with the blood rushing back to her cheeks.

"Your entrance was sufficiently startling, coz! but tell me over again—what was the occasion?"

"That caitiff, Craven Le Noir, has slandered me. Oh, the villain! He is a base slanderer! Percy get up this moment and challenge Le Noir! I cannot breathe freely until it is done!" exclaimed Capitola, impetuously.

"Cousin Cap, duelling is obsolete; scenes are passé; law settles everything; and here there is scarcely ground for action for libel. But be comforted, coz, for if this comes to Uncle Hurricane's ears, he'll make mincemeat of him in no time. It is all in his line; he'll chaw him right up!"

"Percy, do you mean to say that you will not call out that man?" asked Capitola, drawing her breath hardly.

"Yes, coz."

"You won't fight him?"

"No, coz."

"You won't?"

"No."

"Edwin Percy, look me straight in the face!" said Cap, between her closed teeth.

"Well, I *am* looking you straight in the face! straight in the two blazing gray eyes, you little tempest in a teapot!—what then?"

"Do I look as though I should be in earnest in what I am about to speak?"

"I should judge so."

"Then listen, and don't take your eyes off mine until I am done speaking!"

"Very well; don't be long though, for it rather agitates me."

"I will not! hear me, then: You say that you decline to challenge Le Noir. Very good. I, on my part, here renounce all acquaintance with you! I will never sit down at the same table; enter the same room; or breathe the same air with you; never speak to you; listen to you; or recognize you in any manner, until my deep wrongs are avenged in the punishment of my slanderer, so help me——"

"*Hush-sh!* don't swear, Cap; it's profane and unwomanly; and nothing on earth but broken oaths would be the result!"

But Cap was off. In an instant she was down in the yard, where her groom was holding her horse ready, in case she wished to take her usual ride.

"Where is Mr. John Stone?" she asked.

"Down at the kennels, Miss," answered the boy.

She jumped into her saddle, put whip to her horse and flew over to the mansion-house and the kennels.

She pulled up before the door of the main building, sprang from her saddle, threw a bridle to a man in attendance, and rushed into the house and into the presence of Mr. John Stone, who was busy in prescribing for an indisposed pointer.

He looked up in astonishment, exclaiming:

"Hilloe! all the witches! here's Cap! why where on earth did you shoot from? What's up now? You look as if you were in a state of spontaneous combustion and couldn't stand it another minute."

"And I can't! and I won't! John Stone, you must call that man out!"

"What man, Cap—what the deuce do you mean?"

"You know well enough! you do this to provoke me! I mean the man of whom you cautioned me this afternoon! the wretch who slandered *me*, the niece of your host!"

"Whe—ew!"

"*Will you do it?*"

"Where's Percy?"

"On the lounge, with an ice in one hand and a novel in the other! I suppose it is no use mincing the matter, John; he is a——mere epicure! there is no fight in him! It is *you* who must vindicate your cousin's honor!"

"My cousin's honor cannot need vindication! it is unquestioned and unquestionable!"

"No smooth words, if you please, cousin John! Will you, or will you not fight that man?"

"Tut, Cap, no one really questions your honor! That man will get himself knocked into a cocked hat if he goes around talking of an honest girl."

"A likely thing, when her own cousins and guests take it so quietly!"

"What would you have them do, Cap? The longer an affair of this kind is agitated, the more offensive it becomes! Besides, chivalry is out of date. The knights-errant are all dead."

"The MEN are all dead! if any ever really lived!" cried Cap, in a fury. "Heaven knows I am inclined to believe them to have been a fabulous race like that of the mastadon or the centaur! *I* certainly never saw a creature that deserved the name of man! The very first of your race was the meanest fellow that ever was heard of! eat the stolen apple, and when found out, laid one half of the blame on his wife, and the other on his maker——'The WOMAN whom THOU gavest me' did so and so! pah! I don't wonder the Lord took a dislike to the race and sent a flood to sweep them all off the face of the earth!——I will give you one more chance to retrieve your honor! In one word, now——will you fight that man?"

"My dear little cousin, I would do anything in reason to vindicate the assailed manhood of my whole sex, but really, now——"

——"Will you fight that man?—one word—yes or no?"

"Tut, Cap? you are a very reckless young woman! You—it's your nature—you are an incorrigible madcap! You bewitch a poor wretch until he doesn't know his head from his heels; puts his feet into his hat and covers his scalp with his boots! You are a will-o'-the-wisp who lures a poor fellow on through woods, bogs and briars, until you land him in the quicksands! You whirl him around and around until he grows dizzy and delirious, and talks at random, and then you'd have him called out, you blood-thirsty little vixen! I tell you, Cousin Cap, if I were to take up all the quarrels your hoydenism might lead me into, I should have nothing else to do!"

"Then you *won't* fight!"

"Can't little cousin! I have a wife and family, which are powerful checks upon a man's duelling impulses!"

"SILENCE! you are no cousin of mine! no drop of your sluggish blood stagnates in *my* veins! no spark of the liquid fire of *my* life's current burns in your torpid arteries, else at this insult, would it set you in a flame! Never dare to call *me* cousin again, recreant!" And so saying, she flung herself out of the building and into her saddle, put whip to her horse and galloped away home.

Now Mr. Stone had privately resolved to thrash Craven Le Noir; but he did not deem it expedient to take Cap into his confidence. As Capitola reached the horse-block, her own groom came to take the bridle.

"Jem," she said, as she jumped from her saddle,—"put Gyp up and then come to my room, I have a message to send by you."

And then with burning cheeks and flashing eyes, she went to her own sanctum, and after taking off her habit, did the most astounding thing that ever a woman of the nineteenth or any former century attempted—she wrote a challenge to Craven Le Noir—charging him with falsehood in having maligned her honor; demanding from him "the satisfaction of a gentleman;" and requesting him as the challenged party, to name the time, place and weapons with which he would meet her.

By the time she had written, sealed and directed this warlike defiance, her young groom made his appearance.

"Jem," she asked, "do you know the way to the Hidden House?"

"Yes, Miss, sure."

"Then take this note thither, ask for Mr. Le Noir, put it into his hands, and say that you are directed to wait an answer. And listen, you need not mention to any one in this house, where you are going; nor when you return, where you have been; but bring the answer you may get directly to this room, where you will find me."

"Yes, Miss," said the boy, who was off like a flying Mercury.

Capitola threw herself into her chair to spend the slow hours until the boy's return, as well as her fierce impatience and forced inaction would permit.

At tea-time she was summoned; but excused herself from going below upon a plea of indisposition.

"Which is perfectly true," she said to herself, "since I am utterly indisposed to go. And besides, I have sworn never again to sit at the same table with my cousins, until for the wrongs done me, I have received ample satisfaction."

CHAPTER XLVII

CAPITOLA CAPS THE CLIMAX

"Oh! when she's angry, she is keen and shrewd;
She was a vixen when she went to school;
And though she is but little she is fierce."
——*Shakespeare*[1]

IT WAS QUITE late in the evening when Jem, her messenger, returned.

"Have you an answer?" she impetuously demanded, rising to meet him as he entered.

"Yes, Miss, here it is," replied the boy, handing a neatly folded, highly perfumed little note.

"Go," said Cap, curtly, as she received it.

And when the boy had bowed and withdrawn, she threw herself into a chair, and with little respect for the pretty device of the pierced heart with which the note was sealed, she tore it open and devoured its contents.

Why did Capitola's cheeks and lips blanch, white as death? Why did her eyes contract and glitter like stilettos? Why was her breath drawn hard and laboriously through clenched teeth and livid lips?

That note was couched in the most insulting terms.

Capitola's first impulse was to rend the paper to atoms and grind those atoms to powder beneath her heel. But a second inspiration changed her purpose.

"No, no, no, I will not destroy you, precious little note! No legal document involving the ownership of the largest estate, no cherished love-letter filled with vows of undying affection, shall be more carefully guarded! Next to my heart, shall you lie. My shield and buckler, shall you be! my sure defense and justification! I know what to do with you, my precious little jewel! You are the warrant for the punishment of that man, signed by his own hand." And so saying Capitola carefully deposited the note in her bosom.

Then she lighted her chamber lamp, and taking it with her, went down stairs to her uncle's bedroom.

Taking advantage of the time when she knew he would be absorbed in a game of chess with John Stone, and she should be safe from interruption for several hours if she wished, she went to Major Warfield's little armory in the closet adjoining his room, opened his pistol-case and took from it a pair of revolvers, closed and locked the case, and withdrew and hid the key that they might not chance to be missed until she should have time to replace them.

Then she hurried back into her own chamber, locked the pistols up in her own drawer, and wearied out with so much excitement, prepared to go to rest. Here a grave and unexpected obstacle met her; she had always been accustomed to kneel and offer up to Heaven her evening's tribute of praise and thanksgiving for the mercies of the day, and prayers for protection and blessing through the night.

Now she knelt as usual, but thanksgiving and prayer seemed frozen on her lips. How could she praise or pray with such a purpose as she had in her heart?

For the first time Capitola doubted the perfect righteousness of that purpose which was of a character to arrest her prayers upon her lips.

With a start of impatience and a heavy sigh, she sprang up and hurried into bed.

She did not sleep, but lay tossing from side to side in feverish excitement the whole night—having, in fact, a terrible battle between her own fierce passions and her newly-awakened conscience.

Nevertheless, she arose by daybreak in the morning, dressed herself, went and unlocked her drawer, took out the pistols, carefully loaded them, and laid them down for service.

Then she went down stairs, where the servants were only just beginning to stir, and sent for her groom, Jem, whom she ordered to saddle her pony, and also get a horse for himself, to attend her in a morning ride.

After which she returned up stairs, put on her riding-habit, and buckled around her waist a morocco belt, into which she stuck the two revolvers. She then threw around her shoulders a short circular cape that concealed the weapons, and put on her hat and gloves and went below.

She found her little groom already at the door with the horses. She sprang into her saddle, and, bidding Jem follow her, took the road towards Tip-Top.

She knew that Mr. Le Noir was in the habit of riding to the village every morning, and she determined to meet him. She knew, from the early hour of the day, that he could not possibly be ahead of her, and she rode on slowly, to give him an opportunity to overtake her.

Probably Craven Le Noir was later that morning than usual, for Capitola had reached the entrance of the village before she heard the sound of his horse's feet approaching behind her.

She did not wish that their *rencontre* should be in the streets of the village, so she instantly wheeled her horse and galloped back to meet him.

As both were riding at full speed, they soon met.

She first drew rein, and, standing in his way accosted him with:

"Mr. Le Noir!"

"Your most obedient, Miss Black," he said, with a deep bow.

"I happen to be without father or brother to protect me from affront, sir, and my uncle is an invalid veteran whom I will not trouble. I am, therefore, under the novel necessity of fighting my own battles. Yesterday, sir, I sent you a note demanding satisfaction for a heinous slander you circulated against me. You replied by an insulting note. You do not escape punishment so! Here are two pistols; both are loaded; take either one of them: for, sir, we have met, and now we do not part until one of us falls from the horse!"

And so saying, she rode up to him and offered him the choice of the pistols.

He laughed—partly in surprise and partly in admiration as he said, with seeming good humor:

"Miss Black, you are a very charming young woman, and delightfully original and piquant in all your ideas; but you outrage all the laws that govern the duello. You know that, as the challenged party, I have the right to the choice of time, place and arms. I made that choice yesterday. I renew it to-day. When you accede to the terms of the meeting, I shall endeavor to give you all the satisfaction you demand. Good morning, Miss."

And with a deep bow, even to the flaps of his saddle, he rode past her.

"That base insult again!" cried Capitola, with the blood rushing to her face.

Then lifting her voice, she again accosted him:

"Mr. Le Noir!"

He turned, with a smile.

She threw one of the pistols on the ground near him, saying:

"Take that up and defend yourself."

He waved his hand in negation, bowed, smiled, and rode on.

"Mr. Le Noir!" she called in a peremptory tone.

Once more he turned.

She raised her pistol, took deliberate aim at his white forehead, and fired——

Bang! bang! bang! BANG! BANG! BANG!

Six times without an instant's intermission, until her revolver was spent.

When the smoke cleared away, a terrible vision met her eyes.

It was Craven Le Noir with his face covered with blood, reeling in his saddle, from which he soon dropped to the ground.

In falling, his foot remained hanging in the stirrup. The well-trained cavalry horse stood perfectly still, though trembling in a panic of terror, from which he might at any moment start to run, dragging the helpless body after him.

Capitola saw this danger, and not being cruel, she tempered justice with mercy; threw down her spent pistol; dismounted from her horse; went up to the fallen man; disengaged his foot from the stirrup, and taking hold of his shoulders, tried with all her might to drag the still breathing form from the dusty road where it lay in danger of being run over by wagons, to the green bank where it might lie in comparative safety.

But the heavy form was too much for her single strength. And calling her terrified groom to assist her, they removed the body.

Capitola then remounted her horse, and galloped rapidly into the village, and up to the "ladies' entrance" of the hotel, where after sending for the proprietor, she said:

"I have just been shooting Craven Le Noir for slandering me; he lies by the roadside at the entrance of the village; you had better send somebody to pick him up."

"Miss!" cried the astounded inn-keeper.

Capitola distinctly repeated her words, and then leaving the inn-keeper, transfixed with consternation, she crossed the street and entered a magistrate's office, where a little old gentleman, with a pair of green spectacles resting on his hooked nose, sat at a writing-table, giving some directions to a constable, who was standing hat in hand before him.

Capitola waited until this functionary had his orders and a written paper, and had left the office, and the magistrate was alone, before she walked up to the desk and stood before him.

"Well, well, young woman! Well, well, what do you want?" inquired the old gentleman, impatiently looking up from folding his papers.

"I have come to give myself up for shooting Craven Le Noir, who slandered me," answered Capitola, quietly.

The old man let fall his handfuls of papers, raised his head and stared at her over the tops of his green spectacles.

"What did you say, young woman?" he asked, in the tone of one who doubted his own ears.

"I say that I have forestalled an arrest by coming here to give myself up for the shooting of a dastard who slandered, insulted, and refused to give me satisfaction," answered Capitola, very distinctly.

"Am I awake? Do I hear aright? Do you mean to say that *you* have killed a man?" asked the dismayed magistrate.

"Oh! I can't say as to the killing! I shot him off his horse, and then sent Mr. Merry and his men to pick him up, while I came here to answer for myself!"

"Unfortunate girl! and how can you answer for such a dreadful deed!" exclaimed the utterly confounded magistrate.

"Oh, as to the dreadfulness of the deed, that depends on circumstances," said Cap, "and I can answer for it very well. He made addresses to me; I refused him. He slandered me; I challenged him. He insulted me; I shot him."

"Miserable young woman, if this be proved true, I shall have to commit you!"

"Just as you please," said Cap, "but bless your soul, that won't help Craven Le Noir a single bit!"

As she spoke several persons entered the office in a state of high excitement—all talking at once, saying:

"That is the girl!"

"Yes, that is her!"

"She is Miss Black, old Warfield's niece."

"Yes, he said she was," etc., etc., etc.

"What is all this, neighbors, what is all this?" inquired the troubled magistrate, rising in his place.

"Why, sir, there's been a gentleman, Mr. Craven Le Noir, shot. He has been taken to the Antlers, where he lies in *articulus mortis,*[2] and we wish him to be confronted with Miss Capitola Black, the young woman here present, that he may indentify her, whom he accuses of having fired six charges into him, before his death. She needn't deny it, because he is ready to swear to her!" said Mr. Merry, who constituted himself spokesman.

"She accuses herself," said the magistrate in dismay.

"Then, sir, had she not better be taken at once to the presence of Mr. Le Noir, who may not have many minutes to live!"

"Yes, come along," said Cap. "I only gave myself up to wait for this; and as he is already at hand, let's go and have it all over, for I have been riding about in this frosty morning air, for three hours, and I have got a good appetite, and I want to go home to breakfast."

"I am afraid, young woman, you will scarcely get home to breakfast this morning," said Mr. Merry.

"We'll see that presently," answered Cap, composedly, as they all left the office, and crossed the street to the Antlers.

They were conducted by the landlord to a chamber on the first floor, where upon a bed lay stretched, almost without breath or motion, the form of Craven Le Noir. His face was still covered with blood, that the by-standers had scrupulously refused to wash off until the arrival of the magistrate. His complexion as far as could be seen, was very pale. He was thoroughly prostrated, if not actually dying.

Around his bed were gathered the village doctor, the landlady, and several maidservants.

"The squire has come, sir; are you able to speak to him?" asked the landlord, approaching the bed.

"Yes—let him swear me," feebly replied the wounded man, "and then send for a clergyman."

The landlady immediately left to send for Mr. Goodwin, and the magistrate approached the head of the bed, and speaking solemnly, ex-horted the wounded man, as he expected soon to give an account of the works done in his body, to speak the truth, the whole truth, and nothing but the truth, without reserve, malice or exaggeration, both as to the deed, and its provocation.

"I will, I will, for I have sent for a minister and I intend to try to make my peace with Heaven," replied Le Noir.

The magistrate then directed Capitola to come and take her stand at the foot of the bed where the wounded man, who was lying on his back, could see her without turning.

Cap came as she was commanded, and stood there with some irrepressible and incomprehensible mischief gleaming out from under her long eyelashes and from the corners of her dimpled lips.

The magistrate then administered the oath to Craven Le Noir, and bade him look upon Capitola and give his evidence.

He did so, and under the terrors of a guilty conscience and of expected death, his evidence partook more of the nature of a confession than an accusation. He testified that he had addressed Capitola, and had been rejected by her; then, under the influence of evil motives, he had circulated insinuations against her honor, which were utterly unjustifiable by fact; she, seeming to have heard of them, took the strange course of challenging him—just as if she had been a man; he could not of course meet a lady in a duel, but he had taken advantage of the technical phraseology of the challenged party, as to time, place and weapons, to offer her a deep insult; then she had waylaid him on the highway, offered him his choice of a pair of revolvers, and told him, that having met, they should not part until one or the other fell from the horse; he had again laughingly refused the encounter except upon the insulting terms he had before proposed;—she had then thrown him one of the pistols, bidding him defend himself;—he had laughingly passed her when she called him by name, he turned and she fired—six times in succession and he fell. He knew no more until he was brought to his present room. He said in conclusion, he did not wish that the young girl should be prosecuted as she had only avenged her own honor; and that he hoped his death would be taken by her and her friends, as a sufficient expiation of his offenses against her; and lastly, he requested that he might be left alone with the minister.

"Bring that unhappy young woman over to my office, Ketchem," said the magistrate, addressing himself to a constable. Then turning to the landlord, he said:

"Sir, it would be a charity in you to put a messenger on horseback and send him to Hurricane Hall for Major Warfield, who will have to enter into a recognizance for Miss Black's appearance at court."

"Stop," said Cap, "don't be too certain of that! 'Be always sure you're right—then go ahead!' Is not any one here cool enough to reflect that if I had fired six bullets at that man's forehead, and every one had struck, I should have blown his head to the sky?—Will not somebody at once wash his face and see how deep the wounds are?"

The doctor who had been restrained by others now took a sponge and water and cleaned the face of Le Noir, which was found to be well peppered with split peas!

Cap looked around, and seeing the astonished looks of the good people, burst into an irrepressible fit of laughter, saying, as soon as she had got breath enough:

"Upon my word, neighbors, you look more shocked, if not actually more disappointed, to find that, after all, he is not killed, and there'll be no spectacle, than you did at first when you thought murder had been done."

"Will you be good enough to explain this, young woman?" said the magistrate, severely.

"Certainly, for your worship seems as much disappointed as others!" said Cap. Then turning towards the group around the bed, she said:

"You have heard Mr. Le Noir's 'last dying speech and confession,' as he supposed it to be; and you know the maddening provocations that inflamed my temper against him. Last night, after having received his insulting answer to my challenge, there was evil in my heart, I do assure you! I possessed myself of my uncle's revolvers, and resolved to waylay him this morning, and force him to give me satisfaction, or if he refused—well, no matter! I tell you, there was danger in me!—But, before retiring to bed at night it is my habit to say my prayers; now the practice of prayer and the purpose of 'red-handed violence' cannot exist in the same person at the same time. I wouldn't sleep without praying, and I couldn't pray without giving up my thoughts of fatal vengeance upon Craven Le Noir. So at last I made up my mind to spare his life, and teach him a lesson. The next morning I drew the charges of the revolvers, and re-loaded them with poor powder and dried peas. Everything else has happened just as he has told you. He has received no harm, except in being terribly frightened, and in having his beauty spoiled!—and as for that, didn't I offer him one of the pistols, and expose my own face to similar damage?—for I'd scorn to take advantage of any one!" said Cap, laughing.

Craven Le Noir had now raised himself up in a sitting posture, and was looking around with an expression of countenance which was a strange blending of relief at this unexpected respite from the grave and intense mortification at finding himself in the ridiculous position in which the address of Capitola and his own weak nerves, cowardice, and credulity had placed him.

Cap went up to him and said, in a consoling voice:

"Come! thank Heaven that you are not going to die this bout. I'm glad you repented and told the truth; and I hope you may live long enough to offer Heaven a truer repentance than that which is the mere effect of fright. For I tell you plainly that if it had not been for the grace of the Lord acting upon my heart last night, your soul might have been in Hades now."

Craven Le Noir shut his eyes, groaned, and fell back overpowered by the reflection.

"Now, please your Worship, may I go home?" asked Cap, demurely popping down a mock courtesy to the magistrate.

"Yes—go! go! go!" said that officer, with an expression as though he considered our Cap an individual of the animal kingdom whom neither Buffon[3] nor any other natural philosopher had ever classified, and who, as a creature of unknown habits, might sometimes be dangerous.

Cap immediately availed herself of the permission, and went out to look for her servant and horses.

But Jem, the first moment he had found himself unwatched, had put out as fast as he could fly to Hurricane Hall, to inform Major Warfield of what had occurred.

And Capitola, after losing a great deal of time in looking for him, mounted her horse and was just about to start, when who should ride up in hot haste but Old Hurricane, attended by Wool.

"Stop there!" he shouted, as he saw Cap.

She obeyed; and he sprung from his horse with the agility of youth, and helped her to descend from hers.

Then drawing her arm within his own, he led her into the parlor, and putting an unusual restraint upon himself, he ordered her to tell him all about the affair.

Cap sat down and gave him the whole history from beginning to end.

Old Hurricane could not sit still to hear. He strode up and down the room, striking his stick upon the floor, and uttering inarticulate sounds of rage and defiance.

When Cap had finished her story he suddenly stopped before her, brought down the point of his stick with a resounding thump upon the floor, and exclaimed:

"Demmy, you New York newsboy, will you never be a woman? Why the demon didn't you tell *me,* sirrah? *I* would have called the fellow out and chastised him to your heart's consent. Hang it, Miss, answer me and say."

"Because you are on the invalid list and I am in sound condition and capable of taking my own part," said Cap.

"Then, answer me this: while you *were* taking your own part, why the foul fiend didn't you pepper him with something sharper than dried peas?"

"I think he is quite as severely punished in suffering from extreme terror and intense mortification and public ridicule," said Cap.

"And now, uncle, I have not eaten a single blessed mouthful this morning, and I am hungry enough to eat up Gyp, or to satisfy Patty."

Old Hurricane, permitting his excitement to subside in a few expiring grunts, rang the bell and gave orders for breakfast to be served.

And after that meal was over, he set out with his niece for Hurricane Hall.

And upon arriving at home, he addressed a letter to Mr. Le Noir, to the effect that as soon as the latter should have recovered from the effect of his fright and mortification, he, Major Warfield should demand and expect satisfaction.

CHAPTER XLVIII

BLACK DONALD'S LAST ATTEMPT

"Who can express the horror of that night,
   When darkness lent his robes to monster fear?
And heaven's black mantle, banishing the light,
   Made everything in fearful form appear."
   —*Brandon*

LET IT NOT be supposed that Black Donald had forgotten his promise to Colonel Le Noir, or was indifferent to its performance.

But many perilous failures had taught him caution.

He had watched and waylaid Capitola in her rides. But the girl seemed to bear a charmed safety; for never once had he caught sight of her except in company with her groom and with Craven Le Noir. And very soon by eaves-dropping on these occasions, he learned the secret design of the son to forestall the father, and run off with the heiress.

And as Black Donald did not foresee what success Craven Le Noir might have with Capitola, he felt the more urgent necessity for prompt action on his own part.

He might indeed have brought his men and attacked and overcome Capitola's attendants, in open day; but the enterprise must needs have been attended with great bloodshed and loss of life, which would have made a sensation in the neighborhood that Black Donald, in the present state of his fortunes, was by no means ambitious of daring.

In a word, had such an act of unparalleled violence been attempted, the better it succeeded the greater would have been the indignation of the people, and the whole country would probably have risen and armed themselves, and hunted the outlaws, as so many wild beasts, with horses and hounds.

Therefore Black Donald preferred quietly to abduct his victim, so as to leave no trace of her "taking off," but to allow it to be supposed that she had eloped.

He resolved to undertake this adventure alone, though to himself personally this plan was even more dangerous than the other.

He determined to gain access to her chamber, secrete himself anywhere in the room, (except under the bed, where his instincts informed him that Capitola every night looked,) and when the household should be buried in repose, steal out upon her, overpower, gag, and carry her off, in the silence of the night, leaving no trace of his own presence behind.

By means of one of his men, who went about unsuspected among the negroes, buying up mats and baskets, that the latter were in the habit of making for sale, he learned that Capitola occupied the same remote chamber in the oldest part of the house; but that a guest slept in the room next, and another in the one opposite hers. And that the house was besides full of visitors from the city, who had come down to spend the sporting season, and that they were hunting all day and carousing all night from one week's end to another.

On hearing this, Black Donald quickly comprehended that it was no time to attempt the abduction of the maiden with the least probability of success. All would be risked, and most probably lost in the endeavor.

He resolved, therefore, to wait until the house should be clear of company, and the household fallen into their accustomed carelessness and monotony.

He had to wait much longer than he had reckoned upon—through October and through November, when he first heard of and laughed over Cap's "duel" with Craven Le Noir, and congratulated himself upon the fact that *that* rival was no longer to be feared. He had also to wait through two-thirds of the month of December because a party had come down to enjoy a short season of fox-hunting. They went away just before Christmas.

And then at last came Black Donald's opportunity! And a fine opportunity it was! Had Satan himself engaged to furnish him with one to order, it could not have been better!

The reader must know, that throughout Virginia the Christmas week, from the day after Christmas until the day after New Year, is the negroes' saturnalia! there are usually eight days of incessant dancing, feasting and frolicking from quarter to quarter, and from barn to barn. Then the banjo, the fiddle and the "bones,"[1] are heard from morning until night, and from night until morning.

And nowhere was this annual octave of festivity held more sacred

379

than at Hurricane Hall. It was the will of Major Warfield that they should have their full satisfaction out of their seven days' carnival. He usually gave a dinner party on Christmas day, after which his people were free until the third of January.

"Demmy, mum!" he would say to Mrs. Condiment, "they wait on us fifty-one weeks in the year, and it's hard if we can't wait on ourselves the fifty-second!"

Small thanks to Old Hurricane for his self-denial! *He* did nothing for himself or others, and Mrs. Condiment and Capitola had a hot time of it in serving him. Mrs. Condiment had to do all the cooking and housework. And Cap had to perform most of the duties of Major Warfield's valet. And that was the way in which Old Hurricane waited on *himself.*

It happened therefore, that about the middle of the Christmas week, being Wednesday, the twenty-eighth of December, all the house-servants and farm-laborers from Hurricane Hall went off in a body to a banjo break-down given at a farm five miles across the country.

And Major Warfield, Mrs. Condiment and Capitola were the only living beings left in the old house that night.

Black Donald, who had been prowling about the premises evening after evening, watching his opportunity to effect his nefarious object, soon discovered the outward bound stampede of the negroes, and the un-protected state in which the old house, for that night only, would be left. And he determined to take advantage of the circumstances to consummate his wicked purpose.

In its then defenceless condition, he could easily have mustered his force and carried off his prize without immediate personal risk. But, as we said before, he eschewed violence, as being likely to provoke aftereffects of a too fatal character.

He resolved rather at once to risk his own personal safety in the quieter plan of abduction which he had formed.

He determined that as soon as it should be dark, he would watch his opportunity to enter the house, steal to Cap's chamber, secrete himself in a closet, and when all should be quiet, "in the dead waste and middle of the night," he would come out, master her, stop her mouth, and carry her off.

When it became quite dark he approached the house, and hid himself under the steps beneath the back door leading from the hall into the garden, to watch his opportunity of entering. He soon found that his enterprise required great patience as well as courage. He had to wait more than two hours before he heard the door unlocked and opened.

He then peered out from his hiding-place, and saw Old Hurricane taking his way out towards the garden.

Now was his time to slip unperceived into the house. He stealthily came out of this hiding-place, crept up the portico stairs to the back door, noiselessly turned the latch, entered, and closed it behind him. He had just time to open a side door on his right hand, and conceal himself in a wood closet under the stairs, when he heard the footsteps of Old Hurricane returning.

The old man came in, and Black Donald laughed to himself to hear with what caution he locked, bolted and barred the doors to keep out house-breakers!

"Ah, old fellow! you are fastening the stable after the horse has been stolen!" said Black Donald to himself.

As soon as Old Hurricane had passed by the closet in which the outlaw was concealed, and had gone into the parlor, Black Donald determined to risk the ascent into Capitola's chamber. From the description given by his men, who had once succeeded in finding their way thither, he knew very well where to go.

Noiselessly, therefore, he left his place of concealment, and crept out to reconnoitre the hall, which he found deserted.

Old Hurricane's shawl, hat and walking-stick were deposited in one corner. In case of being met on the way, he put the hat on his head, wrapped the shawl around his shoulders, and took the stick in his hand.

His forethought proved to be serviceable. He went through the hall and up the first flight of stairs without interruption; but on going along the hall of the second story he met Mrs. Condiment coming out of Old Hurricane's room.

"Your slippers are on the hearth, your gown is at the fire and the water is boiling to make your punch, Major Warfield," said the old lady, in passing.

"Umph, umph, umph," grunted Black Donald in reply.

The housekeeper then bade him good-night, saying that she was going at once to her room.

"Umph!" assented Black Donald. And so they parted, and this peril was passed.

Black Donald went up the second flight of stairs and then down a back passage and a narrow stair-case and along a corridor and through several untenanted rooms, and into another passage, and finally through a side door leading into Capitola's chamber.

Here he looked around for a safe hiding-place—there was a high bedstead curtained; two deep windows also curtained; two closets; a dressing bureau, work-stand, wash-stand and two arm-chairs. The forethought of little Pitapat had caused her to kindle a fire on the hearth and place a waiter of refreshments on the work-stand, so as to make all comfortable before she had left with the other negroes to go to the banjo breakdown.

Among the edibles, Pitapat had been careful to leave a small bottle of brandy, a pitcher of cream, a few eggs and some spice, saying to herself, "Long as it was Christmas times Miss Caterpillar might want a sup of egg-nog quiet to herself, jes as much as ole marse did his whiskey punch"— and never fancying that her young mistress would require a more delicate lunch than her old master.

Black Donald laughed as he saw this outlay, and remarking that the young occupant of the chamber must have an appetite of her own, he put the neck of the brandy bottle to his lips and took what he called "a hearty swig."

Then vowing that Old Hurricane knew what good liquor was, he replaced the bottle and looked around to find the best place for his concealment.

He soon determined to hide himself behind the thick folds of the window curtain nearest the door, so that immediately after the entrance of Capitola he could glide to the door, lock it, withdraw the key and have the girl at once in his power.

He took a second "swig" at the brandy bottle; and then went into his place of concealment to wait events.

That same hour Capitola was her uncle's partner in a prolonged game of chess. It was near eleven o'clock before Cap heartily tired of the battle, permitted herself to be beaten in order to get to bed.

With a satisfied chuckle, Old Hurricane arose from his seat, lighted two bed-chamber lamps, gave one to Capitola, took the other himself, and started off for his room, followed by Cap as far as the head of the first flight of stairs, where she bade him good-night.

She waited until she saw him enter his room, heard him lock his door on the inside, and throw himself down heavily into his arm-chair, and then she went on her own way.

She hurried up the second flight of stairs, and along the narrow passages, empty rooms, steep steps, and dreary halls, until she reached the door of her dormitory.

She turned the latch and entered the room.

The first thing that met her sight was the waiter of provisions upon the stand. And at this fresh instance of her little maid's forethought, she burst into an uncontrollable fit of laughter.

She did not see a dark figure glide from behind the window curtains, steal to the door, turn the lock and withdraw the key.

But still retaining her prejudice against the presence of food in her bed-chamber, she lifted up the waiter in both hands to carry it out into the passage, turned and stood face to face with—Black Donald!

CHAPTER XLIX

THE AWFUL PERIL OF CAPITOLA

$$\text{寒 寒 寒 寒 寒 寒}$$

"Out of this nettle, danger,
I'll pluck the flower, safety!"
—*Shakespeare*[1]

CAPITOLA'S BLOOD seemed to turn to ice, and her form to stone at the sight! Her first impulse was to scream and let fall the waiter! She controlled herself and repressed the scream, though she was very near dropping the waiter.

Black Donald looked at her and laughed aloud at her consternation, saying with a chuckle:

"You did not expect to see me here to-night, did you now, my dear?"

She gazed at him in a silent panic for a moment.

Then her faculties, that had been suddenly dispersed by the shock, as suddenly rallied to her rescue.

In one moment she understood her real position.

Black Donald had locked her in with himself, and held the key; so she could not hope to get out.

The loudest scream that she might utter would never reach the distant chamber of Major Warfield, or the still more remote apartment of Mrs. Condiment; so she could not hope to bring any one to her assistance.

She was therefore entirely in the power of Black Donald. She fully comprehended this, and said to herself:

"Now, my dear Cap, if you don't look sharp your hour is come! Nothing on earth will save you, Cap, but your own wits! for if ever I saw mischief in any one's face, it is in that fellow's that is eating you up with his great eyes at the same time that he is laughing at you with his big mouth! Now, Cap, my little man, be a woman! don't you stick at trifles! Think of

384

Jael and Sisera![2] Think of Judith and Holofernes![3] And the devil and Doctor Faust,[4] if necessary, and don't you blench! All stratagems are fair in love and war—especially in war, and most especially in such a war as this is likely to be—a contest in close quarters for dear life!"

All this passed through her mind in one moment, and in the next her plan was formed.

Setting her waiter down upon the table, and throwing herself into one of the arm-chairs, she said:

"Well, upon my word, I think a gentleman might let a lady know when he means to pay her a domiciliary visit at midnight!"

"Upon *my* word, *I* think you are very cool!" replied Black Donald, throwing himself into the second arm-chair on the other side of the stand of refreshments.

"People are likely to be cool on a December night, with the thermometer at zero, and the ground three feet under the snow," said Cap, nothing daunted.

"Capitola, I admire you! You are a *cucumber*. That's what you are, a *cucumber.*"

"A pickled one?" asked Cap.

"Yes! and as pickled cucumbers are good to give one an appetite, I think I shall fall to and eat."

"Do so," said Cap, "for Heaven forbid that I should fail in hospitality."

"Why, really, this looks as though you had expected a visitor—doesn't it?" asked Black Donald, helping himself to a huge slice of ham, and stretching his feet out towards the fire.

"Well, yes, rather; though, to say the truth, it was not *your* reverence I expected," said Cap.

"Ah! somebody *else's* reverence, eh? Well, let them come! I'll be ready for them!" said the outlaw, pouring out and quaffing a large glass of brandy. He drank it, set down the glass, and turning to our little heroine, inquired:

"Capitola, did you ever have Craven Le Noir here to supper with you?"

"You insult me! I scorn to reply!" said Cap.

"Whe-ew! what long whiskers our Grimalkin's got! You scorn to reply! Then you really are not afraid of me?" asked the robber, rolling a great piece of cheese in his mouth.

"Afraid of you?—No, I guess not," replied Cap, with a toss of her head.

"Yet, I *might* do you some harm."

"But you won't."

"Why won't I?"

"Because it won't pay."

"Why won't it?"

"Because you couldn't do me any harm, unless you were to kill me, and you would gain nothing by my death, except a few trinkets that you may have without."

"Then, you are really not afraid of me?" he asked, taking another deep draught of brandy.

"Not a bit of it—I rather like you."

"Come, now, you're running a rig upon a fellow," said the outlaw, winking, and depositing a huge chunk of bread in his capacious jaws.

"No, indeed! I liked you long before I saw you! I always *did* like people that made other people's hair stand on end! Don't you remember when you first came here disguised as a peddler, though I did not know who you were, when we were talking of Black Donald, and everybody was abusing him, except myself, I took his part, and said that, for my part, I *liked* Black Donald, and wanted to see him?"

"Sure enough, my jewel, so you did! and didn't I bravely risk my life, by throwing off my disguise, to gratify your laudable wish?"

"So you did, my hero!"

"Ah, but *well* as you liked me, the moment you thought me in your power, didn't you leap upon my shoulders like a catamount, and cling there, shouting to all the world to come and help you, for that you had caught Black Donald, and would die, before you would give him up? Ah! you little vampire, how you thirsted for my blood! And *you* pretended to like me!" said Black Donald, eyeing her from head to foot, with a sly leer.

Cap returned the look with interest. Dropping her head on one side, she glanced upwards, from the corner of her eye, with an expression of "infinite" humor, mischief and roguery, saying:

"Lor! didn't you know why I did *that?*"

"Because you wanted me captured, I suppose."

"No, indeed, but, because——"

"Well, what?"

"Because—I wanted you to carry me off!"

"Well, I declare, I never thought of that!" said the outlaw, dropping his bread and cheese, and staring at the young girl.

"Well, you *might* have thought of it then! I was tired of hum-drum life, and I wanted to see adventures!" said Cap.

Black Donald looked at the mad girl from head to foot, and then said, coolly:

"Miss Black, I am afraid you are not good."

"Yes I am—before folks!" said Cap.

"And so you really wished me to carry you off."

"I should think so! didn't I stick to you until you dropped me?"

"Certainly; and now if you really like me as well as you say you do, come give me a kiss."

"I won't!" said Cap, "until you have done your supper and washed your face. Your beard is full of crumbs!"

"Very well, I can wait awhile! meantime just brew me a bowl of egg-nog, by way of a night-cap, will you?" said the outlaw, drawing off his boots and stretching his legs to the fire.

"Agreed; but it takes two to make egg-nog; you'll have to whisk up the whites of the eggs into a froth, while I beat the yellows, and mix the other ingredients," said Cap.

"Just so," assented the outlaw, standing up and taking off his coat, and flinging it upon the floor.

Cap shuddered, but went on calmly with her preparations. There were two little white bowls sitting one within the other upon the table. Cap took them apart and set them side by side and began to break the eggs, letting the white slip into one bowl and dropping the yellow into the other.

Black Donald sat down in his shirt-sleeves, took one of the bowls from Capitola and began to whisk up the whites with all his might and main.

Capitola beat up the yellows, gradually mixing the sugar with it. In the course of her work she complained that the heat of the fire scorched her face, and she drew her chair farther towards the corner of the chimney, and pulled the stand after her.

"Oh! you are trying to get away from me," said Black Donald, hitching his own chair in the same direction, close to the stand, so that he sat immediately in front of the fireplace.

Cap smiled, and went on beating her eggs and sugar together. Then she stirred in the brandy and poured in the milk, and took the bowl from Black Donald, and laid on the foam. Finally, she filled a goblet with the rich compound and handed it to her uncanny guest.

Black Donald untied his neck cloth, threw it upon the floor, and sipped his egg-nog, all the while looking over the top of the glass at Capitola.

"Miss Black," he said, "it must be past twelve o'clock."

"I suppose it is," said Cap.

"Then it must be long past your usual hour of retiring."

"Of course it is," said Cap.

"Then what are you waiting for?"

"For my company to go home," replied Cap.

"Meaning me?"

"Meaning you."

"Oh, don't mind me, my dear."

"Very well," said Cap. "I shall not trouble myself about you," and her tones were steady though her heart seemed turned into a ball of ice through terror.

Black Donald went on slowly sipping his egg-nog, filling up his goblet when it was empty, and looked at Capitola over the top of his glass. At last he said:

"I have been watching you, Miss Black."

"Little need to tell me that," said Cap.

"And I have been reading you."

"Well, I hope the page was entertaining."

"Well—yes, my dear, it was, rather so. But why don't you *proceed?*"

"Proceed—with what?"

"With what you are thinking of, my darling."

"I don't understand you."

"Why don't you offer to go down stairs and bring up some lemons?"

"Oh, I'll go in a moment," said Cap, "if you wish."

"Ha—ha—ha—ha—ha! Of course you will, my darling! and you'd deliver me into the hands of the Philistines, just as you did my poor men when you fooled them about the victuals! I know your tricks, and all your acting has no other effect on me than to make me admire your wonderful coolness and courage; so, my dear, stop puzzling your little head with schemes to baffle me. You are like the caged starling! You—can't—get—out!" chuckled Black Donald, hitching his chair nearer to hers. He was now right upon the centre of the rug.

Capitola turned very pale, but not with fear, though Black Donald thought she did, and roared with laughter.

"Have you done your supper?" she asked, with a sort of awful calmness.

"Yes, my duck," replied the outlaw, pouring the last of the egg-nog into his goblet, drinking it at a draught, and chuckling as he set down the glass.

Capitola then lifted the stand with the refreshments to remove it to its usual place.

"What are you going to do, my dear?" asked Black Donald.

"Clear away the things and set the room in order," said Capitola, in the same awfully calm tone.

"A nice little housewife you'll make, my duck!" said Black Donald.

Capitola set the stand in its corner, and then removed her own arm-chair to its place before the dressing-bureau.

Nothing now remained upon the rug except Black Donald seated in the arm-chair.

Capitola paused; her blood seemed freezing in her veins; her heart beat thickly; her throat was choked; her head full nearly to bursting, and her eyes were veiled by a blinding film.

"Come, come, my duck—make haste; it is late; haven't you done setting the room in order yet?" said Black Donald, impatiently.

"In one moment," said Capitola, coming behind his chair and leaning upon the back of it.

"Donald," she said, with dreadful calmness, "I will not call you *Black* Donald! I will call you as your poor mother did, when your young soul was as white as your skin, before she ever dreamed her boy would grow black with crime. I will call you simply Donald, and entreat you to hear me for a few minutes."

"Talk on, then, but talk fast, and leave my mother alone. Let the dead rest!" exclaimed the outlaw, with a violent convulsion of his bearded chin and lip that did not escape the notice of Capitola, who hoped some good of this betrayal of feeling.

"Donald," she said, "men call you a man of blood; they say that your hand is red and your soul black with crime."

"They may say what they like; I care not," laughed the outlaw.

"But *I* do not believe all this of you. I believe that there is good in all, and much good in you; that there is hope for all, and strong hope for you."

"Bosh! stop talking poetry! 'Taint in my line, nor yours either!" laughed Black Donald.

389

"But truth is in all our lines. Donald! I repeat it, men call you a man of blood! They say that your hands are red and your soul black with sin. *Black* Donald they call you! But, Donald, you have never yet stained your soul with a crime as black as that which you think of perpetrating to-night!"

"It must be near one o'clock, and I'm tired," replied the outlaw, with a yawn.

"All your former acts," continued Capitola, in the same voice of awful calmness, "have been those of a bold, bad man! this act would be that of a *base one!*"

"Take care, girl! no bad names! You are in my power! at my mercy!"

"I know my position; but I must continue. Hitherto you have robbed mail-coaches and broken into rich men's houses. In doing this, you have always boldly risked your life, often at such fearful odds that men have trembled at their firesides to hear of it. And even women, while deploring your crimes, have admired your courage."

"I thank 'em kindly for it. Women always like men with a spice of the devil in them," laughed the outlaw.

"No, they do not," said Capitola, gravely; "they like men of strength, courage, and spirit—but those qualities do not come from the Evil One, but from the Lord, who is the giver of all good. Your Creator, Donald, gave you the strength, courage, and spirit that all men and women so much admire; but he did not give you these great powers that you might use them in the service of his enemy, the devil."

"I declare there is really something *in that*—I never thought of that before."

"Nor ever thought, perhaps, that however misguided you may have been, there is really something great and good *in yourself* that might yet be used for the good of man and the glory of God," said Capitola, solemnly.

"Ha-ha-ha! Oh, you flatterer. Come—have you done? I tell you it is after one o'clock, and I am tired to death."

"Donald, in all your former acts of lawlessness your antagonists were strong men; and as you boldly risked your life in your depredations, your acts, though bad, were not base. But now your antagonist is a feeble girl, who has been unfortunate from her very birth—to destroy her would be an act of baseness to which you never yet descended."

"Bosh! who talks of destruction? I am tired of all this nonsense. I mean to carry you off, and there's an end of it," said the outlaw, doggedly rising from his seat.

"Stop!" said Capitola, turning ashen pale—"stop, sit down and hear me for just five minutes; I will not tax your patience longer."

The robber, with a loud laugh, sank again into his chair, saying:

"Very well; talk on for just five minutes and not a single second longer; but if you think in that time to persuade me to leave this room to-night without you, you are widely out of your reckoning, my duck, that's all."

"Donald, do not sink your soul to perdition by a crime that Heaven cannot pardon. Listen to me; I have jewels here worth several thousand dollars. If you will consent to go, I will give them all to you, and let you quietly out of the front door, and never say one word to mortal of what has passed here to-night."

"Ha-ha-ha! why, my dear, how green you must think me! What hinders me from possessing myself of your jewels as well as yourself?" said Black Donald, impatiently rising.

"Sit still! the five minutes' grace are not half out yet!" said Capitola, in a breathless voice.

"So they are not! I will keep my promise" replied Black Donald—laughing, and again dropping into his seat.

"Donald, uncle pays me a quarterly sum for pocket-money, which is at least five times as much as I can spend in this quiet country place. It has been accumulating for years until now I have several thousand dollars all of my own. You shall have it if you will only go quietly away and leave me in peace!" prayed Capitola.

"My dear, I intend to take *that* anyhow! take it as your bridal dower, you know. For I'm going to carry you off and make an honest wife of you!"

"Donald, give up this heinous purpose!" cried Capitola, in an agony of supplication, as she leant over the back of the outlaw's chair.

"Yes, you know I will! ha-ha-ha!" laughed the robber.

"Man, for *your own* sake give it up!"

"Ha-ha-ha! for *my* sake!"

"Yes, for *yours!* Black Donald, have you ever reflected on death?" asked Capitola, in a low and terrible voice.

"I have *risked* it often enough; but as to reflecting upon it, it will be time enough to do *that* when it comes. I am a powerful man, in the prime and pride of life," said the athlete, stretching himself exultingly.

"Yet it might come! death might come with sudden, overwhelming power and hurl you to destruction. What a terrible thing for this magnificent frame of yours, this glorious handiwork of the creator, to be hurled to swift destruction, and for the soul that animates it to be cast into hell!"

"Bosh, again! that is a subject for the pulpit, not for a pretty girl's room. If you really think me such a handsome man, why don't you go with me at once and say no more about it," roared the outlaw, laughing.

"Black Donald—WILL you leave my room!" cried Capitola, in an agony of prayer.

"No," answered the outlaw, mocking her tone.

"Is there no inducement that I can hold out to you to leave me?"

"NONE!"

Capitola raised herself from her leaning posture, took a step backward so that she stood entirely free from the trap-door; then slipping her foot under the rug, she placed it lightly on the spring-bolt which she was careful not to press; the ample fall of her dress concealed the position of her foot.

Capitola was now paler than a corpse, for hers was the pallor of a *living* horror! Her heart beat violently, her head throbbed, her voice was broken as she said:

"Man, I will give you one more chance. Oh, man, pity yourself as I pity you, and consent to leave me."

"Ha-ha-ha! it is quite likely that I will! isn't it now? No, my duck! I haven't watched and planned for this chance for this long time past to give it up now that you are in my power. A likely story, indeed! and now the five minutes' grace are quite up."

"STOP! don't move yet! before you stir say, 'Lord have mercy on me!'" said Capitola, solemnly.

"Ha-ha-ha! *that's* a pretty idea! why should I say that?"

"Say it to please me! only say it, Black Donald!"

"But *why* to please you!"

"Because I wish not to kill both your body and soul! because I would not send you prayerless into the presence of your Creator! for, Black Donald, within a few seconds your body will be hurled to swift destruction, and your soul will stand before the bar of God!" said Capitola, with her foot upon the spring of the concealed trap.

She had scarcely ceased speaking before he bounded to his feet, whirled around, and confronted her, like a lion at bay, roaring forth:

"You have a revolver there, girl! move a finger and I shall throw myself on you like an avalanche!"

"I have no revolver! watch my hands as I take them forth and see!" said Capitola, stretching her arms out towards him.

"What do you mean, then, by your talk of sudden destruction!" inquired Black Donald, in a voice of thunder.

"I mean that it hangs over you! that it is imminent! that it is not to be escaped! Oh, man, call on God, for you have not a minute to live!"

The outlaw gazed on her in astonishment.

Well he might, for there she stood, paler than marble! sterner than fate! with no look of human feeling about her but the gleaming light of her terrible eyes, and the beading sweat upon her death-like brow.

For an instant the outlaw gazed on her in consternation, and then recovering himself, he burst into a loud laugh, exclaiming:

"Ha-ha-ha! Well, I suppose this is what people would call a piece of splendid acting. Do you expect to frighten *me,* my dear, as you did Craven Le Noir, with the peas!"

"Say—'Lord have mercy on my soul,' say it Black Donald, say it, I beseech you!" she prayed.

"Ha-ha-ha, my dear! *you* may say it for me! and to reward you, I will give you—*such a kiss!* it will put life into those marble cheeks of yours!" he laughed.

"I *will* say it for you! May the Lord pity and save Black Donald's soul, if that be yet possible, for the Savior's sake!" prayed Capitola, in a broken voice, with her foot upon the concealed and fatal spring.

He laughed aloud, and stretched forth his arms to clasp her.

She pressed the spring.

The drop fell with a tremendous crash!

The outlaw shot downwards! There was an instant's vision of a white and panic-stricken face, and wild uplifted hands as he disappeared, and then a square, black opening was all that remained where the terrible intruder had sat.

No sight or sound came up from that horrible pit to hint of the secrets of the prison house.

One shuddering glance at the awful void, and then Capitola turned and threw herself, face downwards, upon the bed, not daring to rejoice in the safety that had been purchased by such a dreadful deed, feeling that it was an awful, though a complete victory!

CHAPTER L

THE NEXT MORNING

"Oh, such a day
So fought, so followed and so fairly won
Came not till now to dignify the times,
Since Cæsar's fortunes."
—*Shakespeare*[1]

CAPITOLA LAY upon the bed, with her face buried in the pillow, the greater portion of the time from two o'clock until day. An uncontrollable horror prevented her from turning lest she should see the yawning mystery in the middle of the floor, or hear some awful sound from its unknown depths. The very shadows on the walls thrown up wildly by the expiring firelight, were objects of grotesque terror. Never, never, in the whole youth of strange vicissitude, had the nerves of this brave girl been so tremendously shaken and prostrated.

It was late in the morning when at last nature succumbed, and she sank into a deep sleep. She had not slept long when she was aroused from a profound state of insensibility by a loud, impatient knocking at her door.

She started up wildly and gazed around her. For a minute she could not remember what were the circumstances under which she had lain down, or what was that vague feeling of horror and alarm that possessed her. Then the yawning trap-door, the remnants of the supper, and Black Donald's coat, hat and boots upon the floor, drove in upon her reeling brain the memory of the night of terror!

The knocking continued more loudly and impatiently, accompanied by the voice of Mrs. Condiment, crying:

"Miss Capitola! Miss Capitola! why, what can be the matter with her?—Miss Capitola!"

"Eh! what? yes!" answered Capitola, pressing her hands to her feverish forehead, and putting back her disheveled hair.

The Next Morning

"Why, how soundly you sleep, my dear! I've been calling and rapping here for a quarter of an hour! Good gracious, child, what made you over-sleep yourself so?"

"I—did not get to bed till very late," said Capitola, confusedly.

"Well, well, my dear, make haste now, your uncle is none of the patientest, and he has been waiting breakfast for some time! Come, open the door and I will help you to dress, so that you may be ready sooner."

Capitola rose from the side of the bed, where she had been sitting, and went cautiously around that gaping trap-door to her chamber-door, when she missed the key, and suddenly remembered that it had been in Black Donald's pocket when he fell. A shudder thrilled her frame at the thought of that horrible fall.

"Well, well, Miss Capitola, why don't you open the door?" cried the old lady, impatiently.

"Mrs. Condiment, I have lost the key—dropped it down the trap-door. Please ask uncle to send for some one to take the lock off—and don't wait breakfast for me."

"Well, I do think that was very careless, my dear; but I'll go at once," said the old lady, moving away.

She had not been gone more than ten minutes, when Old Hurricane was heard, coming blustering along the hall, and calling:

"What now, you imp of Satan? What mischief have you been at now? Opening the trap-door, you mischievous monkey! I wish from the bottom of my soul you had fallen into it, and I should have got rid of one trial! Losing your key, you careless baggage! I've a great mind to leave you locked up there for ever."

Thus scolding, Old Hurricane reached the spot, and began to ply screw-drivers and chisels until at length the strong lock yielded, and he opened the door.

There a vision met his eyes that arrested his steps upon the very threshold; the remains of a bacchanalian supper; a man's coat and hat and boots upon the floor; in the midst of the room the great, square, black opening; and beyond it, standing upon the hearth, the form of Capitola, with disordered dress, dishevelled hair, and wild aspect.

"Oh, uncle, *see* what I have been obliged to do!" she exclaimed, extending both her arms down towards the opening with a look of blended horror and inspiration, such as might have sat upon the countenance of some sacrificial priestess of the olden time.

"What—what—what!" cried the old man, nearly dumb with amazement.

"Black Donald was in my room last night; he stole from his concealment and locked the door on the inside, and withdrew the key, thus locking me in with himself, and———" she ceased and struck both hands to her face, shuddering from head to foot.

"Go on, girl!" thundered Old Hurricane, in an agony of anxiety.

———"I escaped harmless! oh, I *did,* sir, but at what a fearful price!"

"Explain! Explain!" cried Old Hurricane, in breathless agitation.

"I drew him to sit upon the chair on the rug, and—" again she shuddered from head to foot—"and I sprung the trap and precipitated him to—oh, Heaven of Heavens! where?—I know not!"

"But you—you were unharmed?"

"Yes, yes!"

"Oh, Cap! Oh, my dear Cap! Thank Heaven for that!"

"But, uncle, where—oh, where did he go?" inquired Capitola, almost wildly.

"Who the demon cares? To perdition, I hope and trust, with all my heart and soul!" cried Old Hurricane, with emphasis, as he approached and looked down the opening.

"Uncle, what is below there?" asked Capitola, anxiously pointing down the abyss.

"An old cellar, as I have told you long ago, and Black Donald, as you have just told me. Hillo there! are you killed, as you deserve to be, you atrocious villain?" roared Old Hurricane, stooping down into the opening.

A feeble, distant moan answered him.

"Oh, heaven! he is living! he is living! I have not killed him!" cried Capitola, clasping her hands.

"Why, I do believe you are glad of it!" exclaimed Old Hurricane, in astonishment.

"Oh, yes, yes, yes! for it was a fearful thought that I had been compelled to take a sacred life! to send an immortal soul unprepared to its account!"

"Well! his neck isn't broken, it appears, or he couldn't groan; but I hope and trust that every other bone in his body is! Mrs. Condiment, mum! I'll trouble you to put on your bonnet and walk over to Ezy's and tell him to come here directly! I must send for the constable," said Old Hurricane, going to the door and speaking to his housekeeper, who, with an appalled countenance, had been a silent spectator of all that had passed.

As soon as the old woman had gone to do her errand he turned again, and stooping down the hole, exclaimed:

"I say, you scoundrel down there! What do you think of yourself *now?* Are you much hurt, you knave? Is every one of your bones broken, as they deserve to be, you villain? Answer me, you varlet!"

A low, deep moan was the only response.

"If that means yes, I'm glad to hear it, you wretch. You'll go to the camp-meeting with us again, won't you, you knave! You'll preach against evil passions and profane swearing, looking right straight at me all the time, until you bring the eyes of the whole congregation upon me as a sinner above all sinners, you scoundrel? You'll turn me out of my own bed and away from my own board, won't you, you villain? Won't you, precious Father Gray? Oh, we'll Father Gray you! Demmy, the next time a trap-door falls under you, you rascal, there shall be a rope around your neck to keep you from the ground, precious Father Gray!"

"Uncle! Uncle! that is cowardly!" exclaimed Capitola.

"What is cowardly, Miss Impertinence?"

"To insult and abuse a fallen man who is in your power! The poor man is badly hurt, may be dying, for aught you know, and you stand over him and berate him when he cannot even answer you!"

"Umph, umph, umph; demmy, you're—umph, well, he *is* fallen, fallen pretty badly, eh? and if he should come around after this, the *next* fall he gets will be like to break his neck, eh?—I say, you gentleman below there—Mr. Black Donald—precious Father Gray—you'll keep quiet won't you, while we go and get our breakfast? Do, now! Come, Cap, come down and pour out my coffee, and by the time we get through, old Ezy will be here."

Capitola complied, and they left the room together.

The overseer came in while they were at breakfast, and with his hair standing on end, listened to the account of the capture of the outlaw by our heroine.

"And now saddle Fleetfoot and ride for your life to Tip-Top and bring a pair of constables," were the last orders of Old Hurricane.

While Mr. Ezy was gone on his errand, Major Warfield, Capitola and Mrs. Condiment remained below stairs.

It was several hours before the messenger returned with the constables, and with several neighbors whom interest and curiosity had instigated to join the party.

As soon as they arrived, a long ladder was procured and carried up into Capitola's chamber, and let down through the trap-door. Fortunately it was long enough, for when the foot of the ladder found the floor of the cellar, the head rested securely against the edge of the opening.

In a moment the two constables began singly to descend, the foremost one carrying a lighted candle in his hand.

The remaining members of the party, consisting of Major Warfield, Capitola, Mrs. Condiment, and some half dozen neighbors, remained gathered around the open trapdoor, waiting, watching, and listening for what might next happen.

Presently one of the constables called out:

"Major Warfield, sir!"

"Well!" replied Old Hurricane.

"He's a-breathing still sir; but seems badly hurt, and may be a-dying, seeing as he's unsensible and unspeakable. What shall we do along of him?"

"Bring him up! let's have a look at the fellow, at any rate!" exclaimed Old Hurricane, peremptorily.

"Just so, sir! but some of the gem'men up there'll have to come down on the ladder and give a lift. He's dead weight now, I tell your honor!"

Several of the neighbors immediately volunteered for the service, and two of the strongest descended the ladder to lend their aid.

On attempting to move the injured man he uttered a cry of pain, and fainted, and then it took the united strength and skill of four strong men to raise the huge insensible form of the athlete, and get him up the ladder. No doubt the motion greatly inflamed his inward wounds, but that could not be helped. They got him up at last, and laid out upon the floor, a ghastly, bleeding, insensible form, around which every one gathered to gaze. While they were all looking upon him as upon a slaughtered wild beast, Capitola alone felt compassion.

"Uncle, he is quite crushed by his fall. Make the men lay him upon the bed. Never think of me; I shall never occupy this room again; its associations are too full of horrors. There, uncle, make them at once lay him upon the bed."

"I think the young lady is right, unless we mean to let the fellow die," said one of the neighbors.

"Very well! I have particular reasons of my own for wishing that the man's life should be spared until he could be brought to trial and induced to give up his accomplices," said Old Hurricane. Then turning to his ward, he said:

"Come along, Capitola. Mrs. Condiment will see that your effects are transferred to another apartment."

"And you, friends," he continued, addressing the men present, "be so good, so soon as we have gone, as to undress that fellow and put him to bed, and examine his injuries while I send off for a physician; for I consider it *very* important that his life should be spared sufficiently long to enable him to give up his accomplices." And so saying, Old Hurricane drew the arm of Capitola within his own and left the room.

It was noon before the physician arrived. When he had examined the patient, he pronounced him utterly unfit to be removed, as besides other serious contusions and bruises, his legs were broken and several of his ribs fractured.

In a word, it was several weeks before the strong constitution of the outlaw prevailed over his many injuries, and he was pronounced well enough to be taken before a magistrate and committed to prison to wait his trial. Alas! his life, it was said, was forfeit by an hundred crimes, and there could be no doubt as to his fate. He maintained a self-possessed, good-humored, and laughingly defiant manner, and when asked to give up his accomplices, he answered gaily:

"That treachery was a legal virtue which outlaws could not be expected to know anything about."

Capitola was everywhere lauded for her brave part in the capture of the famous desperado. But Cap was too sincerely sorry for Black Donald to care for the applause.

CHAPTER LI

A FATAL HATRED

"Oh, heaven and all its hosts, he shall not die!"
"By Satan and his fiends, he shall not live!
This is no transient flash of fugitive passion,—
His death hath been my life for years of misery,
Which, else, I had not lived,—
Upon that thought, and not on food, I fed;
Upon that thought, and not on sleep, I rested;
I came to do the deed that must be done,—
Nor thou, nor the sheltering angels could prevent me."
—*Maturin*[1]

THE UNITED STATES army, under General Scott, invested the city of Mexico.

A succession of splendid victories had marked every stage of their advance, from the sea-coast to the capital. Vera Cruz had fallen; Cerro Gordo had been stormed and passed; Xalpa taken; the glorious triumph of Churubusco had been achieved. The names of Scott, Worth, Wool, Quitman, Pillow,[2] and others, were crowned with honor. Others, again, whose humble names and unnoticed heroism has never been recorded, endured as nobly, suffered as patiently, and fought as bravely. Our own young hero, Herbert Greyson, had covered himself with honor.

The war with Mexico witnessed, perhaps, the most rapid promotions of any other in the whole history of military affairs.

The rapid ascent of our young officer was a striking instance of this. In two years from the time he had entered the service with a lieutenant's commission, he held the rank of major in the —— regiment of infantry.

Fortune had not so smiled upon our other young friend, Traverse Rocke; partly, because, being entirely out of his vocation, he had no right to expect success; but, mostly, because he had a powerful enemy in the colonel of his regiment—an unsleeping enemy, whose constant vigilance was directed to prevent the advancement, and insure the degradation and ruin of one whom he contemptuously termed the "gentleman private."

Now, it is known that, by the rules of the military etiquette, a wide social gulf lies between the colonel of the regiment and the private in the ranks.

Yet Colonel Le Noir continually went out of his way to insult Private Rocke, hoping to provoke him to some act of fatal insubordination.

And very heavy was this trial to a high-spirited young man like Traverse Rocke; and very fortunate was it for him that he had early been imbued with that most important truth that "he who ruleth his own spirit is greater than he who taketh a city."[3]

But if Colonel Le Noir crossed the gulf of military etiquette to harass the poor young soldier, Major Greyson did the same thing for the more honorable purpose of soothing and encouraging him.

And both Herbert and Traverse hoped that the designs of their colonel would be still frustrated by the self-command and patience of the young private.

Alas! they did not know the great power of evil—they did not know that nothing less than Divine Providence could meet and overcome it.

They fondly believed that the malignity of Le Noir had resulted in no other practical evil than the preventing the young soldier's well-merited advancement, and in keeping him in the humble position of a private in the ranks.

They were not aware that the discharge of Traverse Rocke had long ago arrived, but that it had been suppressed through the diabolical cunning of Le Noir. That letters, messages, and packets, sent by his friends to the young soldier, had found their way into his colonel's possession, and no further.

And so, believing the hatred of that bad man to have been fruitless of serious, practical evil, Herbert encouraged his friend to be patient for a short time longer, when they should see the end of the campaign, if not the war.

It was now that period of suspense and of false truce, between the glorious 20th of August, and the equally glorious 8th of September, 1847—between the two most brilliant actions of the war, the battle of Churubusco and the storming of Chapultepec.[4]

The General-in-chief of the United States forces in Mexico was at his headquarters in the archiepiscopal palace of Tacubaya, on the suburbs, or in the full sight of the city of the Montezumas,[5] awaiting the issue of the conference between the commissioners of the two hostile governments, met to arrange the terms of a treaty of peace—that every day grew more hopeless.

General Scott, who had had misgivings as to the good faith of the Mexicans, had now his suspicions confirmed by several breaches on the part of the enemy of the terms of the armistice.

Early in September, he despatched a letter to General Santa Anna,[6] complaining of these infractions of the truce, and warning him that, if some satisfactory explanations were not made within forty-eight hours, he should consider the armistice at an end, and renew hostilities.

And, not to lose time, he began on the same night a series of reconnoissances, the object of which was to ascertain the best approach to the city of Mexico—which, in the event of the renewal of the war, he purposed to carry by assault.

It is not my intention to pretend to describe the siege and capture of the capital, which has been so often and eloquently described by grave and wise historians, but rather to follow the fortunes of a humble private in the ranks and relate the events of a certain court martial, as I learned them from the after-dinner talk of a gallant officer, who had officiated on the occasion.

It was during these early days in September, while the illustrious General-in-chief was meditating concluding the war by the assault of the city of Mexico, that Colonel Le Noir also resolved to bring his own private feud to an end, and ruin his enemy by a *coup-de-diable*.[7]

He had an efficient tool for his purpose in the captain of the company to which Traverse Rocke belonged. This man, Captain Zuten, was a vulgar upstart, thrown into his command by the turbulence of war, as the scum is cast up to the surface by the boiling of the cauldron.

He hated Traverse Rocke, for no conceivable reason, unless it was that the young private was a perfect contrast to himself, in the possession of a handsome person, a well-cultivated mind, and a gentlemanly deportment,—cause sufficient for the antagonism of a mean and vulgar nature.

Colonel Le Noir was not slow to see and to take advantage of his hatred.

And Captain Zuten became the willing co-adjutor and instrument of his vengeance. Between them they concocted a plot almost certain to bring the unfortunate young man to an ignominious death.

One morning, about the first of September, Major Greyson, in going his rounds, came upon Traverse, standing sentry near one of the out-posts. The aspect of the young private was so pale, haggard and despairing, that his friend immediately stopped and exclaimed:

"Why Traverse, how ill you look! more fitted for the sick list, than the sentry's duties. What the deuce is the matter!"

The young soldier touched his hat to his superior, and answered sadly, "I am ill, ill in body and mind, sir."

"Pooh!—leave off etiquette when we are alone, Traverse, and call me Herbert, as usual. Heaven knows I shall be glad when all this is over, and we fall back into our relative civil positions towards each other! But what is the matter now, Traverse?—Some of Le Noir's villainy again, of course."

"Of course! but I did not mean to complain, Herbert!—that were childish! I must endure this slavery, these insults, and persecutions patiently, since I have brought them upon myself."

"Take comfort, Traverse! the war is drawing to a close. Either this armistice will end in a permanent peace, or when hostilities are renewed our General will carry the city of Mexico by storm, and dictate the terms of a treaty from the grand square of the capital! In either event the war will soon be over, the troops disbanded, and the volunteers free to go about their business;—and Doctor Traverse Rocke, at liberty to pursue his legitimate profession," said Herbert cheerfully.

"It may be so; I do not know. Oh, Herbert, whether it be from want of sleep, and excessive fatigue,—for I have been on duty for three days and nights,—or whether it be from incipient illness, or all these causes put together, I cannot tell, but my spirits are dreadfully depressed! There seems to be hanging over me a cloud of fate I cannot dispel! Every hour it seems descending lower and blacker over my head, until it feels like some heavy weight, about to suffocate or crush me!" said Traverse, sadly.

"Pooh, pooh! hypochondria! cheer up! remember that in a month we shall probably be disbanded, and in a year—think of it, Traverse Rocke!—Clara Day will be twenty-one, and at liberty to give you her hand! cheer up!"

"Ah, Herbert! all that seems now to be more unsubstantial than the fabric of a dream! I cannot think of Clara or of my mother, without despair! For oh, Herbert, between me and them there seems to yawn *a dishonored grave!* Herbert, they talk, you know, of an attack upon the Molino-del-Rey,[8] and I almost *hope* to fall in that charge!"

"Why?" inquired Major Greyson, in dismay.

"*To escape being forced into a dishonored grave!* Herbert, that man has sworn my ruin, and he will accomplish it!" said Traverse, solemnly.

"For Heaven's sake, explain yourself!" said Herbert.

"I will! listen! I will tell you the history of the last three days," said Traverse; but before he could add another word, the sentry that was to relieve his guard, approached and said:

"Captain Zuten orders you to come to his tent instantly."

With a glance full of significance, Traverse bowed to Herbert, and walked off, while the sentinel took his place.

Herbert saw no more of Traverse that day. At night he went to inquire for him, but learned that he had been sent with a reconnoitering party to the Molino-del-Rey.

The next day, on seeking for Traverse, he understood that the young private had been despatched on a foraging expedition. That night, upon again inquiring for him, he was told that he had been sent in attendance upon the officer who had borne secret despatches to General Quitman, at his quarters on the Acapulco road.

"Traverse is right! They mean to ruin him! I see how it is, exactly. When I saw Traverse on guard, two days ago, he looked like a man exhausted and crazed for want of sleep: and since that time he has been night and day engaged in harassing duty! That demon, Le Noir, with Zuten to help him, has determined to keep Traverse from sleep, until nature is thoroughly exhausted, and then set him upon guard, that he may be found sleeping upon his post. That was what the boy meant, when he talked of the cloud that was hanging over him, and of being forced into a dishonored grave;—and when he hoped, poor fellow, to fall in the approaching assault upon the Molino-del-Rey!—I see it all now! They have decided upon the destruction of Traverse! He can do nothing; a soldier's whole duty is comprised in one word—obedience, even if, as in this instance, he is ordered to commit suicide! Let them hatch their diabolical plots! We will see if the Lord does not still reign, and if the devil is not a fool! It shall go hard, but they are 'hoist with their own petard!'" said Herbert, indignantly.

Early the next morning he went to the tent of Captain Zuten, and requested to see Private Traverse Rocke, in whom, he said, he felt a warm interest.

The answer of Colonel Le Noir's tool confirmed Herbert's worst suspicions.

Touching his cap with an air of deference, he said:

"As you think so much of the young fellow, Major, I am very sorry to inform you, sir, that he is under arrest."

"Upon what charge?" inquired Herbert, calmly, concealing the suspicion and indignation of his bosom.

"Upon a rather bad one, Major—sleeping on his post," replied the officer, masking his exultation with a show of respect.

"Rather bad! the penalty is death," said Herbert, dryly.

"Yes, sir—martial law is rather severe."

"Who charges him?" asked Herbert, curtly.

"The Colonel of our regiment, sir," replied the man, scarcely able to conceal his triumph.

"An accusation from a high quarter. Is his charge supported by *other* testimony?"

"Beg your pardon, Major, but is that necessary?"

"You have answered my question by asking another one, sir. I will trouble you for a direct reply," said Herbert, with dignity.

"Then, Major, I must reply—Yes."

"What testimony? I would know the circumstances?"

"Well, sir, I will tell you all about it," said the officer, with ill-concealed triumph. "Private Traverse Rocke had the early morning watch——"

——"After his return from the night ride to Acapulco?"

"Yes, sir; well, Colonel Le Noir and myself, in going our rounds this morning, just before sunrise, came full upon the young fellow, fast asleep on his post. In fact, sir, it requried a hearty shake to awaken him."

"After ninety-six hours' loss of sleep, I should not wonder!"

"I know nothing about that, sir; I only know that Colonel Le Noir and myself found him fast asleep on his post. He was immediately arrested."

"Where is he now?" inquired Herbert.

"In one of the Colonel's extra tents, under guard," replied the officer.

Herbert immediately went to the tent in question, where he found two sentinels, with loaded muskets, on duty before the door. They grounded arms, on the approach of their superior officer.

"Is Private Traverse Rocke confined within there?" he inquired.

"Yes, sir."

"I must pass in to see him."

"I beg your pardon, sir; but our orders are strict, not even to admit an officer, without a written order from our Colonel," said the sentinel.

"Where is the Colonel?"

"In his tent, sir."

Herbert immediately went on to the fine marquee occupied by Colonel Le Noir.

The sentinel on duty there, at once admitted him, and he passed on into the presence of the Colonel.

He saluted his superior officer with cold military etiquette, and said:

"I have come, sir, to ask of you an order to be admitted to see Private Traverse Rocke, confined under the charge of sleeping on his post."

"I regret to say, Major Greyson, that it cannot be done," replied Le Noir, with ironical politeness.

"Will you have the kindness to inform me, sir, upon what pretext my reasonable request is refused?" asked Herbert, coldly.

"I deem it quite unnecessary to do so, sir," answered the Colonel, haughtily.

"Then, I have no more to do here," replied Herbert, leaving the tent.

He immediately threw himself into his saddle, and rode off to the archiepiscopal palace of Tacubaya, where the General-in-chief had fixed his headquarters.

Here he had to wait some little time before he was admitted to the presence of the gallant Commander, who received him with all the stately courtesy, for which that renowned officer was distinguished.

Herbert mentioned the business that had brought him to the general's presence, the request of a written order to see a prisoner in strict confinement for sleeping on his post.

The Commander, whose kind heart was interested in the welfare of all his soldiers, made some inquiries into the affair, of which Herbert proceeded to give him a short history, without, however, venturing, as yet, directly to charge the Captain or the Colonel with intentional foul play;—indeed, to have attempted to criminate the superior officers of the accused man, would then have been most unwise, useless, and hurtful.

The general immediately wrote the desired order, and passed it to the young officer.

Herbert bowed, and was about to retire from the room, when he was called back by the general, who placed a packet of letters in his hand, saying that they had arrived among his despatches, and were for the prisoner, to whom Major Greyson might as well take them at once.

Herbert received them with avidity, and on his way back to the colonel's tent, he examined their superscription.

There were three letters—all directed to Traverse Rocke; on two of them, he recognized the familiar handwriting of Marah Rocke, on the other, he saw the delicate Italian style of a young lady's hand, which he readily believed to be that of Clara.

In the midst of his anxiety on his friend's account he rejoiced to have this one little ray of comfort to carry him. He knew that many months had elapsed since the young soldier had heard from his friends at home—in fact, Traverse never received a letter unless it happened to come under cover to Herbert Greyson. And well they both knew the reason.

"How *very* fortunate," said Herbert, as he rode on, "that I happened to be at the general's quarters to receive these letters just when I did; for if they had been sent to Colonel Le Noir's quarters, or to Captain Z.'s, poor Traverse would never have heard of them. However, I shall not distract Traverse's attention by showing him these letters until he has told me the full history of his arrest, for I wish him to give me a cool account of the whole thing, so that I may know if I can possibly serve him. Ah, it is very unlikely that any power of mine will be able to save him if indeed, and in truth, he *did* sleep upon his post," ruminated Herbert, as he rode up to the tent where the prisoner was confined.

Another pair of sentinels were on duty in place of those who had refused him admittance.

He alighted from his horse, was challenged, showed his order, and passed into the tent.

There a sight met him that caused the tears to rush to his eyes—for the bravest is always the tenderest heart.

Thrown down on a mat, at the back of the tent, lay Traverse Rocke, pale, haggard, and sunken in the deep, deep sleep of utter exhaustion. Even in that state of perfect abandonment, prostration and insensibility, the expression of great mental anguish remained upon his deathly countenance; a mortal pallor overspread his face; his thick, black curls, matted with perspiration, clung to his hollow temples and cheeks; great drops of sweat beaded upon his corrugated brow; a quiver convulsed his mouth and chin; every circumstance betrayed how severely, even in that swoon-like state, he suffered!

Herbert drew a camp-stool and sat down beside his mat, resolving not to break that greatly needed rest, but to wait patiently until the sleeper should awake.

Again I say that I know nothing about mesmerism, but I have seen strange effects produced quite unconsciously by the presence of one person upon another. And in a few minutes after Herbert took his seat beside Traverse it was noticeable that the face of the sleeper lost its look of pain, and his rest grew deep and calm.

Herbert sat watching that pale, calm, intellectual face, thanking heaven that his mother in her distant home knew nothing of her boy's deadly peril; and praying heaven that its justice might be vindicated in the deliverance of this victim from the snares of those who sought his life.

For more than an hour longer Traverse slept the deep sleep of exhaustion, and then calmly awoke. On seeing Herbert sitting beside him, he smiled sadly, saying:

"You here, Herbert! How kind of you to come! Well, Herbert, you see they have succeeded, as I knew they would; that was what I wished to tell you about, when I was so abruptly ordered away. I do believe it was done on purpose to prevent my telling you. I really think I have been surrounded by spies to report and distort every word and look and gesture. If our company had only watched the enemy with half the vigilance with which they watched *me,* that party of emigrants would not have been cut off on the plains."

"Traverse," said Herbert, solemnly taking the hand of his friend, "*were* you caught sleeping on your post?"

"Ay! sleeping like death, Herbert."

Herbert dropped the hand of his friend, covered his face with his own, and groaned aloud. He could not help it!

"I told you that they had resolved upon my death, Herbert. I told you that I should be pushed into a shameful grave!"

"Oh, no, no, the Lord forbid! but tell me all about it, Traverse, that I may understand and know how to proceed," said Herbert, in a broken voice.

"Well, I need not tell you how I have been insulted, oppressed and persecuted by those two men, for you know that already."

"Yes, yes!"

"It really soon became apparent to me that they were resolved, if possible, to exasperate me to desert, to retort, or to commit some other fatal act of insubordination, or violence. Yet, for the sake of my dear mother and Clara, I did violence only to my own natural manhood, and bore it all with the servility of a slave."

"With the submission of a saint, dear Traverse; and in doing so you followed the divine precept and example of Our Saviour, who, when accused, railed upon and buffeted, 'opened not his mouth.'" And in his forbearance, dear Traverse, there was as much of God-like dignity as there was of saintly patience. Great respect is as often manifested in forbearance as in resentment," said Herbert, soothingly.

"But you see it availed me nothing; here I am under a charge to which I plead guilty, and the penalty of which is—death!" replied Traverse, in despair.

"Tell me how it was, Traverse! Your persecutions and your patience I knew before; but what are the circumstances that led to your present position. That your misfortune is the result of a concerted plan, on the part of Le Noir and his tool, I partly see; but I wish you to put me in possession of all the facts, that I may see in what manner I may be able to assist you."

"Ah, Herbert, I thank you, most faithful of friends; but I doubt whether you can assist me in any other manner than in being kind to my poor mother and my dear Clara when I am gone—for ah, old playmate! the act can be too surely proved upon me, and the penalty is certain—and it is death!" said the poor boy, deeply sighing.

Herbert groaned, and said:

"But tell me at least the history of the four days preceding your arrest."

"I will. Let me see—this is Friday. Well, until this morning's fatal sleep, I had not slept since Sunday night. Monday was passed in the usual routine of military duty. Monday evening I was sent on a reconnoitering expedition to the old castellated Spanish fort of the Casa de Mata, that occupied the whole night. On Tuesday morning I was selected to attend the messenger who went with the flag of truce into the city to carry our general's letter of expostulation to Santa Anna, which employed the whole day. On Tuesday night, without having had an hour's rest in the interval, I was put on guard. Wednesday morning I was sent with a party to escort an emigrant caravan across the marsh to the village of Churubusco. Wednesday afternoon you saw me on guard and I told you that I had not slept one hour for three days and nights!"

"Yes; you looked ill enough to be ordered on the sick list."

"Yet, listen: Thoroughly exhausted as I was, on Wednesday night I was ordered to join a party to go on a secret reconnoitering expedition to the Molino-del-Rey. On Thursday morning I was sent out with another party on a foraging tour. On Thursday night I was sent in attendance upon the officer who carried despatches to General Quitman. On Friday morning I was sent on guard between the hours of four and eight!"

"Oh, heaven! what an infamous abuse of military authority!" exclaimed Herbert, indignantly.

"Herbert, in my life I have sometimes suffered with hunger, cold and pain, and have some idea of what starving, freezing and torture may be; but among all the ills to which flesh is heir, I doubt if there is one so trying to the nerves and brain of a man as enforced and long continued vigilance, when all his failing nature sinks for want of sleep. Insanity and death must soon be the result."

"Humph! go on! tell me about the manner of their finding you," said Herbert, scarcely able to repress his indignation.

"Well, when after—let me see—eighty-four—ninety—ninety-six hours of incessant watching, riding and walking, I was set on guard to keep the morning watch between four o'clock and eight, 'my whole head was sick and my whole heart faint;' my frame was sinking; my soul could scarcely hold my body upright. In addition to this physical suffering was the mental anguish of feeling that these men had resolved upon my death, and thinking of my dear mother and Clara, whose hearts would be broken by my fall. Oh! the thought of them at this moment quite unmans me! I must not reflect! Well, I endeavored with all the faculties of my mind and body to keep awake. I kept steadily pacing to and fro, though I could scarcely drag one limb after the other; or even stand upright; sleep would arrest me while in motion, and I would drop my musket, and wake up in a panic, with the impression of some awful, overhanging ruin appalling my soul. Herbert, will you think me a miserably weak wretch if I tell you that that night was a night of mental and physical *horrors!* Brain and nerves seemed in a state of disorganization; thought and emotion were chaos; the relations of soul and body broken up. I had but one strong, clear idea, namely, that I must keep awake at all costs, or bring shameful death upon myself and disgrace upon my family. And even in the very midst of thinking this I would fall asleep!"

"No power within yourself could have prevented it; indeed you had to drop into *sleep* or *death!*"

"I pinched myself, I cut my flesh, I burned my skin, but all in vain! Nothing could withstand the overwhelming power of sleep that finally conquered me about five o'clock this morning. Then, in the midst of a delightful dream of mother and Clara, and home, I was roused up by a rude shake, and woke to find my musket fallen from my hands, and my captain and colonel standing over me! It was several minutes before I could travel back from the pleasant land of sleep and dreams and realize my real position. When I did, I had nothing to say. The inevitable ruin I felt had come, and crushed me into a sort of dumb despair. Nor did my superior officers reproach me—their revenge was too perfect! The captain called a sergeant to take my gun, and I was marched off to my present prison. And, Herbert, no sooner was I left alone here than sleep overcame me again, like a strong man, and despite all the gloom and terror of my situation, despite all my thoughts of home and mother and Clara, I slept like a tired child! But this awakening! Oh! this awakening, Herbert!"

"Be of good courage! Let us hope that Heaven will enable us to confound the plots of evil, and save you!"

"Ah, Herbert, that will be impossible! The duty of a soldier is clear and stern; his punishment, if he fails in it, swift and sure. At the word of command, he must march into the very jaws of death, as is right! He must die or madden for the want of rest, rather than fall asleep on his post, for if he does, his punishment is certain and shameful death! Oh, my mother! oh, Clara! would to Heaven I had fallen at Vera Cruz or Churubusco, rather than live to bring this dreadful sorrow upon you!" cried Traverse, covering his convulsed face with his hands.

"Cheer up, cheer up, old comrade! All is not lost that is endangered, and we shall save you yet!"

"Herbert you *know* it is impossible!"

"No, I do not know any such thing!"

"You know that I shall be *tried to-day* and *shot to-morrow!*—Oh, Herbert! never let my dear ones at home know how I shall die! Tell them that I fell before Chapultepec—which will be literally true, you know! Oh, my mother! Oh, my dear Clara! shall I never, never see you more! never hear your sweet voices calling me! never feel the kind clasping of your hands again?—Is this the end of a life of aspiration and endeavor? Is this the comfort and happiness I was to bring you?—early bereavement, dishonored names and broken hearts!"

"I tell you, no! You shall be saved! I say it!"

"Ah, it is impossible!"

"No, it is only very difficult—*so very difficult, that I shall be sure to accomplish it!*"

"What a paradox!"

"It is a truth! Things difficult—almost to impossibility can always be accomplished! Write that upon your tablets, for it is a valuable truth! And now cheer up, for I bring you letters from Clara and your mother."

"Letters! from Clara! and mother! Oh, give them to me!" exclaimed the young man, eagerly.

Herbert handed them, and Traverse eagerly broke the seals one after another and devoured the contents.

"They are well! They are well and happy! Oh, thank God they are so! Oh, Herbert, never let them know how I shall die! If they think I fell honorably in battle, they will get over it in time; but if they know I died a convict's death, it will break their hearts! Oh, Herbert! my dear friend! by all our boyhood's love! never let my poor mother and dear Clara know the manner of my death!" cried Traverse, in an imploring voice.

Before he could say another word or Herbert could answer, an orderly sergeant entered and put into Major Greyson's hands a paper that proved to be a summons for him to attend immediately at headquarters to serve upon a court martial, to try Private Traverse Rocke upon the charge of sleeping on his post.

"This is done on purpose to prevent me becoming a witness for the defense!" whispered Herbert to his friend; "but take courage! We will see yet whether they shall succeed!"

CHAPTER LII

THE COURT MARTIAL

☙☙☙☙☙

"I wish I could
Meet all my accusers with as good excuse,
As well as I am certain I can clear
Myself of this."
—*Shakespeare*[1]

PURSUANT WITH the general orders issued from headquarters, the court martial, consisting of thirteen officers, convened at Tacubaya, for the trial of Traverse Rocke, private in the ―― Regiment of Infantry, accused of sleeping on his post.

It was a sultry morning, early in September, and by seven o'clock the drum was heard beating before the archiepiscopal palace, where it was understood the trial involving life or death, would come off.

The two sentinels on guard before the doors and a few officers off duty, loitering about the verandas, were the only persons visible near the well-ordered premises, until the members of the court martial, with the prosecutors and witnesses, began to assemble and pass in.

Within a lofty apartment of the building, which was probably at one time the great dining-hall of the priests, were collected some twenty persons, comprising the court martial and its attendants.

An extension-table covered with green cloth occupied the middle of the long room.

At the head of this table sat General W., the President of the court. On his right and left, at the sides of the table, were arranged the other members according to their rank.

At a small table, near the right hand of the President, stood the Judge Advocate, or prosecutor on behalf of the United States.

At the door stood a sentinel on guard, and near him two or three orderly sergeants, in attendance upon the officers.

413

The Judge Advocate opened the court by calling over the names of the members, beginning with the President and ending with the youngest officer present, and recording them as they responded.

This preliminary settled, orders were despatched to bring the prisoner, prosecutor and witnesses into court.

And in a few minutes entered Colonel Le Noir, Captain Zuten, Lieutenant Adams and Sergeant Baker. They were accommodated with seats near the left hand of the President.

Lastly, the prisoner was brought in, guarded, and placed standing at the foot of the table.

Traverse looked pale, from the severe effects of excessive fatigue and anxiety; but he deported himself with firmness and dignity, bowed respectfully to the court and then drew his stately form up to its fullest height, and stood awaiting the proceedings.

The Judge Advocate, at the order of the President, commenced and read the warrant for holding the court. He then read over the names of the members, commencing as before, with the President, and descending through the gradations of rank to the youngest officer, and demanded of the prisoner whether he had any cause of challenge, or took any exception to any member present, and if so, to declare it, as was his privilege.

Traverse lifted his noble head and keen eyes, and looked slowly around, in turn, upon each officer of the court martial.

They might all be said to be strangers to him, since he knew them only by sight—all except his old acquaintance, Herbert Greyson, who sat first at the left hand of the President, and who returned his look of scrutiny with a gaze full of encouragement.

"I find no cause of challenge, and take no exception to any among the officers composing this court," answered Traverse, again bowing, with such sweetness and dignity in tone and gesture that the officers, in surprise, looked—first at the prisoner, and then at each other. No one could doubt that the accused, in the humble garb of a private soldier, was nevertheless a man of education and refinement—a true man both in birth and breeding.

As no challenge was made, the Judge Advocate proceeded to administer to each of the members of the court the oath prescribed by the Articles of War, to the intent that they should try "the matter before them, between the prisoner and the United States, according to the evidence, without fear, favor, or affection."

This oath was taken by each member holding up his right hand, and repeating the words after the officer.

The court then being regularly constituted, and every preliminary form observed, the Judge Advocate arose and directed the prisoner to listen to the charge brought against him and preferred by the colonel of his regiment, Gabriel Le Noir.

Traverse raised his head and fixed his eagle eyes upon the prosecutor, who stood beside the Judge Advocate; while the latter, in an audible voice, read the accusation, charging the prisoner with willful neglect of duty—in that he, the said Traverse Rocke, on the night of the first of September, being placed upon guard at the north-western outpost of the infantry quarters at Tacubaya, did fall asleep upon his post, thereby endangering the safety of the quarters and violating the 46th Article of War.

To which charge the prisoner, in a firm voice replied:

"Not guilty of willful neglect of duty, though found sleeping upon my post."

The Judge Advocate then cautioned all witnesses to withdraw from the court and come only as they were called. They withdrew; and he then arranged some preliminaries of the examination, and called in Captain Zuten, of the —— regiment of infantry.

This witness was a short, coarse-featured, red-haired person, without intellect enough to enable him to conceal the malignity of his nature.

He testified that on Thursday, the first of September, Traverse Rocke, private in his company, was ordered on guard at the north-western outpost of the quarters, between the hours of four and eight A.M. That about five o'clock on the same morning, he, Joseph Zuten, in making his usual rounds, and being accompanied on that occasion by Colonel Gabriel Le Noir, Lieutenant Adams, and Sergeant Baker, did surprise Private Traverse Rocke asleep on his post, leaning against the sentry-box with his musket at his feet.

This witness was cross-examined by the Judge Advocate—who, it is known, combines in his own person the office of prosecutor on the part of the United States and counsel for the prisoner—or rather, if he be honest, he acts as impartial inquirer and arbiter between the two.

As no new facts were gained by the cross-examination, the Judge Advocate proceeded to call the next witness, Colonel Le Noir.

Here, then, was a gentleman of most prepossessing exterior as well as of most irreproachable reputation!

In brief, his testimony corroborated that of the foregoing witness as to the finding of the prisoner asleep on his post at the time and place specified. In honor of his high social and military standing, this witness was not cross-examined.

The next called was Lieutenant Adams, who corroborated the evidence of former witnesses. The last person examined was Sergeant Baker, whose testimony corresponded exactly to that of all who had gone before him.

The Judge Advocate then briefly summed up the case on the part of the United States—first by reading the 46th Article of War, to wit, that:

"Any sentinel who shall be found sleeping on his post, or shall leave it before he shall be regularly relieved, shall suffer death," etc., etc., etc.

And secondly, by reading the recorded evidence to the effect that—

"Traverse Rocke had been found by competent witnesses sleeping on his post."

And concluded by saying:

"Gentlemen, officers of the court martial, here is the law and here is the fact both proven, and it remains for the court to find a verdict in accordance to both."

The prisoner was then put upon his defense.

Traverse Rocke drew himself up and said, that—the TRUTH, like the blessed sun, must, on its shining forth, dispel all clouds of error; that, trusting in the power of truth, he should briefly relate the history of the preceding seven days. And then he commenced and narrated the facts with which the reader is already acquainted.

Traverse was interrupted several times in the course of his narrative by the President, General W., a severe martinet, who reminded him that an attempt to criminate his superior officers would injure his cause before the court.

Traverse, bowing, as in duty bound, to the President at every fresh interruption, nevertheless proceeded straight on with his narrative to its conclusion.

The defense being closed, the Judge Advocate arose, as was his privilege, to have the last word. He stated that if the prisoner had been oppressed or aggrieved by his superior officer, his remedy lay in the 35th of the Articles of War, providing that any soldier who shall feel himself wronged by his captain, shall complain thereof to the colonel of his regiment.

To this the prisoner begged to reply that he had considered the colonel of his regiment his personal enemy, and as such could have little hope of the issue, even if he had had opportunity afforded him, of appealing to that authority.

The Judge Advocate expressed his belief that this complaint was vexatious and groundless.

And here the evidence was closed, and the prosecutor, prisoner and witnesses dismissed, and the court adjourned to meet again to deliberate with closed doors.

It was a period of awful suspense with Traverse Rocke. The prospect seemed dark for him.

The FACT of the offence, and the LAW affixing the penalty of death to that offence was established, and as the Judge Advocate truly said, nothing remained but for the court to find their verdict, in accordance to both.

Extenuating circumstances there were certainly; but extenuating circumstances were seldom admitted in courts martial, the law and practice of which were severe, to the extent of cruelty.

Another circumstance against him, was the fact that it did not require an unanimous vote to render a legal verdict; but that if a majority of two-thirds should vote for conviction, the fate of the prisoner would be sealed. Traverse had but one friend in the court, and what could his single voice do against so many?—Apparently nothing; yet, as the prisoner on leaving the court-room, raised his eyes to that friend, Herbert Greyson returned the look with a glance of more than encouragement—of triumph!

CHAPTER LIII

THE VERDICT

☙☙☙☙☙☙

"We must not make a scare-crow of the law,
Setting it up to frighten birds of prey;
And let it keep one shape till custom makes it
Their perch and not their terror."
— *Shakespeare* [1]

THE MEMBERS of a court martial sit in the double capacity of jurors and judges; as jurors they find the facts, and as judges they award the punishment. Yet, their session with closed doors was without the solemn formality that the uninitiated might have supposed to attend a grave deliberation upon a matter of guilt or innocence involving a question of life or death.

No sooner were the doors closed that shut out the "vulgar" crowd, than the "high and mighty" officials immediately fell into easy attitudes, and engaged in conversation upon the weather, the climate, yesterday's dinner at General Cushion's quarters, the claret, the cigars and the Mexican signoritas.

They were presently recalled from this easy chat by the President, a severe disciplinarian, who reminded them rather sharply of the business upon which they had convened.

The officers immediately wheeled themselves around in the chairs, facing the table, and fell into order.

The Judge Advocate seated himself at his detached stand, opened his book, called the attention of the court, and commenced and read over the whole record of the evidence and the proceedings up to this time.

The President then said:

"For my own part, gentlemen, I think this quite a simple matter, requiring but little deliberation. Here is the fact of the offence proved, and here is the law upon that offence clearly defined. Nothing seems to remain for us to do but to bring in a verdict in accordance with the law and the fact."

Several of the older officers and sterner disciplinarians agreed with the President, who now said:

"I move that the vote be immediately taken upon this question."

To this also, the elder officers assented. And the Judge Advocate was preparing to take the ballot, when one of the younger members arose and said:

"Mr. President and gentlemen, there are mitigating circumstances attending this offence, which, in my opinion, should be duly weighed before making up our ballot."

"Lieutenant Lovel, when your hair has grown white in the service of your country, as mine has, and when your skin is mottled with the scars of a score of well-fought fields, you will find your soft theories corrected by hard experience, and you will know that in the case of a sentinel sleeping upon his post, there *can* be no mitigating circumstances; that nothing *can* palliate such flagrant and dangerous neglect, involving the safety of the whole army; a crime that martial law and custom has very necessarily made punishable by death," said the President, sternly.

The young lieutenant sat down abashed, under the impression that he had betrayed himself into some act of gross impropriety. This was his first appearance in the character of juror and judge; he was literally "unaccustomed to public speaking," and did not hazard a reply.

"Has any other gentleman any views to advance before we proceed to a general ballot?" inquired the President.

Several of the officers whispered together, and then some one replied that there seemed to be no reason why the vote should not be immediately taken.

Herbert Greyson remained perfectly silent. Why he did not speak *then,* in reply to this adjuration,—why, indeed, he had not spoken *before,* in support of Lieutenant Lovel's views in favor of his friend, I do not know to this day; though I mean to ask him the first time I have the opportunity. Perhaps he was inclined to dramatic effects: but whatever might have been the motive, he continued silent, offering no obstacle to the immediate taking of the vote.

The Judge Advocate then called the court to order for the taking of the ballot, and proceeded to question the members in turn, commencing with the youngest.

"How say you, Lieutenant Lovel, is the prisoner on trial guilty or not guilty of the offence laid to his charge?"

"GUILTY," responded the young officer, as his eyes filled with tears of pity for the other young life against which he had felt obliged to record his vote.

"If that is the opinion of one who seems friendly to him, what will be the votes of the other stern judges?" said Herbert Greyson to himself, in dismay.

"What say you, Lieutenant Jones—is the prisoner guilty or not guilty?" said the Judge Advocate, proceeding with the ballot.

"*Guilty!*"

"Lieutenant Cragin?"

"Guilty!"

"Lieutenant Evans?"

"Guilty!"

"Lieutenant Goffe?"

"Guilty!"

"Lieutenant Hesse?"

"Guilty!"

"Captain Kingsley?"

"Guilty!"

"Captain McConkey?"

"Guilty!"

"Captain Lucas?"

"Guilty!"

"Captain O'Donnelly?"

"Guilty!"

"Captain Rozencrantz?"

"Guilty!"

"Major Greyson?"

"NOT GUILTY!"

Every officer sprang to his feet and gazed in astonishment, consternation and indignant inquiry upon the renderer of this unprecedented vote.

The president was the first to speak, breaking out with:

"Sir! Major Greyson! your vote, sir! in direct defiance of the fact and the law upon it, is *unprecedented,* sir, in the whole history of courts martial!"

"I record it as uttered, nevertheless," replied Herbert.

"And your oath, sir! what becomes of your oath as a judge of this court!"

"I regard my oath in my vote!"

"What, sir," inquired Captain McConkey, "do you mean to say that you have rendered that vote in accordance with the facts elicited in evidence, as by your oath you were bound to do?"

"Yes."

"How, sir! do you mean to say that the prisoner did *not* sleep on his post?"

"Certainly I do not; on the contrary, I grant that he *did* sleep upon his post, and yet I maintain that in doing so he was not guilty!"

"Major Greyson plays with us!" said the President.

"By no means, sir! I never was in more solemn earnest than at present! Your honor, the President, and gentlemen judges of the court, as I am not counsel for the prisoner, nor civil officer, nor lawyer, of whose interference courts martial are proverbially jealous, I beg you will permit me to say a few words in support, or at least, I will say, in explanation of the vote which you have characterized as an opinion in opposition to fact and law, and unprecedented in the whole history of courts martial."

"Yes, it is! it is!" said General W., shifting uneasily in his seat.

"You heard the defense of the prisoner," continued Herbert; "you heard the narrative of his wrongs and sufferings, to the truth of which his very aspect bore testimony. I will not here express a judgment as to the motives that prompted his superior officers. I will merely advert to the facts themselves, in order to prove that the prisoner, under the circumstances, could not, with his human power, have done otherwise than he did."

"Sir, if the prisoner considered himself wronged by his captain, which is very doubtful, he could have appealed to the colonel of his regiment!"

"Sir, the articles of war accord him that privilege. But is it ever taken advantage of? Is there a case on record where a private soldier ventures to make a dangerous enemy of his immediate superior by complaining of his captain to his colonel? Nor in this case would it have been of the least use, inasmuch as this soldier had well-founded reasons for believing the colonel of his regiment his personal enemy, and the captain as the instrument of this enmity."

"And you, Major Greyson, do you coincide in the opinion of the prisoner? Do you think that there could have been anything in common between the colonel of the regiment and the poor private in the ranks, to explain such an equalizing sentiment as enmity?" inquired Captain O'Donnelly.

"I answer distinctly, yes, sir! In the first place, this poor private is a young gentleman of birth and education, the heir of one of the most important estates in Virginia, and the betrothed of one of the most lovely girls in the world. In both these capacities he has stood in the way of Colonel Le Noir, standing between him and the estate on the one hand, and between him and the young lady on the other. He has disappointed Le Noir both in love and ambition. And he has thereby made an enemy of the man who has besides the nearest interest in his destruction. Gentlemen, what I say now in the absence of Colonel Le Noir, I am prepared to repeat in his presence, and maintain at the proper time and place."

"But how came this young gentleman of birth and expectations to be found in the ranks?" inquired Captain Rosencrantz.

"How came we to have headstrong sons of wealthy parents, fast young men of fortune, and runaway students from the universities and colleges of the United States, in our ranks? In a burst of boyish impatience the young man enlisted. Destiny gave him as the colonel of his regiment his mortal enemy. Colonel Le Noir found in Captain Zuten a ready instrument for his malignity. And between them both they have done all that could possibly be effected to defeat the good fortune and insure the destruction of Traverse Rocke. And I repeat, gentlemen, that what I feel constrained to affirm here in the absence of those officers, I shall assuredly re-assert and maintain in their presence, upon the proper occasion. In fact, I shall bring formal charges against Colonel Le Noir and Captain Zuten, of conduct unworthy of officers and gentlemen!"

"But it seems to me that this is not directly to the point at issue," said Captain Kingsley.

"On the contrary, sir, it *is* the point, the *whole* point, and *only* point, as you shall presently see, by attending to the facts that I shall recall to your memory. You and all present must, then, see that there was a deliberate purpose to effect the ruin of this young man. He is accused of having been found sleeping on his post, the penalty of which, in time of war, is death. Now listen to the history of the days that preceded his fault, and tell me if human nature could have withstood the trial.

"Sunday night was the last of repose to the prisoner until Friday morning, when he was found asleep on his post.

"Monday night he was sent with the reconnoitering party to Casa-de-Mata.

"Tuesday he was sent with the officer that carried our General's expostulation to Santa Anna. *At night* he was put on guard.

"Wednesday he was sent with another party to protect a band of emigrants crossing the marshes. *At night* he was sent with still another party to reconnoitre Molino-del-Rey.

"Thursday he was sent in attendance upon the officer that carried despatches to General Quitman, and did not return until after *midnight,* when, thoroughly worn out, driven indeed to the extreme degree of mortal endurance, he was again, on a sultry, oppressive night, in a still, solitary place, set on guard; where a few hours later he was found asleep upon his post—by whom?—the colonel of his regiment and the captain of his company, who seemed bent upon his ruin!—as I hold myself bound to establish before another court martial.

"This result had been intended from the first! If *five* night's loss of sleep would not have effected this, *fifteen* probably *would;* if *fifteen* would not, *thirty* would; or if *thirty* wouldn't, *sixty* would!—and all this Captain Zuten *had the power to enforce* until his doomed victim should fall into the hands of the provost-marshal, and into the arms of death!

"And now, gentlemen, in view of all these circumstances, I ask you—Was Traverse Rocke guilty of willful neglect of duty in dropping asleep on his post? And I move for a reconsideration, and a new ballot!"

"Such a thing is without precedent, sir! These mitigating circumstances may be brought to bear on the Commander-in-Chief, and may be embodied in a recommendation to mercy! they should have no weight in the finding of the verdict," said the President, "which should be in accordance with the fact and the law."

"And with justice and humanity! To find a verdict of guilty against this young man would be to place an unmerited brand upon his spotless name, that no after clemency of the executive could wipe out! Gentlemen, will you do this? No! I am sure that you will not! And again I move for a new ballot!"

"I second the motion!" said Lieutenant Lovel, rising quite encouraged to believe in his own first instincts, which had been so favorable.

"Gentlemen," said the President, sternly, "this thing is without *precedent!* In all the annals of courts martial, without *precedent!*"

"Then, if there *is* no such precedent, it is quite time that such a one were *established!* so that the iron car of literal law should not always roll over and crush justice! Gentlemen, shall we have a new ballot?"

"Yes! yes! yes! yes!" were the answers.

"It is irregular! it is illegal! it is *unprecedented!* a new ballot, never heard of such a thing in forty years of military life! Lord bless my soul, what *is* the service coming to?"

"A new ballot! a new ballot! a new ballot!" was the unanimous cry.

The President groaned in spirit, and recorded a vow never to forgive Herbert Greyson for this departure from routine.

The new ballot demanded by acclamation had to be held.

The Judge Advocate called the court to order and began anew. The votes were taken as before, commencing with the young lieutenant, who now responded sonorously:

"NOT GUILTY!"

And so it ran around the entire circle. "Not guilty!"

"Not guilty!" "Not guilty!" were the hearty responses of the court.

The acquittal was unanimous. The verdict was recorded.

The doors were then thrown open to the public, and the prisoner called in and publicly discharged from custody.

The court then adjourned.

Traverse Rocke threw himself upon the bosom of his friend, exclaiming in a broken voice:

"I cannot sufficiently thank you! My dear mother and Clara will do that!"

"Nonsense!" said Herbert, laughing; "didn't I tell you that the Lord reigns, and that the devil is a fool? This is only the beginning of victories!"

CHAPTER LIV

THE END OF THE WAR

🦂🦂🦂🦂🦂

"Now are our brows bound with victorious wreaths,
Our bruised arms hung up for monuments;
Our stern alarums changed to merry meetings,
Our dreadful marches to delightful measures,
Grim-visaged war hath smoothed his wrinkled front,
And now, instead of mounting barbed steeds,
To fright the souls of fearful adversaries,
He capers nimbly in a lady's chamber,
To the lascivious pleasing of a lute."
　　　—*Shakespeare* [1]

TEN DAYS LATER Molino-del-Rey, Casa-de-Mata and Chapultepec had fallen. The United States forces occupied the city of Mexico. General Scott was in the Grand Plaza, and the American standard waved above the capital of the Montezumas!

Let those who have a taste for swords and muskets, drums and trumpets, blood and fire, describe the desperate battles and splendid victories that led to this final magnificent triumph!

My business lies with the persons of our story, to illustrate whom I must pick out a few isolated instances of heroism in this glorious campaign.

Herbert Greyson's division was a portion of the gallant Eleventh that charged the Mexican batteries on Molino-del-Rey. He covered his name with glory, and qualified himself to merit the command of the regiment, which he afterwards received.

Traverse Rocke fought like a young Paladin. When they were marching into the very mouths of the cannon that were vomiting fire upon them, and when the young ensign of his company was struck down before him, Traverse Rocke took the colors from his falling hand, and crying "Victory!" pressed onwards and upwards over the dead and the dying, and springing upon one of the guns which continued to belch forth fire, he thrice waved the flag over his head, and then planted it upon the battery! Captain Zuten fell in the subsequent assault upon Chapultepec.

Colonel Le Noir entered the city of Mexico with the victorious army, but on the subsequent day, being engaged in a street skirmish with the leperos or liberated convicts, he fell mortally wounded by a copper bullet, and he was now dying by inches at his quarters near the Grand Cathedral.

It was on the evening of the 20th of September, six days from the triumphant entry of General Scott into the capital, that Major Greyson was seated at supper at his quarters, with some of his brother officers, when an orderly entered and handed a note to Herbert, which proved to be a communication from the surgeon of their regiment, begging him to repair without delay to the quarters of Colonel Le Noir, who, being in extremity, desired to see him.

Major Greyson immediately excused himself to his company, and repaired to the quarters of the dying man.

He found Colonel Le Noir stretched upon his bed, in a state of extreme exhaustion and attended by the surgeon and chaplain of his regiment.

As Herbert advanced to the side of his bed, Le Noir stretched out his pale hand, and said:

"You bear no grudge against a dying man, Greyson?"

"Certainly not," said Herbert; "especially when he purposes doing the right thing, as I judge you do, from the fact of your sending for me."

"Yes, I do, I do," replied Le Noir, pressing the hand that Herbert's kindness of heart could not withhold.

Le Noir then beckoned the minister to hand him two sealed packets, which he took and laid upon the bed before him.

Then taking up the larger of the two packets, he placed it in the hands of Herbert Greyson, saying:

"There, Greyson, I wish you to hand that to your friend, young Rocke, who has received his colors, I understand?"

"Yes; he has now the rank of ensign."

"Then give this parcel into the hands of Ensign Rocke, with the request, that being freely yielded up, they may not be used in any manner to harass the last hours of a dying man."

"I promise, on the part of my noble young friend, that they shall not be so used," said Herbert, as he took possession of the parcel.

Le Noir then took up the second packet, which was much smaller, but much more firmly secured than the first, being an envelope of parchment, sealed with three great seals.

Le Noir held it in his hand for a moment, gazing from the surgeon to the chaplain, and thence down upon the mysterious packet, while spasms of pain convulsed his countenance. At length he spoke:

"This second packet, Greyson, contains a—well, I may as well call it a narrative. I confide it to your care upon these conditions—that it shall not be opened until after my death and funeral; and that, when it has served its purpose of restitution, it may be, as far as possible, forgotten. Will you promise me this?"

"On my honor, yes," responded the young man, as he received the second parcel.

"That is all I have to say, except this—that you seemed to me, upon every account, the most proper person to whom I could confide this trust. I thank you for accepting it; and I believe that I may safely promise that you will find the contents of the smaller packet of great importance and advantage to yourself and those dear to you."

Herbert bowed in silence.

"That is all. Good-bye. I wish now to be alone with our chaplain," said Colonel le Noir, extending his hand.

Herbert pressed that wasted hand; silently sent up a prayer for the dying wrong-doer; bowed gravely, and withdrew.

It was almost eight o'clock, and Herbert thought that he would scarcely have time to find Traverse before the drum should beat to quarters.

He was more fortunate than he had anticipated; for he had scarcely turned the Grand Cathedral, when he came full upon the young ensign.

"Ah! Traverse, I am very glad to meet you! I was just going to look for you. Come immediately to my rooms, for I have a very important communication to make to you! Colonel Le Noir is supposed to be dying. He has given me a parcel to be handed to you, which I shrewdly suspect to contain your intercepted correspondence for the last two years," said Herbert.

Traverse started and gazed upon his friend in amazement, and was about to express his astonishment, when Herbert, seeing others approach, drew the arm of his friend within his own, and they hurried silently on toward Major Greyson's quarters.

They had scarcely got in, and closed the door, and stricken a light, before Traverse exclaimed, impatiently:

"Give it me!" and almost snatched the parcel from Herbert's hands.

"Whist! don't be impatient. I dare say it is all stale news!" said Herbert, as he yielded up the prize.

They sat down together, on each side a little stand supporting a light.

Herbert watched with sympathetic interest while Traverse tore open the envelope and examined its contents.

They were, as Herbert had anticipated, letters from the mother and the betrothed of Traverse—letters that had arrived and been intercepted, from time to time, for the preceding two years.

There were blanks, also, directed in a hand strange to Traverse, but familiar to Herbert as that of Old Hurricane; and those blanks enclosed draughts upon a New Orleans bank, payable to the order of Traverse Rocke.

Traverse pushed all these latter aside with scarcely a glance and not a word of inquiry, and began eagerly to examine the long-desired, long-withheld letters from the dear ones at home.

His cheek flamed to see that every seal was broken and the fresh aroma of every heart-breathed word inhaled by others, before they reached himself!

"Look here, Herbert! look here! Is not this insufferable? Every fond word of my mother, every delicate and sacred expression of—of regard from Clara, all read by the profane eyes of that man!"

"That man is on his deathbed, Traverse, and you must forgive him! He has restored your letters."

"Yes, after their sacred privacy has been profaned! Oh!"

Traverse handed his mother's letters over to Herbert, that her foster-son might read them, but Clara's "sacred epistles," were kept to himself.

"What are you laughing at?" inquired Traverse looking up from his page and detecting Herbert with a smile upon his face.

"I am thinking that you are not as generous as you were some few years since, when you would have given me Clara herself; for now you will not even let me have a glimpse of her letters!"

"Have they not been already sufficiently published?" said Traverse, with an almost girlish smile and blush.

When those cherished letters were all read and put away, Traverse stooped down and "fished up," from amidst envelopes, strings, and waste paper, another set of letters, which proved to be the blanks enclosing the checks, of various dates, which Herbert recognized as coming anonymously from Old Hurricane.

"What in the world is the meaning of all this Herbert? Have I a nabob uncle turned up anywhere, do you think? Look here!—a hundred dollars—and a fifty, and another—all draughts upon the Planters' Bank, New Orleans, drawn in my favor and signed by Largent & Dor, Bankers!—I, that haven't had five dollars at a time to call my own for the last two years! Here, Herbert, give me a good sharp pinch to wake me up! I may be sleeping on my post again!" said Traverse, in perplexity.

"You are not sleeping, Traverse!"

"Are you sure?"

"Perfectly," replied Herbert, laughing.

"Well, then, do you think that crack upon the crown of my head that I got upon Chapultepec has not injured my intellect?"

"Not in the slightest degree!" said Herbert, still laughing at his friend's perplexity.

"Then I am the hero of a fairy tale, that is all—a fairy tale in which wastepaper is changed into bank notes, and private soldiers prince-palatines! LOOK HERE!" cried Traverse, desperately, thrusting the bank checks under the nose of his friend; "do you see those things and know what they are, and will you tell me that everything in this castle doesn't 'go by enchantment?'"

"Yes, I see what they are, and it seems to me perfectly natural that you should have them!"

"Humph!" said Traverse, looking at Herbert with an expression that seemed to say that he thought the wits of his friend deranged.

"Traverse," said Major Greyson, "did it never occur to you, that you *must* have other relatives in the world besides your mother? Well, I suspect that those checks were sent by some relative of yours or your mother's, who just begins to remember that he has been neglecting you!"

"Herbert, do *you* know this?" inquired Traverse, anxiously.

"*No,* I do not *know* it; I only suspect this to be the case," said Herbert, evasively. "But what is *that* which you are forgetting?"

"Oh! *this*—yes, I had forgotten it. Let us see what it is!" said Traverse, examining a paper that had rested unobserved upon the stand.

"This is an order for my discharge, signed by the Secretary of War, and dated—ha-ha-ha—two years ago! Here I have been serving two years illegally, and if I had been convicted of neglect of duty in sleeping on my post, I should have been *shot* unlawfully, as that man, when he prosecuted me, knew perfectly well," exclaimed Traverse.

"That man, as I said before, lies upon his deathbed! Remember nothing against him! But that order for a discharge—now that you are in the way of promotion and the war is over—will you take advantage of it?"

"Decidedly, *yes!* for, though I am said to have acquitted myself passably well at Chapultepec———"

"Gloriously, Traverse! You won your colors gloriously."

——"Yet, for all that, my true mission is not to break men's bones, but to set them when broken!—not to take men's lives, but to save them when endangered. So, tomorrow morning, please Providence, I shall present this order to General Butler, and apply for my discharge."

"And you will set out immediately for home?"

The face of Traverse suddenly changed.

"I should like to do so! Oh, how I should like to see my dear mother and Clara, if only for a day; but I must not indulge the longing of my heart. I must not go home until I can do so with honor."

"And can you *not* do so now? You, who have triumphed over all your personal enemies, and won your colors at Chapultepec?"

"No, for all this was in my legitimate profession! Nor will I present myself at home until, by the blessing of the Lord, I have done what I set out to do, and establish myself in a good practice. And so, by the help of Heaven! I hope within one week to be on my way to New Orleans to try my fortune in that city."

"To New Orleans!—And a new, malignant fever, of some horrible, unknown type, raging there!" exclaimed Herbert.

"So much the more need of a physician! Herbert, I am not the least uneasy on the subject of infection! I have a theory for its annihilation."

"I never saw a clever young professional man *without* a theory!" laughed Herbert.

The drum was now heard beating the tattoo, and the friends separated with hearts of full of revived hope.

The next morning Traverse presented the order of the secretary to the commander-in-chief, and received his discharge.

And then, after writing long, loving and hopeful letters to his mother and betrothed, and entreating the former to try to find out who was the secret benefactor who had sent him such timely aid, Traverse took leave of his friends, and set out for the Southern Queen of Cities, once more to seek his fortune.

Meantime the United States army continued to occupy the City of Mexico, through the whole of the autumn and the winter.

General Butler, who temporarily succeeded the illustrious Scott in the chief command, very wisely arranged the terms of an armistice with the enemy, that was intended to last two months from the beginning of February; but which happily lasted until the conclusion of the treaty of peace between the two countries.

Colonel Le Noir had not been destined soon to die, his wound,—an inward canker from a copper bullet, that the surgeon had at length succeeded in extracting—took the form of a chronic fester disease. Since the night upon which he had been so extremely ill, as to be supposed dying, and yet had rallied, the doctors felt no apprehensions of his speedy death, though they gave no hopes of his final recovery.

Under these circumstances, there were hours in which Le Noir bitterly regretted his precipitation in permitting those important documents to go out of his own hands. And he frequently sent for Herbert Greyson in private to require re-assurances that he would not open the packet confided to him before the occurrence of the event specified.

And Herbert always soothed the sufferer by reiterating his promise that so long as Colonel Le Noir should survive, the seal of that packet should not be broken.

Beyond the suspicion that the parcel contained an important confession, Herbert Greyson was entirely ignorant of its contents.

But the life of Gabriel Le Noir was prolonged beyond all human calculus of probabilities.

He was spared to experience a more effectual repentence than that spurious one into which he had been frightened by the seeming rapid approach of death. And after seven months of lingering illness and gradual decline, during the latter portions of which he was comforted by the society of his only son, who had come at his summons to visit him, in May, 1848, Gabriel Le Noir expired, a sincere penitent, reconciled to God and man.

And soon afterwards, in the month of May, the treaty of peace having been ratified by the Mexican Congress at Queretaro, the American army evacuated the city and territory of Mexico.

And our brave soldiers, their "brows crowned with victorious wreaths," set out upon their return to home and friends.

CHAPTER LV

THE FORTUNATE BATH

"Heaven has to all allotted, soon or late,
Some lucky revolution of their fate;
Whose motions if we watch and guide with skill
(For human good depends on human will)
Our fortune rolls as from a smooth descent,
And from the first impression takes its bent,
Now, now she meets you with a glorious prize,
And spreads her locks before her as she flies."
　　　—Dryden[1]

MEANWHILE, WHAT HAD our young adventurer been doing in all these months between September and June?

Traverse with his two hundred dollars had set out for New Orleans about the first of October.

By the time he had paid his traveling expenses and fitted himself out with a respectable suit of professional black, and a few necessary books, his little capital had diminished three quarters.

So that when he found himself settled in his new office, in a highly respectable quarter of the city, he had but fifty dollars and a few dimes left.

A portion of this sum was expended in a cheap sofa-bedstead, a closed wash-stand and a spirit-lamp coffee-boiler, for Traverse determined to lodge in his office and board himself—"which will have this additional advantage," said the cheerful fellow to himself—"for besides saving me from debt, it will keep me always on hand for calls."

The fever, though it was October, had scarcely abated; indeed, on the contrary, it seemed to have revived and increased in virulency in consequence of the premature return of many people who had fled on its first appearance, and who in coming back too soon to the infected atmosphere, were less able to withstand contagion than those who remained.

That Traverse escaped the plague was owing not so much to his favorite "theory" as to his vigorous constitution, pure blood, and regular habits of temperance, cleanliness, and cheerful activity of mind and body.

Just then the demand was greater than the supply of medical service.

Traverse found plenty to do. And his pleasant young face and hopeful and confident manners won him great favor in sick rooms, where, whether it were to be ascribed to his "theory," his "practice," or to the happy influence of his personal presence, or to all these together, with the blessing of the Lord upon them,—it is certain that he was very successful in raising the sick. It is true that he did not earn five dollars in as many days; for his practice, like that of almost every young professional man, was among the indigent.

But what of that?—what if he were not running up heavy accounts against wealthy patrons?—he was "giving to the poor"—not money, for himself was as poor as any of them—but his time, labor and professional skill; he "was giving to the poor," he was "lending to the Lord," and he "liked the security." And the most successful speculator that ever made a fortune on 'Change,² never, never invested time, labor or money to a surer advantage.

And this I would say for the encouragement of all young persons in similar circumstances—do not be impatient if the "returns" are a little while delayed, for they are so sure and so rich that they are quite worth waiting for, nor will the waiting be long. Give your services cheerfully, also, for "the Lord loveth a cheerful giver."³

Traverse managed to keep out of debt; he regularly paid his office rent and his laundress' bill; he daily purchased his mutton chop or pound of beefsteak, and broiled it himself; he made his coffee; swept and dusted his office; put up his sofa-bed; blacked his boots; and oh! miracle of independence, he mended his own gloves and sewed on his own shirt-buttons—for you may depend that the widow's son knew how to do all these things; nor was there a bit of hardship in his having so to wait upon himself, though if his mother and Clara, in their well-provided and comfortable home at Willow Heights, had only known how destitute the young man was of female aid and comfort how they would have cried!

"No one but himself to mend his poor dear gloves! Oh—oh, boo-hoo-oo!"

Traverse never alluded to his straitened circumstances; but boasted of the comfort of his quarters and the extent of his practice, and declared that his income already exceeded his outlay; which was perfectly true, since he was resolved to live within it, whatever it might be.

As the fever began to subside, Traverse's practice declined, and about the middle of November his "occupation was gone."⁴

We said that his office was in the most respectable locality in the city; it was, in fact, on the ground floor of a first-class hotel.

It happened that one night, near the close of winter, Traverse lay awake on his sofa-bedstead, turning over in his mind how he should contrive to make both ends meet, at the conclusion of the present term, and feeling as near despondency as it was possible for his buoyant and God-trusting soul to be, when there came a loud ringing at his office bell.

This reminded him of the stirring days and nights of the preceding autumn. He started up at once to answer the summons.

"Who's there?"

"Is Doctor Rocke in?"

"Yes, what's wanted?"

"A gentleman, sir, in the house here, sir, taken very bad, wants the doctor directly, room number 555."

"Very well, I will be with the gentleman immediately," answered Traverse, plunging his head into a basin of cold water and drying it hastily.

In five minutes Traverse was in the office of the hotel, inquiring for a waiter to show him up to 555.

One was ordered to attend him, who led the way up several flights of stairs, and around divers galleries, until he opened a door and ushered the doctor immediately into the sick room.

There was a little, old, dried-up Frenchman in a blue night-cap, extended on a bed in the middle of the room, and covered with a white counterpane that clung close to his rigid form as to a corpse.

And there was a little, old, dried-up Frenchwoman in a brown merino gown and a high-crowned muslin cap, who hopped and chattered about the bed like a frightened magpie.

"Ou! Monsieur le Docteur!" she screamed, jumping at Traverse in a way to make him start back; "Ou, Monsieur le Docteur! I am vera happy you to see! Voilà mon frère! Behold my brother! He is ill! he is vera ill! he is dead! he is vera dead!"

"I hope not," said Traverse, approaching the bed.

"Voilà! Behold! Mon Dieu, he is vera still! he is vera cold! he is vera dead! what can you, mon frère, my brother to save?"

"Be composed, Madam, if you please, and allow me to examine my patient," said Traverse, taking the wrist of the sick man.

"Ma foi! I know not what you speak 'compose.' What can you my brother to save?"

"Much, I hope, Madam, but you must leave me to examine my patient and not interrupt me," said Traverse, passing his hand over the naked chest of the sick man.

"Mon Dieu! I know not 'exam' and 'interrup!' and I know not what can you mon frère to save!"

"If you don't hush parley-vooing, the doctor can't nothink, mum," said the waiter, in a respectful tone.

Traverse found his patient in a bad condition—in a stupor, if not in a state of positive insensibility. The surface of his body was cold as ice, and apparently without the least vitality. If he was not, as his sister had expressed it, "very dead," he was certainly "next to it."

By close questioning, and by putting his questions in various forms, the doctor learned from the chattering little magpie of a Frenchwoman that the patient had been ill for nine days; that he had been under the care of Monsieur le Docteur Cartiere; that there had been a consultation of physicians; that they had prescribed for him and given him over; that le Docteur Cartiere still attended him, but was at this instant in attendance as accoucheur to a lady in extreme danger, whom he could not leave; but Docteur Cartiere had directed them, in his unavoidable absence, to call in the skilful, the talented, the soon to be illustrious young Docteur Rocke, who was also near at hand.

The heart of Traverse thrilled with joy. The Lord had remembered him. His best skill spent upon the poor and needy who could make him no return, but whose lives he had succeeded in saving, had reached the ears of the celebrated Dr. C., who had with the unobtrusive magnanimity of real genius, quietly recommended him to his own patrons.

Oh! well, he would do his very best, not only to advance his own professional interests, and to please his mother and Clara, but also to do honor to the magnanimous Dr. C.'s recommendation.

Here, too, was an opportunity of putting in practice his favorite theory; but first of all it was necessary to be informed of the preceding mode of treatment and its results.

So he farther questioned the little, restless magpie, and by ingeniously framed inquiries, succeeded in gaining from her the necessary knowledge of his patient's antecedents. He examined all the medicines that had been used, and informed himself of their effects upon the disease. But the most serious difficulty of all seemed to be the impossibility of raising vital action upon the cold, dead skin.

The chattering little woman informed him that the patient had been covered with blisters that would not "pull," that would not "decliniate," that would not, what you call it— "*draw!*"

Traverse could easily believe this, for not only the skin, but the very flesh of the old Frenchman seemed bloodless and lifeless.

Now for his theory! what would kill a healthy man with a perfect circulation, might save the life of this dying one, whose whole surface, inch deep, seemed already dead.

"Put him in a bath of mustard water, as hot as you can bear your own hand in, and continue to raise the temperature slowly, watching the effect, for about five minutes. I will go down and prepare a cordial draught to be taken the moment he gets back to bed," said Doctor Rocke, who immediately left the room.

His directions were all but too well obeyed. The bathing tub was quickly brought into the chamber and filled with water, as hot as the nurse could bear her hand in. Then the invalid was hastily invested in a slight bathing gown and lifted by two servants and laid in the hot bath.

"Now, bring quickly, water boiling," said the little, old woman, imperatively. And when a large copper kettle full was forthcoming, she took it and began to pour a stream of hissing, bubbling water in at the foot of the bath.

The skin of the torpid patient had been redding for a few seconds, so as to prove that its sensibility was returning, and now when the stream from the kettle began to mix with the already very hot bath, the patient, with the agility of youth and health, skipped out of the tub and into his bed, kicking vigorously, and exclaiming:

"Brigands! assassins! you have scalded my legs to death!"

"Glory be to the Lord! he's saved!" cried one of the waiters, a devout Irishman.

"Ciel! he speaks! he moves! he lives! *mon frère!*" cried the little Frenchwoman, going to him.

"Ah, murderers! bandits! you've scalded me to death! I'll have you all before the commissaire!"

"He scolds! he threatens! he swears! he gets well! *mon frère!*" cried the old woman, busying herself to change his clothes and put on his flannel night-gown. They then tucked him up warmly in bed, and put bottles of hot water all around, to keep up this newly stimulated circulation.

At that moment Dr. Rocke came in, put his hand into the bath-tub, and could scarcely repress a cry of pain and of horror—the water scalded his fingers! what must it have done to the sick man!

"Good heaven, Madam? I did not tell you to parboil your patient!" exclaimed Traverse, speaking to the old woman. Traverse was shocked to find how perilously his orders had been executed.

"*Eh bien Monsieur!* he lives! he does well! *Voilà mon frère!*" exclaimed the little old woman.

It was true! the accidental "boiling bath," as it might almost be called, had effected what perhaps no other means in the world could—a restored circulation.

The disease was broken up and the convalescence of the patient was rapid. And as Traverse kept his own secret concerning the accidental high temperature of that bath, which every one considered a fearful and a successful experiment, the fame of Dr. Rocke spread over the whole city and country.

He would soon have made a fortune in New Orleans, had not the hand of destiny beckoned him elsewhere. It happened thus:

The old Frenchman whose life Traverse had partly by accident and partly by design succeeded in saving, comprehended perfectly well how narrow his escape from death had been, and attributed his restoration solely to the genius, skill and boldness of his young physician, and was grateful accordingly with all a Frenchman's noisy demonstration.

He called Traverse his friend, his deliverer, his son!

One day, as soon as he found himself strong enough to think of pursuing his journey, he called his "son" into the room and explained to him that he, Doctor Pierre St. Jean, was the proprietor of a private Insane Asylum, very exclusive, very quiet, very aristocratic, indeed, receiving none but patients of the highest rank; that this retreat was situated on the wooded banks of a charming lake in one of the most healthy and beautiful neighborhoods of East Feliciana; that he had originally come down to the city to engage the services of some young physician of talent as his assistant, and finally, that he would be delighted! enraptured! if "his deliverer! his friend! his son!" would accept the post.

Now, Traverse particularly wished to study the various phases of mental derangement, a department of his professional education that had hitherto been opened to him only through books.

He explained this to his old friend, the French physician, who immediately went off into ecstatic exclamations of joy as, "Good! Great!!

Grand!!!" and "I shall now repay my good child! my dear son! for his so excellent skill!"

The terms of the engagement were soon arranged, and Traverse prepared to accompany his new friend to his "beautiful retreat," the private mad-house. But first Traverse wrote to his mother and to Clara in Virginia, and also to Herbert Greyson in Mexico, to apprise them of his good fortune.

CHAPTER LVI

THE MYSTERIOUS MANIAC

᭄᭄᭄᭄᭄᭄

"Stay, jailer, stay, and hear my woe:
    She is not mad who kneels to thee,
For what I am, full well I know,
    And what I was, and what should be;
I'll rave no more in proud despair—
    My language shall be calm tho' sad;
But yet I'll truly, firmly swear,
    I am not mad! no, no, not mad!"
        —*M. G. Lewis* [1]

IT WAS AT the close of a beautiful day in early spring that Traverse Rocke, accompanying the old doctor and the old sister, reached the grove on the borders of the beautiful lake upon the banks of which was situated the "Calm Retreat."

A large, low, white building, surrounded with piazzas and shaded by fragrant and flowering southern trees, it looked like the luxurious country seat of some wealthy merchant or planter, rather than a prison for the insane.

Doctor St. Jean conducted his young assistant into a broad and cool hall, on each side of which doors opened into spacious rooms, occupied by the proprietor and his household. The cells of the patients, as it appeared, were up stairs. The country doctor and the matron who had been in charge during the absence of the proprietor and his sister, now came forward to welcome the party, and report the state of the institution and its inmates.

All were as usual, the country doctor said, except "Mademoiselle."

"And what of her, how is Mademoiselle?—A patient most interesting, Doctor Rocke." said the old Frenchman, alternately questioning his substitute and addressing Traverse.

"She has stopped her violent ravings, and seems to me to be sinking into a state of stupid despair," replied the substitute.

"A patient most interesting, my young friend! a history most pathetic; you shall hear of it some time. But come into the parlor. And you, Angele, my sister, ring, and order coffee," said the old Frenchman, leading

439

the way into a pleasant apartment on the right of the hall, furnished with straw matting upon the floor, and bamboo settees and chairs around the walls.

Here coffee was presently served to the travelers, who soon after retired for the night.

Traverse's room was a large, pleasant apartment at the end of a wide, long hall, on each side of which were the doors opening into the cells of the patients.

Fatigued by his journey, Traverse slept soundly through the night; but early in the morning he was rudely awakened by the sounds of maniac voices from the cells. Some were crying, some laughing aloud, some groaning and howling, and some holding forth in fancied exhortations.

He dressed himself quickly and left his room, to walk down the length of the long hall and observe the cells on each side. The doors were at regular intervals, and each door had in its centre a small opening to enable the proprietor to look in upon the patients.

As these were all women, and some of them delicate and refined even in their insanity, Traverse felt shocked at this necessary, if it *were* necessary, exposure of their sanctuary.

The cells were in fact small bedrooms, that with their white-washed walls, and white curtained beds and windows, looked excessively neat, clean and cool, but also, it must be confessed, very bare, dreary and cheerless.

"Even a looking-glass would be a great benefit to those poor girls, for I remember that even Clara, in her violent grief, and mother in her life-long sorrow, never neglected their looking-glass, and personal appearance," said Traverse to himself, as he passed down the hall, and resolved that this little indulgence should be afforded the patients.

And except those first involuntary glances, he scrupulously avoided looking in through the gratings upon those helpless women who had no means of secluding themselves.

But as he turned to go down the stairs, his eyes went full into an opposite cell, and fell upon a vision of beauty and sorrow that immediately rivetted his gaze.

It was a small and graceful female figure, clothed in deep black, seated by the window, with her elbow resting upon the sill and her chin supported on her hand. Her eyes were cast down until her eyelashes lay like inky lines upon her snow-white cheek. Her face, of classic regularity and marble whiteness, bore a ghastly contrast to the long eyelashes, arched eyebrows and silken ringlets, black as midnight. She might have been a statue or a picture, so motionless she sat.

Conscious of the wrong of gazing upon this solitary woman, Traverse forced his looks away and passed on down stairs, where he again met the old doctor and Mademoiselle Angele at breakfast.

After breakfast, Doctor St. Jean invited his young assistant to accompany him on a round of visits to the patients, and they went immediately up to the hall, at the end of which Traverse had slept.

"These are our incurables, but they are not violent; incurables never are. Poor Mademoiselle! she has just been conveyed to this ward," said the doctor, opening the door of the first cell on the right at the head of the stairs, and admitting Traverse at once into the presence of the beautiful, black-haired, snow-faced woman, who had so much interested him.

"This is my friend, Doctor Rocke, Mademoiselle; Doctor, this is my friend, Mademoiselle Mont de St. Pierre!"

Traverse bowed profoundly, and the lady arose, curtsied and resumed her seat, saying coldly:

"I have told you, Monsieur, never to address me as Mademoiselle; you persist in doing so; and I shall never notice the insult again."

"Ten thousand pardons, Madame! but if Madame will always look so young! so beautiful! can I ever remember that she is a widow?"

The classic lip of the woman curled in scorn, and she disdained a reply.

"I take an appeal to Monsieur le Docteur—Is not Madame young and beautiful?" asked the Frenchman, turning to Traverse, while the splendid black eyes of the stranger passed from one to the other.

Traverse caught the glance of the lady and bowed gravely. It was the most delicate, and proper reply.

She smiled almost as gravely, and with a much kinder expression than any she had bestowed upon the Frenchman.

"And how has Madame fared during my absence so long? The servants—have they been respectful? have they been observant? have they been obedient to the will of Madame? Madame has but to speak!" said the doctor, bowing politely.

"Why should I speak when every word I utter you believe, or affect to believe, to be the ravings of a maniac? I will speak no more," said the lady, turning away her superb dark eyes and looking out of the window.

"Ah, Madame will not so punish her friend, her servant! her slave!"

A gesture of fierce impatience and disgust was the only reply deigned by the lady.

"Come away; she is angry and may become dangerously excited," said the old doctor, leading the way from the cell.

"Did you tell me this lady is one of the incurables?" inquired Traverse, when they had left her apartment.

"Bah! yes, poor girl, vera incurable, as my sister would say."

"Yet, she appears to me to be perfectly sane, as well as exceedingly beautiful and interesting."

"Ah, bah! my excellent, my admirable, my inexperienced young friend; that is all you know of lunatics. With more or less violence of assertion, they every one insist upon their sanity; just as criminals protest their innocence! Ah, bah! you shall go into every cell in this ward, and not find one lunatic among them," sneered the old doctor, as he led the way into the next little room.

It was indeed as he had foretold, and Traverse Rocke found himself deeply affected by the melancholy, the earnest, and sometimes the violent manner in which the poor unfortunates protested their sanity, and implored or demanded to be restored to home and friends.

"You perceive," said the doctor, with a dry laugh, "that they are none of them crazy!"

"I see," said Traverse, "but I also detect a very great difference between that lovely woman in the south cell and these other inmates."

"Bah! bah! bah! she is more beautiful! more accomplished! more refined than the others, and she is in one of her lucid intervals! that is all! but as to a difference between her insanity and that of other patients, it lies in this, that she is the most hopelessly mad of the whole lot. She has been mad eighteen years!

"Is it possible!" exclaimed Traverse, incredulously.

"She lost her reason at the age of sixteen, and she is now thirty-four—you can calculate!"

"It is amazing and very sorrowful! how beautiful she is!"

"Yes; her beauty was a fatal gift! It is a sad story! Ah, it is a sad story! You shall hear of it when we get through."

"I can connect no idea of woman's frailty with that refined and intellectual face," said Traverse, coldly.

"Ah, bah! you are young! you know not the world! you! my innocent, my excellent, my pious young friend!" said the old doctor, as they crossed

442

the hall to go into the next wing of the building, in which were situated the men's wards.

Traverse found nothing that particularly interested him in this department, and when they had concluded their round of visits, and were seated together in the old doctor's study, Traverse asked him for the story of his beautiful patient.

The doctor shrugged his shoulders.

"It is a story miserable, as I told you before. A gentleman, illustrious, from Virginia, an officer high in the army, and distinguished in the war, he brought this woman to me nearly three years ago. He informed me that— eh bien! I had better tell you the story in my own manner. This young lady, Mademoiselle Mont de St. Pierre, is of a family noble and distinguished—a relative of this officer, illustrious and brave. At fifteen, Mademoiselle met a man, handsome and without honor. Ah, bah! you understand! at sixteen the child became a fallen angel! She lost her reason through sorrow and shame! This relative—this gentleman, illustrious and noble, tender and compassionate—took her to the seclusion of his country house, where she lived in elegance, luxury and honor. But as the years passed her malady increased; her presence became dangerous; in a word, the gentleman, distinguished and noble, saw the advertisement of my 'Calm Retreat,' my institution incomparable, and he wrote to me. In a word, he liked my terms, and brought to me his young relative, so lovely and so unfortunate. Ah! he is a good man, this officer so gallant, so chivalrous; but she is ungrateful!"

"Ungrateful!"

"Ah, bah! yes; it is the way with lunatics! They ever imagine their best friends to be their worst enemies! The poor, crazed creature fancies that she is the sister-in-law of this officer illustrious! she thinks that she is the widow of his elder brother, whom she imagines he murdered, and that she is the mother of children whom she says he has abducted or destroyed, so that he may enjoy the estate that is her widow's dower and their orphans' patrimony! That is the reason why she insists on being called Madame instead of Mademoiselle, and we indulge her when we think of it."

"But all this is very singular!"

"Ah, bah! who can account for a lunatic's fancies? She is the maddest of the whole lot! Sometimes she used to become so violent that we would have to restrain her! But lately, Doctor Wood tells me, she is quite still; *that* we consider a bad sign; there is always hope for lunatics until they begin to sink into this state," said the doctor, with an air of competency.

CHAPTER LVII

THE MANIAC'S STORY

✤✤✤✤✤

"A scheming villain forged the tale
    That chains me in this dreary cell,
My fate unknown, my friends bewail,
    O, doctor, haste that fate to tell?
Oh, haste, my daughter's heart to cheer,
    Her heart, at once, 'twill grieve and glad
To know, tho' chained and captive here,
    I am not mad! I am not mad!"
    —*M. G. Lewis*

THERE IS SOME advantage in having imagination, since that visionary faculty opens the mental eyes to facts that more practical and duller intellects could never see.

Traverse was young and romantic, and deeply interested in the doctor's beautiful patient. He, therefore, did not yield his full credulity to the tale told by the "relative illustrious" to the old doctor, as to the history and cause of the lady's madness, or even take it for granted that she *was* mad. He thought it quite possible that the distinguished officer's story might be a wicked fabrication, to conceal a crime, and that the lady's "crazy fancy" might be the pure truth.

And Traverse had heard to what heinous uses private mad-houses were sometimes put by some unscrupulous men, who wished to get certain women out of their way, yet who shrank from bloodshed.

And he thought it not impossible that this "gentleman so noble, so compassionate, and tender," might be just such a man, and this "fallen angel" such a victim. And he determined to watch and observe. And he farther resolved to treat the interesting patient with all the studious delicacy and respect due to a refined and accomplished woman in the full possession of her faculties. If she were really mad, this demeanor would not hurt her; and if she were not mad, it was the only proper conduct to be observed towards her, as any other must be equally cruel and offensive. Her bodily health certainly required the attendance of a physician, and Traverse had, therefore, a fair excuse for his daily visits to her cell.

444

His respectful manners, his grave bow, and his reverential tone in saying—

"I hope I find you stronger to-day, Madam," seemed to gratify one who had few sources of pleasure.

"I thank you," she would answer, with a softened tone and look, adding "yes," or "no," as the truth might be.

One day, after looking at the young physician some time, she suddenly said:

"*You* never forget! *You* always address me by my proper title of Madam, and without the touch of irony which others indulge in when 'humoring' me as they call it! Now, pray explain to me why, in sober earnest, you give me this title?"

"Because, Madam, I have heard you lay claim to that title, and I think that you, yourself, of all the world, have the best right to know how you should be addressed," said Traverse, respectfully.

The lady looked wistfully at him, and said—

"But my next-door neighbor asserts that *she* is a queen; she insists upon being called 'your majesty.' Has she, then, the best right to know how she should be addressed?"

"Alas! no Madam; and I am pained that you should do yourself the great wrong to draw such comparisons."

"Why? Am not I and the 'queen' inmates of the same ward of incurables, in the same lunatic asylum?"

"Yes, but not with equal justice of cause. The 'queen' is a hopelessly deranged, but happy lunatic. You, Madam, are a lady who has retained the full possession of your faculties amid circumstances and surroundings that must have overwhelmed the reason of a weaker mind."

The lady looked at him in wonder and almost in joy.

"Ah, it was not the strength of my mind, it was the strength of the Almighty upon whom my mind was stayed for time and for eternity, that has saved my reason in all these many years! But how did you know that I was not mad? How do you know that this is anything more than a lucid interval of longer duration than usual?" she asked.

"Madam, you will forgive me for having looked at you so closely and watched you so constantly, but I am your physician, you know——"

"I have nothing to forgive and much to thank you for, young man. You have an honest, truthful, frank young face! the only one such that I have seen in eighteen years of sorrow! But why, then, did you not believe the doctor? Why did you not take the fact of my insanity upon trust, as others did?" she asked, fixing her glorious dark eyes inquiringly upon his face.

"Madam, from the first moment in which I saw you, I disbelieved the story of your insanity and mentioned my doubts to Doctor St. Jean———"

———"Who ridiculed your doubts, of course. I can readily believe that he did. Doctor St. Jean is not a very bad man; but he is a charlatan and a dullard; he received the story of my reported insanity as he received me, as an advantage to his institution; and he never gave himself the unprofitable trouble to investigate the circumstances. I told him the truth about myself as calmly as I now speak to you; but somebody else had told him that this truth was the fiction of a deranged imagination, and he found it more convenient and profitable to believe somebody else! But again I ask you, why were not *you* also, so discreetly obtuse?"

"Madam," said Traverse, blushing ingenuously, "I hope you will forgive me for saying that it is impossible any one could see you without becoming deeply interested in your fate. Your face, Madam, speaks equally of profound sorrows and of saintly resignation. I saw no sign of madness there! In the calm depths of those sad eyes, lady, I know that the fires of insanity never could have burned. Pardon me that I looked at you so closely; I was your physician, and was most deeply anxious concerning my patient."

"I thank you; may the Lord bless you; perhaps He has sent you here for my relief; for you are right, young friend; you are altogether right; I have been wild with grief, frantic with despair, but never for one hour in the whole course of my life have I been insane."

"I believe you, Madam, on my sacred honor, I do!" said Traverse, fervently.

"And yet you could get no one about this place to believe you! They have taken my brother-in-law's false story, endorsed as it is by the doctor-proprietor, for granted. And just so long as I persist in telling my true story, they will consider me a monomaniac, and so often as the thought of my many wrongs and sorrows, combines with the nervous irritability to which every woman is occasionally subject, and makes me rave with impatience and excitement, they will report me a dangerous lunatic, subject to the periodical attacks of violent frenzy; but, young man, even at my worst I am no more mad than any other woman, wild with grief and hysterical through nervous irritation, might at any time become without having her sanity called in question."

"I am sure that you are not, nor ever could have been, Madam. The nervous excitement of which you speak is entirely within the control of medicine, which mania proper is not. You will use the means that I prescribe and your continued calmness will go far to convince even these dullards that they have been wrong."

"I will do everything you recommend; indeed for some weeks before you came, I had put a constraint upon myself and forced myself to be very still; but the effect of that was, that acting upon their theory they said that I was sinking into the last or 'melancholy-mad' state of mania, and they put me in here with the incurables."

"Lady," said Traverse respectfully taking her hand, "now that I am acquainted in some slight degree with the story of your heavy wrongs, do not suppose that I will ever leave you, until I see you restored to your friends."

"Friends! ah! young man, do you really suppose, that if I had friends, I should have been left thus long unsought? I have no friends, Doctor Rocke, except yourself, newly sent me by the Lord! nor any relatives except a young daughter whom I have seen but twice in my life!—once upon the dreadful night when she was born and torn away from my sight, and once about two years ago, when she must have been sixteen years of age. My little daughter does not know that she has a poor mother living, and I have no friends upon earth but you, whom the Lord has sent."

"And not in vain!" said Traverse, fervently; "though you have no other friends, yet you have the law to protect you. I will make your case known, and restore you to liberty! Then lady, listen! I have a good mother to whom suffering has taught sympathy with the unfortunate; and I have a lovely betrothed bride, whom you will forgive her lover for thinking an angel in woman's form; and we have a beautiful home among the hills of Virginia; and you shall add to our happiness by living with us."

The lady looked at Traverse Rocke with astonishment and incredulity.

"Boy," she said, "do you know what you are promising—to assume the whole burden of the support of a useless woman for her whole life! What would your mother or promised wife say to such a proposition?"

"Ah! you do not know my dear mother, nor my Clara, no, nor even me. I tell you the truth when I say that your coming among us would make us happier. Oh, Madam, I myself owe so much to the Lord, and to his instruments, the benevolent of this world, for all that has been done for me, I seize with gratitude the chance to serve in my turn any of His suffering children! Pray believe me!"

447

"I do! I do, Doctor Rocke! I see that life has not deprived you of a generous, youthful enthusiasm," said the lady, with the tears welling up into her glorious black eyes.

After a little, with a smile, she held out her hand to him, saying:

"Young friend, if you should succeed in freeing me from this prison, and establish my sanity before a court of justice, I and my daughter will come into immediate possession of one of the largest estates in your native Virginia! Sit down, Doctor Rocke, while I tell you my true story, and much, very much more of it than I have ever confided to any human being."

"Lady, I am very impatient to hear your history, but I am your physician, and must first consider your health. You have been sufficiently excited for one day; it is late: take your tea and retire early to bed. To-morrow morning, after I have visited the wards and you have taken your breakfast, I will come, and you shall tell me the story of your life."

"I will do whatever you think best," said the lady.

Traverse lifted her hand to his lips, bowed, and retreated from the cell.

That same night Traverse wrote to his friend Herbert Greyson in Mexico, and to his mother and Clara, describing his interesting patient, though as yet he could tell but little of her, not even in fact her real name, but promising fuller particulars next time, and declaring his intention of bringing her home for the present to their house.

CHAPTER LVIII

END OF THE LADY'S STORY

"Of the present naught is bright,
But in the coming years I see
A brilliant and a cheerful light,
Which burns before thee constantly."
—*W. D. Gallagher*[1]

AT THE APPOINTED hour the next morning, Traverse Rocke repaired to the cell of his mysterious patient.

He was pleased to find her up and dressed with more than usual care and taste, and looking, upon the whole, much better in health and spirits than upon the preceding day.

"Ah, my young hero, is it you? You see that I am ready for you," she said, holding out her hand.

"You are looking very well this morning?" said Traverse, smiling.

"Yes, hope is a fine tonic, Doctor Rocke."

She was seated by the same window at which Traverse had first seen her, and she now beckoned the young doctor to come and take a seat near her.

"My story is almost as melo-dramatic as a modern romance, Doctor Rocke," she said.

Traverse bowed gravely and waited.

"My father was a French patriot, who suffered death in the cause of liberty, when I, his only child, was but fourteen years of age. My mother, broken-hearted by his loss, followed him within a few months. I was left an orphan and penniless, for our estate was confiscated."

"Ah, your sorrows came early and heavily indeed," said Traverse.

"Yes; well! a former servant of my father held an humble situation of porter on the ground floor of a house, the several floors of which were let out to different lodgers. This poor man and his wife gave me a temporary home with themselves. Among the lodgers of the house there was a young

Virginian gentleman of fortune, traveling for pleasure and improvement, whose name was Mr. Eugene Le Noir.'

"*Le Noir!* cried Traverse with a violent start.

"Yes! what is the matter?"

"It is a familiar Virginian name, Madam, that is all; pray go on."

"Mr. Le Noir was as good and kind as he was wise and cultivated. He used to stop to gossip with old Cliquot every time he stopped at the porter's room to take or to leave his key. There he heard of the poor little orphan of the guillotine, who had no friend in the world but her father's old servant. He pitied me, and after many consultations with Father and Mother Cliquot, he assumed the position of guardian to me, and placed me at one of the best schools in Paris. He lingered in the city and came to see me very often; but always saw me in the presence of Madam, the directress. I clung to him with the affection for a father or an elder brother, and I knew he loved me with the tender, protecting affection that he would have given a younger sister, had he possessed one. Ah! Doctor Rocke, tell me besides yourself, are there many other men in your state like *him?*"

"I knew but one such; but go on, dear madam."

"When I had been to school some months, he came to me one day scarcely able to conceal his woe! He told me that his father was ill and that he should have to sail in the first packet from Havre, and that in fact he had then come to take leave of me. I was wild with grief, not only upon his account but upon my own, at the prospect of losing him, my only friend! I was but a child, and a French child to boot. I knew nothing of the world; I regarded this noble gentleman, who was so much my superior in years as in everything else, as a father, guardian or elder brother, so in an agony of grief, I threw myself into his arms, sobbing and weeping bitterly, and imploring him not to break my heart by leaving me! It was in vain Madame the Directress exclaimed and expostulated at these improprieties. I am sure I did not hear a word until *he* spoke. Putting me out of his arms he said:

" 'I must go, my child, duty calls me.'

" 'Then take me with you—take your poor little one with you, and do not pull her out of your warm, good heart, or she will wither and die like a poor flower torn up by the roots!' I cried, between my sobs and tears.

"He drew me back to his bosom and whispered:

" 'There is but one way in which I can take you with me, my child. Will you be my wife, little Capitola?' "

"*Capitola!*" cried Traverse, with another great start.

"Yes; why? what is the matter now?"

"Why, it is such an odd name, that is all. Pray proceed, Madam."

"We were married the same day, and sailed the third morning thereafter from Havre for the United States, where we arrived, alas! only to find the noble gentleman, my Eugene's father, laid in his grave. After Mr. Le Noir's natural grief was over, we settled down peaceably to our country life at the Hidden House——"

"*The Hidden House!*" again exclaimed Traverse Rocke.

"Yes; that is another odd name, isn't it. Well I was very happy. At first, when I understood my real position, I had been afraid that my husband had married me only from compassion; but he soon proved to me that his love was as high, as pure, and as noble as himself. I was very happy! But one day, in the midst of my exultant joy, a thunderbolt fell and shattered my peace to destruction forever! Oh, Dr. Rocke, my husband was murdered by some unknown hand in his own woods, in open day. I cannot talk of this!" cried the widow, breaking down, overwhelmed with the rush of terrible recollections.

Traverse poured out a glass of water, and handed it to her.

She drank it, made an effort at self-control, and resumed:

"Thus, scarcely sixteen years of age, I was a widow, helpless, penniless, and entirely dependent upon my brother-in-law, Colonel Gabriel Le Noir; for by the terms of their father's will if Eugene died without issue, the whole property descended to his younger brother, Gabriel. To speak the truth, Colonel Le Noir was exceedingly kind to me after my awful bereavement, until a circumstance was discovered that changed all our relations. It was two months after my husband's death, that I discovered with mingled emotions of joy and sorrow that Heaven had certainly destined me to become a mother. I kept my cherished secret to myself as long as it was possible, but it could not indeed be long concealed from the household. I believe that my brother-in-law was the first to suspect it. He called me into his study one day and I obeyed like a child. And there he rudely questioned me upon the subject of my sacred mother-mystery. He learned the truth, more from my silence than from my replies, for I could not answer him."

"The brute! the miserable hound!" ejaculated Traverse.

"Oh, Dr. Rocke, I could not tell you the avalanche of abuse, insult, and invective that he hurled upon my defenceless head. He accused me of more crimes than I had ever heard talk of. He told me that my condition was an impossible one unless I had been false to the memory of his brother;

that I had dishonored his name, disgraced his house, and brought myself to shame; that I should leave the roof, leave the neighborhood, and die as I deserved to die, in a ditch! I made no reply. I was crushed into silence under the weight of his reproaches."

"The caitiff! the poltroon! Ah, poor stranger, why did you not leave the house at once and throw yourself upon the protection of the minister of your parish, or some other kind neighbor?"

"Alas, I was a child, a widow, and a foreigner, all in one. I did not know your land, or your laws, or your people. I was not hopeful or confident, I had suffered so cruelly, and I was overwhelmed by his abuse."

"But did you not know, dear lady, that all his rage was aroused only by the fact that the birth of your child would disinherit him?"

"Ah, no. I was not aware, at that time, that Gabriel Le Noir was a villain. I thought his anger honest, though unjust; and I was as ignorant as a child—I had no mother nor matronly friend to instruct me. I knew that I had broken no command of God or man—that I had been a faithful wife, but when Gabriel Le Noir accused me with such bitter earnestness, I feared that some strange departure from the usual course of nature had occurred for my destruction. And I was overwhelmed by mortification, terror, and despair."

"Ah, the villain!" exclaimed Traverse, between his teeth.

"He told me at last, that, to save the memory of his dead brother he would hide my dishonor; and he ordered me to seclude myself from the sight of all persons. I obeyed him like a slave, grateful even for the shelter of his roof."

"A roof that was your own as he very well knew. And he knew also, the caitiff, that if the circumstance became known, the whole state would have protected you in your rights, and ejected him like a cur."

"Nay, even in that case no harm should have reached him on my account. He was my husband's brother."

"And worst enemy. But proceed, dear lady."

"Well, I secluded myself as he commanded. For four months I never left the attic to which he had ordered me to retreat. At the end of that time I became the mother of twins—a boy and a girl. The boy only opened his eyes on this world to close them again directly. The girl was living and healthy. The old nurse who attended me had an honest and compassionate face; I persuaded her to secret and save the living child, and to present the dead babe to Colonel Le Noir as the only one; for the suspicions that had never been awakened for myself were alarmed for my child. I instinctively felt that he would have destroyed it."

"The mother's instinct is like inspiration," said Traverse.

"It may be so! well, the old woman pitied me and did as I desired. She took the dead child to Colonel Le Noir, who carried it off, and afterwards buried it as the sole heir of his elder brother. The old woman carried off my living child and my wedding ring, concealed under her ample shawl. Anxiety for the fate of my child caused me to do what nothing else on earth would have tempted me to do—to creep about the halls and passages on tiptoe and under cover of the night, and listen at keyholes," said the lady, blushing deeply at the recollection.

"You—you were perfectly right, Mrs. Le Noir! In a den of robbers, where your life and honor were always at stake, you could have done no otherwise!" exclaimed Traverse, warmly.

"I learned by this means that my poor old nurse had paid with her liberty for her kindness to me. She had been abducted and forced from her native country together with a *child* found in her possession, which they evidently suspected and I knew to be mine. Oh heaven! the agony then of thinking of what might be her unfortunate fate,—worse than death, perhaps! I felt that I had only succeeded in saving her life;—doubtful good!"

Here Mrs. Le Noir paused in thought for a few moments and then resumed.

"It is the memory of a long, dreary and hopeless imprisonment, my recollection of my residence in that house! In the same manner in which I gained all my information, I learned that it was reported in the neighborhood that I had gone mad with grief for the loss of my husband and that I was an inmate of a mad-house in the north! It was altogether false! I never left the Hidden House in all those years until about two years ago. My life there was dreary beyond all conception. I was forbidden to go out or to appear at a window! I had the whole attic, containing some eight or ten rooms to rove over, but I was forbidden to descend. An ill-looking woman, called Dorcas Knight, between whom and the elder le Noir there seemed to have been some sinful bond, was engaged ostensibly as my attendant; but really as my jailer. Nevertheless, when the sense of confinement grew intolerable I sometimes eluded her vigilance and wandered about the house at night."

"Thence no doubt," said Traverse, "giving rise to the report that the house was haunted!"

Mrs. Le Noir smiled, saying:

"I believe the Le Noirs secretly encouraged that report! I'll tell you why. They gave me a chamber-lamp enclosed in an intense blue shade, that cast a strange unearthly light around. Their ostensible reason was to ensure my safety from fire. Their real reason was that this light might be seen from without in what was reputed to be an uninhabited portion of the house, and give color to its bad reputation among the ignorant of being haunted!"

"So much for the origin of *one* authenticated ghost story," said Traverse.

"Yes! and there was still more circumstantial evidence to support this ghostly reputation of the house. As the years passed I had, even in my confined state, gathered knowledge in one way and another—picking up stray books and hearing stray conversation; and so, in the end I learned how gross a deception and how great a wrong had been practised upon me. I was not wise or cunning. I betrayed constantly to my attendant my knowledge of these things. In consequence of which my confinement became still more restricted."

"Yes, they were afraid of you, and fear is always the mother of cruelty," said Traverse.

"Well, from the time that I became enlightened as to my real position, all my faculties were upon the alert to find means of escaping and making my condition known to the authorities. One night they had a guest, Colonel Eglen, of the army. Old Dorcas had her hands full, and forgot her prisoner. My door was left unlocked. So, long after Colonel Eglen had retired to rest, and when all the household were buried in repose, I left my attic and crept down to the chamber of the guest, with no other purpose than to make known my wrongs and appeal to his compassion. I entered his chamber, approached his bed to speak to him, when this hero of a hundred fields started up in a panic, and at the sight of the pale woman who drew his curtains in the dead of night, he shrieked, violently rang his bell, and fainted prone away!"

"Ha! ha! ha! he could brave an army, or march into a cannon's mouth, easier than meet a supposed denizen of another world! Well, Doctor Johnson believed in ghosts," laughed Traverse.

"It remained for me to retreat as fast as possible to my room, to avoid the Le Noirs, who were hurrying with headlong speed to the guest-chamber. *They* knew, of course, that I was the ghost, although they affected to treat their visitor's story as a dream. After that my confinement was so strict that for years I had no opportunity of leaving my attic. At last the strict espionage was relaxed. Sometimes my door would be left unlocked. Upon one such occasion, in creeping about in the dark, I learned, by overhearing a conversation between Le Noir and his housekeeper, that my long-lost daughter, Capitola, had been found, and was living at Hurricane Hall! This was enough to comfort me for years. About three years ago, the surveillance over me was so modified that I was left again to roam about the upper rooms of the house at will, until I learned that they had a new inmate, young Clara Day, a ward of Le Noir! Oh, how I longed to warn that child to fly! But I could not! Alas, again I was restricted to my own room, lest I should be seen by her! But again, upon one occasion, old Dorcas forgot to lock my door at night. I stole forth from my room and learned that a young girl, caught out in the storm, was to stay all night at the Hidden House. Young girls were not plentiful in that neighborhood, I knew! Besides, some secret instinct told me that this was my daughter. I knew that she would sleep in the chamber under mine, because that was the only habitable guest-room in the whole house. In the dead of night I left my room and went below and entered the chamber of the young girl. I went first to the toilet table to see if among her little girlish ornaments, I could find any clue to her identity. I found it in a plain, gold ring—the same that I had entrusted to the old nurse. Some strange impulse caused me to slip the ring upon my finger. Then I went to the bed and threw aside the curtains to gaze upon the sleeper. My girl! my own girl! With what strange sensations I first looked upon her face! Her eyes were open and fixed upon mine in a panic of terror. I stooped to press my lips to hers and she closed her eyes in mortal fear. I carried nothing but terror with me! I withdrew from the room and went back, sobbing, to my chamber. My poor girl, next morning, unconsciously, betrayed her mother. It had nearly cost me my life.

"When the Le Noirs came home, the first night of their arrival they entered my room, seized me in my bed, and dragged me shrieking from it!"

"Good heaven! what punishment is sufficient for such wretches!" exclaimed Traverse, starting up and pacing the narrow limits of the cell.

"Listen! They soon stopped both my shrieks and my breath at once! I lost consciousness for a time, and when I awoke I found myself in a close carriage, rattling over a mountain road, through the night. Late the next morning we reached an uninhabited country-house, where I was again imprisoned, in charge of an old dumb woman whom Le Noir called Mrs. Raven. This I afterwards understood to be Willow Heights, the property of the orphan heiress, Clara Day. And here, also, for the term of my stay, the presence of the unknown inmate got the house the reputation of being haunted. The old dumb woman was a shade kinder to me than Doreas Knight had been; but I did not stay in her charge very long. One night the Le Noirs came in hot haste. The young heiress had been delivered from their charge by a decree of the Orphans' Court, and they had to give up her house. I was drugged and hurried away. Some narcotic sedative must have been insinuated into my food, for I was in a state of semi-insensibility and mild delirium during the whole course of a long journey by land and sea, which passed to me like a dream, and at the end of which I found myself here. No doubt, from the excessive use of narcotics, there was something wild and stupid in my manner and appearance that justified the charge of madness. And when I found that I was a prisoner, in a lunatic asylum, far, far away from the neighborhood where, at least, I had once been known, I gave way to the wilder grief that further confirmed the story of my madness. I have been here two years, occasionally giving way to outbursts of wild despair, that the doctor calls frenzy. I was sinking into an apathy when one day I opened the little Bible that lay upon the table of my cell. I fixed upon the last chapters in the gospel of John. That narrative of meek patience and divine love! It did for me what no power under that of God could have done. It saved me! it saved me from madness! it saved me from despair! There is a time for the second birth of every soul; that time had come for me. From that hour, this book has been my constant companion and comfort. I have learned from its pages how little it matters how or where this fleeting, mortal life is passed, so that it answers its purpose of preparing the soul for another. I have learned patience with sinners, forgiveness of enemies, and confidence in God. In a word, I trust I have learned the way of salvation, and in that have learned everything. Your coming, and your words, young friend, have stirred within my heart the desire to be free, to mingle again on equal terms with my fellow-beings, and, above all, to find and to embrace my child. But not wildly anxious am I even for these earthly blessings. These, as well as all things else, I desire to leave to the Lord, praying that His will may be mine! Young friend, my story is told."

"Madam," said Traverse, after a thoughtful pause, "our fates have been more nearly connected than you could have imagined. Those Le Noirs have been *my* enemies as they are *yours*. That young orphan heiress, who appealed from their cruelty to the Orphans' Court, was my own betrothed. Willow Heights was her patrimony, and is now her quiet home, where she lives with my mother, and where in their name I invite you to come. And take this comfort also; your enemy no longer lives; months ago I left him ill with a mortal wound. This morning the papers announce his death. There remains, therefore, but little for me to do, but to take legal measures to free you from this place, and restore you to your home. Within an hour I shall set out for New Orleans, for the purpose of taking the initiatory steps. Until my return thence, dear lady," said Traverse, respectfully taking her hand—"Farewell, and be of good cheer!"

CHAPTER LIX

PROSPECTS BRIGHTEN

*"Thus far our fortune keeps an onward course,
And we are graced with wreaths of victory."*
—*Shakespeare*[1]

LEAVING MRS. Le Noir, Traverse went down to the stable, saddled the horse that had been allotted to his use, and set off for a long day's journey to New Orleans, where late at night he arrived, and put up at the St. Charles.

He slept deeply from fatigue until late the next morning, when he was awakened by the sound of drums, trumpets and fifes, and by general rejoicing.

He arose and looked from his windows to ascertain the cause, and saw the square full of people in a state of the highest excitement, watching for a military procession coming up the street.

It was the United States troops under their gallant commanders, who had landed from the steamboats that morning and were now marching from the quay up to their quarters at the St. Charles.

As they advanced, Traverse, eagerly upon the lookout, recognized his own regiment, and presently saw Major Greyson himself.

Traverse withdrew from the window, hurriedly completed his toilet, and hastened down stairs, where he soon found himself face to face with Herbert, who warmly grasping his hand, exclaimed:

"*You* here, old friend? Why, I thought you were down in East Feliciana, with your interesting patient!"

"It is for the *interest* of that 'interesting patient' that I am here, Herbert! Did I tell you she was one of the victims of that demon, Le Noir?"

"No; but I know it from another source! I know as much, or more of her, perhaps than you do!"

Prospects Brighten

"Ah!" exclaimed Traverse, in surprise.

"Yes! I know, for instance, that she is Capitola's mother, the long-lost widow of Eugene Le Noir, the mistress of the Hidden House, and the ghost who drew folks' curtains there at night."

"Then you *do* know something about her, but *how* did you arrive at the knowledge?"

"By the 'last dying speech and confession' of Gabriel Le Noir, confided to me, to be used in *restitution* after his decease! But, come! there is the second bell! Our mess are going in to breakfast; join us and afterwards you and I will retire and compare notes," said Herbert, taking the arm of his friend, as they followed the moving crowd into the breakfast parlor.

After the morning meal was concluded the friends withdrew together, to the chamber occupied by Traverse Rocke, where they sat down for mutual explanations.

Herbert first related to Traverse all that had occurred from the time that the latter left the city of Mexico, including the arrival of Craven Le Noir at the dying bed of his father, the subsequent death and funeral of Colonel Le Noir, and the late emigration of Craven, who, to avoid the shame of the approaching revelation, joined a party of explorers bound for the recently discovered gold mines of California.

"The civilized world is then rid of two villains at once," said the uncompromising Traverse.

Herbert took from his pocket the confession of Colonel Le Noir, which he said he was now at liberty to use as he thought proper for the ends of justice. That certain parts of the disclosure intimately concerned Traverse Rocke; to whom he should, therefore, read the whole. The confession may be briefly summed up as follows:

The first item was, that he had sought to win the affections of Marah Rocke, the supposed wife of Major Ira Warfield; he had sedulously waylaid and followed her with his suit during the whole summer; she had constantly repulsed and avoided him; he, listening to his own evil passions, had bribed her maid to admit him in the dark to Marah's cabin, upon a certain night when her husband was to be absent; that the unexpected return of Major Warfield, who had tracked him to the house, had prevented the success of his evil purpose; but had not saved the reputation of the innocent wife, whose infuriated husband would not believe her ignorant of the presence of the villain in her house; that he, Gabriel Le Noir, in hatred as well as in shame, had forborne until now to make the explanation, which he hoped might now, late in life as it was, bring the long severed pair

459

together, and establish Marah Rocke and her son in their legal and social rights.

The second item in the black list of crime was the death of his elder brother, whom he declared he had not intended to kill. He said that, having contracted large debts which he was unable to pay, he had returned secretly from his distant quarters to demand the money from his brother, who had often helped him; that, meeting his brother in the woods, he made this request. Eugene reproached him for his extravagance and folly, and refused to aid him; an encounter ensued, in which Eugene fell. He, Gabriel Le Noir, fled, pursued by the curse of Cain, and reached his own quarters before even his absence had been suspected. His agency in the death of his brother was not suspected even by his accomplice in other crimes. The outlaw called Black Donald, who, thinking to gain an ascendency over one whom he called his patron, falsely pretended to have made away with Eugene Le Noir for the sake of his younger brother!

The third item of confession was the abduction of the nurse and babe of the young widow of Eugene, the circumstances of which are already known to the reader.

The fourth in the dreadful list comprised the deceptions, wrongs and persecutions practiced upon Madam Eugene Le Noir, and the final false imprisonment of that lady under the charge of insanity, in the private madhouse kept by Doctor Pierre St. Jean, in East Feliciana.

In conclusion, he spoke of the wrongs done to Clara Day, whose pardon, with that of others, be begged. And he prayed that in consideration of his son, as little publicity as was possible might be given to these crimes.

During the reading of his confession, the eyes of Traverse Rocke were fixed in wonder and half incredulity upon the face of Herbert, and at its conclusion he said:

"What a mass of crime! But that we may not dare to question the mercy of the Lord, I should ask if these were sins that He would *ever* pardon! Herbert, it appalls me to think of it!"

Then, after deep thought, he added:

"This, then, was the secret of my dear mother's long unhappiness! She was Major Warfield's forsaken wife!—Herbert! I feel as though I never, never, could forgive my father!"

"Traverse, if Major Warfield had *wilfully* and *wantonly* forsaken your mother, I should say that your resentment was natural and right! *Who* should be an honorable woman's champion if not her own son? But Major Warfield, as well as his wife, was more sinned against than sinning! Your parents were both victims of a cruel conspiracy, and he suffered as much in his way, as she did in hers," said Herbert.

"I always thought, somehow, that my dear mother was a forsaken wife. She never told me so; but there was something about her circumstances and manners, her retired life, her condition, so much below her deserts, her never speaking of her husband's death—which would have been natural for her to do, had she been a widow—all, somehow, went to give me the impression that my father had abandoned us. Lately I had suspected that Major Warfield had something to do with the sad affair, though I never once suspected him to be my father!—so much for natural instincts," said Traverse, with a melancholy smile.

"Traverse," said Herbert, with a design of drawing him off from sad remembrances of his mother's early trials. "Traverse, this confession, signed and witnessed as it is, will wonderfully simplify your course of action in regard to the deliverance of Madam Le Noir."

"Yes; so it will," said Traverse, with animation. "There will be no need now of applying to law; especially if you will come down with me to East Feliciana and bring the confession with you."

"I will set out with you this very morning, if you wish, as I am on leave. What! to hasten the release of Capitola's mother! I would set out at midnight, and ride straight on for a week!"

"Ah! there is no need of such extravagant feats of travel. It is now ten o'clock; if we start within an hour we can reach the "Calm Retreat" by eleven o'clock tonight."

"*En avant,* then," exclaimed Herbert, rising and ringing the bell.

Traverse ordered horses, and in twenty minutes the friends were on the road to East Feliciana.

They reached the "Calm Retreat" so late that night, that there was none but the porter awake to admit them.

Traverse took his friend up to his own dormitory, saying, laughingly:

"It is an unappreciable distance of time since you and I occupied the same bed, Herbert."

"Yes; but it is not the first, by five hundred times. Do you remember, Traverse, the low attic where we used to sleep, and how on stormy nights we used to listen to the rain pattering on the roof, within two or three inches of our faces, and how we used to be half afraid to turn over for fear that we should bump our heads against the timbers of the ceiling?"

"Yes, indeed," said Traverse.

And thereupon the two friends launched into a discussion of old times, when the two widows and their sons lived together—the two women occupying one bed, and the two boys the other. And this discussion they kept up until long after they retired, and until sleep overtook them.

The next morning Traverse conducted his friend down to the breakfast parlor, to introduce him to Doctor St. Jean, who, as soon as he perceived his young medical assistant, sprang forward exclaiming:

"*Grand Heaven!* Is this then you? Have you then returned? What for did you run away with my horse?"

"I went to New Orleans in great haste, upon very important business, sir."

"*Grand Dieu!* I should think so, I! when you ride off on my horse without saying a word! If it had been my ambling pony I should have been in despair, I! Your business so hasty and so important was accomplished, I hope?"

"Yes; I did my errand with less trouble than I had anticipated, owing to the happy circumstance of meeting my friend here, who has come down hither connected with the same business."

"Ah, very happy to see your friend. In the medical profession, I suppose?"

"No, sir; in the army. Allow me to present him. Major Herbert Greyson, of the ———th Regiment of Cavalry."

"Oui! ay! Grand ciel! this is the brave, the distinguished, the illustrious officer, so honorably mentioned in the despatches of the invincible Taylor and the mighty Scott!" said the little Frenchman, bowing his nightcapped head down to his slippered toes.

Herbert smiled as he returned the bow. And then the little French doctor, turning to Traverse, said:

"But your business, so important and so hasty, which has brought this officer so illustrious down here;—what is it my friend?"

"We will have the honor of explaining to Monsieur le Docteur, over our coffee, if he will oblige us by ordering the servant to retire," said Traverse, who sometimes adopted in speaking to the old Frenchman his own formal style of politeness.

"Oui, oui, certainment! Allez donc, John! Go, then, John!"

As soon as the man had gone, Traverse said:

"I propose to discuss this business over our coffee, because it will save time without interfering with our morning meal, and I know that immediately afterwards you will go your usual round of visits to your patients."

"Eh bien! proceed, my son! proceed!"

Traverse immediately commenced and related all that was necessary concerning the fraud practiced upon the institution by introducing into it an unfortunate woman, represented to be mad, but really only sorrowful, nervous and excitable. And to prove the truth of his words, Traverse desired Herbert to read from the confession the portion relating to this fraud, and to show the doctor the signature of the principal and the witness.

To have seen the old French doctor then! I rejoice in a Frenchman, for the frank abandon with which he gives himself up to his emotions! Our doctor, after staring at the confession, took hold of the top of his blue tasselled nightcap, pulled it off his head and threw it violently upon the floor! Then remembering that he was exposing a cranium, as bald as a peeled potato, he suddenly caught it up again, clapped it upon his crown and exclaimed:

"Sacre! Diable!" and other ejaculations dreadful to translate, and others again which it would be profane to set down in French or English.

Gabriel Le Noir was no longer an officer illustrious, a gentleman noble and distinguished, compassionate and tender; he was a robber infamous! a villain atrocious! a caitiff, ruthless, and without remorse!

After breakfast the doctor consented that his young hero, his little knight-errant, his dear son, should go to the distressed lady and open the good news to her; while the great Major Greyson, the warrior invincible, should go around with himself to inspect the institution.

Traverse immediately repaired to the chamber of Mrs. Le Noir, whom he found sitting at the window, engaged in some little trifle of needlework, the same pale, patient woman that she had first appeared to him.

"Ah, you have come! I read good news upon your smiling face, my friend! Tell it! I have borne the worst of sorrows! shall I not have strength to bear joy?"

Traverse told her all, and then ended by saying:

"Now, dear Madam, it is necessary that we leave this place within two hours, as Major Greyson's regiment leaves New Orleans for Washington tomorrow, and it is advisable that you go under our protection. We can get you a female attendant from the St. Charles."

"Oh, I can be ready in ten minutes! I have no fine lady's wardrobe to pack up!" replied Mrs. Le Noir, with a smile.

Traverse bowed and went out to procure a carriage from the next village. And in half an hour afterwards the whole party took leave of Doctor Pierre St. Jean and his "institution incomparable," and set forth on their journey to New Orleans, whence in two days afterwards they sailed for the North. And now, dear reader, let you and me take the fast boat, and get home before them to see our little Cap, and find out what adventures she is now engaged in, and how she is getting on.

CHAPTER LX

CAPITOLA A CAPITALIST

"Plumed victory
Is truly painted with a cheerful look,
Equally distant from proud insolence
And sad detection."
—*Massinger*[1]

HOW GLAD I am to get back to my little Cap; for I know very well, reader, just as well as if you had told me, that you have been grumbling for two weeks for the want of Cap. But I could not help it, for, to tell the truth, I was pining after her myself, which was the reason that I could not do half justice to the scenes of the Mexican War.

Well, now let us see what Cap has been doing—what oppressors she has punished—what victims she has delivered—in a word, what new heroic adventures she has achieved.

Well, the trial of Donald Bayne, alias Black Donald, was over. Cap, of course, had been compelled to appear against him. During the whole course of the trial the court-room was crowded with a curious multitude, "from far and near," eager to get sight of the notorious outlaw.

Black Donald, through the whole ordeal, deported himself with a gallant and joyous dignity, that would have better become a triumph than a trial.

He was indicted upon several distinct counts, the most serious of which—the murder of the solitary widow and her daughter in the forest cabin, and the assassination of Eugene Le Noir in the woods near the Hidden House—were sustained only by circumstantial evidence. But the aggregate weight of all these, together with his very bad reputation, was sufficient to convict him, and Black Donald was sentenced to death.

This dreadful doom, most solemnly pronounced by the judge, was received by the prisoner with a loud laugh, and the words:

"You're out o' your reckoning now, cap'n! I never was a saint, the Lord knows, but my hands are free from blood-guiltiness! There's an honest little girl that believes me—don't you?" he said, turning laughingly to our little heroine.

"Yes, I do!" said Cap, bursting into tears; "and I am as sorry for you as ever I can be, Donald Bayne."

"Bother! it was sure to come to this first or last, and I knew it! Now, to prove you do not think this rugged hand of mine stained with blood, give it a friendly shake!" said the condemned man. And before Old Hurricane could prevent her, Capitola had jumped over two or three intervening seats and climbed up to the side of the dock, and reached up her hand to the prisoner saying:

"God help you, Donald Bayne, in your great trouble, and I will do all I can to help you in this world. I will go to the Governor myself, and tell him I know you never did any murder."

"Remove the prisoner," said the judge, peremptorily.

The constables approached and led away Black Donald.

Old Hurricane rushed upon Cap, seized her, and shaking her fiercely, exclaimed, under his breath:

"You—you—you—you New York hurrah boy![2] you foundling! you vagabond! you vagrant! you brat! you beggar! will you never be a lady! to go and shake hands with that ruffian!"

"Sure, uncle, *that's* nothing now; I have shaken hands with *you* often enough!"

"Demmy, you—you—you New York trash, what do you mean by *that?*"

"Of course I mean, uncle, that you are as rough a ruffian as ever Donald Bayne was!"

"Demmy, I'll murder you!"

"Don't uncle; they have an uncivilized way here of hanging murderers," said Cap, shaking herself free of Old Hurricane's grasp, and hastening out of the court-room to mount her horse and ride home.

One night after tea, Capitola and her uncle occupied their usual seats by the little bright wood fire, that the chilly evening and the keen mountain air made agreeable, even in May.

Old Hurricane was smoking his pipe and reading his paper.

Cap was sitting with her slender fingers around her throat, which she, with a shudder, occasionally compressed.

"Well, that demon Black Donald will be hanged the 26th of July," said Old Hurricane, exultingly, "and we shall get rid of one villain, Cap."

"*I* pity Black Donald, and I can't bear to think of his being hanged! It quite breaks my heart to think that I was compelled to bring him to such fate!"

"Oh! that reminds me! The reward offered for the apprehension of Black Donald, to which you were entitled, Cap, was paid over to me for you. I placed it to your account in the Agricultural Bank."

"I don't want it! I won't touch it! The price of blood. It would burn my fingers!" said Cap.

"Oh, very well! a thousand dollars won't go a begging," said Old Hurricane.

"Uncle, it breaks my heart to think of Black Donald's execution! It just does! It must be dreadful, this hanging! I have put my fingers around my throat and squeezed it, to know how it feels, and it is awful! Even a little squeeze makes my head feel as if it would burst, and I have to let go! Oh, it is horrible to think of!"

"Well, Cap, it wasn't intended to be as pleasant as tickling, you know. I wish it was twenty times worse! It would serve him right, the villain! I wish it was lawful to break him on the wheel—I do!"

"Uncle, that is very wicked in you! I declare I won't have it! I'll write a petition to the Governor to commute his sentence, and carry it all around the country myself!"

"You wouldn't get a soul to sign it to save your life, much less his."

"I'll go to the Governor myself, and beg him to pardon Donald Bayne!"

"Ha! ha! ha! the Governor would not do it to save *all* our lives; and if he *were* to do such an outrageous thing, he might whistle for his re-election!"

"I declare, Donald Bayne shall not be hung—and so there!" said Cap, passionately.

"Whe-ew! You'll deliver him by the strength of your arm, my little Donna Quixota."[3]

"I'll save him in one way or another, now mind I tell you! He sinned more against *me* than against anybody else, and so I have the best right of anybody in the world to forgive him, and I *do* forgive him! And he shan't be hung! I say it!"

"*You* say it! ha! ha! ha! Who are *you*, to turn aside the law?"

"I, Capitola Black, say that Donald Bayne, not having deserved to be hung, shall not be hung! And in one way or another I'll keep my word!"

And Cap did her best to keep it. The next morning she mounted Gyp and rode up to Tip-Top, where she employed the village lawyer to draw up a petition to the Governor for the commutation of Donald Bayne's sentence. And then she rode all over the country to try to get signatures to the document. But all in vain! People of every age and condition too thoroughly feared and hated the famous outlaw, and too earnestly wished to be entirely and forever rid of him, to sign any petition for a commutation of his sentence. If a petition for his instant execution had been carried around, it would have stood a much better chance of success!

Cap spent many days in her fruitless enterprise, but at last gave it up—but by no means in despair, for——

"I'll save his life, yet! by one means or another! I can't change clothes with him as I did with Clara, he's too big! but one way or other I'll save him," said Cap, to herself. She said it to no one else, for the more difficult the enterprise, the more determined she was to succeed, and the more secretive she grew as to her measures.

In the meantime the outlaw, double-ironed, was confined in the condemned cell, the strongest portion of the county jail. All persons were strictly prohibited from visiting him, except certain of the clergy.

They did all they could to bring the outlaw to a sense of his condition, to prepare him to meet his fate and to induce him to make a confession and give up the retreat of his band.

And Donald listened to them with respect, acknowledged himself a great sinner, and knelt with them when they knelt to pray for him.

But he denied that he was guilty of the murders for which he had been doomed to die, and he utterly refused to give up his old companions, replying to the ministers in something like these words:

"Poor wretches! they are no more fit to die than *I* am, and a condemned cell, with the thought of the scaffold before him, are not exactly the most favorable circumstances under which a man might experience *sincere* repentance, my masters!"

And so, while the convict listened with docility to all that the ministers had to say, he steadily persisted in asserting his own innocence of the crimes for which he was condemned, and in his refusal to deliver up his companions.

Meantime, Capitola, at Hurricane Hall, was doing all she could to discover or invent means to save the life of Black Donald. But still she said no more about it, even to Old Hurricane.

One evening, while Cap was sitting by the fire with her thoughts busy with this subject, her uncle came in, saying:

"Cap! I have got some curiosities to show you!"

"What are they?" said Cap, languidly.

"A set of burglar's tools, supposed to belong to some member of Black Donald's band! One of my negroes found them in the woods in the neighborhood of the Devil's Punch Bowl! I wrote to the sheriff concerning them, and he requested me to take care of them until he should have occasion to call for them. Look! did you ever see such things?" said Old Hurricane, setting down a canvas bag upon the table, and turning out from it all sorts of strange looking instruments—tiny saws, files, punches, screws, picks, etc., etc., etc.

Cap looked at them with the most curious interest, while Old Hurricane explained their supposed uses.

"It must have been an instrument of *this* sort, Cap, that that blamed demon, Donald, gave to the imprisoned men to file their fetters off with!" he said, showing a thin file of tempered steel.

"That!" said Cap, "hand it here! let me see it!" and she examined it with the deepest interest.

"I wonder what they force locks with?" she inquired.

"Why, this, and this, and this!" said Old Hurricane, producing a burglar's pick, saw and chisel.

Cap took them and scrutinized them so attentively that Old Hurricane burst out in a loud laugh, exclaiming—

"You'll dream of house-breakers to-night, Cap!" and taking the tools he put them all back in the little canvas bag, and put the bag up on a high shelf of the parlor closet.

The next morning, while Cap was arranging flowers on the parlor mantle-piece, Old Hurricane burst in upon her with his hands full of letters and newspapers, and his heart full of exultation—throwing up his hat and cutting an alarming caper for a man of his age, he exclaimed:

"Hurrah, Cap! Hurrah! Peace is at last proclaimed and our victorious troops are on their way home! It's all in the newspapers! and here are letters from Herbert, dated from New Orleans! Here are letters for you, and here are some for me! I have not opened them yet! Hurrah, Cap, Hurrah!"

"Hurrah, uncle! Hurrah!" cried Cap, tossing up her flowers and rushing into his arms!

"Don't squeeze me into an apoplexy, you little bear," said Old Hurricane, turning purple in the face, from the savage hug of Cap's joyful arms. "Come along and sit down with me, at this table, and let us see what the letters have brought us."

They took their seats opposite each other, at a small table, and Old Hurricane threw the whole mail between them, and began to pick out the letters.

"That's for you, Cap. This is for me," he said, pitching out two in the handwriting of Herbert Greyson.

Cap opened hers, and commenced reading. It was in fact Herbert's first downright practical proposal of marriage, in which he begged that their union might take place as soon as he should return, and that as *he* had written to his uncle by the same mail, upon another subject, which he did not wish to mix up with his own marriage, *she* would, upon a proper opportunity, let her uncle know of their plans.

"Upon my word, he takes *my* consent very cooly as a matter of course, and even forces upon me the disagreeable duty of asking myself of my own uncle! Whoever heard of such proceedings! If he were not coming home from the wars, I declare I should get angry; but I won't get upon my dignity with Herbert,—dear, darling, sweet Herbert—if it were anybody else, shouldn't they know the difference between their liege lady and Tom Trotter? However, as it's Herbert, here goes! Now, I suppose the best way to ask myself of uncle, for Herbert, will be just to hand him over this letter. The dear knows it isn't so over and above affectionate that I should hesitate. Uncle," said Cap, pulling Old Hurricane's coat-sleeve.

"Don't bother me, Cap," exclaimed Major Warfield, who sat there holding a large, closely-written document in his hand, with his great round eyes strained from their sockets, as they passed along the lines with devouring interest.

"Well, I do declare! I do believe he has received a proposal of marriage himself," cried Cap, shooting much nearer the truth than she knew.

Old Hurricane did not hear her. Starting up with the document in his hand, he rushed from the room, and went and shut himself up in his own study.

"I vow, some widow has offered to marry him," said Cap, to herself. Old Hurricane did not come to dinner, nor to supper. But after supper, when Capitola's wonder was at its climax, and while she was sitting by the little wood fire that the chilly evening required, Old Hurricane came in, looking very unlike himself, in an humble, confused, deprecating, yet happy manner, like one who had at once a mortifying confession to make, and a happy secret to tell.

"Cap," he said, trying to repress a smile, and growing purple in the face.

——"Oh, yes! you've come to tell me, I suppose, that you're going to put a step-aunt-in-law over my head, only you don't know how to announce it," answered Capitola, little knowing how closely she had come to the truth; when to her unbound astonishment, Old Hurricane answered:

"Yes, my dear, that's just *it!*"

"WHAT! My eyes! Oh crickey!" cried Cap, breaking into her newsboy's slang, from more consternation.

"Yes, my dear, it is perfectly true!" replied the old man, growing furiously red, and rubbing his face.

"Oh! oh! oh! HOLD ME! I'M 'KILT!'" cried Cap, falling back in her chair in an inextinguishable fit of laughter, that shook her whole frame. She laughed until the tears ran down her cheeks. She wiped her eyes and looked at Old Hurricane, and every time she saw his confused happy face, she burst into a fresh paroxysm that seemed to threaten her life or her reason.

"Who is the happy——. Oh, I can't speak! Oh, I'm 'kilt entirely!'" she cried, breaking off in the midst of her question, and falling into fresh convulsions.

"It's no new love, Cap. It's my old wife!" said Old Hurricane, wiping his face.

This brought Capitola up with a jerk! She sat bolt upright, gazing at him with her eyes fixed as if in death.

"Cap," said Old Hurricane, growing more and more confused, "I've been a married man more years than I like to think of! Cap, I've—I've a wife and grown-up son! What do you sit there staring at me for, you little demon? Why don't you say something to encourage me, you little wretch?"

"Go on," said Cap, without removing her eyes.

"Cap, I was—a jealous—passionate—Demmy! confession isn't in my line! A diabolical villain made me believe that my poor little wife wasn't good!"

"There! I knew you'd lay it on somebody else. Men always do that!" said Cap to herself.

"He was mortally wounded in Mexico. He made a confession, and confided it to Herbert, who has just sent me an attested copy. It was Le Noir. My poor wife lived under her girlhood's name of Marah Rocke." Old Hurricane made a gulp, and his voice broke down.

Cap understood all now, as well as if she had known it as long as Old Hurricane had. She comprehended his extreme agitation upon a certain evening, years ago, when Herbert Greyson had mentioned Marah Rocke's name, and his later and more lasting disturbance upon accidentally meeting Marah at the Orphans' Court.

This revelation filled her with strange and contradictory emotions. She was glad; she was angry with him; she was sorry for him; she was divided between divers impulses to hug and kiss him, to cry over him, and to seize him and give him a good shaking! And between them she did nothing at all.

Old Hurricane was again the first to speak.

"What was that you wished to say to me, Cap, when I ran away from you this morning?"

"Why, uncle, that Herbert wants to follow your example, and—and—and———" Cap blushed and broke down.

"I thought as much. Getting married at his age! a boy of twenty-five!" said the veteran in contempt.

"Taking a wife at *your* age, uncle, an infant of sixty-six!"

"Bother, Cap! Let me see the fellow's letter to you."

Cap handed it to him, and the old man read it.

"If I were to object, you'd get married all the same! Demmy! you're both of age. Do as you please."

"Thank you, sir," said Cap, demurely.

"And now, Cap, one thing is to be noticed. Herbert says, both in your letter and in mine, that they were to start to return the day after these letters were posted. These letters have been delayed in the mail. Consequently we may expect our hero here every day. But Cap, my dear, *you* must receive them. For to-morrow morning, please the Lord, I shall set out for Staunton and Willow Heights, and go and kneel down at the feet of my wife, and ask her pardon on my knees!"

Cap was no longer divided between the wish to pull Old Hurricane's gray beard and to cry over him. She threw herself at once into his arms and exclaimed:

"Oh uncle! God bless you! God bless you! God bless you! It has come very late in life, but may you be happy with her through all the ages of eternity."

Old Hurricane was deeply moved by the sympathy of his little mad-cap, and pressed her to his bosom, saying:

"Cap, my dear, if you had not set your heart upon Herbert, I would marry you to my son Traverse, and you two should inherit all that I have in the world! But never mind, Cap, you have an inheritance of your own! Cap, Cap, my dear, did it ever occur to you that you might have had a father and mother?"

"Yes! often! But I used to think _you_ were my father, and that my mother was dead."

"I wish to the Lord that I _had_ been your father, Cap, and that Marah Rocke had been your mother! But Cap, your father was a better man than I, and your mother as good a woman as Marah. And Cap, my dear, you vagabond, you vagrant, you brat, you beggar, you are the sole heiress of the Hidden House estate and all its enormous wealth! What do you think of _that_ now, what do you think of _that,_ you beggar?" cried Old Hurricane.

A shriek pierced the air, and Capitola starting up, stood before Old Hurricane, crying in an impassioned voice:

"Uncle! Uncle! don't mock me! don't overwhelm me! I do not care for wealth or power; but tell me of the parents who possessing _both,_ cast off their unfortunate child—_a girl,_ too! to meet the sufferings and perils of such a life as mine had been, if I had not met you!"

"Cap, my dear, hush! your parents were no more to blame for their seeming abandonment of _you,_ than _I_ was to blame for the desertion of my poor wife. We are all the victims of one villain who has now gone to his account, Capitola. I mean Gabriel Le Noir. Sit down my dear, and I will read the copy of his whole confession, and afterwards, in addition, tell you all _I_ know upon the subject!"

Capitola resumed her seat, and Major Warfield read the confession of Gabriel Le Noir, and afterwards continued the subject by relating the events of that memorable Hallow Eve when he was called out in a snow-storm to take the dying deposition of the nurse who had been abducted with the infant Capitola.

And at the end of his narrative, Cap, knew as much of her own history as the reader has known all along.

"And I have a mother! and I shall even see her soon! you told me she was coming home with the party—did you not, Uncle?" said Capitola.

"Yes, my child. Only think of it? *I* saved the *daughter* from the streets of New York, and *my son* saved the *mother* from her prison at the mad-house! And now my dear Cap, I must bid you good-night and go to bed, for I intend to rise to-morrow morning long before daylight, to ride to Tip-Top to meet the Staunton stage," said the old man, kissing Capitola.

Just as he was about to leave the room, he was arrested by a loud ringing and knocking at the door.

Wool was heard running along the front hall to answer the summons.

"Cap, I shouldn't wonder much if that was our party. I wish it may be, for I should like to welcome them before I leave home to fetch my wife," said Old Hurricane, in a voice of agitation.

And while they were still eagerly listening, the door was thrown open by Wool, who announced:

"Marse Herbert, which I mean to say, Major Herbert Greyson;" and Herbert entered and was grasped by the two hands of Old Hurricane, who exclaimed:

"Ah, Herbert, my lad! I have got your letters. It is all right, Herbert, or going to be so. You shall marry Cap when you like. And I am going to-morrow morning to throw myself at the feet of my wife."

"No need of your going so far, dear sir, no need. Let me speak to my own dear girl a moment, and then I shall have something to say to you," said Herbert, leaving the old man in suspense, and going to salute Capitola, who returned his fervent embrace by an honest, downright frank kiss, that made no secret of itself.

"Capitola! My uncle has told you all?"

"Every single bit! so don't lose time by telling it all over again! *Is* my mother with you?"

"Yes! and I will bring her in, in one moment; but first I must bring in some one else," said Herbert, kissing the hand of Capitola and turning to Old Hurricane, to whom he said:

"You need not travel far to find Marah. We took Staunton in our way, and brought her and Clara along—Traverse!" he said, going to the door—"bring in your mother."

And the next instant, Traverse entered with the wife of Major War-field upon his arm.

Old Hurricane started forward to meet her, exclaiming in a broken voice:

"Marah, my dear Marah, God may forgive me, but can you—can you

474

ever do so!" and he would have sunk at her feet, but that she prevented, by meeting him and silently placing both her hands in his. And so quietly Marah's forgiveness was expressed, and the reconciliation sealed.

Meanwhile Herbert went out, and brought in Mrs. Le Noir and Clara. Mrs. Le Noir with a Frenchwoman's impetuosity, hurried to her daughter, and clasped her to her heart.

Cap gave one hurried glance at the beautiful pale woman that claimed from her a daughter's love, and then, returning the caress, she said:

"Oh, mamma! Oh, mamma! If I were only a boy instead of a girl, I would thrash that Le Noir within an inch of his life! But I forgot! he is gone to his account."

Old Hurricane was at this moment shaking hands with his son, Traverse, who presently took occasion to lead up and introduce his betrothed wife, Clara Day, to her destined father-in-law.

Major Warfield received her with all a soldier's gallantry, a gentleman's courtesy and a father's tenderness.

He next shook hands with his old acquaintance, Mrs. Le Noir.

And then supper was ordered, and the evening was passed in general and comparative reminiscences and cheerful conversation.

CHAPTER LXI

"THERE SHALL BE LIGHT AT THE EVENTIDE"

—*Holy Bible*[1]

᯽᯽᯽᯽᯽

"They shall be blessed exceedingly; their store
   Grow daily, weekly more and more,
And peace so multiply around,
   Their very hearth seems holy ground."
   —*Mary Howitt*[2]

THE MARRIAGE OF Capitola and Herbert, and that of Clara and of Traverse, was fixed to take place upon the first of August, which was the twenty-first birthday of the doctor's daughter, and also the twenty-fifth anniversary of the wedding of Ira Warfield and Marah Rocke.

German husbands and wives have a beautiful custom of keeping the twenty-fifth anniversary of their marriage by a festival which they call the "Silver Wedding." And thus Major Warfield and Marah resolved to keep this first of August, and farther to honor the occasion by uniting the hands of their young people.

There was but one cloud upon the happiness of Capitola; this was the approaching execution of Black Donald.

No one else seemed to care about the matter, until a circumstance occurred which painfully aroused their interest.

This was the fact that the Governor, through the solicitation of certain ministers of the gospel, who represented the condemned as utterly unprepared to meet his fate, had respited him until the first of August, at which time, he wished the prisoner to be made to understand that his sentence would certainly, without farther delay, be carried into effect.

This carried a sort of consternation into the heart of every member of the Hurricane Hall household!

The idea of Black Donald being hung in their immediate neighborhood upon their wedding day was appalling!

Yet there was no help for it, unless their wedding was postponed to

476

another occasion than that upon which Old Hurricane had set his heart. No one knew what to do.

Cap fretted herself almost sick. She had cudgelled her brains to no purpose. She had not been able to think of any plan by which she could deliver Black Donald. Meantime the last days of July were rapidly passing away.

Black Donald in the condemned cell maintained his firmness, resolutely asserting his innocence of any capital crime, and persistently refusing to give up his band. As a last motive of confession, the paper written by Gabriel Le Noir upon his deathbed was shown him. He laughed a loud, crackling laugh, and said *that* was all true, but that he, for his part, never had intended to harm a hair of Capitola's head; that he had taken a fancy to the girl when he had first seen her, and had only wanted to carry her off and force her into a marriage with himself; that he had pretended to consent to her death only for the purpose of saving her life.

When Cap heard this she burst into tears, and said she believed it was true!

The night before the wedding of Capitola and Herbert, and Clara and Traverse, and of the execution of Black Donald, came.

At Hurricane Hall, the two prospective bridegrooms were busy with Old Hurricane over some papers that had to be prepared in the library.

The two intended brides were engaged, under the direction of Mrs. Warfield, in her dressing-room, consulting over certain proprieties of the approaching festival. But Capitola could give only a half attention to the discussion. Her thoughts were with the poor condemned man who was to die the next day.

And suddenly she flew out of the room, summoned her groom, mounted her horse, and rode away.

In his condemned cell Black Donald was bitterly realizing how unprepared he was to die, and how utterly impossible it was for him to prepare in the short hours left. He tried to pray, but could form no other petition than that he might be allowed, if possible, a little longer to fit himself to meet his Creator. From his cell he could hear the striking of the great clock in the prison hall. And as every hour struck, it seemed "a nail driven in his coffin."

At eight o'clock that night the warden sat in his little office, consulting the sheriff about some details of the approaching execution. While they were still in discussion, a turnkey opened the door, saying:

"A lady to see the warden."

And Capitola stood before them!

"Miss Black!" exclaimed both sheriff and warden, rising in surprise, gazing upon our heroine, and addressing her by the name under which they had first known her.

"Yes, gentlemen, it is I. The truth is, I cannot rest to-night without saying a few words of comfort to the poor man who is to die to-morrow. So I came hither, attended by my groom, to know if I may see him for a few minutes."

"Miss Black, here is the sheriff. It is just as *he* pleases. My orders were so strict that had you come to me alone I should have been obliged to refuse you."

"Mr. Keepe, *you* will not refuse me," said Capitola turning to the sheriff.

"Miss Black, my rule is to admit no one but the officers of the prison and the ministers of the gospel, to see the condemned! This we have been obliged to observe as a measure of safety. This convict, as you are aware, is a man of consummate cunning, so that it is really wonderful he has not found means to make his escape, closely as he has been watched and strongly as he has been guarded."

"Ah, but Mr. Keepe, his cunning was no match for mine, you know!" said Capitola, smiling.

"Ha-ha-ha! so it was not! You took him very cleverly! very cleverly, indeed! In fact, if it had not been for you, I doubt if ever we should have captured Black Donald at all. The authorities are entirely indebted to you for the capture of this notorious outlaw. And really that being the case, I do think it would be straining a point to refuse you admittance to see him! So, Miss Black, you have my authority for visiting the condemned man in his cell and giving him all the comfort you can. I would attend you thither myself, but I have got to go to see the captain of a militia company to be on the scene of action to-morrow," said the sheriff, who soon after took leave of the warden and departed.

The warden then called a turnkey and ordered him to attend Miss Black to the condemned cell.

The young turnkey took up a lamp and a great key and walked before, leading the way down stairs to a cell in the interior of the basement, occupied by Black Donald.

He unlocked the door, admitted Capitola, and then walked off to the extremity of the lobby, as he was accustomed to do when he let in the preachers.

Capitola thanked heaven for this chance, for had he not done so she would have had to invent some excuse for getting rid of him.

She entered the cell. It was very dimly lighted from the great lamp that hung in the lobby, nearly opposite the cell door.

By its light she saw Black Donald, not only doubly ironed but confined by a chain and staple to the wall. He was very pale and haggard from long imprisonment and great anxiety.

Cap's heart bled for the poor banned and blighted outlaw, who had not a friend in the world to speak a kind word to him in his trouble.

He also recognized her, and rising and coming to meet her as far as the length of the chain would permit, he held out his hand and said:

"I am very glad you have come, little one; it is very kind of you to come and see a poor fellow in his extremity! You are the first female that has been in my cell since my imprisonment. Think of *that,* child! I wanted to see you too; I wanted to say to you yourself *again,* that I never was guilty of murder, and that I only seemed to consent to your death to save your life! Do you believe this?—On the word of a dying man it is truth!"

"I do believe you, Donald Bayne," said Capitola, in a broken voice.

"I hear that you have come into your estate! I am glad of it. And they tell me that you are going to be married to-morrow! Well! God bless you, little one!"

"Oh, Donald Bayne! Can you say God bless *me,* when it was I who put you here?"

"Tut, child, we outlaws bear no malice! Spite is a civilized vice! It was a fair contest, child, and you conquered! It's well you did! Give me your hand in good will, since I must die to-morrow!"

Capitola gave her hand, and while he held it, she stooped and said:

"Donald! I have done everything in the world to save your life!"

"I know you have, child. May yours be long and happy."

"Donald, may your life be longer and better than you think. I have tried all other means of saving you in vain; there is but one means left."

The outlaw started violently, exclaiming:

"IS THERE ONE?"

"Donald, yes! there is! I bring you the means of deliverance and escape. Heaven knows whether I am doing right—for I do not. I know many people would blame me very much, but I hope that he who forgave the thief upon the cross and the sinful woman at his feet, will not condemn me for following his own compassionate example. For Donald, as *I* was the person whom you injured most of all others, so I consider that *I* of all others have the best right to pardon you and set you free. Oh, Donald! use well the life I am about to give you, else I shall be chargeable with every future sin you commit!"

"In the name of mercy do not hold out a false hope. I had nerved myself to die."

"But you were not prepared to meet your Maker. Oh, Donald! I hold out no false hope! Listen, for I must speak low and quick—I could never be happy again, if, on my wedding day, you should die a felon's death! Here! here are tools with the use of which you must be acquainted, for they were found in the woods near the Hidden House!" said Capitola, producing from her pockets a burglar's lock-pick, saw, chisel, file, etc.

Black Donald seized them as a famished wolf might seize his prey.

"WILL they do?" inquired Capitola, in breathless anxiety.

"Yes! yes! yes! I can file off my irons, pick every lock, drive back every bolt, and dislodge every bar between myself and freedom with these instruments! But, child, there is one thing you have forgotten: suppose a turnkey or a guard should stop me?—you have brought me no revolver!"

Capitola turned pale.

"Donald, I could easily have brought you a revolver; but I would not, even to save you from to-morrow's death. No, Donald! no! I give you the means of freeing yourself, if you can do it, as you may, without bloodshed. But, Donald, though your life is not justly forfeited, *your liberty is,* and so I cannot give you the means of taking any one's life for the sake of saving your own."

"You are right," said the outlaw.

"Listen, further, Donald. Here are a thousand dollars. I thought never to have taken it from the bank, for I would never have used the price of blood. But I drew it to-day for you. Take it—it will help you to live a better life. When you have picked your way out of this place, go to the great elm tree at the back of the old mill, and you will find my horse, Gyp, whom I shall have tied there. He is very swift—mount him and ride for your life to the nearest seaport, and so escape by a vessel to some foreign country. And oh! try to lead a good life, and may God redeem you, Donald Bayne! There! conceal your tools and money quickly, for I hear the guard coming. Good-bye! and again,—God redeem you, Donald Bayne!"

"God bless you, brave and tender girl! And God forsake me if I do not heed your advice!" said the outlaw, pressing the hand she gave him, while the tears rushed to his eyes.

The guard approached, Capitola turned to meet him. They left the cell together, and Black Donald was locked in for the last time.

"O, I hope, I pray that he may get off! O, what shall I do if he doesn't! How can I enjoy my wedding to-morrow! how can I bear the music, and the dancing, and the rejoicing, when I know that a fellow creature is in such a strait! Oh! Lord grant that Black Donald may get clear off to-night, for he isn't fit to die!" said Cap to herself as she hurried out of the prison.

Her young groom was waiting for her, and she mounted her horse and rode until they got to the old haunted church at the end of the village, when, drawing rein, she said:

"Jem, I am very tired. I will wait here, and you must just ride back to the village, to Mr. Cassell's livery stable, and get a gig, and put your horse into it, and come back here to drive me home, for I cannot ride."

Jem, who never questioned his imperious little mistress's orders, rode off at once to do her bidding.

Cap immediately dismounted from her pony, and led him under the deep shadows of the elm tree, where she fastened him. Then taking his face between her hands, and looking him in the eyes, she said:

"Gyp, my son, you and I have had a many a frolic together, but we've got to part now! It almost breaks my heart, Gyp, but it is to save a fellow creature's life, and it can't he helped! He'll treat you well, for my sake, dear Gyp. Gyp! he'll part with his *life* sooner than sell you! Good-bye dear, dear Gyp!"

Gyp took all these caresses in a very nonchalant manner, only snorting and pawing in reply.

Presently the boy came back, bringing the gig. Cap once more hugged Gyp about the neck, pressed her cheek against his mane, and with a whispered "Good-bye, dear Gyp," sprang into the gig, and ordered the boy to drive home.

"An' leab the pony, Miss?"

"Oh yes, for the present; everybody knows Gyp,—no one will steal him. I have left him length of line enough to move around a little and eat grass, drink from the brook, or lie down. You can come after him early to-morrow morning."

The little groom thought this a queer arrangement, but he was not in the habit of criticizing his young mistress's actions.

Capitola got home to a late supper, and to the anxious inquiries of her friends she replied that she had been to the prison to take leave of Black Donald, and begged that they would not pursue so painful a subject.

And, in respect to Cap's sympathies, they changed the conversation.

That night the remnant of Black Donald's band were assembled in their first old haunt, the Old Road Inn. They had met for a two-fold purpose—to bury their old matron, Mother Raven, who, since the death of her patron and the apprehension of her Captain, had returned to the inn to die—and to bewail the fate of their leader, whose execution was expected to come off the next day.

The men laid the poor old woman in her woodland grave, and assembled in the kitchen to keep a death watch in sympathy with their "unfortunate" Captain. They gathered around the table, and foaming mugs of ale were freely quaffed, for "sorrow's dry" they said. But neither laugh, song, nor jest attended their draughts. They were to keep that night's vigil in honor of their Captain, and then were to disband and separate forever.

Suddenly, in the midst of their heavy grief and utter silence, a familiar sound was heard—a ringing footstep under the back windows.

And every man leaped to his feet, with looks of wild delight and questioning.

And the next instant the door was flung wide open, and the outlaw chief stood among them!

Hal leaped forward and flung himself around Black Donald's neck, exclaiming—

"It's you! it's you! it's you! my dear! my darling! my adored! my sweetheart! my prince! my lord! my king! my dear, dear Captain!"

Steve, the lazy mulatto, rolled down upon the floor at his master's feet, and embraced them in silence.

While Demon Dick growled forth—

"How the foul fiend *did* you get out?"

And the anxious faces of all the other men silently repeated the question.

"Not by any help of *yours,* boys! But don't think I reproach you, lads! Well I know that you could do nothing on earth to save me! No one on earth could have helped me except the one who really freed me—Capitola!"

"That girl again!" exclaimed Hal, in the extremity of wonder.

Steve stopped rolling and curling himself around the feet of his master, and gazed up in stupid astonishment.

"It's to be hoped, then, you've got her at last, Captain," said Demon Dick.

"No—Heaven bless her!—she's in better hands. Now listen, lads, for I must talk fast! I have already lost a great deal too much time. I went first to the cave in the Punch Bowl, and not finding you there, came here at a venture, where I am happy to meet you for the last time—for to-night we disband forever!"

"'Twas our intention, Captain," said Hal, in a melancholy voice.

Black Donald then threw himself into a seat at the head of the table, poured out a mug of ale, and invited his band to pledge him. They gathered around the table, filled their mugs, pledged him standing, and then resumed their seats to listen to the last words of their chief.

Black Donald commenced and related the manner of his deliverance by Capitola; and then taking from his bosom a bag of gold, he poured it upon the table and divided it into two equal portions, one of which he handed to "Headlong Hal," saying—

"There, Hal, take that and divide it among your companions, and scatter to distant parts of the country, where you may yet have a chance of earning an honest livelihood! As for me I shall have to quit the country altogether, and it will take nearly half this sum to enable me to do it. Now I shall have not a minute more to give you! So once more pledge your Captain, and away!"

The men filled their mugs, rose to their feet, and pledged their leader in a parting toast, and then—

"Good luck to you all!" exclaimed Black Donald, waving his hat thrice above his head with a valedictory hurrah. And the next moment he was gone!

That night, if any watchman had been on guard near the stables of Hurricane Hall, he might have seen a tall man mounted upon Capitola's pony, ride up in hot haste, dismount and pick the stable lock, take Gyp by the bridle and lead him in, and presently return leading out Fleetfoot, Old Hurricane's racer, upon which he mounted and rode away.

The next morning, while Capitola was dressing, her groom rapped at the door and, in great dismay, begged that he might speak to Miss Cap one minute.

"Well, what is it, Jem?" said Capitola.

"Oh, Miss Cap, you'll kill *me!* I done been got up long afore day and gone to Tip-Top arter Gyp; but somebody done been stole him away afore I got there!"

"Thank Heaven!" cried Capitola, to little Jem's unspeakable amazement. For to Capitola the absence of her horse meant just the escape of Black Donald!

The next minute Cap sighed and said:

"Poor Gyp! I shall never see you again!"

That was all *she* knew of the future!

That morning while they were all at breakfast, a groom from the stable came in, with a little canvas bag in his hand, which he laid, with a bow, before his master.

Major Warfield took it up; it was full of gold, and upon one side was written, in red chalk:

"Three hundred dollars, to pay for Fleetfoot. Black Donald, Reformed Robber."

While Old Hurricane was reading this inscription, the groom said that Fleetfoot was missing from his stall, and that Miss Cap's pony, that was supposed to have been stolen, was found in his place, with this bag of gold tied around his neck!

"It is Black Donald! he has escaped!" cried Old Hurricane, about to fling himself into a rage, when his furious eyes encountered the gentle gaze of Marah, that fell like oil on the waves of his rising passion.

"Let him go! I'll not storm on my silver wedding day," said Major Warfield.

As for Cap, her eyes danced with delight; the only little clouds upon her bright sky were removed. Black Donald had escaped to commence a better life, and Gyp was restored!

That evening a magnificent, old-fashioned wedding came off at Hurricane Hall.

The double ceremony was performed by the bishop of the diocese (then on a visit to the neighborhood), in the great saloon of Hurricane Hall, in the presence of as large and splendid an assembly as could be gathered together from that remote neighborhood.

The two brides, of course, were lovely in white satin and honiton lace, pearls and orange flowers. "Equally," of course, the bridegrooms were handsome and elegant, proud and happy.

To this old-fashioned wedding succeeded a round of dinners and evening parties given by the wedding guests. And when all these old-time customs had been observed for the satisfaction of old friends, the bridal party went upon the new-fashioned tour, for their own delight. They spent a year in traveling over the Eastern Continent, and then returned home to settle upon their patrimonial estates.

Major Warfield and Marah live at Hurricane Hall, and as his heart is satisfied and at rest, his temper is gradually improving. As the lion shall be led by the little child, Old Hurricane is led by the gentlest woman that ever loved or suffered, and she is leading him in his old age to the Saviour's feet.

Clara and Traverse live at Willow Heights, which has been repaired, enlarged and improved, and where Traverse has already an extensive practice, and where both endeavor to emulate the enlightened goodness of the sainted Doctor Day.

Cap and Herbert, with Mrs. Le Noir, live at the Hidden House, which has been turned by wealth and taste into a dwelling of light and beauty. As the bravest are always the gentlest, so the most high-spirited are always the most forgiving. And thus the weak or wicked old Dorcas Knight still finds a home under the roof of Mrs. Le Noir. Her only retribution being the very mild one of having her relations changed in the fact that her temporary prisoner is now her mistress and sovereign lady.

I wish I could say "they all lived happy ever after." But the truth is, I have reason to suppose that even Clara had sometimes occasion to administer to Doctor Rocke dignified curtain lectures; which no doubt did him good. And I know for a positive fact, that our Cap sometimes gives her "dear, darling, sweet Herbert," the benefit of the sharp edge of her tongue, which of course he deserves.

But notwithstanding all this, I am happy to say that they all enjoy a fair amount of human felicity.

EXPLANATORY NOTES

Southworth quoted in a free manner, from memory or to suit her particular purposes in a scene. Therefore her epigraphs and quotations are often far from exact. While I have given sources wherever possible, only in the case of the biblical quotations have I made a concerted effort to reconstruct the original text.

CHAPTER I

1. William Shakespeare (1564–1616), *Macbeth* II.ii.
2. Douglas is a family name in Scottish history, legend, and romance, prominent in the novels of Sir Walter Scott.
3. Halloween.

CHAPTER II

1. *Macbeth* I.iii.
2. "battle, murder, and sudden death" is from *The American Book of Common Prayer* (1789).

CHAPTER III

1. *Hudibras* is a long satirical poem by Samuel Butler (1612–80).

CHAPTER IV

1. Sir Walter Scott (1771–1832), "Marmion."
2. "king of shreds and patches": Shakespeare, *Hamlet* III.iv.
3. a ten-dollar gold coin.
4. First Families of Virginia.

CHAPTER V

1. Scott, "Marmion." This passage is quoted freely from memory. The original reads:

> But, at the prioress' command,
> A monk undid the silken band
>   That tied her tresses fair,
> And raised the bonnet from her head,
> And down her slender form they spread
>   In ringlets rich and rare.

2. var. of cassinette, a lightweight twilled trousering.

CHAPTER VI

1. Ps. 147.9: "He giveth to the beast his food, *and* to the young ravens which cry."

CHAPTER VII

1. Although Southworth attributes this passage to Shakespeare, it does not appear in any of the standard concordances of his work.

Explanatory Notes

CHAPTER VIII

1. Fitz-Greene Halleck (1790–1867), American poet.
2. Shakespeare, *Romeo and Juliet* II.ii: "That which we call a rose / By any other name would smell as sweet."

CHAPTER X

1. *Hamlet* I.ii.
2. John Milton (1608–74), *Paradise Lost* 1: "yet from those flames / No light, but rather darkness visible."

CHAPTER XI

1. George Gordon, Lord Byron (1788–1824), "Parisina."
2. Edward Young (1683–1765), *Night Thoughts,* Night One: "At thirty, man suspects himself a fool; / Knows it at forty and reforms his plan."
3. Numa Pompilius, the legendary second king of Rome, was favored by the nymph Egeria with secret interviews and was taught by her the lessons of wisdom and law which he embodied in the institutions of his nation.

CHAPTER XII

1. John Greenleaf Whittier (1807–92), "Maud Muller."
2. Hagar was the Egyptian servant of Sarah and Abraham who bore Abraham a son, Ishmael, while Sarah remained childless. She was exiled with her son into the wilderness, where their lives were saved by an angel (Gen. 21).

CHAPTER XIII

1. "Maud Muller."
2. *Hamlet* III.ii: "The lady doth protest too much, methinks."
3. Shakespeare, *King Lear* I.i: "Unhappy that I am I cannot heave my heart into my mouth."

The Hidden Hand

CHAPTER XIV

1. "Maud Muller."
2. Reproductions of Thomas Cole's four-part allegorical *Voyage of Life* were extremely popular in nineteenth-century America. The paintings now hang in the National Gallery in Washington.

CHAPTER XV

1. The Man in the Iron Mask was a mysterious French prisoner held for over forty years by Louis XIV. Billy Patterson may be a reference to the influential Baltimore merchant William Patterson (1752–1835).

CHAPTER XVI

1. These lines are the first verse of a traditional French folk song entitled "Compagnon de la marjolaine."

CHAPTER XVII

1. *archaic:* a person who attends to duty only when watched.
2. a person who shapes his or her behavior and ideas to please superiors.

CHAPTER XVIII

1. Elizabeth Barrett Browning (1806–61), "A Portrait."
2. Queen Victoria ascended to the British throne in 1837 at the age of eighteen.

CHAPTER XIX

1. Alexander Pope (1688–1744), "Universal Prayer."
2. *Hamlet* V.ii: "There's a special providence in the fall of a sparrow."

Explanatory Notes

CHAPTER XX

1. Sir Robert Howard (1625?–98), English politician and dramatist.
2. a partisan of the devil.
3. Moloch is a pagan diety whose worship requires the sacrifice of children.

CHAPTER XXI

1. *Macbeth* III.ii.

CHAPTER XXII

1. *The Winter's Tale* IV.iv.

CHAPTER XXIII

1. William Motherwell (1797–1835), Scottish poet.
2. Matt. 6.34: "Take therefore no thought for the morrow: for the morrow shall take thought for the things of itself. Sufficient unto the day is the evil thereof."

CHAPTER XXIV

1. Robert Browning (1812–89), "A Blot in the Scutcheon: A Tragedy."

CHAPTER XXV

1. Robert Burns (1759–96), "I Hae a Wife o' My Ain."
2. Mary Rogers was the victim of a sensational murder in New York City in 1841. Edgar Allan Poe used the incident as the basis for his "Mystery of Marie Roget."

CHAPTER XXVII

1. Galen was a Greek physician and writer (c. 130–200). Benjamin Rush was an American physician (1745?–1813).
2. Matt. 13.57: "A prophet is not without honor, save in his own country."
3. Ps. 137.5: "If I forget thee, O Jerusalem, let my right hand forget her cunning."
4. *Lat.* ever upward.
5. I Cor. 13.13: "And now abideth these three: faith, hope and charity, but the greatest of these is charity."

CHAPTER XXVIII

1. Hannah More (1745–1833) was an English writer, reformer, and philanthropist.
2. George Crabbe (1754–1832), an English poet, known for his realistic descriptions of rural life.
3. Shakespeare, *1 Henry IV* V, iv: "the better part of valor is discretion."
4. II Sam. 1.26: David laments the death of Jonathan, saying, "very pleasant hast thou been unto me: thy love to me was wonderful, passing the love of women."

CHAPTER XXIX

1. "A Vision of Poets."

CHAPTER XXX

1. When Christ's followers went to his tomb after his crucifixion, they were met by two angels who greeted them, saying: "He is not here, but is risen" (Luke 24.6).

Explanatory Notes

CHAPTER XXXII

1. The original of this passage from *Hudibras* reads as follows:

> At this the knight grew high in chase,
> And staring furiously on Ralph,
> He trembled, and looked pale with ire
> Like ashes first, then red as fire.

2. hot, sweetened alcoholic drinks.

CHAPTER XXXIII

1. "Tam O'Shanter": "And sic a night he taks the road in, / As ne'er poor sinner was abroad in."
2. 1 Pet. 5.8: "Be sober, be vigilant; because your adversary the devil, as a roaring lion, walketh about, seeking whom he may devour."

CHAPTER XXXIV

1. Thomas Hood (1799–1845).
2. an eccentric hero created by Miguel de Cervantes. His mind was so affected by reading romances of chivalry that he believed himself called upon to redress the wrongs of the whole world.
3. *Macbeth* III.iv.

CHAPTER XXXV

1. "The Haunted House."

CHAPTER XXXVI

1. Thomas Moore (1779–1852), Irish poet.

CHAPTER XXXVII

1. *Julius Caesar* IV.iii.
2. murdered by suffocation or strangulation by someone who wishes to obtain a body to sell for dissection, after William Burke, Irish criminal executed for this crime.

CHAPTER XXXVIII

1. Hood's "The Haunted House." The original reads:

> Obscurely spotted to the door, and thence
> With mazy doubles to the grated casement—
> Oh what a tale they told of fear intense,
> Of horror and amazement!

CHAPTER XXXIX

1. *Romeo and Juliet* IV.i.
2. Shadrach, Meshach, and Abednego were Jews who refused to obey the order of Nebuchadnezzar, king of Babylon, to worship an image of gold. He had them cast into a furnace, where they were protected by God (Dan. 3).

CHAPTER XL

1. "Marmion."

CHAPTER XLI

1. Prov. 19.17: "He that hath pity upon the poor lendeth unto the Lord; and that which he hath given will he pay him again."

Explanatory Notes

CHAPTER XLII

1. "Epistle to Davie, a Brother Poet."
2. A reference to Washington Irving's "The Legend of Sleepy Hollow," published in 1820.

CHAPTER XLIII

1. "The Corsair: A Tale" 1.
2. Joseph Surface is the scheming and hypocritical older brother in Richard Brinsley Sheridan's comedy of manners, *The School for Scandal* (1777).
3. a mirage.

CHAPTER XLV

1. Pierre Terrail, seigneur de Bayard (1473–1524) was an heroic French soldier known as "the knight without fear and without reproach."

CHAPTER XLVI

1. *Much Ado about Nothing* IV.i.

CHAPTER XLVII

1. *A Midsummer-Night's Dream* III.ii.
2. *in articulo mortis:* at the brink of death.
3. Georges Louis Leclerc, Comte de Buffon (1707–88), was a well-known French writer and naturalist.

CHAPTER XLVIII

1. thin bars of bone, ivory, or wood held in pairs between the fingers and used to produce musical sounds. Often used in minstrel shows.

CHAPTER XLIX

1. *1 Henry IV* II.iii.
2. Sisera was a Canaanite captain who took refuge in the tent of Jael and was killed by her with a tent pin (Judg. 4–5).
3. Judith was the Jewish heroine of the Apocryphal book of Judith. She entered the tent of the Assyrian general Holofernes and slew him in his drunken sleep. Then she showed his head to her countrymen, who put the invading army to rout.
4. Johann Wolfgang von Goeth published his drama *Faust* in 1808, about a scholar who sells his soul to the devil in order to comprehend all experience.

CHAPTER L

1. *2 Henry IV* I.i.

CHAPTER LI

1. Charles Robert Maturin (1787–1824), Irish novelist.
2. Vera Cruz, Cerro Gordo, and Churubusco were decisive battles in the Mexican War. The individuals referred to were all generals in that war: Winfield Scott (1786–1866) was supreme commander of the United States Army; William Jenkens Worth (1794–1849) was first to plant the American flag at the Rio Grande; John Ellis Wool (1784–1869) commanded volunteer troops; John Anthony Quitman (1798–1858) served as governor of Mexico City during its occupation by the Americans; Gideon Johnson Pillow (1806–78) also commanded volunteers.
3. Prov. 16.32: "He that is slow to anger is better than the mighty; and he that ruleth his spirit than he that taketh a city."
4. Chapultepec is a castle-fortress at the edge of Mexico City, captured by U.S. forces in 1847.
5. Montezuma was the last Aztec emperor of Mexico (1502–20).
6. Antonio Lopez de Santa Anna (1794–1876) was president of Mexico and commanding general of his nation's forces during the Mexican War.
7. diabolical stroke.
8. Molino-del-Rey is the site of a Mexican War battle.
9. Isa. 53.7: "He was oppressed, and he was afflicted, yet he opened not his mouth: he is brought as a lamb to the slaughter, and as a sheep before her shearers is dumb, so he openeth not his mouth." This passage prophesizes the sufferings of the Messiah.

Explanatory Notes

CHAPTER LII

1. *1 Henry IV* III.ii.

CHAPTER LIII

1. *Measure for Measure* II.i.

CHAPTER LIV

1. *Richard the Third* I.i.

CHAPTER LV

1. John Dryden (1631–1700), "Absalom and Achitophel."
2. the Stock Market.
3. II Cor. 9.7: "God loveth a cheerful giver."
4. *Othello* III.iii: "Farewell, Othello's occupation's gone."

CHAPTER LVI

1. Matthew Gregory Lewis (1775–1818), English novelist and dramatist.

CHAPTER LVIII

1. William Davis Gallagher (1808–94), American journalist and poet.

CHAPTER LIX

1. Shakespeare, *3 Henry VI* V.iii.

CHAPTER LX

1. Philip Massinger (1583–1640), English dramatist.
2. a nineteenth-century colloquialism meaning a blindly enthusiastic partisan, or a noisy attack or melee.
3. feminization of Don Quixote; see ch. XXXIV, n. 2.

CHAPTER LXI

1. Zech. 14.7: "at evening time it shall be light."
2. Mary Howitt (1799–1888), English poet, storywriter, and essayist.